Andrea Hutchins
'77

WUTHERING HEIGHTS

REVISED

AN AUTHORITATIVE TEXT

WITH ESSAYS IN CRITICISM

NORTON CRITICAL EDITIONS

AUSTEN *Emma* edited by Stephen M. Parrish

AUSTEN *Pride and Prejudice* edited by Donald J. Gray

BRONTË, CHARLOTTE *Jane Eyre* edited by Richard J. Dunn

BRONTË, EMILY *Wuthering Heights*, Revised edited by William M. Sale, Jr.

CARROLL, LEWIS *Alice in Wonderland* edited by Donald J. Gray

CLEMENS *Adventures of Huckleberry Finn* edited by Sculley Bradley, Richmond Croom Beatty, and E. Hudson Long

CONRAD *Heart of Darkness*, Revised edited by Robert Kimbrough

CONRAD *Lord Jim* edited by Thomas Moser

CRANE *The Red Badge of Courage* edited by Sculley Bradley, Richmond Croom Beatty, and E. Hudson Long

Darwin edited by Philip Appleman

DICKENS *Hard Times* edited by George Ford and Sylvère Monod

John Donne's Poetry selected and edited by A. L. Clements

DOSTOEVSKY *Crime and Punishment* (the Coulson translation) edited by George Gibian

DREISER *Sister Carrie* edited by Donald Pizer

FLAUBERT *Madame Bovary* edited with a substantially new translation by Paul de Man

HARDY *The Return of the Native* edited by James Gindin

HARDY *Tess of the D'Urbervilles* edited by Scott Elledge

HAWTHORNE *The House of the Seven Gables* edited by Seymour L. Gross

HAWTHORNE *The Scarlet Letter* edited by Sculley Bradley, Richmond Croom Beatty, and E. Hudson Long

IBSEN *The Wild Duck* translated and edited by Dounia B. Christiani

JAMES *The Ambassadors* edited by S. P. Rosenbaum

JAMES *The Turn of the Screw* edited by Robert Kimbrough

MELVILLE *The Confidence-Man* edited by Hershel Parker

MELVILLE *Moby-Dick* edited by Harrison Hayford and Hershel Parker

NEWMAN *Apologia Pro Vita Sua* edited by David J. DeLaura

The Writings of St. Paul edited by Wayne A. Meeks

SHAKESPEARE *Hamlet* edited by Cyrus Hoy

SHAKESPEARE *Henry IV, Part I*, Revised edited by James L. Sanderson

Bernard Shaw's Plays edited by Warren Sylvester Smith

SOPHOCLES *Oedipus Tyrannus* translated and edited by Luci Berkowitz and Theodore F. Brunner

Edmund Spenser's Poetry selected and edited by Hugh Maclean

STENDHAL *Red and Black* translated and edited by Robert M. Adams

SWIFT *Gulliver's Travels*, Revised edited by Robert A. Greenberg

Tennyson's Poetry selected and edited by Robert W. Hill, Jr.

THOREAU *Walden and Civil Disobedience* edited by Owen Thomas

TOLSTOY *Anna Karenina* (the Maude translation) edited by George Gibian

TOLSTOY *War and Peace* (the Maude translation) edited by George Gibian

TURGENEV *Fathers and Sons* edited with a substantially new translation by Ralph E. Matlaw

VOLTAIRE *Candide* translated and edited by Robert M. Adams

WHITMAN *Leaves of Grass* edited by Sculley Bradley and Harold Blodgett

A Norton Critical Edition of Modern Drama edited by Anthony Caputi

Restoration and Eighteenth-Century Drama edited by Scott McMillin

➤➤➤ A NORTON CRITICAL EDITION ⫷⫷⫷

EMILY BRONTË

WUTHERING HEIGHTS

REVISED

AN AUTHORITATIVE TEXT
WITH ESSAYS IN CRITICISM

➤➤➤ ⫷⫷⫷

Edited by

WILLIAM M. SALE, JR.

PROFESSOR EMERITUS, CORNELL UNIVERSITY

W · W · NORTON & COMPANY · INC · *New York*

W. W. NORTON & COMPANY, INC.
also publishes

THE NORTON ANTHOLOGY OF ENGLISH LITERATURE
edited by M. H. Abrams et al.

THE NORTON ANTHOLOGY OF POETRY
edited by Arthur M. Eastman et al.

WORLD MASTERPIECES
edited by Maynard Mack et al.

THE NORTON READER
edited by Arthur M. Eastman et al.

THE NORTON FACSIMILE OF
THE FIRST FOLIO OF SHAKESPEARE
prepared by Charlton Hinman

and the NORTON CRITICAL EDITIONS

Library of Congress Cataloging in Publication Data

Brontë, Emily Jane, 1818-1848.
    Wuthering Heights, revised.

    (A Norton critical edition)
    Bibliography: p.
    I.   Sale, William Merritt, 1899-   ed.

II. Title.
PZ3.B7902W73 [PR4172]   823'.8   76-38631
ISBN 0-393-09400-6

PRINTED IN THE UNITED STATES OF AMERICA

1 2 3 4 5 6 7 8 9 0

Contents

Preface to the Revised Edition   vii
Preface   ix

The Text of *Wuthering Heights*   1

Biographical Notice of Ellis and Acton Bell (1850)   3
Editor's Preface to the New Edition of *Wuthering Heights* (1850)   9
Wuthering Heights   13
Textual Commentary   267

Contemporary Reviews and Essays in Criticism

CONTEMPORARY REVIEWS   277
From the *Palladium*   279
From the *Examiner*   281
From the *Britannia*   282
From the *North American Review*   283
From the *Leader*   284

ESSAYS IN CRITICISM   286
Charles Percy Sanger · The Structure of *Wuthering Heights*   286
David Cecil · Emily Brontë and *Wuthering Heights*   298
Q. D. Leavis · A Fresh Approach to *Wuthering Heights*   306
Inga-Stina Ewbank · [The Structure and Pattern of the Whole Novel]   322
John K. Mathison · Nelly Dean and the Power of *Wuthering Heights*   333
Carl R. Woodring · The Narrators of *Wuthering Heights*   353
Mary Visick · [Catherine Earnshaw and Edgar Linton]   358
Mark Schorer · Fiction and the "Analogical Matrix"   371
William M. Sale, Jr. · Emily Brontë's History of Gondal   376

Selected Bibliography   381

Preface to the Revised Edition

Significant changes in this edition appear among the Essays in Criticism with the omission of several articles and the inclusion of two pieces that have appeared since the publication of the first edition. Mrs. Leavis's "A Fresh Approach to *Wuthering Heights*" is really a fresh approach, the most far-ranging among recent commentaries. Inga-Stina Ewbank's discussion of the novel's structure seems more reasonably argued than the work of many others who have addressed themselves to this subject. For those curious about the possible relation between Emily Brontë's poems and her novel, I have provided an essay—"Emily Brontë's History of Gondal"— that includes the most convincing conjectures that have been offered.

In my note in the first edition on "Emily Brontë's copy of *Wuthering Heights*" I tentatively concluded that her copy, with some of her revisions, had indeed survived. I am now able to confirm this conjecture, though unfortunately not able to identify the present owner.

WILLIAM M. SALE, JR.

Ithaca, N.Y., 1971

Preface

Wuthering Heights was first published in December, 1847. Emily Brontë died a year later, and the second edition, revised by her sister Charlotte, did not appear until December, 1850. Charlotte Brontë had recognized that revision was required, since the first edition abounded in errors and inconsistencies, for many of which Emily's printer was responsible. But in trying to do justice to her sister's novel, she assumed privileges that now seem unwarranted. Therefore, it seems desirable to return to the first edition as a point of departure. My intention, like Charlotte's, is to provide a readable text, but at the same time to supply for the reader with a more special interest something other than the assurance that editions have been "collated." I have therefore noted all the substantive changes that I have made from the first edition (Notes to the Text, pp. 269–71), and I have indicated in Appendix I the departures made from that edition with respect to spelling and capitalization. Only the incredibly chaotic punctuation and such obvious errors as *to* for *two*, *who's* for *whose*, *Linton's* for *Lintons* have been corrected silently. When a change in punctuation is made to resolve an ambiguity in meaning, the original punctuation is recorded in the textual notes. In order to make clear the responsibilities of a modern editor, I have provided in a section following the text (pp. 267–69) a full account of the difficulties that Emily Brontë met with in the printing and publishing of her novel. To the best of my knowledge, this is the first time that such an account has been provided.

I have glossed at the foot of the appropriate pages those words of the Yorkshire dialect that I think the modern reader may have difficulty in understanding, and I have provided a few notes explaining other matters. This glossary seems to me to be long overdue, and the need in no satisfactory way supplied by Charlotte Brontë's occasional replacing of a word of dialect by its equivalent in standard English. Charlotte justified her changes by saying that Emily's orthography exactly rendered "the Yorkshire dialect to a Yorkshire ear," but "Southerns must find it unintelligible."[1] But she herself was so familiar with the dialect that she never really knew when a "Southern" needed help. Emily is no expert in reproducing dialect, but she is surprisingly good. Hers is at least a literary convention preferable to the hit-or-miss mixture of dialect and standard English which Charlotte produced.

The critical writing following the text includes a sampling of contemporary notices of the novel. These reviews are followed by a number of essays and articles that are designed to represent the critical opinion of this century. These critics have addressed themselves to most of the points that have challenged readers and occasioned controversy, but I have made no attempt to include all the shades of opinion that have emerged during the last twenty years or so. A reader interested in pursuing the subtle and sometimes tenuous course of recent controversy will find a guide to the more lively work of this sort in the Selected Bibliography of books and articles on Emily Brontë and on her novel.

WILLIAM M. SALE, JR.

Ithaca, N.Y.

1. *The Brontës: Their Lives, Friendships and Correspondence,* Oxford, Shakespeare Head Press, ed. Wise and Symington, 4 vols., 1932, III, 165.

The Text of
Wuthering Heights

Biographical Notice of
Ellis and Acton Bell
(1850)[1]

It has been thought that all the works published under the names of Currer, Ellis, and Acton Bell, were, in reality, the production of one person. This mistake I endeavoured to rectify by a few words of disclaimer prefixed to the third edition of *Jane Eyre*. These, too, it appears, failed to gain general credence, and now, on the occasion of a reprint of *Wuthering Heights* and *Agnes Grey*, I am advised distinctly to state how the case really stands.

Indeed, I feel myself that it is time the obscurity attending those two names—Ellis and Acton—was done away. The little mystery, which formerly yielded some harmless pleasure, has lost its interest; circumstances are changed. It becomes, then, my duty to explain briefly the origin and authorship of the books written by Currer, Ellis, and Acton Bell.

About five years ago, my two sisters and myself, after a somewhat prolonged period of separation, found ourselves reunited, and at home. Resident in a remote district where education had made little progress, and where, consequently, there was no inducement to seek social intercourse beyond our own domestic circle, we were wholly dependent on ourselves and each other, on books and study, for the enjoyments and occupations of life. The highest stimulus, as well as the liveliest pleasure we had known from childhood upwards, lay in attempts at literary composition; formerly we used to show each other what we wrote, but of late years this habit of communication and consultation had been discontinued; hence it ensued, that we were mutually ignorant of the progress we might respectively have made.

One day, in the autumn of 1845, I accidentally lighted on a MS. volume of verse in my sister Emily's handwriting. Of course, I was

1. This notice and the preface which follows were written by Charlotte Brontë for the second edition of her sister's novel, 1850, and are reprinted from that edition. Slight changes from this text appear in some later reprintings of the material.

3

not surprised, knowing that she could and did write verse: I looked
it over, and something more than surprise seized me,—a deep conviction that these were not common effusions, nor at all like the
poetry women generally write. I thought them condensed and terse,
vigorous and genuine. To my ear, they had also a peculiar music—
wild, melancholy, and elevating.

My sister Emily was not a person of demonstrative character, nor
one, on the recesses of whose mind and feelings, even those nearest
and dearest to her could, with impunity, intrude unlicensed; it took
hours to reconcile her to the discovery I had made, and days to
persuade her that such poems merited publication. I knew, however, that a mind like hers could not be without some latent spark
of honourable ambition, and refused to be discouraged in my attempts to fan that spark to flame.

Meantime, my younger sister quietly produced some of her own
compositions, intimating that since Emily's had given me pleasure,
I might like to look at hers. I could not but be a partial judge, yet
I thought that these verses too had a sweet sincere pathos of their
own.

We had very early cherished the dream of one day becoming
authors. This dream, never relinquished even when distance divided
and absorbing tasks occupied us, now suddenly acquired strength
and consistency: it took the character of a resolve. We agreed to
arrange a small selection of our poems, and, if possible, get them
printed. Averse to personal publicity, we veiled our own names
under those of Currer, Ellis, and Acton Bell; the ambiguous choice
being dictated by a sort of conscientious scruple at assuming Christian names positively masculine, while we did not like to declare
ourselves women, because—without at that time suspecting that our
mode of writing and thinking was not what is called "feminine"—
we had a vague impression that authoresses are liable to be looked
on with prejudice; we had noticed how critics sometimes use for
their chastisement the weapon of personality, and for their reward,
a flattery, which is not true praise.

The bringing out of our little book was hard work. As was to be
expected, neither we nor our poems were at all wanted; but for this
we had been prepared at the outset; though inexperienced ourselves,
we had read the experience of others. The great puzzle lay in the
difficulty of getting answers of any kind from the publishers to
whom we applied. Being greatly harassed by this obstacle, I ventured to apply to the Messrs. Chambers, of Edinburgh, for a word
of advice; *they* may have forgotten the circumstance, but *I* have
not, for from them I received a brief and business-like but civil
and sensible reply, on which we acted, and at last made a way.

The book was printed: it is scarcely known, and all of it that merits to be known are the poems of Ellis Bell. The fixed conviction I held, and hold, of the worth of these poems has not indeed received the confirmation of much favourable criticism; but I must retain it notwithstanding.

Ill-success failed to crush us: the mere effort to succeed had given a wonderful zest to existence; it must be pursued. We each set to work on a prose tale: Ellis Bell produced *Wuthering Heights*, Acton Bell *Agnes Grey*, and Currer Bell also wrote a narrative in one volume. These MSS. were perseveringly obtruded upon various publishers for the space of a year and a half; usually, their fate was an ignominious and abrupt dismissal.

At last *Wuthering Heights* and *Agnes Grey* were accepted on terms somewhat impoverishing to the two authors; Currer Bell's book found acceptance nowhere, nor any acknowledgment of merit, so that something like the chill of despair began to invade his heart. As a forlorn hope, he tried one publishing house more—Messrs. Smith and Elder. Ere long, in a much shorter space than that on which experience had taught him to calculate—there came a letter, which he opened in the dreary expectation of finding two hard hopeless lines, intimating that Messrs. Smith and Elder "were not disposed to publish the MS.," and, instead, he took out of the envelope a letter of two pages. He read it trembling. It declined, indeed, to publish that tale, for business reasons, but it discussed its merits and demerits so courteously, so considerately, in a spirit so rational, with a discrimination so enlightened, that this very refusal cheered the author better than a vulgarly-expressed acceptance would have done. It was added, that a work in three volumes would meet with careful attention.

I was then just completing *Jane Eyre*, at which I had been working while the one volume tale was plodding its weary round in London: in three weeks I sent it off; friendly and skilful hands took it in. This was in the commencement of September 1847; it came out before the close of October following, while *Wuthering Heights* and *Agnes Grey*, my sisters' works, which had already been in the press for months, still lingered under a different management.

They appeared at last. Critics failed to do them justice. The immature but very real powers revealed in *Wuthering Heights* were scarcely recognised; its import and nature were misunderstood; the identity of its author was misrepresented; it was said that this was an earlier and ruder attempt of the same pen which had produced *Jane Eyre*. Unjust and grievous error! We laughed at it at first, but I deeply lament it now. Hence, I fear, arose a prejudice against the book. That writer who could attempt to palm off an inferior and immature production under cover of one successful effort, must indeed be unduly eager after the secondary and sordid result of authorship, and pitiably indifferent to its true and honourable meed. If reviewers and the public truly believed this, no wonder that they looked darkly on the cheat.

Yet I must not be understood to make these things subject for reproach or complaint; I dare not do so; respect for my sister's memory forbids me. By her any such querulous manifestation would have been regarded as an unworthy, and offensive weakness.

It is my duty, as well as my pleasure, to acknowledge one exception to the general rule of criticism. One writer,[2] endowed with the keen vision and fine sympathies of genius, has discerned the real nature of *Wuthering Heights*, and has, with equal accuracy, noted its beauties and touched on its faults. Too often do reviewers remind us of the mob of Astrologers, Chaldeans, and Soothsayers gathered before the "writing on the wall," and unable to read the characters or make known the interpretation. We have a right to rejoice when a true seer comes at last, some man in whom is an excellent spirit, to whom have been given light, wisdom, and understanding; who can accurately read the "Mene, Mene, Tekel, Upharsin" of an original mind (however unripe, however inefficiently cultured and partially expanded that mind may be); and who can say with confidence, "This is the interpretation thereof."

Yet even the writer to whom I allude shares the mistake about the authorship, and does me the injustice to suppose that there was equivoque in my former rejection of this honour (as an honour, I regard it). May I assure him that I would scorn in this and in every other case to deal in equivoque; I believe language to have been given us to make our meaning clear, and not to wrap it in dishonest doubt.

The Tenant of Wildfell Hall by Acton Bell, had likewise an unfavourable reception. At this I cannot wonder. The choice of subject was an entire mistake. Nothing less congruous with the writer's nature could be conceived. The motives which dictated this choice were pure, but, I think, slightly morbid. She had, in the course of her life, been called on to contemplate, near at hand and for a long time, the terrible effects of talents misused and faculties abused; hers was naturally a sensitive, reserved, and dejected nature; what she saw sank very deeply into her mind; it did her harm. She brooded over it till she believed it to be a duty to reproduce every detail (of course with fictitious characters, incidents, and situations) as a warning to others. She hated her work, but would pursue it. When reasoned with on the subject, she regarded such reasonings as a temptation to self-indulgence. She must be honest; she must not varnish, soften, or conceal. This well-meant resolution brought on her misconstruction and some abuse, which she bore, as it was

2. See the *Palladium* for September 1850. [*Author's note*]

her custom to bear whatever was unpleasant, with mild, steady patience. She was a very sincere and practical Christian, but the tinge of religious melancholy communicated a sad shade to her brief, blameless life.

Neither Ellis nor Acton allowed herself for one moment to sink under want of encouragement; energy nerved the one, and endurance upheld the other. They were both prepared to try again; I would fain think that hope and the sense of power was yet strong within them. But a great change approached: affliction came in that shape which to anticipate is dread; to look back on, grief. In the very heat and burden of the day, the labourers failed over their work.

My sister Emily first declined. The details of her illness are deep-branded in my memory, but to dwell on them, either in thought or narrative, is not in my power. Never in all her life had she lingered over any task that lay before her, and she did not linger now. She sank rapidly. She made haste to leave us. Yet, while physically she perished, mentally, she grew stronger than we had yet known her. Day by day, when I saw with what a front she met suffering, I looked on her with an anguish of wonder and love. I have seen nothing like it; but, indeed, I have never seen her parallel in anything. Stronger than a man, simpler than a child, her nature stood alone. The awful point was, that, while full of ruth for others, on herself she had no pity; the spirit was inexorable to the flesh; from the trembling hand, the unnerved limbs, the faded eyes, the same service was exacted as they had rendered in health. To stand by and witness this, and not dare to remonstrate, was a pain no words can render.

Two cruel months of hope and fear passed painfully by, and the day came at last when the terrors and pains of death were to be undergone by this treasure, which had grown dearer and dearer to our hearts as it wasted before our eyes. Towards the decline of that day, we had nothing of Emily but her mortal remains as consumption left them. She died December 19, 1848.

We thought this enough; but we were utterly and presumptuously wrong. She was not buried ere Anne fell ill. She had not been committed to the grave a fortnight, before we received distinct intimation that it was necessary to prepare our minds to see the younger sister go after the elder. Accordingly, she followed in the same path with slower step, and with a patience that equalled the other's fortitude. I have said that she was religious, and it was by leaning on those Christian doctrines in which she firmly believed, that she found support through her most painful journey. I witnessed their efficacy in her latest hour and greatest trial, and must bear my testimony to the calm triumph with which they brought her through. She died May 28, 1849.

What more shall I say about them? I cannot and need not say much more. In externals, they were two unobtrusive women; a perfectly secluded life gave them retiring manners and habits. In Emily's nature the extremes of vigour and simplicity seemed to meet. Under an unsophisticated culture, inartificial tastes, and an unpretending outside, lay a secret power and fire that might have informed the brain and kindled the veins of a hero; but she had no worldly wisdom; her powers were unadapted to the practical business of life; she would fail to defend her most manifest rights, to consult her most legitimate advantage. An interpreter ought always to have stood between her and the world. Her will was not very flexible, and it generally opposed her interest. Her temper was magnanimous, but warm and sudden; her spirit altogether unbending.

Anne's character was milder and more subdued; she wanted the power, the fire, the originality of her sister, but was well-endowed with quiet virtues of her own. Long-suffering, self-denying, reflective, and intelligent, a constitutional reserve and taciturnity placed and kept her in the shade, and covered her mind, and especially her feelings, with a sort of nun-like veil, which was rarely lifted. Neither Emily nor Anne was learned; they had no thought of filling their pitchers at the well-spring of other minds; they always wrote from the impulse of nature, the dictates of intuition, and from such stores of observation as their limited experience had enabled them to amass. I may sum up all by saying, that for strangers they were nothing, for superficial observers less than nothing; but for those who had known them all their lives in the intimacy of close relationship, they were genuinely good and truly great.

This notice has been written, because I felt it a sacred duty to wipe the dust off their gravestones, and leave their dear names free from soil.

CURRER BELL.

September 19, 1850.

Editor's Preface
to the New Edition of
Wuthering Heights (1850)

I have just read over "Wuthering Heights," and, for the first time, have obtained a clear glimpse of what are termed (and, perhaps, really are) its faults; have gained a definite notion of how it appears to other people—to strangers who knew nothing of the author; who are unacquainted with the locality where the scenes of the story are laid; to whom the inhabitants, the customs, the natural characteristics of the outlying hills and hamlets in the West-Riding of Yorkshire are things alien and unfamiliar.

To all such "Wuthering Heights" must appear a rude and strange production. The wild moors of the north of England can for them have no interest; the language, the manners, the very dwellings and household customs of the scattered inhabitants of those districts, must be to such readers in a great measure unintelligible, and—where intelligible—repulsive. Men and women who, perhaps, naturally very calm, and with feelings moderate in degree, and little marked in kind, have been trained from their cradle to observe the utmost evenness of manner and guardedness of language, will hardly know what to make of the rough, strong utterance, the harshly manifested passions, the unbridled aversions, and headlong partialities of unlettered moorland hinds and rugged moorland squires, who have grown up untaught and unchecked, except by mentors as harsh as themselves. A large class of readers, likewise, will suffer greatly from the introduction into the pages of this work of words printed with all their letters, which it has become the custom to represent by the initial and final letter only—a blank line filling the interval. I may as well say at once that, for this circumstance, it is out of my power to apologize; deeming it, myself, a rational plan to write words at full length. The practice of hinting by single letters those expletives with which profane and violent persons are wont to garnish their discourse, strikes me as a proceeding which, however well meant, is weak and futile. I cannot tell what good it does

9

—what feeling it spares—what horror it conceals.

With regard to the rusticity of "Wuthering Heights," I admit the charge, for I feel the quality. It is rustic all through. It is moorish, and wild, and knotty as a root of heath. Nor was it natural that it should be otherwise; the author being herself a native and nursling of the moors. Doubtless, had her lot been cast in a town, her writings, if she had written at all, would have possessed another character. Even had chance or taste led her to choose a similar subject, she would have treated it otherwise. Had Ellis Bell been a lady or a gentleman accustomed to what is called "the world," her view of a remote and unreclaimed region, as well as of the dwellers therein, would have differed greatly from that actually taken by the homebred country girl. Doubtless it would have been wider—more comprehensive: whether it would have been more original or more truthful is not so certain. As far as the scenery and locality are concerned, it could scarcely have been so sympathetic: Ellis Bell did not describe as one whose eye and taste alone found pleasure in the prospect; her native hills were far more to her than a spectacle; they were what she lived in, and by, as much as the wild birds, their tenants, or as the heather, their produce. Her descriptions, then, of natural scenery, are what they should be, and all they should be.

Where delineation of human character is concerned, the case is different. I am bound to avow that she had scarcely more practical knowledge of the peasantry amongst whom she lived, than a nun has of the country people who sometimes pass her convent gates. My sister's disposition was not naturally gregarious; circumstances favoured and fostered her tendency to seclusion; except to go to church or take a walk on the hills, she rarely crossed the threshold of home. Though her feeling for the people round was benevolent, intercourse with them she never sought; nor, with very few exceptions, ever experienced. And yet she knew them: knew their ways, their language, their family histories; she could hear of them with interest, and talk of them with detail, minute, graphic, and accurate; but *with* them, she rarely exchanged a word. Hence it ensued that what her mind had gathered of the real concerning them, was too exclusively confined to those tragic and terrible traits of which, in listening to the secret annals of every rude vicinage, the memory is sometimes compelled to receive the impress. Her imagination, which was a spirit more sombre than sunny, more powerful than sportive, found in such traits material whence it wrought creations like Heathcliff, like Earnshaw, like Catherine. Having formed these beings, she did not know what she had done. If the auditor of her work when read in manuscript, shuddered under the grinding influence of natures so relentless and implacable, of spirits so lost and fallen; if it was complained that the mere hearing of certain vivid and fearful scenes banished sleep by night, and disturbed mental peace by day, Ellis Bell would wonder what was meant, and suspect the complainant of affectation. Had she but lived, her mind would of itself have grown like a strong tree, loftier, straighter, wider-spreading, and its matured fruits would have attained a mellower ripeness and sunnier bloom; but on that mind time and experience alone could work: to the influence of other intellects, it was not amenable.

Having avowed that over much of "Wuthering Heights" there broods "a horror of great darkness;" that, in its storm-heated and electrical atmosphere, we seem at times to breathe lightning, let me point to those spots where clouded daylight and the eclipsed sun still attest their existence. For a specimen of true benevolence and homely fidelity, look at the character of Nelly Dean; for an example of constancy and tenderness, remark that of Edgar Linton. (Some people will think these qualities do not shine so well incarnate in a man as they would do in a woman, but Ellis Bell could never be brought to comprehend this notion: nothing moved her more than any insinuation that the faithfulness and clemency, the long-suffering and loving-kindness which are esteemed virtues in the daughters of Eve, become foibles in the sons of Adam. She held that mercy and forgiveness are the divinest attributes of the Great Being who made both man and woman, and that what clothes the Godhead in glory, can disgrace no form of feeble humanity.) There is a dry saturnine humour in the delineation of old Joseph, and some glimpses of grace and gaiety animate the younger Catherine. Nor is even the first heroine of the name destitute of a certain strange beauty in her fierceness, or of honesty in the midst of perverted passion and passionate perversity.

Heathcliff, indeed, stands unredeemed; never once swerving in his arrow-straight course to perdition, from the time when "the little black-haired, swarthy thing, as dark as if it came from the Devil," was first unrolled out of the bundle and set on its feet in the farm-house kitchen, to the hour when Nelly Dean found the grim, stalwart corpse laid on its back in the panel-enclosed bed, with wide-gazing eyes that seemed "to sneer at her attempt to close them, and parted lips and sharp white teeth that sneered too."

Heathcliff betrays one solitary human feeling, and that is *not* his love for Catherine; which is a sentiment fierce and inhuman: a passion such as might boil and glow in the bad essence of some evil genius; a fire that might form the tormented centre—the ever-suffering soul of a magnate of the infernal world: and by its quenchless and ceaseless ravage effect the execution of the decree which dooms him to carry Hell with him wherever he wanders. No; the single link that connects Heathcliff with humanity is his rudely confessed regard for Hareton Earnshaw—-the young man whom he has ruined; and then his half-implied esteem for Nelly Dean. These solitary traits omitted, we should say he was child neither of Lascar nor gipsy, but a man's shape animated by demon life—a Ghoul—an Afreet.

Whether it is right or advisable to create beings like Heathcliff, I do not know: I scarcely think it is. But this I know; the writer who possesses the creative gift owns something of which he is not always master—something that at times strangely wills and works for itself. He may lay down rules and devise principles, and to rules and principles it will perhaps for years lie in subjection; and then, haply without any warning of revolt, there comes a time when it will no longer consent "to harrow the vallies, or be bound with a band in the furrow"—when it "laughs at the multitude of the city, and regards not the crying of the driver"—when, refusing absolutely to make ropes out of sea-sand any longer, it sets to work on statue-hewing, and you have a Pluto or a Jove, a Tisiphone or a Psyche, a Mermaid or a Madonna, as Fate or Inspiration direct. Be the work grim or glorious, dread or divine, you have little choice left but quiescent adoption. As for you—the nominal artist—your share in it has been to work passively under dictates you neither delivered nor could question—that would not be uttered at your prayer, nor suppressed nor changed at your caprice. If the result be attractive, the World will praise you, who little deserve praise; if it be repulsive, the same World will blame you, who almost as little deserve blame.

"Wuthering Heights" was hewn in a wild workshop, with simple tools, out of homely materials. The statuary found a granite block on a solitary moor: gazing thereon, he saw how from the crag might be elicited a head, savage, swart, sinister; a form moulded with at least one element of grandeur—power. He wrought with a rude chisel, and from no model but the vision of his meditations. With time and labour, the crag took human shape; and there it stands colossal, dark, and frowning, half statue, half rock: in the former sense, terrible and goblin-like; in the latter, almost beautiful, for its colouring is of mellow grey, and moorland moss clothes it; and heath, with its blooming bells and balmy fragrance, grows faithfully close to the giant's foot.

CURRER BELL.

Wuthering Heights

Chapter I

1801——I have just returned from a visit to my landlord—the solitary neighbour that I shall be troubled with. This is certainly a beautiful country! In all England, I do not believe that I could have fixed on a situation so completely removed from the stir of society. A perfect misanthropist's heaven—and Mr. Heathcliff and I are such a suitable pair to divide the desolation between us. A capital fellow! He little imagined how my heart warmed towards him when I beheld his black eyes withdraw so suspiciously under their brows, as I rode up, and when his fingers sheltered themselves, with a jealous resolution, still further in his waistcoat, as I announced my name.

"Mr. Heathcliff?" I said.

A nod was the answer.

"Mr. Lockwood, your new tenant, sir. I do myself the honour of calling as soon as possible after my arrival, to express the hope that I have not inconvenienced you by my perseverance in soliciting the occupation of Thrushcross Grange: I heard, yesterday, you had had some thoughts—"

"Thrushcross Grange is my own, sir," he interrupted, wincing, "I should not allow any one to inconvenience me, if I could hinder it—walk in!"

The "walk in," was uttered with closed teeth and expressed the sentiment, "Go to the Deuce!". Even the gate over which he leant manifested no sympathizing movement to the words, and I think that circumstance determined me to accept the invitation: I felt interested in a man who seemed more exaggeratedly reserved than myself.

When he saw my horse's breast fairly pushing the barrier, he did pull out his hand to unchain it, and then sullenly preceded me up the causeway, calling, as we entered the court—

"Joseph, take Mr. Lockwood's horse; and bring up some wine."

"Here we have the whole establishment of domestics, I suppose," was the reflection, suggested by this compound order. "No wonder the grass grows up between the flags, and cattle are the only hedge-cutters."

Joseph was an elderly, nay, an old man, very old, perhaps, though hale and sinewy.

"The Lord help us!" he soliloquized in an undertone of peevish displeasure, while relieving me of my horse: looking, meantime, in my face so sourly that I charitably conjectured he must have need of divine aid to digest his dinner, and his pious ejaculation had no reference to my unexpected advent.

Wuthering Heights is the name of Mr. Heathcliff's dwelling. "Wuthering" being a significant provincial adjective, descriptive of the atmospheric tumult to which its station is exposed in stormy weather. Pure, bracing ventilation they must have up there, at all times, indeed: one may guess the power of the north wind, blowing over the edge, by the excessive slant of a few stunted firs at the end of the house; and by a range of gaunt thorns all stretching their limbs one way, as if craving alms of the sun. Happily, the architect had foresight to build it strong: the narrow windows are deeply set in the wall, and the corners defended with large jutting stones.

Before passing the threshold, I paused to admire a quantity of grotesque carving lavished over the front, and especially about the principal door, above which, among a wilderness of crumbling griffins and shameless little boys, I detected the date "1500," and the name "Hareton Earnshaw." I would have made a few comments, and requested a short history of the place from the surly owner, but his attitude at the door appeared to demand my speedy entrance, or complete departure, and I had no desire to aggravate his impatience, previous to inspecting the penetralium.

One step brought us into the family sitting-room, without any introductory lobby or passage: they call it here "the house" preeminently. It includes kitchen and parlour, generally, but I believe at Wuthering Heights the kitchen is forced to retreat altogether into another quarter; at least I distinguished a chatter of tongues, and a clatter of culinary utensils deep within; and I observed no signs of roasting, boiling, or baking about the huge fire-place; nor any glitter of copper saucepans and tin cullenders on the walls. One end, indeed, reflected splendidly both light and heat from ranks of immense pewter dishes, interspersed with silver jugs and tankards, towering row after row, in a vast oak dresser, to the very roof. The latter had never been underdrawn: its entire anatomy lay bare to an inquiring eye, except where a frame of wood laden with oatcakes, and clusters of legs of beef, mutton, and ham, concealed it. Above the chimney were sundry villanous old guns, and a couple of horse-pistols, and, by way of ornament, three gaudily-painted canisters disposed along its ledge. The floor was of smooth, white stone; the chairs, high-backed, primitive structures, painted green, one or two heavy black ones lurking in the shade. In an arch under the dresser, reposed a huge, liver-coloured bitch pointer surrounded by a swarm of squealing puppies, and other dogs haunted other recesses.

The apartment and furniture would have been nothing extraordinary as belonging to a homely, northern farmer, with a stubborn countenance, and stalwart limbs set out to advantage in knee-breeches and gaiters. Such an individual, seated in his arm-chair, his mug of ale frothing on the round table before him, is to be seen in any circuit of five or six miles among these hills, if you go at the right time, after dinner. But Mr. Heathcliff forms a singular contrast to his abode and style of living. He is a dark-skinned gypsy in aspect, in dress and manners a gentleman, that is, as much a gentleman as many a country squire: rather slovenly, perhaps, yet not looking amiss with his negligence, because he has an erect and handsome figure—and rather morose. Possibly, some people might suspect him of a degree of under-bred pride; I have a sympathetic chord within that tells me it is nothing of the sort: I know, by instinct, his reserve springs from an aversion to showy displays of feeling—to manifestations of mutual kindliness. He'll love and hate, equally under cover, and esteem it a species of impertinence to be loved or hated again—No, I'm running on too fast—I bestow my own attributes over-liberally on him. Mr. Heath-cliff may have entirely dissimilar reasons for keeping his hand out of the way when he meets a would-be acquaintance, to those which actuate me. Let me hope my constitution is almost peculiar: my dear mother used to say I should never have a comfortable home, and only last summer I proved myself perfectly unworthy of one.

While enjoying a month of fine weather at the sea-coast, I was thrown into the company of a most fascinating creature, a real goddess in my eyes, as long as she took no notice of me. I "never told my love" vocally; still, if looks have language, the merest idiot might have guessed I was over head and ears: she understood me at last, and looked a return—the sweetest of all imaginable looks. And what did I do? I confess it with shame—shrunk icily into myself, like a snail; at every glance retired colder and farther; till, finally, the poor innocent was led to doubt her own senses, and, overwhelmed with confusion at her supposed mistake, persuaded her mamma to decamp.

By this curious turn of disposition I have gained the reputation of deliberate heartlessness, how undeserved, I alone can appreciate.

I took a seat at the end of the hearthstone opposite that towards which my landlord advanced, and filled up an interval of silence by attempting to caress the canine mother, who had left her nursery and was sneaking wolfishly to the back of my legs, her lip curled up, and her white teeth watering for a snatch.

My caress provoked a long, guttural gnarl.

"You'd better let the dog alone," growled Mr. Heathcliff in unison, checking fiercer demonstrations with a punch of his foot. "She's not accustomed to be spoiled—not kept for a pet."

Then, striding to a side-door, he shouted again—

"Joseph!"

Joseph mumbled indistinctly in the depths of the cellar, but gave no intimation of ascending; so his master dived down to him, leaving me *vis-à-vis* the ruffianly bitch and a pair of grim, shaggy sheep dogs, who shared with her a jealous guardianship over all my movements.

Not anxious to come in contact with their fangs, I sat still; but, imagining they would scarcely understand tacit insults, I unfortunately indulged in winking and making faces at the trio, and some turn of my physiognomy so irritated madam, that she suddenly broke into a fury and leapt on my knees. I flung her back, and hastened to interpose the table between us. This proceeding roused the whole hive. Half-a-dozen four-footed fiends, of various sizes and ages, issued from hidden dens to the common centre. I felt my heels and coat-laps peculiar subjects of assault; and, parrying off the larger combatants as effectually as I could with the poker, I was constrained to demand, aloud, assistance from some of the household in re-establishing peace.

Mr. Heathcliff and his man climbed the cellar steps with vexatious phlegm. I don't think they moved one second faster than usual, though the hearth was an absolute tempest of worrying and yelping.

Happily, an inhabitant of the kitchen made more dispatch; a lusty dame, with tucked-up gown, bare arms, and fire-flushed cheeks, rushed into the midst of us flourishing a frying-pan; and used that weapon, and her tongue, to such purpose, that the storm subsided magically, and she only remained, heaving like a sea after a high wind, when her master entered on the scene.

"What the devil is the matter?" he asked, eyeing me in a manner that I could ill endure after this inhospitable treatment.

"What the devil, indeed!" I muttered. "The herd of possessed swine could have had no worse spirits in them than those animals of yours, sir. You might as well leave a stranger with a brood of tigers!"

"They won't meddle with persons who touch nothing," he remarked, putting the bottle before me, and restoring the displaced table. "The dogs do right to be vigilant. Take a glass of wine?"

"No, thank you."

"Not bitten, are you?"

"If I had been, I would have set my signet on the biter."

Heathcliff's countenance relaxed into a grin.

"Come, come," he said, "you are flurried, Mr. Lockwood. Here, take a little wine. Guests are so exceedingly rare in this house that I and my dogs, I am willing to own, hardly know how to receive them. Your health, sir!"

I bowed and returned the pledge, beginning to perceive that it would be foolish to sit sulking for the misbehaviour of a pack of curs: besides, I felt loath to yield the fellow further amusement, at my expense, since his humour took that turn.

He—probably swayed by prudential considerations of the folly of offending a good tenant—relaxed a little, in the laconic style of chipping off his pronouns and auxiliary verbs, and introduced what he supposed would be a subject of interest to me, a discourse on the advantages and disadvantages of my present place of retirement.

I found him very intelligent on the topics we touched; and, before I went home, I was encouraged so far as to volunteer another visit to-morrow.

He evidently wished no repetition of my intrusion. I shall go, notwithstanding. It is astonishing how sociable I feel myself compared with him.

Chapter II

Yesterday afternoon set in misty and cold. I had half a mind to spend it by my study fire, instead of wading through heath and mud to Wuthering Heights.

On coming up from dinner, however (N. B. I dine between twelve and one o'clock; the housekeeper, a matronly lady taken as a fixture along with the house, could not, or would not comprehend my request that I might be served at five.)—on mounting the stairs with this lazy intention, and stepping into the room, I saw a servant-girl on her knees, surrounded by brushes and coal-scuttles, and raising an infernal dust as she extinguished the flames with heaps of cinders. This spectacle drove me back immediately; I took my hat, and, after a four miles' walk, arrived at Heathcliff's garden gate just in time to escape the first feathery flakes of a snow shower.

On that bleak hill-top the earth was hard with a black frost, and the air made me shiver through every limb. Being unable to remove the chain, I jumped over, and, running up the flagged causeway bordered with straggling gooseberry bushes, knocked vainly for admittance, till my knuckles tingled and the dogs howled.

"Wretched inmates!" I ejaculated, mentally, "you deserve perpetual isolation from your species for your churlish inhospitality. At least, I would not keep my doors barred in the day time. I don't care—I will get in!"

So resolved, I grasped the latch and shook it vehemently. Vinegar-faced Joseph projected his head from a round window of the barn.

"Whet are ye for?" he shouted. "T' maister's dahn i' t'fowld. Goa rahnd by th' end ut' laith, if yah went tuh spake tull him."[3]

"Is there nobody inside to open the door?" I hallooed, responsively.

"They's nobbut t' missis; and shoo'll nut oppen't an ye mak yer flaysome dins till neeght."[4]

"Why? cannot you tell her who I am, eh, Joseph?"

"Nor-ne me![5] Aw'll hae noa hend wi't," muttered the head vanishing.

The snow began to drive thickly. I seized the handle to essay another trial, when a young man, without coat, and shouldering a pitchfork, appeared in the yard behind. He hailed me to follow him, and, after marching through a washhouse and a paved area containing a coal-shed, pump, and pigeon cote, we at length arrived in the large, warm, cheerful apartment where I was formerly received.

It glowed delightfully in the radiance of an immense fire, compounded of coal, peat, and wood; and near the table, laid for a plentiful evening meal, I was pleased to observe the "missis," an individual whose existence I had never previously suspected.

I bowed and waited, thinking she would bid me take a seat. She looked at me, leaning back in her chair, and remained motionless and mute.

"Rough weather!" I remarked. "I'm afraid, Mrs. Heathcliff, the door must bear the consequence of your servants' leisure attendance: I had hard work to make them hear me!"

She never opened her mouth. I stared—she stared also. At any rate, she kept her eyes on me, in a cool, regardless manner, exceedingly embarrassing and disagreeable.

"Sit down," said the young man, gruffly. "He'll be in soon."

I obeyed; and hemmed, and called the villain Juno, who deigned, at this second interview, to move the extreme tip of her tail, in token of owning my acquaintance.

"A beautiful animal!" I commenced again. "Do you intend parting with the little ones, madam?"

"They are not mine," said the amiable hostess more repellingly than Heathcliff himself could have replied.

"Ah, your favourites are among these!" I continued, turning to an obscure cushion full of something like cats.

3. See p. 272 for some general comments on Emily Brontë's transcription of dialect; *t'fowld:* the fold; *ut' laith:* of the barn.

4. *Nobbut:* only; *shoo'll:* she'll; *flaysome:* terrible.

5. *Nor-ne me:* not me.

"A strange choice of favourites," she observed scornfully.

Unluckily, it was a heap of dead rabbits. I hemmed once more, and drew closer to the hearth, repeating my comment on the wildness of the evening.

"You should not have come out," she said, rising and reaching from the chimney-piece two of the painted canisters.

Her position before was sheltered from the light; now, I had a distinct view of her whole figure and countenance. She was slender, and apparently scarcely past girlhood: an admirable form, and the most exquisite little face that I have ever had the pleasure of beholding: small features, very fair; flaxen ringlets, or rather golden, hanging loose on her delicate neck; and eyes—had they been agreeable in expression, they would have been irresistible. Fortunately for my susceptible heart, the only sentiment they evinced hovered between scorn and a kind of desperation, singularly unnatural to be detected there.

The canisters were almost out of her reach; I made a motion to aid her; she turned upon me as a miser might turn if any one attempted to assist him in counting his gold.

"I don't want your help," she snapped, "I can get them for myself."

"I beg your pardon," I hastened to reply.

"Were you asked to tea?" she demanded, tying an apron over her neat black frock, and standing with a spoonful of the leaf poised over the pot.

"I shall be glad to have a cup," I answered.

"Were you asked?" she repeated.

"No," I said, half smiling. "You are the proper person to ask me."

She flung the tea back, spoon and all, and resumed her chair in a pet, her forehead corrugated, and her red under-lip pushed out, like a child's, ready to cry.

Meanwhile, the young man had slung onto his person a decidedly shabby upper garment, and, erecting himself before the blaze, looked down on me from the corner of his eyes, for all the world as if there were some mortal feud unavenged between us. I began to doubt whether he were a servant or not; his dress and speech were both rude, entirely devoid of the superiority observable in Mr. and Mrs. Heathcliff; his thick, brown curls were rough and uncultivated, his whiskers encroached bearishly over his cheeks, and his hands were embrowned like those of a common labourer. Still his bearing was free, almost haughty, and he showed none of a domestic's assiduity in attending on the lady of the house.

In the absence of clear proofs of his condition, I deemed it best to abstain from noticing his curious conduct, and, five minutes afterwards, the entrance of Heathcliff relieved me, in some measure, from my uncomfortable state.

"You see, sir, I am come according to promise!" I exclaimed, assuming the cheerful; "and I fear I shall be weather-bound for half an hour, if you can afford me shelter during that space."

"Half an hour?" he said, shaking the white flakes from his clothes; "I wonder you should select the thick of a snow-storm to ramble about in. Do you know that you run a risk of being lost in the marshes? People familiar with these moors often miss their road on such evenings, and, I can tell you, there is no chance of a change at present."

"Perhaps I can get a guide among your lads, and he might stay at the Grange till morning—could you spare me one?"

"No, I could not."

"Oh, indeed! Well, then, I must trust to my own sagacity."

"Umph."

"Are you going to mak th' tea?" demanded he of the shabby coat, shifting his ferocious gaze from me to the young lady.

"Is *he* to have any?" she asked, appealing to Heathcliff.

"Get it ready, will you?" was the answer, uttered so savagely that I started. The tone in which the words were said revealed a genuine bad nature. I no longer felt inclined to call Heathcliff a capital fellow.

When the preparations were finished, he invited me with—

"Now, sir, bring forward your chair." And we all, including the rustic youth, drew round the table, an austere silence prevailing while we discussed our meal.

I thought, if I had caused the cloud, it was my duty to make an effort to dispel it. They could not every day sit so grim and taciturn, and it was impossible, however ill-tempered they might be, that the universal scowl they wore was their every day countenance.

"It is strange," I began in the interval of swallowing one cup of tea and receiving another, "it is strange how custom can mould our tastes and ideas; many could not imagine the existence of happiness in a life of such complete exile from the world as you spend, Mr. Heathcliff; yet, I'll venture to say, that, surrounded by your family, and with your amiable lady as the presiding genius over your home and heart—"

"My amiable lady!" he interrupted, with an almost diabolical sneer on his face. "Where is she—my amiable lady?"

"Mrs. Heathcliff, your wife, I mean."

"Well, yes—Oh! you would intimate that her spirit has taken the post of ministering angel, and guards the fortunes of Wuthering Heights, even when her body is gone. Is that it?"

Perceiving myself in a blunder, I attempted to correct it. I might have seen there was too great a disparity between the ages of the parties to make it likely that they were man and wife. One was about forty, a period of mental vigour at which men seldom cherish the delusion of being married for love, by girls: that dream is reserved for the solace of our declining years. The other did not look seventeen.

Then it flashed upon me—"The clown at my elbow, who is drinking his tea out of a basin and eating his bread with unwashed hands, may be her husband. Heathcliff, junior, of course. Here is the consequence of being buried alive: she has thrown herself away upon that boor, from sheer ignorance that better individuals existed! A sad pity—I must beware how I cause her to regret her choice."

The last reflection may seem conceited; it was not. My neighbour struck me as bordering on repulsive. I knew, through experience, that I was tolerably attractive.

"Mrs. Heathcliff is my daughter-in-law," said Heathcliff, corroborating my surmise. He turned, as he spoke, a peculiar look in her direction, a look of hatred, unless he has a most perverse set of facial muscles that will not, like those of other people, interpret the language of his soul.

"Ah, certainly—I see now; you are the favoured possessor of the beneficent fairy," I remarked, turning to my neighbour.

This was worse than before: the youth grew crimson, and clenched his fist with every appearance of a meditated assault. But he seemed to recollect himself, presently, and smothered the storm in a brutal curse, muttered on my behalf, which, however, I took care not to notice.

"Unhappy in your conjectures, sir!" observed my host; "we neither of us have the privilege of owning your good fairy; her mate is dead. I said she was my daughter-in-law, therefore, she must have married my son."

"And this young man is—"

"Not my son, assuredly!"

Heathcliff smiled again, as if it were rather too bold a jest to attribute the paternity of that bear to him.

"My name is Hareton Earnshaw," growled the other; "and I'd counsel you to respect it!"

"I have shown no disrespect," was my reply, laughing internally at the dignity with which he announced himself.

He fixed his eye on me longer than I cared to return the stare, for fear I might be tempted either to box his ears, or render my hilarity audible. I began to feel unmistakably out of place in that pleasant family circle. The dismal spiritual atmosphere overcame, and more than neutralized the glowing physical comforts round me; and I resolved to be cautious how I ventured under those rafters a third time.

The business of eating being concluded, and no one uttering a word of sociable conversation, I approached a window to examine the weather.

A sorrowful sight I saw: dark night coming down prematurely, and sky and hills mingled in one bitter whirl of wind and suffocating snow.

"I don't think it possible for me to get home now, without a guide," I could not help exclaiming. "The roads will be buried already; and, if they were bare, I could scarcely distinguish a foot in advance."

"Hareton, drive those dozen sheep into the barn porch. They'll be covered if left in the fold all night; and put a plank before them," said Heathcliff.

"How must I do?" I continued, with rising irritation.

There was no reply to my question; and, on looking round, I saw only Joseph bringing in a pail of porridge for the dogs, and Mrs. Heathcliff, leaning over the fire, diverting herself with burning a bundle of matches which had fallen from the chimney-piece as she restored the tea-canister to its place.

The former, when he had deposited his burden, took a critical survey of the room, and, in cracked tones, grated out—

"Aw woonder hagh yah can faishion tuh stand thear i' idleness un war, when all on 'em's goan aght! Bud yah're a nowt, and it's noa use talking—yah'll niver mend uh yer ill ways; bud goa raight tuh t' divil, like yer mother afore ye!"[6]

I imagined, for a moment, that this piece of eloquence was addressed to me; and, sufficiently enraged, stepped towards the aged rascal with an intention of kicking him out of the door.

Mrs. Heathcliff, however, checked me by her answer.

"You scandalous old hypocrite!" she replied. "Are you not afraid of being carried away bodily, whenever you mention the devil's name? I warn you to refrain from provoking me, or I'll ask your abduction as a special favour. Stop, look here, Joseph," she continued, taking a long, dark book from a shelf. "I'll show you how far I've progressed in the Black Art—I shall soon be competent to make a clear house of it. The red cow didn't die by chance; and your rheumatism can hardly be reckoned among providential visitations!"

"Oh, wicked, wicked!" gasped the elder, "may the Lord deliver us from evil!"

"No, reprobate! you are a castaway—be off, or I'll hurt you seriously! I'll have you all modelled in wax and clay; and the first who passes the limits I fix, shall—I'll not say what he shall be done to—

6. *Faishion:* bring yourself; *un war:* and worse; *yah're a nowt:* you're a nothing.

but, you'll see! Go, I'm looking at you!"

The little witch put a mock malignity into her beautiful eyes, and Joseph, trembling with sincere horror, hurried out praying and ejaculating "wicked" as he went.

I thought her conduct must be prompted by a species of dreary fun; and, now that we were alone, I endeavoured to interest her in my distress.

"Mrs. Heathcliff," I said, earnestly, "you must excuse me for troubling you—I presume, because, with that face, I'm sure you cannot help being good-hearted. Do point out some landmarks by which I may know my way home. I have no more idea how to get there than you would have how to get to London!"

"Take the road you came," she answered, ensconcing herself in a chair, with a candle, and the long book open before her. "It is brief advice, but as sound as I can give."

"Then, if you hear of me being discovered dead in a bog, or a pit full of snow, your conscience won't whisper that it is partly your fault?"

"How so? I cannot escort you. They wouldn't let me go to the end of the garden-wall."

"*You!* I should be sorry to ask you to cross the threshold, for my convenience, on such a night," I cried. "I want you to *tell* me my way, not to *show* it; or else to persuade Mr. Heathcliff to give me a guide."

"Who? There is himself, Earnshaw, Zillah, Joseph, and I. Which would you have?"

"Are there no boys at the farm?"

"No, those are all."

"Then it follows that I am compelled to stay."

"That you may settle with your host. I have nothing to do with it."

"I hope it will be a lesson to you, to make no more rash journeys on these hills," cried Heathcliff's stern voice from the kitchen entrance. "As to staying here, I don't keep accommodations for visitors; you must share a bed with Hareton, or Joseph, if you do."

"I can sleep on a chair in this room," I replied.

"No, no! A stranger is a stranger, be he rich or poor—it will not suit me to permit any one the range of the place while I am off guard!" said the unmannerly wretch.

With this insult my patience was at an end. I uttered an expression of disgust, and pushed past him into the yard, running against Earnshaw in my haste. It was so dark that I could not see the means of exit, and, as I wandered round, I heard another specimen of their civil behaviour amongst each other.

At first, the young man appeared about to befriend me.

"I'll go with him as far as the park," he said.

"You'll go with him to hell!" exclaimed his master, or whatever relation he bore. "And who is to look after the horses, eh?"

"A man's life is of more consequence than one evening's neglect of the horses; somebody must go," murmured Mrs. Heathcliff, more kindly than I expected.

"Not at your command!" retorted Hareton. "If you set store on him, you'd better be quiet."

"Then I hope his ghost will haunt you; and I hope Mr. Heathcliff will never get another tenant, till the Grange is a ruin!" she answered sharply.

"Hearken, hearken, shoo's[7] cursing on em!" muttered Joseph, towards whom I had been steering.

He sat within earshot, milking the cows by the aid of a lantern which I seized unceremoniously, and, calling out that I would send it back on the morrow, rushed to the nearest postern.

"Maister, maister, he's staling t' lantern!" shouted the ancient, pursuing my retreat. "Hey, Gnasher! Hey, dog! Hey, Wolf, holld him, holld him!"

On opening the little door, two hairy monsters flew at my throat, bearing me down and extinguishing the light, while a mingled guffaw, from Heathcliff and Hareton, put the copestone on my rage and humiliation.

Fortunately, the beasts seemed more bent on stretching their paws, and yawning and flourishing their tails, than devouring me alive; but they would suffer no resurrection, and I was forced to lie till their malignant masters pleased to deliver me: then hatless, and trembling with wrath, I ordered the miscreants to let me out—on their peril to keep me one minute longer—with several incoherent threats of retaliation that, in their indefinite depth of virulency, smacked of King Lear.

The vehemence of my agitation brought on a copious bleeding at the nose, and still Heathcliff laughed, and still I scolded. I don't know what would have concluded the scene had there not been one person at hand rather more rational than myself, and more benevolent than my entertainer. This was Zillah, the stout housewife, who at length issued forth to inquire into the nature of the uproar. She thought that some of them had been laying violent hands on me, and, not daring to attack her master, she turned her vocal artillery against the younger scoundrel.

"Well, Mr. Earnshaw," she cried, "I wonder what you'll have agait[8] next! Are we going to murder folk on our very door-stones? I see this house will never do for me—look at t' poor lad, he's fair choking! Wisht, wisht![9] you mun'n't go on so—come in, and I'll

7. She's.
8. A-going.

9. Hush.

cure that. There now, hold ye still."

With these words she suddenly splashed a pint of icy water down my neck, and pulled me into the kitchen. Mr. Heathcliff followed, his accidental merriment expiring quickly in his habitual moroseness.

I was sick exceedingly, and dizzy and faint; and thus compelled, perforce, to accept lodgings under his roof. He told Zillah to give me a glass of brandy, and then passed on to the inner room, while she condoled with me on my sorry predicament, and having obeyed his orders, whereby I was somewhat revived, ushered me to bed.

Chapter III

While leading the way upstairs, she recommended that I should hide the candle, and not make a noise, for her master had an odd notion about the chamber she would put me in, and never let anybody lodge there willingly.

I asked the reason.

She did not know, she answered; she had only lived there a year or two; and they had so many queer goings on, she could not begin to be curious.

Too stupified to be curious myself, I fastened my door and glanced round for the bed. The whole furniture consisted of a chair, a clothes-press, and a large oak case, with squares cut out near the top, resembling coach windows.

Having approached this structure, I looked inside, and perceived it to be a singular sort of old-fashioned couch, very conveniently designed to obviate the necessity for every member of the family having a room to himself. In fact, it formed a little closet, and the ledge of a window, which it enclosed, served as a table.

I slid back the panelled sides, got in with my light, pulled them together again, and felt secure against the vigilance of Heathcliff, and every one else.

The ledge, where I placed my candle, had a few mildewed books piled up in one corner; and it was covered with writing scratched on the paint. This writing, however, was nothing but a name repeated in all kinds of characters, large and small—*Catherine Earnshaw*, here and there varied to *Catherine Heathcliff*, and then again to *Catherine Linton*.

In vapid listlessness I leant my head against the window, and continued spelling over Catherine Earnshaw—Heathcliff—Linton, till my eyes closed; but they had not rested five minutes when a glare of white letters started from the dark, as vivid as spectres—the air swarmed with Catherines; and rousing myself to dispel the obtrusive name, I discovered my candle wick reclining on one of the antique volumes, and perfuming the place with an odour of roasted calf-skin.

I snuffed it off, and, very ill at ease under the influence of cold and lingering nausea, sat up, and spread open the injured tome on my knee. It was a Testament, in lean type, and smelling dreadfully musty: a fly-leaf bore the inscription—"Catherine Earnshaw, her book," and a date some quarter of a century back.

I shut it, and took up another, and another, till I had examined all. Catherine's library was select, and its state of dilapidation proved it to have been well used, though not altogether for a legitimate purpose; scarcely one chapter had escaped a pen and ink commentary—at least, the appearance of one—covering every morsel of blank that the printer had left.

Some were detached sentences; other parts took the form of a regular diary, scrawled in an unformed, childish hand. At the top of an extra page, quite a treasure probably when first lighted on, I was greatly amused to behold an excellent caricature of my friend Joseph, rudely yet powerfully sketched.

An immediate interest kindled within me for the unknown Catherine, and I began, forthwith, to decypher her faded hieroglyphics.

"An awful Sunday!" commenced the paragraph beneath. "I wish my father were back again. Hindley is a detestable substitute—his conduct to Heathcliff is atrocious—H. and I are going to rebel—we took our initiatory step this evening.

"All day had been flooding with rain; we could not go to church, so Joseph must needs get up a congregation in the garret; and, while Hindley and his wife basked downstairs before a comfortable fire—doing anything but reading their Bibles, I'll answer for it—Heathcliff, myself, and the unhappy plough-boy were commanded to take our Prayer-books, and mount. We were ranged in a row, on a sack of corn, groaning and shivering, and hoping that Joseph would shiver too, so that he might give us a short homily for his own sake. A vain idea! The service lasted precisely three hours; and yet my brother had the face to exclaim, when he saw us descending—

" 'What, done already?'

"On Sunday evenings we used to be permitted to play, if we did not make much noise; now a mere titter is sufficient to send us into corners!

" 'You forget you have a master here,' says the tyrant. 'I'll demolish the first who puts me out of temper! I insist on perfect sobriety and silence. Oh, boy! was that you? Frances, darling, pull his hair as you go by; I heard him snap his fingers.'

"Frances pulled his hair heartily; and then went and seated herself on her husband's knee, and there they were, like two babies, kissing and talking nonsense by the hour—foolish palaver that we should be ashamed of.

"We made ourselves as snug as our means allowed in the arch of the dresser. I had just fastened our pinafores together, and hung them up for a curtain, when in comes Joseph, on an errand from the stables. He tears down my handywork, boxes my ears, and croaks—

" 'T' maister nobbut just buried, and Sabbath nut oe'red, und t'sahnd uh't gospel still i' yer lugs, and yah darr be laiking! shame on ye! sit ye dahn, ill childer! they's good books eneugh if ye'll read 'em; sit ye dahn, and think uh yer sowls!' [1]

"Saying this, he compelled us so to square our positions that we might receive, from the far-off fire, a dull ray to show us the text of the lumber he thrust upon us.

"I could not bear the employment. I took my dingy volume by the scroop,[2] and hurled it into the dog-kennel, vowing I hated a good book.

"Heathcliff kicked his to the same place.

"Then there was a hubbub!

" 'Maister Hindley!' shouted our chaplain. 'Maister, coom hither! Miss Cathy's riven th' back off "Th' Helmet uh Salvation," un' Heathcliff's pawsed his fit intuh t' first part uh "T' Brooad Way to Destruction!" It's fair flaysome ut yah let 'em goa on this gait.[3] Ech! th' owd man ud uh laced 'em properly—bud he's goan!'

"Hindley hurried up from his paradise on the hearth, and seizing one of us by the collar, and the other by the arm, hurled both into the back-kitchen, where, Joseph asseverated, 'owd Nick' would fetch us as sure as we were living; and, so comforted, we each sought a separate nook to await his advent.

"I reached this book, and a pot of ink from a shelf, and pushed the house-door ajar to give me light, and I have got the time on with writing for twenty minutes; but my companion is impatient and proposes that we should appropriate the dairy woman's cloak, and have a scamper on the moors, under its shelter. A pleasant suggestion—and then, if the surly old man come in, he may believe his prophesy verified—we cannot be damper, or colder, in the rain than we are here."

I suppose Catherine fulfilled her project, for the next sentence took up another subject; she waxed lachrymose.

"How little did I dream that Hindley would ever make me cry so!" she wrote. "My head aches, till I cannot keep it on the pillow;

1. *Nobbut:* only; *oe'red:* gone by, got past; *t'sahnd:* the sound; *lugs:* ears; *darr be laiking:* dare be playing; *ill childer:* bad children.

2. The back of the cover of a book.
3. *Riven:* torn; *pawsed his fit:* made a hole with his foot; *flaysome:* terrible; *gait:* way.

and still I can't give over. Poor Heathcliff! Hindley calls him a
vagabond, and won't let him sit with us, nor eat with us any more;
and, he says, he and I must not play together, and threatens to turn
him out of the house if we break his orders.

"He has been blaming our father (how dared he?) for treating
H. too liberally; and swears he will reduce him to his right place—"

I began to nod drowsily over the dim page; my eye wandered
from manuscript to print. I saw a red ornamented title—"Seventy
Times Seven, and the First of the Seventy-First. A Pious Discourse
delivered by the Reverend Jabes Branderham, in the Chapel of
Gimmerden Sough." And while I was, half consciously, worrying
my brain to guess what Jabes Branderham would make of his subject, I sank back in bed, and fell asleep.

Alas, for the effects of bad tea and bad temper! what else could
it be that made me pass such a terrible night? I don't remember
another that I can at all compare with it since I was capable of
suffering.

I began to dream, almost before I ceased to be sensible of my
locality. I thought it was morning, and I had set out on my way
home, with Joseph for a guide. The snow lay yards deep in our
road; and, as we floundered on, my companion wearied me with
constant reproaches that I had not brought a pilgrim's staff, telling
me I could never get into the house without one, and boastfully
flourishing a heavy-headed cudgel, which I understood to be so
denominated.

For a moment I considered it absurd that I should need such a
weapon to gain admittance into my own residence. Then, a new
idea flashed across me. I was not going there; we were journeying
to hear the famous Jabes Branderham preach from the text—
"Seventy Times Seven"; and either Joseph, the preacher, or I had
committed the "First of the Seventy-First," and were to be publicly
exposed and excommunicated.

We came to the chapel. I have passed it really in my walks,
twice or thrice; it lies in a hollow, between two hills—an elevated
hollow, near a swamp, whose peaty moisture is said to answer all
the purposes of embalming on the few corpses deposited there.
The roof has been kept whole hitherto, but, as the clergyman's
stipend is only twenty pounds per annum, and a house with two
rooms, threatening speedily to determine into one, no clergyman will
undertake the duties of pastor, especially as it is currently reported
that his flock would rather let him starve than increase the living
by one penny from their own pockets. However, in my dream,
Jabes had a full and attentive congregation: and he preached—
good God—what a sermon! Divided into *four hundred and ninety*

parts, each fully equal to an ordinary address from the pulpit, and each discussing a separate sin! Where he searched for them, I cannot tell; he had his private manner of interpreting the phrase, and it seemed necessary the brother should sin different sins on every occasion.

They were of the most curious character—odd trangressions that I never imagined previously.

Oh, how weary I grew. How I writhed, and yawned, and nodded, and revived! How I pinched and pricked myself, and rubbed my eyes, and stood up, and sat down again, and nudged Joseph to inform me if he would *ever* have done!

I was condemned to hear all out; finally, he reached the "*First of the Seventy-First.*" At that crisis, a sudden inspiration descended on me; I was moved to rise and denounce Jabes Branderham as the sinner of the sin that no Christian need pardon.

"Sir," I exclaimed, "sitting here, within these four walls, at one stretch, I have endured and forgiven the four hundred and ninety heads of your discourse. Seventy times seven times have I plucked up my hat and been about to depart—Seventy times seven times have you preposterously forced me to resume my seat. The four hundred and ninety-first is too much. Fellow martyrs, have at him! Drag him down, and crush him to atoms, that the place which knows him may know him no more!"

"*Thou art the Man!*" cried Jabes, after a solemn pause, leaning over his cushion. "Seventy times seven times didst thou gapingly contort thy visage—seventy times seven did I take counsel with my soul—Lo, this is human weakness; this also may be absolved! The First of the Seventy-First is come. Brethren, execute upon him the judgment written! such honour have all His saints!"

With that concluding word, the whole assembly, exalting their pilgrim's staves, rushed round me in a body, and I, having no weapon to raise in self-defence, commenced grappling with Joseph, my nearest and most ferocious assailant, for his. In the confluence of the multitude, several clubs crossed; blows, aimed at me, fell on other sconces. Presently the whole chapel resounded with rappings and counter-rappings. Every man's hand was against his neighbour; and Branderham, unwilling to remain idle, poured forth his zeal in a shower of loud taps on the boards of the pulpit, which responded so smartly that, at last, to my unspeakable relief, they woke me.

And what was it that had suggested the tremendous tumult, what had played Jabes's part in the row? Merely the branch of a fir tree that touched my lattice, as the blast wailed by, and rattled its dry cones against the panes!

I listened doubtingly an instant; detected the disturber, then turned and dozed, and dreamt again; if possible, still more dis-agreebly than before.

This time, I remembered I was lying in the oak closet, and I heard distinctly the gusty wind, and the driving of the snow; I heard, also, the fir-bough repeat its teasing sound, and ascribed it to the right cause; but it annoyed me so much, that I resolved to silence it, if possible; and, I thought, I rose and endeavoured to unhasp the casement. The hook was soldered into the staple, a circumstance observed by me when awake, but forgotten.

"I must stop it, nevertheless!" I muttered, knocking my knuckles through the glass, and stretching an arm out to seize the importu-nate branch: instead of which, my fingers closed on the fingers of a little, ice-cold hand!

The intense horror of nightmare came over me; I tried to draw back my arm, but the hand clung to it, and a most melancholy voice sobbed—

"Let me in—let me in!"

"Who are you?" I asked, struggling, meanwhile, to disengage myself.

"Catherine Linton," it replied, shiveringly (why did I think of *Linton?* I had read *Earnshaw* twenty times for Linton). "I'm come home, I'd lost my way on the moor!"

As it spoke, I discerned, obscurely, a child's face looking through the window. Terror made me cruel; and, finding it useless to at-tempt shaking the creature off, I pulled its wrist on to the broken pane, and rubbed it to and fro till the blood ran down and soaked the bed-clothes: still it wailed, "Let me in!" and maintained its tenacious gripe, almost maddening me with fear.

"How can I?" I said at length. "Let *me* go, if you want me to let you in!"

The fingers relaxed, I snatched mine through the hole, hurriedly piled the books up in a pyramid against it, and stopped my ears to exclude the lamentable prayer.

I seemed to keep them closed above a quarter of an hour, yet, the instant I listened again, there was the doleful cry moaning on!

"Begone!" I shouted, "I'll never let you in, not if you beg for twenty years!"

"It's twenty years," mourned the voice, "twenty years, I've been a waif for twenty years!"

Thereat began a feeble scratching outside, and the pile of books moved as if thrust forward.

I tried to jump up, but could not stir a limb; and so yelled aloud, in a frenzy of fright.

To my confusion, I discovered the yell was not ideal. Hasty footsteps approached my chamber door; somebody pushed it open, with a vigorous hand, and a light glimmered through the squares at the top of the bed. I sat shuddering yet, and wiping the perspiration from my forehead: the intruder appeared to hesitate, and muttered to himself.

At last, he said in a half-whisper, plainly not expecting an answer—

"Is any one here?"

I considered it best to confess my presence, for I knew Heathcliff's accents, and feared he might search further, if I kept quiet.

With this intention, I turned and opened the panels. I shall not soon forget the effect my action produced.

Heathcliff stood near the entrance, in his shirt and trousers, with a candle dripping over his fingers, and his face as white as the wall behind him. The first creak of the oak startled him like an electric shock: the light leaped from his hold to a distance of some feet, and his agitation was so extreme that he could hardly pick it up.

"It is only your guest, sir," I called out, desirous to spare him the humiliation of exposing his cowardice further. "I had the misfortune to scream in my sleep, owing to a frightful nightmare. I'm sorry I disturbed you."

"Oh, God confound you, Mr. Lockwood! I wish you were at the—" commenced my host, setting the candle on a chair, because he found it impossible to hold it steady.

"And who showed you up to this room?" he continued, crushing his nails into his palms, and grinding his teeth to subdue the maxillary convulsions. "Who was it? I've a good mind to turn them out of the house this moment!"

"It was your servant, Zillah," I replied, flinging myself on to the floor, and rapidly resuming my garments. "I should not care if you did, Mr. Heathcliff; she richly deserves it. I suppose that she wanted to get another proof that the place was haunted, at my expense. Well, it is—swarming with ghosts and goblins! You have reason in shutting it up, I assure you. No one will thank you for a doze in such a den!"

"What do you mean?" asked Heathcliff, "and what are you doing? Lie down and finish out the night, since you *are* here; but, for heaven's sake! don't repeat that horrid noise. Nothing could excuse it, unless you were having your throat cut!"

"If the little fiend had got in at the window, she probably would have strangled me!" I returned. "I'm not going to endure the persecutions of your hospitable ancestors again. Was not the Reverend Jabes Branderham akin to you on the mother's side? And that minx, Catherine Linton, or Earnshaw, or however she was called—she must have been a changeling—wicked little soul! She told me she had been walking the earth these twenty years: a just punishment for her mortal transgressions, I've no doubt!"

Scarcely were these words uttered, when I recollected the association of Heathcliff's with Catherine's name in the book, which had completely slipped from my memory till thus awakened. I blushed at my inconsideration; but, without showing further consciousness of the offence, I hastened to add—

"The truth is, sir, I passed the first part of the night in—" here, I stopped afresh—I was about to say "perusing those old volumes;" then it would have revealed my knowledge of their written, as well as their printed contents; so, correcting myself, I went on—"in spelling over the name scratched on that window-ledge. A monotonous occupation, calculated to set me asleep, like counting, or—"

"What *can* you mean by talking in this way to *me!*" thundered Heathcliff with savage vehemence. "How—how *dare* you, under my roof—God! he's mad to speak so!" And he struck his forehead with rage.

I did not know whether to resent this language, or pursue my explanation; but he seemed so powerfully affected that I took pity and proceeded with my dreams, affirming I had never heard the appellation of "Catherine Linton" before, but reading it often over produced an impression which personified itself when I had no longer my imagination under control.

Heathcliff gradually fell back into the shelter of the bed as I spoke, finally sitting down almost concealed behind it. I guessed, however, by his irregular and intercepted breathing, that he struggled to vanquish an access of violent emotion.

Not liking to show him that I heard the conflict, I continued my toilette rather noisily, looked at my watch, and soliloquized on the length of the night—

"Not three o'clock yet! I could have taken oath it had been six. Time stagnates here—we must surely have retired to rest at eight!"

"Always at nine in winter, and always rise at four," said my host, suppressing a groan, and, as I fancied, by the motion of his shadow's arm, dashing a tear from his eyes.

"Mr. Lockwood," he added, "you may go into my room; you'll only be in the way, coming downstairs so early; and your childish outcry has sent sleep to the devil for me."

"And for me, too," I replied. "I'll walk in the yard till daylight, and then I'll be off; and you need not dread a repetition of my intrusion. I am now quite cured of seeking pleasure in society, be it country or town. A sensible man ought to find sufficient company in himself."

"Delightful company!" muttered Heathcliff. "Take the candle, and go where you please. I shall join you directly. Keep out of the yard, though; the dogs are unchained, and the house—Juno mounts sentinel there, and—nay, you can only ramble about the steps and passages. But, away with you! I'll come in two minutes."

I obeyed, so far as to quit the chamber; when, ignorant where the narrow lobbies led, I stood still, and was witness, involuntarily, to a piece of superstition on the part of my landlord, which belied, oddly, his apparent sense.

He got on to the bed and wrenched open the lattice, bursting, as he pulled at it, into an uncontrollable passion of tears.

"Come in! come in!" he sobbed. "Cathy, do come. Oh, do— once more! Oh! my heart's darling, hear me *this* time—Catherine, at last!"

The spectre showed a spectre's ordinary caprice; it gave no sign of being; but the snow and wind whirled wildly through, even reaching my station, and blowing out the light.

There was such anguish in the gush of grief that accompanied this raving, that my compassion made me overlook its folly, and I drew off, half angry to have listened at all, and vexed at having related my ridiculous nightmare, since it produced that agony, though *why*, was beyond my comprehension.

I descended cautiously to the lower regions and landed in the back-kitchen, where a gleam of fire, raked compactly together, enabled me to rekindle my candle.

Nothing was stirring except a brindled, grey cat, which crept from the ashes and saluted me with a querulous mew.

Two benches, shaped in sections of a circle, nearly enclosed the hearth; on one of these I stretched myself, and Grimalkin mounted the other. We were both of us nodding, ere any one invaded our retreat; and then it was Joseph shuffling down a wooden ladder that vanished in the roof, through a trap: the ascent to his garret, I suppose.

He cast a sinister look at the little flame which I had enticed to play between the ribs, swept the cat from its elevation, and bestowing himself in the vacancy, commenced the operation of stuffing a three-inch pipe with tobacco; my presence in his sanctum was evidently esteemed a piece of impudence too shameful for remark. He silently applied the tube to his lips, folded his arms, and puffed away.

I let him enjoy the luxury, unannoyed; and after sucking out the last wreath, and heaving a profound sigh, he got up, and departed as solemnly as he came.

A more elastic footstep entered next, and now I opened my mouth for a "good morning," but closed it again, the salutation unachieved; for Hareton Earnshaw was performing his orisons, *sotto voce*, in a series of curses directed against every object he touched, while he rummaged a corner for a spade or shovel to dig through the drifts. He glanced over the back of the bench, dilating his nostrils, and thought as little of exchanging civilities with me as with my companion, the cat.

I guessed by his preparations that egress was allowed, and leaving my hard couch, made a movement to follow him. He noticed this, and thrust at an inner door with the end of his spade, intimating by an inarticulate sound, that there was the place where I must go, if I changed my locality.

It opened into the house, where the females were already astir, Zillah, urging flakes of flame up the chimney with a colossal bellows, and Mrs. Heathcliff, kneeling on the hearth, reading a book by the aid of the blaze.

She held her hand interposed between the furnace-heat and her eyes, and seemed absorbed in her occupation; desisting from it only to chide the servant for covering her with sparks, or to push away a dog, now and then, that snoozled its nose over-forwardly into her face.

I was surprised to see Heathcliff there also. He stood by the fire, his back towards me, just finishing a stormy scene to poor Zillah, who ever and anon interrupted her labour to pluck up the corner of her apron, and heave an indignant groan.

"And you, you worthless—" he broke out as I entered, turning to his daughter-in-law, and employing an epithet as harmless as duck, or sheep, but generally represented by a dash—"there you are at your idle tricks again! The rest of them do earn their bread —you live on my charity! Put your trash away, and find something to do. You shall pay me for the plague of having you eternally in my sight—do you hear, damnable jade?"

"I'll put my trash away, because you can make me, if I refuse," answered the young lady, closing her book, and throwing it on a chair. "But I'll not do anything, though you should swear your tongue out, except what I please!"

Heathcliff lifted his hand, and the speaker sprang to a safer distance, obviously acquainted with its weight.

Having no desire to be entertained by a cat and dog combat, I stepped forward briskly, as if eager to partake the warmth of the hearth, and innocent of any knowledge of the interrupted dispute. Each had enough decorum to suspend further hostilities: Heathcliff placed his fists, out of temptation, in his pockets; Mrs. Heathcliff curled her lip and walked to a seat far off, where she kept her word by playing the part of a statue during the remainder of my stay.

That was not long. I declined joining their breakfast, and, at the first gleam of dawn, took an opportunity of escaping into the free air, now clear and still, and cold as impalpable ice.

My landlord hallooed for me to stop, ere I reached the bottom of the garden, and offered to accompany me across the moor. It was well he did, for the whole hill-back was one billowy, white ocean, the swells and falls not indicating corresponding rises and depressions in the ground: many pits, at least, were filled to a level; and entire ranges of mounds, the refuse of the quarries, blotted from the chart which my yesterday's walk left pictured in my mind.

I had remarked on one side of the road, at intervals of six or seven yards, a line of upright stones, continued through the whole length of the barren: these were erected, and daubed with lime, on purpose to serve as guides in the dark, and also, when a fall, like the present, confounded the deep swamps on either hand with the firmer path: but, excepting a dirty dot pointing up here and there, all traces of their existence had vanished; and my companion found it necessary to warn me frequently to steer to the right or left, when I imagined I was following, correctly, the windings of the road.

We exchanged little conversation, and he halted at the entrance of Thrushcross park, saying, I could make no error there. Our adieux were limited to a hasty bow, and then I pushed forward, trusting to my own resources, for the porter's lodge is untenanted as yet.

The distance from the gate to the Grange is two miles: I believe I managed to make it four, what with losing myself among the trees, and sinking up to the neck in snow, a predicament which only those who have experienced it can appreciate. At any rate, whatever were my wanderings, the clock chimed twelve as I entered the house; and that gave exactly an hour for every mile of the usual way from Wuthering Heights.

My human fixture and her satellites rushed to welcome me; exclaiming, tumultuously, they had completely given me up: everybody conjectured that I perished last night; and they were wondering how they must set about the search for my remains.

I bid them be quiet, now that they saw me returned, and, benumbed to my very heart, I dragged upstairs, whence, after putting on dry clothes, and pacing to and fro thirty or forty minutes, to restore the animal heat, I am adjourned to my study, feeble as a kitten, almost too much so to enjoy the cheerful fire and smoking coffee which the servant has prepared for my refreshment.

Chapter IV

What vain weather-cocks we are! I, who had determined to hold myself independent of all social intercourse, and thanked my stars that, at length, I had lighted on a spot where it was next to impracticable—I, weak wretch, after maintaining till dusk a struggle with low spirits and solitude, was finally compelled to strike my colours; and, under pretence of gaining information concerning the necessities of my establishment, I desired Mrs. Dean, when she brought in supper, to sit down while I ate it, hoping sincerely she would prove a regular gossip, and either rouse me to animation, or lull me to sleep by her talk.

"You have lived here a considerable time," I commenced; "did you not say sixteen years?"

"Eighteen, sir; I came, when the mistress was married, to wait on her; after she died, the master retained me for his house-keeper."

"Indeed."

There ensued a pause. She was not a gossip, I feared, unless about her own affairs, and those could hardly interest me.

However, having studied for an interval, with a fist on either knee, and a cloud of meditation over her ruddy countenance, she ejaculated—

"Ah, times are greatly changed since then!"

"Yes," I remarked, "you've seen a good many alterations, I suppose?"

"I have: and troubles too," she said.

"Oh, I'll turn the talk on my landlord's family!" I thought to myself. "A good subject to start—and that pretty girl-widow, I should like to know her history: whether she be a native of the country, or, as is more probable, an exotic that the surly *indigenae* will not recognise for kin."

With this intention I asked Mrs. Dean why Heathcliff let Thrushcross Grange, and preferred living in a situation and residence so much inferior.

"Is he not rich enough to keep the estate in good order?" I enquired.

"Rich, sir!" she returned. "He has, nobody knows what money, and every year it increases. Yes, yes, he's rich enough to live in a finer house than this, but he's very near—close-handed; and, if he had meant to flit to Thrushcross Grange, as soon as he heard of a good tenant he could not have borne to miss the chance of getting a few hundreds more. It is strange people should be so greedy, when they are alone in the world!"

"He had a son, it seems?"

"Yes, he had one—he is dead."

"And that young lady, Mrs. Heathcliff, is his widow?"

"Yes."

"Where did she come from originally?"

"Why, sir, she is my late master's daughter; Catherine Linton was her maiden name. I nursed her, poor thing! I did wish Mr.

Heathcliff would remove here, and then we might have been together again."

"What, Catherine Linton!" I exclaimed, astonished. But a minute's reflection convinced me it was not my ghostly Catherine. "Then," I continued, "my predecessor's name was Linton?"

"It was."

"And who is that Earnshaw, Hareton Earnshaw, who lives with Mr. Heathcliff? are they relations?"

"No; he is the late Mrs. Linton's nephew."

"The young lady's cousin, then?"

"Yes; and her husband was her cousin also—one, on the mother's —the other, on the father's side. Heathcliff married Mr. Linton's sister."

"I see the house at Wuthering Heights has 'Earnshaw' carved over the front door. Are they an old family?"

"Very old, sir; and Hareton is the last of them, as our Miss Cathy is of us—I mean, of the Lintons. Have you been to Wuthering Heights? I beg pardon for asking; but I should like to hear how she is!"

"Mrs. Heathcliff? She looked very well, and very handsome; yet, I think, not very happy."

"Oh dear, I don't wonder! And how did you like the master?"

"A rough fellow, rather, Mrs. Dean. Is not that his character?"

"Rough as a saw-edge, and hard as whinstone! The less you meddle with him the better."

"He must have had some ups and downs in life to make him such a churl. Do you know anything of his history?"

"It's a cuckoo's, sir—I know all about it, except where he was born, and who were his parents, and how he got his money, at first. And Hareton has been cast out like an unfledged dunnock! The unfortunate lad is the only one, in all this parish, that does not guess how he has been cheated!"

"Well, Mrs. Dean, it will be a charitable deed to tell me something of my neighbours—I feel I shall not rest, if I go to bed; so, be good enough to sit and chat an hour."

"Oh, certainly, sir! I'll just fetch a little sewing, and then I'll sit as long as you please. But you've caught cold; I saw you shivering, and you must have some gruel to drive it out."

The worthy woman bustled off; and I crouched nearer the fire; my head felt hot, and the rest of me chill: moreover, I was excited, almost to a pitch of foolishness, through my nerves and brain. This caused me to feel, not uncomfortable, but rather fearful, as I am still, of serious effects from the incidents of today and yesterday.

She returned presently, bringing a smoking basin, and a basket of work; and, having placed the former on the hob, drew in her seat, evidently pleased to find me so companionable.

———

Before I came to live here, she commenced, waiting no further invitation to her story, I was almost always at Wuthering Heights, because my mother had nursed Mr. Hindley Earnshaw, that was Hareton's father, and I got used to playing with the children. I ran errands too, and helped to make hay, and hung about the farm ready for anything that anybody would set me to.

One fine summer morning—it was the beginning of harvest, I remember—Mr. Earnshaw, the old master, came downstairs, dressed for a journey; and, after he had told Joseph what was to be done during the day, he turned to Hindley, and Cathy, and me—for I sat eating my porridge with them—and he said, speaking to his son—

"Now, my bonny man, I'm going to Liverpool, to-day. What shall I bring you? You may choose what you like; only let it be little, for I shall walk there and back; sixty miles each way, that is a long spell!"

Hindley named a fiddle, and then he asked Miss Cathy; she was hardly six years old, but she could ride any horse in the stable, and she chose a whip.

He did not forget me, for he had a kind heart, though he was rather severe, sometimes. He promised to bring me a pocketful of apples and pears, and then he kissed his children good-bye, and set off.

It seemed a long while to us all—the three days of his absence—and often did little Cathy ask when he would be home. Mrs. Earnshaw expected him by supper-time, on the third evening; and she put the meal off hour after hour; there were no signs of his coming, however, and at last the children got tired of running down to the gate to look. Then it grew dark; she would have had them to bed, but they begged sadly to be allowed to stay up; and, just about eleven o'clock, the door-latch was raised quietly and in stept the master. He threw himself into a chair, laughing and groaning, and bid them all stand off, for he was nearly killed—he would not have such another walk for the three kingdoms.

"And at the end of it, to be flighted [4] to death!" he said, opening his great coat, which he held bundled up in his arms, "See here, wife; I was never so beaten with anything in my life; but you must e'en take it as a gift of God, though it's as dark almost as if it came from the devil."

We crowded round, and, over Miss Cathy's head, I had a peep

4. Frightened.

at a dirty, ragged, black-haired child; big enough both to walk and talk—indeed, its face looked older than Catherine's—yet, when it was set on its feet, it only stared round, and repeated over and over again some gibberish that nobody could understand. I was frightened, and Mrs. Earnshaw was ready to fling it out of doors: she did fly up—asking how he could fashion to bring that gipsy brat into the house, when they had their own bairns to feed and fend for? What he meant to do with it, and whether he were mad?

The master tried to explain the matter; but he was really half dead with fatigue, and all that I could make out, amongst her scolding, was a tale of his seeing it starving, and houseless, and as good as dumb in the streets of Liverpool, where he picked it up and inquired for its owner. Not a soul knew to whom it belonged, he said, and his money and time being both limited, he thought it better to take it home with him at once, than run into vain expenses there; because he was determined he would not leave it as he found it.

Well, the conclusion was that my mistress grumbled herself calm; and Mr. Earnshaw told me to wash it, and give it clean things, and let it sleep with the children.

Hindley and Cathy contented themselves with looking and listening till peace was restored; then, both began searching their father's pockets for the presents he had promised them. The former was a boy of fourteen, but when he drew out what had been a fiddle, crushed to morsels in the great coat, he blubbered aloud, and Cathy, when she learnt the master had lost her whip in attending on the stranger, showed her humour by grinning and spitting at the stupid little thing, earning for her pains a sound blow from her father to teach her cleaner manners.

They entirely refused to have it in bed with them, or even in their room, and I had no more sense, so I put it on the landing of the stairs, hoping it might be gone on the morrow. By chance, or else attracted by hearing his voice, it crept to Mr. Earnshaw's door and there he found it on quitting his chamber. Inquiries were made as to how it got there; I was obliged to confess, and in recompense for my cowardice and inhumanity was sent out of the house.

This was Heathcliff's first introduction to the family. On coming back a few days afterwards, for I did not consider my banishment perpetual, I found they had christened him "Heathcliff"; it was the name of a son who died in childhood, and it has served him ever since, both for Christian and surname.

Miss Cathy and he were now very thick; but Hindley hated him, and to say the truth I did the same; and we plagued and went on with him shamefully, for I wasn't reasonable enough to feel my injustice, and the mistress never put in a word on his behalf when she saw him wronged.

He seemed a sullen, patient child, hardened, perhaps, to ill-treatment: he would stand Hindley's blows without winking or shedding a tear, and my pinches moved him only to draw in a breath, and open his eyes as if he had hurt himself by accident, and nobody was to blame.

This endurance made old Earnshaw furious when he discovered his son persecuting the poor, fatherless child, as he called him. He took to Heathcliff strangely, believing all he said (for that matter, he said precious little, and generally the truth) and petting him up far above Cathy, who was too mischievous and wayward for a favourite.

So, from the very beginning, he bred bad feeling in the house; and at Mrs. Earnshaw's death, which happened in less than two years after, the young master had learnt to regard his father as an oppressor rather than a friend, and Heathcliff as a usurper of his parent's affections and his privileges, and he grew bitter with brooding over these injuries.

I sympathised a while, but, when the children fell ill of the measles and I had to tend them, and take on me the cares of a woman at once, I changed my ideas. Heathcliff was dangerously sick, and while he lay at the worst he would have me constantly by his pillow; I suppose he felt I did a good deal for him, and he hadn't wit to guess that I was compelled to do it. However, I will say this, he was the quietest child that ever nurse watched over. The difference between him and the others forced me to be less partial. Cathy and her brother harassed me terribly; *he* was as uncomplaining as a lamb, though hardness, not gentleness, made him give little trouble.

He got through, and the doctor affirmed it was in a great measure owing to me, and praised me for my care. I was vain of his commendations, and softened towards the being by whose means I earned them, and thus Hindley lost his last ally; still I couldn't dote on Heathcliff, and I wondered often what my master saw to admire so much in the sullen boy who never, to my recollection, repaid his indulgence by any sign of gratitude. He was not insolent to his benefactor; he was simply insensible, though knowing perfectly the hold he had on his heart, and conscious he had only to speak and all the house would be obliged to bend to his wishes.

As an instance, I remember Mr. Earnshaw once bought a couple of colts at the parish fair, and gave the lads each one. Heathcliff took the handsomest, but it soon fell lame, and when he discovered it, he said to Hindley—

"You must exchange horses with me; I don't like mine, and if you won't I shall tell your father of the three thrashings you've given me this week, and show him my arm, which is black to the shoulder."

Hindley put out his tongue, and cuffed him over the ears.

"You'd better do it at once," he persisted, escaping to the porch (they were in the stable); "you will have to, and if I speak of these blows, you'll get them again with interest."

"Off, dog!" cried Hindley, threatening him with an iron weight, used for weighing potatoes and hay.

"Throw it," he replied, standing still, "and then I'll tell how you boasted that you would turn me out of doors as soon as he died, and see whether he will not turn you out directly."

Hindley threw it, hitting him on the breast, and down he fell, but staggered up immediately, breathless and white, and had not I prevented it, he would have gone just so to the master, and got full revenge by letting his condition plead for him, intimating who had caused it.

"Take my colt, gipsy, then!" said young Earnshaw. "And I pray that he may break your neck; take him, and be damned, you beggarly interloper! and wheedle my father out of all he has, only afterwards show him what you are, imp of Satan—And take that, I hope he'll kick out your brains!"

Heathcliff had gone to loose the beast, and shift it to his own stall. He was passing behind it, when Hindley finished his speech by knocking him under its feet, and without stopping to examine whether his hopes were fulfilled, ran away as fast as he could.

I was surprised to witness how coolly the child gathered himself up, and went on with his intention, exchanging saddles and all, and then sitting down on a bundle of hay to overcome the qualm which the violent blow occasioned, before he entered the house.

I persuaded him easily to let me lay the blame of his bruises on the horse; he minded little what tale was told since he had what he wanted. He complained so seldom, indeed, of such stirs as these, that I really thought him not vindictive—I was deceived completely, as you will hear.

Chapter V

In the course of time, Mr. Earnshaw began to fail. He had been active and healthy, yet his strength left him suddenly; and when he was confined to the chimney-corner he grew grievously irritable. A nothing vexed him, and suspected slights of his authority nearly threw him into fits.

This was especially to be remarked if any one attempted to impose upon, or domineer over, his favourite: he was painfully jealous lest a word should be spoken amiss to him, seeming to have got into his head the notion that, because he liked Heathcliff, all hated, and longed to do him an ill-turn.

It was a disadvantage to the lad, for the kinder among us did not wish to fret the master, so we humoured his partiality; and that humouring was rich nourishment to the child's pride and black tempers. Still it became in a manner necessary; twice, or thrice, Hindley's manifestations of scorn, while his father was near, roused the old man to a fury. He seized his stick to strike him, and shook with rage that he could not do it.

At last, our curate (we had a curate then who made the living answer by teaching the little Lintons and Earnshaws, and farming his bit of land himself) he advised that the young man should be sent to college, and Mr. Earnshaw agreed, though with a heavy spirit, for he said—

"Hindley was naught, and would never thrive as where he wandered."

I hoped heartily we should have peace now. It hurt me to think the master should be made uncomfortable by his own good deed. I fancied the discontent of age and disease arose from his family disagreements, as he would have it that it did; really, you know, sir, it was in his sinking frame.

We might have got on tolerably, notwithstanding, but for two people, Miss Cathy and Joseph, the servant; you saw him, I dare say, up yonder. He was, and is yet, most likely, the wearisomest, self-righteous pharisee that ever ransacked a Bible to rake the promises to himself, and fling the curses on his neighbours. By his knack of sermonizing and pious discoursing, he contrived to make a great impression on Mr. Earnshaw, and the more feeble the master became, the more influence he gained.

He was relentless in worrying him about his soul's concerns, and about ruling his children rigidly. He encouraged him to regard Hindley as a reprobate; and, night after night, he regularly grumbled out a long string of tales against Heathcliff and Catherine; always minding to flatter Earnshaw's weakness by heaping the heaviest blame on the last.

Certainly, she had ways with her such as I never saw a child take up before; and she put all of us past our patience fifty times and oftener in a day: from the hour she came downstairs, till the hour she went to bed, we had not a minute's security that she wouldn't be in mischief. Her spirits were always at high-water mark, her tongue always going—singing, laughing, and plaguing everybody who would not do the same. A wild, wicked slip she was —but she had the bonniest eye, and sweetest smile, and lightest

foot in the parish; and, after all, I believe she meant no harm;
for when once she made you cry in good earnest, it seldom happened that she would not keep you company, and oblige you to
be quiet that you might comfort her.

She was much too fond of Heathcliff. The greatest punishment
we could invent for her was to keep her separate from him: yet she
got chided more than any of us on his account.

In play, she liked, exceedingly, to act the little mistress; using
her hands freely, and commanding her companions: she did so to
me, but I would not bear slapping and ordering; and so I let her
know.

Now, Mr. Earnshaw did not understand jokes from his children:
he had always been strict and grave with them; and Catherine, on
her part, had no idea why her father should be crosser and less
patient in his ailing condition, than he was in his prime.

His peevish reproofs wakened in her a naughty delight to provoke him; she was never so happy as when we were all scolding her
at once, and she defying us with her bold, saucy look, and her
ready words; turning Joseph's religious curses into ridicule, baiting me, and doing just what her father hated most, showing how
her pretended insolence, which he thought real, had more power
over Heathcliff than his kindness; how the boy would do *her*
bidding in anything, and *his* only when it suited his own inclination.

After behaving as badly as possible all day, she sometimes came
fondling to make it up at night.

"Nay, Cathy," the old man would say, "I cannot love thee;
thou'rt worse than thy brother. Go, say thy prayers, child, and ask
God's pardon. I doubt thy mother and I must rue that we ever
reared thee!"

That made her cry, at first; and then, being repulsed continually
hardened her, and she laughed if I told her to say she was sorry
for her faults, and beg to be forgiven.

But the hour came, at last, that ended Mr. Earnshaw's troubles
on earth. He died quietly in his chair one October evening, seated
by the fire-side.

A high wind blustered round the house, and roared in the
chimney: it sounded wild and stormy, yet it was not cold, and we
were all together—I, a little removed from the hearth, busy at
my knitting, and Joseph reading his Bible near the table (for the
servants generally sat in the house then, after their work was done).
Miss Cathy had been sick, and that made her still; she leant
against her father's knee, and Heathcliff was lying on the floor
with his head in her lap.

I remember the master, before he fell into a doze, stroking her bonny hair—it pleased him rarely[5] to see her gentle—and saying—

"Why canst thou not always be a good lass, Cathy?"

And she turned her face up to his, and laughed, and answered—

"Why cannot you always be a good man, father?"

But as soon as she saw him vexed again, she kissed his hand, and said she would sing him to sleep. She began singing very low, till his fingers dropped from hers, and his head sank on his breast. Then I told her to hush, and not stir, for fear she should wake him. We all kept as mute as mice a full half-hour, and should have done so longer, only Joseph, having finished his chapter, got up and said that he must rouse the master for prayers and bed. He stepped forward, and called him by name, and touched his shoulder, but he would not move—so he took the candle and looked at him.

I thought there was something wrong as he set down the light; and seizing the children each by an arm, whispered them to "frame[6] upstairs, and make little din—they might pray alone that evening—he had summut to do."

"I shall bid father good-night first," said Catherine, putting her arms round his neck, before we could hinder her.

The poor thing discovered her loss directly—she screamed out—

"Oh, he's dead, Heathcliff! he's dead!"

And they both set up a heart-breaking cry.

I joined my wail to theirs, loud and bitter; but Joseph asked what we could be thinking of to roar in that way over a saint in heaven.

He told me to put on my cloak and run to Gimmerton for the doctor and the parson. I could not guess the use that either would be of, then. However, I went, through wind and rain, and brought one, the doctor, back with me; the other said he would come in the morning.

Leaving Joseph to explain matters, I ran to the children's room; their door was ajar, I saw they had never laid down, though it was past midnight; but they were calmer, and did not need me to console them. The little souls were comforting each other with better thoughts than I could have hit on; no parson in the world ever pictured heaven so beautifully as they did, in their innocent talk; and, while I sobbed and listened, I could not help wishing we were all there safe together.

5. Exceedingly.   6. Go.

Chapter VI

Mr. Hindley came home to the funeral; and—a thing that amazed us, and set the neighbours gossipping right and left—he brought a wife with him.

What she was, and where she was born he never informed us; probably, she had neither money nor name to recommend her, or he would scarcely have kept the union from his father.

She was not one that would have disturbed the house much on her own account. Every object she saw, the moment she crossed the threshold, appeared to delight her; and every circumstance that took place about her, except the preparing for the burial, and the presence of the mourners.

I thought she was half silly, from her behaviour while that went on; she ran into her chamber, and made me come with her, though I should have been dressing the children; and there she sat shivering and clasping her hands, and asking repeatedly—

"Are they gone yet?"

Then she began describing with hysterical emotion the effect it produced on her to see black; and started, and trembled, and, at last, fell a weeping—and when I asked what was the matter? answered, she didn't know; but she felt so afraid of dying!

I imagined her as little likely to die as myself. She was rather thin, but young, and fresh complexioned, and her eyes sparkled as bright as diamonds. I did remark, to be sure, that mounting the stairs made her breathe very quick, that the least sudden noise set her all in a quiver, and that she coughed troublesomely sometimes: but I knew nothing of what these symptoms portended, and had no impulse to sympathize with her. We don't in general take to foreigners here, Mr. Lockwood, unless they take to us first.

Young Earnshaw was altered considerably in the three years of his absence. He had grown sparer, and lost his colour, and spoke and dressed quite differently; and, on the very day of his return, he told Joseph and me we must thenceforth quarter ourselves in the back-kitchen, and leave the house for him. Indeed, he would have carpeted and papered a small spare room for a parlour; but his wife expressed such pleasure at the white floor, and huge glowing fire-place, at the pewter dishes, and delf-case, and dog-kennel, and the wide space there was to move about in, where they usually sat, that he thought it unnecessary to her comfort, and so dropped the intention.

She expressed pleasure, too, at finding a sister among her new acquaintance, and she prattled to Catherine, and kissed her, and ran about with her, and gave her quantities of presents, at the beginning. Her affection tired very soon, however, and when she grew peevish, Hindley became tyrannical. A few words from her, evincing a dislike to Heathcliff, were enough to rouse in him all his old hatred of the boy. He drove him from their company to the servants, deprived him of the instructions of the curate, and insisted that he should labour out of doors instead, compelling him to do so, as hard as any other lad on the farm.

Heathcliff bore his degradation pretty well at first, because Cathy taught him what she learnt, and worked or played with him in the fields. They both promised fair to grow up as rude as savages, the young master being entirely negligent how they behaved, and what they did, so they kept clear of him. He would not even have seen after their going to church on Sundays, only Joseph and the curate reprimanded his carelessness when they absented themselves, and that reminded him to order Heathcliff a flogging, and Catherine a fast from dinner or supper.

But it was one of their chief amusements to run away to the moors in the morning and remain there all day, and the after-punishment grew a mere thing to laugh at. The curate might set as many chapters as he pleased for Catherine to get by heart, and Joseph might thrash Heathcliff till his arm ached; they forgot everything the minute they were together again, at least the minute they had contrived some naughty plan of revenge; and many a time I've cried to myself to watch them growing more reckless daily, and I not daring to speak a syllable for fear of losing the small power I still retained over the unfriended creatures.

One Sunday evening, it chanced that they were banished from the sitting-room, for making a noise, or a light offence of the kind, and when I went to call them to supper, I could discover them nowhere.

We searched the house, above and below, and the yard and stables; they were invisible; and, at last, Hindley in a passion told us to bolt the doors, and swore nobody should let them in that night.

The household went to bed; and I, too anxious to lie down, opened my lattice and put my head out to hearken, though it rained, determined to admit them in spite of the prohibition, should they return.

In a while, I distinguished steps coming up the road, and the light of a lantern glimmered through the gate.

I threw a shawl over my head and ran to prevent them from waking Mr. Earnshaw by knocking. There was Heathcliff, by himself; it gave me a start to see him alone.

"Where is Miss Catherine?" I cried hurriedly. "No accident, I hope?"

"At Thrushcross Grange," he answered, "and I would have been there too, but they had not the manners to ask me to stay."

"Well, you will catch it!" I said, "you'll never be content till you're sent about your business. What in the world led you wandering to Thrushcross Grange?"

"Let me get off my wet clothes, and I'll tell you all about it, Nelly," he replied.

I bid him beware of rousing the master, and while he undressed, and I waited to put out the candle, he continued—

"Cathy and I escaped from the wash-house to have a ramble at liberty, and getting a glimpse of the Grange lights, we thought we would just go and see whether the Lintons passed their Sunday evenings standing shivering in corners, while their father and mother sat eating and drinking, and singing and laughing, and burning their eyes out before the fire. Do you think they do? Or reading sermons, and being catechised by their man-servant, and set to learn a column of Scripture names, if they don't answer properly?"

"Probably not," I responded. "They are good children, no doubt, and don't deserve the treatment you receive, for your bad conduct."

"Don't you cant, Nelly," he said. "Nonsense! We ran from the top of the Heights to the park, without stopping—Catherine completely beaten in the race, because she was barefoot. You'll have to seek for her shoes in the bog to-morrow. We crept through a broken hedge, groped our way up the path, and planted ourselves on a flower-plot under the drawing-room window. The light came from thence; they had not put up the shutters, and the curtains were only half closed. Both of us were able to look in by standing on the basement, and clinging to the ledge, and we saw—ah! it was beautiful—a splendid place carpeted with crimson, and crimson-covered chairs and tables, and a pure white ceiling bordered by gold, a shower of glass-drops hanging in silver chains from the centre, and shimmering with little soft tapers. Old Mr. and Mrs. Linton were not there. Edgar and his sister had it entirely to themselves; shouldn't they have been happy? We should have thought ourselves in heaven! And now, guess what your good children were doing? Isabella—I believe she is eleven, a year younger than Cathy—lay screaming at the farther end of the room, shrieking as if witches were running red hot needles into her. Edgar stood on the hearth weeping silently, and in the middle of the table sat a little dog shaking its paw and yelping, which, from their mutual accusations, we understood they had nearly pulled in two between them. The idiots! That was their pleasure! to quarrel who should hold a heap of warm hair, and each begin to cry because both, after struggling to get it, refused to take it. We laughed outright at the petted things, we did despise them! When would you catch me wishing to have what Catherine wanted? or find us by ourselves, seeking entertainment in yelling, and sobbing, and rolling on the ground, divided by the whole room? I'd not exchange, for a thousand lives, my condition here, for Edgar Linton's at Thrushcross Grange—not if I might have the privilege of flinging Joseph off the highest gable, and painting the house-front with Hindley's blood!"

"Hush, hush!" I interrupted. "Still you have not told me, Heathcliff, how Catherine is left behind?"

"I told you we laughed," he answered. "The Lintons heard us, and with one accord, they shot like arrows to the door; there was silence, and then a cry, 'Oh, mamma, mamma! Oh, papa! Oh, mamma, come here. Oh, papa, oh!' They really did howl out, something in that way. We made frightful noises to terrify them still more, and then we dropped off the ledge, because somebody was drawing the bars, and we felt we had better flee. I had Cathy by the hand, and was urging her on, when all at once she fell down.

" 'Run, Heathcliff, run!' she whispered. 'They have let the bull-dog loose, and he holds me!'

"The devil had seized her ankle, Nelly; I heard his abominable snorting. She did not yell out—no! She would have scorned to do it, if she had been spitted on the horns of a mad cow. I did, though; I vociferated curses enough to annihilate any fiend in Christendom, and I got a stone and trust it between his jaws, and tried with all my might to cram it down his throat. A beast of a servant came up with a lantern, at last, shouting—

" 'Keep fast, Skulker, keep fast!'

"He changed his note, however, when he saw Skulker's game. The dog was throttled off, his huge, purple tongue hanging half a foot out of his mouth, and his pendant lips streaming with bloody slaver.

"The man took Cathy up; she was sick, not from fear, I'm certain, but from pain. He carried her in; I followed, grumbling execrations and vengeance.

" 'What prey, Robert?' hallooed Linton from the entrance.

" 'Skulker has caught a little girl, sir,' he replied, 'and there's a lad here,' he added, making a clutch at me, 'who looks an out-and-outer! Very like, the robbers were for putting them through the window, to open the doors to the gang after all were asleep, that they might murder us at their ease. Hold your tongue, you foul-mouthed thief, you! you shall go to the gallows for this. Mr.

Linton, sir, don't lay by your gun!'

" 'No, no, Robert!' said the old fool. 'The rascals knew that yesterday was my rent-day; they thought to have me cleverly. Come in; I'll furnish them a reception. There, John, fasten the chain. Give Skulker some water, Jenny. To beard a magistrate in his strong-hold, and on the Sabbath, too! Where will their insolence stop? Oh, my dear Mary, look here! Don't be afraid, it is but a boy—yet the villain scowls so plainly in his face, would it not be a kindness to the country to hang him at once, before he shows his nature in acts, as well as features?'

"He pulled me under the chandelier, and Mrs. Linton placed her spectacles on her nose and raised her hands in horror. The cowardly children crept nearer also, Isabella lisping—

" 'Frightful thing! Put him in the cellar, papa. He's exactly like the son of the fortune-teller that stole my tame pheasant. Isn't he, Edgar?'

"While they examined me, Cathy came round; she heard the last speech, and laughed. Edgar Linton, after an inquisitive stare, collected sufficient wit to recognise her. They see us at church, you know, though we seldom meet them elsewhere.

" 'That's Miss Earnshaw!' he whispered to his mother, 'and look how Skulker has bitten her—how her foot bleeds!'

" 'Miss Earnshaw? Nonsense!' cried the dame, 'Miss Earnshaw scouring the country with a gipsy! And yet, my dear, the child is in mourning—surely it is—and she may be lamed for life!'

" 'What culpable carelessness in her brother!' exclaimed Mr. Linton, turning from me to Catherine. 'I've understood from Shielders' (that was the curate, sir) 'that he lets her grow up in absolute heathenism. But who is this? Where did she pick up this companion? Oho! I declare he is that strange acquisition my late neighbour made in his journey to Liverpool—a little Lascar, or an American or Spanish castaway.'

" 'A wicked boy, at all events,' remarked the old lady, 'and quite unfit for a decent house! Did you notice his language, Linton? I'm shocked that my children should have heard it.'

"I recommended cursing—don't be angry, Nelly—and so Robert was ordered to take me off. I refused to go without Cathy; he dragged me into the garden, pushed the lantern into my hand, assured me that Mr. Earnshaw should be informed of my behaviour, and bidding me march directly, secured the door again.

"The curtains were still looped up at one corner; and I resumed my station as spy, because, if Catherine had wished to return, I intended shattering their great glass panes to a million fragments, unless they let her out.

"She sat on the sofa quietly. Mrs. Linton took off the grey cloak of the dairy maid which we had borrowed for our excursion, shaking her head, and expostulating with her, I suppose; she was a young lady and they made a distinction between her treatment and mine. Then the woman servant brought a basin of warm water, and washed her feet; and Mr. Linton mixed a tumbler of negus, and Isabella emptied a plateful of cakes into her lap, and Edgar stood gaping at a distance. Afterwards, they dried and combed her beautiful hair, and gave her a pair of enormous slippers, and wheeled her to the fire, and I left her, as merry as she could be, dividing her food between the little dog and Skulker whose nose she pinched as he ate; and kindling a spark of spirit in the vacant blue eyes of the Lintons—a dim reflection from her own enchanting face. I saw they were full of stupid admiration; she is so immeasurably superior to them—to everybody on earth, is she not, Nelly?"

"There will more come of this business than you reckon on," I answered, covering him up and extinguishing the light. "You are incurable, Heathcliff, and Mr. Hindley will have to proceed to extremities, see if he won't."

My words came truer than I desired. The luckless adventure made Earnshaw furious. And then Mr. Linton, to mend matters, paid us a visit himself on the morrow; and read the young master such a lecture on the road he guided his family, that he was stirred to look about him, in earnest.

Heathcliff received no flogging, but he was told that the first word he spoke to Miss Catherine should ensure a dismissal; and Mrs. Earnshaw undertook to keep her sister-in-law in due restraint, when she returned home; employing art, not force—with force she would have found it impossible.

Chapter VII

Cathy stayed at Thrushcross Grange five weeks, till Christmas. By that time her ankle was thoroughly cured, and her manners much improved. The mistress visited her often, in the interval, and commenced her plan of reform by trying to raise her self-respect with fine clothes and flattery, which she took readily: so that, instead of a wild, hatless little savage jumping into the house, and rushing to squeeze us all breathless, there alighted from a handsome black pony a very dignified person with brown ringlets falling from the cover of a feathered beaver, and a long cloth habit which she was obliged to hold up with both hands that she might sail in.

Hindley lifted her from her horse, exclaiming delightedly—

"Why, Cathy, you are quite a beauty! I should scarcely have

known you—you look like a lady now. Isabella Linton is not to be compared with her, is she, Frances?"

"Isabella has not her natural advantages," replied his wife, "but she must mind and not grow wild again here. Ellen, help Miss Catherine off with her things. Stay, dear, you will disarrange your curls—let me untie your hat."

I removed the habit, and there shone forth beneath, a grand plaid silk frock, white trousers, and burnished shoes; and, while her eyes sparkled joyfully when the dogs came bounding up to welcome her, she dare hardly touch them lest they should fawn upon her splendid garments.

She kissed me gently—I was all flour making the Christmas cake, and it would not have done to give me a hug—and then she looked round for Heathcliff. Mr. and Mrs. Earnshaw watched anxiously their meeting, thinking it would enable them to judge, in some measure, what grounds they had for hoping to succeed in separating the two friends.

Heathcliff was hard to discover, at first. If he were careless and uncared for, before Catherine's absence, he had been ten times more so, since.

Nobody but I even did him the kindness to call him a dirty boy, and bid him wash himself, once a week; and children of his age seldom have a natural pleasure in soap and water. Therefore, not to mention his clothes, which had seen three months' service in mire and dust, and his thick uncombed hair, the surface of his face and hands was dismally beclouded. He might well skulk behind the settle, on beholding such a bright, graceful damsel enter the house, instead of a rough-headed counterpart of himself, as he expected.

"Is Heathcliff not here?" she demanded, pulling off her gloves, and displaying fingers wonderfully whitened with doing nothing, and staying indoors.

"Heathcliff, you may come forward," cried Mr. Hindley, enjoying his discomfiture and gratified to see what a forbidding young blackguard he would be compelled to present himself. "You may come and wish Miss Catherine welcome, like the other servants."

Cathy, catching a glimpse of her friend in his concealment, flew to embrace him; she bestowed seven or eight kisses on his cheek within the second, and then stopped, and drawing back, burst into a laugh, exclaiming—

"Why, how very black and cross you look! and how—how funny and grim! But that's because I'm used to Edgar and Isabella Linton. Well, Heathcliff, have you forgotten me?"

She had some reason to put the question, for shame and pride threw double gloom over his countenance, and kept him immovable.

"Shake hands, Heathcliff," said Mr. Earnshaw, condescendingly; "once in a way, that is permitted."

"I shall not!" replied the boy, finding his tongue at last, "I shall not stand to be laughed at, I shall not bear it!"

And he would have broken from the circle, but Miss Cathy seized him again.

"I did not mean to laugh at you," she said, "I could not hinder myself. Heathcliff, shake hands, at least! What are you sulky for? It was only that you looked odd. If you wash your face and brush your hair, it will be all right. But you are so dirty!"

She gazed concernedly at the dusky fingers she held in her own, and also at her dress, which she feared had gained no embellishment from its contact with his.

"You needn't have touched me!" he answered, following her eye and snatching away his hand. "I shall be as dirty as I please, and I like to be dirty, and I will be dirty."

With that he dashed head foremost out of the room, amid the merriment of the master and mistress, and to the serious disturbance of Catherine, who could not comprehend how her remarks should have produced such an exhibition of bad temper.

After playing lady's maid to the new-comer, and putting my cakes in the oven, and making the house and kitchen cheerful with great fires befitting Christmas eve, I prepared to sit down and amuse myself by singing carols, all alone, regardless of Joseph's affirmations that he considered the merry tunes I chose as next door to songs.

He had retired to private prayer in his chamber, and Mr. and Mrs. Earnshaw were engaging Missy's attention by sundry gay trifles bought for her to present to the little Lintons, as an acknowledgment of their kindness.

They had invited them to spend the morrow at Wuthering Heights, and the invitation had been accepted, on one condition: Mrs. Linton begged that her darlings might be kept carefully apart from that "naughty, swearing boy."

Under these circumstances I remained solitary. I smelt the rich scent of the heating spices; and admired the shining kitchen utensils, the polished clock, decked in holly, the silver mugs ranged on a tray ready to be filled with mulled ale for supper; and, above all, the speckless purity of my particular care—the scoured and well-swept floor.

I gave due inward applause to every object, and then I remembered how old Earnshaw used to come in when all was tidied, and call me a cant lass,[7] and slip a shilling into my hand, as a

7. Lively girl.

Christmas box; and from that I went on to think of his fondness for Heathcliff, and his dread lest he should suffer neglect after death had removed him; and that naturally led me to consider the poor lad's situation now, and from singing I changed my mind to crying. It struck me soon, however, there would be more sense in endeavouring to repair some of his wrongs than shedding tears over them. I got up and walked into the court to seek him.

He was not far; I found him smoothing the glossy coat of the new pony in the stable, and feeding the other beasts, according to custom.

"Make haste, Heathcliff!" I said, "the kitchen is so comfortable —and Joseph is upstairs; make haste, and let me dress you smart before Miss Cathy comes out, and then you can sit together, with the whole hearth to yourselves, and have a long chatter till bed-time."

He proceeded with his task and never turned his head towards me.

"Come—are you coming?" I continued. "There's a little cake for each of you, nearly enough; and you'll need half an hour's donning."

I waited five minutes, but getting no answer left him. Catherine supped with her brother and sister-in-law: Joseph and I joined at an unsociable meal seasoned with reproofs on one side and sauci-ness on the other. His cake and cheese remained on the table all night for the fairies. He managed to continue work till nine o'clock, and then marched dumb and dour to his chamber.

Cathy sat up late, having a world of things to order for the reception of her new friends: she came into the kitchen, once, to speak to her old one, but he was gone, and she only stayed to ask what was the matter with him, and then went back.

In the morning, he rose early; and, as it was a holiday, carried his ill-humour onto the moors, not re-appearing till the family were departed for church. Fasting and reflection seemed to have brought him to a better spirit. He hung about me for a while, and having screwed up his courage, exclaimed abruptly—

"Nelly, make me decent, I'm going to be good."

"High time, Heathcliff," I said, "you *have* grieved Catherine; she's sorry she ever came home, I dare say! It looks as if you envied her, because she is more thought of than you."

The notion of *envying* Catherine was incomprehensible to him, but the notion of grieving her he understood clearly enough.

"Did she say she was grieved?" he inquired, looking very serious.

"She cried when I told her you were off again this morning."

"Well, *I* cried last night," he returned, "and I had more reason to cry than she."

"Yes, you had the reason of going to bed with a proud heart and an empty stomach," said I. "Proud people breed sad sorrows for themselves. But, if you be ashamed of your touchiness, you must ask pardon, mind, when she comes in. You must go up and offer to kiss her, and say—you know best what to say, only do it heartily, and not as if you thought her converted into a stranger by her grand dress. And now, though I have dinner to get ready, I'll steal time to arrange you so that Edgar Linton shall look quite a doll beside you: and that he does. You are younger, and yet, I'll be bound, you are taller and twice as broad across the shoulders—you could knock him down in a twinkling. Don't you feel that you could?"

Heathcliff's face brightened a moment; then it was overcast afresh, and he sighed.

"But, Nelly, if I knocked him down twenty times, that wouldn't make him less handsome, or me more so. I wish I had light hair and a fair skin, and was dressed and behaved as well, and had a chance of being as rich as he will be!"

"And cried for mamma, at every turn," I added, "and trembled if a country lad heaved his fist against you, and sat at home all day for a shower of rain. O, Heathcliff, you are showing a poor spirit! Come to the glass, and I'll let you see what you should wish. Do you mark those two lines between your eyes; and those thick brows, that instead of rising arched, sink in the middle; and that couple of black fiends, so deeply buried, who never open their windows boldly, but lurk glinting under them, like devil's spies? Wish and learn to smooth away the surly wrinkles, to raise your lids frankly, and change the fiends to confident, innocent angels, suspecting and doubting nothing, and always seeing friends where they are not sure of foes. Don't get the expression of a vicious cur that appears to know the kicks it gets are its desert, and yet hates all the world, as well as the kicker, for what it suffers."

"In other words, I must wish for Edgar Linton's great blue eyes, and even forehead," he replied. "I do—and that won't help me to them."

"A good heart will help you to a bonny face, my lad," I continued, "if you were a regular black; and a bad one will turn the bonniest into something worse than ugly. And now that we've done washing, and combing, and sulking—tell me whether you don't think yourself rather handsome? I'll tell you, I do. You're fit for a prince in disguise. Who knows but your father was Emperor of China, and your mother an Indian queen, each of them able to buy up, with one week's income, Wuthering Heights and Thrushcross Grange together? And you were kidnapped by wicked sailors, and brought to England. Were I in your place, I would frame high notions of my birth; and the thoughts of what I was should give me courage and dignity to support the oppressions of a little farmer!"

So I chattered on; and Heathcliff gradually lost his frown, and began to look quite pleasant, when, all at once, our conversation was interrupted by a rumbling sound moving up the road and entering the court. He ran to the window, and I to the door, just in time to behold the two Lintons descend from the family carriage, smothered in cloaks and furs, and the Earnshaws dismount from their horses—they often rode to church in winter. Catherine took a hand of each of the children, and brought them into the house, and set them before the fire, which quickly put colour into their white faces.

I urged my companion to hasten now, and show his amiable humour, and he willingly obeyed; but ill luck would have it that, as he opened the door leading from the kitchen on one side, Hindley opened it on the other. They met, and the master, irritated at seeing him clean and cheerful, or, perhaps, eager to keep his promise to Mrs. Linton, shoved him back with a sudden thrust, and angrily bade Joseph "keep the fellow out of the room —send him into the garret till dinner is over. He'll be cramming his fingers in the tarts, and stealing the fruit, if left alone with them a minute."

"Nay, sir," I could not avoid answering, "he'll touch nothing, not he—and, I suppose, he must have his share of the dainties as well as we."

"He shall have his share of my hand, if I catch him downstairs again till dark," cried Hindley. "Begone, you vagabond! What! you are attempting the coxcomb, are you? Wait till I get hold of those elegant locks—see if I won't pull them a bit longer!"

"They are long enough already," observed Master Linton, peeping from the door-way; "I wonder they don't make his head ache. It's like a colt's mane over his eyes!"

He ventured this remark without any intention to insult; but Heathcliff's violent nature was not prepared to endure the appearance of impertinence from one whom he seemed to hate, even then, as a rival. He seized a tureen of hot apple-sauce, the first thing that came under his gripe, and dashed it full against the speaker's face and neck—who instantly commenced a lament that brought Isabella and Catherine hurrying to the place.

Mr. Earnshaw snatched up the culprit directly and conveyed him to his chamber, where, doubtless, he administered a rough remedy to cool the fit of passion, for he reappeared red and breathless. I got the dishcloth, and, rather spitefully, scrubbed Edgar's nose and mouth, affirming it served him right for meddling. His sister began weeping to go home, and Cathy stood by, confounded, blushing for all.

"You should not have spoken to him!" she expostulated with Master Linton. "He was in a bad temper, and now you've spoilt your visit, and he'll be flogged—I hate him to be flogged! I can't eat my dinner. Why did you speak to him, Edgar?"

"I didn't," sobbed the youth, escaping from my hands, and finishing the remainder of the purification with his cambric pocket-handkerchief. "I promised mamma that I wouldn't say one word to him, and I didn't!"

"Well, don't cry!" replied Catherine, contemptuously. "You're not killed. Don't make more mischief—my brother is coming—be quiet! Give over, Isabella! Has anybody hurt *you?*"

"There, there, children—to your seats!" cried Hindley, bustling in. "That brute of a lad has warmed me nicely. Next time, Master Edgar, take the law into your own fists—it will give you an appetite!"

The little party recovered its equanimity at sight of the fragrant feast. They were hungry after their ride, and easily consoled, since no real harm had befallen them.

Mr. Earnshaw carved bountiful platefuls; and the mistress made them merry with lively talk. I waited behind her chair, and was pained to behold Catherine, with dry eyes and an indifferent air, commence cutting up the wing of a goose before her.

"An unfeeling child," I thought to myself, "how lightly she dismisses her old playmate's troubles. I could not have imagined her to be so selfish."

She lifted a mouthful to her lips; then she set it down again: her cheeks flushed, and the tears gushed over them. She slipped her fork to the floor, and hastily dived under the cloth to conceal her emotion. I did not call her unfeeling long, for I perceived she was in purgatory throughout the day, and wearying to find an opportunity of getting by herself, or paying a visit to Heathcliff, who had been locked up by the master, as I discovered on endeavouring to introduce to him a private mess of victuals.

In the evening we had a dance. Cathy begged that he might be liberated then, as Isabella Linton had no partner; her entreaties were vain, and I was appointed to supply the deficiency.

We got rid of all gloom in the excitement of the exercise, and our pleasure was increased by the arrival of the Gimmerton band, mustering fifteen strong: a trumpet, a trombone, clarionets, bassoons, French horns, and a bass viol, besides singers. They go the rounds of all the respectable houses, and receive contributions every Christmas, and we esteemed it a first-rate treat to hear them.

After the usual carols had been sung, we set them to songs

and glees. Mrs. Earnshaw loved the music, and so they gave us plenty.

Catherine loved it too; but she said it sounded sweetest at the top of the steps, and she went up in the dark; I followed. They shut the house door below, never noting our absence, the place was so full of people. She made no stay at the stairs' head, but mounted farther, to the garret where Heathcliff was confined, and called him. He stubbornly declined answering for a while; she persevered, and finally persuaded him to hold communion with her through the boards.

I let the poor things converse unmolested, till I supposed the songs were going to cease, and the singers to get some refreshment: then, I clambered up the ladder to warn her.

Instead of finding her outside, I heard her voice within. The little monkey had crept by the skylight of one garret, along the roof, into the skylight of the other, and it was with the utmost difficulty I could coax her out again.

When she did come, Heathcliff came with her; and she insisted that I should take him into the kitchen, as my fellow-servant had gone to a neighbour's to be removed from the sound of our "devil's psalmody," as it pleased him to call it.

I told them I intended, by no means, to encourage their tricks; but as the prisoner had never broken his fast since yesterday's dinner, I would wink at his cheating Mr. Hindley that once.

He went down; I set him a stool by the fire, and offered him a quantity of good things; but he was sick and could eat little, and my attempts to entertain him were thrown away. He leant his two elbows on his knees, and his chin on his hands, and remained wrapt in dumb meditation. On my inquiring the subject of his thoughts, he answered gravely—

"I'm trying to settle how I shall pay Hindley back. I don't care how long I wait, if I can only do it, at last. I hope he will not die before I do!"

"For shame, Heathcliff!" said I. "It is for God to punish wicked people; we should learn to forgive."

"No, God won't have the satisfaction that I shall," he returned. "I only wish I knew the best way! Let me alone, and I'll plan it out: while I'm thinking of that, I don't feel pain."

But, Mr. Lockwood, I forget these tales cannot divert you. I'm annoyed how I should dream of chattering on at such a rate; and your gruel cold, and you nodding for bed! I could have told Heathcliff's history, all that you need hear, in half-a-dozen words.

Thus interrupting herself, the housekeeper rose, and proceeded to lay aside her sewing; but I felt incapable of moving from the hearth, and I was very far from nodding.

"Sit still, Mrs. Dean," I cried, "do sit still, another half hour! You've done just right to tell the story leisurely. That is the method I like; and you must finish in the same style. I am interested in every character you have mentioned, more or less."

"The clock is on the stroke of eleven, sir."

"No matter—I'm not accustomed to go to bed in the long hours. One or two is early enough for a person who lies till ten."

"You shouldn't lie till ten. There's the very prime of the morning gone long before that time. A person who has not done one half his day's work by ten o'clock runs a chance of leaving the other half undone."

"Nevertheless, Mrs. Dean, resume your chair; because to-morrow I intend lengthening the night till afternoon. I prognosticate for myself an obstinate cold, at least."

"I hope not, sir. Well, you must allow me to leap over some three years; during that space Mrs. Earnshaw—"

"No, no, I'll allow nothing of the sort! Are you acquainted with the mood of mind in which, if you were seated alone, and the cat licking its kitten on the rug before you, you would watch the operation so intently that puss's neglect of one ear would put you seriously out of temper?"

"A terribly lazy mood, I should say."

"On the contrary, a tiresomely active one. It is mine, at present, and, therefore, continue minutely. I perceive that people in these regions acquire over people in towns the value that a spider in a dungeon does over a spider in a cottage, to their various occupants; and yet the deepened attraction is not entirely owing to the situation of the looker-on. They *do* live more in earnest, more in themselves, and less in surface change, and frivolous external things. I could fancy a love for life here almost possible; and I was a fixed unbeliever in any love of a year's standing. One state resembles setting a hungry man down to a single dish on which he may concentrate his entire appetite, and do it justice; the other, introducing him to a table laid out by French cooks. He can perhaps extract as much enjoyment from the whole, but each part is a mere atom in his regard and remembrance."

"Oh! here we are the same as anywhere else, when you get to know us," observed Mrs. Dean, somewhat puzzled at my speech.

"Excuse me," I responded; "you, my good friend, are a striking evidence against that assertion. Excepting a few provincialisms of slight consequence, you have no marks of the manners that I am habituated to consider as peculiar to your class. I am sure you have thought a great deal more than the generality of servants think. You have been compelled to cultivate your reflective faculties, for want of occasions for frittering your life away in silly trifles."

Mrs. Dean laughed.

"I certainly esteem myself a steady, reasonable kind of body," she said, "not exactly from living among the hills and seeing one set of faces, and one series of actions, from year's end to year's end; but I have undergone sharp discipline which has taught me wisdom; and then, I have read more than you would fancy, Mr. Lockwood. You could not open a book in this library that I have not looked into, and got something out of also, unless it be that range of Greek and Latin, and that of French—and those I know one from another: it is as much as you can expect of a poor man's daughter."

"However, if I am to follow my story in true gossip's fashion, I had better go on; and instead of leaping three years, I will be content to pass to the next summer—the summer of 1778, that is, nearly twenty-three years ago."

Chapter VIII

On the morning of a fine June day, my first bonny little nursling, and the last of the ancient Earnshaw stock, was born.

We were busy with the hay in a far-away field, when the girl that usually brought our breakfasts came running, an hour too soon, across the meadow and up the lane, calling me as she ran.

"Oh, such a grand bairn!" she panted out. "The finest lad that ever breathed! But the doctor says missis must go; he says she's been in a consumption these many months. I heard him tell Mr. Hindley: and now she has nothing to keep her, and she'll be dead before winter. You must come home directly. You're to nurse it, Nelly—to feed it with sugar and milk, and take care of it, day and night. I wish I were you, because it will be all yours when there is no missis!"

"But is she very ill?" I asked, flinging down my rake, and tying my bonnet.

"I guess she is; yet she looks bravely," replied the girl, "and she talks as if she thought of living to see it grow a man. She's out of her head for joy, it's such a beauty! If I were her, I'm certain I should not die. I should get better at the bare sight of it, in spite of Kenneth. I was fairly mad at him. Dame Archer brought the cherub down to master, in the house, and his face just began to light up, when the old croaker steps forward, and, says he—'Earnshaw, it's a blessing your wife has been spared to leave you this son. When she came, I felt convinced we shouldn't keep her long; and now, I must tell you, the winter will probably finish her. Don't take on, and fret about it too much, it can't be helped. And besides, you should have known better than to choose such a rush of a lass!' "[8]

"And what did the master answer?" I enquired.

"I think he swore—but I didn't mind him, I was straining tc see the bairn," and she began again to describe it rapturously. I, as zealous as herself, hurried eagerly home to admire, on my part, though I was very sad for Hindley's sake; he had room in his heart only for two idols—his wife and himself: he doted on both, and adored one, and I couldn't conceive how he would bear the loss.

When we got to Wuthering Heights, there he stood at the front door; and, as I passed in, I asked, how was the baby?

"Nearly ready to run about, Nell!" he replied, putting on a cheerful smile.

"And the mistress?" I ventured to inquire, "the doctor says she's—"

"Damn the doctor!" he interrupted, reddening. "Frances is quite right—she'll be perfectly well by this time next week. Are you going upstairs? will you tell her that I'll come, if she'll promise not to talk? I left her because she would not hold her tongue; and she must—tell her Mr. Kenneth says she must be quiet."

I delivered this message to Mrs. Earnshaw; she seemed in flighty spirits, and replied merrily—

"I hardly spoke a word, Ellen, and there he has gone out twice, crying. Well, say I promise I won't speak; but that does not bind me not to laugh at him!"

Poor soul! Till within a week of her death that gay heart never failed her; and her husband persisted doggedly, nay, furiously, in affirming her health improved every day. When Kenneth warned him that his medicines were useless at that stage of the malady, and he needn't put him to further expense by attending her, he retorted—

"I know you need not—she's well—she does not want any more attendance from you! She never was in a consumption. It was a fever; and it is gone—her pulse is as slow as mine now, and her cheek as cool."

He told his wife the same story, and she seemed to believe him; but one night, while leaning on his shoulder, in the act of saying she thought she should be able to get up to-morrow, a fit of coughing took her—a very slight one. He raised her in his arms; she put her two hands about his neck, her face changed, and she was dead.

As the girl had anticipated, the child Hareton fell wholly into my hands. Mr. Earnshaw, provided he saw him healthy, and never heard him cry, was contented, as far as regarded him. For

8. *Rush of a lass:* slender, delicate, like a rush.

himself, he grew desperate; his sorrow was of that kind that will not lament. He neither wept nor prayed—he cursed and defied—execrated God and man, and gave himself up to reckless dissipation.

The servants could not bear his tyrannical and evil conduct long: Joseph and I were the only two that would stay. I had not the heart to leave my charge; and besides, you know, I had been his foster sister, and excused his behaviour more readily than a stranger would.

Joseph remained to hector over tenants and labourers, and because it was his vocation to be where there was plenty of wickedness to reprove.

The master's bad ways and bad companions formed a pretty example for Catherine and Heathcliff. His treatment of the latter was enough to make a fiend of a saint. And, truly, it appeared as if the lad *were* possessed of something diabolical at that period. He delighted to witness Hindley degrading himself past redemption; and became daily more notable for savage sullenness and ferocity.

I could not half tell what an infernal house we had. The curate dropped calling, and nobody decent came near us, at last, unless Edgar Linton's visits to Miss Cathy might be an exception. At fifteen she was the queen of the country-side; she had no peer, and she did turn out a haughty, headstrong creature! I own I did not like her after her infancy was past; and I vexed her frequently by trying to bring down her arrogance; she never took an aversion to me, though. She had a wondrous constancy to old attachments; even Heathcliff kept his hold on her affections unalterably, and young Linton, with all his superiority, found it difficult to make an equally deep impression.

He was my late master; that is his portrait over the fireplace. It used to hang on one side, and his wife's on the other; but hers has been removed, or else you might see something of what she was. Can you make that out?

Mrs. Dean raised the candle, and I discerned a soft-featured face, exceedingly resembling the young lady at the Heights, but more pensive and amiable in expression. It formed a sweet picture. The long light hair curled slightly on the temple; the eyes were large and serious; the figure almost too graceful. I did not marvel how Catherine Earnshaw could forget her first friend for such an individual. I marvelled much how he, with a mind to correspond with his person, could fancy my idea of Catherine Earnshaw.

"A very agreeable portrait," I observed to the housekeeper. "Is it like?"

"Yes," she answered; "but he looked better when he was animated; that is his every day countenance; he wanted spirit in general."

Catherine had kept up her acquaintance with the Lintons since her five weeks' residence among them; and as she had no temptation to show her rough side in their company, and had the sense to be ashamed of being rude where she experienced such invariable courtesy, she imposed unwittingly on the old lady and gentleman, by her ingenious cordiality; gained the admiration of Isabella, and the heart and soul of her brother—acquisitions that flattered her from the first, for she was full of ambition, and led her to adopt a double character without exactly intending to deceive anyone.

In the place where she heard Heathcliff termed a "vulgar young ruffian," and "worse than a brute," she took care not to act like him; but at home she had small inclination to practise politeness that would only be laughed at, and restrain an unruly nature when it would bring her neither credit nor praise.

Mr. Edgar seldom mustered courage to visit Wuthering Heights openly. He had a terror of Earnshaw's reputation, and shrunk from encountering him, and yet he was always received with our best attempts at civility: the master himself avoided offending him, knowing why he came, and if he could not be gracious, kept out of the way. I rather think his appearance there was distasteful to Catherine; she was not artful, never played the coquette, and had evidently an objection to her two friends meeting at all; for when Heathcliff expressed contempt of Linton, in his presence, she could not half coincide, as she did in his absence; and when Linton evinced disgust and antipathy to Heathcliff, she dare not treat his sentiments with indifference, as if depreciation of her playmate were of scarcely any consequence to her.

I've had many a laugh at her perplexities and untold troubles, which she vainly strove to hide from my mockery. That sounds ill-natured—but she was so proud, it became really impossible to pity her distresses, till she should be chastened into more humility.

She did bring herself, finally, to confess, and confide in me. There was not a soul else that she might fashion into an adviser.

Mr. Hindley had gone from home, one afternoon, and Heathcliff presumed to give himself a holiday on the strength of it. He had reached the age of sixteen then, I think, and without having bad features or being deficient in intellect, he contrived to convey an impression of inward and outward repulsiveness that his present aspect retains no traces of.

In the first place, he had, by that time, lost the benefit of his early education: continual hard work, begun soon and concluded late, had extinguished any curiosity he once possessed in pursuit of knowledge, and any love for books or learning. His childhood's sense of superiority, instilled into him by the favours of old Mr. Earnshaw, was faded away. He struggled long to keep up an equality with Catherine in her studies and yielded with poignant though silent regret: but he yielded completely; and there was no prevailing on him to take a step in the way of moving upward, when he found he must, necessarily, sink beneath his former level. Then personal appearance sympathised with mental deterioration; he acquired a slouching gait, and ignoble look; his naturally reserved disposition was exaggerated into an almost idiotic excess of unsociable moroseness; and he took a grim pleasure, apparently, in exciting the aversion rather than the esteem of his few acquaintance.

Catherine and he were constant companions still, at his seasons of respite from labour; but he had ceased to express his fondness for her in words, and recoiled with angry suspicion from her girlish caresses, as if conscious there could be no gratification in lavishing such marks of affection on him. On the before-named occasion he came into the house to announce his intention of doing nothing, while I was assisting Miss Cathy to arrange her dress: she had not reckoned on his taking it into his head to be idle, and imagining she would have the whole place to herself, she managed, by some means, to inform Mr. Edgar of her brother's absence, and was then preparing to receive him.

"Cathy, are you busy, this afternoon?" asked Heathcliff. "Are you going anywhere?"

"No, it is raining," she answered.

"Why have you that silk frock on, then?" he said. "Nobody coming here, I hope?"

"Not that I know of," stammered Miss, "but you should be in the field now, Heathcliff. It is an hour past dinner time; I thought you were gone."

"Hindley does not often free us from his accursed presence," observed the boy. "I'll not work any more to-day, I'll stay with you."

"O, but Joseph will tell," she suggested. "You'd better go!"

"Joseph is loading lime on the farther side of Pennistow Crag; it will take him till dark, and he'll never know."

So saying he lounged to the fire, and sat down. Catherine reflected an instant, with knitted brows—she found it needful to smooth the way for an intrusion.

"Isabella and Edgar Linton talked of calling this afternoon," she said, at the conclusion of a minute's silence. "As it rains, I hardly expect them; but they may come, and if they do, you run the risk of being scolded for no good."

"Order Ellen to say you are engaged, Cathy," he persisted. "Don't turn me out for those pitiful, silly friends of yours! I'm on the point, sometimes, of complaining that they—but I'll not—"

"That they what?" cried Catherine, gazing at him with a troubled countenance. "Oh, Nelly!" she added petulantly, jerking her head away from my hands, "you've combed my hair quite out of curl! That's enough, let me alone. What are you on the point of complaining about, Heathcliff?"

"Nothing—only look at the almanack on that wall." He pointed to a framed sheet hanging near the window, and continued—

"The crosses are for the evenings you have spent with the Lintons, the dots for those spent with me. Do you see? I've marked every day."

"Yes—very foolish; as if I took notice!" replied Catherine in a peevish tone. "And where is the sense of that?"

"To show that I *do* take notice," said Heathcliff.

"And should I always be sitting with you?" she demanded, growing more irritated. "What good do I get? What do you talk about? You might be dumb or a baby for anything you say to amuse me, or for anything you do, either!"

"You never told me before that I talked too little, or that you disliked my company, Cathy!" exclaimed Heathcliff in much agitation.

"It is no company at all, when people know nothing and say nothing," she muttered.

Her companion rose up, but he hadn't time to express his feelings further, for a horse's feet were heard on the flags, and, having knocked gently, young Linton entered, his face brilliant with delight at the unexpected summons he had received.

Doubtless Catherine marked the difference between her friends as one came in, and the other went out. The contrast resembled what you see in exchanging a bleak, hilly, coal country, for a beautiful fertile valley; and his voice and greeting were as opposite as his aspect. He had a sweet, low manner of speaking, and pronounced his words as you do: that's less gruff than we talk here, and softer.

"I'm not come too soon, am I?" he said, casting a look at me. I had begun to wipe the plate, and tidy some drawers at the far end in the dresser.

"No," answered Catherine. "What are you doing there, Nelly?"

"My work, Miss," I replied. (Mr. Hindley had given me directions to make a third party in any private visits Linton chose to pay.)

She stepped behind me and whispered crossly, "Take yourself and your dusters off; when company are in the house, servants don't commence scouring and cleaning in the room where they are!"

"It's a good opportunity, now that master is away," I answered aloud: "he hates me to be fidgetting over these things in his presence. I'm sure Mr. Edgar will excuse me."

"I hate you to be fidgetting in *my* presence," exclaimed the young lady imperiously, not allowing her guest time to speak. She had failed to recover her equanimity since the little dispute with Heathcliff.

"I'm sorry for it, Miss Catherine!" was my response; and I proceeded assiduously with my occupation.

She, supposing Edgar could not see her, snatched the cloth from my hand, and pinched me, with a prolonged wrench, very spitefully on the arm.

I've said I did not love her, and rather relished mortifying her vanity, now and then; besides, she hurt me extremely, so I started up from my knees, and screamed out—

"O, Miss, that's a nasty trick! you have no right to nip me, and I'm not going to bear it!"

"I didn't touch you, you lying creature!" cried she, her fingers tingling to repeat the act, and her ears red with rage. She never had power to conceal her passion, it always set her whole complexion in a blaze.

"What's that, then?" I retorted, showing a decided purple witness to refute her.

She stamped her foot, wavered a moment, and then, irresistibly impelled by the naughty spirit within her, slapped me on the cheek a stinging blow that filled both eyes with water.

"Catherine, love! Catherine!" interposed Linton, greatly shocked at the double fault of falsehood and violence which his idol had committed.

"Leave the room, Ellen!" she repeated, trembling all over.

Little Hareton, who followed me everywhere, and was sitting near me on the floor, at seeing my tears commenced crying himself, and sobbed out complaints against "wicked Aunt Cathy," which drew her fury on to his unlucky head: she seized his shoulders, and shook him till the poor child waxed livid, and Edgar thoughtlessly laid hold of her hands to deliver him. In an instant one was wrung free, and the astonished young man felt it applied over his own ear in a way that could not be mistaken for jest.

He drew back in consternation. I lifted Hareton in my arms, and walked off to the kitchen with him, leaving the door of communication open, for I was curious to watch how they would settle their disagreement.

The insulted visitor moved to the spot where he had laid his hat, pale and with a quivering lip.

"That's right!" I said to myself. "Take warning and begone! It's a kindness to let you have a glimpse of her genuine disposition."

"Where are you going?" demanded Catherine, advancing to the door.

He swerved aside and attempted to pass.

"You must not go!" she exclaimed energetically.

"I must and shall!" he replied in a subdued voice.

"No," she persisted, grasping the handle; "not yet, Edgar Linton —sit down; you shall not leave me in that temper. I should be miserable all night, and I won't be miserable for you!"

"Can I stay after you have struck me?" asked Linton.

Catherine was mute.

"You've made me afraid, and ashamed of you," he continued; "I'll not come here again!"

Her eyes began to glisten and her lids to twinkle.

"And you told a deliberate untruth!" he said.

"I didn't!" she cried, recovering her speech. "I did nothing deliberately—Well, go, if you please—get away! And now I'll cry— I'll cry myself sick!"

She dropped down on her knees by a chair and set to weeping in serious earnest.

Edgar persevered in his resolution as far as the court; there he lingered. I resolved to encourage him.

"Miss is dreadfully wayward, sir!" I called out. "As bad as any marred child⁹—you'd better be riding home, or else she will be sick, only to grieve us."

The soft thing looked askance through the window: he possessed the power to depart, as much as a cat possesses the power to leave a mouse half killed, or a bird half eaten.

Ah, I thought, there will be no saving him—He's doomed, and flies to his fate!

And so it was; he turned abruptly, hastened into the house again, shut the door behind him; and, when I went in a while after to inform them that Earnshaw had come home rabid drunk, ready to pull the old place about our ears (his ordinary frame of mind in that condition), I saw the quarrel had merely effected a closer intimacy—had broken the outworks of youthful timidity, and enabled them to forsake the disguise of friendship, and confess themselves lovers.

Intelligence of Mr. Hindley's arrival drove Linton speedily to his horse, and Catherine to her chamber. I went to hide little Hareton, and to take the shot out of the master's fowling piece, which he was fond of playing with in his insane excitement, to the hazard of the lives of any who provoked, or even attracted his notice too much; and I had hit upon the plan of removing it, that he might do less mischief, if he did go the length of firing the gun.

9. Spoiled child.

Chapter IX

He entered, vociferating oaths dreadful to hear; and caught me in the act of stowing his son away in the kitchen cupboard. Hareton was impressed with a wholesome terror of encountering either his wild beast's fondness or his madman's rage; for in one he ran a chance of being squeezed and kissed to death, and in the other of being flung into the fire, or dashed against the wall; and the poor thing remained perfectly quiet wherever I chose to put him.

"There, I've found it out at last!" cried Hindley, pulling me back by the skin of the neck, like a dog. "By heaven and hell, you've sworn between you to murder that child! I know how it is, now, that he is always out of my way. But, with the help of Satan, I shall make you swallow the carving knife, Nelly! You needn't laugh; for I've just crammed Kenneth, head-downmost, in the Blackhorse marsh; and two is the same as one—and I want to kill some of you, I shall have no rest till I do!"

"But I don't like the carving knife, Mr. Hindley," I answered; "it has been cutting red herrings. I'd rather be shot, if you please."

"You'd rather be damned!" he said, "and so you shall. No law in England can hinder a man from keeping his house decent, and mine's abominable! open your mouth."

He held the knife in his hand, and pushed its point between my teeth: but, for my part, I was never much afraid of his vagaries. I spat out, and affirmed it tasted detestably—I would not take it on any account.

"Oh!" said he, releasing me, "I see that hideous little villain is not Hareton: I beg your pardon, Nell. If it be, he deserves flaying alive for not running to welcome me, and for screaming as if I were a goblin. Unnatural cub, come hither! I'll teach thee to impose on a good-hearted, deluded father. Now, don't you think the lad would be handsomer cropped? It makes a dog fiercer, and I love something fierce—get me a scissors—something fierce and trim! Besides, it's infernal affectation—devilish conceit it is—to cherish our ears: we're asses enough without them. Hush, child, hush! well, then, it is my darling! wisht,[1] dry thy eyes—there's a joy; kiss me; what! it won't? kiss me, Hareton! Damn thee, kiss me! By God, as if I would rear such a monster! As sure as I'm living, I'll break the brat's neck."

Poor Hareton was squalling and kicking in his father's arms with all his might, and redoubled his yells when he carried him upstairs and lifted him over the banister. I cried out that he would frighten the child into fits, and ran to rescue him.

As I reached them, Hindley leant forward on the rails to listen

1. Be quiet.

to a noise below, almost forgetting what he had in his hands.

"Who is that?" he asked, hearing some one approaching the stair's foot.

I leant forward also, for the purpose of signing to Heathcliff, whose step I recognized, not to come further; and, at the instant when my eye quitted Hareton, he gave a sudden spring, delivered himself from the careless grasp that held him, and fell.

There was scarcely time to experience a thrill of horror before we saw that the little wretch was safe. Heathcliff arrived underneath just at the critical moment; by a natural impulse, he arrested his descent, and setting him on his feet, looked up to discover the author of the accident.

A miser who has parted with a lucky lottery ticket for five shillings, and finds next day he has lost in the bargain five thousand pounds, could not show a blanker countenance than he did on beholding the figure of Mr. Earnshaw above. It expressed, plainer than words could do, the intensest anguish at having made himself the instrument of thwarting his own revenge. Had it been dark, I dare say, he would have tried to remedy the mistake by smashing Hareton's skull on the steps; but we witnessed his salvation; and I was presently below with my precious charge pressed to my heart.

Hindley descended more leisurely, sobered and abashed.

"It is your fault, Ellen," he said, "you should have kept him out of sight; you should have taken him from me! Is he injured anywhere?"

"Injured!" I cried angrily, "If he's not killed, he'll be an idiot! Oh! I wonder his mother does not rise from her grave to see how you use him. You're worse than a heathen—treating your own flesh and blood in that manner!"

He attempted to touch the child, who, on finding himself with me, sobbed off his terror directly. At the first finger his father laid on him, however, he shrieked again louder than before, and struggled as if he would go into convulsions.

"You shall not meddle with him!" I continued, "He hates you —they all hate you—that's the truth! A happy family you have; and a pretty state you're come to!"

"I shall come to a prettier, yet, Nelly!" laughed the misguided man, recovering his hardness. "At present, convey yourself and him away. And, hark you, Heathcliff! clear you too, quite from my reach and hearing. I wouldn't murder you to-night, unless, perhaps, I set the house on fire; but that's as my fancy goes—"

While saying this he took a pint bottle of brandy from the dresser, and poured some into a tumbler.

"Nay, don't!" I entreated, "Mr. Hindley, do take warning. Have mercy on this unfortunate boy, if you care nothing for yourself!"

"Any one will do better for him than I shall," he answered.

"Have mercy on your own soul!" I said, endeavouring to snatch the glass from his hand.

"Not I! on the contrary, I shall have great pleasure in sending it to perdition, to punish its Maker," exclaimed the blasphemer. "Here's to its hearty damnation!"

He drank the spirits, and impatiently bade us go; terminating his command with a sequel of horrid imprecations, too bad to repeat or remember.

"It's a pity he cannot kill himself with drink," observed Heathcliff, muttering an echo of curses back when the door was shut. "He's doing his very utmost; but his constitution defies him. Mr. Kenneth says he would wager his mare, that he'll outlive any man on this side Gimmerton, and go to the grave a hoary sinner; unless some happy chance out of the common course befall him."

I went into the kitchen and sat down to lull my little lamb to sleep. Heathcliff, as I thought, walked through to the barn. It turned out, afterwards, that he only got as far as the other side the settle, when he flung himself on a bench by the wall, removed from the fire, and remained silent.

I was rocking Hareton on my knee, and humming a song that began—·

"It was far in the night, and the bairnies grat,
The mither beneath the mools heard that,"[2]

when Miss Cathy, who had listened to the hubbub from her room, put her head in, and whispered—

"Are you alone, Nelly?"

"Yes, Miss," I replied.

She entered and approached the hearth. I, supposing she was going to say something, looked up. The expression of her face seemed disturbed and anxious. Her lips were half asunder as if she meant to speak; and she drew a breath, but it escaped in a sigh, instead of a sentence.

I resumed my song, not having forgotten her recent behaviour.

"Where's Heathcliff?" she said, interrupting me.

"About his work in the stable," was my answer.

He did not contradict me; perhaps he had fallen into a doze.

There followed another long pause, during which I perceived a drop or two trickle from Catherine's cheek to the flags.

Is she sorry for her shameful conduct? I asked myself. That will be a novelty, but she may come to the point as she will—I shan't help her!

No, she felt small trouble regarding any subject, save her own

2. *Bairnies grat:* little ones wept; *mools:* earth of a grave.

concerns.

"Oh, dear!" she cried at last. "I'm very unhappy!"

"A pity," observed I. "You're hard to please—so many friends and so few cares, and can't make yourself content!"

"Nelly, will you keep a secret for me?" she pursued, kneeling down by me, and lifting her winsome eyes to my face with that sort of look which turns off bad temper, even when one has all the right in the world to indulge it.

"Is it worth keeping?" I inquired, less sulkily.

"Yes, and it worries me, and I must let it out! I want to know what I should do. To-day, Edgar Linton has asked me to marry him, and I've given him an answer. Now, before I tell you whether it was a consent, or denial, you tell me which it ought to have been."

"Really, Miss Catherine, how can I know?" I replied. "To be sure, considering the exhibition you performed in his presence this afternoon, I might say it would be wise to refuse him: since he asked you after that, he must either be hopelessly stupid or a venturesome fool."

"If you talk so, I won't tell you any more," she returned, peevishly, rising to her feet, "I accepted him, Nelly. Be quick, and say whether I was wrong!"

"You accepted him? then, what good is it discussing the matter? You have pledged your word, and cannot retract."

"But, say whether I should have done so—do!" she exclaimed in an irritated tone, chafing her hands together, and frowning.

"There are many things to be considered before that question can be answered properly," I said sententiously. "First and foremost, do you love Mr. Edgar?"

"Who can help it? Of course I do," she answered.

Then I put her through the following catechism: for a girl of twenty-two, it was not injudicious.

"Why do you love him, Miss Cathy?"

"Nonsense, I do—that's sufficient."

"By no means; you must say why."

"Well, because he is handsome, and pleasant to be with."

"Bad," was my commentary.

"And because he is young and cheerful."

"Bad, still."

"And because he loves me."

"Indifferent, coming there."

"And he will be rich, and I shall like to be the greatest woman of the neighbourhood, and I shall be proud of having such a husband."

"Worst of all! And now, say how you love him."

"As everybody loves—You're silly, Nelly."

"Not at all—Answer."

"I love the ground under his feet, and the air over his head, and everything he touches, and every word he says—I love all his looks, and all his actions, and him entirely, and altogether. There now!"

"And why?"

"Nay—you are making a jest of it; it is exceedingly ill-natured! It's no jest to me!" said the young lady, scowling, and turning her face to the fire.

"I'm very far from jesting, Miss Catherine," I replied. "You love Mr. Edgar, because he is handsome, and young, and cheerful, and rich, and loves you. The last, however, goes for nothing. You would love him without that, probably; and with it, you wouldn't, unless he possessed the four former attractions."

"No, to be sure not: I should only pity him—hate him, perhaps, if he were ugly, and a clown."

"But there are several other handsome, rich young men in the world; handsomer, possibly, and richer than he is. What should hinder you from loving them?"

"If there be any, they are out of my way. I've seen none like Edgar."

"You may see some; and he won't always be handsome, and young, and may not always be rich."

"He is now; and I have only to do with the present. I wish you would speak rationally."

"Well, that settles it—if you have only to do with the present, marry Mr. Linton."

"I don't want your permission for that—I *shall* marry him; and yet you have not told me whether I'm right."

"Perfectly right; if people be right to marry only for the present. And now, let us hear what you are unhappy about. Your brother will be pleased; the old lady and gentleman will not object, I think; you will escape from a disorderly, comfortless home into a wealthy, respectable one; and you love Edgar, and Edgar loves you. All seems smooth and easy—where is the obstacle?"

"*Here!* and *here!*" replied Catherine, striking one hand on her forehead, and the other on her breast. "In whichever place the soul lives—in my soul, and in my heart, I'm convinced I'm wrong!"

"That's very strange! I cannot make it out."

"It's my secret; but if you will not mock at me, I'll explain it; I can't do it distinctly, but I'll give you a feeling of how I feel."

She seated herself by me again: her countenance grew sadder and graver, and her clasped hands trembled.

"Nelly, do you never dream queer dreams?" she said, suddenly, after some minutes' reflection.

"Yes, now and then," I answered.

"And so do I. I've dreamt in my life dreams that have stayed with me ever after, and changed my ideas; they've gone through and through me, like wine through water, and altered the colour of my mind. And this is one—I'm going to tell it—but take care not to smile at any part of it."

"Oh! don't, Miss Catherine!" I cried. "We're dismal enough without conjuring up ghosts and visions to perplex us. Come, come, be merry, and like yourself! Look at little Hareton—*he's* dreaming nothing dreary. How sweetly he smiles in his sleep!"

"Yes; and how sweetly his father curses in his solitude! You remember him, I dare say, when he was just such another as that chubby thing—nearly as young and innocent. However, Nelly, I shall oblige you to listen—it's not long; and I've no power to be merry to-night."

"I won't hear it, I won't hear it!" I repeated, hastily.

I was superstitious about dreams then, and am still; and Catherine had an unusual gloom in her aspect, that made me dread something from which I might shape a prophecy, and foresee a fearful catastrophe.

She was vexed, but she did not proceed. Apparently taking up another subject, she recommenced in a short time.

"If I were in heaven, Nelly, I should be extremely miserable."

"Because you are not fit to go there," I answered. "All sinners would be miserable in heaven."

"But it is not for that. I dreamt, once, that I was there."

"I tell you I won't harken to your dreams, Miss Catherine! I'll go to bed," I interrupted again.

She laughed, and held me down, for I made a motion to leave my chair.

"This is nothing," cried she; "I was only going to say that heaven did not seem to be my home; and I broke my heart with weeping to come back to earth; and the angels were so angry that they flung me out, into the middle of the heath on the top of Wuthering Heights; where I woke sobbing for joy. That will do to explain my secret, as well as the other. I've no more business to marry Edgar Linton than I have to be in heaven; and if the wicked man in there had not brought Heathcliff so low, I shouldn't have thought of it. It would degrade me to marry Heathcliff now; so he shall never know how I love him; and that, not because he's handsome, Nelly, but because he's more myself than I am. Whatever our souls are made of, his and mine are the same, and Linton's is as different as a moonbeam from lightning, or frost from fire."

Ere this speech ended, I became sensible of Heathcliff's presence. Having noticed a slight movement, I turned my head, and saw him rise from the bench, and steal out, noiselessly. He had listened till he heard Catherine say it would degrade her to marry him, and then he stayed to hear no farther.

My companion, sitting on the ground, was prevented by the back of the settle from remarking his presence or departure; but I started, and bade her hush!

"Why?" she asked, gazing nervously round.

"Joseph is here," I answered, catching, opportunely, the roll of his cartwheels up the road; "and Heathcliff will come in with him. I'm not sure whether he were not at the door this moment."

"Oh, he couldn't overhear me at the door!" said she. "Give me Hareton, while you get the supper, and when it is ready ask me to sup with you. I want to cheat my uncomfortable conscience, and be convinced that Heathcliff has no notion of these things. He has not, has he? He does not know what being in love is?"

"I see no reason that he should not know, as well as you," I returned; "and if *you* are his choice, he'll be the most unfortunate creature that ever was born! As soon as you become Mrs. Linton, he loses friend, and love, and all! Have you considered how you'll bear the separation, and how he'll bear to be quite deserted in the world? Because, Miss Catherine—"

"He quite deserted! we separated!" she exclaimed, with an accent of indignation. "Who is to separate us, pray? They'll meet the fate of Milo![3] Not as long as I live, Ellen—for no mortal creature. Every Linton on the face of the earth might melt into nothing, before I could consent to forsake Heathcliff. Oh, that's not what I intend—that's not what I mean! I shouldn't be Mrs. Linton were such a price demanded! He'll be as much to me as he has been all his lifetime. Edgar must shake off his antipathy, and tolerate him, at least. He will when he learns my true feelings towards him. Nelly, I see now, you think me a selfish wretch, but, did it never strike you that if Heathcliff and I married, we should be beggars? whereas, if I marry Linton, I can aid Heathcliff to rise, and place him out of my brother's power."

"With your husband's money, Miss Catherine?" I asked. "You'll find him not so pliable as you calculate upon: and, though I'm hardly a judge, I think that's the worst motive you've given yet for being the wife of young Linton."

"It is not," retorted she, "it is the best! The others were the satisfaction of my whims; and for Edgar's sake, too, to satisfy him. This is for the sake of one who comprehends in his person my feelings to Edgar and myself. I cannot express it; but surely you and everybody have a notion that there is, or should be, an exist-

3. An athlete of Crotona, who, caught by the tree he was trying to split, was eaten up by wild beasts.

ence of yours beyond you. What were the use of my creation if I were entirely contained here? My great miseries in this world have been Heathcliff's miseries, and I watched and felt each from the beginning; my great thought in living is himself. If all else perished, and *he* remained, I should still continue to be; and, if all else remained, and he were annihilated, the Universe would turn to a mighty stranger. I should not seem a part of it. My love for Linton is like the foliage in the woods. Time will change it, I'm well aware, as winter changes the trees. My love for Heathcliff resembles the eternal rocks beneath—a source of little visible delight, but necessary. Nelly, I *am* Heathcliff—he's always, always in my mind —not as a pleasure, any more than I am always a pleasure to myself—but as my own being—so, don't talk of our separation again—it is impracticable; and—"

She paused, and hid her face in the folds of my gown; but I jerked it forcibly away. I was out of patience with her folly!

"If I can make any sense of your nonsense, Miss," I said, "it only goes to convince me that you are ignorant of the duties you undertake in marrying; or else that you are a wicked, unprincipled girl. But trouble me with no more secrets. I'll not promise to keep them."

"You'll keep that?" she asked, eagerly.

"No, I'll not promise," I repeated.

She was about to insist, when the entrance of Joseph finished our conversation; and Catherine removed her seat to a corner, and nursed Hareton, while I made the supper.

After it was cooked, my fellow servant and I began to quarrel who should carry some to Mr. Hindley; and we didn't settle it till all was nearly cold. Then we came to the agreement that we would let him ask, if he wanted any, for we feared particularly to go into his presence when he had been some time alone.

"Und hah isn't that nowt comed in frough th' field, be this time?[4] What is he abaht? girt eedle seeght!" demanded the old man, looking round for Heathcliff.

"I'll call him," I replied. "He's in the barn, I've no doubt."

I went and called, but got no answer. On returning, I whispered to Catherine that he had heard a good part of what she said, I was sure; and told how I saw him quit the kitchen just as she complained of her brother's conduct regarding him.

She jumped up in a fine fright, flung Hareton onto the settle, and ran to seek for her friend herself, not taking leisure to consider why she was so flurried, or how her talk would have affected him. e was absent such a while that Joseph proposed we should

ow isn't that nothing come in from the field by this time? *Girt eedle at idle sight.*

wait no longer. He cunningly conjectured they were staying away in order to avoid hearing his protracted blessing. They were "ill eneugh for ony fahl manners," he affirmed. And, on their behalf, he added that night a special prayer to the usual quarter of an hour's supplication before meat, and would have tacked another to the end of the grace, had not his young mistress broken in upon him with a hurried command that he must run down the road, and, wherever Heathcliff had rambled, find and make him re-enter directly!

"I want to speak to him, and I *must*, before I go upstairs," she said. "And the gate is open, he is somewhere out of hearing; for he would not reply, though I shouted at the top of the fold as loud as I could."

Joseph objected at first; she was too much in earnest, however, to suffer contradiction; and at last he placed his hat on his head, and walked grumbling forth.

Meantime, Catherine paced up and down the floor, exclaiming—

"I wonder where he is—I wonder where he *can* be! What did I say, Nelly? I've forgotten. Was he vexed at my bad humour this afternoon? Dear! tell me what I've said to grieve him. I do wish he'd come. I do wish he would!"

"What a noise for nothing!" I cried, though rather uneasy myself. "What a trifle scares you! It's surely no great cause of alarm that Heathcliff should take a moonlight saunter on the moors, or even lie too sulky to speak to us, in the hay-loft. I'll engage he's lurking there. See if I don't ferret him out!"

I departed to renew my search; its result was disappointment, and Joseph's quest ended in the same.

"Yon lad gets war un war!" observed he on re-entering. "He's left th' yate ut t' full swing, and Miss's pony has trodden dahn two rigs uh corn, un plottered through, raight o'er intuh t' meadow! Hahsomdiver, t' maister 'ull play t' divil to-morn, and he'll do weel. He's patience itsseln wi' sich careless, offald craters—patience itsseln, he is! Bud he'll nut be soa allus—yah's see, all on ye! Yah mumn't drive him aht uf his heead fur nowt!"[5]

"Have you found Heathcliff, you ass?" interrupted Catherine. "Have you been looking for him, as I ordered?"

"Aw sud more likker look for th' horse," he replied. "It 'ud be tuh more sense. Bud Aw can look for norther horse, nur man uf a neeght loike this—as black as t' chimbley![6] und Hathecliff's noan t' chap tuh coom ut *maw* whistle—happen he'll be less hard uh hearing wi' *ye!*"

5. *War un war:* worse and worse; *yate:* gate; *rigs:* ridges; *plottered:* scrambled; *hahsomdiver:* howsoever; *offald:* worthless, good-for-nothing.

6. *Sud:* should; *likker:* comparative of like; *norther . . . nur:* neither . . . nor; *neeght:* night.

It *was* a very dark evening for summer: the clouds appeared inclined to thunder, and I said we had better all sit down; the approaching rain would be certain to bring him home without further trouble.

However, Catherine would not be persuaded into tranquillity. She kept wandering to and fro, from the gate to the door, in a state of agitation which permitted no repose; and at length took up a permanent situation on one side of the wall, near the road, where, heedless of my expostulations, and the growling thunder, and the great drops that began to plash around her, she remained, calling at intervals, and then listening, and then crying outright. She beat Hareton, or any child, at a good, passionate fit of crying.

About midnight, while we still sat up, the storm came rattling over the Heights in full fury. There was a violent wind, as well as thunder, and either one or the other split a tree off at the corner of the building; a huge bough fell across the roof, and knocked down a portion of the east chimney-stack, sending a clatter of stones and soot into the kitchen fire.

We thought a bolt had fallen in the middle of us, and Joseph swung onto his knees, beseeching the Lord to remember the Patriarchs Noah and Lot; and, as in former times, spare the righteous, though he smote the ungodly. I felt some sentiment that it must be a judgment on us also. The Jonah, in my mind, was Mr. Earnshaw, and I shook the handle of his den that I might ascertain if he were yet living. He replied audibly enough, in a fashion which made my companion vociferate more clamorously than before that a wide distinction might be drawn between saints like himself, and sinners like his master. But the uproar passed away in twenty minutes, leaving us all unharmed, excepting Cathy, who got thoroughly drenched for her obstinacy in refusing to take shelter, and standing bonnetless and shawlless to catch as much water as she could with her hair and clothes.

She came in and lay down on the settle, all soaked as she was, turning her face to the back, and putting her hands before it.

"Well, Miss!" I exclaimed, touching her shoulder; "you are not bent on getting your death, are you? Do you know what o'clock it is? Half-past twelve. Come! come to bed; there's no use waiting longer on that foolish boy—he'll be gone to Gimmerton, and he'll stay there now. He guesses we shouldn't wake[7] for him till this late hour; at least, he guesses that only Mr. Hindley would be up; and he'd rather avoid having the door opened by the master."

"Nay, nay, he's noan at Gimmerton!" said Joseph. "Aw's niver wonder, bud he's at t' bothom uf a bog-hoile.[8] This visitation worn't for nowt, und Aw wod hev ye tuh look aht, Miss—yah muh

7. Wait up.   8. Bottom of a bog-hole.

be t' next. Thank Hivin for all! All warks togither for gooid tuh them as is chozzen and piked aht froo' th' rubbidge![9] Yah knaw whet t' Scripture ses—"

And he began quoting several texts; referring us to the chapters and verses where we might find them.

I, having vainly begged the wilful girl to rise and remove her wet things, left him preaching and her shivering, and betook myself to bed with little Hareton, who slept as fast as if every one had been sleeping round him.

I heard Joseph read on a while afterwards; then I distinguished his slow step on the ladder, and then I dropt asleep.

Coming down somewhat later than usual, I saw, by the sunbeams piercing the chinks of the shutters, Miss Catherine still seated near the fire-place. The house door was ajar, too; light entered from its unclosed windows; Hindley had come out, and stood on the kitchen hearth, haggard and drowsy.

"What ails you, Cathy?" he was saying when I entered; "you look as dismal as a drowned whelp. Why are you so damp and pale, child?"

"I've been wet," she answered reluctantly, "and I'm cold, that's all."

"Oh, she is naughty!" I cried, perceiving the master to be tolerably sober. "She got steeped in the shower of yesterday evening, and there she has sat the night through, and I couldn't prevail on her to stir."

Mr. Earnshaw stared at us in surprise. "The night through," he repeated. "What kept her up, not fear of the thunder, surely? That was over, hours since."

Neither of us wished to mention Heathcliff's absence, as long as we could conceal it; so I replied, I didn't know how she took it into her head to sit up; and she said nothing.

The morning was fresh and cool; I threw back the lattice, and presently the room filled with sweet scents from the garden; but Catherine called peevishly to me—

"Ellen, shut the window. I'm starving!" And her teeth chattered as she shrunk closer to the almost extinguished embers.

"She's ill," said Hindley, taking her wrist, "I suppose that's the reason she would not go to bed. Damn it! I don't want to be troubled with more sickness here. What took you into the rain?"

"Running after t'lads, as usuald!" croaked Joseph, catching an opportunity, from our hesitation, to thrust in his evil tongue. "If Aw wur yah, maister, Aw'd just slam t'boards i' their faces all on 'em, gentle and simple! Never a day ut yah're off, but yon cat uh Linton comes sneaking hither; and Miss Nelly shoo's a fine

9. Picked out from the rubbish.

lass! shoo sits watching for ye i' t'kitchen; and as yah're in at one door, he's aht at t'other; und, then, wer grand lady goes a coorting uf hor side![1] It's bonny behaviour, lurking amang t'flields, after twelve ut' night, wi that fahl, flaysome divil uf a gipsy, Heathcliff! They think *Aw'm* blind; but Aw'm noan, nowt ut t'soart! Aw seed young Linton, boath coming and going, and Aw seed *yah*" (directing his discourse to me), "yah gooid fur nowt, slattenly witch! nip up und bolt intuh th' hahs, t' minute yah heard t'maister's horse fit clatter up t' road."[2]

"Silence, eavesdropper!" cried Catherine. "None of your insolence before me! Edgar Linton came yesterday, by chance, Hindley; and it was *I* who told him to be off, because I knew you would not like to have met him as you were."

"You lie, Cathy, no doubt," answered her brother, "and you are a confounded simpleton! But never mind Linton, at present. Tell me, were you not with Heathcliff last night? Speak the truth, now. You need not be afraid of harming him: though I hate him as much as ever, he did me a good turn a short time since, that will make my conscience tender of breaking his neck. To prevent it, I shall send him about his business this very morning; and after he's gone, I'd advise you all to look sharp, I shall only have the more humour for you!"

"I never saw Heathcliff last night," answered Catherine, beginning to sob bitterly: "and if you do turn him out of doors, I'll go with him. But, perhaps, you'll never have an opportunity—perhaps, he's gone." Here she burst into uncontrollable grief, and the remainder of her words were inarticulate.

Hindley lavished on her a torrent of scornful abuse, and bid her get to her room immediately, or she shouldn't cry for nothing! I obliged her to obey; and I shall never forget what a scene she acted, when we reached her chamber. It terrified me. I thought she was going mad, and I begged Joseph to run for the doctor.

It proved the commencement of delirium; Mr. Kenneth, as soon as he saw her, pronounced her dangerously ill; she had a fever.

He bled her, and he told me to let her live on whey and water-gruel, and take care she did not throw herself downstairs, or out of the window; and then he left, for he had enough to do in the parish where two or three miles was the ordinary distance between cottage and cottage.

Though I cannot say I made a gentle nurse, and Joseph and the master were no better; and though our patient was as wearisome and headstrong as a patient could be, she weathered it through.

Old Mrs. Linton paid us several visits, to be sure, and set things

1. *T'boards:* the doors; *cat:* a term of contempt; *shoo's:* she's; *wer grand lady:* our grand lady.

2. *Nowt ut t'soart:* nothing of the sort; *slattenly:* slovenly; *hahs:* house; *horse fit:* horse feet.

to rights, and scolded and ordered us all; and when Catherine was convalescent, she insisted on conveying her to Thrushcross Grange: for which deliverance we were very grateful. But the poor dame had reason to repent of her kindness; she and her husband both took the fever, and died within a few days of each other.

Our young lady returned to us, saucier and more passionate, and haughtier than ever. Heathcliff had never been heard of since the evening of the thunder-storm, and, one day, I had the misfortune, when she had provoked me exceedingly, to lay the blame of his disappearance on her (where indeed it belonged, as she well knew). From that period, for several months, she ceased to hold any communication with me, save in the relation of a mere servant. Joseph fell under a ban also; he *would* speak his mind, and lecture her all the same as if she were a little girl; and she esteemed herself a woman, and our mistress, and thought that her recent illness gave her a claim to be treated with consideration. Then the doctor had said that she would not bear crossing much, she ought to have her own way; and it was nothing less than murder, in her eyes, for any one to presume to stand up and contradict her.

From Mr. Earnshaw and his companions she kept aloof; and tutored by Kenneth, and serious threats of a fit that often attended her rages, her brother allowed her whatever she pleased to demand, and generally avoided aggravating her fiery temper. He was rather *too* indulgent in humouring her caprices; not from affection, but from pride, he wished earnestly to see her bring honour to the family by an alliance with the Lintons, and, as long as she let him alone, she might trample us like slaves for ought he cared!

Edgar Linton, as multitudes have been before and will be after him, was infatuated; and believed himself the happiest man alive on the day he led her to Gimmerton chapel, three years subsequent to his father's death.

Much against my inclination, I was persuaded to leave Wuthering Heights and accompany her here. Little Hareton was nearly five years old, and I had just begun to teach him his letters. We made a sad parting, but Catherine's tears were more powerful than ours. When I refused to go, and when she found her entreaties did not move me, she went lamenting to her husband and brother. The former offered me munificent wages; the latter ordered me to pack up. He wanted no women in the house, he said, now that there was no mistress; and as to Hareton, the curate should take him in hand, by and by. And so I had but one choice left, to do as I was ordered. I told the master he got rid of all decent people only to run to ruin a little faster; I kissed Hareton good-bye; and, since then, he has been a stranger, and it's very queer to think it, but I've no doubt he has completely forgotten all about Ellen

Dean and that he was ever more than all the world to her, and she to him!

At this point of the housekeeper's story, she chanced to glance towards the time-piece over the chimney; and was in amazement on seeing the minute-hand measure half-past one. She would not hear of staying a second longer. In truth, I felt rather disposed to defer the sequel of her narrative myself: and now that she is vanished to her rest, and I have meditated for another hour or two, I shall summon courage to go, also, in spite of aching laziness of head and limbs.

Chapter X

A charming introduction to a hermit's life! Four weeks' torture, tossing and sickness! Oh, these bleak winds, and bitter, northern skies, and impassable roads, and dilatory country surgeons! And, oh, this dearth of the human physiognomy, and, worse than all, the terrible intimation of Kenneth that I need not expect to be out of doors till spring!

Mr. Heathcliff has just honoured me with a call. About seven days ago he sent me a brace of grouse—the last of the season. Scoundrel! He is not altogether guiltless in this illness of mine; and that I had a great mind to tell him. But, alas! how could I offend a man who was charitable enough to sit at my bedside a good hour, and talk on some other subject than pills and draughts, blisters and leeches?

This is quite an easy interval. I am too weak to read, yet I feel as if I could enjoy something interesting. Why not have up Mrs. Dean to finish her tale? I can recollect its chief incidents, as far as she had gone. Yes, I remember her hero had run off, and never been heard of for three years; and the heroine was married. I'll ring; she'll be delighted to find me capable of talking cheerfully.

Mrs. Dean came.

"It wants twenty minutes, sir, to taking the medicine," she commenced.

"Away, away with it!" I replied; "I desire to have—"

"The doctor says you must drop the powders."

"With all my heart! Don't interrupt me. Come and take your seat here. Keep your fingers from that bitter phalanx of vials. Draw your knitting out of your pocket—that will do—now continue the history of Mr. Heathcliff, from where you left off, to the present day. Did he finish his education on the Continent, and come back a gentleman? or did he get a sizer's place at college? or escape to America, and earn honours by drawing blood from his foster country? or make a fortune more promptly, on the English highways?"

"He may have done a little in all these vocations, Mr. Lockwood; but I couldn't give my word for any. I stated before that I didn't know how he gained his money; neither am I aware of the means he took to raise his mind from the savage ignorance into which it was sunk; but, with your leave, I'll proceed in my own fashion, if you think it will amuse and not weary you. Are you feeling better this morning?"

"Much."

"That's good news."

I got Miss Catherine and myself to Thrushcross Grange; and to my agreeable disappointment, she behaved infinitely better than I dared to expect. She seemed almost over-fond of Mr. Linton; and even to his sister, she showed plenty of affection. They were both very attentive to her comfort, certainly. It was not the thorn bending to the honeysuckles, but the honeysuckles embracing the thorn. There were no mutual concessions; one stood erect, and the others yielded; and who *can* be ill-natured and bad-tempered, when they encounter neither opposition nor indifference?

I observed that Mr. Edgar had a deep-rooted fear of ruffling her humour. He concealed it from her; but if ever he heard me answer sharply, or saw any other servant grow cloudy at some imperious order of hers, he would show his trouble by a frown of displeasure that never darkened on his own account. He, many a time, spoke sternly to me about my pertness; and averred that the stab of a knife could not inflict a worse pang than he suffered at seeing his lady vexed.

Not to grieve a kind master, I learnt to be less touchy; and, for the space of half a year, the gunpowder lay as harmless as sand, because no fire came near to explode it. Catherine had seasons of gloom and silence, now and then: they were respected with sympathizing silence by her husband, who ascribed them to an alteration in her constitution, produced by her perilous illness, as she was never subject to depression of spirits before. The return of sunshine was welcomed by answering sunshine from him. I believe I may assert that they were really in possession of deep and growing happiness.

It ended. Well, we *must* be for ourselves in the long run; the mild and generous are only more justly selfish than the domineering; and it ended when circumstances caused each to feel that the one's interest was not the chief consideration in the other's thoughts.

On a mellow evening in September, I was coming from the garden with a heavy basket of apples which I had been gathering.

It had got dusk, and the moon looked over the high wall of the court, causing undefined shadows to lurk in the corners of the numerous projecting portions of the building. I set my burden on the house steps by the kitchen door, and lingered to rest and draw in a few more breaths of the soft, sweet air; my eyes were on the moon, and my back to the entrance, when I heard a voice behind me say—

"Nelly, is that you?"

It was a deep voice, and foreign in tone; yet there was something in the manner of pronouncing my name which made it sound familiar. I turned about to discover who spoke, fearfully, for the doors were shut, and I had seen nobody on approaching the steps.

Something stirred in the porch; and moving nearer, I distinguished a tall man dressed in dark clothes, with dark face and hair. He leant against the side, and held his fingers on the latch, as if intending to open for himself.

"Who can it be?" I thought. "Mr. Earnshaw? Oh, no! The voice has no resemblance to his."

"I have waited here an hour," he resumed, while I continued staring; "and the whole of that time all round has been as still as death. I dared not enter. You do not know me? Look, I'm not a stranger!"

A ray fell on his features; the cheeks were sallow, and half covered with black whiskers; the brows lowering, the eyes deep set and singular. I remembered the eyes.

"What!" I cried, uncertain whether to regard him as a worldly visitor, and I raised my hands in amazement. "What! you come back? Is it really you? Is it?"

"Yes, Heathcliff," he replied, glancing from me up to the windows, which reflected a score of glittering moons, but showed no lights from within. "Are they at home—where is she? Nelly, you are not glad—you needn't be so disturbed. Is she here? Speak! I want to have one word with her—your mistress. Go, and say some person from Gimmerton desires to see her."

"How will she take it?" I exclaimed. "What will she do? The surprise bewilders me—it will put her out of her head! And you *are* Heathcliff? But altered! Nay, there's no comprehending it. Have you been for a soldier?"

"Go, and carry my message," he interrupted impatiently; "I'm in hell till you do!"

He lifted the latch, and I entered; but when I got to the parlour where Mr. and Mrs. Linton were, I could not persuade myself to proceed.

At length, I resolved on making an excuse to ask if they would have the candles lighted, and I opened the door.

They sat together in a window whose lattice lay back against the wall, and displayed, beyond the garden trees and the wild green park, the valley of Gimmerton, with a long line of mist winding nearly to its top (for very soon after you pass the chapel, as you may have noticed, the sough that runs from the marshes joins a beck which follows the bend of the glen). Wuthering Heights rose above this silvery vapour; but our old house was invisible—it rather dips down on the other side.

Both the room and its occupants, and the scene they gazed on, looked wondrously peaceful. I shrank reluctantly from performing my errand, and was actually going away, leaving it unsaid, after having put my question about the candles, when a sense of my folly compelled me to return, and mutter—

"A person from Gimmerton wishes to see you, ma'am."

"What does he want?" asked Mrs. Linton.

"I did not question him," I answered.

"Well, close the curtains, Nelly," she said; "and bring up tea. I'll be back again directly."

She quitted the apartment; Mr. Edgar inquired carelessly, who it was?

"Some one the mistress does not expect," I replied. "That Heathcliff, you recollect him, sir, who used to live at Mr. Earnshaw's."

"What, the gipsy—the plough-boy?" he cried. "Why did you not say so to Catherine?"

"Hush! you must not call him by those names, master," I said. "She'd be sadly grieved to hear you. She was nearly heart-broken when he ran off; I guess his return will make a jubilee to her."

Mr. Linton walked to a window on the other side of the room that overlooked the court. He unfastened it, and leant out. I suppose they were below, for he exclaimed, quickly—

"Don't stand there, love! Bring the person in, if it be any one particular."

Ere long, I heard the click of the latch, and Catherine flew upstairs, breathless and wild, too excited to show gladness; indeed, by her face, you would rather have surmised an awful calamity.

"Oh, Edgar, Edgar!" she panted, flinging her arms round his neck. "Oh, Edgar, darling! Heathcliff's come back—he is!" And she tightened her embrace to a squeeze.

"Well, well," cried her husband, crossly, "don't strangle me for that! He never struck me as such a marvellous treasure. There is no need to be frantic!"

"I know you didn't like him," she answered, repressing a little the intensity of her delight. "Yet, for my sake, you must be friends now. Shall I tell him to come up?"

"Here?" he said, "into the parlour?"

"Where else?" she asked.

He looked vexed, and suggested the kitchen as a more suitable place for him.

Mrs. Linton eyed him with a droll expression—half angry, half laughing at his fastidiousness.

"No," she added, after a while; "I cannot sit in the kitchen. Set two tables here, Ellen; one for your master and Miss Isabella, being gentry; the other for Heathcliff and myself, being of the lower orders. Will that please you, dear? Or must I have a fire lighted elsewhere? If so, give directions. I'll run down and secure my guest. I'm afraid the joy is too great to be real!"

She was about to dart off again; but Edgar arrested her.

"*You* bid him step up," he said, addressing me; "and, Catherine, try to be glad, without being absurd! The whole household need not witness the sight of your welcoming a runaway servant as a brother."

I descended and found Heathcliff waiting under the porch, evidently anticipating an invitation to enter. He followed my guidance without waste of words, and I ushered him into the presence of the master and mistress, whose flushed cheeks betrayed signs of warm talking. But the lady's glowed with another feeling when her friend appeared at the door; she sprang forward, took both his hands, and led him to Linton; and then she seized Linton's reluctant fingers and crushed them into his.

Now fully revealed by the fire and candlelight, I was amazed, more than ever, to behold the transformation of Heathcliff. He had grown a tall, athletic, well-formed man, beside whom my master seemed quite slender and youth-like. His upright carriage suggested the idea of his having been in the army. His countenance was much older in expression and decision of feature than Mr. Linton's; it looked intelligent, and retained no marks of former degradation. A half-civilized ferocity lurked yet in the depressed brows and eyes full of black fire, but it was subdued; and his manner was even dignified, quite divested of roughness, though too stern for grace.

My master's surprise equalled or exceeded mine: he remained for a minute at a loss how to address the ploughboy, as he had called him. Heathcliff dropped his slight hand, and stood looking at him coolly till he chose to speak.

"Sit down, sir," he said, at length. "Mrs. Linton, recalling old times, would have me give you a cordial reception, and, of course, I am gratified when anything occurs to please her."

"And I also," answered Heathcliff, "especially if it be anything in which I have a part. I shall stay an hour or two willingly."

He took a seat opposite Catherine, who kept her gaze fixed on him as if she feared he would vanish were she to remove it. He did not raise his to her often; a quick glance now and then sufficed; but it flashed back, each time more confidently, the undisguised delight he drank from hers.

They were too much absorbed in their mutual joy to suffer embarrassment. Not so Mr. Edgar; he grew pale with pure annoyance, a feeling that reached its climax when his lady rose, and stepping across the rug, seized Heathcliff's hands again, and laughed like one beside herself.

"I shall think it a dream to-morrow!" she cried. "I shall not be able to believe that I have seen, and touched, and spoken to you once more—and yet, cruel Heathcliff! you don't deserve this welcome. To be absent and silent for three years, and never to think of me!"

"A little more than you have thought of me!" he murmured. "I heard of your marriage, Cathy, not long since; and, while waiting in the yard below, I meditated this plan: just to have one glimpse of your face, a stare of surprise, perhaps, and pretended pleasure; afterwards settle my score with Hindley; and then prevent the law by doing execution on myself. Your welcome has put these ideas out of my mind; but beware of meeting me with another aspect next time! Nay, you'll not drive me off again. You were really sorry for me, were you? Well, there was cause. I've fought through a bitter life since I last heard your voice, and you must forgive me, for I struggled only for you."

"Catherine, unless we are to have cold tea, please to come to the table," interrupted Linton, striving to preserve his ordinary tone, and a due measure of politeness. "Mr. Heathcliff will have a long walk, wherever he may lodge to-night; and I'm thirsty."

She took her post before the urn; and Miss Isabella came, summoned by the bell; then, having handed their chairs forward, I left the room.

The meal hardly endured ten minutes. Catherine's cup was never filled, she could neither eat nor drink. Edgar had made a slop in his saucer, and scarcely swallowed a mouthful.

Their guest did not protract his stay that evening above an hour longer. I asked, as he departed, if he went to Gimmerton?

"No, to Wuthering Heights," he answered, "Mr. Earnshaw invited me when I called this morning."

Mr. Earnshaw invited *him!* and *he* called on Mr. Earnshaw! I pondered this sentence painfully after he was gone. Is he turning out a bit of a hypocrite, and coming into the country to work mischief under a cloak? I mused—I had a presentiment, in the bottom of my heart, that he had better have remained away.

About the middle of the night, I was wakened from my first nap by Mrs. Linton gliding into my chamber, taking a seat on my bed-side, and pulling me by the hair to rouse me.

"I cannot rest, Ellen," she said by way of apology. "And I want some living creature to keep me company in my happiness! Edgar is sulky, because I'm glad of a thing that does not interest him. He refuses to open his mouth, except to utter pettish, silly speeches; and he affirmed I was cruel and selfish for wishing to talk when he was so sick and sleepy. He always contrives to be sick at the least cross! I gave a few sentences of commendation to Heathcliff, and he, either for a headache or a pang of envy, began to cry: so I got up and left him."

"What use is it praising Heathcliff to him?" I answered. "As lads they had an aversion to each other, and Heathcliff would hate just as much to hear him praised—it's human nature. Let Mr. Linton alone about him, unless you would like an open quarrel between them."

"But does it not show great weakness?" pursued she. "I'm not envious: I never feel hurt at the brightness of Isabella's yellow hair, and the whiteness of her skin; at her dainty elegance, and the fondness all the family exhibit for her. Even you, Nelly, if we have a dispute sometimes, you back Isabella, at once; and I yield like a foolish mother—I call her a darling, and flatter her into a good temper. It pleases her brother to see us cordial, and that pleases me. But they are very much alike; they are spoiled children, and fancy the world was made for their accommodation; and, though I humour both, I think a smart chastisement might improve them, all the same."

"You're mistaken, Mrs. Linton," said I. "They humour you: I know what there would be to do if they did not! You can well afford to indulge their passing whims, as long as their business is to anticipate all your desires. You may, however, fall out, at last, over something of equal consequence to both sides; and then those you term weak are very capable of being as obstinate as you!"

"And then we shall fight to the death, shan't we, Nelly?" she returned laughing. "No! I tell you, I have such faith in Linton's love that I believe I might kill him, and he wouldn't wish to retaliate."

I advised her to value him the more for his affection.

"I do," she answered, "but he needn't resort to whining for trifles. It is childish; and, instead of melting into tears because I said that Heathcliff was now worthy of any one's regard, and it would honour the first gentleman in the country to be his friend, he ought to have said it for me, and been delighted from sympathy. He must get accustomed to him, and he may as well like him. Considering how Heathcliff has reason to object to him, I'm sure he behaved excellently!"

"What do you think of his going to Wuthering Heights?" I inquired. "He is reformed in every respect, apparently—quite a Christian—offering the right hand of fellowship to his enemies all round!"

"He explained it," she replied. "I wondered as much as you. He said he called to gather information concerning me, from you, supposing you resided there still; and Joseph told Hindley, who came out and fell to questioning him of what he had been doing, and how he had been living; and finally, desired him to walk in. There were some persons sitting at cards; Heathcliff joined them; my brother lost some money to him; and, finding him plentifully supplied, he requested that he would come again in the evening, to which he consented. Hindley is too reckless to select his acquaintance prudently; he doesn't trouble himself to reflect on the causes he might have for mistrusting one whom he has basely injured. But Heathcliff affirms his principal reason for resuming a connection with his ancient persecutor is a wish to install himself in quarters at walking distance from the Grange, and an attachment to the house where we lived together, and likewise a hope that I shall have more opportunities of seeing him there than I could have if he settled in Gimmerton. He means to offer liberal payment for permission to lodge at the Heights; and doubtless my brother's covetousness will prompt him to accept the terms; he was always greedy, though what he grasps with one hand, he flings away with the other."

"It's a nice place for a young man to fix his dwelling in!" said I. "Have you no fear of the consequences, Mrs. Linton?"

"None for my friend," she replied. "His strong head will keep him from danger; a little for Hindley, but he can't be made morally worse than he is; and I stand between him and bodily harm. The event of this evening has reconciled me to God and humanity! I had risen in angry rebellion against providence. Oh, I've endured very, very bitter misery, Nelly! If that creature knew how bitter, he'd be ashamed to cloud its removal with idle petulance. It was kindness for him which induced me to bear it alone: had I expressed the agony I frequently felt, he would have been taught to long for its alleviation as ardently as I. However, it's over, and I'll take no revenge on his folly; I can afford to suffer anything, hereafter! Should the meanest thing alive slap me on the cheek, I'd not only turn the other, but I'd ask pardon for provoking it; and, as a proof, I'll go make my peace with Edgar instantly. Good-night—I'm an angel!"

In this self-complacent conviction she departed; and the success of her fulfilled resolution was obvious on the morrow: Mr. Linton had not only abjured his peevishness (though his spirits seemed still subdued by Catherine's exuberance of vivacity), but he ventured no objection to her taking Isabella with her to Wuthering Heights in the afternoon; and she rewarded him with such a summer of sweetness and affection in return, as made the house a paradise for several days; both master and servants profiting from the perpetual sunshine.

Heathcliff—Mr. Heathcliff I should say in future—used the liberty of visiting at Thrushcross Grange cautiously, at first: he seemed estimating how far its owner would bear his intrusion. Catherine, also, deemed it judicious to moderate her expressions of pleasure in receiving him; and he gradually established his right to be expected.

He retained a great deal of the reserve for which his boyhood was remarkable, and that served to repress all startling demonstrations of feeling. My master's uneasiness experienced a lull, and further circumstances diverted it into another channel for a space.

His new source of trouble sprang from the not anticipated misfortune of Isabella Linton evincing a sudden and irresistible attraction towards the tolerated guest. She was at that time a charming young lady of eighteen; infantile in manners, though possessed of keen wit, keen feelings, and a keen temper, too, if irritated. Her brother, who loved her tenderly, was appalled at this fantastic preference. Leaving aside the degradation of an alliance with a nameless man, and the possible fact that his property, in default of heirs male, might pass into such a one's power, he had sense to comprehend Heathcliff's disposition—to know that, though his exterior was altered, his mind was unchangeable, and unchanged. And he dreaded that mind; it revolted him; he shrank forebodingly from the idea of committing Isabella to its keeping.

He would have recoiled still more had he been aware that her attachment rose unsolicited, and was bestowed where it awakened no reciprocation of sentiment; for the minute he discovered its existence, he laid the blame on Heathcliff's deliberate designing.

We had all remarked, during some time, that Miss Linton fretted and pined over something. She grew cross and wearisome, snapping at and teasing Catherine continually, at the imminent risk of exhausting her limited patience. We excused her to a certain extent, on the plea of ill health—she was dwindling and fading before our eyes. But one day, when she had been peculiarly wayward, rejecting her breakfast, complaining that the servants did not do what she told them; that the mistress would allow her to be nothing in the house, and Edgar neglected her; that she had caught a cold with the doors being left open, and we let the parlour fire go out on purpose to vex her; with a hundred yet more frivolous accusations, Mrs. Linton peremptorily insisted that she should get to bed; and, having scolded her heartily, threatened to send for the doctor.

Mention of Kenneth caused her to exclaim, instantly, that her health was perfect, and it was only Catherine's harshness which made her unhappy.

"How can you say I am harsh, you naughty fondling?" cried the mistress, amazed at the unreasonable assertion. "You are surely losing your reason. When have I been harsh, tell me?"

"Yesterday," sobbed Isabella, "and now!"

"Yesterday!" said her sister-in-law. "On what occasion?"

"In our walk along the moor; you told me to ramble where I pleased, while you sauntered on with Mr. Heathcliff!"

"And that's your notion of harshness?" said Catherine, laughing. "It was no hint that your company was superfluous; we didn't care whether you kept with us or not; I merely thought Heathcliff's talk would have nothing entertaining for your ears."

"Oh, no," wept the young lady; "you wished me away, because you knew I liked to be there!"

"Is she sane?" asked Mrs. Linton, appealing to me. "I'll repeat our conversation, word for word, Isabella; and you point out any charm it could have had for you."

"I don't mind the conversation," she answered. "I wanted to be with—"

"Well!" said Catherine, perceiving her hesitate to complete the sentence.

"With him; and I won't be always sent off!" she continued, kindling up. "You are a dog in the manger, Cathy, and desire no one to be loved but yourself!"

"You are an impertinent little monkey!" exclaimed Mrs. Linton, in surprise. "But I'll not believe this idiocy! It is impossible that you can covet the admiration of Heathcliff—that you can consider him an agreeable person! I hope I have misunderstood you, Isabella?"

"No, you have not," said the infatuated girl. "I love him more than ever you loved Edgar; and he might love me if you would let him!"

"I wouldn't be you for a kingdom, then!" Catherine declared, emphatically—and she seemed to speak sincerely. "Nelly, help me to convince her of her madness. Tell her what Heathcliff is—an unreclaimed creature, without refinement, without cultivation; an arid wilderness of furze and whinstone. I'd as soon put that little canary into the park on a winter's day as recommend you to bestow your heart on him! It is deplorable ignorance of his character, child, and nothing else, which makes that dream enter your head. Pray don't imagine that he conceals depths of benevolence and affection beneath a stern exterior! He's not a rough diamond—a pearl-containing oyster of a rustic; he's a fierce, pitiless, wolfish man. I never say to him, 'Let this or that enemy alone, because it would be ungenerous or cruel to harm them'; I say, 'Let them alone, because *I* should hate them to be wronged': and he'd crush you, like a sparrow's egg, Isabella, if he found you a troublesome charge. I know he couldn't love a Linton; and yet he'd be quite capable of marrying your fortune and expectations. Avarice is growing with him a besetting sin. There's my picture; and I'm his friend—so much so, that had he thought seriously to catch you, I should, perhaps, have held my tongue, and let you fall into his trap."

Miss Linton regarded her sister-in-law with indignation.

"For shame! for shame!" she repeated, angrily. "You are worse than twenty foes, you poisonous friend!"

"Ah! you won't believe me, then?" said Catherine. "You think I speak from wicked selfishness?"

"I'm certain you do," retorted Isabella; "and I shudder at you!"

"Good!" cried the other. "Try for yourself, if that be your spirit; I have done, and yield the argument to your saucy insolence."

"And I must suffer for her egotism!" she sobbed, as Mrs. Linton left the room. "All, all is against me; she has blighted my single consolation. But she uttered falsehoods, didn't she? Mr. Heathcliff is not a fiend; he has an honourable soul, and a true one, or how could he remember her?"

"Banish him from your thoughts, Miss," I said. "He's a bird of bad omen; no mate for you. Mrs. Linton spoke strongly, and yet I can't contradict her. She is better acquainted with his heart than I, or any one besides; and she never would represent him as worse than he is. Honest people don't hide their deeds. How has he been living? how has he got rich? why is he staying at Wuthering Heights, the house of a man whom he abhors? They say Mr. Earnshaw is worse and worse since he came. They sit up all night together continually; and Hindley has been borrowing money on his land, and does nothing but play and drink: I heard only a week ago—it was Joseph who told me—I met him at Gimmerton."

" 'Nelly,' he said, 'we's hae a Crahnr's 'quest enah, at ahr folks. One on 'em's a'most getten his finger cut off wi' hauding t'other froo' sticking hisseln loike a cawlf. That's maister, yah knaw, ut's soa up uh going tuh t'grand 'sizes. He's noan feard uh t' Bench uh judges, norther Paul, nur Peter, nur John, nor Mathew, nor noan on 'em, nut he! He fair like's—he langs tuh set his brazened face agean 'em! And yon bonny lad Heathcliff, yah mind, he's a rare un! He cau girn a laugh,[3] as weel's onybody at a raight divil's jest. Does he niver say nowt of his fine living amang us, when he goas tuh t' Grange? This is t' way on't—up at sun-dahn; dice, brandy, cloised shutters, und can'le lught till next day, at nooin —then, t'fooil gangs banning un raving tuh his cham'er, makking dacent fowks dig thur fingers i' thur lugs fur varry shaume; un' the' knave, wah, he carn cahnt his brass, un ate, un' sleep, un' off tuh his neighbour's tuh gossip wi' t' wife. I' course, he tells Dame Catherine hah hor father's goold runs intuh his pocket, and her fathur's son gallops dahn t' broad road, while he flees afore tuh oppen t' pikes.'[4] Now, Miss Linton, Joseph is an old rascal, but no liar; and, if his account of Heathcliff's conduct be true, you would never think of desiring such a husband, would you?"

"You are leagued with the rest, Ellen!" she replied. "I'll not listen to your slanders. What malevolence you must have to wish to convince me that there is no happiness in the world!"

Whether she would have got over this fancy if left to herself, or persevered in nursing it perpetually, I cannot say; she had little time to reflect. The day after, there was a justice-meeting at the next town; my master was obliged to attend; and Mr. Heathcliff, aware of his absence, called rather earlier than usual.

Catherine and Isabella were sitting in the library, on hostile terms, but silent. The latter, alarmed at her recent indiscretion, and the disclosure she had made of her secret feelings in a transient fit of passion; the former, on mature consideration, really offended with her companion; and, if she laughed again at her pertness, inclined to make it no laughing matter to *her*.

She did laugh as she saw Heathcliff pass the window. I was sweeping the hearth, and I noticed a mischievous smile on her lips. Isabella, absorbed in her meditations, or a book, remained till the door opened, and it was too late to attempt an escape, which she would gladly have done had it been practicable.

"Come in, that's right!" exclaimed the mistress, gaily, pulling a chair to the fire. "Here are two people sadly in need of a third to thaw the ice between them, and you are the very one we should both of us choose. Heathcliff, I'm proud to show you, at last, somebody that dotes on you more than myself. I expect you to feel flattered. Nay, it's not Nelly; don't look at her! My poor little sister-in-law is breaking her heart by mere contemplation of

3. *Crahnr's 'quest:* coroner's inquest; *enah:* soon; *hauding:* holding; *soa:* therefore; *t'grand 'sizes:* the grand assizes (sessions of court in English counties); *girn a laugh:* show the teeth in laughing.

4. *Sun-dahn:* sundown; *lught:* light; *gangs banning:* goes cursing; *lugs:* ears; *wah, he carn cahnt his brass:* why, he can count his money; *oppen t' pikes:* open the tollgates (i.e., hasten him to his ruin).

your physical and moral beauty. It lies in your own power to be Edgar's brother! No, no, Isabella, you shan't run off," she continued, arresting, with feigned playfulness, the confounded girl who had risen indignantly. "We were quarrelling like cats about you, Heathcliff; and I was fairly beaten in protestations of devotion and admiration; and, moreover, I was informed that if I would but have the manners to stand aside, my rival, as she will have herself to be, would shoot a shaft into your soul that would fix you for ever, and send my image into eternal oblivion!"

"Catherine," said Isabella, calling up her dignity, and disdaining to struggle from the tight grasp that held her, "I'd thank you to adhere to the truth and not slander me, even in joke! Mr. Heathcliff, be kind enough to bid this friend of yours release me: she forgets that you and I are not intimate acquaintances, and what amuses her is painful to me beyond expression."

As the guest answered nothing, but took his seat, and looked thoroughly indifferent what sentiments she cherished concerning him, she turned, and whispered an earnest appeal for liberty to her tormentor.

"By no means!" cried Mrs. Linton in answer. "I won't be named a dog in the manger again. You *shall* stay: now then, Heathcliff, why don't you evince satisfaction at my pleasant news? Isabella swears that the love Edgar has for me is nothing to that she entertains for you. I'm sure she made some speech of the kind, did she not, Ellen? And she has fasted ever since the day before yesterday's walk, from sorrow and rage that I despatched her out of your society, under the idea of its being unacceptable."

"I think you belie her," said Heathcliff, twisting his chair to face them. "She wishes to be out of my society now, at any rate!"

And he stared hard at the object of discourse, as one might do at a strange repulsive animal, a centipede from the Indies, for instance, which curiosity leads one to examine in spite of the aversion it raises.

The poor thing couldn't bear that; she grew white and red in rapid succession, and, while tears beaded her lashes, bent the strength of her small fingers to loosen the firm clutch of Catherine, and perceiving that as fast as she raised one finger off her arm, another closed down, and she could not remove the whole together, she began to make use of her nails, and their sharpness presently ornamented the detainer's with crescents of red.

"There's a tigress!" exclaimed Mrs. Linton, setting her free, and shaking her hand with pain. "Begone, for God's sake, and hide your vixen face! How foolish to reveal those talons to *him*. Can't you fancy the conclusions he'll draw? Look, Heathcliff! they are instruments that will do execution—you must beware of your eyes."

"I'd wrench them off her fingers, if they ever menaced me," he answered brutally, when the door had closed after her. "But what did you mean by teasing the creature in that manner, Cathy? You were not speaking the truth, were you?"

"I assure you I was," she returned. "She has been pining for your sake several weeks; and raving about you this morning, and pouring forth a deluge of abuse, because I represented your failings in a plain light for the purpose of mitigating her adoration. But don't notice it further. I wished to punish her sauciness, that's all. I like her too well, my dear Heathcliff, to let you absolutely seize and devour her up."

"And I like her too ill to attempt it," said he, "except in a very ghoulish fashion. You'd hear of odd things, if I lived alone with that mawkish, waxen face; the most ordinary would be painting on its white the colours of the rainbow, and turning the blue eyes black, every day or two; they detestably resemble Linton's."

"Delectably," observed Catherine. "They are dove's eyes—angel's!"

"She's her brother's heir, is she not?" he asked, after a brief silence.

"I should be sorry to think so," returned his companion. "Half-a-dozen nephews shall erase her title, please Heaven! Abstract your mind from the subject, at present. You are too prone to covet your neighbour's goods: remember *this* neighbour's goods are mine."

"If they were *mine*, they would be none the less that," said Heathcliff, "but though Isabella Linton may be silly, she is scarcely mad; and, in short, we'll dismiss the matter, as you advise."

From their tongues, they did dismiss it; and Catherine, probably, from her thoughts. The other, I felt certain, recalled it often in the course of the evening; I saw him smile to himself—grin rather—and lapse into ominous musing whenever Mrs. Linton had occasion to be absent from the apartment.

I determined to watch his movements. My heart invariably cleaved to the master's, in preference to Catherine's side; with reason, I imagined, for he was kind, and trustful, and honourable: and she—she could not be called the *opposite*, yet she seemed to allow herself such wide latitude that I had little faith in her principles, and still less sympathy for her feelings. I wanted something to happen which might have the effect of freeing both Wuthering Heights and the Grange of Mr. Heathcliff, quietly, leaving us as we had been prior to his advent. His visits were a continual nightmare to me; and, I suspected, to my master also. His abode at the Heights was an oppression past explaining. I felt that God had forsaken the stray sheep there to its own wicked wanderings, and an evil beast prowled between it and the fold, waiting his time to spring and destroy.

Chapter XI

Sometimes, while meditating on these things in solitude, I've got up in a sudden terror, and put on my bonnet to go see how all was at the farm; I've persuaded my conscience that it was a duty to warn him how people talked regarding his ways; and then I've recollected his confirmed bad habits, and, hopeless of bene-fiting him, have flinched from re-entering the dismal house, doubt-ing if I could bear to be taken at my word.

One time I passed the old gate, going out of my way, on a journey to Gimmerton. It was about the period that my narrative has reached—a bright, frosty afternoon, the ground bare, and the road hard and dry.

I came to a stone where the highway branches off on to the moor at your left hand; a rough sand-pillar, with the letters W. H. cut on its north side, on the east, G., and on the south-west, T. G. It serves as guide-post to the Grange, and Heights, and village.

The sun shone yellow on its grey head, reminding me of sum-mer; and I cannot say why, but all at once, a gush of child's sensa-tions flowed into my heart. Hindley and I held it a favourite spot twenty years before.

I gazed long at the weather-worn block; and, stooping down, perceived a hole near the bottom still full of snail-shells and pebbles, which we were fond of storing there with more perishable things; and, as fresh as reality, it appeared that I beheld my early playmate seated on the withered turf, his dark, square head bent forward, and his little hand scooping out the earth with a piece of slate.

"Poor Hindley!" I exclaimed, involuntarily.

I started—my bodily eye was cheated into a momentary be-lief that the child lifted its face and stared straight into mine! It vanished in a twinkling; but, immediately, I felt an irresistible yearning to be at the Heights. Superstition urged me to comply with this impulse. Supposing he should be dead! I thought—or should die soon!—supposing it were a sign of death!

The nearer I got to the house the more agitated I grew; and on catching sight of it, I trembled every limb. The apparition had out-stripped me; it stood looking through the gate. That was my first idea on observing an elf-locked, brown-eyed boy setting his ruddy countenance against the bars. Further reflection suggested this must be Hareton, *my* Hareton, not altered greatly since I left him, ten months since.

"God bless thee, darling!" I cried, forgetting instantaneously my foolish fears. "Hareton, it's Nelly—Nelly, thy nurse."

He retreated out of arm's length, and picked up a large flint.

"I am come to see thy father, Hareton," I added, guessing from the action that Nelly, if she lived in his memory at all, was not recognised as one with me.

He raised his missile to hurl it; I commenced a soothing speech, but could not stay his hand. The stone struck my bonnet; and then ensued, from the stammering lips of the little fellow, a string of curses, which, whether he comprehended them or not, were delivered with practised emphasis, and distorted his baby features into a shocking expression of malignity.

You may be certain this grieved more than angered me. Fit to cry, I took an orange from my pocket, and offered it to propitiate him.

He hesitated, and then snatched it from my hold, as if he fancied I only intended to tempt and disappoint him.

I showed another, keeping it out of his reach.

"Who has taught you those fine words, my barn,"[5] I inquired. "The curate?"

"Damn the curate, and thee! Gie me that," he replied.

"Tell us where you got your lessons, and you shall have it," said I. "Who's your master?"

"Devil daddy," was his answer.

"And what do you learn from Daddy?" I continued.

He jumped at the fruit; I raised it higher. "What does he teach you?" I asked.

"Naught," said he, "but to keep out of his gait.[6] Daddy cannot bide me, because I swear at him."

"Ah! and the devil teaches you to swear at Daddy?" I observed.

"Aye—nay," he drawled.

"Who then?"

"Heathcliff."

I asked if he liked Mr. Heathcliff?

"Aye!" he answered again.

Desiring to have his reasons for liking him, I could only gather the sentences—"I known't—he pays Dad back what he gies to me —he curses Daddy for cursing me—he says I mun do as I will."

"And the curate does not teach you to read and write, then?" I pursued.

"No, I was told the curate should have his —— teeth dashed down his —— throat, if he stepped over the threshold. Heathcliff had promised that!"

5. Child (bairn).   6. Way.

I put the orange in his hand, and bade him tell his father that a woman called Nelly Dean was waiting to speak with him, by the garden gate.

He went up the walk, and entered the house; but, instead of Hindley, Heathcliff appeared on the door stones, and I turned directly and ran down the road as hard as ever I could race, making no halt till I gained the guide post, and feeling as scared as if I had raised a goblin.

This is not much connected with Miss Isabella's affair; except that it urged me to resolve further on mounting vigilant guard, and doing my utmost to check the spread of such bad influence at the Grange, even though I should wake a domestic storm by thwarting Mrs. Linton's pleasure.

The next time Heathcliff came, my young lady chanced to be feeding some pigeons in the court. She had never spoken a word to her sister-in-law for three days; but she had likewise dropped her fretful complaining, and we found it a great comfort.

Heathcliff had not the habit of bestowing a single unnecessary civility on Miss Linton, I knew. Now, as soon as he beheld her, his first precaution was to take a sweeping survey of the house-front. I was standing by the kitchen window, but I drew out of sight. He then stept across the pavement to her, and said something: she seemed embarrassed, and desirous of getting away; to prevent it, he laid his hand on her arm. She averted her face; he apparently put some question which she had no mind to answer. There was another rapid glance at the house, and supposing himself unseen, the scoundrel had the impudence to embrace her.

"Judas! Traitor!" I ejaculated. "You are a hypocrite too, are you? A deliberate deceiver."

"Who is, Nelly?" said Catherine's voice at my elbow. I had been over-intent on watching the pair outside to mark her entrance.

"Your worthless friend!" I answered warmly; "the sneaking rascal yonder. Ah, he has caught a glimpse of us—he is coming in! I wonder will he have the art to find a plausible excuse for making love to Miss, when he told you he hated her?"

Mrs. Linton saw Isabella tear herself free, and run into the garden; and a minute after, Heathcliff opened the door.

I couldn't withhold giving some loose to my indignation; but Catherine angrily insisted on silence, and threatened to order me out of the kitchen, if I dared be so presumptuous as to put in my insolent tongue.

"To hear you, people might think *you* were the mistress!" she cried. "You want setting down in your right place! Heathcliff, what are you about, raising this stir? I said you must let Isabella alone!—I beg you will, unless you are tired of being received here, and wish Linton to draw the bolts against you!"

"God forbid that he should try!" answered the black villain. I detested him just then. "God keep him meek and patient! Every day I grow madder after sending him to heaven!"

"Hush!" said Catherine, shutting the inner door. "Don't vex me. Why have you disregarded my request? Did she come across you on purpose?"

"What is it to you?" he growled. "I have a right to kiss her, if she chooses, and you have no right to object. I'm not *your* husband: *you* needn't be jealous of me!"

"I'm not jealous *of* you," replied the mistress, "I'm jealous *for* you. Clear your face, you shan't scowl at me! If you like Isabella, you shall marry her. But do you like her? Tell the truth, Heathcliff! There, you won't answer. I'm certain you don't!"

"And would Mr. Linton approve of his sister marrying that man?" I inquired.

"Mr. Linton should approve," returned my lady decisively.

"He might spare himself the trouble," said Heathcliff; "I could do as well without his approbation. And as to you, Catherine, I have a mind to speak a few words now, while we are at it. I want you to be aware that I *know* you have treated me infernally—infernally! Do you hear? And if you flatter yourself that I don't perceive it, you are a fool; and if you think I can be consoled by sweet words you are an idiot; and if you fancy I'll suffer unrevenged, I'll convince you of the contrary, in a very little while! Meantime, thank you for telling me your sister-in-law's secret. I swear I'll make the most of it. And stand you aside!"

"What new phase of his character is this?" exclaimed Mrs. Linton, in amazement. "I've treated you infernally—and you'll take revenge! How will you take it, ungrateful brute? How have I treated you infernally?"

"I seek no revenge on you," replied Heathcliff less vehemently. "That's not the plan. The tyrant grinds down his slaves and they don't turn against him, they crush those beneath them. You are welcome to torture me to death for your amusement, only allow me to amuse myself a little in the same style, and refrain from insult, as much as you are able. Having levelled my palace, don't erect a hovel and complacently admire your own charity in giving me that for a home. If I imagined you really wished me to marry Isabella, I'd cut my throat!"

"Oh, the evil is that I am *not* jealous, is it?" cried Catherine. "Well, I won't repeat my offer of a wife: it is as bad as offering Satan a lost soul. Your bliss lies, like his, in inflicting misery. You prove it. Edgar is restored from the ill-temper he gave way to at your coming; I begin to be secure and tranquil; and you, restless to know us at peace, appear resolved on exciting a quarrel. Quarrel with Edgar, if you please, Heathcliff, and deceive his sister; you'll hit on exactly the most efficient method of revenging yourself on me."

The conversation ceased. Mrs. Linton sat down by the fire, flushed and gloomy. The spirit which served her was growing intractable: she could neither lay nor control it. He stood on the hearth, with folded arms, brooding on his evil thoughts; and in this position I left them to seek the master, who was wondering what kept Catherine below so long.

"Ellen," said he, when I entered, "have you seen your mistress?"

"Yes, she's in the kitchen, sir," I answered. "She's sadly put out by Mr. Heathcliff's behaviour: and, indeed, I do think it's time to arrange his visits on another footing. There's harm in being too soft, and now it's come to this—" And I related the scene in the court, and, as near as I dared, the whole subsequent dispute. I fancied it could not be very prejudicial to Mrs. Linton, unless she made it so afterwards, by assuming the defensive for her guest.

Edgar Linton had difficulty in hearing me to the close. His first words revealed that he did not clear his wife of blame.

"This is insufferable!" he exclaimed. "It is disgraceful that she should own him for a friend, and force his company on me! Call me two men out of the hall, Ellen. Catherine shall linger no longer to argue with the low ruffian—I have humoured her enough."

He descended, and bidding the servants wait in the passage, went, followed by me, to the kitchen. Its occupants had recommenced their angry discussion; Mrs. Linton, at least, was scolding with renewed vigour; Heathcliff had moved to the window, and hung his head, somewhat cowed by her violent rating apparently.

He saw the master first, and made a hasty motion that she should be silent; which she obeyed, abruptly, on discovering the reason of his intimation.

"How is this?" said Linton, addressing her; "what notion of propriety must you have to remain here, after the language which has been held to you by that blackguard? I suppose, because it is his ordinary talk, you think nothing of it—you are habituated to his baseness, and, perhaps, imagine I can get used to it too!"

"Have you been listening at the door, Edgar?" asked the mistress, in a tone particularly calculated to provoke her husband, implying both carelessness and contempt of his irritation.

Heathcliff, who had raised his eyes at the former speech, gave a sneering laugh at the latter, on purpose, it seemed, to draw Mr.

Linton's attention to him.

He succeeded; but Edgar did not mean to entertain him with any high flights of passion.

"I have been so far forbearing with you, sir," he said, quietly; "not that I was ignorant of your miserable, degraded character, but I felt you were only partly responsible for that; and Catherine wishing to keep up your acquaintance, I acquiesced—foolishly. Your presence is a moral poison that would contaminate the most virtuous: for that cause, and to prevent worse consequences, I shall deny you, hereafter, admission into this house, and give notice, now, that I require your instant departure. Three minutes' delay will render it involuntary and ignominious."

Heathcliff measured the height and breadth of the speaker with an eye full of derision.

"Cathy, this lamb of yours threatens like a bull!" he said. "It is in danger of splitting its skull against my knuckles. By God, Mr. Linton, I'm mortally sorry that you are not worth knocking down!"

My master glanced towards the passage, and signed me to fetch the men: he had no intention of hazarding a personal encounter.

I obeyed the hint; but Mrs. Linton, suspecting something, followed, and when I attempted to call them, she pulled me back, slammed the door to, and locked it.

"Fair means!" she said, in answer to her husband's look of angry surprise. "If you have not the courage to attack him, make an apology, or allow yourself to be beaten. It will correct you of feigning more valour than you possess. No, I'll swallow the key before you shall get it! I'm delightfully rewarded for my kindness to each! After constant indulgence of one's weak nature, and the other's bad one, I earn, for thanks, two samples of blind ingratitude, stupid to absurdity! Edgar, I was defending you and yours; and I wish Heathcliff may flog you sick, for daring to think an evil thought of me!"

It did not need the medium of a flogging to produce that effect on the master. He tried to wrest the key from Catherine's grasp; and for safety she flung it into the hottest part of the fire; whereupon Mr. Edgar was taken with a nervous trembling, and his countenance grew deadly pale. For his life he could not avert that access of emotion: mingled anguish and humiliation overcame him completely. He leant on the back of a chair, and covered his face.

"Oh, heavens! In old days this would win you knighthood!" exclaimed Mrs. Linton. "We are vanquished! we are vanquished! Heathcliff would as soon lift a finger at you as the king would march his army against a colony of mice. Cheer up, you shan't be hurt! Your type is not a lamb, it's a sucking leveret."

"I wish you joy of the milk-blooded coward, Cathy!" said her friend. "I compliment you on your taste: and that is the slavering, shivering thing you preferred to me! I would not strike him with my fist, but I'd kick him with my foot, and experience considerable satisfaction. Is he weeping, or is he going to faint for fear?"

The fellow approached and gave the chair on which Linton rested a push. He'd better have kept his distance: my master quickly sprang erect, and struck him full on the throat a blow that would have levelled a slighter man.

It took his breath for a minute; and, while he choked, Mr. Linton walked out by the back door into the yard, and from thence, to the front entrance.

"There! you've done with coming here," cried Catherine. "Get away, now; he'll return with a brace of pistols, and half a dozen assistants. If he did overhear us, of course, he'd never forgive you. You've played me an ill turn, Heathcliff! But go—make haste! I'd rather see Edgar at bay than you."

"Do you suppose I'm going with that blow burning in my gullet?" he thundered. "By hell, no! I'll crush his ribs in like a rotten hazel-nut, before I cross the threshold! If I don't floor him now, I shall murder him sometime, so, as you value his existence, let me get at him!"

"He is not coming," I interposed, framing a bit of a lie. "There's the coachman, and the two gardeners; you'll surely not wait to be thrust into the road by them! Each has a bludgeon, and master will, very likely, be watching from the parlour windows to see that they fulfil his orders."

The gardeners and coachman *were* there; but Linton was with them. They had already entered the court. Heathcliff, on second thoughts, resolved to avoid a struggle against three underlings; he seized the poker, smashed the lock from the inner door, and made his escape as they tramped in.

Mrs. Linton, who was very much excited, bid me accompany her upstairs. She did not know my share in contributing to the disturbance, and I was anxious to keep her in ignorance.

"I'm nearly distracted, Nelly!" she exclaimed, throwing herself on the sofa. "A thousand smiths' hammers are beating in my head! Tell Isabella to shun me—this uproar is owing to her; and should she or any one else aggravate my anger at present, I shall get wild. And, Nelly, say to Edgar, if you see him again to-night, that I'm in danger of being seriously ill. I wish it may prove true. He has startled and distressed me shockingly! I want to frighten him. Besides, he might come and begin a string of abuse, or complainings; I'm certain I should recriminate, and God knows where we should end! Will you do so, my good Nelly? You are aware that I am no way blameable in this matter. What possessed him to turn listener? Heathcliff's talk was outrageous, after you left us; but I could soon have diverted him from Isabella, and the rest meant nothing. Now, all is dashed wrong by the fool's-craving to hear evil of self that haunts some people like a demon! Had Edgar never gathered our conversation, he would never have been the worse for it. Really, when he opened on me in that unreasonable tone of displeasure, after I had scolded Heathcliff till I was hoarse for *him*, I did not care, hardly, what they did to each other, especially as I felt that, however the scene closed, we should all be driven asunder for nobody knows how long! Well, if I cannot keep Heathcliff for my friend, if Edgar will be mean and jealous, I'll try to break their hearts by breaking my own. That will be a prompt way of finishing all, when I am pushed to extremity! But it's a deed to be reserved for a forlorn hope; I'd not take Linton by surprise with it. To this point he has been discreet in dreading to provoke me; you must represent the peril of quitting that policy, and remind him of my passionate temper, verging, when kindled, on frenzy. I wish you could dismiss that apathy out of your countenance, and look rather more anxious about me!"

The stolidity with which I received these instructions was, no doubt, rather exasperating, for they were delivered in perfect sincerity; but I believed a person who could plan the turning of her fits of passion to account, beforehand, might, by exerting her will, manage to control herself tolerably even while under their influence; and I did not wish to "frighten" her husband, as she said, and multiply his annoyances for the purpose of serving her selfishness.

Therefore I said nothing when I met the master coming towards the parlour; but I took the liberty of turning back to listen whether they would resume their quarrel together.

He began to speak first.

"Remain where you are, Catherine," he said, without any anger in his voice, but with much sorrowful despondency. "I shall not stay. I am neither come to wrangle, nor be reconciled; but I wish just to learn whether, after this evening's events, you intend to continue your intimacy with—"

"Oh, for mercy's sake," interrupted the mistress, stamping her foot, "for mercy's sake, let us hear no more of it now! Your cold blood cannot be worked into a fever; your veins are full of ice-water, but mine are boiling, and the sight of such chillness makes them dance."

"To get rid of me, answer my question," persevered Mr. Linton.

"You *must* answer it; and that violence does not alarm me. I have found that you can be as stoical as any one, when you please. Will you give up Heathcliff hereafter, or will you give up me? It is impossible for you to be *my* friend and *his* at the same time; and I absolutely *require* to know which you choose."

"I require to be let alone!" exclaimed Catherine, furiously. "I demand it! Don't you see I can scarcely stand? Edgar, you—you leave me!"

She rung the bell till it broke with a twang: I entered leisurely. It was enough to try the temper of a saint, such senseless, wicked rages! There she lay dashing her head against the arm of the sofa, and grinding her teeth, so that you might fancy she would crash them to splinters!

Mr. Linton stood looking at her in sudden compunction and fear. He told me to fetch some water. She had no breath for speaking.

I brought a glass full; and, as she would not drink, I sprinkled it on her face. In a few seconds she stretched herself out stiff, and turned up her eyes, while her cheeks, at once blanched and livid, assumed the aspect of death.

Linton looked terrified.

"There is nothing in the world the matter," I whispered. I did not want him to yield, though I could not help being afraid in my heart.

"She has blood on her lips!" he said, shuddering.

"Never mind!" I answered, tartly. And I told him how she had resolved, previous to his coming, on exhibiting a fit of frenzy.

I incautiously gave the account aloud, and she heard me, for she started up—her hair flying over her shoulders, her eyes flashing, the muscles of her neck and arms standing out preternaturally. I made up my mind for broken bones, at least; but she only glared about her for an instant, and then rushed from the room.

The master directed me to follow; I did, to her chamber door; she hindered me from going farther by securing it against me.

As she never offered to descend to breakfast next morning, I went to ask whether she would have some carried up.

"No!" she replied, peremptorily.

The same question was repeated at dinner and tea; and again on the morrow after, and received the same answer.

Mr. Linton, on his part, spent his time in the library, and did not inquire concerning his wife's occupations. Isabella and he had had an hour's interview, during which he tried to elicit from her some sentiment of proper horror for Heathcliff's advances; but he could make nothing of her evasive replies, and was obliged to close the examination unsatisfactorily; adding, however, a solemn warning, that if she were so insane as to encourage that worthless suitor, it would dissolve all bonds of relationship between herself and him.

Chapter XII

While Miss Linton moped about the park and garden, always silent, and almost always in tears; and her brother shut himself up among books that he never opened—wearying, I guessed, with a continual vague expectation that Catherine, repenting her conduct, would come of her own accord to ask pardon, and seek a reconciliation—and while *she* fasted pertinaciously, under the idea, probably, that at every meal, Edgar was ready to choke for her absence, and pride alone held him from running to cast himself at her feet, I went about my household duties, convinced that the Grange had but one sensible soul in its walls, and that lodged in my body.

I wasted no condolences on Miss, nor any expostulations on my mistress, nor did I pay attention to the sighs of my master, who yearned to hear his lady's name, since he might not hear her voice.

I determined they should come about as they pleased for me; and though it was a tiresomely slow process, I began to rejoice at length in a faint dawn of its progress, as I thought at first.

Mrs. Linton, on the third day, unbarred her door; and having finished the water in her pitcher and decanter, desired a renewed supply, and a basin of gruel, for she believed she was dying. That I set down as a speech meant for Edgar's ears; I believed no such thing, so I kept it to myself, and brought her some tea and dry toast.

She ate and drank eagerly; and sank back on her pillow again, clenching her hands and groaning.

"Oh, I will die," she exclaimed, "since no one cares anything about me. I wish I had not taken that."

Then a good while after I heard her murmur—

"No, I'll not die—he'd be glad—he does not love me at all—he would never miss me!"

"Did you want anything, ma'am?" I enquired, still preserving my external composure, in spite of her ghastly countenance and strange exaggerated manner.

"What is that apathetic being doing?" she demanded, pushing the thick entangled locks from her wasted face. "Has he fallen into a lethargy, or is he dead?"

"Neither," replied I; "if you mean Mr. Linton. He's tolerably well, I think, though his studies occupy him rather more than they ought; he is continually among his books, since he has no other society."

I should not have spoken so, if I had known her true condition, but I could not get rid of the notion that she acted a part of her disorder.

"Among his books!" she cried, confounded. "And I dying! I on the brink of the grave! My God! does he know how I'm altered?" continued she, staring at her reflection in a mirror, hanging against the opposite wall. "Is that Catherine Linton? He imagines me in a pet—in play, perhaps. Cannot you inform him that it is frightful earnest? Nelly, if it be not too late, as soon as I learn how he feels, I'll choose between these two: either to starve at once—that would be no punishment unless he had a heart—or to recover and leave the country. Are you speaking the truth about him now? Take care. Is he actually so utterly indifferent for my life?"

"Why, ma'am," I answered, "the master has no idea of your being deranged; and, of course, he does not fear that you will let yourself die of hunger."

"You think not? Cannot you tell him I will?" she returned. "Persuade him—speak of your own mind—say you are certain I will!"

"No, you forget, Mrs. Linton," I suggested, "that you have eaten some food with a relish this evening, and to-morrow you will perceive its good effects."

"If I were only sure it would kill him," she interrupted, "I'd kill myself directly! These three awful nights, I've never closed my lids—and oh, I've been tormented! I've been haunted, Nelly! But I begin to fancy you don't like me. How strange! I thought, though everybody hated and despised each other, they could not avoid loving me—and they have all turned to enemies in a few hours. *They* have, I'm positive; the people *here*. How dreary to meet death, surrounded by their cold faces! Isabella, terrified and repelled, afraid to enter the room, it would be so dreadful to watch Catherine go. And Edgar standing solemnly by to see it over; then offering prayers of thanks to God for restoring peace to his house, and going back to his *books!* What, in the name of all that feels, has he to do with *books*, when I am dying?"

She could not bear the notion which I had put into her head of Mr. Linton's philosophical resignation. Tossing about, she increased her feverish bewilderment to madness, and tore the pillow with her teeth; then raising herself up all burning, desired that I would open the window. We were in the middle of winter, the wind blew strong from the northeast, and I objected.

Both the expressions flitting over her face, and the changes of her moods, began to alarm me terribly; and brought to my recollection her former illness, and the doctor's injunction that she should not be crossed.

A minute previously she was violent; now, supported on one arm, and not noticing my refusal to obey her, she seemed to find childish diversion in pulling the feathers from the rents she had just made, and ranging them on the sheet according to their different species: her mind had strayed to other associations.

"That's a turkey's," she murmured to herself; "and this is a wild-duck's; and this is a pigeon's. Ah, they put pigeons' feathers in the pillows—no wonder I couldn't die! Let me take care to throw it on the floor when I lie down. And here is a moor-cock's; and this—I should know it among a thousand—it's a lapwing's. Bonny bird; wheeling over our heads in the middle of the moor. It wanted to get to its nest, for the clouds touched the swells, and it felt rain coming. This feather was picked up from the heath, the bird was not shot; we saw its nest in the winter, full of little skeletons. Heathcliff set a trap over it, and the old ones dare not come. I made him promise he'd never shoot a lapwing after that, and he didn't. Yes, here are more! Did he shoot my lapwings, Nelly? Are they red, any of them? Let me look."

"Give over with that baby-work!" I interrupted, dragging the pillow away, and turning the holes towards the mattress, for she was removing its contents by handfuls. "Lie down and shut your eyes, you're wandering. There's a mess! The down is flying about like snow!"

I went here and there collecting it.

"I see in you, Nelly," she continued, dreamily, "an aged woman —you have grey hair, and bent shoulders. This bed is the fairy cave under Penistone Crag, and you are gathering elf-bolts[5] to hurt our heifers; pretending, while I am near, that they are only locks of wool. That's what you'll come to fifty years hence; I know you are not so now. I'm not wandering: you're mistaken, or else I should believe you really *were* that withered hag, and I should think I *was* under Penistone Crag, and I'm conscious it's night, and there are two candles on the table making the black press shine like jet."

"The black press? where is that?" I asked. "You are talking in your sleep!"

"It's against the wall, as it always is," she replied. "It *does* appear odd—I see a face in it!"

"There is no press in the room, and never was," said I, resuming my seat, and looping up the curtain that I might watch her.

"Don't *you* see that face?" she enquired, gazing earnestly at the

5. Flint arrowheads.

mirror.

And say what I could, I was incapable of making her comprehend it to be her own; so I rose and covered it with a shawl.

"It's behind there still!" she pursued, anxiously. "And it stirred. Who is it? I hope it will not come out when you are gone! Oh! Nelly, the room is haunted! I'm afraid of being alone!"

I took her hand in mine, and bid her be composed, for a succession of shudders convulsed her frame, and she *would* keep straining her gaze towards the glass.

"There's nobody here!" I insisted. "It was *yourself*, Mrs. Linton; you knew it a while since."

"Myself," she gasped, "and the clock is striking twelve! It's true, then; that's dreadful!"

Her fingers clutched the clothes, and gathered them over her eyes. I attempted to steal to the door with an intention of calling her husband; but I was summoned back by a piercing shriek. The shawl had dropped from the frame.

"Why, what *is* the matter?" cried I. "Who is coward now? Wake up! That is the glass—the mirror, Mrs. Linton; and you see yourself in it, and there am I too, by your side."

Trembling and bewildered, she held me fast, but the horror gradually passed from her countenance; its paleness gave place to a glow of shame.

"Oh, dear! I thought I was at home," she sighed. "I thought I was lying in my chamber at Wuthering Heights. Because I'm weak, my brain got confused, and I screamed unconsciously. Don't say anything; but stay with me. I dread sleeping, my dreams appal me."

"A sound sleep would do you good, ma'am," I answered; "and I hope this suffering will prevent your trying starving again."

"Oh, if I were but in my own bed in the old house!" she went on bitterly, wringing her hands. "And that wind sounding in the firs by the lattice. Do let me feel it—it comes straight down the moor—do let me have one breath!"

To pacify her, I held the casement ajar, a few seconds. A cold blast rushed through; I closed it, and returned to my post.

She lay still now, her face bathed in tears. Exhaustion of body had entirely subdued her spirit; our fiery Catherine was no better than a wailing child!

"How long is it since I shut myself in here?" she asked, suddenly reviving.

"It was Monday evening," I replied, "and this is Thursday night, or rather Friday morning, at present."

"What! of the same week?" she exclaimed. "Only that brief time?"

"Long enough to live on nothing but cold water and ill-temper," observed I.

"Well, it seems a weary number of hours," she muttered doubtfully; "it must be more. I remember being in the parlour after they had quarrelled; and Edgar being cruelly provoking, and me running into this room desperate. As soon as ever I had barred the door, utter blackness overwhelmed me, and I fell on the floor. I couldn't explain to Edgar how certain I felt of having a fit, or going raging mad, if he persisted in teasing me! I had no command of tongue, or brain, and he did not guess my agony, perhaps; it barely left me sense to try to escape from him and his voice. Before I recovered sufficiently to see and hear, it began to be dawn; and, Nelly, I'll tell you what I thought, and what has kept recurring and recurring till I feared for my reason. I thought as I lay there with my head against that table leg, and my eyes dimly discerning the grey square of the window, that I was enclosed in the oak-panelled bed at home; and my heart ached with some great grief which, just waking, I could not recollect. I pondered, and worried myself to discover what it could be; and, most strangely, the whole last seven years of my life grew a blank! I did not recall that they had been at all. I was a child; my father was just buried, and my misery arose from the separation that Hindley had ordered between me and Heathcliff. I was laid alone, for the first time, and, rousing from a dismal doze after a night of weeping, I lifted my hand to push the panels aside: it struck the table-top! I swept it along the carpet, and then memory burst in—my late anguish was swallowed in a paroxysm of despair. I cannot say why I felt so wildly wretched—it must have been temporary derangement, for there is scarcely cause. But, supposing at twelve years old, I had been wrenched from the Heights, and every early association, and my all in all, as Heathcliff was at that time, and been converted at a stroke into Mrs. Linton, the lady of Thrushcross Grange, and the wife of a stranger; an exile, and outcast, thenceforth, from what had been my world. You may fancy a glimpse of the abyss where I grovelled! Shake your head as you will, Nelly, *you* have helped to unsettle me! You should, have spoken to Edgar, indeed you should, and compelled him to leave me quiet! Oh, I'm burning! I wish I were out of doors—I wish I were a girl again, half savage, and hardy, and free; and laughing at injuries, not maddening under them! Why am I so changed? why does my blood rush into a hell of tumult at a few words? I'm sure I should be myself were I once among the heather on those hills. Open the window again wide, fasten it open! Quick, why don't you move?"

"Because I won't give you your death of cold," I answered.

"You won't give me a chance of life, you mean," she said sullenly. "However, I'm not helpless yet, I'll open it myself."

And sliding from the bed before I could hinder her, she crossed the room, walking very uncertainly, threw it back, and bent out, careless of the frosty air that cut about her shoulders as keen as a knife.

I entreated, and finally attempted to force her to retire. But I soon found her delirious strength much surpassed mine (she *was* delirious, I became convinced by her subsequent actions, and ravings).

There was no moon, and everything beneath lay in misty darkness; not a light gleamed from any house, far or near; all had been extinguished long ago; and those at Wuthering Heights were never visible—still she asserted she caught their shining.

"Look!" she cried eagerly, "that's my room, with the candle in it, and the trees swaying before it; and the other candle is in Joseph's garret. Joseph sits up late, doesn't he? He's waiting till I come home that he may lock the gate. Well, he'll wait a while yet. It's a rough journey, and a sad heart to travel it; and we must pass by Gimmerton Kirk, to go that journey! We've braved its ghosts often together, and dared each other to stand among the graves and ask them to come. But Heathcliff, if I dare you now, will you venture? If you do, I'll keep you. I'll not lie there by myself; they may bury me twelve feet deep, and throw the church down over me, but I won't rest till you are with me. I never will!"

She paused, and resumed with a strange smile, "He's considering—he'd rather I'd come to him! Find a way, then! not through that Kirkyard. You are slow! Be content, you always followed me!"

Perceiving it vain to argue against her insanity, I was planning how I could reach something to wrap about her, without quitting my hold of herself, for I could not trust her alone by the gaping lattice, when, to my consternation, I heard the rattle of the doorhandle, and Mr. Linton entered. He had only then come from the library; and, in passing through the lobby, had noticed our talking and been attracted by curiosity, or fear, to examine what it signified at that late hour.

"Oh, sir!" I cried, checking the exclamation risen to his lips at the sight which met him, and the bleak atmosphere of the chamber. "My poor mistress is ill, and she quite masters me; I cannot manage her at all; pray, come and persuade her to go to bed. Forget your anger, for she's hard to guide any way but her own."

"Catherine ill?" he said, hastening to us. "Shut the window, Ellen! Catherine! why—"

He was silent; the haggardness of Mrs. Linton's appearance

smote him speechless, and he could only glance from her to me in horrified astonishment.

"She's been fretting here," I continued, "and eating scarcely anything, and never complaining; she would admit none of us till this evening, and so we couldn't inform you of her state, as we were not aware of it ourselves, but it is nothing."

I felt I uttered my explanations awkwardly; the master frowned. "It is nothing, is it, Ellen Dean?" he said sternly. "You shall account more clearly for keeping me ignorant of this!" And he took his wife in his arms, and looked at her with anguish.

At first she gave him no glance of recognition—he was invisible to her abstracted gaze. The delirium was not fixed, however; having weaned her eyes from contemplating the outer darkness, by degrees she centred her attention on him, and discovered who it was that held her.

"Ah! you are come, are you, Edgar Linton?" she said, with angry animation. "You are one of those things that are ever found when least wanted, and when you are wanted, never! I suppose we shall have plenty of lamentations, now—I see we shall—but they can't keep me from my narrow home out yonder, my resting place where I'm bound before spring is over! There it is, not among the Lintons, mind, under the chapel-roof; but in the open air with a head-stone, and you may please yourself, whether you go to them, or come to me!"

"Catherine, what have you done?" commenced the master. "Am I nothing to you, any more? Do you love that wretch, Heath—"

"Hush!" cried Mrs. Linton. "Hush, this moment! You mention that name and I end the matter instantly, by a spring from the window! What you touch at present, you may have; but my soul will be on that hilltop before you lay hands on me again. I don't want you, Edgar; I'm past wanting you. Return to your books. I'm glad you possess a consolation, for all you had in me is gone."

"Her mind wanders, sir," I interposed. "She has been talking nonsense the whole evening; but, let her have quiet and proper attendance, and she'll rally. Hereafter, we must be cautious how we vex her."

"I desire no further advice from you," answered Mr. Linton. "You knew your mistress's nature, and you encouraged me to harass her. And not to give me one hint of how she has been these three days! It was heartless! Months of sickness could not cause such a change!"

I began to defend myself, thinking it too bad to be blamed for another's wicked waywardness!

"I knew Mrs. Linton's nature to be headstrong and domineering," cried I; "but I didn't know that you wished to foster her

fierce temper! I didn't know that, to humour her, I should wink at
Mr. Heathcliff. I performed the duty of a faithful servant in telling
you, and I have got a faithful servant's wages! Well, it will teach
me to be careful next time. Next time you may gather intelligence
for yourself!"

"The next time you bring a tale to me, you shall quit my service,
Ellen Dean," he replied.

"You'd rather hear nothing about it, I suppose, then, Mr.
Linton?" said I. "Heathcliff has your permission to come a-court-
ing to Miss, and to drop in at every opportunity your absence offers,
on purpose to poison the mistress against you?"

Confused as Catherine was, her wits were alert at applying our
conversation.

"Ah! Nelly has played traitor," she exclaimed, passionately.
"Nelly is my hidden enemy. You witch! So you do seek elf-bolts
to hurt us! Let me go, and I'll make her rue! I'll make her howl a
recantation!"

A maniac's fury kindled under her brows; she struggled desperately to disengage herself from Linton's arms. I felt no inclination to tarry the event; and, resolving to seek medical aid on my
own responsibility, I quitted the chamber.

In passing the garden to reach the road, at a place where a
bridle hook is driven into the wall, I saw something white moved
irregularly, evidently by another agent than the wind. Notwithstanding my hurry, I stayed to examine it, lest ever after I should
have the conviction impressed on my imagination that it was a
creature of the other world.

My surprise and perplexity were great to discover, by touch
more than vision, Miss Isabella's springer, Fanny, suspended by a
handkerchief, and nearly at its last gasp.

I quickly released the animal, and lifted it into the garden. I
had seen it follow its mistress upstairs, when she went to bed,
and wondered much how it could have got out there, and what
mischievous person had treated it so.

While untying the knot round the hook, it seemed to me that
I repeatedly caught the beat of horses' feet galloping at some
distance; but there were such a number of things to occupy my
reflections that I hardly gave the circumstance a thought, though
it was a strange sound, in that place, at two o'clock in the
morning.

Mr. Kenneth was fortunately just issuing from his house to see a
patient in the village as I came up the street; and my account of
Catherine Linton's malady induced him to accompany me back
immediately.

He was a plain, rough man; and he made no scruple to speak

his doubts of her surviving this second attack, unless she were more submissive to his directions than she had shown herself before.

"Nelly Dean," said he, "I can't help fancying there's an extra cause for this. What has there been to do at the Grange? We've odd reports up here. A stout, hearty lass like Catherine does not fall ill for a trifle; and that sort of people should not either. It's hard work bringing them through fevers, and such things. How did it begin?"

"The master will inform you," I answered; "but you are acquainted with the Earnshaws' violent dispositions, and Mrs. Linton caps them all. I may say this; it commenced in a quarrel. She was struck during a tempest of passion with a kind of fit. That's her account, at least; for she flew off in the height of it, and locked herself up. Afterwards, she refused to eat, and now she alternately raves and remains in a half dream, knowing those about her, but having her mind filled with all sorts of strange ideas and illusions."

"Mr. Linton will be sorry?" observed Kenneth, interrogatively.

"Sorry? He'll break his heart should anything happen!" I replied. "Don't alarm him more than necessary."

"Well, I told him to beware," said my companion, "and he must bide the consequences of neglecting my warning! Hasn't he been thick with Mr. Heathcliff lately?"

"Heathcliff frequently visits at the Grange," answered I, "though more on the strength of the mistress having known him when a boy, than because the master likes his company. At present, he's discharged from the trouble of calling; owing to some presumptuous aspirations after Miss Linton which he manifested. I hardly think he'll be taken in again."

"And does Miss Linton turn a cold shoulder on him?" was the doctor's next question.

"I'm not in her confidence," returned I, reluctant to continue the subject.

"No, she's a sly one," he remarked, shaking his head. "She keeps her own counsel! But she's a real little fool. I have it from good authority that last night (and a pretty night it was!) she and Heathcliff were walking in the plantation at the back of your house, above two hours; and he pressed her not to go in again, but just mount his horse and away with him! My informant said she could only put him off by pledging her word of honour to be prepared on their first meeting after that: when it was to be, he didn't hear, but you urge Mr. Linton to look sharp!"

This news filled me with fresh fears; I outstripped Kenneth, and ran most of the way back. The little dog was yelping in the garden yet. I spared a minute to open the gate for it, but instead of going to the house door, it coursed up and down snuffing the grass, and would have escaped to the road, had I not seized and conveyed it in with me.

On ascending to Isabella's room, my suspicions were confirmed: it was empty. Had I been a few hours sooner, Mrs. Linton's illness might have arrested her rash step. But what could be done now? There was a bare possibility of overtaking them if pursued instantly. I could not pursue them, however; and I dare not rouse the family, and fill the place with confusion; still less unfold the business to my master, absorbed as he was in his present calamity, and having no heart to spare for a second grief!

I saw nothing for it but to hold my tongue, and suffer matters to take their course; and Kenneth being arrived, I went with a badly composed countenance to announce him.

Catherine lay in a troubled sleep; her husband had succeeded in soothing the access of frenzy; he now hung over her pillow, watching every shade, and every change of her painfully expressive features.

The doctor, on examining the case for himself, spoke hopefully to him of its having a favourable termination, if we could only preserve around her perfect and constant tranquillity. To me, he signified the threatening danger was not so much death, as permanent alienation of intellect.

I did not close my eyes that night, nor did Mr. Linton; indeed, we never went to bed; and the servants were all up long before the usual hour, moving through the house with stealthy tread, and exchanging whispers as they encountered each other in their vocations. Every one was active but Miss Isabella; and they began to remark how sound she slept. Her brother too asked if she had risen, and seemed impatient for her presence, and hurt that she showed so little anxiety for her sister-in-law.

I trembled lest he should send me to call her; but I was spared the pain of being the first proclaimant of her flight. One of the maids, a thoughtless girl, who had been on an early errand to Gimmerton, came panting upstairs, open-mouthed, and dashed into the chamber, crying—

"Oh, dear, dear! What mun[6] we have next? Master, master, our young lady—"

"Hold your noise!" cried I hastily, enraged at her clamorous manner.

"Speak lower, Mary—What is the matter?" said Mr. Linton. "What ails your young lady?"

"She's gone, she's gone! Yon' Heathcliff's run off wi' her!" gasped the girl.

6. Must.

"That is not true!" exclaimed Linton, rising in agitation. "It cannot be—how has the idea entered your head? Ellen Dean, go and seek her—it is incredible—it cannot be."

As he spoke he took the servant to the door, and then repeated his demand to know her reasons for such an assertion.

"Why, I met on the road a lad that fetches milk here," she stammered, "and he asked whether we wern't in trouble at the Grange. I thought he meant for Missis's sickness, so I answered, yes. Then, says he, 'They's somebody gone after 'em, I guess?' I stared. He saw I knew naught about it, and he told how a gentleman and lady had stopped to have a horse's shoe fastened at a blacksmith's shop, two miles out of Gimmerton, not very long after midnight! and how the blacksmith's lass had got up to spy who they were: she knew them both directly. And she noticed the man—Heathcliff it was, she felt certain, nob'dy could mistake him, besides—put a sovereign in her father's hand for payment. The lady had a cloak about her face; but having desired a sup of water, while she drank, it fell back, and she saw her very plain. Heathcliff held both bridles as they rode on, and they set their faces from the village, and went as fast as the rough roads would let them. The lass said nothing to her father, but she told it all over Gimmerton this morning."

I ran and peeped, for form's sake, into Isabella's room: confirming, when I returned, the servant's statement. Mr. Linton had resumed his seat by the bed; on my re-entrance, he raised his eyes, read the meaning of my blank aspect, and dropped them without giving an order, or uttering a word.

"Are we to try any measures for overtaking and bringing her back?" I inquired. "How should we do?"

"She went of her own accord," answered the master; "she had a right to go if she pleased. Trouble me no more about her. Hereafter she is only my sister in name, not because I disown her, but because she has disowned me."

And that was all he said on the subject; he did not make a single inquiry further, or mention her in any way, except directing me to send what property she had in the house to her fresh home, wherever it was, when I knew it.

Chapter XIII

For two months the fugitives remained absent; in those two months, Mrs. Linton encountered and conquered the worst shock of what was denominated a brain fever. No mother could have nursed an only child more devotedly than Edgar tended her. Day and night, he was watching, and patiently enduring all the annoyances that irritable nerves and a shaken reason could inflict; and, though Kenneth remarked that what he saved from the grave would only recompense his care by forming the source of constant future anxiety—in fact, that his health and strength were being sacrificed to preserve a mere ruin of humanity—he knew no limits in gratitude and joy when Catherine's life was declared out of danger; and hour after hour he would sit beside her, tracing the gradual return to bodily health, and flattering his too sanguine hopes with the illusion that her mind would settle back to its right balance also, and she would soon be entirely her former self.

The first time she left her chamber was at the commencement of the following March. Mr. Linton had put on her pillow, in the morning, a handful of golden crocuses; her eye, long stranger to any gleam of pleasure, caught them in waking, and shone delighted as she gathered them eagerly together.

"These are the earliest flowers at the Heights!" she exclaimed. "They remind me of soft thaw winds, and warm sunshine, and nearly melted snow. Edgar, is there not a south wind, and is not the snow almost gone?"

"The snow is quite gone down here, darling," replied her husband, "and I only see two white spots on the whole range of moors. The sky is blue, and the larks are singing, and the becks and brooks are all brim full. Catherine, last spring at this time, I was longing to have you under this roof; now, I wish you were a mile or two up those hills; the air blows so sweetly, I feel that it would cure you."

"I shall never be there, but once more!" said the invalid; "and then you'll leave me, and I shall remain for ever. Next spring you'll long again to have me under this roof, and you'll look back and think you were happy to-day."

Linton lavished on her the kindest caresses, and tried to cheer her by the fondest words; but, vaguely regarding the flowers, she let the tears collect on her lashes and stream down her cheeks unheeding.

We knew she was really better, and, therefore, decided that long confinement to a single place produced much of this despondency, and it might be partially removed by a change of scene.

The master told me to light a fire in the many-weeks-deserted parlour, and to set an easy-chair in the sunshine by the window; and then he brought her down, and she sat a long while enjoying the genial heat, and, as we expected, revived by the objects round her, which, though familiar, were free from the dreary associations investing her hated sickchamber. By evening, she seemed greatly exhausted; yet no arguments could persuade her to return to that apartment, and I had to arrange the parlour sofa for her bed, till another room could be prepared.

To obviate the fatigue of mounting and descending the stairs, we fitted up this, where you lie at present, on the same floor with the parlour; and she was soon strong enough to move from one to the other, leaning on Edgar's arm.

Ah, I thought myself, she might recover, so waited on as she was. And there was double cause to desire it, for on her existence depended that of another; we cherished the hope that in a little while Mr. Linton's heart would be gladdened, and his lands secured from a stranger's gripe, by the birth of an heir.

I should mention that Isabella sent to her brother, some six weeks from her departure, a short note, announcing her marriage with Heathcliff. It appeared dry and cold; but at the bottom was dotted in with pencil an obscure apology, and an entreaty for kind remembrance and reconciliation, if her proceeding had offended him; asserting that she could not help it then, and being done, she had now no power to repeal it.

Linton did not reply to this, I believe; and, in a fortnight more, I got a long letter, which I considered odd coming from the pen of a bride just out of the honeymoon. I'll read it, for I keep it yet. Any relic of the dead is precious, if they were valued living.

Dear Ellen, it begins.

I came last night to Wuthering Heights, and heard, for the first time, that Catherine has been, and is yet, very ill. I must not write to her, I suppose, and my brother is either too angry or too distressed to answer what I send him. Still, I must write to somebody, and the only choice left me is you.

Inform Edgar that I'd give the world to see his face again—that my heart returned to Thrushcross Grange in twenty-four hours after I left it, and is there at this moment, full of warm feelings for him, and Catherine! *I can't follow it, though*—(those words are underlined)—they need not expect me, and they may draw what conclusions they please; taking care, however, to lay nothing at the door of my weak will or deficient affection.

The remainder of the letter is for yourself alone. I want to ask you two questions: the first is—

How did you contrive to preserve the common sympathies of human nature when you resided here? I cannot recognise any sentiment which those around share with me.

The second question, I have great interest in; it is this—

Is Mr. Heathcliff a man? If so, is he mad? And if not, is he a devil? I shan't tell my reasons for making this inquiry; but I beseech you to explain, if you can, what I have married—that is, when you call to see me; and you must call, Ellen, very soon. Don't write, but come, and bring me something from Edgar.

Now, you shall hear how I have been received in my new home, as I am led to imagine the Heights will be. It is to amuse myself that I dwell on such subjects as the lack of external comforts; they never occupy my thoughts, except at the moment when I miss them. I should laugh and dance for joy, if I found their absence was the total of my miseries, and the rest was an unnatural dream!

The sun set behind the Grange, as we turned on to the moors; by that, I judged it to be six o'clock; and my companion halted half-an-hour, to inspect the park, and the gardens, and, probably, the place itself, as well as he could; so it was dark when we dismounted in the paved yard of the farmhouse, and your old fellow-servant, Joseph, issued out to receive us by the light of a dip candle. He did it with a courtesy that redounded to his credit. His first act was to elevate his torch to a level with my face, squint malignantly, project his under-lip, and turn away.

Then he took the two horses, and led them into the stables; reappearing for the purpose of locking the outer gate, as if we lived in an ancient castle.

Heathcliff stayed to speak to him, and I entered the kitchen— a dingy, untidy hole; I dare say you would not know it, it is so changed since it was in your charge.

By the fire stood a ruffianly child, strong in limb and dirty in garb, with a look of Catherine in his eyes and about his mouth. "This is Edgar's legal nephew," I reflected—"mine in a manner; I must shake hands, and—yes—I must kiss him. It is right to establish a good understanding at the beginning."

I approached, and, attempting to take his chubby fist, said—
"How do you do, my dear?"

He replied in a jargon I did not comprehend.

"Shall you and I be friends, Hareton?" was my next essay at conversation.

An oath, and a threat to set Throttler on me if I did not "frame off,"[7] rewarded my perseverance.

"Hey, Throttler, lad!" whispered the little wretch, rousing a half-bred bull-dog from its lair in a corner. "Now, wilt tuh be ganging?"[8] he asked authoritatively.

Love for my life urged a compliance; I stepped over the threshold to wait till the others should enter. Mr. Heathcliff was nowhere visible; and Joseph, whom I followed to the stables and requested to accompany me in, after staring and muttering to himself, screwed up his nose and replied—

7. Be gone.   8. Will you be going?

"Mim! mim! mim! Did iver Christian body hear owt like it? Minching un' munching! Hah can Aw tell whet ye say?"[9]

"I say, I wish you to come with me into the house!" I cried, thinking him deaf, yet highly disgusted at his rudeness.

"Nor nuh me![1] Aw getten summut else to do," he answered, and continued his work, moving his lantern jaws meanwhile, and surveying my dress and countenance (the former a great deal too fine, but the latter, I'm sure, as sad as he could desire) with sovereign contempt.

I walked round the yard, and through a wicket, to another door, at which I took the liberty of knocking, in hopes some more civil servant might shew himself.

After a short suspense, it was opened by a tall, gaunt man, without neckerchief, and otherwise extremely slovenly; his features were lost in masses of shaggy hair that hung on his shoulders; and *his* eyes, too, were like a ghostly Catherine's, with all their beauty annihilated.

"What's your business here?" he demanded, grimly. "Who are you?"

"My name *was* Isabella Linton," I replied. "You've seen me before, sir. I'm lately married to Mr. Heathcliff; and he has brought me here—I suppose by your permission."

"Is he come back, then?" asked the hermit, glaring like a hungry wolf.

"Yes—we came just now," I said; "but he left me by the kitchen door; and when I would have gone in, your little boy played sentinel over the place, and frightened me off by the help of a bull-dog."

"It's well the hellish villain has kept his word!" growled my future host, searching the darkness beyond me in expectation of discovering Heathcliff; and then he indulged in a soliloquy of execrations, and threats of what he would have done had the "fiend" deceived him.

I repented having tried this second entrance, and was almost inclined to slip way before he finished cursing, but ere I could execute that intention, he ordered me in, and shut and re-fastened the door.

There was a great fire, and that was all the light in the huge apartment, whose floor had grown a uniform grey; and the once brilliant pewter dishes, which used to attract my gaze when I was a girl, partook of a similar obscurity, created by tarnish and dust.

I inquired whether I might call the maid, and be conducted to a bed-room? Mr. Earnshaw vouchsafed no answer. He walked up

9. *Owt:* aught; *minching un' munching:*   1. Not me.
mincing and mouthing.

and down, with his hands in his pockets, apparently quite forgetting my presence; and his abstraction was evidently so deep, and his whole aspect so misanthropical, that I shrank from disturbing him again.

You'll not be surprised, Ellen, at my feeling particularly cheerless, seated in worse than solitude on that inhospitable hearth, and remembering that four miles distant lay my delightful home, containing the only people I loved on earth; and there might as well be the Atlantic to part us, instead of those four miles: I could not overpass them!

I questioned with myself—where must I turn for comfort? and —mind you don't tell Edgar, or Catherine—above every sorrow beside, this rose pre-eminent—despair at finding nobody who could or would be my ally against Heathcliff!

I had sought shelter at Wuthering Heights, almost gladly, because I was secured by that arrangement from living alone with him; but he knew the people we were coming amongst, and he did not fear their intermeddling.

I sat and thought a doleful time; the clock struck eight, and nine, and still my companion paced to and fro, his head bent on his breast, and perfectly silent, unless a groan or a bitter ejaculation forced itself out at intervals.

I listened to detect a woman's voice in the house, and filled the interim with wild regrets and dismal anticipations, which, at last, spoke audibly in irrepressible sighing and weeping.

I was not aware how openly I grieved, till Earnshaw halted opposite, in his measured walk, and gave me a stare of newly awakened surprise. Taking advantage of his recovered attention, I exclaimed—

"I'm tired with my journey, and I want to go to bed! Where is the maid-servant? Direct me to her, as she won't come to me!"

"We have none," he answered; "you must wait on yourself!"

"Where must I sleep, then?" I sobbed—I was beyond regarding self-respect, weighed down by fatigue and wretchedness.

"Joseph will show you Heathcliff's chamber," said he; "open that door—he's in there."

I was going to obey, but he suddenly arrested me, and added in the strangest tone—

"Be so good as to turn your lock, and draw your bolt—don't omit it!"

"Well!" I said. "But why, Mr. Earnshaw?" I did not relish the notion of deliberately fastening myself in with Heathcliff.

"Look here!" he replied, pulling from his waistcoat a curiously constructed pistol, having a double-edged spring knife attached to the barrel. "That's a great tempter to a desperate man, is it not?

I cannot resist going up with this, every night, and trying his door. If once I find it open, he's done for! I do it invariably, even though the minute before I have been recalling a hundred reasons that should make me refrain: it is some devil that urges me to thwart my own schemes by killing him. You fight against that devil, for love, as long as you may; when the time comes, not all the angels in heaven shall save him!"

I surveyed the weapon inquisitively; a hideous notion struck me. How powerful I should be possessing such an instrument! I took it from his hand, and touched the blade. He looked astonished at the expression my face assumed during a brief second. It was not horror, it was covetousness. He snatched the pistol back, jealously; shut the knife, and returned it to its concealment.

"I don't care if you tell him," said he. "Put him on his guard, and watch for him. You know the terms we are on, I see; his danger does not shock you."

"What has Heathcliff done to you?" I asked. "In what has he wronged you to warrant this appalling hatred? Wouldn't it be wiser to bid him quit the house?"

"No," thundered Earnshaw; "should he offer to leave me, he's a dead man: persuade him to attempt it, and you are a murderess! Am I to lose *all*, without a chance of retrieval? Is Hareton to be a beggar? Oh, damnation! I *will* have it back; and I'll have *his* gold too; and then his blood; and hell shall have his soul! It will be ten times blacker with that guest than ever it was before!"

You've acquainted me, Ellen, with your old master's habits. He is clearly on the verge of madness—he was so last night, at least. I shuddered to be near him, and thought on the servant's ill-bred moroseness as comparatively agreeable.

He now recommenced his moody walk, and I raised the latch, and escaped into the kitchen.

Joseph was bending over the fire, peering into a large pan that swung above it; and a wooden bowl of oatmeal stood on the settle close by. The contents of the pan began to boil, and he turned to plunge his hand into the bowl; I conjectured that this preparation was probably for our supper, and, being hungry, I resolved it should be eatable; so, crying out sharply, "*I'll* make the porridge!" I removed the vessel out of his reach, and proceeded to take off my hat and riding habit. "Mr. Earnshaw," I continued, "directs me to wait on myself: I will. I'm not going to act the lady among you, for fear I should starve."

"Gooid Lord!" he muttered, sitting down, and stroking his ribbed stockings from the knee to the ankle. "If they's tuh be fresh orther-ings—just when Aw getten used tuh two maisters, if Aw mun hev a *mistress* set o'er my heead, it's loike time tuh be flitting. Aw niver *did* think tuh say t' day ut Aw mud lave th' owld place—but Aw daht it's nigh at hend!'"[2]

This lamentation drew no notice from me; I went briskly to work, sighing to remember a period when it would have been all merry fun, but compelled speedily to drive off the remembrance. It racked me to recall past happiness, and the greater peril there was of conjuring up its apparition, the quicker the thible[3] ran round, and the faster the handfuls of meal fell into the water.

Joseph beheld my style of cookery with growing indignation.

"Thear!" he ejaculated. "Hareton, thah willut sup thy porridge tuh neeght; they'll be nowt bud lumps as big as maw nave. Thear, agean! Aw'd fling in bowl un all, if Aw wer yah! Thear, pale t' guilp off, un' then yah'll hae done wi't. Bang, bang. It's a marcy t' bothom isn't deaved aht!"[4]

It *was* rather a rough mess, I own, when poured into the basins; four had been provided, and a gallon pitcher of new milk was brought from the dairy, which Hareton seized and commenced drinking and spilling from the expansive lip.

I expostulated, and desired that he should have his in a mug; affirming that I could not taste the liquid treated so dirtily. The old cynic chose to be vastly offended at this nicety; assuring me, repeatedly, that "the barn was every bit as gooid" as I, "and every bit as wollsome,"[5] and wondering how I could fashion to be so conceited; meanwhile, the infant ruffian continued sucking; and glowered up at me defyingly, as he slavered into the jug.

"I shall have my supper in another room," I said. "Have you no place you call a parlour?"

"*Parlour!*" he echoed, sneeringly, "*parlour!* Nay, we've noa *parlours.* If yah dunnut loike wer company,[6] they's maister's; un' if yah dunnut loike maister, they's us."

"Then I shall go upstairs," I answered; "shew me a chamber!"

I put my basin on a tray, and went myself to fetch some more milk.

With great grumblings, the fellow rose and preceded me in my ascent: we mounted to the garrets, he opening a door, now and then, to look into the apartments we passed.

"Here's a rahm," he said, at last, flinging back a cranky board on hinges. "It's weel eneugh tuh ate a few porridge in. They's a pack uh corn i' t' corner, thear, meeterly clane; if yah're feared uh muckying yer grand silk cloes, spread yer hankerchir ut t' top

2. *Ortherings:* orders; *flitting:* moving out; *mud lave:* must leave; *daht:* doubt (i.e., don't doubt); *at hend:* at hand.
3. A smooth stick for stirring broth, porridge, etc.
4. *Willut:* will not; *nave:* fist; *pale t' guilp off:* cool the iron pot (of porridge) by taking out a ladleful and dropping it in again; *deaved:* broken violently.
5. *Barn:* child; *wollsome:* healthy.
6. Our company.

on't."[7]

The "rahm" was a kind of lumber-hole smelling strong of malt and grain; various sacks of which articles were piled around, leaving a wide, bare space in the middle.

"Why, man!" I exclaimed, facing him angrily, "this is not a place to sleep in. I wish to see my bed-room."

"*Bed-rume!*" he repeated, in a tone of mockery. "Yah's see all t' *bed-rumes* thear is—yon's mine."

He pointed into the second garret, only differing from the first in being more naked about the walls, and having a large, low, curtainless bed, with an indigo-coloured quilt, at one end.

"What do I want with yours?" I retorted. "I suppose Mr. Heathcliff does not lodge at the top of the house, does he?"

"Oh! it's Maister *Hathecliff's* yah're wenting?" cried he, as if making a new discovery. "Couldn't ye uh said soa, at onst? un then, Aw mud uh telled ye, 'baht all this wark,[8] ut that's just one yah cannut sea—he allas keeps it locked, un' nob'dy iver mells[9] on't but hisseln."

"You've a nice house, Joseph," I could not refrain from observing, "and pleasant inmates; and I think the concentrated essence of all the madness in the world took up its abode in my brain the day I linked my fate with theirs! However, that is not to the present purpose—there are other rooms. For heaven's sake, be quick, and let me settle somewhere!"

He made no reply to this adjuration; only plodding doggedly down the wooden steps, and halting before an apartment which, from that halt and the superior quality of its furniture, I conjectured to be the best one.

There was a carpet, a good one; but the pattern was obliterated by dust; a fire-place hung with cut paper, dropping to pieces; a handsome oak-bedstead with ample crimson curtains of rather expensive material and modern make. But they had evidently experienced rough usage; the valances hung in festoons, wrenched from their rings, and the iron rod supporting them was bent in an arc on one side, causing the drapery to trail upon the floor. The chairs were also damaged, many of them severely; and deep indentations deformed the panels of the walls.

I was endeavouring to gather resolution for entering, and taking possession, when my fool of a guide announced—

"This here is t' maister's."

My supper by this time was cold, my appetite gone, and my patience exhausted. I insisted on being provided instantly with a

7. *Rahm:* room; *meeterly clane:* fairly clean; *muckying:* dirtying.
8. *'Baht all this wark:* without all this work.
9. *Mells:* meddles.

place of refuge, and means of repose.

"Whear the divil—" began the religious elder. "The Lord bless us! The Lord forgie us! Whear the *hell* wold ye gang? ye marred, wearisome nowt! Yah seen all bud Hareton's bit uf a cham'er. They's nut another hoile tuh lig dahn in i' th' hahse!"[1]

I was so vexed, I flung my tray and its contents on the ground; and then seated myself at the stairs-head, hid my face in my hands, and cried.

"Ech! ech!" exclaimed Joseph. "Weel done, Miss Cathy! weel done, Miss Cathy! Hahsiver, t' maister sall just tum'le o'er them brocken pots, un' then we's hear summut; we's hear hah it's tuh be. Gooid-fur-nowt madling! yah desarve pining froo this tuh Churstmas, flinging t' precious gifts uh God under fooit i' yer flaysome rages! Bud Aw'm mista'em if yah shew yer sperrit lang. Will Hathecliff bide sich bonny ways, think ye? Aw nobbut wish he muh cotch ye i' that plisky. Aw nobbut wish he may."[2]

And so he went scolding to his den beneath, taking the candle with him, and I remained in the dark.

The period of reflection succeeding this silly action compelled me to admit the necessity of smothering my pride, and choking my wrath, and bestirring myself to remove its effects.

An unexpected aid presently appeared in the shape of Throttler, whom I now recognised as a son of our old Skulker; it had spent its whelphood at the Grange, and was given by my father to Mr. Hindley. I fancy it knew me: it pushed its nose against mine by way of salute, and then hastened to devour the porridge, while I groped from step to step, collecting the shattered earthenware, and drying the spatters of milk from the banister with my pocket-handkerchief.

Our labours were scarcely over when I heard Earnshaw's tread in the passage; my assistant tucked in his tail, and pressed to the wall; I stole into the nearest doorway. The dog's endeavour to avoid him was unsuccessful, as I guessed by a scutter downstairs, and a prolonged, piteous yelping. I had better luck. He passed on, entered his chamber, and shut the door.

Directly after, Joseph came up with Hareton, to put him to bed. I had found shelter in Hareton's room, and the old man, on seeing me, said—

"'They's rahm fur boath yah un yer pride, nah, Aw sud think i' th' hahse. It's empty; yah muh hev it all tuh yerseln, un Him[3] as allas maks a third, i' sich ill company!"

Gladly did I take advantage of this intimation; and the minute

---

1. *Marred, wearisome nowt:* spoiled, wearisome nothing; *hoile:* room; *lig:* lie.

2. *Pining:* starving; *nobbut wish:* only wish; *plisky:* rage.

3. God.

I flung myself into a chair, by the fire, I nodded, and slept.

My slumber was deep and sweet, though over far too soon. Mr. Heathcliff awoke me; he had just come in, and demanded, in his loving manner, what I was doing there?

I told him the cause of my staying up so late—that he had the key of our room in his pocket.

The adjective *our* gave mortal offence. He swore it was not, nor ever should be mine; and he'd—but I'll not repeat his language, nor describe his habitual conduct; he is ingenious and unresting in seeking to gain my abhorrence! I sometimes wonder at him with an intensity that deadens my fear: yet, I assure you, a tiger or a venomous serpent could not rouse terror in me equal to that which he wakens. He told me of Catherine's illness, and accused my brother of causing it; promising that I should be Edgar's proxy in suffering, till he could get a hold of him.

I do hate him—I am wretched—I have been a fool! Beware of uttering one breath of this to any one at the Grange. I shall expect you every day—don't disappoint me!

                                                      Isabella.

Chapter XIV

As soon as I had perused this epistle, I went to the master, and informed him that his sister had arrived at the Heights, and sent me a letter expressing her sorrow for Mrs. Linton's situation, and her ardent desire to see him; with a wish that he would transmit to her, as early as possible, some token of forgiveness by me.

"Forgiveness!" said Linton. "I have nothing to forgive her, Ellen. You may call at Wuthering Heights this afternoon, if you like, and say that I am not *angry*, but I'm *sorry* to have lost her: especially as I can never think she'll be happy. It is out of the question my going to see her, however; we are eternally divided; and should she really wish to oblige me, let her persuade the villain she has married to leave the country."

"And you won't write her a little note, sir?" I asked, imploringly.

"No," he answered. "It is needless. My communication with Heathcliff's family shall be as sparing as his with mine. It shall not exist!"

Mr. Edgar's coldness depressed me exceedingly; and all the way from the Grange I puzzled my brains how to put more heart into what he said, when I repeated it; and how to soften his refusal of even a few lines to console Isabella.

I dare say she had been on the watch for me since morning: I saw her looking through the lattice, as I came up the garden causeway, and I nodded to her; but she drew back, as if afraid of being observed.

I entered without knocking. There never was such a dreary, dismal scene as the formerly cheerful house presented! I must confess that, if I had been in the young lady's place, I would, at least, have swept the hearth and wiped the tables with a duster. But she already partook of the pervading spirit of neglect which encompassed her. Her pretty face was wan and listless; her hair uncurled, some locks hanging lankly down, and some carelessly twisted round her head. Probably she had not touched her dress since yester evening.

Hindley was not there. Mr. Heathcliff sat at a table, turning over some papers in his pocket-book; but he rose when I appeared, asked me how I did, quite friendly, and offered me a chair.

He was the only thing there that seemed decent, and I thought he never looked better. So much had circumstances altered their positions, that he would certainly have struck a stranger as a born and bred gentleman, and his wife as a thorough little slattern!

She came forward eagerly to greet me; and held out one hand to take the expected letter.

I shook my head. She wouldn't understand the hint, but followed me to a sideboard, where I went to lay my bonnet, and importuned me in a whisper to give her directly what I had brought.

Heathcliff guessed the meaning of her manœuvres, and said—

"If you have got anything for Isabella, as no doubt you have, Nelly, give it to her. You needn't make a secret of it; we have no secrets between us."

"Oh, I have nothing," I replied, thinking it best to speak the truth at once. "My master bid me tell his sister that she must not expect either a letter or a visit from him at present. He sends his love, ma'am, and his wishes for your happiness, and his pardon for the grief you have occasioned; but he thinks that after this time, his household, and the household here, should drop intercommunication, as nothing good could come of keeping it up."

Mrs. Heathcliff's lip quivered slightly, and she returned to her seat in the window. Her husband took his stand on the hearthstone, near me, and began to put questions concerning Catherine.

I told him as much as I thought proper of her illness, and he extorted from me, by cross-examination, most of the facts connected with its origin.

I blamed her, as she deserved, for bringing it all on herself; and ended by hoping that he would follow Mr. Linton's example, and avoid future interference with his family, for good or evil.

"Mrs. Linton is now just recovering," I said; "she'll never be like she was, but her life is spared, and if you really have a regard for her, you'll shun crossing her way again. Nay, you'll move out of this country entirely; and that you may not regret it, I'll inform you Catherine Linton is as different now from your old friend Catherine Earnshaw, as that young lady is different from me! Her appearance is changed greatly, her character much more so; and the person who is compelled, of necessity, to be her companion, will only sustain his affection hereafter by the remembrance of what she once was, by common humanity, and a sense of duty!"

"That is quite possible," remarked Heathcliff, forcing himself to seem calm, "quite possible that your master should have nothing but common humanity, and a sense of duty to fall back upon. But do you imagine that I shall leave Catherine to his *duty* and *humanity*? and can you compare my feelings respecting Catherine, to his? Before you leave this house, I must exact a promise from you, that you'll get me an interview with her: consent, or refuse, I *will* see her! What do you say?"

"I say, Mr. Heathcliff," I replied, "you must not—you never shall, through my means. Another encounter between you and the master would kill her altogether!"

"With your aid that may be avoided," he continued, "and should there be danger of such an event—should he be the cause of adding a single trouble more to her existence—why, I think, I shall be justified in going to extremes! I wish you had sincerity enough to tell me whether Catherine would suffer greatly from his loss. The fear that she would restrains me: and there you see the distinction between our feelings. Had he been in my place, and I in his, though I hated him with a hatred that turned my life to gall, I never would have raised a hand against him. You may look incredulous, if you please! I never would have banished him from her society, as long as she desired his. The moment her regard ceased, I would have torn his heart out, and drank his blood! But, till then—if you don't believe me, you don't know me—till then, I would have died by inches before I touched a single hair of his head!"

"And yet," I interrupted, "you have no scruples in completely ruining all hopes of her perfect restoration, by thrusting yourself into her remembrance, now, when she has nearly forgotten you, and involving her in a new tumult of discord and distress."

"You suppose she has nearly forgotten me?" he said. "Oh, Nelly! you know she has not! You know as well as I do, that for every thought she spends on Linton, she spends a thousand on me! At a most miserable period of my life, I had a notion of the kind; it haunted me on my return to the neighbourhood last summer, but only her own assurance could make me admit the horrible idea again. And then, Linton would be nothing, nor Hindley, nor all the dreams that ever I dreamt. Two words would comprehend my future—*death* and *hell*; existence, after losing her, would be hell.

"Yet I was a fool to fancy for a moment that she valued Edgar Linton's attachment more than mine. If he loved with all the powers of his puny being, he couldn't love as much in eighty years as I could in a day. And Catherine has a heart as deep as I have; the sea could be as readily contained in that horse-trough, as her whole affection be monopolized by him. Tush! He is scarcely a degree dearer to her than her dog, or her horse. It is not in him to be loved like me: how can she love in him what he has not?"

"Catherine and Edgar are as fond of each other as any two people can be!" cried Isabella, with sudden vivacity. "No one has a right to talk in that manner, and I won't hear my brother depreciated in silence!"

"Your brother is wondrous fond of you too, isn't he?" observed Heathcliff scornfully. "He turns you adrift on the world with surprising alacrity."

"He is not aware of what I suffer," she replied. "I didn't tell him that."

"You have been telling him something, then—you have written, have you?"

"To say that I was married, I did write—you saw the note."

"And nothing since?"

"No."

"My young lady is looking sadly the worse for her change of condition," I remarked. "Somebody's love comes short in her case, obviously—whose I may guess; but, perhaps, I shouldn't say."

"I should guess it was her own," said Heathcliff. "She degenerates into a mere slut! She is tired of trying to please me, uncommonly early. You'd hardly credit it, but the very morrow of our wedding, she was weeping to go home. However, she'll suit this house so much the better for not being over nice, and I'll take care she does not disgrace me by rambling abroad."

"Well, sir," returned I, "I hope you'll consider that Mrs. Heathcliff is accustomed to be looked after and waited on; and that she has been brought up like an only daughter, whom every one was ready to serve. You must let her have a maid to keep things tidy about her, and you must treat her kindly. Whatever be your notion of Mr. Edgar, you cannot doubt that she has a capacity for strong attachments, or she wouldn't have abandoned the elegancies, and comforts, and friends of her former home, to fix contentedly, in such a wilderness as this, with you."

"She abandoned them under a delusion," he answered, "picturing in me a hero of romance, and expecting unlimited indulgences from my chivalrous devotion. I can hardly regard her in the light of a rational creature, so obstinately has she persisted in forming a fabulous notion of my character, and acting on the false impressions she cherished. But, at last, I think she begins to know me. I don't perceive the silly smiles and grimaces that provoked me at first; and the senseless incapability of discerning that I was in earnest when I gave her my opinion of her infatuation, and herself. It was a marvellous effort of perspicacity to discover that I did not love her. I believed, at one time, no lessons could teach her that! And yet it is poorly learnt; for this morning she announced, as a piece of appalling intelligence, that I had actually succeeded in making her hate me! A positive labour of Hercules, I assure you! If it be achieved, I have cause to return thanks. Can I trust your assertion, Isabella? Are you sure you hate me? If I let you alone for half-a-day, won't you come sighing and wheedling to me again? I dare say she would rather I had seemed all tenderness before you; it wounds her vanity, to have the truth exposed. But I don't care who knows that the passion was wholly on one side, and I never told her a lie about it. She cannot accuse me of showing one bit of deceitful softness. The first thing she saw me do, on coming out of the Grange, was to hang up her little dog; and when she pleaded for it the first words I uttered were a wish that I had the hanging of every being belonging to her, except one: possibly she took that exception for herself. But no brutality disgusted her. I suppose she has an innate admiration of it, if only her precious person were secure from injury! Now, was it not the depth of absurdity—of genuine idiocy—for that pitiful, slavish, mean-minded brach[4] to dream that I could love her? Tell your master, Nelly, that I never, in all my life, met with such an abject thing as she is. She even disgraces the name of Linton; and I've sometimes relented, from pure lack of invention, in my experiments on what she could endure, and still creep shamefully cringing back! But tell him, also, to set his fraternal and magisterial heart at ease, that I keep strictly within the limits of the law. I have avoided, up to this period, giving her the slightest right to claim a separation; and, what's more, she'd thank nobody for dividing us. If she desired to go she might: the nuisance of her presence outweighs the gratification to be derived from tormenting her!"

"Mr. Heathcliff," said I, "this is the talk of a madman, and your wife, most likely, is convinced you are mad; and, for that reason, she has borne with you hitherto: but now that you say she may go, she'll doubtless avail herself of the permission. You are not so bewitched, ma'am, are you, as to remain with him of your own accord?"

"Take care, Ellen!" answered Isabella, her eyes sparkling irefully; there was no misdoubting by their expression, the full success of

4. Bitch-hound.

her partner's endeavours to make himself detested. "Don't put faith in a single word he speaks. He's a lying fiend, a monster, and not a human being! I've been told I might leave him before; and I've made the attempt, but I dare not repeat it! Only, Ellen, promise you'll not mention a syllable of his infamous conversation to my brother or Catherine. Whatever he may pretend, he wishes to provoke Edgar to desperation: he says he has married me on purpose to obtain power over him; and he shan't obtain it —I'll die first! I just hope, I pray, that he may forget his diabolical prudence, and kill me! The single pleasure I can imagine is to die, or to see him dead!"

"There—that will do for the present!" said Heathcliff. "If you are called upon in a court of law, you'll remember her language, Nelly! And take a good look at that countenance—she's near the point which would suit me. No, you're not fit to be your own guardian, Isabella, now; and I, being your legal protector, must retain you in my custody, however distasteful the obligation may be. Go upstairs; I have something to say to Ellen Dean in private. That's not the way—upstairs, I tell you! Why, this is the road upstairs, child!"

He seized, and thrust her from the room; and returned muttering—

"I have no pity! I have no pity! The more the worms writhe, the more I yearn to crush out their entrails! It is a moral teething, and I grind with greater energy, in proportion to the increase of pain."

"Do you understand what the word pity means?" I said, hastening to resume my bonnet. "Did you ever feel a touch of it in your life?"

"Put that down!" he interrupted, perceiving my intention to depart. "You are not going yet. Come here now, Nelly: I must either persuade or compel you to aid me in fulfilling my determination to see Catherine, and that without delay. I swear that I meditate no harm; I don't desire to cause any disturbance, or to exasperate or insult Mr. Linton; I only wish to hear from herself how she is, and why she has been ill; and to ask if anything that I could do would be of use to her. Last night, I was in the Grange garden six hours, and I'll return there to-night; and every night I'll haunt the place, and every day, till I find an opportunity of entering. If Edgar Linton meets me, I shall not hesitate to knock him down, and give him enough to ensure his quiescence while I stay. If his servants oppose me, I shall threaten them off with these pistols. But wouldn't it be better to prevent my coming in contact with them, or their master? And you could do it so easily! I'd warn you when I came, and then you might let me in unobserved, as soon as she was alone, and watch till I departed, your conscience quite calm: you would be hindering mischief."

I protested against playing that treacherous part in my employer's house; and besides, I urged the cruelty and selfishness of his destroying Mrs. Linton's tranquillity, for his satisfaction.

"The commonest occurrence startles her painfully," I said. "She's all nerves, and she couldn't bear the surprise, I'm positive. Don't persist, sir! or else, I shall be obliged to inform my master of your designs, and he'll take measures to secure his house and its inmates from any such unwarrantable intrusions!"

"In that case, I'll take measures to secure you, woman!" exclaimed Heathcliff; "you shall not leave Wuthering Heights till to-morrow morning. It is a foolish story to assert that Catherine could not bear to see me; and as to surprising her, I don't desire it: you must prepare her—ask her if I may come. You say she never mentions my name, and that I am never mentioned to her. To whom should she mention me if I am a forbidden topic in the house? She thinks you are all spies for her husband. Oh, I've no doubt she's in hell among you! I guess by her silence, as much as any thing, what she feels. You say she is often restless, and anxious-looking—is that a proof of tranquillity? You talk of her mind being unsettled. How the devil could it be otherwise, in her frightful isolation. And that insipid, paltry creature attending her from *duty* and *humanity!* From *pity* and *charity!* He might as well plant an oak in a flowerpot, and expect it to thrive, as imagine he can restore her to vigour in the soil of his shallow cares! Let us settle it at once; will you stay here, and am I to fight my way to Catherine over Linton and his footmen? Or will you be my friend, as you have been hitherto, and do what I request? Decide! because there is no reason for my lingering another minute, if you persist in your stubborn ill-nature!"

Well, Mr. Lockwood, I argued and complained, and flatly refused him fifty times; but in the long run he forced me to an agreement. I engaged to carry a letter from him to my mistress; and should she consent, I promised to let him have intelligence of Linton's next absence from home, when he might come, and get in as he was able. I wouldn't be there, and my fellow servants should be equally out of the way.

Was it right or wrong? I fear it was wrong, though expedient. I thought I prevented another explosion by my compliance; and I thought, too, it might create a favourable crisis in Catherine's mental illness: and then I remembered Mr. Edgar's stern rebuke of my carrying tales; and I tried to smooth away all disquietude on the subject, by affirming, with frequent iteration, that that betrayal of trust, if it merited so harsh an appellation, should be the last.

Notwithstanding, my journey homeward was sadder than my journey thither; and many misgivings I had, ere I could prevail on myself to put the missive into Mrs. Linton's hand.

But here is Kenneth; I'll go down, and tell him how much better you are. My history is *dree*[5] as we say, and will serve to wile away another morning.

Dree, and dreary! I reflected as the good woman descended to receive the doctor; and not exactly of the kind which I should have chosen to amuse me. But never mind! I'll extract wholesome medicines from Mrs. Dean's bitter herbs; and firstly, let me beware of the fascination that lurks in Catherine Heathcliff's brilliant eyes. I should be in a curious taking if I surrendered my heart to that young person, and the daughter turned out a second edition of the mother!

Chapter XV

Another week over—and I am so many days nearer health, and spring! I have now heard all my neighbour's history, at different sittings, as the housekeeper could spare time from more important occupations. I'll continue it in her own words, only a little condensed. She is, on the whole, a very fair narrator and I don't think I could improve her style.

In the evening, she said, the evening of my visit to the Heights, I knew, as well as if I saw him, that Mr. Heathcliff was about the place; and I shunned going out, because I still carried his letter in my pocket, and didn't want to be threatened, or teased any more.

I had made up my mind not to give it till my master went somewhere, as I could not guess how its receipt would affect Catherine. The consequence was, that it did not reach her before the lapse of three days. The fourth was Sunday, and I brought it into her room after the family were gone to church.

There was a man-servant left to keep the house with me, and we generally made a practice of locking the doors during the hours of service; but on that occasion the weather was so warm and pleasant that I set them wide open, and, to fulfil my engagement, as I knew who would be coming, I told my companion that the mistress wished very much for some oranges, and he must run over to the village and get a few, to be paid for on the morrow. He departed, and I went upstairs.

Mrs. Linton sat in a loose, white dress, with a light shawl over her shoulders, in the recess of the open window, as usual. Her thick, long hair had been partly removed at the beginning of her

5. Sad.

illness, and now she wore it simply combed in its natural tresses over her temples and neck. Her appearance was altered, as I had told Heathcliff, but when she was calm, there seemed unearthly beauty in the change.

The flash of her eyes had been succeeded by a dreamy and melancholy softness; they no longer gave the impression of looking at the objects around her; they appeared always to gaze beyond, and far beyond—you would have said out of this world. Then, the paleness of her face—its haggard aspect having vanished as she recovered flesh—and the peculiar expression arising from her mental state, though painfully suggestive of their causes, added to the touching interest which she wakened, and—invariably to me, I know, and to any person who saw her, I should think—refuted more tangible proofs of convalescence and stamped her as one doomed to decay.

A book lay spread on the sill before her, and the scarcely perceptible wind fluttered its leaves at intervals. I believe Linton had laid it there, for she never endeavoured to divert herself with reading, or occupation of any kind, and he would spend many an hour in trying to entice her attention to some subject which had formerly been her amusement.

She was conscious of his aim, and in her better moods endured his efforts placidly, only showing their uselessness by now and then suppressing a wearied sigh, and checking him at last with the saddest of smiles and kisses. At other times, she would turn petulantly away, and hide her face in her hands, or even push him off angrily; and then he took care to let her alone, for he was certain of doing no good.

Gimmerton chapel bells were still ringing; and the full, mellow flow of the beck in the valley came soothingly on the ear. It was a sweet substitute for the yet absent murmur of the summer foliage, which drowned that music about the Grange when the trees were in leaf. At Wuthering Heights it always sounded on quiet days, following a great thaw or a season of steady rain; and of Wuthering Heights, Catherine was thinking as she listened—that is, if she thought, or listened, at all—but she had the vague, distant look I mentioned before, which expressed no recognition of material things either by ear or eye.

"There's a letter for you, Mrs. Linton," I said, gently inserting it in one hand that rested on her knee. "You must read it immediately, because it wants an answer. Shall I break the seal?"

"Yes," she answered, without altering the direction of her eyes. I opened it—it was very short.

"Now," I continued, "read it."

She drew away her hand, and let it fall. I replaced it in her lap, and stood waiting till it should please her to glance down; but that movement was so long delayed that at last I resumed—

"Must I read it, ma'am? It is from Mr. Heathcliff."

There was a start, and a troubled gleam of recollection, and a struggle to arrange her ideas. She lifted the letter, and seemed to peruse it; and when she came to the signature she sighed; yet still I found she had not gathered its import, for, upon my desiring to hear her reply, she merely pointed to the name, and gazed at me with mournful and questioning eagerness.

"Well, he wishes to see you," said I, guessing her need of an interpreter. "He's in the garden by this time, and impatient to know what answer I shall bring."

As I spoke, I observed a large dog, lying on the sunny grass beneath, raise its ears, as if about to bark, and then smoothing them back, announce by a wag of the tail that some one approached whom it did not consider a stranger.

Mrs. Linton bent forward, and listened breathlessly. The minute after, a step traversed the hall; the open house was too tempting for Heathcliff to resist walking in: most likely he supposed that I was inclined to shirk my promise, and so resolved to trust to his own audacity.

With straining eagerness Catherine gazed towards the entrance of her chamber. He did not hit the right room directly; she motioned me to admit him; but he found it out, ere I could reach the door, and in a stride or two was at her side, and had her grasped in his arms.

He neither spoke, nor loosed his hold, for some five minutes, during which period he bestowed more kisses than ever he gave in his life before, I dare say; but then my mistress had kissed him first, and I plainly saw that he could hardly bear, for downright agony, to look into her face! The same conviction had stricken him as me, from the instant he beheld her, that there was no prospect of ultimate recovery there—she was fated, sure to die.

"Oh, Cathy! Oh, my life! how can I bear it?" was the first sentence he uttered, in a tone that did not seek to disguise his despair.

And now he stared at her so earnestly that I thought the very intensity of his gaze would bring tears into his eyes; but they burned with anguish, they did not melt.

"What now?" said Catherine, leaning back, and returning his look with a suddenly clouded brow: her humour was a mere vane for constantly varying caprices. "You and Edgar have broken my heart, Heathcliff! And you both come to bewail the deed to me, as if *you* were the people to be pitied! I shall not pity you, not I. You have killed me—and thriven on it, I think. How strong you are! How many years do you mean to live after I am gone?"

Heathcliff had knelt on one knee to embrace her; he attempted to rise, but she seized his hair, and kept him down.

"I wish I could hold you," she continued, bitterly, "till we were both dead! I shouldn't care what you suffered. I care nothing for your sufferings. Why shouldn't you suffer? I do! Will you forget me—will you be happy when I am in the earth? Will you say twenty years hence, 'That's the grave of Catherine Earnshaw. I loved her long ago, and was wretched to lose her; but it is past. I've loved many others since—my children are dearer to me than she was, and, at death, I shall not rejoice that I am going to her, I shall be sorry that I must leave them!' Will you say so, Heathcliff?"

"Don't torture me till I'm as mad as yourself," cried he, wrenching his head free, and grinding his teeth.

The two, to a cool spectator, made a strange and fearful picture. Well might Catherine deem that heaven would be a land of exile to her, unless, with her mortal body, she cast away her mortal character also. Her present countenance had a wild vindictiveness in its white cheek, and a bloodless lip and scintillating eye; and she retained in her closed fingers a portion of the locks she had been grasping. As to her companion, while raising himself with one hand, he had taken her arm with the other; and so inadequate was his stock of gentleness to the requirements of her condition, that on his letting go, I saw four distinct impressions left blue in the colourless skin.

"Are you possessed with a devil," he pursued, savagely, "to talk in that manner to me, when you are dying? Do you reflect that all those words will be branded in my memory, and eating deeper eternally, after you have left me? You know you lie to say I have killed you; and, Catherine, you know that I could as soon forget you as my existence! Is it not sufficient for your infernal selfishness, that while you are at peace I shall writhe in the torments of hell?"

"I shall not be at peace," moaned Catherine, recalled to a sense of physical weakness by the violent, unequal throbbing of her heart, which beat visibly and audibly under this excess of agitation.

She said nothing further till the paroxysm was over; then she continued, more kindly—

"I'm not wishing you greater torment than I have, Heathcliff! I only wish us never to be parted—and should a word of mine distress you hereafter, think I feel the same distress underground, and for my own sake, forgive me! Come here and kneel down again! You never harmed me in your life. Nay, if you nurse anger, that will be worse to remember than my harsh words! Won't you come here again? Do!"

Heathcliff went to the back of her chair, and leant over, but not so far as to let her see his face, which was livid with emotion. She bent round to look at him; he would not permit it; turning abruptly, he walked to the fire-place, where he stood, silent, with his back towards us.

Mrs. Linton's glance followed him suspiciously: every movement woke a new sentiment in her. After a pause, and a prolonged gaze, she resumed, addressing me in accents of indignant disappointment—

"Oh, you see, Nelly! he would not relent a moment, to keep me out of the grave! *That* is how I'm loved! Well, never mind! That is not *my* Heathcliff. I shall love mine yet; and take him with me—he's in my soul. And," added she, musingly, "the thing that irks me most is this shattered prison, after all. I'm tired, tired of being enclosed here. I'm wearying to escape into that glorious world, and to be always there; not seeing it dimly through tears, and yearning for it through the walls of an aching heart; but really with it, and in it. Nelly, you think you are better and more fortunate than I; in full health and strength. You are sorry for me—very soon that will be altered. I shall be sorry for *you*. I shall be incomparably beyond and above you all. I *wonder* he won't be near me!" She went on to herself. "I thought he wished it. Heathcliff, dear! you should not be sullen now. Do come to me, Heathcliff."

In her eagerness she rose and supported herself on the arm of the chair. At that earnest appeal, he turned to her, looking absolutely desperate. His eyes wide, and wet at last, flashed fiercely on her; his breast heaved convulsively. An instant they held asunder; and then how they met I hardly saw, but Catherine made a spring, and he caught her, and they were locked in an embrace from which I thought my mistress would never be released alive. In fact, to my eyes, she seemed directly insensible. He flung himself into the nearest seat, and on my approaching hurriedly to ascertain if she had fainted, he gnashed at me, and foamed like a mad dog, and gathered her to him with greedy jealousy. I did not feel as if I were in the company of a creature of my own species; it appeared that he would not understand, though I spoke to him; so I stood off, and held my tongue, in great perplexity.

A movement of Catherine's relieved me a little presently: she put up her hand to clasp his neck, and bring her cheek to his, as he held her; while he, in return, covering her with frantic caresses, said wildly—

"You teach me now how cruel you've been—cruel and false. *Why* did you despise me? *Why* did you betray your own heart, Cathy? I have not one word of comfort. You deserve this. You

have killed yourself. Yes, you may kiss me, and cry; and wring
out my kisses and tears. They'll blight you—they'll damn you.
You loved me—then what *right* had you to leave me? What right
—answer me—for the poor fancy you felt for Linton? Because
misery, and degradation, and death, and nothing that God or Satan
could inflict would have parted us, *you*, of your own will, did it.
I have not broken your heart—*you* have broken it—and in breaking it, you have broken mine. So much the worse for me, that
I am strong. Do I want to live? What kind of living will it be
when you—oh, God! would *you* like to live with your soul in the
grave?"

"Let me alone. Let me alone," sobbed Catherine. "If I've done
wrong, I'm dying for it. It is enough! You left me too; but I won't
upbraid you! I forgive you. Forgive me!"

"It is hard to forgive, and to look at those eyes, and feel those
wasted hands," he answered. "Kiss me again; and don't let me
see your eyes! I forgive what you have done to me. I love *my*
murderer—but *yours!* How can I?"

They were silent—their faces hid against each other, and washed
by each other's tears. At least, I suppose the weeping was on both
sides; as it seemed Heathcliff *could* weep on a great occasion like
this.

I grew very uncomfortable, meanwhile; for the afternoon wore
fast away, the man whom I had sent off returned from his errand,
and I could distinguish, by the shine of the westering sun up the
valley, a concourse thickening outside Gimmerton chapel porch.

"Service is over," I announced. "My master will be here in half-
an-hour."

Heathcliff groaned a curse, and strained Catherine closer—she
never moved.

Ere long I perceived a group of the servants passing up the
road towards the kitchen wing. Mr. Linton was not far behind; he
opened the gate himself, and sauntered slowly up, probably enjoying the lovely afternoon that breathed as soft as summer.

"Now he is here," I exclaimed. "For heaven's sake, hurry down!
You'll not meet any one on the front stairs. Do be quick; and
stay among the trees till he is fairly in."

"I must go, Cathy," said Heathcliff, seeking to extricate himself from his companion's arms. "But, if I live, I'll see you again
before you are asleep. I won't stray five yards from your window."

"You must not go!" she answered, holding him as firmly as her
strength allowed. "You shall not, I tell you."

"For one hour," he pleaded, earnestly.

"Not for one minute," she replied.

"I *must*—Linton will be up immediately," persisted the alarmed intruder.

He would have risen, and unfixed her fingers by the act—she clung fast, gasping; there was mad resolution in her face.

"No!" she shrieked. "Oh, don't, don't go. It is the last time! Edgar will not hurt us. Heathcliff, I shall die! I shall die!"

"Damn the fool. There he is," cried Heathcliff, sinking back into his seat. "Hush, my darling! Hush, hush, Catherine! I'll stay. If he shot me so, I'd expire with a blessing on my lips."

And there they were fast again. I heard my master mounting the stairs—the cold sweat ran from my forehead; I was horrified.

"Are you going to listen to her ravings?" I said, passionately. "She does not know what she says. Will you ruin her, because she has not wit to help herself? Get up! You could be free instantly. That is the most diabolical deed that ever you did. We are all done for—master, mistress, and servant."

I wrung my hands, and cried out; and Mr. Linton hastened his step at the noise. In the midst of my agitation, I was sincerely glad to observe that Catherine's arms had fallen relaxed, and her head hung down.

"She's fainted or dead," I thought, "so much the better. Far better that she should be dead, than lingering a burden and a misery-maker to all about her."

Edgar sprang to his unbidden guest, blanched with astonishment and rage. What he meant to do, I cannot tell; however, the other stopped all demonstrations, at once, by placing the lifeless-looking form in his arms.

"Look there," he said. "Unless you be a fiend, help her first—then you shall speak to me!"

He walked into the parlour, and sat down. Mr. Linton summoned me, and with great difficulty, and after resorting to many means, we managed to restore her to sensation; but she was all bewildered; she sighed, and moaned, and knew nobody. Edgar, in his anxiety for her, forgot her hated friend. I did not. I went at the earliest opportunity, and besought him to depart, affirming that Catherine was better, and he should hear from me in the morning, how she passed the night.

"I shall not refuse to go out of doors," he answered; "but I shall stay in the garden; and, Nelly, mind you keep your word tomorrow. I shall be under those larch trees. Mind! or I pay another visit, whether Linton be in or not."

He sent a rapid glance through the half-open door of the chamber, and ascertaining that what I stated was apparently true, delivered the house of his luckless presence.

Chapter XVI

About twelve o'clock that night was born the Catherine you saw at Wuthering Heights, a puny, seven months' child; and two hours after, the mother died, having never recovered sufficient consciousness to miss Heathcliff, or know Edgar.

The latter's distraction at his bereavement is a subject too painful to be dwelt on; its after effects showed how deep the sorrow sunk.

A great addition, in my eyes, was his being left without an heir. I bemoaned that, as I gazed on the feeble orphan; and I mentally abused old Linton for—what was only natural partiality—the securing his estate to his own daughter, instead of his son's.

An unwelcomed infant it was, poor thing! It might have wailed out of life, and nobody cared a morsel, during those first hours of existence. We redeemed the neglect afterwards; but its beginning was as friendless as its end is likely to be.

Next morning—bright and cheerful out of doors—stole softened in through the blinds of the silent room, and suffused the couch and its occupant with a mellow, tender glow.

Edgar Linton had his head laid on the pillow, and his eyes shut. His young and fair features were almost as death-like as those of the form beside him, and almost as fixed; but *his* was the hush of exhausted anguish, and *hers* of perfect peace. Her brow smooth, her lids closed, her lips wearing the expression of a smile. No angel in heaven could be more beautiful than she appeared; and I partook of the infinite calm in which she lay. My mind was never in a holier frame than while I gazed on that untroubled image of Divine rest. I instinctively echoed the words she had uttered, a few hours before. "Incomparably beyond, and above us all! Whether still on earth or now in heaven, her spirit is at home with God!"

I don't know if it be a peculiarity in me, but I am seldom otherwise than happy while watching in the chamber of death, should no frenzied or despairing mourner share the duty with me. I see a repose that neither earth nor hell can break; and I feel an assurance of the endless and shadowless hereafter—the Eternity they have entered—where life is boundless in its duration, and love in its sympathy, and joy in its fulness. I noticed on that occasion how much selfishness there is even in a love like Mr. Linton's, when he so regretted Catherine's blessed release!

To be sure, one might have doubted, after the wayward and impatient existence she had led, whether she merited a haven of peace at last. One might doubt in seasons of cold reflection, but not then, in the presence of her corpse. It asserted its own tranquillity, which seemed a pledge of equal quiet to its former inhabitant.

"Do you believe such people *are* happy in the other world, sir? I'd give a great deal to know."

I declined answering Mrs. Dean's question, which struck me as something heterodox. She proceeded—

"Retracing the course of Catherine Linton, I fear we have no right to think she is: but we'll leave her with her Maker."

The master looked asleep, and I ventured soon after sunrise to quit the room and steal out to the pure, refreshing air. The servants thought me gone to shake off the drowsiness of my protracted watch; in reality, my chief motive was seeing Mr. Heathcliff. If he had remained among the larches all night, he would have heard nothing of the stir at the Grange, unless, perhaps, he might catch the gallop of the messenger going to Gimmerton. If he had come nearer, he would probably be aware, from the lights flitting to and fro, and the opening and shutting of the outer doors, that all was not right within.

I wished, yet feared, to find him. I felt the terrible news must be told, and I longed to get it over, but *how* to do it I did not know.

He was there—at least a few yards further in the park; leant against an old ash tree, his hat off, and his hair soaked with the dew that had gathered on the budded branches, and fell pattering round him. He had been standing a long time in that position, for I saw a pair of ousels passing and repassing scarcely three feet from him, busy in building their nest, and regarding his proximity no more than that of a piece of timber. They flew off at my approach, and he raised his eyes and spoke—

"She's dead!" he said; "I've not waited for you to learn that. Put your handkerchief away—don't snivel before me. Damn you all! she wants none of *your* tears!"

I was weeping as much for him as her: we do sometimes pity creatures that have none of the feeling either for themselves or others; and when I first looked into his face, I perceived that he had got intelligence of the catastrophe; and a foolish notion struck me that his heart was quelled and he prayed, because his lips moved and his gaze was bent on the ground.

"Yes, she's dead!" I answered, checking my sobs and drying my cheeks. "Gone to heaven, I hope, where we may, everyone, join her, if we take due warning, and leave our evil ways to follow good!"

"Did *she* take due warning, then?" asked Heathcliff, attempt-

Chapter XVI · 139

ing a sneer. "Did she die like a saint? Come, give me a true history of the event. How did—"

He endeavoured to pronounce the name, but could not manage it; and compressing his mouth, he held a silent combat with his inward agony, defying, meanwhile, my sympathy with an unflinching, ferocious stare.

"How did she die?" he resumed, at last—fain, notwithstanding his hardihood, to have a support behind him, for, after the struggle, he trembled, in spite of himself, to his very finger-ends.

"Poor wretch!" I thought; "you have a heart and nerves the same as your brother men! Why should you be so anxious to conceal them? Your pride cannot blind God! You tempt Him to wring them, till He forces a cry of humiliation!"

"Quietly as a lamb!" I answered, aloud. "She drew a sigh, and stretched herself, like a child reviving, and sinking again to sleep; and five minutes after I felt one little pulse at her heart, and nothing more!"

"And—and did she ever mention me?" he asked, hesitating, as if he dreaded the answer to his question would introduce details that he could not bear to hear.

"Her senses never returned—she recognised nobody from the time you left her," I said. "She lies with a sweet smile on her face; and her latest ideas wandered back to pleasant early days. Her life closed in a gentle dream—may she wake as kindly in the other world!"

"May she wake in torment!" he cried, with frightful vehemence, stamping his foot, and groaning in a sudden paroxysm of ungovernable passion. "Why, she's a liar to the end! Where is she? Not *there*—not in heaven—not perished—where? Oh! you said you cared nothing for my sufferings! And I pray one prayer—I repeat it till my tongue stiffens—Catherine Earnshaw, may you not rest, as long as I am living! You said I killed you—haunt me, then! The murdered *do* haunt their murderers, I believe. I know that ghosts *have* wandered on earth. Be with me always—take any form—drive me mad! only *do* not leave me in this abyss, where I cannot find you! Oh, God! it is unutterable! I *cannot* live without my life! I *cannot* live without my soul!"

He dashed his head against the knotted trunk; and, lifting up his eyes, howled, not like a man, but like a savage beast getting goaded to death with knives and spears.

I observed several splashes of blood about the bark of the tree, and his hand and forehead were both stained; probably the scene I witnessed was a repetition of others acted during the night. It hardly moved my compassion—it appalled me; still I felt reluctant to quit him so. But the moment he recollected himself

enough to notice me watching, he thundered a command for me
to go, and I obeyed. He was beyond my skill to quiet or console!

Mrs. Linton's funeral was appointed to take place on the Friday
following her decease; and till then her coffin remained uncovered,
and strewn with flowers and scented leaves, in the great drawing-
room. Linton spent his days and nights there, a sleepless guardian;
and—a circumstance concealed from all but me—Heathcliff spent
his nights, at least, outside, equally a stranger to repose.

I held no communication with him; still I was conscious of his
design to enter, if he could; and on the Tuesday, a little after dark,
when my master, from sheer fatigue, had been compelled to retire a
couple of hours, I went and opened one of the windows, moved
by his perseverance to give him a chance of bestowing on the
fading image of his idol one final adieu.

He did not omit to avail himself of the opportunity, cautiously
and briefly—too cautiously to betray his presence by the slightest
noise; indeed, I shouldn't have discovered that he had been there,
except for the disarrangement of the drapery about the corpse's
face, and for observing on the floor a curl of light hair, fastened
with a silver thread, which, on examination, I ascertained to have
been taken from a locket hung round Catherine's neck. Heathcliff
had opened the trinket and cast out its contents, replacing them
by a black lock of his own. I twisted the two, and enclosed them
together.

Mr. Earnshaw was, of course, invited to attend the remains of
his sister to the grave; he sent no excuse, but he never came; so
that besides her husband, the mourners were wholly composed of
tenants and servants. Isabella was not asked.

The place of Catherine's interment, to the surprise of the villagers, was neither in the chapel, under the carved monument of
the Lintons, nor yet by the tombs of her own relations, outside.
It was dug on a green slope, in a corner of the kirkyard, where the
wall is so low that heath and bilberry plants have climbed over it
from the moor; and peat mould almost buries it. Her husband lies
in the same spot, now; and they have each a simple headstone
above, and a plain grey block at their feet, to mark the graves.

Chapter XVII

That Friday made the last of our fine days, for a month. In
the evening, the weather broke; the wind shifted from south to
northeast, and brought rain first, and then sleet and snow.

On the morrow one could hardly imagine that there had been
three weeks of summer: the primroses and crocuses were hidden
under wintry drifts; the larks were silent, the young leaves of the

early trees smitten and blackened. And dreary, and chill, and dismal that morrow did creep over! My master kept his room. I took possession of the lonely parlour, converting it into a nursery; and there I was sitting, with the moaning doll of a child laid on my knee, rocking it to and fro, and watching, meanwhile, the still driving flakes build up the uncurtained window, when the door opened, and some person entered, out of breath and laughing!

My anger was greater than my astonishment for a minute; I supposed it one of the maids, and I cried—

"Have done! How dare you show your giddiness here? What would Mr. Linton say if he heard you?"

"Excuse me!" answered a familiar voice, "but I know Edgar is in bed, and I cannot stop myself."

With that, the speaker came forward to the fire, panting and holding her hand to her side.

"I have run the whole way from Wuthering Heights!" she continued, after a pause. "Except where I've flown. I couldn't count the number of falls I've had. Oh, I'm aching all over! Don't be alarmed. There shall be an explanation as soon as I can give it— only just have the goodness to step out and order the carriage to take me on to Gimmerton, and tell a servant to seek up a few clothes in my wardrobe."

The intruder was Mrs. Heathcliff. She certainly seemed in no laughing predicament: her hair streamed on her shoulders, dripping with snow and water; she was dressed in the girlish dress she commonly wore, befitting her age more than her position—a low frock, with short sleeves, and nothing on either head or neck. The frock was of light silk, and clung to her with wet; and her feet were protected merely by thin slippers; add to this a deep cut under one ear, which only the cold prevented from bleeding profusely, a white face scratched and bruised, and a frame hardly able to support itself through fatigue, and you may fancy my first fright was not much allayed when I had leisure to examine her.

"My dear young lady," I exclaimed, "I'll stir nowhere, and hear nothing, till you have removed every article of your clothes, and put on dry things; and certainly you shall not go to Gimmerton to-night; so it is needless to order the carriage."

"Certainly, I shall," she said; "walking or riding; yet I've no objection to dress myself decently; and—ah, see how it flows down my neck now! The fire does make it smart."

She insisted on my fulfilling her directions, before she would let me touch her; and not till after the coachman had been instructed to get ready, and a maid set to pack up some necessary attire, did I obtain her consent for binding the wound and helping to change her garments.

"Now, Ellen," she said, when my task was finished, and she was seated in an easy chair on the hearth, with a cup of tea before her, "you sit down opposite me, and put poor Catherine's baby away—I don't like to see it! You mustn't think I care little for Catherine, because I behaved so foolishly on entering. I've cried too, bitterly—yes, more than any one else has reason to cry. We parted unreconciled, you remember, and I shan't forgive myself. But for all that, I was not going to sympathise with him— the brute beast! O, give me the poker! This is the last thing of his I have about me." She slipped the gold ring from her third finger, and threw it on the floor. "I'll smash it!" she continued, striking with childish spite. "And then I'll burn it!" and she took and dropped the misused article among the coals. "There! he shall buy another, if he gets me back again. He'd be capable of coming to seek me, to tease Edgar—I dare not stay, lest that notion should possess his wicked head! And besides, Edgar has not been kind, has he? And I won't come suing for his assistance; nor will I bring him into more trouble. Necessity compelled me to seek shelter here; though, if I had not learnt he was out of the way, I'd have halted at the kitchen, washed my face, warmed myself, got you to bring what I wanted, and departed again to anywhere out of the reach of my accursed—of that incarnate goblin! Ah, he was in such a fury! If he had caught me! It's a pity Earnshaw is not his match in strength—I wouldn't have run till I'd seen him all but demolished, had Hindley been able to do it!"

"Well, don't talk so fast, Miss!" I interrupted, "you'll disorder the handkerchief I have tied round your face, and make the cut bleed again. Drink your tea, and take breath and give over laughing. Laughter is sadly out of place under this roof, and in your condition!"

"An undeniable truth," she replied. "Listen to that child! It maintains a constant wail—send it out of my hearing, for an hour; I shan't stay any longer."

I rang the bell, and committed it to a servant's care; and then I inquired what had urged her to escape from Wuthering Heights in such an unlikely plight, and where she meant to go, as she refused remaining with us.

"I ought, and I wish to remain," answered she, "to cheer Edgar and take care of the baby, for two things, and because the Grange is my right home. But I tell you, he wouldn't let me! Do you think he could bear to see me grow fat and merry; and could bear to think that we were tranquil, and not resolve on poisoning our comfort? Now, I have the satisfaction of being sure that he detests me to the point of its annoying him seriously to have me within ear-shot, or eye-sight. I notice, when I enter his presence, the muscles of his countenance are involuntarily distorted into an expression of hatred; partly arising from his knowledge of the good causes I have to feel that sentiment for him, and partly from original aversion. It is strong enough to make me feel pretty certain that he would not chase me over England, supposing I contrived a clear escape; and therefore I must get quite away. I've recovered from my first desire to be killed by him. I'd rather he'd kill himself! He has extinguished my love effectually, and so I'm at my ease. I can recollect yet how I loved him; and can dimly imagine that I could still be loving him, if—no, no! Even if he had doted on me, the devilish nature would have revealed its existence somehow. Catherine had an awfully perverted taste to esteem him so dearly, knowing him so well. Monster! would that he could be blotted out of creation, and out of my memory!"

"Hush, hush! He's a human being," I said. "Be more charitable; there are worse men than he is yet!"

"He's not a human being," she retorted; "and he has no claim on my charity. I gave him my heart, and he took and pinched it to death; and flung it back to me. People feel with their hearts, Ellen, and since he has destroyed mine, I have not power to feel for him, and I would not, though he groaned from this to his dying day, and wept tears of blood for Catherine! No, indeed, indeed, I wouldn't!" And here Isabella began to cry; but, immediately dashing the water from her lashes, she recommenced.

"You asked, what has driven me to flight at last? I was compelled to attempt it, because I had succeeded in rousing his rage a pitch above his malignity. Pulling out the nerves with red hot pincers requires more coolness than knocking on the head. He was worked up to forget the fiendish prudence he boasted of, and proceeded to murderous violence. I experienced pleasure in being able to exasperate him: the sense of pleasure woke my instinct of self-preservation, so I fairly broke free, and if ever I come into his hands again he is welcome to a signal revenge.

"Yesterday, you know, Mr. Earnshaw should have been at the funeral. He kept himself sober for the purpose—tolerably sober; not going to bed mad at six o'clock and getting up drunk at twelve. Consequently, he rose, in suicidal low spirits, as fit for the church as for a dance; and instead, he sat down by the fire and swallowed gin or brandy by tumblerfuls.

"Heathcliff—I shudder to name him!—has been a stranger in the house from last Sunday till to-day. Whether the angels have fed him, or his kin beneath, I cannot tell; but he has not eaten a meal with us for nearly a week. He has just come home at dawn, and gone upstairs to his chamber; locking himself in—as if anybody dreamt of coveting his company! There he has continued, praying like a Methodist; only the deity he implored is senseless dust and ashes; and God, when addressed, was curiously confounded with his own black father! After concluding these precious orisons—and they lasted generally till he grew hoarse, and his voice was strangled in his throat—he would be off again; always straight down to the Grange! I wonder Edgar did not send for a constable, and give him into custody! For me, grieved as I was about Catherine, it was impossible to avoid regarding this season of deliverance from degrading oppression as a holiday.

"I recovered spirits sufficient to hear Joseph's eternal lectures without weeping; and to move up and down the house, less with the foot of a frightened thief than formerly. You wouldn't think that I should cry at anything Joseph could say, but he and Hareton are detestable companions. I'd rather sit with Hindley, and hear his awful talk, than with 't' little maister,' and his staunch supporter, that odious old man!

"When Heathcliff is in, I'm often obliged to seek the kitchen and their society, or starve among the damp, uninhabited chambers; when he is not, as was the case this week, I establish a table and chair at one corner of the house fire, and never mind how Mr. Earnshaw may occupy himself; and he does not interfere with my arrangements. He is quieter now than he used to be, if no one provokes him; more sullen and depressed, and less furious. Joseph affirms he's sure he's an altered man; that the Lord has touched his heart, and he is saved 'so as by fire.' I'm puzzled to detect signs of the favourable change, but it is not my business.

"Yester-evening, I sat in my nook reading some old books till late on towards twelve. It seemed so dismal to go upstairs, with the wild snow blowing outside, and my thoughts continually reverting to the kirkyard and the new made grave! I dared hardly lift my eyes from the page before me, that melancholy scene so instantly usurped its place.

"Hindley sat opposite, his head leant on his hand, perhaps meditating on the same subject. He had ceased drinking at a point below irrationality, and had neither stirred nor spoken during two or three hours. There was no sound through the house but the moaning wind which shook the windows every now and then, the faint crackling of the coals, and the click of my snuffers as I removed at intervals the long wick of the candle. Hareton and Joseph were probably fast asleep in bed. It was very, very sad, and while I read, I sighed, for it seemed as if all joy had vanished from the world, never to be restored.

"The doleful silence was broken at length by the sound of the kitchen latch. Heathcliff had returned from his watch earlier than usual, owing, I suppose, to the sudden storm.

"That entrance was fastened, and we heard him coming round to get in by the other. I rose with an irrepressible expression of what I felt on my lips, which induced my companion, who had been staring towards the door, to turn and look at me.

" 'I'll keep him out five minutes,' he exclaimed. 'You won't object?'

" 'No, you may keep him out the whole night, for me,' I answered. 'Do! put the key in the lock, and draw the bolts.'

"Earnshaw accomplished this ere his guest reached the front; he then came and brought his chair to the other side of my table, leaning over it, and searching in my eyes for a sympathy with the burning hate that gleamed from his: as he both looked and felt like an assassin, he couldn't exactly find that; but he discovered enough to encourage him to speak.

" 'You and I,' he said, 'have each a great debt to settle with the man out yonder! If we were neither of us cowards, we might combine to discharge it. Are you as soft as your brother? Are you willing to endure to the last, and not once attempt a repayment?'

" 'I'm weary of enduring now,' I replied, 'and I'd be glad of a retaliation that wouldn't recoil on myself; but treachery and violence are spears pointed at both ends—they wound those who resort to them, worse than their enemies.'

" 'Treachery and violence are a just return for treachery and violence!' cried Hindley. 'Mrs. Heathcliff, I'll ask you to do nothing but sit still and be dumb. Tell me now, can you? I'm sure you would have as much pleasure as I in witnessing the conclusion of the fiend's existence; he'll be *your* death unless you overreach him —and he'll be *my* ruin. Damn the hellish villain! He knocks at the door as if he were master here already! Promise to hold your tongue, and before that clock strikes—it wants three minutes of one—you're a free woman!'

"He took the implements which I described to you in my letter from his breast, and would have turned down the candle. I snatched it away, however, and seized his arm.

" 'I'll not hold my tongue!' I said; 'you mustn't touch him. Let the door remain shut and be quiet!'

" 'No! I've formed my resolution, and by God, I'll execute it!' cried the desperate being. 'I'll do you a kindness in spite of yourself, and Hareton justice! And you needn't trouble your head to screen me; Catherine is gone. Nobody alive would regret me, or be ashamed, though I cut my throat this minute—and it's time to make an end!'

"I might as well have struggled with a bear, or reasoned with a lunatic. The only resource left me was to run to a lattice, and warn his intended victim of the fate which awaited him.

" 'You'd better seek shelter somewhere else to-night!' I exclaimed in a rather triumphant tone. 'Mr. Earnshaw has a mind to shoot you, if you persist in endeavouring to enter.'

" 'You'd better open the door, you—' he answered, addressing me by some elegant term that I don't care to repeat.

" 'I shall not meddle in the matter,' I retorted again. 'Come in, and get shot, if you please! I've done my duty.'

"With that I shut the window, and returned to my place by the fire, having too small a stock of hypocrisy at my command to pretend any anxiety for the danger that menaced him.

"Earnshaw swore passionately at me, affirming that I loved the villain yet, and calling me all sorts of names for the base spirit I evinced. And I, in my secret heart (and conscience never reproached me) thought what a blessing it would be for *him*, should Heathcliff put him out of misery; and what a blessing for *me*, should he send Heathcliff to his right abode! As I sat nursing these reflections, the casement behind me was banged on to the floor by a blow from the latter individual, and his black countenance looked blightingly through. The stanchions stood too close to suffer his shoulders to follow, and I smiled, exulting in my fancied security. His hair and clothes were whitened with snow, and his sharp cannibal teeth, revealed by cold and wrath, gleamed through the dark.

" 'Isabella, let me in, or I'll make you repent!' he 'girned,'[6] as Joseph calls it.

" 'I cannot commit murder,' I replied. 'Mr. Hindley stands sentinel with a knife and loaded pistol.'

" 'Let me in by the kitchen door!' he said.

" 'Hindley will be there before me,' I answered. 'And that's a poor love of yours that cannot bear a shower of snow! We were left at peace in our beds as long as the summer moon shone, but the moment a blast of winter returns, you must run for shelter! Heathcliff, if I were you, I'd go stretch myself over her grave and die like a faithful dog. The world is surely not worth living in now, is it? You had distinctly impressed on me the idea that Catherine was the whole joy of your life. I can't imagine how you think of surviving her loss.'

" 'He's there, is he?' exclaimed my companion, rushing to the gap. 'If I can get my arm out I can hit him!'

"I'm afraid, Ellen, you'll set me down as really wicked; but you don't know all, so don't judge! I wouldn't have aided or abetted an attempt on even *his* life, for anything. Wish that he were dead, I must; and therefore I was fearfully disappointed, and

6. Snarled.

unnerved by terror for the consequences of my taunting speech, when he flung himself on Earnshaw's weapon and wrenched it from his grasp.

"The charge exploded, and the knife, in springing back, closed into its owner's wrist. Heathcliff pulled it away by main force, slitting up the flesh as it passed on, and thrust it dripping into his pocket. He then took a stone, struck down the division between two windows, and sprung in. His adversary had fallen senseless with excessive pain and the flow of blood that gushed from an artery, or a large vein.

"The ruffian kicked and trampled on him, and dashed his head repeatedly against the flags, holding me with one hand, meantime, to prevent me summoning Joseph.

"He exerted preter-human self-denial in abstaining from finishing him completely; but getting out of breath, he finally desisted, and dragged the apparently inanimate body onto the settle.

"There he tore off the sleeve of Earnshaw's coat, and bound up the wound with brutal roughness, spitting and cursing during the operation, as energetically as he had kicked before.

"Being at liberty, I lost no time in seeking the old servant, who, having gathered by degrees the purport of my hasty tale, hurried below, gasping, as he descended the steps two at once.

" 'Whet is thur tuh do, nah? whet is thur tuh do, nah?'

" 'There's this to do,' thundered Heathcliff, 'that your master's mad; and should he last another month, I'll have him to an asylum. And how the devil did you come to fasten me out, you toothless hound? Don't stand muttering and mumbling there. Come, I'm not going to nurse him. Wash that stuff away; and mind the sparks of your candle—it is more than half brandy!'

" 'Und soa, yah been murthering on him!' exclaimed Joseph, lifting his hands and eyes in horror. 'If iver Aw seed a seeght loike this! May the Lord—'

"Heathcliff gave him a push onto his knees in the middle of the blood, and flung a towel to him; but instead of proceeding to dry it up, he joined his hands, and began a prayer which excited my laughter from its odd phraseology. I was in the condition of mind to be shocked at nothing; in fact, I was as reckless as some malefactors show themselves at the foot of the gallows.

" 'Oh, I forgot you,' said the tyrant. 'You shall do that. Down with you. And you conspire with him against me, do you, viper? There, that is work fit for you!'

"He shook me till my teeth rattled, and pitched me beside Joseph, who steadily concluded his supplications and then rose, vowing he would set off for the Grange directly. Mr. Linton was a magistrate, and though he had fifty wives dead, he should inquire into this.

"He was so obstinate in his resolution that Heathcliff deemed it expedient to compel from my lips a recapitulation of what had taken place; standing over me, heaving with malevolence, as I reluctantly delivered the account in answer to his questions.

"It required a great deal of labour to satisfy the old man that Heathcliff was not the aggressor; especially with my hardly wrung replies. However, Mr. Earnshaw soon convinced him that he was alive still; he hastened to administer a dose of spirits, and by their succour his master presently regained motion and consciousness.

"Heathcliff, aware that his opponent was ignorant of the treatment received while insensible, called him deliriously intoxicated; and said he should not notice his atrocious conduct further, but advised him to get to bed. To my joy, he left us after giving this judicious counsel, and Hindley stretched himself on the hearthstone. I departed to my own room, marvelling that I had escaped so easily.

"This morning, when I came down, about half-an-hour before noon, Mr. Earnshaw was sitting by the fire, deadly sick; his evil genius, almost as gaunt and ghastly, leant against the chimney. Neither appeared inclined to dine, and having waited till all was cold on the table, I commenced alone.

"Nothing hindered me from eating heartily; and I experienced a certain sense of satisfaction and superiority, as, at intervals, I cast a look towards my silent companions, and felt the comfort of a quiet conscience within me.

"After I had done, I ventured on the unusual liberty of drawing near the fire, going round Earnshaw's seat, and kneeling in the corner beside him.

"Heathcliff did not glance my way, and I gazed up and contemplated his features almost as confidently as if they had been turned to stone. His forehead, that I once thought so manly, and that I now think so diabolical, was shaded with a heavy cloud; his basilisk eyes were nearly quenched by sleeplessness, and weeping, perhaps, for the lashes were wet then; his lips devoid of their ferocious sneer, and sealed in an expression of unspeakable sadness. Had it been another, I would have covered my face in the presence of such grief. In *his* case, I was gratified; and ignoble as it seems to insult a fallen enemy, I couldn't miss this chance of sticking in a dart; his weakness was the only time when I could taste the delight of paying wrong for wrong."

"Fie, fie, Miss!" I interrupted. "One might suppose you had never opened a Bible in your life. If God afflict your enemies, surely that ought to suffice you. It is both mean and presumptuous to add your torture to his!"

"In general, I'll allow that it would be, Ellen," she continued. "But what misery laid on Heathcliff could content me, unless I have a hand in it? I'd rather he suffered *less*, if I might cause his sufferings and he might *know* that I was the cause. Oh, I owe him so much. On only one condition can I hope to forgive him. It is, if I may take an eye for an eye, a tooth for a tooth; for every wrench of agony, return a wrench, reduce him to my level. As he was the first to injure, make him the first to implore pardon; and then—why then, Ellen, I might show you some generosity. But it is utterly impossible I can ever be revenged, and therefore I cannot forgive him. Hindley wanted some water, and I handed him a glass, and asked him how he was.

" 'Not as ill as I wish,' he replied. 'But leaving out my arm, every inch of me is as sore as if I had been fighting with a legion of imps!'

" 'Yes, no wonder,' was my next remark. 'Catherine used to boast that she stood between you and bodily harm: she meant that certain persons would not hurt you, for fear of offending her. It's well people don't *really* rise from their grave, or, last night, she might have witnessed a repulsive scene! Are not you bruised, and cut over your chest and shoulders?'

" 'I can't say,' he answered; 'but what do you mean? Did he dare to strike me when I was down?'

" 'He trampled on, and kicked you, and dashed you on the ground,' I whispered. 'And his mouth watered to tear you with his teeth; because he's only half a man—not so much.'

"Mr. Earnshaw looked up, like me, to the countenance of our mutual foe, who, absorbed in his anguish, seemed insensible to anything around him; the longer he stood, the plainer his reflections revealed their blackness through his features.

" 'Oh, if God would but give me strength to strangle him in my last agony, I'd go to hell with joy,' groaned the impatient man, writhing to rise, and sinking back in despair, convinced of his inadequacy for the struggle.

" 'Nay, it's enough that he has murdered one of you,' I observed aloud. 'At the Grange, every one knows your sister would have been living now, had it not been for Mr. Heathcliff. After all, it is preferable to be hated than loved by him. When I recollect how happy we were—how happy Catherine was before he came—I'm fit to curse the day.'

"Most likely, Heathcliff noticed more the truth of what was said, than the spirit of the person who said it. His attention was roused, I saw, for his eyes rained down tears among the ashes, and he drew his breath in suffocating sighs.

"I stared full at him, and laughed scornfully. The clouded windows of hell flashed a moment towards me; the fiend which usually looked out, however, was so dimmed and drowned that I did not fear to hazard another sound of derision.

" 'Get up, and begone out of my sight,' said the mourner.

"I guessed he uttered those words, at least, though his voice was hardly intelligible.

" 'I beg your pardon,' I replied. 'But I loved Catherine too; and her brother requires attendance which, for her sake, I shall supply. Now that she's dead, I see her in Hindley; Hindley has exactly her eyes, if you had not tried to gouge them out and made them black and red, and her—'

" 'Get up, wretched idiot, before I stamp you to death!' he cried, making a movement that caused me to make one also.

" 'But then,' I continued, holding myself ready to flee, 'if poor Catherine had trusted you, and assumed the ridiculous, contemptible, degrading title of Mrs. Heathcliff, she would soon have presented a similar picture! *She* wouldn't have borne your abominable behaviour quietly; her detestation and disgust must have found voice.'

"The back of the settle and Earnshaw's person interposed between me and him; so instead of endeavouring to reach me, he snatched a dinner knife from the table and flung it at my head. It struck beneath my ear, and stopped the sentence I was uttering; but, pulling it out, I sprang to the door and delivered another which I hope went a little deeper than his missile.

"The last glimpse I caught of him was a furious rush on his part, checked by the embrace of his host; and both fell locked together on the hearth.

"In my flight through the kitchen I bid Joseph speed to his master; I knocked over Hareton, who was hanging a litter of puppies from a chair-back in the doorway; and, blest as a soul escaped from purgatory, I bounded, leaped, and flew down the steep road; then, quitting its windings, shot direct across the moor, rolling over banks, and wading through marshes; precipitating myself, in fact, towards the beacon light of the Grange. And far rather would I be condemned to a perpetual dwelling in the infernal regions, than even for one night abide beneath the roof of Wuthering Heights again."

Isabella ceased speaking, and took a drink of tea; then she rose, and bidding me put on her bonnet and a great shawl I had brought, and turning a deaf ear to my entreaties for her to remain another hour, she stepped onto a chair, kissed Edgar's and Catherine's portraits, bestowed a similar salute on me, and descended to the carriage accompanied by Fanny, who yelped wild with joy at recovering her mistress. She was driven away, never to revisit this neighbourhood;

but a regular correspondence was established between her and my master when things were more settled.

I believe her new abode was in the south, near London; there she had a son born, a few months subsequent to her escape. He was christened Linton, and, from the first, she reported him to be an ailing, peevish creature.

Mr. Heathcliff, meeting me one day in the village, inquired where she lived. I refused to tell. He remarked that it was not of any moment, only she must beware of coming to her brother; she should not be with him, if he had to keep her himself.

Though I would give no information, he discovered, through some of the other servants, both her place of residence and the existence of the child. Still he didn't molest her; for which forbearance she might thank his aversion, I suppose.

He often asked about the infant, when he saw me; and on hearing its name, smiled grimly, and observed—

"They wish me to hate it too, do they?"

"I don't think they wish you to know any thing about it," I answered.

"But I'll have it," he said, "when I want it. They may reckon on that!"

Fortunately, its mother died before the time arrived, some thirteen years after the decease of Catherine, when Linton was twelve, or a little more.

On the day succeeding Isabella's unexpected visit, I had no opportunity of speaking to my master: he shunned conversation, and was fit for discussing nothing. When I could get him to listen, I saw it pleased him that his sister had left her husband, whom he abhorred with an intensity which the mildness of his nature would scarcely seem to allow. So deep and sensitive was his aversion, that he refrained from going anywhere where he was likely to see or hear of Heathcliff. Grief, and that together, transformed him into a complete hermit: he threw up his office of magistrate, ceased even to attend church, avoided the village on all occasions, and spent a life of entire seclusion within the limits of his park and grounds, only varied by solitary rambles on the moors, and visits to the grave of his wife, mostly at evening, or early morning before other wanderers were abroad.

But he was too good to be thoroughly unhappy long. *He* didn't pray for Catherine's soul to haunt him. Time brought resignation, and a melancholy sweeter than common joy. He recalled her memory with ardent, tender love, and hopeful aspiring to the better world, where, he doubted not, she was gone.

And he had earthly consolation and affections, also. For a few days, I said, he seemed regardless of the puny successor to the departed: that coldness melted as fast as snow in April, and ere the tiny thing could stammer a word or totter a step, it wielded a despot's sceptre in his heart.

It was named Catherine, but he never called it the name in full, as he had never called the first Catherine short, probably because Heathcliff had a habit of doing so. The little one was always Cathy; it formed to him a distinction from the mother, and yet, a connection with her; and his attachment sprang from its relation to her, far more than from its being his own.

I used to draw a comparison between him and Hindley Earnshaw, and perplex myself to explain satisfactorily why their conduct was so opposite in similar circumstances. They had both been fond husbands, and were both attached to their children; and I could not see how they shouldn't both have taken the same road, for good or evil. But, I thought in my mind, Hindley, with apparently the stronger head, has shown himself sadly the worse and the weaker man. When his ship struck, the captain abandoned his post; and the crew, instead of trying to save her, rushed into riot and confusion, leaving no hope for their luckless vessel. Linton, on the contrary, displayed the true courage of a loyal and faithful soul: he trusted God; and God comforted him. One hoped, and the other despaired: they chose their own lots, and were righteously doomed to endure them.

But you'll not want to hear my moralizing, Mr. Lockwood: you'll judge as well as I can, all these things; at least, you'll think you will, and that's the same.

The end of Earnshaw was what might have been expected; it followed fast on his sister's: there were scarcely six months between them. We, at the Grange, never got a very succinct account of his state preceding it; all that I did learn was on occasion of going to aid in the preparations for the funeral. Mr. Kenneth came to announce the event to my master.

"Well, Nelly," said he, riding into the yard one morning, too early not to alarm me with an instant presentiment of bad news. "It's yours and my turn to go into mourning at present. Who's given us the slip now, do you think?"

"Who?" I asked in a flurry.

"Why, guess!" he returned, dismounting, and slinging his bridle on a hook by the door. "And nip up the corner of your apron; I'm certain you'll need it."

"Not Mr. Heathcliff, surely?" I exclaimed.

"What! would you have tears for him?" said the doctor. "No, Heathcliff's a tough young fellow; he looks blooming to-day—I've just seen him. He's rapidly regaining flesh since he lost his better half."

"Who is it, then, Mr. Kenneth?" I repeated impatiently.

"Hindley Earnshaw! Your old friend Hindley," he replied, "and my wicked gossip; though he's been too wild for me this long while. There! I said we should draw water. But cheer up! He died true to his character, drunk as a lord. Poor lad; I'm sorry, too. One can't help missing an old companion, though he had the worst tricks with him that ever man imagined, and has done me many a rascally turn. He's barely twenty-seven, it seems; that's your own age; who would have thought you were born in one year!"

I confess this blow was greater to me than the shock of Mrs. Linton's death: ancient associations lingered round my heart; I sat down in the porch and wept as for a blood relation, desiring Kenneth to get another servant to introduce him to the master.

I could not hinder myself from pondering on the question—"Had he had fair play?" Whatever I did, that idea would bother me: it was so tiresomely pertinacious that I resolved on requesting leave to go to Wuthering Heights, and assist in the last duties to the dead. Mr. Linton was extremely reluctant to consent, but I pleaded eloquently for the friendless condition in which he lay; and I said my old master and foster brother had a claim on my services as strong as his own. Besides, I reminded him that the child, Hareton, was his wife's nephew, and, in the absence of nearer kin, he ought to act as its guardian; and he ought to and must inquire how the property was left, and look over the concerns of his brother-in-law.

He was unfit for attending to such matters then, but he bid me speak to his lawyer; and at length permitted me to go. His lawyer had been Earnshaw's also: I called at the village, and asked him to accompany me. He shook his head, and advised that Heathcliff should be let alone, affirming, if the truth were known, Hareton would be found little else than a beggar.

"His father died in debt," he said; "the whole property is mortgaged, and the sole chance for the natural heir is to allow him an opportunity of creating some interest in the creditor's heart, that he may be inclined to deal leniently towards him."

When I reached the Heights, I explained that I had come to see everything carried on decently, and Joseph, who appeared in sufficient distress, expressed satisfaction at my presence. Mr. Heathcliff said he did not perceive that I was wanted, but I might stay and order the arrangements for the funeral, if I chose.

"Correctly," he remarked, "that fool's body should be buried at the cross-roads, without ceremony of any kind. I happened to leave him ten minutes, yesterday afternoon; and, in that interval, he fastened the two doors of the house against me, and he has spent the night in drinking himself to death deliberately! We broke in this morning, for we heard him snorting like a horse; and there he was, laid over the settle: flaying and scalping would not have wakened him. I sent for Kenneth, and he came; but not till the beast had changed into carrion: he was both dead and cold and stark; and so you'll allow, it was useless making more stir about him!"

The old servant confirmed this statement, but muttered—

"Aw'd rayther he'd goan hisseln fur t'doctor! Aw sud uh taen tent uh t'maister better nur him—un he warn't deead when Aw left, nowt uh t'soart!"[7]

I insisted on the funeral being respectable. Mr. Heathcliff said I might have my own way there too; only, he desired me to re-member that the money for the whole affair came out of his pocket.

He maintained a hard, careless deportment, indicative of neither joy nor sorrow; if anything, it expressed a flinty gratification at a piece of difficult work successfully executed. I observed once, in-deed, something like exultation in his aspect: it was just when the people were bearing the coffin from the house. He had the hypoc-risy to represent a mourner; and previous to following with Hareton, he lifted the unfortunate child on to the table and muttered, with peculiar gusto—

"Now, my bonny lad, you are *mine*! And we'll see if one tree won't grow as crooked as another, with the same wind to twist it!"

The unsuspecting thing was pleased at this speech; he played with Heathcliff's whiskers, and stroked his cheek, but I divined its meaning and observed tartly—

"That boy must go back with me to Thrushcross Grange, sir. There is nothing in the world less yours than he is!"

"Does Linton say so?" he demanded.

"Of course—he has ordered me to take him," I replied.

"Well," said the scoundrel, "we'll not argue the subject now; but I have a fancy to try my hand at rearing a young one, so inti-mate to your master that I must supply the place of this with my own, if he attempt to remove it. I don't engage to let Hareton go, undisputed; but I'll be pretty sure to make the other come! Re-member to tell him."

This hint was enough to bind our hands. I repeated its substance on my return, and Edgar Linton, little interested at the commence-ment, spoke no more of interfering. I'm not aware that he could have done it to any purpose, had he been ever so willing.

The guest was now the master of Wuthering Heights: he held firm possession, and proved to the attorney, who, in his turn, proved it to Mr. Linton, that Earnshaw had mortgaged every yard of land he owned for cash to supply his mania for gaming; and he,

7. *Sud uh taen tent:* should have taken care; *nur him:* than him; *nowt uh t'soart:* nothing of the sort.

Heathcliff, was the mortgagee.

In that manner, Hareton, who should now be the first gentleman in the neighbourhood, was reduced to a state of complete dependence on his father's inveterate enemy; and lives in his own house as a servant deprived of the advantage of wages, and quite unable to right himself, because of his friendlessness, and his ignorance that he has been wronged.

Chapter XVIII

The twelve years, continued Mrs. Dean, following that dismal period, were the happiest of my life: my greatest troubles, in their passage, rose from our little lady's trifling illnesses, which she had to experience in common with all children, rich and poor.

For the rest, after the first six months, she grew like a larch, and could walk and talk too, in her own wav, before the heath blossomed a second time over Mrs. Linton's dust.

She was the most winning thing that ever brought sunshine into a desolate house—a real beauty in face, with the Earnshaws' handsome dark eyes, but the Lintons' fair skin, and small features, and yellow curling hair. Her spirit was high, though not rough, and qualified by a heart sensitive and lively to excess in its affections. That capacity for intense attachments reminded me of her mother; still she did not resemble her, for she could be soft and mild as a dove, and she had a gentle voice, and pensive expression: her anger was never furious; her love never fierce; it was deep and tender.

However, it must be acknowledged, she had faults to foil her gifts. A propensity to be saucy was one; and a perverse will that indulged children invariably acquire, whether they be good tempered or cross. If a servant chanced to vex her, it was always: "I shall tell papa!" And if he reproved her, even by a look, you would have thought it a heartbreaking business: I don't believe he ever did speak a harsh word to her.

He took her education entirely on himself, and made it an amusement. Fortunately, curiosity and a quick intellect urged her into an apt scholar; she learnt rapidly and eagerly, and did honour to his teaching.

Till she reached the age of thirteen, she had not once been beyond the range of the park by herself. Mr. Linton would take her with him a mile or so outside, on rare occasions; but he trusted her to no one else. Gimmerton was an unsubstantial name in her ears; the chapel, the only building she had approached or entered, except her own home. Wuthering Heights and Mr. Heathcliff did not exist for her; she was a perfect recluse, and, apparently, perfectly contented. Sometimes, indeed, while surveying the country from her nursery window, she would observe—

"Ellen, how long will it be before I can walk to the top of those hills? I wonder what lies on the other side—is it the sea?"

"No, Miss Cathy," I would answer, "it is hills again just like these."

"And what are those golden rocks like, when you stand under them?" she once asked.

The abrupt descent of Penistone Crags particularly attracted her notice, especially when the setting sun shone on it and the topmost heights, and the whole extent of landscape besides lay in shadow.

I explained that they were bare masses of stone, with hardly enough earth in their clefts to nourish a stunted tree.

"And why are they bright so long after it is evening here?" she pursued.

"Because they are a great deal higher up than we are," replied I; "you could not climb them, they are too high and steep. In winter the frost is always there before it comes to us; and, deep into summer, I have found snow under that black hollow on the north-east side!"

"Oh, you have been on them!" she cried, gleefully. "Then I can go, too, when I am a woman. Has papa been, Ellen?"

"Papa would tell you, Miss," I answered, hastily, "that they are not worth the trouble of visiting. The moors, where you ramble with him, are much nicer; and Thrushcross park is the finest place in the world."

"But I know the park, and I don't know those," she murmured to herself. "And I should delight to look round me from the brow of that tallest point—my little pony, Minny, shall take me some time."

One of the maids mentioning the Fairy cave quite turned her head with a desire to fulfil this project; she teased Mr. Linton about it; and he promised she should have the journey when she got older. But Miss Catherine measured her age by months, and—

"Now, am I old enough to go to Penistone Crags?" was the constant question in her mouth.

The road thither wound close by Wuthering Heights. Edgar had not the heart to pass it; so she received as constantly the answer—

"Not yet, love, not yet."

I said Mrs. Heathcliff lived above a dozen years after quitting her husband. Her family were of a delicate constitution: she and Edgar both lacked the ruddy health that you will generally meet in these parts. What her last illness was, I am not certain; I conjecture they died of the same thing, a kind of fever, slow at its commencement, but incurable, and rapidly consuming life towards the close.

She wrote to inform her brother of the probable conclusion of a four months' indisposition under which she had suffered; and entreated him to come to her, if possible, for she had much to settle, and she wished to bid him adieu, and deliver Linton safely into his hands. Her hope was, that Linton might be left with him, as he had been with her; his father, she would fain convince herself, had no desire to assume the burden of his maintenance or education.

My master hesitated not a moment in complying with her request; reluctant as he was to leave home at ordinary calls, he flew to answer this; commending Catherine to my peculiar vigilance in his absence, with reiterated orders that she must not wander out of the park, even under my escort: he did not calculate on her going unaccompanied.

He was away three weeks: the first day or two, my charge sat in a corner of the library, too sad for either reading or playing: in that quiet state she caused me little trouble; but it was succeeded by an interval of impatient, fretful weariness; and being too busy, and too old then, to run up and down amusing her, I hit on a method by which she might entertain herself.

I used to send her on her travels round the grounds—now on foot, and now on a pony; indulging her with a patient audience of all her real and imaginary adventures, when she returned.

The summer shone in full prime; and she took such a taste for this solitary rambling that she often contrived to remain out from breakfast till tea; and then the evenings were spent in recounting her fanciful tales. I did not fear her breaking bounds, because the gates were generally locked, and I thought she would scarcely venture forth alone, if they had stood wide open.

Unluckily, my confidence proved misplaced. Catherine came to me, one morning, at eight o'clock, and said she was that day an Arabian merchant, going to cross the Desert with his caravan; and I must give her plenty of provision for herself and beasts, a horse and three camels, personated by a large hound and a couple of pointers.

I got together good store of dainties, and slung them in a basket on one side of the saddle; and she sprang up as gay as a fairy, sheltered by her wide-brimmed hat and gauze veil from the July sun, and trotted off with a merry laugh, mocking my cautious counsel to avoid galloping, and come back early.

The naughty thing never made her appearance at tea. One traveller, the hound, being an old dog and fond of its ease, returned; but neither Cathy, nor the pony, nor the two pointers were visible in any direction; and I despatched emissaries down this path, and that path, and, at last, went wandering in search of her myself.

There was a labourer working at a fence round a plantation, on the borders of the grounds. I enquired of him if he had seen our young lady.

"I saw her at morn," he replied; "she would have me to cut her a hazel switch, and then she leapt her galloway[8] over the hedge yonder, where it is lowest, and galloped out of sight."

You may guess how I felt at hearing this news. It struck me directly she must have started for Penistone Crags.

"What will become of her?" I ejaculated, pushing through a gap which the man was repairing, and making straight to the high road.

I walked as if for a wager, mile after mile, till a turn brought me in view of the Heights, but no Catherine could I detect, far or near.

The Crags lie about a mile and a half beyond Mr. Heathcliff's place, and that is four from the Grange, so I began to fear night would fall ere I could reach them.

"And what if she should have slipped in, clambering among them," I reflected, "and been killed, or broken some of her bones?"

My suspense was truly painful; and, at first, it gave me delightful relief to observe, in hurrying by the farm-house, Charlie, the fiercest of the pointers, lying under a window, with swelled head and bleeding ear.

I opened the wicket and ran to the door, knocking vehemently for admittance. A woman whom I knew, and who formerly lived at Gimmerton, answered: she had been servant there since the death of Mr Earnshaw.

"Ah," said she, "you are come a seeking your little mistress! don't be frightened. She's here safe—but I'm glad it isn't the master."

"He is not at home then, is he?" I panted, quite breathless with quick walking and alarm.

"No, no," she replied, "both he and Joseph are off, and I think they won't return this hour or more. Step in and rest you a bit."

I entered, and beheld my stray lamb seated on the hearth, rocking herself in a little chair that had been her mother's, when a child. Her hat was hung against the wall, and she seemed perfectly at home, laughing and chattering, in the best spirits imaginable, to Hareton, now a great, strong lad of eighteen, who stared at her with considerable curiosity and astonishment; comprehending precious little of the fluent succession of remarks and questions which her tongue never ceased pouring forth.

"Very well, Miss," I exclaimed, concealing my joy under an

8. One of a small but strong breed of horses peculiar to Galloway.

angry countenance. "This is your last ride, till papa comes back. I'll not trust you over the threshold again, you naughty, naughty girl."

"Aha, Ellen!" she cried gaily, jumping up, and running to my side. "I shall have a pretty story to tell to-night—and so you've found me out. Have you ever been here in your life before?"

"Put that hat on, and home at once," said I. "I'm dreadfully grieved at you, Miss Cathy, you've done extremely wrong! It's no use pouting and crying; that won't repay the trouble I've had, scouring the country after you. To think how Mr. Linton charged me to keep you in; and you stealing off so; it shows you are a cunning little fox, and nobody will put faith in you any more."

"What have I done?" sobbed she, instantly checked. "Papa charged me nothing: he'll not scold me, Ellen—he's never cross, like you!"

"Come, come!" I repeated. "I'll tie the riband. Now, let us have no petulance. Oh, for shame. You thirteen years old, and such a baby!"

This exclamation was caused by her pushing the hat from her head, and retreating to the chimney out of my reach.

"Nay," said the servant, "don't be hard on the bonny lass, Mrs. Dean. We made her stop—she'd fain have ridden forwards, afeard you should be uneasy. Hareton offered to go with her, and I thought he should. It's a wild road over the hills."

Hareton, during the discussion, stood with his hands in his pockets, too awkward to speak, though he looked as if he did not relish my intrusion.

"How long am I to wait?" I continued, disregarding the woman's interference. "It will be dark in ten minutes. Where is the pony, Miss Cathy? And where is Phœnix? I shall leave you, unless you be quick, so please yourself."

"The pony is in the yard," she replied, "and Phœnix is shut in there. He's bitten—and so is Charlie. I was going to tell you all about it; but you are in a bad temper, and don't deserve to hear."

I picked up her hat, and approached to reinstate it; but perceiving that the people of the house took her part, she commenced capering round the room; and, on my giving chase, ran like a mouse, over and under and behind the furniture, rendering it ridiculous for me to pursue.

Hareton and the woman laughed, and she joined them, and waxed more impertinent still; till I cried, in great irritation—

"Well, Miss Cathy, if you were aware whose house this is, you'd be glad enough to get out."

"It's *your* father's, isn't it?" said she, turning to Hareton.

"Nay," he replied, looking down, and blushing bashfully.

He could not stand a steady gaze from her eyes, though they were just his own.

"Whose, then—your master's?" she asked.

He coloured deeper, with a different feeling, muttered an oath, and turned away.

"Who is his master?" continued the tiresome girl, appealing to me. "He talked about 'our house,' and 'our folk.' I thought he had been the owner's son. And he never said, Miss; he should have done, shouldn't he, if he's a servant?"

Hareton grew black as a thunder-cloud, at this childish speech. I silently shook my questioner, and, at last, succeeded in equipping her for departure.

"Now, get my horse," she said, addressing her unknown kinsman as she would one of the stable-boys at the Grange. "And you may come with me. I want to see where the goblin hunter rises in the marsh, and to hear about the *fairishes,* as you call them—but make haste! What's the matter? Get my horse, I say."

"I'll see thee damned, before I be *thy* servant!" growled the lad.

"You'll see me *what?*" asked Catherine in surprise.

"Damned—thou saucy witch!" he replied.

"There, Miss Cathy! you see you have got into pretty company," I interposed. "Nice words to be used to a young lady! Pray don't begin to dispute with him. Come, let us seek for Minny ourselves, and begone."

"But, Ellen," cried she, staring, fixed in astonishment. "How dare he speak so to me? Mustn't he be made to do as I ask him? You wicked creature, I shall tell papa what you said—Now then!"

Hareton did not appear to feel this threat; so the tears sprung into her eyes with indignation. "You bring the pony," she exclaimed, turning to the woman, "and let my dog free this moment!"

"Softly, Miss," answered the addressed. "You'll lose nothing by being civil. Though Mr. Hareton, there, be not the master's son, he's your cousin; and I was never hired to serve you."

"*He* my cousin!" cried Cathy with a scornful laugh.

"Yes, indeed," responded her reprover.

"Oh, Ellen! don't let them say such things," she pursued in great trouble. "Papa is gone to fetch my cousin from London—my cousin is a gentleman's son. That my—" she stopped, and wept outright; upset at the bare notion of relationship with such a clown.

"Hush, hush!" I whispered, "people can have many cousins and of all sorts, Miss Cathy, without being any the worse for it; only they needn't keep their company, if they be disagreeable and bad."

"He's not, he's not my cousin, Ellen!" she went on, gathering fresh grief from reflection, and flinging herself into my arms for refuge from the idea.

I was much vexed at her and the servant for their mutual revelations; having no doubt of Linton's approaching arrival, communicated by the former, being reported to Mr. Heathcliff; and feeling as confident that Catherine's first thought on her father's return would be to seek an explanation of the latter's assertion concerning her rude-bred kindred.

Hareton, recovering from his disgust at being taken for a servant, seemed moved by her distress; and, having fetched the pony round to the door, he took, to propitiate her, a fine crooked-legged terrier whelp from the kennel, and putting it into her hand, bid her wisht[9] for he meant naught.

Pausing in her lamentations, she surveyed him with a glance of awe and horror, then burst forth anew.

I could scarcely refrain from smiling at this antipathy to the poor fellow, who was a well-made, athletic youth, good-looking in features, and stout and healthy, but attired in garments befitting his daily occupations of working on the farm, and lounging among the moors after rabbits and game. Still, I thought I could detect in his physiognomy a mind owning better qualities than his father ever possessed. Good things lost amid a wilderness of weeds, to be sure, whose rankness far over-topped their neglected growth; yet, notwithstanding, evidence of a wealthy soil that might yield luxuriant crops under other and favourable circumstances. Mr. Heathcliff, I believe, had not treated him physically ill; thanks to his fearless nature, which offered no temptation to that course of oppression; it had none of the timid susceptibility that would have given zest to ill-treatment, in Heathcliff's judgment. He appeared to have bent his malevolence on making him a brute: he was never taught to read or write; never rebuked for any bad habit which did not annoy his keeper; never led a single step towards virtue, or guarded by a single precept against vice. And from what I heard, Joseph contributed much to his deterioration by a narrow-minded partiality which prompted him to flatter and pet him, as a boy, because he was the head of the old family. And as he had been in the habit of accusing Catherine Earnshaw and Heathcliff, when children, of putting the master past his patience, and compelling him to seek solace in drink, by what he termed their "offald[1] ways," so at present he laid the whole burden of Hareton's faults on the shoulders of the usurper of his property.

If the lad swore, he wouldn't correct him; nor however culpably he behaved. It gave Joseph satisfaction, apparently, to watch him go the worst lengths. He allowed that he was ruined; that his soul was abandoned to perdition; but then, he reflected that Heathcliff

9. Hush.   1. Disreputable.

must answer for it. Hareton's blood would be required at his hands; and there lay immense consolation in that thought.

Joseph had instilled into him a pride of name, and of his lineage; he would, had he dared, have fostered hate between him and the present owner of the Heights, but his dread of that owner amounted to superstition; and he confined his feelings regarding him to muttered innuendoes and private comminations.

I don't pretend to be intimately acquainted with the mode of living customary in those days at Wuthering Heights. I only speak from hearsay; for I saw little. The villagers affirmed Mr. Heathcliff was *near*,[2] and a cruel hard landlord to his tenants; but the house, inside, had regained its ancient aspect of comfort under female management; and the scenes of riot common in Hindley's time were not now enacted within its walls. The master was too gloomy to seek companionship with any people, good or bad, and he is yet.

This, however, is not making progress with my story. Miss Cathy rejected the peace-offering of the terrier, and demanded her own dogs, Charlie and Phœnix. They came limping, and hanging their heads; and we set out for home, sadly out of sorts, every one of us.

I could not wring from my little lady how she had spent the day; except that, as I supposed, the goal of her pilgrimage was Penistone Crags; and she arrived without adventure to the gate of the farmhouse, when Hareton happened to issue forth, attended by some canine followers who attacked her train.

They had a smart battle, before their owners could separate them: that formed an introduction. Catherine told Hareton who she was, and where she was going; and asked him to show her the way, finally beguiling him to accompany her.

He opened the mysteries of the Fairy cave, and twenty other queer places; but, being in disgrace, I was not favoured with a description of the interesting objects she saw.

I could gather, however, that her guide had been a favourite till she hurt his feelings by addressing him as a servant; and Heathcliff's housekeeper hurt hers by calling him her cousin.

Then the language he had held to her rankled in her heart; she who was always "love," and "darling," and "queen," and "angel," with everybody at the Grange, to be insulted so shockingly by a stranger! She did not comprehend it; and hard work I had to obtain a promise that she would not lay the grievance before her father.

I explained how he objected to the whole household at the Heights, and how sorry he would be to find she had been there; but I insisted most on the fact, that if she revealed my negligence

2. Niggardly.

of his orders, he would perhaps be so angry that I should have to leave; and Cathy couldn't bear that prospect: she pledged her word, and kept it, for my sake—after all, she was a sweet little girl.

Chapter XIX

A letter, edged with black, announced the day of my master's return. Isabella was dead; and he wrote to bid me get mourning for his daughter, and arrange a room and other accommodations for his youthful nephew.

Catherine ran wild with joy at the idea of welcoming her father back, and indulged most sanguine anticipations of the innumerable excellencies of her "real" cousin.

The evening of their expected arrival came. Since early morning, she had been busy, ordering her own small affairs; and now, attired in her new black frock—poor thing! her aunt's death impressed her with no definite sorrow—she obliged me, by constant worrying, to walk with her down through the grounds to meet them.

"Linton is just six months younger than I am," she chattered, as we strolled leisurely over the swells and hollows of mossy turf, under shadow of the trees. "How delightful it will be to have him for a playfellow! Aunt Isabella sent papa a beautiful lock of his hair; it was lighter than mine—more flaxen, and quite as fine. I have it carefully preserved in a little glass box; and I've often thought what pleasure it would be to see its owner. Oh! I am happy—and papa, dear, dear papa! Come, Ellen, let us run! come run!"

She ran, and returned and ran again, many times before my sober footsteps reached the gate, and then she seated herself on the grassy bank beside the path, and tried to wait patiently, but that was impossible; she couldn't be still a minute.

"How long they are!" she exclaimed. "Ah, I see some dust on the road—they are coming! No! When will they be here? May we not go a little way—half a mile, Ellen, only just half a mile? Do say yes, to that clump of birches at the turn!"

I refused staunchly; and, at length, her suspense was ended: the travelling carriage rolled in sight.

Miss Cathy shrieked, and stretched out her arms, as soon as she caught her father's face, looking from the window. He descended, nearly as eager as herself; and a considerable interval elapsed ere they had a thought to spare for any but themselves.

While they exchanged caresses, I took a peep in to see after Linton. He was asleep in a corner, wrapped in a warm, fur-lined cloak, as if it had been winter. A pale, delicate, effeminate boy, who might have been taken for my master's younger brother, so strong was the resemblance; but there was a sickly peevishness in his aspect that Edgar Linton never had.

The latter saw me looking; and having shaken hands, advised me to close the door, and leave him undisturbed; for the journey had fatigued him.

Cathy would fain have taken one glance; but her father told her to come on, and they walked together up the park, while I hastened before to prepare the servants.

"Now, darling," said Mr. Linton, addressing his daughter, as they halted at the bottom of the front steps, "your cousin is not so strong or so merry as you are, and he has lost his mother, remember, a very short time since; therefore, don't expect him to play and run about with you directly. And don't harass him much by talking—let him be quiet this evening, at least, will you?"

"Yes, yes, papa," answered Catherine; "but I do want to see him; and he hasn't once looked out."

The carriage stopped; and the sleeper, being roused, was lifted to the ground by his uncle.

"This is your cousin Cathy, Linton," he said, putting their little hands together. "She's fond of you already; and mind you don't grieve her by crying to-night. Try to be cheerful now; the travelling is at an end, and you have nothing to do but rest and amuse yourself as you please."

"Let me go to bed, then," answered the boy, shrinking from Catherine's salute; and he put his fingers to his eyes to remove incipient tears.

"Come, come, there's a good child," I whispered, leading him in. "You'll make her weep too—see how sorry she is for you!"

I do not know whether it were sorrow for him, but his cousin put on as sad a countenance as himself, and returned to her father. All three entered, and mounted to the library, where tea was laid ready.

I proceeded to remove Linton's cap and mantle, and placed him on a chair by the table; but he was no sooner seated than he began to cry afresh. My master inquired what was the matter.

"I can't sit on a chair," sobbed the boy.

"Go to the sofa, then, and Ellen shall bring you some tea," answered his uncle, patiently.

He had been greatly tried during the journey, I felt convinced, by his fretful, ailing charge.

Linton slowly trailed himself off, and lay down. Cathy carried a foot-stool and her cup to his side.

At first she sat silent; but that could not last; she had resolved to make a pet of her little cousin, as she would have him to be; and she commenced stroking his curls, and kissing his cheek, and offering him tea in her saucer, like a baby. This pleased him, for he was not much better; he dried his eyes, and lightened into a faint smile.

"Oh, he'll do very well," said the master to me, after watching them a minute. "Very well, if we can keep him, Ellen. The company of a child of his own age will instil new spirit into him soon, and by wishing for strength he'll gain it."

"Aye, if we can keep him!" I mused to myself; and sore misgivings came over me that there was slight hope of that. And then, I thought, however will that weakling live at Wuthering Heights, between his father and Hareton? What playmates and instructors they'll be.

Our doubts were presently decided—even earlier than I expected. I had just taken the children upstairs, after tea was finished, and seen Linton asleep—he would not suffer me to leave him till that was the case. I had come down, and was standing by the table in the hall, lighting a bed-room candle for Mr. Edgar, when a maid stepped out of the kitchen and informed me that Mr. Heathcliff's servant, Joseph, was at the door, and wished to speak with the master.

"I shall ask him what he wants first," I said, in considerable trepidation. "A very unlikely hour to be troubling people, and the instant they have returned from a long journey. I don't think the master can see him."

Joseph had advanced through the kitchen, as I uttered these words, and now presented himself in the hall. He was donned in his Sunday garments, with his most sanctimonious and sourest face; and holding his hat in one hand and his stick in the other, he proceeded to clean his shoes on the mat.

"Good evening, Joseph," I said, coldly. "What business brings you here to-night?"

"It's Maister Linton Aw mun spake tull,"[3] he answered, waving me disdainfully aside.

"Mr. Linton is going to bed; unless you have something particular to say, I'm sure he won't hear it now," I continued. "You had better sit down in there, and entrust your message to me."

"Which is his rahm?" pursued the fellow, surveying the range of closed doors.

I perceived he was bent on refusing my mediation; so very reluctantly I went up to the library, and announced the unseasonable visitor, advising that he should be dismissed till next day.

Mr. Linton had no time to empower me to do so, for he mounted close at my heels, and, pushing into the apartment, planted himself at the far side of the table, with his two fists clapped on the head of his stick, and began in an elevated tone, as

3. Speak to.

if anticipating opposition—

"Hathecliff has send me for his lad, un Aw 'munn't goa back 'baht him."[4]

Edgar Linton was silent a minute; an expression of exceeding sorrow overcast his features; he would have pitied the child on his own account; but, recalling Isabella's hopes and fears, and anxious wishes for her son, and her commendations of him to his care, he grieved bitterly at the prospect of yielding him up, and searched in his heart how it might be avoided. No plan offered itself: the very exhibition of any desire to keep him would have rendered the claimant more peremptory: there was nothing left but to resign him. However, he was not going to rouse him from his sleep.

"Tell Mr. Heathcliff," he answered, calmly, "that his son shall come to Wuthering Heights to-morrow. He is in bed, and too tired to go the distance now. You may also tell him that the mother of Linton desired him to remain under my guardianship; and, at present, his health is very precarious."

"Noa!" said Joseph, giving a thud with his prop on the floor, and assuming an authoritative air. "Noa! that manes nowt—Hathecliff maks noa 'cahnt uh t' mother, nur yah norther—bud he'll hev his lad; und Aw mun tak him—soa nah yah knaw!"[5]

"You shall not to-night!" answered Linton, decisively. "Walk down stairs at once, and repeat to your master what I have said. Ellen, show him down. Go—"

And, aiding the indignant elder with a lift by the arm, he rid the room of him, and closed the door.

"Varrah weel!" shouted Joseph, as he slowly drew off. "Tuh morn, he's come hisseln, un' thrust *him* aht, if yah darr!"

Chapter XX

To obviate the danger of this threat being fulfilled, Mr. Linton commissioned me to take the boy home early, on Catherine's pony, and, said he—

"As we shall now have no influence over his destiny, good or bad, you must say nothing of where he is gone to my daughter; she cannot associate with him hereafter, and it is better for her to remain in ignorance of his proximity, lest she should be restless, and anxious to visit the Heights. Merely tell her, his father sent for him suddenly, and he has been obliged to leave us."

Linton was very reluctant to be roused from his bed at five o'clock, and astonished to be informed that he must prepare for further travelling; but I softened off the matter by stating that he

4. Without him.
5. *Manes nowt:* means nothing; *maks* noa *'cahnt:* takes no account; *norther:* neither.

was going to spend some time with his father, Mr. Heathcliff, who wished to see him so much, he did not like to defer the pleasure till he should recover from his late journey.

"My father?" he cried, in strange perplexity. "Mamma never told me I had a father. Where does he live? I'd rather stay with uncle."

"He lives a little distance from the Grange," I replied, "just beyond those hills—not so far but you may walk over here, when you get hearty. And you should be glad to go home, and to see him. You must try to love him, as you did your mother, and then he will love you."

"But why have I not heard of him before?" asked Linton; "why didn't mamma and he live together, as other people do?"

"He had business to keep him in the north," I answered; "and your mother's health required her to reside in the south."

"And why didn't mamma speak to me about him?" persevered the child. "She often talked of uncle, and I learnt to love him long ago. How am I to love papa? I don't know him."

"Oh, all children love their parents," I said. "Your mother, perhaps, thought you would want to be with him, if she mentioned him often to you. Let us make haste. An early ride on such a beautiful morning is much preferable to an hour's more sleep."

"Is *she* to go with us?" he demanded. "The little girl I saw yesterday?"

"Not now," replied I.

"Is uncle?" he continued.

"No, I shall be your companion there," I said.

Linton sank back on his pillow, and fell into a brown study.

"I won't go without uncle," he cried at length; "I can't tell where you mean to take me."

I attempted to persuade him of the naughtiness of showing reluctance to meet his father; still he obstinately resisted any progress towards dressing, and I had to call for my master's assistance in coaxing him out of bed.

The poor thing was finally got off with several delusive assurances that his absence should be short; that Mr. Edgar and Cathy would visit him; and other promises, equally ill-founded, which I invented and reiterated at intervals throughout the way.

The pure heather-scented air, and the bright sunshine, and the gentle canter of Minny relieved his despondency, after a while. He began to put questions concerning his new home, and its inhabitants, with greater interest and liveliness.

"Is Wuthering Heights as pleasant a place as Thrushcross Grange?" he inquired, turning to take a last glance into the valley, whence a light mist mounted and formed a fleecy cloud on the skirts of the blue.

"It is not so buried in trees," I replied, "and it is not quite so large, but you can see the country beautifully, all round; and the air is healthier for you—fresher and dryer. You will, perhaps, think the building old and dark at first—though it is a respectable house, the next best in the neighbourhood. And you will have such nice rambles on the moors! Hareton Earnshaw—that is Miss Cathy's other cousin, and so yours in a manner—will show you all the sweetest spots; and you can bring a book in fine weather, and make a green hollow your study; and, now and then, your uncle may join you in a walk: he does, frequently, walk out on the hills."

"And what is my father like?" he asked. "Is he as young and handsome as uncle?"

"He's as young," said I, "but he has black hair and eyes, and looks sterner, and he is taller and bigger altogether. He'll not seem to you so gentle and kind at first, perhaps, because it is not his way —still, mind you be frank and cordial with him; and naturally he'll be fonder of you than any uncle, for you are his own."

"Black hair and eyes!" mused Linton. "I can't fancy him. Then I am not like him, am I?"

"Not much," I answered. Not a morsel, I thought, surveying with regret the white complexion and slim frame of my companion, and his large languid eyes—his mother's eyes, save that, unless a morbid touchiness kindled them a moment, they had not a vestige of her sparkling spirit.

"How strange that he should never come to see mamma and me," he murmured. "Has he ever seen me? If he have, I must have been a baby—I remember not a single thing about him!"

"Why, Master Linton," said I, "three hundred miles is a great distance; and ten years seem very different in length to a grown up person, compared with what they do to you. It is probable Mr. Heathcliff proposed going, from summer to summer, but never found a convenient opportunity; and now it is too late. Don't trouble him with questions on the subject: it will disturb him for no good."

The boy was fully occupied with his own cogitations for the remainder of the ride, till we halted before the farm-house garden gate. I watched to catch his impressions in his countenance. He surveyed the carved front and low-browed lattices, the straggling gooseberry bushes and crooked firs, with solemn intentness, and then shook his head: his private feelings entirely disapproved of the exterior of his new abode; but he had sense to postpone complaining—there might be compensation within.

Before he dismounted, I went and opened the door. It was half-past six; the family had just finished breakfast; the servant was clearing and wiping down the table. Joseph stood by his master's chair telling some tale concerning a lame horse; and Hareton was preparing for the hay-field.

"Hallo, Nelly!" cried Mr. Heathcliff, when he saw me. "I feared I should have to come down and fetch my property myself. You've brought it, have you? Let us see what we can make of it."

He got up and strode to the door: Hareton and Joseph followed in gaping curiosity. Poor Linton ran a frightened eye over the faces of the three.

"Sure-ly," said Joseph after a grave inspection, "he's swopped wi' ye, maister, an' yon's his lass!"

Heathcliff, having stared his son into an ague of confusion, uttered a scornful laugh.

"God! what a beauty! what a lovely, charming thing!" he exclaimed. "Haven't they reared it on snails and sour milk, Nelly? Oh, damn my soul! but that's worse than I expected—and the devil knows I was not sanguine!"

I bid the trembling and bewildered child get down, and enter. He did not thoroughly comprehend the meaning of his father's speech, or whether it were intended for him: indeed, he was not yet certain that the grim, sneering stranger was his father; but he clung to me with growing trepidation, and on Mr. Heathcliff's taking a seat, and bidding him "come hither," he hid his face on my shoulder, and wept.

"Tut, tut!" said Heathcliff, stretching out a hand and dragging him roughly between his knees, and then holding up his head by the chin. "None of that nonsense! We're not going to hurt thee, Linton—isn't that thy name? Thou art thy mother's child, entirely! Where is *my* share in thee, puling chicken?"

He took off the boy's cap and pushed back his thick flaxen curls, felt his slender arms, and his small fingers; during which examination, Linton ceased crying, and lifted his great blue eyes to inspect the inspector.

"Do you know me?" asked Heathcliff, having satisfied himself that the limbs were all equally frail and feeble.

"No!" said Linton, with a gaze of vacant fear.

"You've heard of me, I dare say?"

"No," he replied again.

"No? What a shame of your mother, never to waken your filial regard for me! You are my son, then, I'll tell you; and your mother was a wicked slut to leave you in ignorance of the sort of father you possessed. Now, don't wince, and colour up! Though it *is* something to see you have not white blood. Be a good lad; and I'll do for you. Nelly, if you be tired you may sit down; if not get home again. I guess you'll report what you hear and see, to the cipher at the Grange; and this thing won't be settled while you linger about it."

"Well," replied I, "I hope you'll be kind to the boy, Mr. Heathcliff, or you'll not keep him long, and he's all you have akin in the wide world that you will ever know—remember."

"I'll be *very* kind to him, you needn't fear!" he said, laughing. "Only nobody else must be kind to him—I'm jealous of monopolizing his affection. And, to begin my kindness, Joseph! bring the lad some breakfast. Hareton, you infernal calf, begone to your work. Yes, Nell," he added when they were departed, "my son is prospective owner of your place, and I should not wish him to die till I was certain of being his successor. Besides, he's *mine*, and I want the triumph of seeing *my* descendent fairly lord of their estates; my child hiring their children to till their fathers' lands for wages. That is the sole consideration which can make me endure the whelp—I despise him for himself, and hate him for the memories he revives! But that consideration is sufficient; he's as safe with me, and shall be tended as carefully as your master tends his own. I have a room upstairs, furnished for him in handsome style; I've engaged a tutor, also, to come three times a week, from twenty miles distance, to teach him what he pleases to learn. I've ordered Hareton to obey him; and in fact I've arranged everything with a view to preserve the superior and the gentleman in him, above his associates. I do regret, however, that he so little deserves the trouble. If I wished any blessing in the world, it was to find him a worthy object of pride, and I'm bitterly disappointed with the whey-faced whining wretch!"

While he was speaking, Joseph returned, bearing a basin of milk-porridge, and placed it before Linton. He stirred round the homely mess with a look of aversion, and affirmed he could not eat it.

I saw the old man-servant shared largely in his master's scorn of the child, though he was compelled to retain the sentiment in his heart, because Heathcliff plainly meant his underlings to hold him in honour.

"Cannot ate it?" repeated he, peering in Linton's face, and subduing his voice to a whisper, for fear of being overheard. "But Maister Hareton nivir ate nowt else, when he wer a little un: und what wer gooid eneugh fur him's gooid eneugh fur yah, Aw's rayther think!"

"I *shan't* eat it!" answered Linton, snappishly. "Take it away." Joseph snatched up the food indignantly, and brought it to us.

"Is there owt ails th' victuals?" he asked, thrusting the tray under Heathcliff's nose.

"What should ail them?" he said.

"Wah!" answered Joseph, "yon dainty chap says he cannut ate

'em. Bud Aw guess it's raight! His mother wer just soa—we wer a'most too mucky⁶ tuh sow t' corn fur makking her breead."

"Don't mention his mother to me," said the master, angrily. "Get him something that he can eat, that's all. What is his usual food, Nelly?"

I suggested boiled milk or tea; and the housekeeper received instructions to prepare some.

Come, I reflected, his father's selfishness may contribute to his comfort. He perceives his delicate constitution, and the necessity of treating him tolerably. I'll console Mr. Edgar by acquainting him with the turn Heathcliff's humour has taken.

Having no excuse for lingering longer, I slipped out, while Linton was engaged in timidly rebuffing the advances of a friendly sheep-dog. But he was too much on the alert to be cheated: as I closed the door, I heard a cry, and a frantic repetition of the words—

"Don't leave me! I'll not stay here! I'll not stay here!"

Then the latch was raised and fell: they did not suffer him to come forth. I mounted Minny, and urged her to a trot; and so my brief guardianship ended.

Chapter XXI

We had sad work with little Cathy that day: she rose in high glee, eager to join her cousin; and such passionate tears and lamentations followed the news of his departure, that Edgar himself was obliged to sooth her, by affirming he should come back soon; he added, however, "if I can get him"; and there were no hopes of that.

This promise poorly pacified her, but time was more potent; and though still, at intervals, she inquired of her father when Linton would return, before she did see him again, his features had waxed so dim in her memory that she did not recognise him.

When I chanced to encounter the housekeeper of Wuthering Heights, in paying business-visits to Gimmerton, I used to ask how the young master got on; for he lived almost as secluded as Catherine herself, and was never to be seen. I could gather from her that he continued in weak health, and was a tiresome inmate. She said Mr. Heathcliff seemed to dislike him ever longer and worse, though he took some trouble to conceal it. He had an antipathy to the sound of his voice, and could not do at all with his sitting in the same room with him many minutes together.

There seldom passed much talk between them; Linton learnt his lessons, and spent his evenings in a small apartment they called

6. Dirty.

the parlour; or else lay in bed all day, for he was constantly getting coughs, and colds, and aches, and pains of some sort.

"And I never knew such a faint-hearted creature," added the woman; "nor one so careful of hisseln. He *will* go on, if I leave the window open, a bit late in the evening. Oh! it's killing, a breath of night air! And he must have a fire in the middle of summer; and Joseph's 'bacca pipe is poison; and he must always have sweets and dainties, and always milk, milk for ever—heeding naught how the rest of us are pinched in winter; and there he'll sit, wrapped in his furred cloak in his chair by the fire, and some toast and water, or other slop on the hob to sip at; and if Hareton, for pity, comes to amuse him—Hareton is not bad-natured, though he's rough— they're sure to part, one swearing and the other crying. I believe the master would relish Earnshaw's thrashing him to a mummy, if he were not his son; and I'm certain he would be fit to turn him out of doors, if he knew half the nursing he gives hisseln. But then, he won't go into danger of temptation; he never enters the parlour, and should Linton show those ways in the house where he is, he sends him upstairs directly."

I divined, from this account, that utter lack of sympathy had rendered young Heathcliff selfish and disagreeable, if he were not so originally; and my interest in him, consequently, decayed, though still I was moved with a sense of grief at his lot, and a wish that he had been left with us.

Mr. Edgar encouraged me to gain information; he thought a great deal about him, I fancy, and would have run some risk to see him; and he told me once to ask the housekeeper whether he ever came into the village?

She said he had only been twice, on horseback, accompanying his father; and both times he pretended to be quite knocked up for three or four days afterwards.

That housekeeper left, if I recollect rightly, two years after he came; and another, whom I did not know, was her successor: she lives there still.

Time wore on at the Grange in its former pleasant way, till Miss Cathy reached sixteen. On the anniversary of her birth we never manifested any signs of rejoicing, because it was also the anniversary of my late mistress's death. Her father invariably spent that day alone in the library; and walked, at dusk, as far as Gimmerton kirkyard, where he would frequently prolong his stay beyond midnight. Therefore Catherine was thrown on her own resources for amusement.

This twentieth of March was a beautiful spring day, and when her father had retired, my young lady came down dressed for going out, and said she had asked to have a ramble on the edge of the moors with me; and Mr. Linton had given her leave, if we went only a short distance and were back within the hour.

"So make haste, Ellen!" she cried. "I know where I wish to go; where a colony of moor game are settled. I want to see whether they have made their nests yet."

"That must be a good distance up," I answered; "they don't breed on the edge of the moor."

"No, it's not," she said. "I've gone very near with papa."

I put on my bonnet and sallied out, thinking nothing more of the matter. She bounded before me, and returned to my side, and was off again like a young greyhound; and, at first, I found plenty of entertainment in listening to the larks singing far and near, and enjoying the sweet, warm sunshine, and watching her, my pet and my delight, with her golden ringlets flying loose behind, and her bright cheek, as soft and pure in its bloom as a wild rose, and her eyes radiant with cloudless pleasure. She was a happy creature, and an angel, in those days. It's a pity she could not be content.

"Well," said I, "where are your moor game, Miss Cathy? We should be at them—the Grange park-fence is a great way off now."

"Oh, a little further—only a little further, Ellen," was her answer, continually. "Climb to that hillock, pass that bank, and by the time you reach the other side, I shall have raised the birds."

But there were so many hillocks and banks to climb and pass, that, at length, I began to be weary, and told her we must halt, and retrace our steps.

I shouted to her, as she had outstripped me, a long way; she either did not hear or did not regard, for she still sprang on, and I was compelled to follow. Finally, she dived into a hollow; and before I came in sight of her again, she was two miles nearer Wuthering Heights than her own home; and I beheld a couple of persons arrest her, one of whom I felt convinced was Mr. Heathcliff himself.

Cathy had been caught in the fact of plundering, or, at least, hunting out the nests of the grouse.

The Heights were Heathcliff's land, and he was reproving the poacher.

"I've neither taken any nor found any," she said, as I toiled to them, expanding her hands in corroboration of the statement. "I didn't mean to take them; but papa told me there were quantities up here, and I wished to see the eggs."

Heathcliff glanced at me with an ill-meaning smile, expressing his acquaintance with the party, and, consequently, his malevolence towards it, and demanded who "papa" was?

"Mr. Linton of Thrushcross Grange," she replied. "I thought you did not know me, or you wouldn't have spoken in that way."

"You suppose papa is highly esteemed and respected then?" he said, sarcastically.

"And what are you?" inquired Catherine, gazing curiously on the speaker. "That man I've seen before. Is he your son?"

She pointed to Hareton, the other individual, who had gained nothing but increased bulk and strength by the addition of two years to his age: he seemed as awkward and rough as ever.

"Miss Cathy," I interrupted, "it will be three hours instead of one that we are out, presently. We really must go back."

"No, that man is not my son," answered Heathcliff, pushing me aside. "But I have one, and you have seen him before, too; and, though your nurse is in a hurry, I think both you and she would be the better for a little rest. Will you just turn this nab of heath,[7] and walk into my house? You'll get home earlier for the ease; and you shall receive a kind welcome."

I whispered Catherine that she mustn't, on any account, accede to the proposal; it was entirely out of the question.

"Why?" she asked, aloud. "I'm tired of running, and the ground is dewy—I can't sit here. Let us go, Ellen! Besides, he says I have seen his son. He's mistaken, I think; but I guess where he lives— at the farm-house I visited in coming from Penistone Crags. Don't you?"

"I do. Come, Nelly, hold your tongue—it will be a treat for her to look in on us. Hareton, get forwards with the lass. You shall walk with me, Nelly."

"No, she's not going to any such place," I cried, struggling to release my arm which he had seized; but she was almost at the doorstones already, scampering round the brow at full speed. Her appointed companion did not pretend to escort her; he shyed off by the road-side, and vanished.

"Mr. Heathcliff, it's very wrong," I continued; "you know you mean no good. And there she'll see Linton, and all will be told, as soon as ever we return; and I shall have the blame."

"I want her to see Linton," he answered; "he's looking better these few days; it's not often he's fit to be seen. And we'll soon persuade her to keep the visit secret—where is the harm of it?"

"The harm of it is, that her father would hate me if he found I suffered her to enter your house; and I am convinced you have a bad design in encouraging her to do so," I replied.

"My design is as honest as possible. I'll inform you of its whole scope," he said. "That the two cousins may fall in love, and get married. I'm acting generously to your master; his young chit has

7. A *nab* is an abrupt termination of a range of uplands. Emily Brontë probably has in mind the bold escarpment of Millstone Grit from which one could see the whole of the Haworth moorlands. It was known as the "Nab." She capitalizes the word on p. 265.

no expectations, and should she second my wishes, she'll be provided for, at once, as joint successor with Linton."

"If Linton died," I answered, "and his life is quite uncertain, Catherine would be the heir."

"No, she would not," he said. "There is no clause in the will to secure it so; his property would go to me; but, to prevent disputes, I desire their union, and am resolved to bring it about."

"And I'm resolved she shall never approach your house with me again," I returned, as we reached the gate, where Miss Cathy waited our coming.

Heathcliff bid me be quiet; and, preceding us up the path, hastened to open the door. My young lady gave him several looks, as if she could not exactly make up her mind what to think of him; but now he smiled when he met her eye, and softened his voice in addressing her, and I was foolish enough to imagine the memory of her mother might disarm him from desiring her injury.

Linton stood on the hearth. He had been out walking in the fields, for his cap was on, and he was calling to Joseph to bring him dry shoes.

He had grown tall of his age, still wanting some months of sixteen. His features were pretty yet, and his eye and complexion brighter than I remembered them, though with merely temporary lustre borrowed from the salubrious air and genial sun.

"Now, who is that?" asked Mr. Heathcliff, turning to Cathy. "Can you tell?"

"Your son?" she said, having doubtfully surveyed first one and then the other.

"Yes, yes," answered he; "but is this the only time you have beheld him? Think! Ah! you have a short memory. Linton, don't you recall your cousin, that you used to tease us so with wishing to see?"

"What, Linton!" cried Cathy, kindling into joyful surprise at the name. "Is that little Linton? He's taller than I am! Are you Linton?"

The youth stepped forward, and acknowledged himself: she kissed him fervently, and they gazed with wonder at the change time had wrought in the appearance of each.

Catherine had reached her full height; her figure was both plump and slender, elastic as steel, and her whole aspect sparkling with health and spirits. Linton's looks and movements were very languid, and his form extremely slight; but there was a grace in his manner that mitigated these defects, and rendered him not unpleasing.

After exchanging numerous marks of fondness with him, his cousin went to Mr. Heathcliff, who lingered by the door, dividing his attention between the objects inside and those that lay without, pretending, that is, to observe the latter, and really noting the former alone.

"And you are my uncle, then!" she cried, reaching up to salute him. "I thought I liked you, though you were cross, at first. Why don't you visit at the Grange with Linton? To live all these years such close neighbours, and never see us, is odd; what have you done so for?"

"I visited it once or twice too often before you were born," he answered. "There—damn it! If you have any kisses to spare, give them to Linton—they are thrown away on me."

"Naughty Ellen!" exclaimed Catherine, flying to attack me next with her lavish caresses. "Wicked Ellen! to try to hinder me from entering. But I'll take this walk every morning in future. May I, uncle—and sometimes bring papa? Won't you be glad to see us?"

"Of course!" replied the uncle, with a hardly supressed grimace, resulting from his deep aversion to both the proposed visitors. "But stay," he continued, turning towards the young lady. "Now I think of it, I'd better tell you. Mr. Linton has a prejudice against me; we quarrelled at one time of our lives, with unchristian ferocity; and, if you mention coming here to him, he'll put a veto on your visits altogether. Therefore, you must not mention it, unless you be careless of seeing your cousin hereafter. You may come, if you will, but you must not mention it."

"Why did you quarrel?" asked Catherine, considerably crestfallen.

"He thought me too poor to wed his sister," answered Heathcliff," and was grieved that I got her. His pride was hurt, and he'll never forgive it."

"That's wrong!" said the young lady: "some time, I'll tell him so. But Linton and I have no share in your quarrel. I'll not come here, then; he shall come to the Grange."

"It will be too far for me," murmured her cousin; "to walk four miles would kill me. No, come here, Miss Catherine, now and then, not every morning, but once or twice a week."

The father launched towards his son a glance of bitter contempt.

"I am afraid, Nelly, I shall lose my labour," he muttered to me. "Miss Catherine, as the ninny calls her, will discover his value, and send him to the devil. Now, if it had been Hareton—do you know that, twenty times a day, I covet Hareton, with all his degradation? I'd have loved the lad had he been some one else. But I think he's safe from *her* love. I'll pit him against that paltry creature, unless it bestir itself briskly. We calculate it will scarcely last till it is eighteen. Oh, confound the vapid thing. He's absorbed in drying his feet, and never looks at her—Linton!"

"Yes, father," answered the boy.

"Have you nothing to show your cousin, anywhere about; not even a rabbit, or a weasel's nest? Take her into the garden, before you change your shoes; and into the stable to see your horse."

"Wouldn't you rather sit here?" asked Linton, addressing Cathy in a tone which expressed reluctance to move again.

"I don't know," she replied, casting a longing look to the door, and evidently eager to be active.

He kept his seat, and shrank closer to the fire.

Heathcliff rose, and went into the kitchen, and from thence to the yard, calling out for Hareton.

Hareton responded, and presently the two re-entered. The young man had been washing himself, as was visible by the glow on his cheeks, and his wetted hair.

"Oh, I'll ask *you*, uncle," cried Miss Cathy, recollecting the housekeeper's assertion. "That's not my cousin, is he?"

"Yes," he replied, "Your mother's nephew. Don't you like him?"

Catherine looked queer.

"Is he not a handsome lad?" he continued.

The uncivil little thing stood on tiptoe, and whispered a sentence in Heathcliff's ear.

He laughed; Hareton darkened; I perceived he was very sensitive to suspected slights, and had obviously a dim notion of his inferiority. But his master or guardian chased the frown by exclaiming—

"You'll be the favourite among us, Hareton! She says you are a—what was it? Well, something very flattering. Here! you go with her round the farm. And behave like a gentleman, mind! Don't use any bad words; and don't stare, when the young lady is not looking at you, and be ready to hide your face when she is; and, when you speak, say your words slowly, and keep your hands out of your pockets. Be off, and entertain her as nicely as you can."

He watched the couple walking past the window. Earnshaw had his countenance completely averted from his companion. He seemed studying the familiar landscape with a stranger's and an artist's interest.

Catherine took a sly look at him, expressing small admiration. She then turned her attention to seeking out objects of amusement for herself, and tripped merrily on, lilting a tune to supply the lack of conversation.

"I've tied his tongue," observed Heathcliff. "He'll not venture a single syllable, all the time! Nelly, you recollect me at his age—nay, some years younger. Did I ever look so stupid, so 'gaumless,'[8] as Joseph calls it?"

8. Witless, lacking in understanding.

"Worse," I replied, "because more sullen with it."

"I've a pleasure in him," he continued reflecting aloud. "He has satisfied my expectations. If he were a born fool I should not enjoy it half so much. But he's no fool; and I can sympathise with all his feelings, having felt them myself. I know what he suffers now, for instance, exactly—it is merely a beginning of what he shall suffer, though. And he'll never be able to emerge from his bathos of coarseness and ignorance. I've got him faster than his scoundrel of a father secured me, and lower; for he takes a pride in his brutishness. I've taught him to scorn everything extra-animal as silly and weak. Don't you think Hindley would be proud of his son, if he could see him? almost as proud as I am of mine. But there's this difference; one is gold put to the use of paving stones, and the other is tin polished to ape a service of silver. *Mine* has nothing valuable about it; yet I shall have the merit of making it go as far as such poor stuff can go. *His* had first-rate qualities, and they are lost—rendered worse than unavailing. I have nothing to regret; he would have more than any but I are aware of. And the best of it is, Hareton is damnably fond of me! You'll own that I've out-matched Hindley there. If the dead villain could rise from his grave to abuse me for his offspring's wrongs, I should have the fun of seeing the said offspring fight him back again, indignant that he should dare to rail at the one friend he has in the world!"

Heathcliff chuckled a fiendish laugh at the idea; I made no reply, because I saw that he expected none.

Meantime, our young companion, who sat too removed from us to hear what was said, began to evince symptoms of uneasiness, probably repenting that he had denied himself the treat of Catherine's society for fear of a little fatigue.

His father remarked the restless glances wandering to the window, and the hand irresolutely extended towards his cap.

"Get up, you idle boy!" he exclaimed with assumed heartiness. "Away after them! they are just at the corner, by the stand of hives."

Linton gathered his energies, and left the hearth. The lattice was open, and, as he stepped out, I heard Cathy inquiring of her unsociable attendant, what was that inscription over the door?

Hareton stared up, and scratched his head like a true clown.

"It's some damnable writing," he answered. "I cannot read it."

"Can't read it?" cried Catherine; "I can read it: it's English. But I want to know why it is there."

Linton giggled—the first appearance of mirth he had exhibited.

"He does not know his letters," he said to his cousin. "Could you believe in the existence of such a colossal dunce?"

"Is he all as he should be?" asked Miss Cathy seriously, "or is he simple—not right? I've questioned him twice now, and each time he looked so stupid I think he does not understand me; I can hardly understand *him*, I'm sure!"

Linton repeated his laugh, and glanced at Hareton tauntingly, who certainly did not seem quite clear of comprehension at that moment.

"There's nothing the matter but laziness, is there, Earnshaw?" he said. "My cousin fancies you are an idiot. There you experience the consequence of scorning 'book-larning,' as you would say. Have you noticed, Catherine, his frightful Yorkshire pronunciation?"

"Why, where the devil is the use on't?" growled Hareton, more ready in answering his daily companion. He was about to enlarge further, but the two youngsters broke into a noisy fit of merriment; my giddy Miss being delighted to discover that she might turn his strange talk to matter of amusement.

"Where is the use of the devil in that sentence?" tittered Linton. "Papa told you not to say any bad words, and you can't open your mouth without one. Do try to behave like a gentleman, now do!"

"If thou weren't more a lass than a lad, I'd fell thee this minute, I would; pitiful lath of a crater!" retorted the angry boor, retreating, while his face burnt with mingled rage and mortification; for he was conscious of being insulted, and embarrassed how to resent it.

Mr. Heathcliff, having overheard the conversation as well as I, smiled when he saw him go, but immediately afterwards cast a look of singular aversion on the flippant pair, who remained chattering in the door-way: the boy finding animation enough while discussing Hareton's faults and deficiencies, and relating anecdotes of his goings on; and the girl relishing his pert and spiteful sayings, without considering the ill-nature they evinced. But I began to dislike, more than to compassionate, Linton, and to excuse his father, in some measure, for holding him cheap.

We stayed till afternoon: I could not tear Miss Cathy away, before: but happily my master had not quitted his apartment, and remained ignorant of our prolonged absence.

As we walked home, I would fain have enlightened my charge on the characters of the people we had quitted; but she got it into her head that I was prejudiced against them.

"Aha!" she cried, "you take papa's side, Ellen—you are partial, I know, or else you wouldn't have cheated me so many years into the notion that Linton lived a long way from here. I'm really extremely angry, only I'm so pleased, I can't show it! But you must hold your tongue about my uncle: he's *my* uncle, remember, and I'll scold papa for quarrelling with him."

And so she ran on, till I dropped endeavouring to convince her of her mistake.

She did not mention the visit that night, because she did not see Mr. Linton. Next day it all came out, sadly to my chagrin; and still I was not altogether sorry: I thought the burden of directing and warning would be more efficiently borne by him than me, but he was too timid in giving satisfactory reasons for his wish that she would shun connection with the household of the Heights, and Catherine liked good reasons for every restraint that harassed her petted will.

"Papa!" she exclaimed, after the morning's salutations, "guess whom I saw yesterday, in my walk on the moors. Ah, papa, you started! you've not done right, have you, now? I saw—But listen, and you shall hear how I found you out, and Ellen, who is in league with you, and yet pretended to pity me so, when I kept hoping, and was always disappointed about Linton's coming back!"

She gave a faithful account of her excursion and its consequences; and my master, though he cast more than one reproachful look at me, said nothing till she had concluded. Then he drew her to him, and asked if she knew why he had concealed Linton's near neighbourhood from her? Could she think it was to deny her a pleasure that she might harmlessly enjoy?

"It was because you disliked Mr. Heathcliff," she answered.

"Then you believe I care more for my own feelings than yours, Cathy?" he said. "No, it was not because I disliked Mr. Heathcliff, but because Mr. Heathcliff dislikes me; and is a most diabolical man, delighting to wrong and ruin those he hates, if they give him the slightest opportunity. I knew that you could not keep up an acquaintance with your cousin, without being brought into contact with him; and I knew he would detest you, on my account; so, for your own good, and nothing else, I took precautions that you should not see Linton again. I meant to explain this some time as you grew older, and I'm sorry I delayed it!"

"But Mr. Heathcliff was quite cordial, papa," observed Catherine, not at all convinced; "and *he* didn't object to our seeing each other: he said I might come to his house when I pleased, only I must not tell you, because you had quarrelled with him, and would not forgive him for marrying Aunt Isabella. And you won't—*you* are the one to be blamed. He is willing to let *us* be friends—at least Linton and I—and you are not."

My master, perceiving that she would not take his word for her uncle-in-law's evil disposition, gave a hasty sketch of his conduct to Isabella, and the manner in which Wuthering Heights became his property. He could not bear to discourse long upon the topic, for though he spoke little of it, he still felt the same horror and detestation of his ancient enemy that had occupied his heart ever since Mrs. Linton's death. "She might have been living yet, if it had not been for him!" was his constant bitter reflection; and, in his eyes, Heathcliff seemed a murderer.

Miss Cathy, conversant with no bad deeds except her own slight acts of disobedience, in justice and passion, rising from hot temper and thoughtlessness, and repented of on the day they were committed, was amazed at the blackness of spirit that could brood on and cover revenge for years, and deliberately prosecute its plans, without a visitation of remorse. She appeared so deeply impressed and shocked at this new view of human nature—excluded from all her studies and all her ideas till now—that Mr. Edgar deemed it unnecessary to pursue the subject. He merely added—

"You will know hereafter, darling, why I wish you to avoid his house and family; now, return to your old employments and amusements, and think no more about them!"

Catherine kissed her father, and sat down quietly to her lessons for a couple of hours, according to custom; then she accompanied him into the grounds, and the whole day passed as usual: but in the evening, when she had retired to her room, and I went to help her to undress, I found her crying, on her knees by the bedside.

"Oh, fie, silly child!" I exclaimed. "If you had any real griefs, you'd be ashamed to waste a tear on this little contrariety. You never had one shadow of substantial sorrow, Miss Catherine. Suppose, for a minute, that master and I were dead, and you were by yourself in the world—how would you feel, then? Compare the present occasion with such an affliction as that, and be thankful for the friend you have, instead of coveting more."

"I'm not crying for myself, Ellen," she answered, "it's for him. He expected to see me again to-morrow, and there, he'll be so disappointed—and he'll wait for me, and I shan't come!"

"Nonsense!" said I, "do you imagine he has thought as much of you as you have of him? Hasn't he Hareton for a companion? Not one in a hundred would weep at losing a relation they had just seen twice, for two afternoons. Linton will conjecture how it is, and trouble himself no further about you."

"But may I not write a note to tell him why I cannot come?" she asked, rising to her feet. "And just send those books I promised to lend him? His books are not as nice as mine, and he wanted to have them extremely, when I told him how interesting they were. May I not, Ellen?"

"No, indeed, no, indeed!" replied I with decision. "Then he would write to you, and there'd never be an end of it. No, Miss Catherine, the acquaintance must be dropped entirely—so papa expects, and I shall see that it is done!"

"But how can one little note—" she recommenced, putting on an imploring countenance.

"Silence!" I interrupted. "We'll not begin with your little notes.

Get into bed!"

She threw at me a very naughty look, so naughty that I would not kiss her good-night at first: I covered her up, and shut her door, in great displeasure; but, repenting half-way, I returned softly, and lo! there was Miss, standing at the table with a bit of blank paper before her and a pencil in her hand, which she guiltily slipped out of sight, on my re-entrance.

"You'll get nobody to take that, Catherine," I said, "if you write it; and at present I shall put out your candle."

I set the extinguisher on the flame, receiving as I did so a slap on my hand, and a petulant "cross thing!" I then quitted her again, and she drew the bolt in one of her worst, most peevish humours.

The letter was finished and forwarded to its destination by a milk-fetcher who came from the village, but that I didn't learn till some time afterwards. Weeks passed on, and Cathy recovered her temper, though she grew wondrous fond of stealing off to corners by herself, and often, if I came near her suddenly while reading, she would start, and bend over the book, evidently desirous to hide it; and I detected edges of loose paper sticking out beyond the leaves.

She also got a trick of coming down early in the morning, and lingering about the kitchen, as if she were expecting the arrival of something; and she had a small drawer in a cabinet in the library, which she would trifle over for hours, and whose key she took special care to remove when she left it.

One day, as she inspected this drawer, I observed that the play-things and trinkets, which recently formed its contents, were trans-muted into bits of folded paper.

My curiosity and suspicions were roused; I determined to take a peep at her mysterious treasures; so, at night, as soon as she and my master were safe upstairs, I searched and readily found among my house keys, one that would fit the lock. Having opened, I emptied the whole contents into my apron, and took them with me to examine at leisure in my own chamber.

Though I could not but suspect, I was still surprised to discover that they were a mass of correspondence—daily almost, it must have been—from Linton Heathcliff, answers to documents for-warded by her. The earlier dated were embarrassed and short; gradually, however, they expanded into copious love letters, foolish as the age of the writer rendered natural, yet with touches, here and there, which I thought were borrowed from a more experienced source.

Some of them struck me as singularly odd compounds of ardour and flatness; commencing in strong feeling, and concluding in the affected, wordy way that a schoolboy might use to a fancied, incorporeal sweetheart.

Whether they satisfied Cathy, I don't know, but they appeared very worthless trash to me.

After turning over as many as I thought proper, I tied them in a handkerchief and set them aside, re-locking the vacant drawer.

Following her habit, my young lady descended early, and visited the kitchen: I watched her go to the door, on the arrival of a certain little boy; and, while the dairy maid filled his can, she tucked something into his jacket pocket, and plucked something out.

I went round by the garden, and laid wait for the messenger, who fought valorously to defend his trust, and we spilt the milk between us; but I succeeded in abstracting the epistle, and, threatening serious consequences if he did not look sharp home, I remained under the wall, and perused Miss Cathy's affectionate composition. It was more simple and more eloquent than her cousin's—very pretty and very silly. I shook my head, and went meditating into the house.

The day being wet, she could not divert herself with rambling about the park; so, at the conclusion of her morning studies, she resorted to the solace of the drawer. Her father sat reading at the table; and I, on purpose, had sought a bit of work in some unripped fringes of the window curtain, keeping my eye steadily fixed on her proceedings.

Never did any bird flying back to a plundered nest which it had left brim-ful of chirping young ones, express more complete despair in its anguished cries and flutterings, than she by her single "Oh!" and the change that transfigured her late happy countenance. Mr. Linton looked up.

"What is the matter, love? Have you hurt yourself?" he said.

His tone and look assured her *he* had not been the discoverer of the hoard.

"No, papa—" she gasped. "Ellen! Ellen! come upstairs—I'm sick!"

I obeyed her summons, and accompanied her out.

"Oh, Ellen! you have got them," she commenced immediately, dropping on her knees, when we were enclosed alone. "O, give them to me, and I'll never never do so again! Don't tell papa. You have not told papa, Ellen, say you have not! I've been exceedingly naughty, but I won't do it any more!"

With a grave severity in my manner, I bid her stand up.

"So," I exclaimed, "Miss Catherine, you are tolerably far on, it seems—you may well be ashamed of them! A fine bundle of trash you study in your leisure hours, to be sure: why, it's good enough to be printed! And what do you suppose the master will think, when I display it before him? I haven't shown it yet, but you needn't imagine I shall keep your ridiculous secrets. For shame! And you must have led the way in writing such absurdities; he would not have thought of beginning, I'm certain."

"I didn't! I didn't!" sobbed Cathy, fit to break her heart. "I didn't once think of loving him till—"

"*Loving!*" cried I, as scornfully as I could utter the word. "*Loving!* Did anybody ever hear the like! I might just as well talk of loving the miller who comes once a year to buy our corn. Pretty loving, indeed, and both times together you have seen Linton hardly four hours in your life! Now here is the babyish trash. I'm going with it to the library; and we'll see what your father says to such *loving.*"

She sprang at her precious epistles, but I held them above my head; and then she poured out further frantic entreaties that I would burn them—do anything rather than show them. And being really fully as inclined to laugh as scold, for I esteemed it all girlish vanity, I at length relented in a measure, and asked—

"If I consent to burn them, will you promise faithfully, neither to send nor receive a letter again, nor a book—for I perceive you have sent him books—nor locks of hair, nor rings, nor playthings?"

"We don't send playthings!" cried Catherine, her pride overcoming her shame.

"Nor anything at all, then, my lady!" I said. "Unless you will, here I go."

"I promise, Ellen!" she cried, catching my dress. "Oh, put them in the fire, do, do!"

But when I proceeded to open a place with the poker, the sacrifice was too painful to be borne. She earnestly supplicated that I would spare her one or two.

"One or two, Ellen, to keep for Linton's sake!"

I unknotted the handkerchief, and commenced dropping them in from an angle, and the flame curled up the chimney.

"I will have one, you cruel wretch!" she screamed, darting her hand into the fire, and drawing forth some half consumed fragments, at the expense of her fingers.

"Very well—and I will have some to exhibit to papa!" I answered, shaking back the rest into the bundle, and turning anew to the door.

She emptied her blackened pieces into the flames, and motioned me to finish the immolation. It was done; I stirred up the ashes, and interred them under a shovel-full of coals; and she mutely, and with a sense of intense injury, retired to her private apartment. I descended to tell my master that the young lady's qualm of sickness was almost gone, but I judged it best for her to lie down a while.

She wouldn't dine; but she re-appeared at tea, pale and red about the eyes, and marvellously subdued in outward aspect.

Next morning, I answered the letter by a slip of paper inscribed, "Master Heathcliff is requested to send no more notes to Miss Linton, as she will not receive them." And, thenceforth, the little boy came with vacant pockets.

Chapter XXII

Summer drew to an end, and early Autumn: it was past Michaelmas, but the harvest was late that year, and a few of our fields were still uncleared.

Mr. Linton and his daughter would frequently walk out among the reapers; at the carrying of the last sheaves, they stayed till dusk, and the evening happening to be chill and damp, my master caught a bad cold, that, settling obstinately on his lungs, confined him indoors throughout the whole of the winter, nearly without intermission.

Poor Cathy, frightened from her little romance, had been considerably sadder and duller since its abandonment; and her father insisted on her reading less, and taking more exercise. She had his companionship no longer; I esteemed it a duty to supply its lack, as much as possible, with mine: an inefficient substitute, for I could only spare two or three hours, from my numerous diurnal occupations, to follow her footsteps, and then my society was obviously less desirable than his.

On an afternoon in October, or the beginning of November— a fresh watery afternoon, when the turf and paths were rustling with moist, withered leaves, and the cold, blue sky was half hidden by clouds, dark grey streamers, rapidly mounting from the west, and boding abundant rain—I requested my young lady to forego her ramble because I was certain of showers. She refused; and I unwillingly donned a cloak, and took my umbrella to accompany her on a stroll to the bottom of the park: a formal walk which she generally affected if low-spirited—and that she invariably was when Mr. Edgar had been worse than ordinary; a thing never known from his confession, but guessed both by her and me from his increased silence, and the melancholy of his countenance.

She went sadly on: there was no running or bounding now, though the chill wind might well have tempted her to a race. And often, from the side of my eye, I could detect her raising a hand, and brushing something off her cheek.

I gazed round for a means of diverting her thoughts. On one side of the road rose a high, rough bank, where hazels and stunted oaks, with their roots half exposed, held uncertain tenure: the soil was too loose for the latter; and strong winds had blown some nearly horizontal. In summer, Miss Catherine delighted to climb along these trunks, and sit in the branches, swinging twenty feet above the ground; and I, pleased with her agility, and her light, childish heart, still considered it proper to scold every time I caught her at such an elevation, but so that she knew there was no necessity for descending. From dinner to tea she would lie in her breeze-rocked cradle, doing nothing except singing old songs—my nursery lore— to herself, or watching the birds, joint tenants, feed and entice their young ones to fly, or nestling with closed lids, half thinking, half dreaming, happier than words can express.

"Look, Miss!" I exclaimed, pointing to a nook under the roots of one twisted tree. "Winter is not here yet. There's a little flower, up yonder, the last bud from the multitude of blue-bells that clouded those turf steps in July with a lilac mist. Will you clamber up, and pluck it to show to papa?"

Cathy stared a long time at the lonely blossom trembling in its earthy shelter, and replied, at length—

"No, I'll not touch it—but it looks melancholy, does it not, Ellen?"

"Yes," I observed, "about as starved and sackless [9] as you— your cheeks are bloodless; let us take hold of hands and run. You're so low, I dare say I shall keep up with you."

"No," she repeated, and continued sauntering on, pausing, at intervals, to muse over a bit of moss, or a tuft of blanched grass, or a fungus spreading its bright orange among the heaps of brown foliage; and, ever and anon, her hand was lifted to her averted face.

"Catherine, why are you crying, love?" I asked, approaching and putting my arm over her shoulder. "You mustn't cry because papa has a cold; be thankful it is nothing worse."

She now put no further restraint on her tears; her breath was stifled by sobs.

"Oh, it *will* be something worse," she said. "And what shall I do when papa and you leave me, and I am by myself? I can't forget your words, Ellen, they are always in my ear. How life will be changed, how dreary the world will be, when papa and you are dead."

"None can tell, whether you won't die before us," I replied. "It's wrong to anticipate evil. We'll hope there are years and years to come before any of us go: master is young, and I am strong, and hardly forty-five. My mother lived till eighty, a canty [1] dame to the last. And suppose Mr. Linton were spared till he saw sixty, that would be more years than you have counted, Miss. And would

9. Feeble.   1. Brisk, lively.

it not be foolish to mourn a calamity above twenty years before-hand?"

"But Aunt Isabella was younger than papa," she remarked, gaz-ing up with timid hope to seek further consolation.

"Aunt Isabella had not you and me to nurse her," I replied. "She wasn't as happy as master; she hadn't as much to live for. All you need do, is to wait well on your father, and cheer him by letting him see you cheerful; and avoid giving him anxiety on any sub-ject—mind that, Cathy! I'll not disguise but you might kill him, if you were wild and reckless, and cherished a foolish, fanciful af-fection for the son of a person who would be glad to have him in his grave; and allowed him to discover that you fretted over the separation he has judged it expedient to make."

"I fret about nothing on earth except papa's illness," answered my companion. "I care for nothing in comparison with papa. And I'll never—never—oh, never, while I have my senses, do an act, or say a word to vex him. I love him better than myself, Ellen; and I know it by this: I pray every night that I may live after him, because I would rather be miserable than that he should be —that proves I love him better than myself."

"Good words," I replied. "But deeds must prove it also; and after he is well, remember you don't forget resolutions formed in the hour of fear."

As we talked, we neared a door that opened on the road; and my young lady, lightening into sunshine again, climbed up, and seated herself on the top of the wall, reaching over to gather some hips that bloomed scarlet on the summit branches of the wild rose trees, shadowing the highway side; the lower fruit had disappeared, but only birds could touch the upper, except from Cathy's present station.

In stretching to pull them, her hat fell off; and as the door was locked, she proposed scrambling down to recover it. I bid her be cautious lest she got a fall, and she nimbly disappeared.

But the return was no such easy matter; the stones were smooth and neatly cemented, and the rosebushes and blackberry stragglers could yield no assistance in re-ascending. I, like a fool, didn't rec-ollect that till I heard her laughing, and exclaiming—

"Ellen! you'll have to fetch the key, or else I must run round to the porter's lodge. I can't scale the ramparts on this side!"

"Stay where you are," I answered, "I have my bundle of keys in my pocket; perhaps I may manage to open it; if not, I'll go."

Catherine amused herself with dancing to and fro before the door, while I tried all the large keys in succession. I had applied the last, and found that none would do; so, repeating my desire that she would remain there, I was about to hurry home as fast as

I could, when an approaching sound arrested me. It was the trot of a horse; Cathy's dance stopped, and in a minute the horse stopped also.

"Who is that?" I whispered.

"Ellen, I wish you could open the door," whispered back my companion, anxiously.

"Ho, Miss Linton!" cried a deep voice (the rider's). "I'm glad to meet you. Don't be in haste to enter, for I have an explanation to ask and obtain."

"I shan't speak to you, Mr. Heathcliff!" answered Catherine. "Papa says you are a wicked man, and you hate both him and me; and Ellen says the same."

"That is nothing to the purpose," said Heathcliff. (He it was.) "I don't hate my son, I suppose, and it is concerning him that I demand your attention. Yes! you have cause to blush. Two or three months since, were you not in the habit of writing to Linton? making love in play, eh? You deserved, both of you, flogging for that! You especially, the elder, and less sensitive, as it turns out. I've got your letters, and if you give me any pertness, I'll send them to your father. I presume you grew weary of the amusement, and dropped it, didn't you? Well, you dropped Linton with it, into a Slough of Despond. He was in earnest—in love—really. As true as I live, he's dying for you—breaking his heart at your fickleness, not figuratively, but actually. Though Hareton has made him a standing jest for six weeks, and I have used more serious measures, and attempted to frighten him out of his idiocy, he gets worse daily, and he'll be under the sod before summer, unless you restore him!"

"How can you lie so glaringly to the poor child!" I called from the inside. "Pray ride on! How can you deliberately get up such paltry falsehoods? Miss Cathy, I'll knock the lock off with a stone. You won't believe that vile nonsense. You can feel in yourself, it is impossible that a person should die for love of a stranger."

"I was not aware there were eaves-droppers," muttered the detected villain. "Worthy Mrs. Dean, I like you, but I don't like your double dealing," he added, aloud. "How could *you* lie so glaringly, as to affirm I hated the 'poor child'? And invent bugbear stories to terrify her from my door-stones? Catherine Linton (the very name warms me), my bonny lass, I shall be from home all this week; go and see if I have not spoken truth; do, there's a darling! Just imagine your father in my place, and Linton in yours; then think how you would value your careless lover, if he refused to stir a step to comfort you, when your father, himself, entreated him; and don't, from pure stupidity, fall into the same error. I swear, on my salvation, he's going to his grave, and none but you can save him!"

The lock gave way, and I issued out.

"I swear Linton is dying," repeated Heathcliff, looking hard at me. "And grief and disappointment are hastening his death. Nelly, if you won't let her go, you can walk over yourself. But I shall not return till this time next week; and I think your master would scarcely object to her visiting her cousin!"

"Come in," said I, taking Cathy by the arm and half forcing her to re-enter, for she lingered, viewing with troubled eyes, the features of the speaker, too stern to express his inward deceit.

He pushed his horse close, and, bending down, observed—

"Miss Catherine, I'll own to you that I have little patience with Linton—and Hareton and Joseph have less. I'll own that he's with a harsh set. He pines for kindness, as well as love; and a kind word from you would be his best medicine. Don't mind Mrs. Dean's cruel cautions, but be generous, and contrive to see him. He dreams of you day and night, and cannot be persuaded that you don't hate him, since you neither write nor call."

I closed the door, and rolled a stone to assist the loosened lock in holding it; and spreading my umbrella, I drew my charge underneath, for the rain began to drive through the moaning branches of the trees, and warned us to avoid delay.

Our hurry prevented any comment on the encounter with Heathcliff, as we stretched towards home; but I divined instinctively that Catherine's heart was clouded now in double darkness. Her features were so sad, they did not seem hers: she evidently regarded what she had heard as every syllable true.

The master had retired to rest before we came in. Cathy stole to his room to inquire how he was; he had fallen asleep. She returned, and asked me to sit with her in the library. We took our tea together; and afterwards she lay down on the rug, and told me not to talk, for she was weary.

I got a book, and pretended to read. As soon as she supposed me absorbed in my occupation, she recommenced her silent weeping: it appeared, at present, her favourite diversion. I suffered her to enjoy it a while; then I expostulated, deriding and ridiculing all Mr. Heathcliff's assertions about his son, as if I were certain she would coincide. Alas! I hadn't the skill to counteract the effect his account had produced; it was just what he intended.

"You may be right, Ellen," she answered; "but I shall never feel at ease till I know. And I must tell Linton it is not my fault that I don't write; and convince him that I shall not change."

What use were anger and protestations against her silly credulity? We parted that night hostile; but next day beheld me on the road to Wuthering Heights, by the side of my wilful young mistress's pony. I couldn't bear to witness her sorrow, to see her pale, dejected countenance, and heavy eyes; and I yielded in the faint hope that Linton himself might prove, by his reception of us, how little of the tale was founded on fact.

Chapter XXIII

The rainy night had ushered in a misty morning—half frost, half drizzle—and temporary brooks crossed our path, gurgling from the uplands. My feet were thoroughly wetted; I was cross and low, exactly the humour suited for making the most of these disagreeable things.

We entered the farm-house by the kitchen way to ascertain whether Mr. Heathcliff were really absent, because I put slight faith in his own affirmation.

Joseph seemed sitting in a sort of elysium alone, beside a roaring fire; a quart of ale on the table near him, bristling with large pieces of toasted oat cake, and his black, short pipe in his mouth.

Catherine ran to the hearth to warm herself. I asked if the master were in?

My question remained so long unanswered, that I thought the old man had grown deaf, and repeated it louder.

"Na—ay!" he snarled, or rather screamed through his nose. "Na—ay! yah muh goa back whear yah coom frough."

"Joseph!" cried a peevish voice, simultaneously with me, from the inner room. "How often am I to call you? There are only a few red ashes now. Joseph! come this moment."

Vigorous puffs, and a resolute stare into the grate, declared he had no ear for this appeal. The housekeeper and Hareton were invisible; one gone on an errand, and the other at his work, probably. We knew Linton's tones and entered.

"Oh, I hope you'll die in a garret! starved to death," said the boy, mistaking our approach for that of his negligent attendant.

He stopped, on observing his error; his cousin flew to him.

"Is that you, Miss Linton?" he said, raising his head from the arm of the great chair in which he reclined. "No—don't kiss me. It takes my breath—dear me! Papa said you would call," continued he, after recovering a little from Catherine's embrace, while she stood by looking very contrite. "Will you shut the door, if you please? you left it open, and those—those *detestable* creatures won't bring coals to the fire. It's so cold!"

I stirred up the cinders, and fetched a scuttle-full myself. The invalid complained of being covered with ashes; but he had a tiresome cough, and looked feverish and ill, so I did not rebuke his temper.

"Well, Linton," murmured Catherine, when his corrugated brow relaxed. "Are you glad to see me? Can I do you any good?"

"Why didn't you come before?" he said. "You should have come, instead of writing. It tired me dreadfully, writing those long letters. I'd far rather have talked to you. Now, I can neither bear to talk, nor anything else. I wonder where Zillah is! Will you (looking at me) step into the kitchen and see?"

I had received no thanks for my other service; and being unwilling to run to and fro at his behest, I replied—

"Nobody is out there but Joseph."

"I want to drink," he exclaimed, fretfully, turning away. "Zillah is constantly gadding off to Gimmerton since papa went. It's miserable! And I'm obliged to come down here—they resolved never to hear me upstairs."

"Is your father attentive to you, Master Heathcliff?" I asked, perceiving Catherine to be checked in her friendly advances.

"Attentive? He makes *them* a little more attentive, at least," he cried. "The wretches! Do you know, Miss Linton, that brute Hareton laughs at me. I hate him—indeed, I hate them all—they are odious beings."

Cathy began searching for some water; she lighted on a pitcher in the dresser, filled a tumbler, and brought it. He bid her add a spoonful of wine from a bottle on the table; and, having swallowed a small portion, appeared more tranquil, and said she was very kind.

"And are you glad to see me?" asked she, reiterating her former question, and pleased to detect the faint dawn of a smile.

"Yes, I am. It's something new to hear a voice like yours!" he replied, "but I *have* been vexed, because you wouldn't come. And papa swore it was owing to me; he called me a pitiful, shuffling, worthless thing; and said you despised me; and if he had been in my place, he would be more the master of the Grange than your father, by this time. But you don't despise me, do you, Miss—"

"I wish you would say Catherine, or Cathy!" interrupted my young lady. "Despise you? No! Next to papa, and Ellen, I love you better than anybody living. I don't love Mr. Heathcliff, though; and I dare not come when he returns; will he stay away many days?"

"Not many," answered Linton, "but he goes onto the moors frequently, since the shooting season commenced, and you might spend an hour or two with me, in his absence. Do! say you will! I think I should not be peevish with you; you'd not provoke me, and you'd always be ready to help me, wouldn't you?"

"Yes," said Catherine, stroking his long soft hair; "if I could only get papa's consent, I'd spend half my time with you. Pretty Linton! I wish you were my brother!"

"And then you would like me as well as your father?" observed he, more cheerfully. "But papa says you would love me better than him and all the world, if you were my wife—so I'd rather you were that!"

"No! I should never love anybody better than papa," she returned gravely. "And people hate their wives, sometimes; but not their sisters and brothers, and if you were the latter, you would live with us, and papa would be as fond of you as he is of me."

Linton denied that people ever hated their wives; but Cathy affirmed they did, and in her wisdom, instanced his own father's aversion to her aunt.

I endeavoured to stop her thoughtless tongue. I couldn't succeed till everything she knew was out. Master Heathcliff, much irritated, asserted her relation was false.

"Papa told me; and papa does not tell falsehoods!" she answered pertly.

"*My* papa scorns yours!" cried Linton. "He calls him a sneaking fool!"

"Yours is a wicked man," retorted Catherine, "and you are very naughty to dare to repeat what he says. He must be wicked, to have made Aunt Isabella leave him as she did!"

"She didn't leave him," said the boy; "you shan't contradict me!"

"She did!" cried my young lady.

"Well, I'll tell *you* something!" said Linton. "Your mother hated your father, now then."

"Oh!" exclaimed Catherine, too enraged to continue.

"And she loved mine!" added he.

"You little liar! I hate you now," she panted, and her face grew red with passion.

"She did! she did!" sang Linton, sinking into the recess of his chair, and leaning back his head to enjoy the agitation of the other disputant, who stood behind.

"Hush, Master Heathcliff!" I said; "that's your father's tale too, I suppose."

"It isn't—you hold your tongue!" he answered. "She did, she did, Catherine, she did, she did!"

Cathy, beside herself, gave the chair a violent push, and caused him to fall against one arm. He was immediately seized by a suffocating cough that soon ended his triumph.

It lasted so long that it frightened even me. As to his cousin, she wept with all her might, aghast at the mischief she had done, though she said nothing.

I held him till the fit exhausted itself. Then he thrust me away, and leant his head down, silently. Catherine quelled her lamentations also, took a seat opposite, and looked solemnly into the fire.

"How do you feel now, Master Heathcliff?" I inquired, after

waiting ten minutes.

"I wish *she* felt as I do," he replied, "spiteful, cruel thing! Hareton never touches me, he never struck me in his life. And I was better to-day—and there—" his voice died in a whimper.

"*I* didn't strike you!" muttered Cathy, chewing her lip to prevent another burst of emotion.

He sighed and moaned like one under great suffering, and kept it up for a quarter of an hour, on purpose to distress his cousin, apparently, for whenever he caught a stifled sob from her, he put renewed pain and pathos into the inflexions of his voice.

"I'm sorry I hurt you, Linton!" she said at length, racked beyond endurance. "But *I* couldn't have been hurt by that little push; and I had no idea that you could, either—you're not much, are you, Linton? Don't let me go home thinking I've done you harm! Answer, speak to me."

"I can't speak to you," he murmured, "you've hurt me so, that I shall lie awake all night, choking with this cough! If you had it you'd know what it was; but *you'll* be comfortably asleep, while I'm in agony—and nobody near me! I wonder how you would like to pass those fearful nights!" And he began to wail aloud for very pity of himself.

"Since you are in the habit of passing dreadful nights," I said, "it won't be Miss who spoils your ease; you'd be the same, had she never come. However, she shall not disturb you again—and perhaps you'll get quieter when we leave you."

"Must I go?" asked Catherine dolefully, bending over him. "Do you want me to go, Linton?"

"You can't alter what you're done," he replied pettishly, shrinking from her, "unless you alter it for the worse, by teasing me into a fever."

"Well, then I must go?" she repeated.

"Let me alone, at least," said he; "I can't bear your talking!"

She lingered, and resisted my persuasions to departure, a tiresome while, but as he neither looked up nor spoke, she finally made a movement to the door and I followed.

We were recalled by a scream. Linton had slid from his seat on to the hearthstone, and lay writhing in the mere perverseness of an indulged plague of a child, determined to be as grievous and harassing as it can.

I thoroughly gauged his disposition from his behaviour, and saw at once it would be folly to attempt humouring him. Not so my companion: she ran back in terror, knelt down, and cried, and soothed, and entreated, till he grew quiet from lack of breath, by no means from compunction at distressing her.

"I shall lift him on to the settle," I said, "and he may roll about as he pleases; we can't stop to watch him. I hope you are satisfied, Miss Cathy, that *you* are not the person to benefit him, and that his condition of health is not occasioned by attachment to you. Now then, there he is! Come away; as soon as he knows there is nobody by to care for his nonsense, he'll be glad to lie still!"

She placed a cushion under his head, and offered him some water; he rejected the latter, and tossed uneasily on the former, as if it were a stone, or a block of wood.

She tried to put it more comfortably.

"I can't do with that," he said, "it's not high enough!"

Catherine brought another to lay above it.

"That's *too* high!" murmured the provoking thing.

"How must I arrange it, then?" she asked despairingly.

He twined himself up to her, as she half knelt by the settle, and converted her shoulder into a support.

"No, that won't do!" I said. "You'll be content with the cushion, Master Heathcliff! Miss has wasted too much time on you already; we cannot remain five minutes longer."

"Yes, yes, we can!" replied Cathy. "He's good and patient, now. He's beginning to think I shall have far greater misery than he will to-night, if I believe he is the worse for my visit; and then, I dare not come again. Tell the truth about it, Linton, for I mustn't come, if I have hurt you."

"You must come, to cure me," he answered. "You ought to come because you have hurt me. You know you have, extremely! I was not as ill when you entered, as I am at present—was I?"

"But you've made yourself ill by crying, and being in a passion."

"I didn't do it all," said his cousin. "However, we'll be friends now. And you want me—you would wish to see me sometimes, really?"

"I told you I did!" he replied impatiently. "Sit on the settle and let me lean on your knee. That's as mamma used to do, whole afternoons together. Sit quite still, and don't talk, but you may sing a song if you can sing, or you may say a nice, long interesting ballad —one of those you promised to teach me—or a story. I'd rather have a ballad, though: begin."

Catherine repeated the longest she could remember. The employment pleased both mightily. Linton would have another, and after that another, notwithstanding my strenuous objections; and so they went on until the clock struck twelve, and we heard Hareton in the court, returning for his dinner.

"And to-morrow, Catherine, will you be here to-morrow?" asked young Heathcliff, holding her frock, as she rose reluctantly.

"No!" I answered, "nor next day neither." She, however, gave a different response, evidently, for his forehead cleared as she stooped and whispered in his ear.

"You won't go to-morrow, recollect, Miss!" I commenced, when we were out of the house. "You are not dreaming of it, are you?"

She smiled.

"Oh, I'll take good care!" I continued; "I'll have that lock mended, and you can escape by no way else."

"I can get over the wall," she said, laughing. "The Grange is not a prison, Ellen, and you are not my jailer. And besides, I'm almost seventeen. I'm a woman—and I'm certain Linton would recover quickly if he had me to look after him. I'm older than he is, you know, and wiser, less childish, am I not? And he'll soon do as I direct him with some slight coaxing. He's a pretty little darling when he's good. I'd make such a pet of him, if he were mine. We should never quarrel, should we, after we were used to each other? Don't you like him, Ellen?"

"Like him?" I exclaimed. "The worst-tempered bit of a sickly slip that ever struggled into its teens! Happily, as Mr. Heathcliff conjectured, he'll not win twenty! I doubt whether he'll see spring, indeed—and small loss to his family, whenever he drops off; and lucky it is for us that his father took him. The kinder he was treated, the more tedious and selfish he'd be! I'm glad you have no chance of having him for a husband, Miss Catherine!"

My companion waxed serious at hearing this speech. To speak of his death so regardlessly wounded her feelings.

"He's younger than I," she answered, after a protracted pause of meditation, "and he ought to live the longest; he will—he must live as long as I do. He's as strong now as when he first came into the North, I'm positive of that! It's only a cold that ails him, the same as papa has. You say papa will get better, and why shouldn't he?"

"Well, well," I cried, "after all, we needn't trouble ourselves; for listen, Miss—and mind, I'll keep my word—if you attempt going to Wuthering Heights again, with or without me, I shall inform Mr. Linton, and, unless he allow it, the intimacy with your cousin must not be revived."

"It has been revived!" muttered Cathy sulkily.

"Must not be continued, then!" I said.

"We'll see!" was her reply, and she set off at a gallop, leaving me to toil in the rear.

We both reached home before our dinnertime; my master supposed we had been wandering through the park, and therefore he demanded no explanation of our absence. As soon as I entered, I hastened to change my soaked shoes and stockings; but sitting such a while at the Heights had done the mischief. On the succeeding morning, I was laid up; and during three weeks I remained incapacitated for attending to my duties—a calamity never experienced prior to that period, and never, I am thankful to say, since.

My little mistress behaved like an angel in coming to wait on me, and cheer my solitude: the confinement brought me exceedingly low. It is wearisome, to a stirring active body, but few have slighter reasons for complaint than I had. The moment Catherine left Mr. Linton's room, she appeared at my bed-side. Her day was divided between us; no amusement usurped a minute: she neglected her meals, her studies, and her play; and she was the fondest nurse that ever watched. She must have had a warm heart, when she loved her father so, to give so much to me!

I said her days were divided between us; but the master retired early, and I generally needed nothing after six o'clock, thus the evening was her own.

Poor thing, I never considered what she did with herself after tea. And though frequently, when she looked in to bid me goodnight, I remarked a fresh colour in her cheeks, and a pinkness over her slender fingers; instead of fancying the hue borrowed from a cold ride across the moors, I laid it to the charge of a hot fire in the library.

Chapter XXIV

At the close of three weeks, I was able to quit my chamber, and move about the house. And on the first occasion of my sitting up in the evening, I asked Catherine to read to me, because my eyes were weak. We were in the library, the master having gone to bed: she consented, rather unwillingly, I fancied; and imagining my sort of books did not suit her, I bid her please herself in the choice of what she perused.

She selected one of her own favourites, and got forward steadily about an hour; then came frequent questions.

"Ellen, are not you tired? Hadn't you better lie down now? You'll be sick, keeping up so long, Ellen."

"No, no, dear, I'm not tired," I returned, continually.

Perceiving me immovable, she essayed another method of showing her dis-relish for her occupation. It changed to yawning, and stretching, and—

"Ellen, I'm tired."

"Give over then and talk," I answered.

That was worse: she fretted and sighed, and looked at her watch till eight; and finally went to her room, completely overdone with sleep, judging by her peevish, heavy look, and the constant rubbing she inflicted on her eyes.

The following night she seemed more impatient still; and on the third from recovering my company, she complained of a head-ache, and left me.

I thought her conduct odd; and having remained alone a long while, I resolved on going, and inquiring whether she were better, and asking her to come and lie on the sofa, instead of upstairs, in the dark.

No Catherine could I discover upstairs, and none below. The servants affirmed they had not seen her. I listened at Mr. Edgar's door—all was silence. I returned to her apartment, extinguished my candle, and seated myself in the window.

The moon shone bright; a sprinkling of snow covered the ground, and I reflected that she might, possibly, have taken it into her head to walk about the garden, for refreshment. I did detect a figure creeping along the inner fence of the park, but it was not my young mistress; on its emerging into the light, I recognised one of the grooms.

He stood a considerable period, viewing the carriage-road through the grounds; then started off at a brisk pace, as if he had detected something, and reappeared presently, leading Miss's pony; and there she was, just dismounted, and walking by its side.

The man took his charge stealthily across the grass towards the stable. Cathy entered by the casement-window of the drawing-room, and glided noiselessly up to where I awaited her.

She put the door gently to, slipped off her snowy shoes, untied her hat, and was proceeding, unconscious of my espionage, to lay aside her mantle, when I suddenly rose and revealed myself. The surprise petrified her an instant: she uttered an inarticulate exclamation, and stood fixed.

"My dear Miss Catherine," I began, too vividly impressed by her recent kindness to break into a scold, "where have you been riding out at this hour? And why should you try to deceive me, by telling a tale? Where have you been? Speak!"

"To the bottom of the park," she stammered. "I didn't tell a tale."

"And nowhere else?" I demanded.

"No," was the muttered reply.

"Oh, Catherine," I cried, sorrowfully. "You know you have been doing wrong, or you wouldn't be driven to uttering an untruth to me. That does grieve me. I'd rather be three months ill, than hear you frame a deliberate lie."

She sprang forward, and bursting into tears, threw her arms round my neck.

"Well, Ellen, I'm so afraid of you being angry," she said. "Promise not to be angry, and you shall know the very truth. I hate to hide it."

We sat down in the window-seat; I assured her I would not scold, whatever her secret might be, and I guessed it, of course; so she commenced—

"I've been to Wuthering Heights, Ellen, and I've never missed going a day since you fell ill; except thrice before, and twice after you left your room. I gave Michael books and pictures to prepare Minny every evening, and to put her back in the stable; you mustn't scold *him* either, mind. I was at the Heights by half-past six, and generally stayed till half-past eight, and then galloped home. It was not to amuse myself that I went; I was often wretched all the time. Now and then, I was happy, once in a week perhaps. At first, I expected there would be sad work persuading you to let me keep my word to Linton, for I had engaged to call again next day, when we quitted him; but, as you stayed upstairs on the morrow, I escaped that trouble; and while Michael was refastening the lock of the park door in the afternoon, I got possession of the key, and told him how my cousin wished me to visit him, because he was sick, and couldn't come to the Grange; and how papa would object to my going. And then I negotiated with him about the pony. He is fond of reading, and he thinks of leaving soon to get married, so he offered, if I would lend him books out of the library, to do what I wished; but I preferred giving him my own, and that satisfied him better.

"On my second visit, Linton seemed in lively spirits; and Zillah— that is their housekeeper—made us a clean room and a good fire, and told us that, as Joseph was out at a prayer-meeting and Hareton Earnshaw was off with his dogs—robbing our woods of pheasants, as I heard afterwards—we might do what we liked.

"She brought me some warm wine and gingerbread, and appeared exceedingly good-natured; and Linton sat in the arm-chair, and I in the little rocking chair on the hearthstone, and we laughed and talked so merrily, and found so much to say; we planned where we would go, and what we would do in summer. I needn't repeat that, because you would call it silly.

"One time, however, we were near quarrelling. He said the pleasantest manner of spending a hot July day was lying from morning till evening on a bank of heath in the middle of the moors, with the bees humming dreamily about among the bloom, and the larks singing high up over head, and the blue sky and bright sun shining steadily and cloudlessly. That was his most perfect idea of heaven's happiness. Mine was rocking in a rustling green tree, with a west wind blowing, and bright, white clouds flitting rapidly above; and not only larks, but throstles, and blackbirds, and linnets, and cuckoos pouring out music on every side, and the moors seen at a distance, broken into cool dusky dells; but close by, great swells of

long grass undulating in waves to the breeze; and woods and sounding water, and the whole world awake and wild with joy. He wanted
all to lie in an ecstacy of peace; I wanted all to sparkle, and dance
in a glorious jubilee.

"I said his heaven would be only half alive, and he said mine
would be drunk; I said I should fall asleep in his, and he said he
could not breathe in mine, and began to grow very snappish. At
last, we agreed to try both as soon as the right weather came; and
then we kissed each other and were friends. After sitting still an
hour, I looked at the great room with its smooth, uncarpeted floor,
and thought how nice it would be to play in, if we removed the
table; and I asked Linton to call Zillah in to help us, and we'd
have a game at blind-man's buff—she should try to catch us; you
used to, you know, Ellen. He wouldn't; there was no pleasure in
it, he said, but he consented to play at ball with me. We found
two in a cupboard, among a heap of old toys: tops, and hoops, and
battledores, and shuttlecocks. One was marked C., and the other
H.; I wished to have the C., because that stood for Catherine, and
the H. might be for Heathcliff, his name; but the bran came out of
H., and Linton didn't like it.

"I beat him constantly; and he got cross again, and coughed, and
returned to his chair. That night, though, he easily recovered his
good humour; he was charmed with two or three pretty songs—
your songs, Ellen; and when I was obliged to go, he begged and entreated me to come the following evening, and I promised.

"Minny and I went flying home as light as air: and I dreamt of
Wuthering Heights, and my sweet, darling cousin, till morning.

"On the morrow, I was sad; partly because you were poorly, and
partly that I wished my father knew, and approved of my excur-
sions: but it was beautiful moonlight after tea; and, as I rode on,
the gloom cleared.

"I shall have another happy evening, I thought to myself, and
what delights me more, my pretty Linton will.

"I trotted up their garden, and was turning round to the back,
when that fellow Earnshaw met me, took my bridle, and bid me
go in by the front entrance. He patted Minny's neck, and said she
was a bonny beast, and appeared as if he wanted me to speak to
him. I only told him to leave my horse alone, or else it would kick
him.

"He answered in his vulgar accent.

" 'It wouldn't do mitch hurt if it did'; and surveyed its legs with
a smile.

"I was half inclined to make it try; however, he moved off to open
the door, and, as he raised the latch, he looked up to the inscription above, and said, with a stupid mixture of awkwardness and

elation—

" 'Miss Catherine! I can read yon, nah.'

" 'Wonderful,' I exclaimed. 'Pray let us hear you—you *are* grown clever!'

"He spelt, and drawled over by syllables, the name—

" 'Hareton Earnshaw.'

" 'And the figures?' I cried, encouragingly, perceiving that he came to a dead halt.

" 'I cannot tell them yet,' he answered.

" 'Oh, you dunce!' I said, laughing heartily at his failure.

"The fool stared, with a grin hovering about his lips, and a scowl gathering over his eyes, as if uncertain whether he might not join in my mirth; whether it were not pleasant familiarity, or what it really was, contempt.

"I settled his doubts by suddenly retrieving my gravity, and desiring him to walk away, for I came to see Linton, not him.

"He reddened—I saw that by the moonlight—dropped his hand from the latch, and skulked off, a picture of mortified vanity. He imagined himself to be as accomplished as Linton, I suppose, because he could spell his own name; and was marvellously discomfited that I didn't think the same."

"Stop, Miss Catherine, dear!" I interrupted. "I shall not scold, but I don't like your conduct there. If you had remembered that Hareton was your cousin as much as Master Heathcliff, you would have felt how improper it was to behave in that way. At least, it was praiseworthy ambition for him to desire to be as accomplished as Linton; and probably he did not learn merely to show off; you had made him ashamed of his ignorance before, I have no doubt; and he wished to remedy it and please you. To sneer at his imperfect attempt was very bad breeding. Had *you* been brought up in his circumstances, would you be less rude? He was as quick and as intelligent a child as ever you were, and I'm hurt that he should be despised now, because that base Heathcliff has treated him so unjustly."

"Well, Ellen, you won't cry about it, will you?" she exclaimed, surprised at my earnestness. "But wait, and you shall hear if he conned his A B C to please me; and if it were worth while being civil to the brute. I entered; Linton was lying on the settle, and half got up to welcome me.

" 'I'm ill to-night, Catherine, love,' he said, 'and you must have all the talk, and let me listen. Come, and sit by me. I was sure you wouldn't break your word, and I'll make you promise again, before you go.'

"I knew now that I mustn't tease him, as he was ill; and I spoke softly and put no questions, and avoided irritating him in any way.

I had brought some of my nicest books for him; he asked me to read a little of one, and I was about to comply, when Earnshaw burst the door open, having gathered venom with reflection. He advanced direct to us, seized Linton by the arm, and swung him off the seat.

" 'Get to thy own room!' he said in a voice almost inarticulate with passion, and his face looked swelled and furious. 'Take her there if she comes to see thee—thou shalln't keep me out of this. Begone, wi' ye both!'

"He swore at us, and left Linton no time to answer, nearly throwing him into the kitchen; and he clenched his fist, as I followed, seemingly longing to knock me down. I was afraid, for a moment, and I let one volume fall; he kicked it after me, and shut us out.

"I heard a malignant, crackly laugh by the fire, and turning, beheld that odious Joseph, standing rubbing his bony hands, and quivering.

" 'Aw wer sure he'd sarve ye eht! He's a grand lad! He's getten t'raight sperrit in him! *He* knaws—Aye, he knaws, as weel as Aw do, who sud be t'maister yonder. Ech, ech, ech! He mad ye skift properly! Ech, ech, ech!'[2]

" 'Where must we go?' I said to my cousin, disregarding the old wretch's mockery.

"Linton was white and trembling. He was not pretty then, Ellen. Oh, no! he looked frightful! for his thin face and large eyes were wrought into an expression of frantic, powerless fury. He grasped the handle of the door, and shook it—it was fastened inside.

" 'If you don't let me in, I'll kill you! If you don't let me in, I'll kill you!' he rather shrieked than said. 'Devil! devil! I'll kill you, I'll kill you!'

"Joseph uttered his croaking laugh again.

" 'Thear, that's t'father!' he cried. 'That's father! We've allas summut uh orther side[3] in us. Niver heed Hareton, lad—dunnut be 'feard—he cannot get at thee!'

"I took hold of Linton's hands, and tried to pull him away; but he shrieked so shockingly that I dared not proceed. At last, his cries were choked by a dreadful fit of coughing; blood gushed from his mouth, and he fell on the ground.

"I ran into the yard, sick with terror; and called for Zillah, as loud as I could. She soon heard me; she was milking the cows in a shed behind the barn, and hurrying from her work, she inquired what there was to do?

"I hadn't breath to explain; dragging her in, I looked about for Linton. Earnshaw had come out to examine the mischief he had

2. *Sarve ye eht:* punish you, give you what's coming; *skift:* move.

3. Something of (the) other side (i.e., something inherited from Heathcliff).

caused, and he was then conveying the poor thing upstairs. Zillah and I ascended after him; but he stopped me at the top of the steps, and said I shouldn't go in, I must go home.

"I exclaimed that he had killed Linton and I *would* enter.

"Joseph locked the door, and declared I should do 'no sich stuff,' and asked me whether I were 'bahn[4] to be as mad as him.'

"I stood crying, till the housekeeper re-appeared; she affirmed he would be better in a bit, but he couldn't do with that shrieking and din, and she took me, and nearly carried me into the house.

"Ellen, I was ready to tear my hair off my head! I sobbed and wept so that my eyes were almost blind; and the ruffian you have such sympathy with stood opposite, presuming every now and then to bid me 'wisht,' and denying that it was his fault; and finally, frightened by my assertions that I would tell papa, and that he should be put in prison and hanged, he commenced blubbering himself, and hurried out to hide his cowardly agitation.

"Still, I was not rid of him: when at length they compelled me to depart, and I had got some hundred yards off the premises, he suddenly issued from the shadow of the road-side, and checked Minny and took hold of me.

"'Miss Catherine, I'm ill grieved,' he began, 'but it's rayther too bad—'

"I gave him a cut with my whip, thinking perhaps he would murder me. He let go, thundering one of his horrid curses, and I galloped home more than half out of my senses.

"I didn't bid you good-night, that evening; and I didn't go to Wuthering Heights, the next. I wished to, exceedingly; but I was strangely excited, and dreaded to hear that Linton was dead, sometimes; and sometimes shuddered at the thoughts of encountering Hareton.

"On the third day I took courage; at least, I couldn't bear longer suspense and stole off once more. I went at five o'clock, and walked, fancying I might manage to creep into the house, and up to Linton's room, unobserved. However, the dogs gave notice of my approach: Zillah received me, and saying 'the lad was mending nicely,' showed me into a small, tidy, carpeted apartment, where, to my inexpressible joy, I beheld Linton laid on a little sofa, reading one of my books. But he would neither speak to me nor look at me, through a whole hour, Ellen. He has such an unhappy temper—and what quite confounded me, when he did open his mouth it was to utter the falsehood that I had occasioned the uproar, and Hareton was not to blame!

"Unable to reply, except passionately, I got up and walked from the room. He sent after me a faint 'Catherine!' He did not reckon

4. Born.

on being answered so, but I wouldn't turn back; and the morrow was the second day on which I stayed at home, nearly determined to visit him no more.

"But it was so miserable going to bed, and getting up, and never hearing anything about him, that my resolution melted into air before it was properly formed. It *had* appeared wrong to take the journey once; now it seemed wrong to refrain. Michael came to ask if he must saddle Minny; I said 'Yes,' and considered myself doing a duty as she bore me over the hills.

"I was forced to pass the front windows to get to the court; it was no use trying to conceal my presence.

" 'Young master is in the house,' said Zillah, as she saw me making for the parlour.

"I went in; Earnshaw was there also, but he quitted the room directly. Linton sat in the great arm chair half asleep; walking up to the fire, I began in a serious tone, partly meaning it to be true—

" 'As you don't like me, Linton, and as you think I come on purpose to hurt you, and pretend that I do so every time, this is our last meeting—let us say good-bye; and tell Mr. Heathcliff that you have no wish to see me, and that he mustn't invent any more falsehoods on the subject.'

" 'Sit down and take your hat off, Catherine,' he answered. 'You are so much happier than I am, you ought to be better. Papa talks enough of my defects, and shows enough scorn of me, to make it natural I should doubt myself. I doubt whether I am not altogether as worthless as he calls me, frequently; and then I feel so cross and bitter, I hate everybody! I *am* worthless, and bad in temper, and bad in spirit, almost always—and if you choose, you *may* say good-bye. You'll get rid of an annoyance. Only, Catherine, do me this justice; believe that if I might be as sweet, and as kind, and as good as you are, I would be, as willingly and more so, than as happy and as healthy. And believe that your kindness has made me love you deeper than if I deserved your love, and though I couldn't, and cannot help showing my nature to you, I regret it and repent it, and shall regret and repent it, till I die!'

"I felt he spoke the truth; and I felt I must forgive him; and, though he should quarrel the next moment, I must forgive him again. We were reconciled, but we cried, both of us, the whole time I stayed. Not entirely for sorrow, yet I *was* sorry Linton had that distorted nature. He'll never let his friends be at ease, and he'll never be at ease himself!

"I have always gone to his little parlour, since that night; because his father returned the day after. About three times, I think, we have been merry and hopeful, as we were the first evening; the rest of my visits were dreary and troubled—now, with his selfishness and spite; and now, with his sufferings: but I've learnt to endure the former with nearly as little resentment as the latter.

"Mr. Heathcliff purposely avoids me. I have hardly seen him at all. Last Sunday, indeed, coming earlier than usual, I heard him abusing poor Linton, cruelly, for his conduct of the night before. I can't tell how he knew of it, unless he listened. Linton had certainly behaved provokingly; however, it was the business of nobody but me; and I interrupted Mr. Heathcliff's lecture by entering and telling him so. He burst into a laugh, and went away, saying he was glad I took that view of the matter. Since then, I've told Linton he must whisper his bitter things.

"Now, Ellen, you have heard all; and I can't be prevented from going to Wuthering Heights, except by inflicting misery on two people; whereas, if you'll only not tell papa, my going need disturb the tranquillity of none. You'll not tell, will you? It will be very heartless if you do."

"I'll make up my mind on that point by to-morrow, Miss Catherine," I replied. "It requires some study; and so I'll leave you to your rest, and go think it over."

I thought it over aloud, in my master's presence; walking straight from her room to his, and relating the whole story, with the exception of her conversations with her cousin, and any mention of Hareton.

Mr. Linton was alarmed and distressed more than he would acknowledge to me. In the morning, Catherine learnt my betrayal of her confidence, and she learnt also that her secret visits were to end.

In vain she wept and writhed against the interdict, and implored her father to have pity on Linton: all she got to comfort her was a promise that he would write, and give him leave to come to the Grange when he pleased; but explaining that he must no longer expect to see Catherine at Wuthering Heights. Perhaps, had he been aware of his nephew's disposition and state of health, he would have seen fit to withhold even that slight consolation.

Chapter XXV

"These things happened last winter, sir," said Mrs. Dean; "hardly more than a year ago. Last winter, I did not think, at another twelve months' end, I should be amusing a stranger to the family with relating them! Yet, who knows how long you'll be a stranger? You're too young to rest always contented, living by yourself; and I some way fancy no one could see Catherine Linton, and not love her. You smile; but why do you look so lively and interested, when

I talk about her? and why have you asked me to hang her picture over your fireplace? and why—"

"Stop, my good friend!" I cried. "It may be very possible that I should love her; but would she love me? I doubt it too much to venture my tranquillity by running into temptation; and then my home is not here. I'm of the busy world, and to its arms I must return. Go on. Was Catherine obedient to her father's commands?"

"She was," continued the housekeeper. "Her affection for him was still the chief sentiment in her heart; and he spoke without anger. He spoke in the deep tenderness of one about to leave his treasures amid perils and foes, where his remembered words would be the only aid that he could bequeath to guide her.

He said to me, a few days afterwards—

"I wish my nephew would write, Ellen, or call. Tell me, sincerely, what you think of him—is he changed for the better, or is there a prospect of improvement, as he grows a man?"

"He's very delicate, sir," I replied; "and scarcely likely to reach manhood; but this I can say, he does not resemble his father; and if Miss Catherine had the misfortune to marry him, he would not be beyond her control, unless she were extremely and foolishly indulgent. However, master, you'll have plenty of time to get acquainted with him, and see whether he would suit her: it wants four years and more to his being of age."

Edgar sighed; and, walking to the window, looked out towards Gimmerton Kirk. It was a misty afternoon, but the February sun shone dimly, and we could just distinguish the two fir trees in the yard, and the sparely scattered gravestones.

"I've prayed often," he half soliloquized, "for the approach of what is coming; and now I begin to shrink, and fear it. I thought the memory of the hour I came down that glen a bridegroom would be less sweet than the anticipation that I was soon, in a few months, or, possibly, weeks, to be carried up, and laid in its lonely hollow! Ellen, I've been very happy with my little Cathy. Through winter nights and summer days she was a living hope at my side. But I've been as happy musing by myself among those stones, under that old church—lying, through the long June evenings, on the green mound of her mother's grave, and wishing, yearning for the time when I might lie beneath it. What can I do for Cathy? How must I quit her? I'd not care one moment for Linton being Heathcliff's son; nor for his taking her from me, if he could console her for my loss. I'd not care that Heathcliff gained his ends, and triumphed in robbing me of my last blessing! But should Linton be unworthy —only a feeble tool to his father—I cannot abandon her to him! And, hard though it be to crush her buoyant spirit, I must persevere in making her sad while I live, and leaving her solitary when I die. Darling! I'd rather resign her to God, and lay her in the earth before me."

"Resign her to God, as it is, sir," I answered, "and if we should lose you—which may He forbid—under His providence, I'll stand her friend and counsellor to the last. Miss Catherine is a good girl; I don't fear that she will go wilfully wrong; and people who do their duty are always finally rewarded."

Spring advanced; yet my master gathered no real strength, though he resumed his walks in the grounds with his daughter. To her inexperienced notions, this itself was a sign of convalescence; and then his cheek was often flushed, and his eyes were bright: she felt sure of his recovering.

On her seventeenth birthday, he did not visit the churchyard; it was raining, and I observed—

"You'll surely not go out to-night, sir?"

He answered—

"No, I'll defer it this year, a little longer."

He wrote again to Linton, expressing his great desire to see him; and, had the invalid been presentable, I've no doubt his father would have permitted him to come. As it was, being instructed, he returned an answer, intimating that Mr. Heathcliff objected to his calling at the Grange; but his uncle's kind remembrance delighted him, and he hoped to meet him, sometimes, in his rambles, and personally to petition that his cousin and he might not remain long so utterly divided.

That part of his letter was simple, and probably his own. Heathcliff knew he could plead eloquently enough for Catherine's company, then—

"I do not ask," he said, "that she may visit here; but am I never to see her, because my father forbids me to go to her home, and you forbid her to come to mine? Do, now and then, ride with her towards the Heights; and let us exchange a few words, in your presence! We have done nothing to deserve this separation; and you are not angry with me—you have no reason to dislike me, you allow, yourself. Dear uncle! send me a kind note to-morrow; and leave to join you anywhere you please, except at Thrushcross Grange. I believe an interview would convince you that my father's character is not mine; he affirms I am more your nephew than his son; and though I have faults which render me unworthy of Catherine, she has excused them, and, for her sake, you should also. You inquire after my health—it is better; but while I remain cut off from all hope, and doomed to solitude, or the society of those who never did, and never will like me, how can I be cheerful and well?"

Edgar, though he felt for the boy, could not consent to grant his request; because he could not accompany Catherine.

He said, in summer, perhaps, they might meet: meantime, he wished him to continue writing at intervals, and engaged to give him what advice and comfort he was able by letter; being well aware of his hard position in his family.

Linton complied; and had he been unrestrained, would probably have spoiled all by filling his epistles with complaints and lamentations; but his father kept a sharp watch over him; and, of course, insisted on every line that my master sent being shown; so, instead of penning his peculiar personal sufferings and distresses, the themes constantly uppermost in his thoughts, he harped on the cruel obligation of being held asunder from his friend and love; and gently intimated that Mr. Linton must allow an interview soon, or he should fear he was purposely deceiving him with empty promises.

Cathy was a powerful ally at home; and, between them, they at length persuaded my master to acquiesce in their having a ride or a walk together, about once a week, under my guardianship, and on the moors nearest the Grange, for June found him still declining; and, though he had set aside, yearly, a portion of his income for my young lady's fortune, he had a natural desire that she might retain—or, at least, return in a short time to—the house of her ancestors; and he considered her only prospect of doing that was by a union with his heir; he had no idea that the latter was failing almost as fast as himself; nor had any one, I believe: no doctor visited the Heights, and no one saw Master Heathcliff to make report of his condition, among us.

I, for my part, began to fancy my forebodings were false, and that he must be actually rallying, when he mentioned riding and walking on the moors, and seemed so earnest in pursuing his object.

I could not picture a father treating a dying child as tyrannically and wickedly as I afterwards learnt Heathcliff had treated him, to compel this apparent eagerness; his efforts redoubling the more imminently his avaricious and unfeeling plans were threatened with defeat by death.

Chapter XXVI

Summer was already past its prime, when Edgar reluctantly yielded his assent to their entreaties, and Catherine and I set out on our first ride to join her cousin.

It was a close, sultry day, devoid of sunshine, but with a sky too dappled and hazy to threaten rain; and our place of meeting had been fixed at the guide-stone, by the crossroads. On arriving there, however, a little herd-boy, despatched as a messenger, told us that—

"Maister Linton wer just ut this side th' Heights: and he'd be mitch obleeged to us to gang on a bit further."

"Then Master Linton has forgot the first injunction of his uncle," I observed: "he bid us keep on the Grange land, and here we are, off at once."

"Well, we'll turn our horses' heads round, when we reach him," answered my companion; "our excursion shall lie towards home."

But when we reached him, and that was scarcely a quarter of a mile from his own door, we found he had no horse, and we were forced to dismount, and leave ours to graze.

He lay on the heath, awaiting our approach, and did not rise till we came within a few yards. Then he walked so feebly, and looked so pale, that I immediately exclaimed—

"Why, Master Heathcliff, you are not fit for enjoying a ramble this morning. How ill you do look!"

Catherine surveyed him with grief and astonishment; she changed the ejaculation of joy on her lips, to one of alarm, and the congratulation on their long postponed meeting, to an anxious inquiry, whether he were worse than usual?

"No—better—better!" he panted, trembling, and retaining her hand as if he needed its support, while his large blue eyes wandered timidly over her; the hollowness round them, transforming to haggard wildness the languid expression they once possessed.

"But you have been worse," persisted his cousin, "worse than when I saw you last—you are thinner, and—"

"I'm tired," he interrupted, hurriedly. "It is too hot for walking, let us rest here. And, in the morning, I often feel sick—papa says I grow so fast."

Badly satisfied, Cathy sat down, and he reclined beside her.

"This is something like your paradise," said she, making an effort at cheerfulness. "You recollect the two days we agreed to spend in the place and way each thought pleasantest? This is nearly yours, only there are clouds; but then, they are so soft and mellow, it is nicer than sunshine. Next week, if you can, we'll ride down to the Grange Park, and try mine."

Linton did not appear to remember what she talked of; and he had evidently great difficulty in sustaining any kind of conversation. His lack of interest in the subjects she started, and his equal incapacity to contribute to her entertainment, were so obvious that she could not conceal her disappointment. An indefinite alteration had come over his whole person and manner. The pettishness that might be caressed into fondness, had yielded to a listless apathy; there was less of the peevish temper of a child which frets and teases on purpose to be soothed, and more of the self-absorbed moroseness of a confirmed invalid, repelling consolation, and ready to regard the good-humoured mirth of others as an insult.

Catherine perceived, as well as I did, that he held it rather a punishment, than a gratification, to endure our company; and she made no scruple of proposing, presently, to depart.

That proposal, unexpectedly, roused Linton from his lethargy, and threw him into a strange state of agitation. He glanced fearfully towards the Heights, begging she would remain another half-hour, at least.

"But, I think," said Cathy, "you'd be more comfortable at home than sitting here; and I cannot amuse you to-day, I see, by my tales, and songs, and chatter; you have grown wiser than I, in these six months; you have little taste for my diversions now; or else, if I could amuse you, I'd willingly stay."

"Stay to rest yourself," he replied. "And, Catherine, don't think, or say that I'm *very* unwell—it is the heavy weather and heat that make me dull; and I walked about, before you came, a great deal, for me. Tell uncle, I'm in tolerable health, will you?"

"I'll tell him that *you* say so, Linton. I couldn't affirm that you are," observed my young lady, wondering at his pertinacious assertion of what was evidently an untruth.

"And be here again next Thursday," continued he, shunning her puzzled gaze. "And give him my thanks for permitting you to come —my best thanks, Catherine. And—and if you *did* meet my father, and he asked you about me, don't lead him to suppose that I've been extremely silent and stupid; don't look sad and downcast, as you *are* doing—he'll be angry."

"I care nothing for his anger," exclaimed Cathy, imagining she would be its object.

"But I do," said her cousin, shuddering. "*Don't* provoke him against me, Catherine, for he is very hard."

"Is he severe to you, Master Heathcliff?" I inquired. "Has he grown weary of indulgence, and passed from passive, to active hatred?"

Linton looked at me, but did not answer; and, after keeping her seat by his side another ten minutes, during which his head fell drowsily on his breast, and he uttered nothing except suppressed moans of exhaustion or pain, Cathy began to seek solace in looking for bilberries, and sharing the produce of her researches with me: she did not offer them to him, for she saw further notice would only weary and annoy.

"Is it half an hour now, Ellen?" she whispered in my ear, at last. "I can't tell why we should stay. He's asleep, and papa will be wanting us back."

"Well, we must not leave him asleep," I answered; "wait till he wakes and be patient. You were mighty eager to set off, but your longing to see poor Linton has soon evaporated!"

"Why did *he* wish to see me?" returned Catherine. "In his crossest humours, formerly, I liked him better than I do in his present curious mood. It's just as if it were a task he was compelled to perform—this interview—for fear his father should scold him. But I'm hardly going to come to give Mr. Heathcliff pleasure, whatever reason he may have for ordering Linton to undergo this penance. And, though I'm glad he's better in health, I'm sorry he's so much less pleasant, and so much less affectionate to me."

"You think *he is* better in health, then?" I said.

"Yes," she answered; "because he always made such a great deal of his sufferings, you know. He is not tolerably well, as he told me to tell papa, but he's better, very likely."

"Then you differ with me, Miss Cathy," I remarked; "I should conjecture him to be far worse."

Linton here started from his slumber in bewildered terror, and asked if any one had called his name.

"No," said Catherine; "unless in dreams. I cannot conceive how you manage to doze, out of doors, in the morning."

"I thought I heard my father," he gasped, glancing up to the frowning nab[5] above us. "You are sure nobody spoke?"

"Quite sure," replied his cousin. "Only Ellen and I were disputing concerning your health. Are you truly stronger, Linton, than when we separated in winter? If you be, I'm certain one thing is not stronger—your regard for me—speak, are you?"

The tears gushed from Linton's eyes as he answered—

"Yes, yes, I am!"

And, still under the spell of the imaginary voice, his gaze wandered up and down to detect its owner.

Cathy rose.

"For to-day we must part," she said. "And I won't conceal that I have been sadly disappointed with our meeting, though I'll mention it to nobody but you—not that I stand in awe of Mr. Heathcliff!"

"Hush," murmured Linton; "for God's sake, hush! He's coming." And he clung to Catherine's arm, striving to detain her; but, at that announcement, she hastily disengaged herself, and whistled to Minny, who obeyed her like a dog.

"I'll be here next Thursday," she cried, springing to the saddle. "Good-bye. Quick, Ellen!"

And so we left him, scarcely conscious of our departure, so absorbed was he in anticipating his father's approach.

Before we reached home, Catherine's displeasure softened into a perplexed sensation of pity and regret largely blended with vague, uneasy doubts about Linton's actual circumstances, physical and

5. See p. 174.

social; in which I partook, though I counselled her not to say much, for a second journey would make us better judges.

My master requested an account of our ongoings: his nephew's offering of thanks was duly delivered, Miss Cathy gently touching on the rest: I also threw little light on his inquiries, for I hardly knew what to hide, and what to reveal.

Chapter XXVII

Seven days glided away, every one marking its course by the henceforth rapid alteration of Edgar Linton's state. The havoc that months had previously wrought was now emulated by the inroads of hours.

Catherine, we would fain have deluded yet, but her own quick spirit refused to delude her. It divined, in secret, and brooded on the dreadful probability, gradually ripening into certainty.

She had not the heart to mention her ride, when Thursday came round; I mentioned it for her, and obtained permission to order her out of doors; for the library, where her father stopped a short time daily—the brief period he could bear to sit up—and his chamber had become her whole world. She grudged each moment that did not find her bending over his pillow, or seated by his side. Her countenance grew wan with watching and sorrow, and my master gladly dismissed her to what he flattered himself would be a happy change of scene and society, drawing comfort from the hope that she would not now be left entirely alone after his death.

He had a fixed idea, I guessed by several observations he let fall, that as his nephew resembled him in person, he would resemble him in mind; for Linton's letters bore few or no indications of his defective character. And I, through pardonable weakness, refrained from correcting the error; asking myself what good there would be in disturbing his last moments with information that he had neither power nor opportunity to turn to account.

We deferred our excursion till the afternoon; a golden afternoon of August—every breath from the hills so full of life, that it seemed whoever respired it, though dying, might revive.

Catherine's face was just like the landscape—shadows and sunshine flitting over it, in rapid succession; but the shadows rested longer and the sunshine was more transient, and her poor little heart reproached itself for even that passing forgetfulness of its cares.

We discerned Linton watching at the same spot he had selected before. My young mistress alighted, and told me that as she was resolved to stay a very little while, I had better hold the pony and remain on horseback; but I dissented; I wouldn't risk losing sight of the charge committed to me a minute; so we climbed the slope of heath together.

Master Heathcliff received us with greater animation on this occasion; not the animation of high spirits though, nor yet of joy; it looked more like fear.

"It is late!" he said, speaking short, and with difficulty. "Is not your father very ill? I thought you wouldn't come."

"*Why* won't you be candid?" cried Catherine, swallowing her greeting. "Why cannot you say at once, you don't want me? It is strange, Linton, that for the second time, you have brought me here on purpose, apparently, to distress us both, and for no reason besides!"

Linton shivered, and glanced at her, half supplicating, half ashamed, but his cousin's patience was not sufficient to endure this enigmatical behaviour.

"My father *is* very ill," she said, "and why am I called from his bedside—why didn't you send to absolve me from my promise, when you wished I wouldn't keep it? Come! I desire an explanation; playing and trifling are completely banished out of my mind, and I can't dance attendance on your affectations, now!"

"My affectations!" he murmured; "what are they? For heaven's sake, Catherine, don't look so angry! Despise me as much as you please; I am a worthless, cowardly wretch—I can't be scorned enough! but I'm too mean for your anger—hate my father, and spare me, for contempt!"

"Nonsense!" cried Catherine in a passion. "Foolish, silly boy! And there! he trembles, as if I were really going to touch him! You needn't bespeak contempt, Linton; anybody will have it spontaneously, at your service. Get off! I shall return home; it is folly dragging you from the hearth-stone, and pretending—what do we pretend? Let go my frock! If I pitied you for crying and looking so very frightened, you should spurn such pity. Ellen, tell him how disgraceful this conduct is. Rise, and don't degrade yourself into an abject reptile—*don't.*"

With streaming face and an expression of agony, Linton had thrown his nerveless frame along the ground; he seemed convulsed with exquisite terror.

"Oh!" he sobbed, "I cannot bear it! Catherine, Catherine, I'm a traitor too, and I dare not tell you! But leave me and I shall be killed! *Dear* Catherine, my life is in your hands; and you have said you loved me—and if you did, it wouldn't harm you. You'll not go, then? kind, sweet, good Catherine! And perhaps you *will* consent—and he'll let me die with you!"

My young lady, on witnessing his intense anguish, stooped to raise him. The old feeling of indulgent tenderness overcame her vexation, and she grew thoroughly moved and alarmed.

"Consent to what?" she asked. "To stay? Tell me the meaning of this strange talk, and I will. You contradict your own words, and distract me! Be calm and frank, and confess at once all that weighs on your heart. You wouldn't injure me, Linton, would you? You wouldn't let any enemy hurt me, if you could prevent it? I'll believe you are a coward, for yourself, but not a cowardly betrayer of your best friend."

"But my father threatened me," gasped the boy, clasping his attenuated fingers, "and I dread him—I dread him! I *dare* not tell!"

"Oh well!" said Catherine, with scornful compassion, "keep your secret, *I'm* no coward—save yourself, I'm not afraid!"

Her magnanimity provoked his tears; he wept wildly, kissing her supporting hands, and yet could not summon courage to speak out.

I was cogitating what the mystery might be, and determined Catherine should never suffer to benefit him or any one else, by my good will; when hearing a rustle among the ling,[6] I looked up, and saw Mr. Heathcliff almost close upon us, descending the Heights. He didn't cast a glance towards my companions, though they were sufficiently near for Linton's sobs to be audible; but hailing me in the almost hearty tone he assumed to none besides, and the sincerity of which I couldn't avoid doubting, he said—

"It is something to see you so near to my house, Nelly! How are you at the Grange? Let us hear! The rumour goes," he added in a lower tone, "that Edgar Linton is on his death-bed—perhaps they exaggerate his illness?"

"No; my master is dying," I replied; "it is true enough. A sad thing it will be for us all, but a blessing for him!"

"How long will he last, do you think?" he asked.

"I don't know," I said.

"Because," he continued, looking at the two young people, who were fixed under his eye—Linton appeared as if he could not venture to stir, or raise his head, and Catherine could not move, on his account—"Because that lad yonder seems determined to beat me—and I'd thank his uncle to be quick, and go before him. Hallo! Has the whelp been playing that game long? I *did* give him some lessons about snivelling. Is he pretty lively with Miss Linton generally?"

"Lively? no—he has shown the greatest distress," I answered. "To see him, I should say, that instead of rambling with his sweetheart on the hills, he ought to be in bed, under the hands of a doctor."

"He shall be, in a day or two," muttered Heathcliff. "But first

6. Heather.

—get up, Linton! Get up!" he shouted. "Don't grovel **on the** ground, there—up this moment!"

Linton had sunk prostrate again in another paroxysm of helpless fear, caused by his father's glance towards him, I suppose: there was nothing else to produce such humiliation. He made several efforts to obey, but his little strength was annihilated for the time, and he fell back again with a moan.

Mr. Heathcliff advanced, and lifted him to lean against a ridge of turf.

"Now," said he with curbed ferocity, "I'm getting angry—and if you don't command that paltry spirit of yours—*Damn* you! Get up, directly!"

"I will, father!" he panted. "Only, let me alone, or I shall faint! I've done as you wished, I'm sure. Catherine will tell you that— that I—have been cheerful. Ah! keep by me, Catherine; give me your hand."

"Take mine," said his father; "stand on your feet! There now— she'll lend you her arm. That's right, look at *her*. You would imagine I was the devil himself, Miss Linton, to excite such horror. Be so kind as to walk home with him, will you? He shudders, if I touch him."

"Linton, dear!" whispered Catherine, "I can't go to Wuthering Heights—papa has forbidden me. He'll not harm you, why are you so afraid?"

"I can never re-enter that house," he answered. "I am *not* to re-enter it without you!"

"Stop!" cried his father. "We'll respect Catherine's filial scruples. Nelly, take him in, and I'll follow your advice concerning the doctor, without delay."

"You'll do well," replied I, "but I must remain with my mistress. To mind your son is not my business."

"You are very stiff!" said Heathcliff; "I know that—but you'll force me to pinch the baby, and make it scream, before it moves your charity. Come then, my hero. Are you willing to return, escorted by me?"

He approached once more, and made as if he would seize the fragile being; but shrinking back, Linton clung to his cousin, and implored her to accompany him, with a frantic importunity that admitted no denial.

However I disapproved, I couldn't hinder her; indeed, how could she have refused him herself? What was filling him with dread, we had no means of discerning, but there he was, powerless under its gripe, and any addition seemed capable of shocking him into idiocy.

We reached the threshold; Catherine walked in; and I stood waiting till she had conducted the invalid to a chair, expecting her out immediately; when Mr. Heathcliff, pushing me forward, exclaimed—

"My house is not stricken with the plague, Nelly; and I have a mind to be hospitable to-day; sit down, and allow me to shut the door."

He shut and locked it also. I started.

"You shall have tea, before you go home," he added. "I am by myself. Hareton is gone with some cattle to the Lees—and Zillah and Joseph are off on a journey of pleasure. And, though I'm used to being alone, I'd rather have some interesting company, if I can get it. Miss Linton, take your seat by *him*. I give you what I have; the present is hardly worth accepting; but I have nothing else to offer. It is Linton, I mean. How she does stare! It's odd what a savage feeling I have to anything that seems afraid of me! Had I been born where laws are less strict, and tastes less dainty, I should treat myself to a slow vivisection of those two, as an evening's amusement."

He drew in his breath, struck the table, and swore to himself—

"By hell! I hate them."

"I'm not afraid of you!" exclaimed Catherine, who could not hear the latter part of his speech.

She stepped close up, her black eyes flashing with passion and resolution.

"Give me that key—I will have it!" she said. "I wouldn't eat or drink here, if I were starving."

Heathcliff had the key in his hand that remained on the table. He looked up, seized with a sort of surprise at her boldness, or, possibly, reminded by her voice and glance, of the person from whom she inherited it.

She snatched at the instrument, and half succeeded in getting it out of his loosened fingers; but her action recalled him to the present; he recovered it speedily.

"Now, Catherine Linton," he said, "stand off, or I shall knock you down; and that will make Mrs. Dean mad."

Regardless of this warning, she captured his closed hand and its contents again.

"We *will* go!" she repeated, exerting her utmost efforts to cause the iron muscles to relax; and finding that her nails made no impression, she applied her teeth pretty sharply.

Heathcliff glanced at me a glance that kept me from interfering a moment. Catherine was too intent on his fingers to notice his face. He opened them suddenly, and resigned the object of dispute; but, ere she had well secured it, he seized her with the liberated hand, and, pulling her on his knee, administered with the other a shower of terrific slaps on both sides of the head, each sufficient to have fulfilled his threat, had she been able to fall.

At this diabolical violence, I rushed on him furiously.

"You villain!" I began to cry, "you villain!"

A touch on the chest silenced me; I am stout, and soon put out of breath; and, what with that and the rage, I staggered dizzily back, and felt ready to suffocate, or to burst a blood-vessel.

The scene was over in two minutes; Catherine, released, put her two hands to her temples, and looked just as if she were not sure whether her ears were off or on. She trembled like a reed, poor thing, and leant against the table perfectly bewildered.

"I know how to chastise children, you see," said the scoundrel, grimly, as he stooped to repossess himself of the key, which had dropped to the floor. "Go to Linton now, as I told you; and cry at your ease! I shall be your father to-morrow—all the father you'll have in a few days—and you shall have plenty of that—you can bear plenty—you're no weakling—you shall have a daily taste, if I catch such a devil of a temper in your eyes again!"

Cathy ran to me instead of Linton, and knelt down, and put her burning cheek on my lap, weeping aloud. Her cousin had shrunk into a corner of the settle, as quiet as a mouse, congratulating himself, I dare say, that the correction had lighted on another than him.

Mr. Heathcliff, perceiving us all confounded, rose, and expeditiously made the tea himself. The cups and saucers were laid ready. He poured it out, and handed me a cup.

"Wash away your spleen," he said. "And help your own naughty pet and mine. It is not poisoned, though I prepared it. I'm going out to seek your horses."

Our first thought, on his departure, was to force an exit somewhere. We tried the kitchen door, but that was fastened outside; we looked at the windows—they were too narrow for even Cathy's little figure.

"Master Linton," I cried, seeing we were regularly imprisoned, "you know what your diabolical father is after, and you shall tell us, or I'll box your ears, as he has done your cousin's."

"Yes, Linton; you must tell," said Catherine. "It was for your sake I came; and it will be wickedly ungrateful if you refuse."

"Give me some tea, I'm thirsty, and then I'll tell you," he answered. "Mrs. Dean, go away. I don't like you standing over me. Now, Catherine, you are letting your tears fall into my cup! I won't drink that. Give me another."

Catherine pushed another to him, and wiped her face. I felt disgusted at the little wretch's composure, since he was no longer in terror for himself. The anguish he had exhibited on the moor subsided as soon as ever he entered Wuthering Heights; so I guessed he had been menaced with an awful visitation of wrath if he failed in decoying us there; and, that accomplished, he had no further immediate fears.

"Papa wants us to be married," he continued, after sipping some of the liquid. "And he knows your papa wouldn't let us marry now; and he's afraid of my dying, if we wait; so we are to be married in the morning, and you are to stay here all night; and, if you do as he wishes, you shall return home next day, and take me with you."

"Take you with her, pitiful changeling?" I exclaimed. "*You* marry? Why, the man is mad, or he thinks us fools, every one. And do you imagine that beautiful young lady, that healthy, hearty girl, will tie herself to a little perishing monkey like you? Are you cherishing the notion that *anybody*, let alone Miss Catherine Linton, would have you for a husband? You want whipping for bringing us in here at all, with your dastardly, puling tricks; and—don't look so silly now! I've a very good mind to shake you severely, for your contemptible treachery, and your imbecile conceit."

I did give him a slight shaking, but it brought on the cough, and he took to his ordinary resource of moaning and weeping, and Catherine rebuked me.

"Stay all night? No!" she said, looking slowly round. "Ellen, I'll burn that door down, but I'll get out."

And she would have commenced the execution of her threat directly, but Linton was up in alarm, for his dear self, again. He clasped her in his two feeble arms, sobbing—

"Won't you have me, and save me? Not let me come to the Grange? Oh! darling Catherine! you mustn't go, and leave me, after all. You *must* obey my father, you *must*!"

"I must obey my own," she replied, "and relieve him from this cruel suspense. The whole night! What would he think? he'll be distressed already. I'll either break or burn a way out of the house. Be quiet! You're in no danger—but, if you hinder me—Linton, I love papa better than you!"

The mortal terror he felt of Mr. Heathcliff's anger restored to the boy his coward's eloquence. Catherine was near distraught; still, she persisted that she must go home, and tried entreaty, in her turn, persuading him to subdue his selfish agony.

While they were thus occupied, our jailer re-entered.

"Your beasts have trotted off," he said, "and—Now, Linton! snivelling again? What has she been doing to you? Come, come—have done, and get to bed. In a month or two, my lad, you'll be able to pay her back her present tyrannies, with a vigorous hand. You're pining for pure love, are you not? nothing else in the world —and she shall have you! There, to bed! Zillah won't be here to-night; you must undress yourself. Hush! hold your noise! Once in your own room, I'll not come near you, you needn't fear. By chance, you've managed tolerably. I'll look to the rest."

He spoke these words, holding the door open for his son to pass; and the latter achieved his exit exactly as a spaniel might, which suspected the person who attended on it of designing a spiteful squeeze.

The lock was re-secured. Heathcliff approached the fire, where my mistress and I stood silent. Catherine looked up, and instinctively raised her hand to her cheek: his neighbourhood revived a painful sensation. Anybody else would have been incapable of regarding the childish act with sternness, but he scowled on her, and muttered—

"Oh, you are not afraid of me? Your courage is well disguised— you *seem* damnably afraid!"

"I *am* afraid now," she replied; "because if I stay, papa will be miserable; and how can I endure making him miserable—when he —when he—Mr. Heathcliff, *let* me go home! I promise to marry Linton—papa would like me to, and I love him—and why should you wish to force me to do what I'll willingly do of myself?"

"Let him dare to force you!" I cried. "There's law in the land, thank God, there is! though we *be* in an out-of-the-way place. I'd inform, if he were my own son, and it's felony without benefit of clergy!"

"Silence!" said the ruffian. "To the devil with your clamour! I don't want *you* to speak. Miss Linton, I shall enjoy myself remarkably in thinking your father will be miserable; I shall not sleep for satisfaction. You could have hit on no surer way of fixing your residence under my roof, for the next twenty-four hours, than informing me that such an event would follow. As to your promise to marry Linton, I'll take care you shall keep it, for you shall not quit the place till it is fulfilled."

"Send Ellen then, to let papa know I'm safe!" exclaimed Catherine, weeping bitterly. "Or marry me now. Poor papa! Ellen, he'll think we're lost. What shall we do?"

"Not he! He'll think you are tired of waiting on him, and run off, for a little amusement," answered Heathcliff. "You cannot deny that you entered my house of your own accord, in contempt of his injunctions to the contrary. And it is quite natural that you should desire amusement at your age; and that you should weary of nursing a sick man, and that man *only* your father. Catherine, his happiest days were over when your days began. He cursed you, I dare say, for coming into the world (I did, at least). And it would just do if he cursed you as *he* went out of it. I'd join him. I don't love you! How should I? Weep away. As far as I can see, it will be your chief diversion hereafter, unless Linton make amends for other losses; and your provident parent appears to fancy he may. His letters of advice and consolation entertained me vastly. In his last, he recommended my jewel to be careful of his; and kind to her when he got her. Careful and kind—that's paternal! But Linton requires his whole stock of care and kindness for himself. Linton can play the little tyrant well. He'll undertake to torture any number of cats if their teeth be drawn, and their claws pared. You'll be able to tell his uncle fine tales of his *kindness*, when you get home again, I assure you."

"You're right there!" I said; "explain your son's character. Show his resemblance to yourself; and then, I hope, Miss Cathy will think twice before she takes the cockatrice!"

"I don't much mind speaking of his amiable qualities now," he answered, "because she must either accept him, or remain a prisoner, and you along with her, till your master dies. I can detain you both, quite concealed, here. If you doubt, encourage her to retract her word, and you'll have an opportunity of judging!"

"I'll not retract my word," said Catherine. "I'll marry him, within this hour, if I may go to Thrushcross Grange afterwards. Mr. Heathcliff, you're a cruel man, but you're not a fiend; and you won't, from *mere* malice, destroy, irrevocably, all my happiness. If papa thought I had left him on purpose, and if he died before I returned, could I bear to live? I've given over crying; but I'm going to kneel here, at your knee; and I'll not get up, and I'll not take my eyes from your face, till you look back at me! No, don't turn away! *do* look! You'll see nothing to provoke you. I don't hate you. I'm not angry that you struck me. Have you never loved *anybody*, in all your life, uncle? *never?* Ah! you must look once—I'm so wretched—you can't help being sorry and pitying me."

"Keep your eft's fingers off; and move, or I'll kick you!" cried Heathcliff, brutally repulsing her. "I'd rather be hugged by a snake. How the devil can you dream of fawning on me? I *detest* you!"

He shrugged his shoulders—shook himself, indeed, as if his flesh crept with aversion, and thrust back his chair, while I got up, and opened my mouth, to commence a downright torrent of abuse; but I was rendered dumb in the middle of the first sentence, by a threat that I should be shown into a room by myself, the very next syllable I uttered.

It was growing dark—we heard a sound of voices at the garden gate. Our host hurried out, instantly; *he* had his wits about him; *we* had not. There was a talk of two or three minutes, and he returned alone.

"I thought it had been your cousin Hareton," I observed to Catherine. "I wish he would arrive! Who knows but he might take our part?"

"It was three servants sent to seek you from the Grange," said Heathcliff, overhearing me. "You should have opened a lattice and called out; but I could swear that chit is glad you didn't. She's glad to be obliged to stay, I'm certain."

At learning the chance we had missed, we both gave vent to our grief without control, and he allowed us to wail on till nine o'clock; then he bid us go upstairs, through the kitchen, to Zillah's chamber, and I whispered my companion to obey; perhaps we might contrive to get through the window there, or into a garret, and out by its skylight.

The window, however, was narrow like those below, and the garret trap was safe from our attempts; for we were fastened in as before.

We neither of us lay down: Catherine took her station by the lattice, and watched anxiously for morning—a deep sigh being the only answer I could obtain to my frequent entreaties that she would try to rest.

I seated myself in a chair, and rocked, to and fro, passing harsh judgment on my many derelictions of duty; from which, it struck me then, all the misfortunes of all my employers sprang. It was not the case, in reality, I am aware; but it was, in my imagination, that dismal night, and I thought Heathcliff himself less guilty than I.

At seven o'clock he came, and inquired if Miss Linton had risen. She ran to the door immediately, and answered—

"Yes."

"Here, then," he said, opening it, and pulling her out.

I rose to follow, but he turned the lock again. I demanded my release.

"Be patient," he replied; "I'll send up your breakfast in a while."

I thumped on the panels, and rattled the latch angrily; and Catherine asked why I was still shut up? He answered, I must try to endure it another hour, and they went away.

I endured it two or three hours; at length, I heard a footstep, not Heathcliff's.

"I've brought you something to eat," said a voice; "oppen t' door!"

Complying eagerly, I beheld Hareton, laden with food enough to last me all day.

"Tak it," he added, thrusting the tray into my hand.

"Stay one minute," I began.

"Nay!" cried he, and retired, regardless of any prayers I could pour forth to detain him.

And there I remained enclosed, the whole day, and the whole of the next night; and another, and another. Five nights and four days I remained, altogether, seeing nobody but Hareton, once every morning, and he was a model of a jailer—surly, and dumb, and deaf to every attempt at moving his sense of justice or compassion.

Chapter XXVIII

On the fifth morning, or rather afternoon, a different step approached—lighter and shorter—and, this time, the person entered the room. It was Zillah, donned in her scarlet shawl, with a black silk bonnet on her head, and a willow basket swung to her arm.

"Eh, dear! Mrs. Dean," she exclaimed. "Well! there is a talk about you at Gimmerton. I never thought but you were sunk in the Blackhorse marsh, and Missy with you, till master told me you'd been found, and he'd lodged you here! What, and you must have got on an island, sure? And how long were you in the hole? Did master save you, Mrs. Dean? But you're not so thin—you've not been so poorly, have you?"

"Your master is a true scoundrel!" I replied. "But he shall answer for it. He needn't have raised that tale—it shall all be laid bare!"

"What do you mean?" asked Zillah. "It's not his tale: they tell that in the village—about your being lost in the marsh; and I calls to Earnshaw, when I come in—"

" 'Eh, they's queer things, Mr. Hareton, happened since I went off. It's a sad pity of that likely young lass, and cant [7] Nelly Dean.'

"He stared. I thought he had not heard aught, so I told him the rumour.

"The master listened, and he just smiled to himself, and said—

" 'If they have been in the marsh, they are out now, Zillah. Nelly Dean is lodged, at this minute, in your room. You can tell her to flit, when you go up; here is the key. The bog-water got into her head, and she would have run home, quite flighty, but I fixed her, till she came round to her senses. You can bid her go to the Grange, at once, if she be able, and carry a message from me, that her young lady will follow in time to attend the Squire's funeral."

"Mr. Edgar is not dead?" I gasped. "Oh! Zillah, Zillah!"

"No, no—sit you down, my good mistress," she replied; "you're right sickly yet. He's not dead: Doctor Kenneth thinks he may last another day. I met him on the road and asked."

Instead of sitting down, I snatched my outdoor things, and hastened below, for the way was free.

On entering the house, I looked about for some one to give information of Catherine.

The place was filled with sunshine, and the door stood wide

7. Brisk.

open, but nobody seemed at hand.

As I hesitated whether to go off at once, or return and seek my mistress, a slight cough drew my attention to the hearth.

Linton lay on the settle, sole tenant, sucking a stick of sugar-candy, and pursuing my movements with apathetic eyes.

"Where is Miss Catherine?" I demanded, sternly, supposing I could frighten him into giving intelligence, by catching him thus, alone.

He sucked on like an innocent.

"Is she gone?" I said.

"No," he replied; "she's upstairs—she's not to go; we won't let her."

"You won't let her, little idiot!" I exclaimed. "Direct me to her room immediately, or I'll make you sing out sharply."

"Papa would make you sing out, if you attempted to get there," he answered. "He says I'm not to be soft with Catherine; she's my wife, and it's shameful that she should wish to leave me! He says, she hates me, and wants me to die, that she may have my money, but she shan't have it; and she shan't go home! She never shall! she may cry, and be sick as much as she pleases!"

He resumed his former occupation, closing his lids, as if he meant to drop asleep.

"Master Heathcliff," I resumed, "have you forgotten all Catherine's kindness to you, last winter, when you affirmed you loved her, and when she brought you books, and sung you songs, and came many a time through wind and snow to see you? She wept to miss one evening, because you would be disappointed; and you felt then, that she was a hundred times too good to you; and now you believe the lies your father tells, though you know he detests you both! And you join him against her. That's fine gratitude, is it not?"

The corner of Linton's mouth fell, and he took the sugar-candy from his lips.

"Did she come to Wuthering Heights, because she hated you?" I continued. "Think for yourself! As to your money, she does not even know that you will have any. And you say she's sick; and yet, you leave her alone, up there in a strange house! *You*, who have felt what it is to be so neglected! You could pity your own sufferings, and she pitied them, too, but you won't pity hers! I shed tears, Master Heathcliff, you see—an elderly woman, and a servant merely —and you, after pretending such affection, and having reason to worship her almost, store every tear you have for yourself, and lie there quite at ease. Ah! you're a heartless, selfish boy!"

"I can't stay with her," he answered crossly. "I'll not stay, by myself. She cries so I can't bear it. And she won't give over, though

I say I'll call my father. I did call him once; and he threatened to strangle her, if she was not quiet, but she began again, the instant he left the room; moaning and grieving, all night long, though I screamed for vexation that I couldn't sleep."

"Is Mr. Heathcliff out?" I inquired, perceiving that the wretched creature had no power to sympathise with his cousin's mental tortures.

"He's in the court," he replied, "talking to Doctor Kenneth, who says uncle is dying, truly, at last. I'm glad, for I shall be master of the Grange after him—and Catherine always spoke of it as *her* house. It isn't hers! It's mine—papa says everything she has is mine. All her nice books are mine; she offered to give me them, and her pretty birds, and her pony Minny, if I would get the key of our room, and let her out; but I told her she had nothing to give, they were all, all mine. And then she cried, and took a little picture from her neck, and said I should have that—two pictures in a gold case, on one side her mother, and on the other, uncle, when they were young. That was yesterday—I said *they* were mine, too; and tried to get them from her. The spiteful thing wouldn't let me; she pushed me off, and hurt me. I shrieked out—that frightens her —she heard papa coming, and she broke the hinges, and divided the case and gave me her mother's portrait; the other she attempted to hide; but papa asked what was the matter and I explained it. He took the one I had away; and ordered her to resign hers to me; she refused, and he—he struck her down, and wrenched it off the chain, and crushed it with his foot."

"And were you pleased to see her struck?" I asked, having my designs in encouraging his talk.

"I winked," he answered. "I wink to see my father strike a dog, or a horse, he does it so hard. Yet I was glad at first—she deserved punishing for pushing me: but when papa was gone, she made me come to the window and showed me her cheek cut on the inside, against her teeth, and her mouth filling with blood; and then she gathered up the bits of the picture, and went and sat down with her face to the wall, and she has never spoken to me since, and I sometimes think she can't speak for pain. I don't like to think so! but she's a naughty thing for crying continually; and she looks so pale and wild, I'm afraid of her!"

"And you can get the key if you choose?" I said.

"Yes, when I am upstairs," he answered; "but I can't walk upstairs now."

"In what apartment is it?" I asked.

"Oh," he cried, "I shan't tell *you* where it is! It is our secret. Nobody, neither Hareton, nor Zillah are to know. There! you've tired me—go away, go away!" And he turned his face onto his arm, and shut his eyes, again.

I considered it best to depart without seeing Mr. Heathcliff; and bring a rescue for my young lady, from the Grange.

On reaching it, the astonishment of my fellow servants to see me, and their joy also, was intense; and when they heard that their little mistress was safe, two or three were about to hurry up, and shout the news at Mr. Edgar's door: but I bespoke the announcement of it, myself.

How changed I found him, even in those few days! He lay an image of sadness, and resignation, waiting his death. Very young he looked: though his actual age was thirty-nine, one would have called him ten years younger, at least. He thought of Catherine, for he murmured her name. I touched his hand, and spoke.

"Catherine is coming, dear master!" I whispered; "she is alive, and well; and will be here I hope to-night."

I trembled at the first effects of this intelligence: he half rose up, looked eagerly round the apartment, and then sunk back in a swoon.

As soon as he recovered, I related our compulsory visit, and detention at the Heights. I said Heathcliff forced me to go in, which was not quite true; I uttered as little as possible against Linton; nor did I describe all his father's brutal conduct, my intentions being to add no bitterness, if I could help it, to his already overflowing cup.

He divined that one of his enemy's purposes was to secure the personal property, as well as the estate, to his son, or rather himself; yet why he did not wait till his decease, was a puzzle to my master, because ignorant how nearly he and his nephew would quit the world together.

However, he felt his will had better be altered. Instead of leaving Catherine's fortune at her own disposal, he determined to put it in the hands of trustees, for her use during life, and for her children, if she had any, after her. By that means, it could not fall to Mr. Heathcliff should Linton die.

Having received his orders, I despatched a man to fetch the attorney, and four more, provided with serviceable weapons, to demand my young lady of her jailer. Both parties were delayed very late. The single servant returned first.

He said Mr. Green, the lawyer, was out when he arrived at his house, and he had to wait two hours for his re-entrance: and then Mr. Green told him he had a little business in the village that must be done, but he would be at Thrushcross Grange before morning.

The four men came back unaccompanied, also. They brought word that Catherine was ill, too ill to quit her room, and Heathcliff would not suffer them to see her.

I scolded the stupid fellows well, for listening to that tale, which I would not carry to my master; resolving to take a whole bevy up to the Heights, at daylight, and storm it, literally, unless the prisoner were quietly surrendered to us.

Her father *shall* see her, I vowed, and vowed again, if that devil be killed on his own doorstones in trying to prevent it!

Happily, I was spared the journey, and the trouble.

I had gone downstairs at three o'clock to fetch a jug of water; and was passing through the hall with it in my hand, when a sharp knock at the front door made me jump.

"Oh! it is Green," I said, recollecting myself, "—only Green," and I went on, intending to send somebody else to open it; but the knock was repeated, not loud, and still importunately.

I put the jug on the banister, and hastened to admit him myself.

The harvest moon shone clear outside. It was not the attorney. My own sweet little mistress sprung on my neck sobbing—

"Ellen! Ellen! Is papa alive?"

"Yes!" I cried, "yes, my angel, he is! God be thanked, you are safe with us again!"

She wanted to run, breathless as she was, upstairs to Mr. Linton's room; but I compelled her to sit down on a chair, and made her drink, and washed her pale face, chafing it into a faint colour with my apron. Then I said I must go first, and tell of her arrival; imploring her to say, she should be happy with young Heathcliff. She stared, but soon comprehending why I counselled her to utter the falsehood, she assured me she would not complain.

I couldn't abide to be present at their meeting. I stood outside the chamber-door a quarter of an hour, and hardly ventured near the bed, then.

All was composed, however; Catherine's despair was as silent as her father's joy. She supported him calmly, in appearance; and he fixed on her features his raised eyes, that seemed dilating with ecstasy.

He died blissfully, Mr. Lockwood; he died so. Kissing her cheek, he murmured—

"I am going to her, and you, darling child, shall come to us"; and never stirred or spoke again, but continued that rapt, radiant gaze, till his pulse imperceptibly stopped, and his soul departed. None could have noticed the exact minute of his death, it was so entirely without a struggle.

Whether Catherine had spent her tears, or whether the grief were too weighty to let them flow, she sat there dry-eyed till the sun rose; she sat till noon, and would still have remained, brooding over that death-bed, but I insisted on her coming away, and taking some repose.

It was well I succeeded in removing her, for at dinner-time appeared the lawyer, having called at Wuthering Heights to get his instructions how to behave. He had sold himself to Mr. Heathcliff, and that was the cause of his delay in obeying my master's summons. Fortunately, no thought of worldly affairs crossed the latter's mind, to disturb him, after his daughter's arrival.

Mr. Green took upon himself to order everything and everybody about the place. He gave all the servants but me, notice to quit. He would have carried his delegated authority to the point of insisting that Edgar Linton should not be buried beside his wife, but in the chapel, with his family. There was the will, however, to hinder that, and my loud protestations against any infringement of its directions.

The funeral was hurried over; Catherine, Mrs. Linton Heathcliff now, was suffered to stay at the Grange, till her father's corpse had quitted it.

She told me that her anguish had at last spurred Linton to incur the risk of liberating her. She heard the men I sent, disputing at the door, and she gathered the sense of Heathcliff's answer. It drove her desperate. Linton, who had been conveyed up to the little parlour soon after I left, was terrified into fetching the key before his father re-ascended.

He had the cunning to unlock, and re-lock the door, without shutting it; and when he should have gone to bed, he begged to sleep with Hareton, and his petition was granted, for once.

Catherine stole out before break of day. She dare not try the doors, lest the dogs should raise an alarm; she visited the empty chambers, and examined their windows; and, luckily, lighting on her mother's, she got easily out of its lattice, and onto the ground, by means of the fir tree, close by. Her accomplice suffered for his share in the escape, notwithstanding his timid contrivances.

Chapter XXIX

The evening after the funeral, my young lady and I were seated in the library; now musing mournfully, one of us despairingly, on our loss, now venturing conjectures as to the gloomy future.

We had just agreed the best destiny which could await Catherine, would be a permission to continue resident at the Grange, at least during Linton's life: he being allowed to join her there, and I to remain as housekeeper. That seemed rather too favourable an arrangement to be hoped for, and yet I did hope, and began to cheer up under the prospect of retaining my home, and my employment, and, above all, my beloved young mistress, when a servant—one of the discarded ones, not yet departed—rushed hastily in, and said, "that devil Heathcliff" was coming through the court: should he fasten the door in his face?

If we had been mad enough to order that proceeding, we had not time. He made no ceremony of knocking, or announcing his name; he was master, and availed himself of the master's privilege to walk straight in, without saying a word.

The sound of our informant's voice directed him to the library; he entered, and motioning him out, shut the door.

It was the same room into which he had been ushered, as a guest, eighteen years before: the same moon shone through the window; and the same autumn landscape lay outside. We had not yet lighted a candle, but all the apartment was visible, even to the portraits on the wall—the splendid head of Mrs. Linton, and the graceful one of her husband.

Heathcliff advanced to the hearth. Time had little altered his person either. There was the same man, his dark face rather sallower, and more composed, his frame a stone or two heavier, perhaps, and no other difference.

Catherine had risen with an impulse to dash out, when she saw him.

"Stop!" he said, arresting her by the arm. "No more runnings away! Where would you go? I'm come to fetch you home; and I hope you'll be a dutiful daughter, and not encourage my son to further disobedience. I was embarrassed how to punish him, when I discovered his part in the business—he's such a cobweb, a pinch would annihilate him—but you'll see by his look that he has received his due! I brought him down one evening, the day before yesterday, and just set him in a chair, and never touched him afterwards. I sent Hareton out, and we had the room to ourselves. In two hours, I called Joseph to carry him up again; and, since then, my presence is as potent on his nerves as a ghost; and I fancy he sees me often, though I am not near. Hareton says he wakes and shrieks in the night by the hour together; and calls you to protect him from me; and, whether you like your precious mate or not, you must come—he's your concern now; I yield all my interest in him to you."

"Why not let Catherine continue here?" I pleaded, "and send Master Linton to her. As you hate them both, you'd not miss them; they *can* only be a daily plague to your unnatural heart."

"I'm seeking a tenant for the Grange," he answered; "and I want my children about me, to be sure—besides, that lass owes me her services for her bread; I'm not going to nurture her in luxury and idleness after Linton is gone. Make haste and get ready now. And don't oblige me to compel you."

"I shall," said Catherine. "Linton is all I have to love in the world, and, though you have done what you could to make him hateful to me, and me to him, you *cannot* make us hate each other! and I defy you to hurt him when I am by, and I defy you to frighten me."

"You are a boastful champion!" replied Heathcliff; "but I don't like you well enough to hurt him: you shall get the full benefit of the torment, as long as it lasts. It is not I who will make him hateful to you—it is his own sweet spirit. He's as bitter as gall at your desertion, and its consequences; don't expect thanks for this noble devotion. I heard him draw a pleasant picture to Zillah of what he would do, if he were as strong as I. The inclination is there, and his very weakness will sharpen his wits to find a substitute for strength."

"I know he has a bad nature," said Catherine; "he's your son. But I'm glad I've a better, to forgive it; and I know he loves me and for that reason I love him. Mr. Heathcliff, *you* have *nobody* to love you; and, however miserable you make us, we shall still have the revenge of thinking that your cruelty rises from your greater misery! You *are* miserable, are you not? Lonely, like the devil, and envious like him? *Nobody* loves you—*nobody* will cry for you, when you die! I wouldn't be you!"

Catherine spoke with a kind of dreary triumph: she seemed to have made up her mind to enter into the spirit of her future family, and draw pleasure from the griefs of her enemies.

"You shall be sorry to be yourself presently," said her father-in-law, "if you stand there another minute. Begone, witch, and get your things."

She scornfully withdrew.

In her absence, I began to beg for Zillah's place at the Heights, offering to resign her mine; but he would suffer it on no account. He bid me be silent, and then, for the first time, allowed himself a glance round the room, and a look at the pictures. Having studied Mrs. Linton, he said—

"I shall have that at home. Not because I need it, but—"

He turned abruptly to the fire, and continued, with what, for lack of a better word, I must call a smile—

"I'll tell you what I did yesterday! I got the sexton, who was digging Linton's grave, to remove the earth off her coffin lid, and I opened it. I thought, once, I would have stayed there, when I saw her face again—it is hers yet—he had hard work to stir me; but he said it would change, if the air blew on it, and so I struck one side of the coffin loose, and covered it up—not Linton's side, damn him! I wish he'd been soldered in lead—and I bribed the sexton to pull it away, when I'm laid there, and slide mine out too. I'll have it made so, and then, by the time Linton gets to us, he'll not know which is which!"

"You were very wicked, Mr. Heathcliff!" I exclaimed; "were you not ashamed to disturb the dead?"

"I disturbed nobody, Nelly," he replied; "and I gave some ease to myself. I shall be a great deal more comfortable now; and you'll have a better chance of keeping me underground, when I get there. Disturbed her? No! she has disturbed me, night and day, through eighteen years—incessantly—remorselessly—till yesternight; and yesternight, I was tranquil. I dreamt I was sleeping the last sleep, by that sleeper, with my heart stopped, and my cheek frozen against hers."

"And if she had been dissolved into earth, or worse, what would you have dreamt of then?" I said.

"Of dissolving with her, and being more happy still!" he answered. "Do you suppose I dread any change of that sort? I expected such a transformation on raising the lid, but I'm better pleased that it should not commence till I share it. Besides, unless I had received a distinct impression of her passionless features, that strange feeling would hardly have been removed. It began oddly. You know, I was wild after she died, and eternally, from dawn to dawn, praying her to return to me—her spirit. I have a strong faith in ghosts; I have a conviction that they can, and do exist, among us!

"The day she was buried there came a fall of snow. In the evening I went to the churchyard. It blew bleak as winter—all round was solitary: I didn't fear that her fool of a husband would wander up the den so late; and no one else had business to bring them there.

"Being alone, and conscious two yards of loose earth was the sole barrier between us, I said to myself—

" 'I'll have her in my arms again! If she be cold, I'll think it is this north wind that chills *me*; and if she be motionless, it is sleep.'

"I got a spade from the toolhouse, and began to delve with all my might—it scraped the coffin; I fell to work with my hands; the wood commenced cracking about the screws, I was on the point of attaining my object, when it seemed that I heard a sigh from some one above, close at the edge of the grave, and bending down. 'If I can only get this off,' I muttered, 'I wish they may shovel in the earth over us both!' and I wrenched at it more desperately still. There was another sigh, close at my ear. I appeared to feel the warm breath of it displacing the sleet-laden wind. I knew no living thing in flesh and blood was by; but as certainly as you perceive the approach to some substantial body in the dark, though it cannot be discerned, so certainly I felt that Cathy was there, not under me, but on the earth.

"A sudden sense of relief flowed from my heart through every limb. I relinquished my labour of agony, and turned consoled at once, unspeakably consoled. Her presence was with me; it remained while I re-filled the grave, and led me home. You may laugh, if you will, but I was sure I should see her there. I was sure she was with me, and I could not help talking to her.

"Having reached the Heights, I rushed eagerly to the door. It was fastened; and, I remember, that accursed Earnshaw and my wife opposed my entrance. I remember stopping to kick the breath out of him, and then hurrying upstairs, to my room, and hers. I looked round impatiently—I felt her by me—I could *almost* see her, and yet I *could not!* I ought to have sweat blood then, from the anguish of my yearning, from the fervour of my supplications to have but one glimpse! I had not one. She showed herself, as she often was in life, a devil to me! And, since then, sometimes more, and sometimes less, I've been the sport of that intolerable torture! Infernal—keeping my nerves at such a stretch, that, if they had not resembled catgut, they would, long ago, have relaxed to the feebleness of Linton's.

"When I sat in the house with Hareton, it seemed that on going out, I should meet her; when I walked on the moors I should meet her coming in. When I went from home, I hastened to return; she *must* be somewhere at the Heights, I was certain! And when I slept in her chamber—I was beaten out of that—I couldn't lie there; for the moment I closed my eyes, she was either outside the window, or sliding back the panels, or entering the room, or even resting her darling head on the same pillow as she did when a child. And I must open my lids to see. And so I opened and closed them a hundred times a night—to be always disappointed! It racked me! I've often groaned aloud, till that old rascal Joseph no doubt believed that my conscience was playing the fiend inside of me.

"Now since I've seen her, I'm pacified—a little. It was a strange way of killing, not by inches, but by fractions of hair-breadths, to beguile me with the spectre of a hope, through eighteen years!"

Mr. Heathcliff paused and wiped his forehead. His hair clung to it, wet with perspiration; his eyes were fixed on the red embers of the fire; the brows not contracted, but raised next the temples, diminishing the grim aspect of his countenance, but imparting a peculiar look of trouble, and a painful appearance of mental tension towards one absorbing subject. He only half addressed me, and I maintained silence—I didn't like to hear him talk!

After a short period, he resumed his meditation on the picture, took it down, and leant it against the sofa to contemplate it at better advantage; and while so occupied Catherine entered, announcing that she was ready, when her pony should be saddled.

"Send that over to-morrow," said Heathcliff to me, then turning to her he added, "You may do without your pony; it is a fine evening, and you'll need no ponies at Wuthering Heights, for what journeys you take, your own feet will serve you—Come along."

"Good-bye, Ellen!" whispered my dear little mistress. As she kissed me, her lips felt like ice. "Come and see me, Ellen, don't forget."

"Take care you do no such thing, Mrs. Dean!" said her new father. "When I wish to speak to you I'll come here. I want none of your prying at my house!"

He signed her to precede him; and casting back a look that cut my heart, she obeyed.

I watched them from the window walk down the garden. Heathcliff fixed Catherine's arm under his, though she disputed the act, at first, evidently, and with rapid strides, he hurried her into the alley, whose trees concealed them.

Chapter XXX

I have paid a visit to the Heights, but I have not seen her since she left; Joseph held the door in his hand, when I called to ask after her, and wouldn't let me pass. He said Mrs. Linton was "thrang,"[8] and the master was not in. Zillah has told me something of the way they go on, otherwise I should hardly know who was dead, and who living.

She thinks Catherine haughty, and does not like her, I can guess by her talk. My young lady asked some aid of her, when she first came, but Mr. Heathcliff told her to follow her own business, and let his daughter-in-law look after herself, and Zillah willingly acquiesced, being a narrow-minded, selfish woman. Catherine evinced a child's annoyance at this neglect; repaid it with contempt, and thus enlisted my informant among her enemies, as securely as if she had done her some great wrong.

I had a long talk with Zillah, about six weeks ago, a little before you came, one day when we foregathered on the moor; and this is what she told me.

"The first thing Mrs. Linton did," she said, "on her arrival at the Heights, was to run upstairs without even wishing good-evening to me and Joseph; she shut herself into Linton's room, and remained till morning. Then, while the master and Earnshaw were at breakfast, she entered the house and asked all in a quiver if the doctor might be sent for? her cousin was very ill."

" 'We know that!' answered Heathcliff, 'but his life is not worth

8. Busy.

a farthing, and I won't spend a farthing on him.'

" 'But I cannot tell how to do,' she said, 'and if nobody will help me, he'll die!'

" 'Walk out of the room!' cried the master, 'and let me never hear a word more about him! None here care what becomes of him; if you do, act the nurse; if you do not, lock him up and leave him.'

"Then she began to bother me, and I said I'd had enough plague with the tiresome thing; we each had our tasks, and hers was to wait on Linton; Mr. Heathcliff bid me leave that labour to her.

"How they managed together, I can't tell. I fancy he fretted a great deal, and moaned hisseln,[9] night and day; and she had precious little rest, one could guess by her white face, and heavy eyes. She sometimes came into the kitchen all wildered like, and looked as if she would fain beg assistance: but I was not going to disobey the master. I never dare disobey him, Mrs. Dean, and though I thought it wrong that Kenneth should not be sent for, it was no concern of mine, either to advise or complain; and I always refused to meddle.

"Once or twice, after we had gone to bed, I've happened to open my door again, and seen her sitting crying, on the stairs' top; and then I've shut myself in, quick, for fear of being moved to interfere. I did pity her then, I'm sure; still, I didn't wish to lose my place, you know!

"At last, one night she came boldly into my chamber, and frightened me out of my wits, by saying—

" 'Tell Mr. Heathcliff that his son is dying—I'm sure he is, this time. Get up, instantly, and tell him!'

"Having uttered this speech, she vanished again. I lay a quarter of an hour listening and trembling. Nothing stirred—the house was quiet.

" 'She's mistaken,' I said to myself. 'He's got over it. I needn't disturb them.' And I began to doze. But my sleep was marred a second time, by a sharp ringing of the bell—the only bell we have, put up on purpose for Linton; and the master called to me, to see what was the matter, and inform them that he wouldn't have that noise repeated.

"I delivered Catherine's message. He cursed to himself, and in a few minutes, came out with a lighted candle, and proceeded to their room. I followed. Mrs. Heathcliff was seated by the bedside, with her hands folded on her knees. Her father-in-law went up, held the light to Linton's face, looked at him, and touched him; afterwards he turned to her.

" 'Now—Catherine,' he said, 'how do you feel?'

9. Himself.

"She was dumb.

" 'How do you feel, Catherine?' he repeated.

" 'He's safe, and I'm free,' she answered, 'I should feel well—but,' she continued with a bitterness she couldn't conceal, 'you have left me so long to struggle against death, alone, that I feel and see only death! I feel like death!'

"And she looked like it, too! I gave her a little wine. Hareton and Joseph, who had been wakened by the ringing and the sound of feet, and heard our talk from outside, now entered. Joseph was fain, I believe, of the lad's removal: Hareton seemed a thought bothered, though he was more taken up with staring at Catherine than thinking of Linton. But the master bid him get off to bed again—we didn't want his help. He afterwards made Joseph remove the body to his chamber, and told me to return to mine, and Mrs. Heathcliff remained by herself.

"In the morning, he sent me to tell her she must come down to breakfast. She had undressed, and appeared going to sleep, and said she was ill; at which I hardly wondered. I informed Mr. Heathcliff, and he replied—

" 'Well, let her be till after the funeral; and go up now and then to get her what is needful; and as soon as she seems better, tell me.'

Cathy stayed upstairs a fortnight, according to Zillah, who visited her twice a day, and would have been rather more friendly, but her attempts at increasing kindness were proudly and promptly repelled.

Heathcliff went up once, to show her Linton's will. He had bequeathed the whole of his, and what had been her, moveable property to his father. The poor creature was threatened, or coaxed, into that act during her week's absence, when his uncle died. The lands, being a minor, he could not meddle with. However, Mr. Heathcliff has claimed and kept them in his wife's right, and his also, I suppose legally. At any rate Catherine, destitute of cash and friends, cannot disturb his possession.

"Nobody," said Zillah, "ever approached her door, except that once, but I; and nobody asked anything about her. The first occasion of her coming down into the house, was on a Sunday afternoon.

"She had cried out, when I carried up her dinner, that she couldn't bear any longer being in the cold; and I told her the master was going to Thrushcross Grange; and Earnshaw and I needn't hinder her from descending; so, as soon as she heard Heathcliff's horse trot off, she made her appearance, donned in black, and her yellow curls combed back behind her ears, as plain as a Quaker; she couldn't comb them out.

"Joseph and I generally go to chapel on Sundays," (the Kirk, you know, has no minister now, explained Mrs. Dean, and they call the Methodists' or Baptists' place, I can't say which it is, at Gimmerton, a chapel). "Joseph had gone," she continued, "but I thought proper to bide at home. Young folks are always the better for an elder's over-looking, and Hareton, with all his bashfulness, isn't a model of nice behaviour. I let him know that his cousin would very likely sit with us, and she had been always used to see the Sabbath respected, so he had as good leave his guns and bits of in-door work alone, while she stayed.

"He coloured up at the news, and cast his eyes over his hands and clothes. The train-oil[1] and gunpowder were shoved out of sight in a minute. I saw he meant to give her his company; and I guessed, by his way, he wanted to be presentable; so, laughing, as I durst not laugh when the master is by, I offered to help him, if he would, and joked at his confusion. He grew sullen, and began to swear.

"Now, Mrs. Dean," she went on, seeing me not pleased by her manner, "you happen think your young lady too fine for Mr. Hareton, and happen you're right; but, I own, I should love well to bring her pride a peg lower. And what will all her learning and her daintiness do for her, now? She's as poor as you or I—poorer, I'll be bound; you're saving, and I'm doing my little all, that road."[2]

Hareton allowed Zillah to give him her aid; and she flattered him into a good humour; so, when Catherine came, half forgetting her former insults, he tried to make himself agreeable, by the housekeeper's account.

"Missis walked in," she said, "as chill as an icicle, and as high as a princess. I got up and offered her my seat in the arm-chair. No, she turned up her nose at my civility. Earnshaw rose too, and bid her come to the settle, and sit close by the fire; he was sure she was starved.

" 'I've been starved a month and more,' she answered, resting on the word, as scornful as she could.

"And she got a chair for herself, and placed it at a distance from both of us.

"Having sat till she was warm, she began to look round, and discovered a number of books in the dresser; she was instantly upon her feet again, stretching to reach them, but they were too high up.

"Her cousin, after watching her endeavours a while, at last summoned courage to help her; she held her frock, and he filled it with the first that came to hand.

"That was a great advance for the lad. She didn't thank him; still, he felt gratified that she had accepted his assistance, and ventured to stand behind as she examined them, and even to stoop and point out what struck his fancy in certain old pictures which they contained; nor was he daunted by the saucy style in which she jerked

1. Oil from whales or seals.   2. That way.

the page from his finger; he contented himself with going a bit farther back, and looking at her instead of the book.

"She continued reading, or seeking for something to read. His attention became, by degrees, quite centred in the study of her thick, silky curls; her face he couldn't see, and she couldn't see him. And, perhaps, not quite awake to what he did, but attracted like a child to a candle, at last he proceeded from staring to touching; he put out his hand and stroked one curl, as gently as if it were a bird. He might have stuck a knife into her neck, she started round in such a taking.

" 'Get away, this moment! How dare you touch me? Why are you stopping there?' she cried, in a tone of disgust. 'I can't endure you! I'll go up stairs again, if you come near me.'

"Mr. Hareton recoiled, looking as foolish as he could do; he sat down in the settle, very quiet, and she continued turning over her volumes, another half hour; finally, Earnshaw crossed over, and whispered to me—

" 'Will you ask her to read to us, Zillah? I'm stalled of doing naught; and I do like—I could like to hear her! Dunnot say I wanted it, but ask of yourseln.'

" 'Mr. Hareton wishes you would read to us, ma'am,' I said, immediately. 'He'd take it very kind—he'd be much obliged.'

"She frowned; and, looking up, answered—

" 'Mr. Hareton, and the whole set of you, will be good enough to understand that I reject any pretence at kindness you have the hypocrisy to offer! I despise you, and will have nothing to say to any of you! When I would have given my life for one kind word, even to see one of your faces, you all kept off. But I won't complain to you! I'm driven down here by the cold, not either to amuse you, or enjoy your society.'

" 'What could I ha' done?' began Earnshaw. 'How was I to blame?'

" 'Oh! you are an exception,' answered Mrs. Heathcliff. 'I never missed such a concern as you.'

" 'But I offered more than once, and asked,' he said, kindling up at her pertness, 'I asked Mr. Heathcliff to let me wake for[3] you—'

" 'Be silent! I'll go out of doors, or anywhere, rather than have your disagreeable voice in my ear!' said my lady.

"Hareton muttered, she might go to hell, for him! and unslinging his gun, restrained himself from his Sunday occupations no longer.

"He talked now, freely enough; and she presently saw fit to retreat to her solitude: but the frost had set in, and, in spite of her pride, she was forced to condescend to our company, more and

3. Watch, guard.

more. However, I took care there should be no further scorning at
my good nature. Ever since, I've been as stiff as herself; and she has
no lover, or liker among us—and she does not deserve one—for, let
them say the least word to her, and she'll curl back without respect
of any one! She'll snap at the master himself, and as good as dares
him to thrash her; and the more hurt she gets, the more venomous
she grows."

At first, on hearing this account from Zillah, I determined to leave
my situation, take a cottage, and get Catherine to come and live
with me; but Mr. Heathcliff would as soon permit that, as he would
set up Hareton in an independent house; and I can see no remedy,
at present, unless she could marry again; and that scheme, it does
not come within my province to arrange.

Thus ended Mrs. Dean's story. Notwithstanding the doctor's
prophecy, I am rapidly recovering strength, and, though it be only
the second week in January, I propose getting out on horseback, in
a day or two, and riding over to Wuthering Heights, to inform my
landlord that I shall spend the next six months in London; and, if
he likes, he may look out for another tenant to take the place, after
October—I would not pass another winter here, for much.

Chapter XXXI

Yesterday was bright, calm, and frosty. I went to the Heights
as I proposed; my housekeeper entreated me to bear a little note
from her to her young lady, and I did not refuse, for the worthy
woman was not conscious of anything odd in her request.

The front door stood open, but the jealous gate was fastened, as
at my last visit; I knocked and invoked Earnshaw from among the
garden beds; he unchained it, and I entered. The fellow is as handsome a rustic as need be seen. I took particular notice of him this
time; but then he does his best, apparently, to make the least of his
advantages.

I asked if Mr. Heathcliff were at home? He answered, no; but he
would be in at dinner-time. It was eleven o'clock, and I announced
my intention of going in, and waiting for him, at which he immediately flung down his tools and accompanied me, in the office
of watchdog, not as a substitute for the host.

We entered together; Catherine was there, making herself useful
in preparing some vegetables for the approaching meal; she looked
more sulky, and less spirited than when I had seen her first. She
hardly raised her eyes to notice me, and continued her employment
with the same disregard to common forms of politeness, as before;
never returning my bow and good morning by the slightest acknowl-

edgment.

"She does not seem so amiable," I thought, "as Mrs. Dean would persuade me to believe. She's a beauty, it is true; but not an angel."

Earnshaw surlily bid her remove her things to the kitchen.

"Remove them yourself," she said, pushing them from her, as soon as she had done, and retiring to a stool by the window, where she began to carve figures of birds and beasts, out of the turnip parings in her lap.

I approached her, pretending to desire a view of the garden; and, as I fancied, adroitly dropped Mrs. Dean's note onto her knee, unnoticed by Hareton—but she asked aloud—

"What is that?" And chucked it off.

"A letter from your old acquaintance, the housekeeper at the Grange," I answered, annoyed at her exposing my kind deed, and fearful lest it should be imagined a missive of my own.

She would gladly have gathered it up at this information, but Hareton beat her; he seized, and put it in his waistcoat, saying Mr. Heathcliff should look at it first.

Thereat, Catherine silently turned her face from us, and, very stealthily, drew out her pocket-handkerchief and applied it to her eyes; and her cousin, after struggling a while to keep down his softer feelings, pulled out the letter and flung it on the floor beside her as ungraciously as he could.

Catherine caught and perused it eagerly; then she put a few questions to me concerning the inmates, rational and irrational, of her former home; and gazing towards the hills, murmured in soliloquy—

"I should like to be riding Minny down there! I should like to be climbing up there—Oh! I'm tired—I'm *stalled*, Hareton!"

And she leant her pretty head back against the sill, with half a yawn and half a sigh, and lapsed into an aspect of abstracted sadness, neither caring nor knowing whether we remarked her.

"Mrs. Heathcliff," I said, after sitting some time mute, "you are not aware that I am an acquaintance of yours? so intimate, that I think it strange you won't come and speak to me. My housekeeper never wearies of talking about and praising you; and she'll be greatly disappointed if I return with no news of, or from you, except that you received her letter, and said nothing!"

She appeared to wonder at this speech and asked—

"Does Ellen like you?"

"Yes, very well," I replied unhesitatingly.

"You must tell her," she continued, "that I would answer her letter, but I have no materials for writing, not even a book from which I might tear a leaf."

"No books!" I exclaimed. "How do you contrive to live here

without them, if I may take the liberty to inquire? Though provided with a large library, I'm frequently very dull at the Grange; take my books away, and I should be desperate!"

"I was always reading, when I had them," said Catherine, "and Mr. Heathcliff never reads; so he took it into his head to destroy my books. I have not had a glimpse of one, for weeks. Only once, I searched through Joseph's store of theology, to his great irritation; and once, Hareton, I came upon a secret stock in your room— some Latin and Greek, and some tales and poetry; all old friends. I brought the last here—and you gathered them, as a magpie gathers silver spoons, for the mere love of stealing! They are of no use to you; or else you concealed them in the bad spirit, that as you cannot enjoy them, nobody else shall. Perhaps *your* envy counselled Mr. Heathcliff to rob me of my treasures? But I've most of them written on my brain and printed in my heart, and you cannot deprive me of those!"

Earnshaw blushed crimson, when his cousin made this revelation of his private literary accumulations, and stammered an indignant denial of her accusations.

"Mr. Hareton is desirous of increasing his amount of knowledge," I said, coming to his rescue. "He is not *envious* but *emulous* of your attainments. He'll be a clever scholar in a few years!"

"And he wants *me* to sink into a dunce, meantime," answered Catherine. "Yes, I hear him trying to spell and read to himself, and pretty blunders he makes! I wish you would repeat Chevy Chase, as you did yesterday; it was extremely funny! I heard you—and I heard you turning over the dictionary, to seek out the hard words, and then cursing, because you couldn't read their explanations!"

The young man evidently thought it too bad that he should be laughed at for his ignorance, and then laughed at for trying to remove it. I had a similar notion, and, remembering Mrs. Dean's anecdote of his first attempt at enlightening the darkness in which he had been reared, I observed—

"But, Mrs. Heathcliff, we have each had a commencement, and each stumbled and tottered on the threshold, and had our teachers scorned, instead of aiding us, we should stumble and totter yet."

"Oh!" she replied, "I don't wish to limit his acquirements. Still, he has no right to appropriate what is mine, and make it ridiculous to me with his vile mistakes and mis-pronunciations! Those books, both prose and verse, were consecrated to me by other associations, and I hate to have them debased and profaned in his mouth! Besides, of all, he has selected my favourite pieces that I love the most to repeat, as if out of deliberate malice!"

Hareton's chest heaved in silence a minute; he laboured under a severe sense of mortification and wrath, which it was no easy task to suppress.

I rose, and, from a gentlemanly idea of relieving his embarrassment, took up my station in the door-way, surveying the external prospect, as I stood.

He followed my example, and left the room, but presently reappeared, bearing half-a-dozen volumes in his hands, which he threw into Catherine's lap, exclaiming—

"Take them! I never want to hear, or read, or think of them again!"

"I won't have them, now!" she answered. "I shall connect them with you, and hate them."

She opened one that had obviously been often turned over, and read a portion in the drawling tone of a beginner; then laughed, and threw it from her.

"And listen!" she continued provokingly, commencing a verse of an old ballad in the same fashion.

But his self-love would endure no further torment. I heard, and not altogether disapprovingly, a manual check given to her saucy tongue. The little wretch had done her utmost to hurt her cousin's sensitive though uncultivated feelings, and a physical argument was the only mode he had of balancing the account and repaying its effects on the inflicter.

He afterwards gathered the books and hurled them on the fire. I read in his countenance what anguish it was to offer that sacrifice to spleen. I fancied that as they consumed, he recalled the pleasure they had already imparted, and the triumph and ever increasing pleasure he had anticipated from them; and, I fancied, I guessed the incitement to his secret studies, also. He had been content with daily labour and rough animal enjoyments, till Catherine crossed his path. Shame at her scorn, and hope of her approval were his first prompters to higher pursuits; and instead of guarding him from one, and winning him the other, his endeavours to raise himself had produced just the contrary result.

"Yes, that's all the good that such a brute as you can get from them!" cried Catherine, sucking her damaged lip, and watching the conflagration with indignant eyes.

"You'd *better* hold your tongue, now!" he answered fiercely.

And his agitation precluding further speech, he advanced hastily to the entrance, where I made way for him to pass. But, ere he had crossed the door-stones, Mr. Heathcliff, coming up the causeway, encountered him and laying hold of his shoulder, asked—

"What's to do now, my lad?"

"Naught, naught!" he said, and broke away, to enjoy his grief and anger in solitude.

Heathcliff gazed after him, and sighed.

"It will be odd, if I thwart myself!" he muttered, unconscious that I was behind him. "But, when I look for his father in his face, I find *her* every day more! How the devil is he so like? I can hardly bear to see him."

He bent his eyes to the ground, and walked moodily in. There was a restless, anxious expression in his countenance I had never remarked there before, and he looked sparer in person.

His daughter-in-law, on perceiving him through the window, immediately escaped to the kitchen, so that I remained alone.

"I'm glad to see you out of doors again, Mr. Lockwood," he said in reply to my greeting, "from selfish motives partly; I don't think I could readily supply your loss in this desolation. I've wondered, more than once, what brought you here."

"An idle whim, I fear, sir," was my answer, "or else an idle whim is going to spirit me away. I shall set out for London next week, and I must give you warning, that I feel no disposition to retain Thrushcross Grange, beyond the twelvemonths I agreed to rent it. I believe I shall not live there any more."

"Oh, indeed! you're tired of being banished from the world, are you?" he said. "But, if you be coming to plead off paying for a place you won't occupy, your journey is useless. I never relent in exacting my due, from any one."

"I'm coming to plead off nothing about it!" I exclaimed, considerably irritated. "Should you wish it, I'll settle with you now," and I drew my notebook from my pocket.

"No, no," he replied coolly; "you'll leave sufficient behind, to cover your debts, if you fail to return. I'm not in such a hurry—sit down and take your dinner with us; a guest that is safe from repeating his visit, can generally be made welcome. Catherine! bring the things in—where are you?"

Catherine re-appeared, bearing a tray of knives and forks.

"You may get your dinner with Joseph," muttered Heathcliff aside, "and remain in the kitchen till he is gone."

She obeyed his directions very punctually; perhaps she had no temptation to transgress. Living among clowns and misanthropists, she probably cannot appreciate a better class of people, when she meets them.

With Mr. Heathcliff, grim and saturnine, on one hand, and Hareton, absolutely dumb, on the other, I made a somewhat cheerless meal, and bid adieu early. I would have departed by the back way to get a last glimpse of Catherine, and annoy old Joseph; but Hareton received orders to lead up my horse, and my host himself escorted me to the door, so I could not fulfil my wish.

"How dreary life gets over in that house!" I reflected, while riding down the road. "What a realization of something more romantic than a fairy tale it would have been for Mrs. Linton Heathcliff, had she and I struck up an attachment, as her good nurse desired, and migrated together into the stirring atmosphere of the town!"

Chapter XXXII

1802.—This September, I was invited to devastate the moors of a friend, in the North; and, on my journey to his abode, I unexpectedly came within fifteen miles of Gimmerton. The hostler at a roadside public-house was holding a pail of water to refresh my horses, when a cart of very green oats, newly reaped, passed by, and he remarked—

"Yon's frough Gimmerton, nah! They're allas three wick' after other folk wi' ther harvest."

"Gimmerton?" I repeated—my residence in that locality had already grown dim and dreamy. "Ah! I know! How far is it from this?"

"Happen fourteen mile' o'er th' hills, and a rough road," he answered.

A sudden impulse seized me to visit Thrushcross Grange. It was scarcely noon, and I conceived that I might as well pass the night under my own roof, as in an inn. Besides, I could spare a day easily, to arrange matters with my landlord, and thus save myself the trouble of invading the neighbourhood again.

Having rested a while, I directed my servant to inquire the way to the village; and, with great fatigue to our beasts, we managed the distance in some three hours.

I left him there, and proceeded down the valley alone. The grey church looked greyer, and the lonely churchyard lonelier. I distinguished a moor sheep cropping the short turf on the graves. It was sweet, warm weather—too warm for travelling; but the heat did not hinder me from enjoying the delightful scenery above and below; had I seen it nearer August, I'm sure it would have tempted me to waste a month among its solitudes. In winter, nothing more dreary, in summer, nothing more divine, than those glens shut in by hills, and those bluff, bold swells of heath.

I reached the Grange before sunset, and knocked for admittance; but the family had retreated into the back premises, I judged by one thin, blue wreath curling from the kitchen chimney, and they did not hear.

I rode into the court. Under the porch, a girl of nine or ten sat knitting, and an old woman reclined on the horse-steps, smoking a meditative pipe.

"Is Mrs. Dean within?" I demanded of the dame.

"Mistress Dean? Nay!" she answered, "shoo doesn't bide here;

shoo's up at th' Heights."

"Are you the housekeeper, then?" I continued.

"Eea, Aw keep th' hause," she replied.

"Well, I'm Mr. Lockwood, the master. Are there any rooms to lodge me in, I wonder? I wish to stay here all night."

"'T' maister!'" she cried in astonishment. "Whet, whoiver knew yah wur coming? Yah sud ha' send word! They's nowt norther dry, nor mensful[4] abaht t' place—nowt there isn't!"

She threw down her pipe and bustled in, the girl followed, and I entered too; soon perceiving that her report was true, and, moreover, that I had almost upset her wits by my unwelcome apparition.

I bid her be composed—I would go out for a walk; and, meantime, she must try to prepare a corner of a sitting-room for me to sup in, and a bed-room to sleep in. No sweeping and dusting, only good fires and dry sheets were necessary.

She seemed willing to do her best; though she thrust the hearthbrush into the grates in mistake for the poker, and mal-appropriated several other articles of her craft; but I retired, confiding in her energy for a resting-place against my return.

Wuthering Heights was the goal of my proposed excursion. An after-thought brought me back, when I had quitted the court.

"All well at the Heights?" I enquired of the woman.

"Eea, f'r owt Ee knaw!" she answered, skurrying away with a pan of hot cinders.

I would have asked why Mrs. Dean had deserted the Grange; but it was impossible to delay her at such a crisis, so I turned away and made my exit, rambling leisurely along with the glow of a sinking sun behind, and the mild glory of a rising moon in front—one fading, and the other brightening, as I quitted the park, and climbed the stony by-road branching off to Mr. Heathcliff's dwelling.

Before I arrived in sight of it, all that remained of day was a beamless, amber light along the west; but I could see every pebble on the path, and every blade of grass by that splendid moon.

I had neither to climb the gate, nor to knock—it yielded to my hand.

That is an improvement! I thought. And I noticed another, by the aid of my nostrils; a fragrance of stocks and wall flowers, wafted on the air, from amongst the homely fruit trees.

Both doors and lattices were open; and yet, as is usually the case in a coal district, a fine, red fire illumined the chimney; the comfort which the eye derives from it, renders the extra heat endurable. But the house of Wuthering Heights is so large, that the inmates have plenty of space for withdrawing out of its influence; and, accordingly, what inmates there were had stationed themselves not

4. Neither dry nor proper.

far from one of the windows. I could both see them and hear them talk before I entered, and looked and listened in consequence, being moved thereto by a mingled sense of curiosity and envy that grew as I lingered.

"Con-*trary!*" said a voice, as sweet as a silver bell—"That for the third time, you dunce! I'm not going to tell you, again—Recollect, or I pull your hair!"

"Contrary, then," answered another, in deep, but softened tones. "And now, kiss me, for minding so well."

"No, read it over first correctly, without a single mistake."

The male speaker began to read. He was a young man, respectably dressed, and seated at a table, having a book before him. His handsome features glowed with pleasure, and his eyes kept impatiently wandering from the page to a small white hand over his shoulder, which recalled him by a smart slap on the cheek, whenever its owner detected such signs of inattention.

Its owner stood behind; her light shining ringlets blending, at intervals, with his brown locks, as she bent to superintend his studies; and her face—it was lucky he could not see her face, or he would never have been so steady. I could, and I bit my lip, in spite, at having thrown away the chance I might have had of doing something besides staring at its smiting beauty.

The task was done, not free from further blunders, but the pupil claimed a reward, and received at least five kisses, which, however, he generously returned. Then, they came to the door, and from their conversation, I judged they were about to issue out and have a walk on the moors. I supposed I should be condemned in Hareton Earnshaw's heart, if not by his mouth, to the lowest pit in the infernal regions if I showed my unfortunate person in his neighbourhood then, and feeling very mean and malignant, I skulked round to seek refuge in the kitchen.

There was unobstructed admittance on that side also; and, at the door, sat my old friend, Nelly Dean, sewing and singing a song, which was often interrupted from within, by harsh words of scorn and intolerance, uttered in far from musical accents.

"Aw'd rayther, by th' haulf, hev 'em swearing i' my lugs frough morn tuh neeght, nur hearken yah, hahsiver!" said the tenant of the kitchen, in answer to an unheard speech of Nelly's. "It's a blazing shaime, ut Aw cannut oppen t' Blessed Book, bud yah set up them glories tuh Sattan, un' all t' flaysome wickednesses ut iver wer born intuh t' warld! Oh! yah're a raight nowt, un' shoo's another; un' that poor lad 'ull be lost, atween ye. Poor lad!" he added, with a groan; "he's witched, Aw'm sartin on't! O, Lord, judge 'em, for they's norther law nur justice amang wer rullers!"[5]

5. *lugs:* ears; *Sattan:* Satan; *amang wer rullers:* among our rulers.

"No! or we should be sitting in flaming fagots, I suppose," retorted the singer. "But wisht, old man, and read your Bible, like a Christian, and never mind me. This is 'Fairy Annie's Wedding'— a bonny tune—it goes to a dance."

Mrs. Dean was about to recommence, when I advanced, and recognising me directly, she jumped to her feet, crying—

"Why, bless you, Mr. Lockwood! How could you think of returning in this way? All's shut up at Thrushcross Grange. You should have given us notice!"

"I've arranged to be accommodated there, for as long as I shall stay," I answered. "I depart again to-morrow. And how are you transplanted here, Mrs. Dean? tell me that."

"Zillah left, and Mr. Heathcliff wished me to come, soon after you went to London, and stay till you returned. But, step in, pray! Have you walked from Gimmerton this evening?"

"From the Grange," I replied; "and, while they make me lodging room there, I want to finish my business with your master, because I don't think of having another opportunity in a hurry."

"What business, sir?" said Nelly, conducting me into the house. "He's gone out, at present, and won't return soon."

About the rent," I answered.

"Oh! then it is with Mrs. Heathcliff you must settle," she observed, "or rather with me. She has not learnt to manage her affairs yet, and I act for her; there's nobody else."

I looked surprised.

"Ah! you have not heard of Heathcliff's death, I see!" she continued.

"Heathcliff dead?" I exclaimed, astonished. "How long ago?"

"Three months since—but, sit down, and let me take your hat, and I'll tell you all about it. Stop, you have had nothing to eat, have you?"

"I want nothing. I have ordered supper at home. You sit down too. I never dreamt of his dying! Let me hear how it came to pass. You say you don't expect them back for some time—the young people?"

"No—I have to scold them every evening, for their late rambles, but they don't care for me. At least, have a drink of our old ale; it will do you good—you seem weary."

She hastened to fetch it, before I could refuse, and I heard Joseph asking whether "it warn't a crying scandal that she should have fellies at her time of life? And then, to get them jocks out uh t' Maister's cellar! He fair shaamed to 'bide still and see it."[6]

She did not stay to retaliate, but re-entered, in a minute, bearing a reaming, silver pint, whose contents I lauded with becoming ear-

6. *Fellies:* fellows; *jocks:* jugs.

nestness. And afterwards she furnished me with the sequel of Heath-cliff's history. He had a "queer" end, as she expressed it.

I was summoned to Wuthering Heights, within a fortnight of your leaving us, she said; and I obeyed joyfully, for Catherine's sake.

My first interview with her grieved and shocked me! she had altered so much since our separation. Mr. Heathcliff did not explain his reasons for taking a new mind about my coming here; he only told me he wanted me, and he was tired of seeing Catherine; I must make the little parlour my sitting room, and keep her with me. It was enough if he were obliged to see her once or twice a day.

She seemed pleased at this arrangement; and, by degrees, I smuggled over a great number of books and other articles, that had formed her amusement at the Grange; and flattered myself we should get on in tolerable comfort.

The delusion did not last long. Catherine, contented at first, in a brief space grew irritable and restless. For one thing, she was forbidden to move out of the garden, and it fretted her sadly to be confined to its narrow bounds, as Spring drew on; for another, in following the house, I was forced to quit her frequently, and she complained of loneliness; she preferred quarrelling with Joseph in the kitchen, to sitting at peace in her solitude.

I did not mind their skirmishes; but Hareton was often obliged to seek the kitchen also, when the master wanted to have the house to himself; and, though, in the beginning, she either left it at his approach, or quietly joined in my occupations, and shunned remarking, or addressing him—and though he was always as sullen and silent as possible—after a while, she changed her behaviour, and became incapable of letting him alone: talking at him; commenting on his stupidity and idleness; expressing her wonder how he could endure the life he lived—how he could sit a whole evening staring into the fire, and dozing.

"He's just like a dog, is he not, Ellen?" she once observed, "or a cart-horse? He does his work, eats his food, and sleeps, eternally! What a blank, dreary mind he must have! Do you ever dream, Hareton? And, if you do, what is it about? But you can't speak to me!"

Then she looked at him; but he would neither open his mouth, nor look again.

"He's perhaps dreaming now," she continued. "He twitched his shoulder as Juno twitches hers. Ask him, Ellen."

"Mr. Hareton will ask the master to send you upstairs, if you don't behave!" I said. He had not only twitched his shoulder, but clenched his fist, as if tempted to use it.

"I know why Hareton never speaks, when I am in the kitchen," she exclaimed, on another occasion. "He is afraid I shall laugh at him. Ellen, what do you think? He began to teach himself to read once; and, because I laughed, he burned his books, and dropped it—was he not a fool?"

"Were not you naughty?" I said; "answer me that."

"Perhaps I was," she went on, "but I did not expect him to be so silly. Hareton, if I gave you a book, would you take it now? I'll try!"

She placed one she had been perusing on his hand; he flung it off, and muttered, if she did not give over, he would break her neck.

"Well, I shall put it here," she said, "in the table drawer, and I'm going to bed."

Then she whispered me to watch whether he touched it, and departed. But he would not come near it, and so I informed her in the morning, to her great disappointment. I saw she was sorry for his persevering sulkiness and indolence. Her conscience reproved her for frightening him off improving himself; she had done it effectually.

But her ingenuity was at work to remedy the injury; while I ironed, or pursued other stationary employments I could not well do in the parlour, she would bring some pleasant volume, and read it aloud to me. When Hareton was there, she generally paused in an interesting part, and left the book lying about—that she did repeatedly; but he was as obstinate as a mule, and, instead of snatching at her bait, in wet weather he took to smoking with Joseph, and they sat like automatons, one on each side of the fire, the elder happily too deaf to understand her wicked nonsense, as he would have called it, the younger doing his best to seem to disregard it. On fine evenings the latter followed his shooting expeditions, and Catherine yawned and sighed, and teased me to talk to her, and ran off into the court or garden, the moment I began; and, as a last resource, cried and said she was tired of living, her life was useless.

Mr. Heathcliff, who grew more and more disinclined to society, had almost banished Earnshaw out of his apartment. Owing to an accident, at the commencement of March, he became for some days a fixture in the kitchen. His gun burst while out on the hills by himself; a splinter cut his arm, and he lost a good deal of blood before he could reach home. The consequence was, that, perforce, he was condemned to the fire-side and tranquillity, till he made it up again.

It suited Catherine to have him there: at any rate, it made her hate her room upstairs more than ever; and she would compel me to find out business below, that she might accompany me.

On Easter Monday, Joseph went to Gimmerton fair with some cattle; and, in the afternoon, I was busy getting up linen in the kitchen. Earnshaw sat, morose as usual, at the chimney corner, and my little mistress was beguiling an idle hour with drawing pictures on the window panes, varying her amusement by smothered bursts of songs, and whispered ejaculations, and quick glances of annoyance and impatience in the direction of her cousin, who steadfastly smoked, and looked into the grate.

At a notice that I could do with her no longer intercepting my light, she removed to the hearthstone. I bestowed little attention on her proceedings, but, presently, I heard her begin—

"I've found out, Hareton, that I want—that I'm glad—that I should like you to be my cousin, now, if you had not grown so cross to me, and so rough."

Hareton returned no answer.

"Hareton, Hareton, Hareton! do you hear?" she continued.

"Get off wi' ye!" he growled, with uncompromising gruffness.

"Let me take that pipe," she said, cautiously advancing her hand, and abstracting it from his mouth.

Before he could attempt to recover it, it was broken, and behind the fire. He swore at her and seized another.

"Stop," she cried, "you must listen to me, first; and I can't speak while those clouds are floating in my face."

"Will you go to the devil!" he exclaimed, ferociously, "and let me be!"

"No," she persisted, "I won't—I can't tell what to do to make you talk to me, and you are determined not to understand. When I call you stupid, I don't mean anything—I don't mean that I despise you. Come, you shall take notice of me, Hareton—you are my cousin, and you shall own me."

"I shall have naught to do wi' you, and your mucky pride, and your damned, mocking tricks!" he answered. "I'll go to hell, body and soul, before I look sideways after you again! Side out of t' gait,[7] now; this minute!"

Catherine frowned, and retreated to the window-seat, chewing her lip, and endeavouring, by humming an eccentric tune, to conceal a growing tendency to sob.

"You should be friends with your cousin, Mr. Hareton," I interrupted, "since she repents of her sauciness! It would do you a great deal of good—it would make you another man, to have her for a companion."

"A companion!" he cried; "when she hates me, and does not think me fit to wipe her shoon! Nay, if it made me a king, I'd not be scorned for seeking her good will any more."

"It is not I who hate you, it is you who hate me!" wept Cathy, no longer disguising her trouble. "You hate me as much as Mr.

7. Get out of the way.

Heathcliff does, and more."

"You're a damned liar," began Earnshaw; "why have I made him angry, by taking your part then, a hundred times? and that, when you sneered at, and despised me, and—Go on plaguing me, and I'll step in yonder, and say you worried me out of the kitchen!"

"I didn't know you took my part," she answered, drying her eyes; "and I was miserable and bitter at everybody; but, now I thank you and beg you to forgive me, what can I do besides?"

She returned to the hearth, and frankly extended her hand.

He blackened, and scowled like a thunder cloud, and kept his fists resolutely clenched, and his gaze fixed on the ground.

Catherine, by instinct, must have divined it was obdurate perversity, and not dislike, that prompted this dogged conduct; for, after remaining an instant undecided, she stooped, and impressed on his cheek a gentle kiss.

The little rogue thought I had not seen her, and, drawing back, she took her former station by the window, quite demurely.

I shook my head reprovingly; and then she blushed, and whispered—

"Well! what should I have done, Ellen? He wouldn't shake hands, and he wouldn't look. I must show him some way that I like him, that I want to be friends."

Whether the kiss convinced Hareton, I cannot tell; he was very careful, for some minutes, that his face should not be seen; and when he did raise it, he was sadly puzzled where to turn his eyes.

Catherine employed herself in wrapping a handsome book neatly in white paper; and having tied it with a bit of riband, and addressed it to "Mr. Hareton Earnshaw," she desired me to be her ambassadress, and convey the present to its destined recipient.

"And tell him, if he'll take it, I'll come and teach him to read it right," she said, "and, if he refuse it, I'll go upstairs, and never tease him again."

I carried it, and repeated the message, anxiously watched by my employer. Hareton would not open his fingers, so I laid it on his knee. He did not strike it off either. I returned to my work. Catherine leaned her head and arms on the table, till she heard the slight rustle of the covering being removed; then she stole away, and quietly seated herself beside her cousin. He trembled, and his face glowed. All his rudeness and all his surly harshness had deserted him—he could not summon courage, at first, to utter a syllable, in reply to her questioning look, and her murmured petition.

"Say you forgive me, Hareton, do! You can make me so happy, by speaking that little word."

He muttered something inaudible.

"And you'll be my friend?" added Catherine, interrogatively.

"Nay! you'll be ashamed of me every day of your life," he answered. "And the more, the more you know me, and I cannot bide it."

"So, you won't be my friend?" she said, smiling as sweet as honey, and creeping close up.

I overheard no further distinguishable talk; but, on looking round again, I perceived two such radiant countenances bent over the page of the accepted book, that I did not doubt the treaty had been ratified on both sides, and the enemies were, thenceforth, sworn allies.

The work they studied was full of costly pictures; and those, and their position, had charm enough to keep them unmoved, till Joseph came home. He, poor man, was perfectly aghast at the spectacle of Catherine seated on the same bench with Hareton Earnshaw, leaning her hand on his shoulder; and confounded at his favourite's endurance of her proximity. It affected him too deeply to allow an observation on the subject that night. His emotion was only revealed by the immense sighs he drew, as he solemnly spread his large Bible on the table, and overlaid it with dirty bank-notes from his pocket-book, the produce of the day's transactions. At length, he summoned Hareton from his seat.

"Tak' these in tuh t' maister, lad," he said, "un' bide theare; Aw's gang up tuh my awn rahm. This hoile's norther mensful, nor seemly fur us—we mun side aht, and search another!"[8]

"Come, Catherine," I said, "we must 'side out,' too—I've done my ironing, are you ready to go?"

"It is not eight o'clock!" she answered, rising unwillingly, "Hareton, I'll leave this book upon the chimney-piece, and I'll bring some more to-morrow."

"Ony books ut yah leave, Aw suall tak' intuh th' hahse," said Joseph, "un' it 'ull be mitch[9] if yah find 'em agean; soa, yah muh plase yourseln!"

Cathy threatened that his library should pay for hers; and, smiling as she passed Hareton, went singing upstairs, lighter of heart, I venture to say, than ever she had been under that roof before, except, perhaps, during her earliest visits to Linton.

The intimacy, thus commenced, grew rapidly, though it encountered temporary interruptions. Earnshaw was not to be civilized with a wish; and my young lady was no philosopher, and no paragon of patience; but both their minds tending to the same point—one loving and desiring to esteem, and the other loving and desiring to be esteemed—they contrived in the end to reach it.

You see, Mr. Lockwood, it was easy enough to win Mrs. Heath-

---

8. *Hoile:* room or house (probably house in this context); *mensful:* proper; *side aht:* get out.
9. A strange thing, a marvel.

cliff's heart; but now, I'm glad you did not try. The crown of all my wishes will be the union of those two; I shall envy no one on their wedding-day—there won't be a happier woman than myself in England!

Chapter XXXIII

On the morrow of that Monday, Earnshaw being still unable to follow his ordinary employments, and, therefore, remaining about the house, I speedily found it would be impracticable to retain my charge beside me, as heretofore.

She got downstairs before me, and out into the garden, where she had seen her cousin performing some easy work; and when I went to bid them come to breakfast, I saw she had persuaded him to clear a large space of ground from currant and gooseberry bushes, and they were busy planning together an importation of plants from the Grange.

I was terrified at the devastation which had been accomplished in a brief half hour; the black currant trees were the apple of Joseph's eye, and she had just fixed her choice of a flower bed in the midst of them!

"There! That will be all shewn to the master," I exclaimed, "the minute it is discovered. And what excuse have you to offer for taking such liberties with the garden? We shall have a fine explosion on the head of it: see if we don't! Mr. Hareton, I wonder you should have no more wit, than to go and make that mess at her bidding!"

"I'd forgotten they were Joseph's," answered Earnshaw, rather puzzled, "but I'll tell him I did it."

We always ate our meals with Mr. Heathcliff. I held the mistress's post in making tea and carving; so I was indispensable at table. Catherine usually sat by me; but to-day, she stole nearer to Hareton, and I presently saw she would have no more discretion in her friendship, than she had in her hostility.

"Now, mind you don't talk with and notice your cousin too much," were my whispered instructions as we entered the room. "It will certainly annoy Mr. Heathcliff, and he'll be mad at you both."

"I'm not going to," she answered.

The minute after, she had sidled to him, and was sticking primroses in his plate of porridge.

He dared not speak to her, there; he dared hardly look, and yet she went on teasing, till he was twice on the point of being provoked to laugh; and I frowned, and then she glanced towards the master, whose mind was occupied on other subjects than his company, as his countenance evinced, and she grew serious for an instant, scrutinizing him with deep gravity. Afterwards she turned, and re-commenced her nonsense; at last, Hareton uttered a smothered laugh.

Mr. Heathcliff started; his eye rapidly surveyed our faces. Catherine met it with her accustomed look of nervousness, and yet defiance, which he abhorred.

"It is well you are out of my reach"; he exclaimed. "What fiend possesses you to stare back at me, continually, with those infernal eyes? Down with them! and don't remind me of your existence again. I thought I had cured you of laughing!"

"It was me," muttered Hareton.

"What do you say?" demanded the master.

Hareton looked at his plate, and did not repeat the confession.

Mr. Heathcliff looked at him a bit, and then silently resumed his breakfast, and his interrupted musing.

We had nearly finished, and the two young people prudently shifted wider asunder, so I anticipated no further disturbance during that sitting, when Joseph appeared at the door, revealing by his quivering lip and furious eyes, that the outrage committed on his precious shrubs was detected.

He must have seen Cathy and her cousin about the spot before he examined it, for while his jaws worked like those of a cow chewing its cud, and rendered his speech difficult to understand, he began—

"Aw mun hev my wage, and Aw mun goa! Aw *hed* aimed tuh dee,[1] wheare Aw'd sarved fur sixty year; un' Aw thowt Aw'd lug my books up intuh t' garret, un' all my bits uh stuff, un' they sud hev t' kitchen tuh theirseln; fur t' sake uh quietness. It wur hard tuh gie up my awn hearthstun, bud Aw thowt Aw *could* do that! Bud nah, shoo's taan my garden frough me, un' by th' heart, Maister, Aw cannot stand it! Yah muh bend[2] tuh th' yoak, an ye will— Aw' noan used to't and an ow'd man doesn't sooin get used tuh new barthens.[3] Aw'd rayther arn my bite an' my sup, wi' a hammer in th' road!"

"Now, now, idiot!" interrupted Heathcliff, "cut it short! What's your grievance? I'll interfere in no quarrels between you and Nelly. She may thrust you into the coal-hole for anything I care."

"It's noan Nelly!" answered Joseph. "Aw sudn't shift fur Nelly— nasty, ill nowt as shoo is. Thank God! *shoo* cannot stale t'sowl uh nob'dy! Shoo wer niver soa handsome, bud whet a body mud look at her 'baht winking. It's yon flaysome, graceless quean, ut's witched ahr lad, wi' her bold een, un' her forrard ways till—Nay! It fair

---

1. Die.
2. May bend.

3. *Barthens* (*barth*): literally, a warm place for cattle.

brusts my heart! He's forgetten all E done for him, un made on him, un' goan un' riven up a whole row ut t' grandest currant trees i' t' garden!"[4] And here he lamented outright, unmanned by a sense of his bitter injuries, and Earnshaw's ingratitude and dangerous condition.

"Is the fool drunk?" asked Mr. Heathcliff. "Hareton, is it you he's finding fault with?"

"I've pulled up two or three bushes," replied the young man, "but I'm going to set 'em again."

"And why have you pulled them up?" said the master.

Catherine wisely put in her tongue.

"We wanted to plant some flowers there," she cried. "I'm the only person to blame, for I wished him to do it."

"And who the devil gave *you* leave to touch a stick about the place?" demanded her father-in-law, much surprised. "And who ordered *you* to obey her?" he added, turning to Hareton.

The latter was speechless; his cousin replied—

"You shouldn't grudge a few yards of earth for me to ornament, when you have taken all my land!"

"Your land, insolent slut? you never had any!" said Heathcliff.

"And my money," she continued, returning his angry glare, and, meantime, biting a piece of crust, the remnant of her breakfast.

"Silence!" he exclaimed. "Get done, and begone!"

"And Hareton's land, and his money," pursued the reckless thing. "Hareton and I are friends now; and I shall tell him all about you!"

The master seemed confounded a moment; he grew pale, and rose up, eyeing her all the while, with an expression of mortal hate.

"If you strike me, Hareton will strike you!" she said; "so you may as well sit down."

"If Hareton does not turn you out of the room, I'll strike him to hell," thundered Heathcliff. "Damnable witch! dare you pretend to rouse him against me? Off with her! Do you hear? Fling her into the kitchen! I'll kill her, Ellen Dean, if you let her come into my sight again!"

Hareton tried under his breath to persuade her to go.

"Drag her away!" he cried savagely. "Are you staying to talk?" And he approached to execute his own command.

"He'll not obey you, wicked man, any more!" said Catherine, "and he'll soon detest you, as much as I do!"

"Wisht! wisht!" muttered the young man reproachfully. "I will not hear you speak so to him. Have done!"

"But *y*ou won't let him strike me?" she cried.

"Come then!" he whispered earnestly.

---

4. *Sudn't shift fur Nelly:* shouldn't leave on Nelly's account; *nasty, ill nowt as shoo is:* nasty, evil nothing as she is; *t'sowl:* the soul; *'baht:* without; *brusts:* breaks; *E:* I; *riven up:* torn up.

It was too late—Heathcliff had caught hold of her.

"Now *you* go!" he said to Earnshaw. "Accursed witch! this time she has provoked me, when I could not bear it; and I'll make her repent it for ever!"

He had his hand in her hair; Hareton attempted to release the locks, entreating him not to hurt her that once. His black eyes flashed; he seemed ready to tear Catherine in pieces, and I was just worked up to risk coming to the rescue, when of a sudden, his fingers relaxed, he shifted his grasp from her head to her arm, and gazed intently in her face. Then, he drew his hand over his eyes, stood a moment to collect himself apparently, and turning anew to Catherine, said with assumed calmness—

"You must learn to avoid putting me in a passion, or I shall really murder you, some time! Go with Mrs. Dean, and keep with her, and confine your insolence to her ears. As to Hareton Earnshaw, if I see him listen to you, I'll send him seeking his bread where he can get it! Your love will make him an outcast, and a beggar. Nelly, take her, and leave me, all of you! Leave me!"

I led my young lady out; she was too glad of her escape, to resist; the other followed, and Mr. Heathcliff had the room to himself, till dinner.

I had counselled Catherine to get her upstairs; but, as soon as he perceived her vacant seat, he sent me to call her. He spoke to none of us, ate very little, and went out directly afterwards, intimating that he should not return before evening.

The two new friends established themselves in the house, during his absence, where I heard Hareton sternly check his cousin, on her offering a revelation of her father-in-law's conduct to his father.

He said he wouldn't suffer a word to be uttered to him, in his disparagement; if he were the devil, it didn't signify; he would stand by him; and he'd rather she would abuse himself, as she used to, than begin on Mr. Heathcliff.

Catherine was waxing cross at this; but he found means to make her hold her tongue, by asking, how she would like *him* to speak ill of her father? and then she comprehended that Earnshaw took the master's reputation home to himself, and was attached by ties stronger than reason could break—chains, forged by habit, which it would be cruel to attempt to loosen.

She showed a good heart, thenceforth, in avoiding both complaints and expressions of antipathy concerning Heathcliff, and confessed to me her sorrow that she had endeavoured to raise a bad spirit between him and Hareton; indeed, I don't believe she has ever breathed a syllable, in the latter's hearing, against her oppressor, since.

When this slight disagreement was over, they were thick again, and as busy as possible, in their several occupations, of pupil and teacher. I came in to sit with them, after I had done my work, and I felt so soothed and comforted to watch them, that I did not notice how time got on. You know, they both appeared, in a measure, my children: I had long been proud of one, and now, I was sure, the other would be a source of equal satisfaction. His honest, warm, and intelligent nature shook off rapidly the clouds of ignorance and degradation in which it had been bred; and Catherine's sincere commendations acted as a spur to his industry. His brightening mind brightened his features, and added spirit and nobility to their aspect. I could hardly fancy it the same individual I had beheld on the day I discovered my little lady at Wuthering Heights, after her expedition to the Crags.

While I admired, and they laboured, dusk drew on, and with it returned the master. He came upon us quite unexpectedly, entering by the front way, and had a full view of the whole three, ere we could raise our heads to glance at him.

Well, I reflected, there was never a pleasanter, or more harmless sight; and it will be a burning shame to scold them. The red fire-light glowed on their two bonny heads, and revealed their faces, animated with the eager interest of children; for, though he was twenty-three, and she eighteen, each had so much of novelty to feel and learn, that neither experienced nor evinced the sentiments of sober disenchanted maturity.

They lifted their eyes together, to encounter Mr. Heathcliff. Perhaps you have never remarked that their eyes are precisely similar, and they are those of Catherine Earnshaw. The present Catherine has no other likeness to her, except a breadth of forehead, and a certain arch of the nostril that makes her appear rather haughty, whether she will or not. With Hareton the resemblance is carried farther; it is singular, at all times—then, it was particularly striking, because his senses were alert, and his mental faculties wakened to unwonted activity.

I suppose this resemblance disarmed Mr. Heathcliff: he walked to the hearth in evident agitation, but it quickly subsided, as he looked at the young man; or, I should say, altered its character, for it was there yet.

He took the book from his hand, and glanced at the open page, then returned it without any observation, merely signing Catherine away. Her companion lingered very little behind her, and I was about to depart also, but he bid me sit still.

"It is a poor conclusion, is it not," he observed, having brooded a while on the scene he had just witnessed. "An absurd termination to my violent exertions? I get levers and mattocks to demolish the two houses, and train myself to be capable of working like Hercules, and when everything is ready, and in my power, I find the will to lift a slate off either roof has vanished! My old enemies have not beaten me; now would be the precise time to revenge myself on their representatives: I could do it; and none could hinder me. But where is the use? I don't care for striking, I can't take the trouble to raise my hand! That sounds as if I had been labouring the whole time, only to exhibit a fine trait of magnanimity. It is far from being the case—I have lost the faculty of enjoying their destruction, and I am too idle to destroy for nothing.

"Nelly, there is a strange change approaching—I'm in its shadow at present. I take so little interest in my daily life, that I hardly remember to eat, and drink. Those two, who have left the room, are the only objects which retain a distinct material appearance to me; and that appearance causes me pain, amounting to agony. About *her* I won't speak; and I don't desire to think; but I earnestly wish she were invisible—her presence invokes only maddening sensations. *He* moves me differently; and yet if I could do it without seeming insane, I'd never see him again! You'll perhaps think me rather inclined to become so," he added, making an effort to smile, "if I try to describe the thousand forms of past associations and ideas he awakens, or embodies—But you'll not talk of what I tell you, and my mind is so eternally secluded in itself, it is tempting, at last, to turn it out to another.

"Five minutes ago, Hareton seemed a personification of my youth, not a human being. I felt to him in such a variety of ways, that it would have been impossible to have accosted him rationally.

"In the first place, his startling likeness to Catherine connected him fearfully with her. That, however, which you may suppose the most potent to arrest my imagination, is actually the least, for what is not connected with her to me? and what does not recall her? I cannot look down to this floor, but her features are shaped on the flags! In every cloud, in every tree—filling the air at night, and caught by glimpses in every object by day, I am surrounded with her image! The most ordinary faces of men and women—my own features—mock me with a resemblance. The entire world is a dreadful collection of memoranda that she did exist, and that I have lost her!

"Well, Hareton's aspect was the ghost of my immortal love, of my wild endeavours to hold my right, my degradation, my pride, my happiness, and my anguish—

"But it is frenzy to repeat these thoughts to you; only it will let you know why, with a reluctance to be always alone, his society is no benefit, rather an aggravation of the constant torment I suffer; and it partly contributes to render me regardless how he and his cousin go on together. I can give them no attention, any more."

"But what do you mean by a *change*, Mr. Heathcliff?" I said, alarmed at his manner, though he was neither in danger of losing his senses, nor dying; according to my judgment he was quite strong and healthy; and, as to his reason, from childhood he had a delight in dwelling on dark things, and entertaining odd fancies. He might have had a monomania on the subject of his departed idol; but on every other point his wits were as sound as mine.

"I shall not know that, till it comes," he said, "I'm only half conscious of it now."

"You have no feeling of illness, have you?" I asked.

"No, Nelly, I have not," he answered.

"Then, you are not afraid of death?" I pursued.

"Afraid? No!" he replied. "I have neither a fear, nor a presentiment, nor a hope of death. Why should I? With my hard constitution, and temperate mode of living, and unperilous occupations, I ought to, and probably *shall* remain above ground, till there is scarcely a black hair on my head. And yet I cannot continue in this condition! I have to remind myself to breathe—almost to remind my heart to beat! And it is like bending back a stiff spring; it is by compulsion that I do the slightest act not prompted by one thought, and by compulsion, that I notice anything alive, or dead, which is not associated with one universal idea. I have a single wish, and my whole being and faculties are yearning to attain it. They have yearned towards it so long, and so unwaveringly, that I'm convinced it *will* be reached—and *soon*—because it has devoured my existence. I am swallowed in the anticipation of its fulfilment.

"My confessions have not relieved me, but they may account for some otherwise unaccountable phases of humour, which I show. O, God! It is a long fight, I wish it were over!"

He began to pace the room, muttering terrible things to himself, till I was inclined to believe, as he said Joseph did, that conscience had turned his heart to an earthly hell. I wondered greatly how it would end.

Though he seldom before had revealed this state of mind, even by looks, it was his habitual mood, I had no doubt: he asserted it himself; but not a soul, from his general bearing, would have conjectured the fact. You did not, when you saw him, Mr. Lockwood; and at the period of which I speak, he was just the same as then, only fonder of continued solitude, and perhaps still more laconic in company.

Chapter XXXIV

For some days after that evening, Mr. Heathcliff shunned meeting us at meals; yet he would not consent, formally, to exclude

Hareton and Cathy. He had an aversion to yielding so completely to his feelings, choosing rather to absent himself; and eating once in twenty-four hours seemed sufficient sustenance for him.

One night, after the family were in bed, I heard him go downstairs, and out at the front door: I did not hear him re-enter and, in the morning, I found he was still away.

We were in April then: the weather was sweet and warm, the grass as green as showers and sun could make it, and the two dwarf apple trees, near the southern wall, in full bloom.

After breakfast, Catherine insisted on my bringing a chair, and sitting with my work under the fir trees at the end of the house; and she beguiled Hareton, who had perfectly recovered from his accident, to dig and arrange her little garden, which was shifted to that corner by the influence of Joseph's complaints.

I was comfortably revelling in the spring fragrance around, and the beautiful soft blue overhead, when my young lady, who had run down near the gate to procure some primrose roots for a border, returned only half laden, and informed us that Mr. Heathcliff was coming in.

"And he spoke to me," she added with a perplexed countenance.

"What did he say?" asked Hareton.

"He told me to begone as fast as I could," she answered. "But he looked so different from his usual look that I stopped a moment to stare at him."

"How?" he enquired.

"Why, almost bright and cheerful—No, almost nothing—*very much* excited, and wild and glad!" she replied.

"Night-walking amuses him, then," I remarked, affecting a careless manner. In reality, as surprised as she was, and, anxious to ascertain the truth of her statement, for to see the master looking glad would not be an every day spectacle, I framed an excuse to go in.

Heathcliff stood at the open door; he was pale, and he trembled; yet, certainly, he had a strange joyful glitter in his eyes that altered the aspect of his whole face.

"Will you have some breakfast?" I said, "You must be hungry rambling about all night!"

I wanted to discover where he had been; but I did not like to ask directly.

"No, I'm not hungry," he answered, averting his head, and speaking rather contemptuously, as if he guessed I was trying to divine the occasion of his good humour.

I felt perplexed: I didn't know whether it were not a proper opportunity to offer a bit of admonition.

"I don't think it right to wander out of doors," I observed, "instead of being in bed: it is not wise, at any rate, this moist season. I dare say you'll catch a bad cold, or a fever—you have something the matter with you now!"

"Nothing but what I can bear," he replied, "and with the greatest pleasure, provided you'll leave me alone. Get in, and don't annoy me."

I obeyed; and, in passing, I noticed he breathed as fast as a cat.

"Yes!" I reflected to myself, "we shall have a fit of illness. I cannot conceive what he has been doing!"

That noon, he sat down to dinner with us, and received a heaped-up plate from my hands, as if he intended to make amends for previous fasting.

"I've neither cold, nor fever, Nelly," he remarked, in allusion to my morning's speech. "And I'm ready to do justice to the food you give me."

He took his knife and fork, and was going to commence eating, when the inclination appeared to become suddenly extinct. He laid them on the table, looked eagerly towards the window, then rose and went out.

We saw him walking, to and fro, in the garden, while we concluded our meal; and Earnshaw said he'd go and ask why he would not dine; he thought we had grieved him some way.

"Well, is he coming?" cried Catherine, when her cousin returned.

"Nay," he answered, "but he's not angry; he seemed rare and pleased[5] indeed; only, I made him impatient by speaking to him twice; and then he bid me be off to you; he wondered how I could want the company of any body else."

I set his plate, to keep warm, on the fender: and after an hour or two, he re-entered, when the room was clear, in no degree calmer: the same unnatural—it was unnatural—appearance of joy under his black brows; the same bloodless hue, and his teeth visible, now and then, in a kind of smile; his frame shivering, not as one shivers with chill or weakness, but as a tight-stretched cord vibrates—a strong thrilling, rather than trembling.

I will ask what is the matter, I thought, or who should? And I exclaimed—

"Have you heard any good news, Mr. Heathcliff? You look uncommonly animated."

"Where should good news come from, to me?" he said. "I'm animated with hunger; and, seemingly, I must not eat."

"Your dinner is here," I returned; "why won't you get it?"

"I don't want it now," he muttered, hastily. "I'll wait till supper. And, Nelly, once for all, let me beg you to warn Hareton and the

5. Very pleased.

other away from me. I wish to be troubled by nobody—I wish to have this place to myself."

"Is there some new reason for this banishment?" I inquired. "Tell me why you are so queer, Mr. Heathcliff? Where were you last night? I'm not putting the question through idle curiosity, but—"

"You are putting the question through very idle curiosity," he interrupted, with a laugh. "Yet, I'll answer it. Last night, I was on the threshold of hell. To-day, I am within sight of my heaven. I have my eyes on it—hardly three feet to sever me! And now you'd better go. You'll neither see nor hear anything to frighten you, if you refrain from prying."

Having swept the hearth and wiped the table, I departed more perplexed than ever.

He did not quit the house again that afternoon, and no one intruded on his solitude, till, at eight o'clock, I deemed it proper, though unsummoned, to carry a candle and his supper to him.

He was leaning against the ledge of an open lattice, but not looking out; his face was turned to the interior gloom. The fire had smouldered to ashes; the room was filled with the damp, mild air of the cloudy evening, and so still, that not only the murmur of the beck down Gimmerton was distinguishable, but its ripples and its gurgling over the pebbles, or through the large stones which it could not cover.

I uttered an ejaculation of discontent at seeing the dismal grate, and commenced shutting the casements, one after another, till I came to his.

"Must I close this?" I asked, in order to rouse him, for he would not stir.

The light flashed on his features, as I spoke. Oh, Mr. Lockwood, I cannot express what a terrible start I got, by the momentary view! Those deep black eyes! That smile, and ghastly paleness! It appeared to me, not Mr. Heathcliff, but a goblin; and, in my terror, I let the candle bend towards the wall, and it left me in darkness.

"Yes, close it," he replied, in his familiar voice. "There, that is pure awkwardness! Why did you hold the candle horizontally? Be quick, and bring another."

I hurried out in a foolish state of dread, and said to Joseph—

"The master wishes you to take him a light, and rekindle the fire." For I dared not go in myself again just then.

Joseph rattled some fire into the shovel, and went; but he brought it back, immediately, with the supper tray in his other hand, explaining that Mr. Heathcliff was going to bed, and he wanted nothing to eat till morning.

We heard him mount the stairs directly; he did not proceed to his ordinary chamber, but turned into that with the panelled bed. Its window, as I mentioned before, is wide enough for anybody to get through, and it struck me that he plotted another midnight excursion, which he had rather we had no suspicion of.

"Is he a ghoul, or a vampire?" I mused. I had read of such hideous, incarnate demons. And then I set myself to reflect how I had tended him in infancy; and watched him grow to youth; and followed him almost through his whole course; and what absurd nonsense it was to yield to that sense of horror.

"But where did he come from, the little dark thing, harboured by a good man to his bane?" muttered superstition, as I dozed into unconsciousness. And I began, half dreaming, to weary myself with imaging some fit parentage for him; and repeating my waking meditations, I tracked his existence over again, with grim variations; at last, picturing his death and funeral; of which, all I can remember is, being exceedingly vexed at having the task of dictating an inscription for his monument, and consulting the sexton about it; and, as he had no surname, and we could not tell his age, we were obliged to content ourselves with the single word, "Heathcliff." That came true; we were. If you enter the kirkyard, you'll read on his headstone only that, and the date of his death.

Dawn restored me to common sense. I rose, and went into the garden, as soon as I could see, to ascertain if there were any footmarks under his window. There were none.

"He has stayed at home," I thought, "and he'll be all right, to-day!"

I prepared breakfast for the household, as was my usual custom, but told Hareton and Catherine to get theirs ere the master came down, for he lay late. They preferred taking it out of doors, under the trees, and I set a little table to accommodate them.

On my re-entrance, I found Mr. Heathcliff below. He and Joseph were conversing about some farming business; he gave clear, minute directions concerning the matter discussed, but he spoke rapidly, and turned his head continually aside, and had the same excited expression, even more exaggerated.

When Joseph quitted the room, he took his seat in the place he generally chose, and I put a basin of coffee before him. He drew it nearer, and then rested in his arms on the table, and looked at the opposite wall, as I supposed, surveying one particular portion, up and down, with glittering, restless eyes, and with such eager interest, that he stopped breathing, during half a minute together.

"Come now," I exclaimed, pushing some bread against his hand. "Eat and drink that, while it is hot. It has been waiting near an hour."

He didn't notice me, and yet he smiled. I'd rather have seen him gnash his teeth than smile so.

"Mr. Heathcliff! master!" I cried. "Don't, for God's sake, stare as if you saw an unearthly vision."

"Don't, for God's sake, shout so loud," he replied. "Turn round, and tell me, are we by ourselves?"

"Of course," was my answer, "of course, we are!"

Still, I involuntarily obeyed him, as if I were not quite sure.

With a sweep of his hand, he cleared a vacant space in front among the breakfast things, and leant forward to gaze more at his ease.

Now, I perceived he was not looking at the wall, for when I regarded him alone, it seemed exactly that he gazed at something within two yards distance. And, whatever it was, it communicated, apparently, both pleasure and pain, in exquisite extremes; at least, the anguished, yet raptured expression of his countenance suggested that idea.

The fancied object was not fixed, either; his eyes pursued it with unwearied vigilance, and, even in speaking to me, were never weaned away.

I vainly reminded him of his protracted abstinence from food; if he stirred to touch anything in compliance with my entreaties, if he stretched his hand out to get a piece of bread, his fingers clenched, before they reached it, and remained on the table, forgetful of their aim.

I sat, a model of patience, trying to attract his absorbed attention from its engrossing speculation, till he grew irritable, and got up, asking why I would not allow him to have his own time in taking his meals? and saying that, on the next occasion, I needn't wait; I might set the things down, and go.

Having uttered these words, he left the house, slowly sauntered down the garden path, and disappeared through the gate.

The hours crept anxiously by: another evening came. I did not retire to rest till late, and when I did, I could not sleep. He returned after midnight, and, instead of going to bed, shut himself into the room beneath. I listened, and tossed about; and, finally, dressed and descended. It was too irksome to lie up there, harassing my brain with a hundred idle misgivings.

I distinguished Mr. Heathcliff's step, restlessly measuring the floor; and he frequently broke the silence by a deep inspiration, resembling a groan. He muttered detached words also; the only one I could catch was the name of Catherine, coupled with some wild term of endearment or suffering, and spoken as one would speak to a person present—low and earnest, and wrung from the depth of his soul.

I had not courage to walk straight into the apartment; but I desired to divert him from his reverie, and, therefore fell foul of the kitchen fire, stirred it, and began to scrape the cinders. It drew him forth sooner than I expected. He opened the door immediately, and said—

"Nelly, come here—is it morning? Come in with your light."

"It is striking four," I answered; "you want a candle to take upstairs—you might have lit one at this fire."

"No, I don't wish to go upstairs," he said. "Come in, and kindle *me* a fire, and do anything there is to do about the room."

"I must blow the coals red first, before I can carry any," I replied, getting a chair and the bellows.

He roamed to and fro, meantime, in a state approaching distraction; his heavy sighs succeeding each other so thick as to leave no space for common breathing between.

"When day breaks, I'll send for Green," he said; "I wish to make some legal inquiries of him while I can bestow a thought on those matters, and while I can act calmly. I have not written my will yet, and how to leave my property, I cannot determine! I wish I could annihilate it from the face of the earth."

"I would not talk so, Mr. Heathcliff," I interposed. "Let your will be, a while—you'll be spared to repent of your many injustices, yet! I never expected that your nerves would be disordered: they are, at present, marvellously so, however; and, almost entirely, through your own fault. The way you've passed these three last days might knock up a Titan. Do take some food, and some repose. You need only look at yourself in a glass to see how you require both. Your cheeks are hollow, and your eyes blood-shot, like a person starving with hunger, and going blind with loss of sleep."

"It is not my fault, that I cannot eat or rest," he replied. "I assure you it is through no settled designs. I'll do both, as soon as I possibly can. But you might as well bid a man struggling in the water, rest within arms-length of the shore! I must reach it first, and then I'll rest. Well, never mind Mr. Green; as to repenting of my injustices, I've done no injustice, and I repent of nothing— I'm too happy, and yet I'm not happy enough. My soul's bliss kills my body, but does not satisfy itself."

"Happy, master?" I cried. "Strange happiness! If you would hear me without being angry, I might offer some advice that would make you happier.

"What is that?" he asked. "Give it."

"You are aware, Mr. Heathcliff," I said, "that from the time you were thirteen years old, you have lived a selfish, unchristian life; and probably hardly had a Bible in your hands during all that period. You must have forgotten the contents of the book, and you may not have space to search it now. Could it be hurtful to send for some one—some minister of any denomination, it does not matter which, to explain it, and show you how very far you have erred from its precepts, and how unfit you will be for its heaven, unless a change takes place before you die?"

"I'm rather obliged than angry, Nelly," he said, "for you remind me of the manner that I desire to be buried in. It is to be carried to the churchyard, in the evening. You and Hareton may, if you please accompany me—and mind, particularly, to notice that the sexton obeys my directions concerning the two coffins! No minister need come; nor need anything be said over me. I tell you, I have nearly attained *my* heaven; and that of others is altogether un-valued and uncoveted by me!"

"And supposing you persevered in your obstinate fast, and died by that means, and they refused to bury you in the precincts of the Kirk?" I said, shocked at his godless indifference. "How would you like it?"

"They won't do that," he replied; "if they did, you must have me removed secretly; and if you neglect it, you shall prove, prac-tically, that the dead are not annihilated!"

As soon as he heard the other members of the family stirring he retired to his den, and I breathed freer. But in the afternoon, while Joseph and Hareton were at their work, he came into the kitchen again, and with a wild look, bid me come, and sit in the house—he wanted somebody with him.

I declined, telling him plainly that his strange talk and manner frightened me, and I had neither the nerve nor the will to be his companion, alone.

"I believe you think me a fiend!" he said, with his dismal laugh, "something too horrible to live under a decent roof!"

Then turning to Catherine, who was there, and who drew behind me at his approach, he added, half sneeringly—

"Will *you* come, chuck? I'll not hurt you. No! to you, I've made myself worse than the devil. Well, there is *one* who won't shrink from my company! By God! she's relentless. Oh, damn it! It's unutterably too much for flesh and blood to bear, even mine."

He solicited the society of no one more. At dusk, he went into his chamber. Through the whole night, and far into the morning, we heard him groaning, and murmuring to himself. Hareton was anxious to enter, but I bid him fetch Mr. Kenneth, and he should go in and see him.

When he came, and I requested admittance and tried to open the door, I found it locked; and Heathcliff bid us be damned. He was better, and would be left alone; so the doctor went away.

The following evening was very wet; indeed it poured down, till day-dawn; and, as I took my morning walk round the house, I observed the master's window swinging open, and the rain driving straight in.

He cannot be in bed, I thought; those showers would drench him through! He must either be up, or out. But I'll make no more ado, I'll go boldly and look!

Having succeeded in obtaining entrance with another key, I ran to unclose the panels, for the chamber was vacant; quickly pushing them aside, I peeped in. Mr. Heathcliff was there—laid on his back. His eyes met mine so keen and fierce, I started; and then he seemed to smile.

I could not think him dead, but his face and throat were washed with rain; the bedclothes dripped, and he was perfectly still. The lattice, flapping to and fro, had grazed one hand that rested on the sill; no blood trickled from the broken skin, and when I put my fingers to it, I could doubt no more—he was dead and stark!

I hasped the window; I combed his black long hair from his forehead; I tried to close his eyes—to extinguish, if possible, that frightful, life-like gaze of exultation, before any one else beheld it. They would not shut; they seemed to sneer at my attempts, and his parted lips and sharp, white teeth sneered too! Taken with another fit of cowardice, I cried out for Joseph. Joseph shuffled up and made a noise, but resolutely refused to meddle with him.

"Th' divil's harried off his soul," he cried, "and he muh hev his carcass intuh t' bargin, for ow't Aw care! Ech! what a wicked un he looks girnning[6] at death!" and the old sinner grinned in mockery.

I thought he intended to cut a caper round the bed; but suddenly composing himself, he fell on his knees, and raised his hands, and returned thanks that the lawful master and the ancient stock were restored to their rights.

I felt stunned by the awful event; and my memory unavoidably recurred to former times with a sort of oppressive sadness. But poor Hareton, the most wronged, was the only one that really suffered much. He sat by the corpse all night, weeping in bitter earnest. He pressed its hand, and kissed the sarcastic, savage face that every one else shrank from contemplating; and bemoaned him with that strong grief which springs naturally from a generous heart, though it be tough as tempered steel.

Kenneth was perplexed to pronounce of what disorder the master died. I concealed the fact of his having swallowed nothing for four days, fearing it might lead to trouble, and then, I am persuaded he did not abstain on purpose; it was the consequence of his strange illness, not the cause.

6. Grinning.

We buried him, to the scandal of the whole neighbourhood, as he had wished. Earnshaw, and I, the sexton and six men to carry the coffin, comprehended the whole attendance.

The six men departed when they had let it down into the grave: we stayed to see it covered. Hareton, with a streaming face, dug green sods, and laid them over the brown mould himself. At present it is as smooth and verdant as its companion mounds—and I hope its tenant sleeps as soundly. But the country folks, if you asked them, would swear on their Bible that he *walks*. There are those who speak to having met him near the church, and on the moor, and even within this house. Idle tales, you'll say, and so say I. Yet that old man by the kitchen fire affirms he has seen two on 'em looking out of his chamber window, on every rainy night, since his death—and an odd thing happened to me about a month ago.

I was going to the Grange one evening—a dark evening threatening thunder—and, just at the turn of the Heights, I encountered a little boy with a sheep and two lambs before him; he was crying terribly, and I supposed the lambs were skittish, and would not be guided.

"What is the matter, my little man?" I asked.

"They's Heathcliff and a woman, yonder, under t' Nab,"[7] he blubbered, "un' Aw darnut pass 'em."

I saw nothing; but neither the sheep nor he would go on, so I bid him take the road lower down.

He probably raised the phantoms from thinking, as he traversed the moors alone, on the nonsense he had heard his parents and companions repeat—yet still, I don't like being out in the dark, now; and I don't like being left by myself in this grim house. I cannot help it, I shall be glad when they leave it, and shift to the Grange!

"They are going to the Grange, then?" I said.

"Yes," answered Mrs. Dean, "as soon as they are married; and that will be on New Year's day."

"And who will live here then?"

"Why, Joseph will take care of the house, and, perhaps, a lad to keep him company. They will live in the kitchen, and the rest will be shut up."

"For the use of such ghosts as choose to inhabit it," I observed.

"No, Mr. Lockwood," said Nelly, shaking her head. "I believe the dead are at peace, but it is not right to speak of them with levity."

At that moment the garden gate swung to; the ramblers were returning.

"*They* are afraid of nothing," I grumbled, watching their ap-

7. Nab: See p. 174.

proach through the window. "Together they would brave Satan and all his legions."

As they stepped onto the door-stones, and halted to take a last look at the moon, or, more correctly, at each other, by her light, I felt irresistibly impelled to escape them again; and, pressing a remembrance into the hand of Mrs. Dean, and disregarding her expostulations at my rudeness, I vanished through the kitchen, as they opened the house-door, and so should have confirmed Joseph in his opinion of his fellow-servant's gay indiscretions, had he not, fortunately, recognised me for a respectable character by the sweet ring of a sovereign at his feet.

My walk home was lengthened by a diversion in the direction of the Kirk. When beneath its walls, I perceived decay had made progress, even in seven months: many a window showed black gaps deprived of glass; and slates jutted off, here and there, beyond the right line of the roof, to be gradually worked off in coming autumn storms.

I sought, and soon discovered, the three head-stones on the slope next the moor—the middle one, grey, and half buried in heath—Edgar Linton's only harmonized by the turf, and moss creeping up its foot—Heathcliff's still bare.

I lingered round them, under that benign sky; watched the moths fluttering among the heath and hare-bells; listened to the soft wind breathing through the grass; and wondered how any one could ever imagine unquiet slumbers for the sleepers in that quiet earth.

THE END.

Textual Commentary

An account of the printing and publishing of *Wuthering Heights* helps to make clear the problems that an editor must face, but the available facts have not hitherto been brought together. We know that each of the three Brontë sisters had written first novels and had had a discouraging experience in finding a publisher. After a prolonged search, Emily and her sister Anne finally had to come to terms with Thomas C. Newby, who seems to have been primarily a printer, but sometimes undertook to publish the books he printed.[1] Newby agreed to print their novels only if they shared the risk, and demanded £50 as advance payment.[2] *Wuthering Heights* finally appeared as Volumes I and II of a three-volume set (the third volume contained Anne Brontë's *Agnes Grey*), but in dealing with Newby the two sisters had had their troubles. He was to print 350 copies but printed only 250; he was dilatory in supplying proof-sheets; and he was indifferent to corrections in proof made by the author.[3]

Charlotte Brontë, whose *Jane Eyre* had been published by Smith, Elder, and Company shortly before *Wuthering Heights*, wrote to her publisher that "the orthography and punctuation of the books [*Wuthering Heights* and *Agnes Grey*] are mortifying to a degree: almost all the errors that were corrected in the proof-sheets appear intact in what should have been the fair copies. If Mr. Newby always does business in this way, few authors would like to have him for their publisher a second time."[4] Charlotte's judgment that the novels "abound in errors of the press" is clearly corroborated by even a casual examination of the text of the first edition, but it seems impossible to deny that some of the errors and inconsistencies in matters of form were the responsibility of Emily herself. Charlotte is thought to have been more meticulous about such matters than her sister, but she wrote to her far more responsible publisher to thank him for "punctuating the sheets" of *Jane Eyre*, "as I found the task very puzzling, and, besides, I consider your mode of punctuation a great deal more correct and rational than my own."[5] Thus we can see that even Charlotte was uncertain about formal matters and gave evidence of continued uncertainty in the large number of changes she made between the first edition of *Jane Eyre* (1847) and the second and third (1848).[6] When she came to revise *Wuthering Heights* for the second edition two years after Emily's death (1850), she made changes of the same sort in Emily's text. But if Charlotte had much to learn about these matters, Emily surely had as much or more.

Newby, however, is certainly responsible for many of the errors in Emily's text. Typographical errors abound (*modlled* for *modelled*, *had'nt* for *hadn't*, *wick* for *wicked*); letters are transposed and out of alignment; ellipsis dots are sometimes used in place of dashes; hyphens are occasionally omitted at the ends of lines when words are divided. Some of the mispunctuation is hard to account for except as a consequence of Newby's ignorance or carelessness. But the degree to which printer and author should share in the responsibility for the state of the text can never be exactly determined. The manuscript of the novel has never been discovered and probably was destroyed before or shortly after Emily's death. A copy of the first volume of the first edition, said to have been her own copy and to contain a few revisions in her handwriting, provides little help, for the emendations are too few to make clear the nature and degree of her dissatisfaction with the text.[7] Consequently the responsibility of an editor of this novel is serious if he wants to respect at the same time the text of the author and the needs of the modern reader.

Faced with this responsibility, most of those who have undertaken to make the book available solved their problem by simply reprinting, more or less accurately, the second edition, elaborately revised by Charlotte Brontë and apparently so paragraphed that *Wuthering Heights* and *Agnes Grey*, originally containing 1,127 pages, might be issued in one volume of 504 pages.[8] In this century, however, beginning with Clement Shorter's edition in 1911, there has been a growing tendency to reject Charlotte Brontë's version of the text—a version perhaps justly stigmatized by H. W. Garrod in 1930 as frequently indicating "misunderstanding or defective appreciation of the original."[9] But no editor or publisher who has decided to return to the text of the first edition has contemplated reprinting that edition with all its errors. Among modern reprints the nature and the number of retained errors varies radically, however, and, with one exception, the editing has been done silently. It is particularly unfortunate that the handsomely printed Shakespeare Head Edition of *Wuthering Heights* (Vol. III of the nineteen-volume works of all the Brontës, edited by Thomas J. Wise and John Alexander Symington) should have laid itself open to the charge of having retained "variant spellings of proper names" and a host of "unnecessary and misleading commas."[10] It is true that in a note to this edition of the novel the editors promised that the "chief variations [between the first and second editions] will be noted in the bibliography to be printed in a later volume." The failure to provide this information was perhaps due to Wise's death, which occurred shortly before the publication of the last volume of this work, but in any case, it would be more interesting to have had a note indicating why certain changes were *not* made.

If, however, Charlotte Brontë's edition should not be used as the basis for the text, and Emily Brontë's first edition must be edited, how ought an editor proceed? I do not believe that Charlotte's painstaking efforts should be rejected in toto, especially when we know that she was aware of the printer's failure to make corrections proposed by the author in her proof-sheets, nor do I believe that an editor need be scrupulous to retain the erratic punctuation of the first edition under the impression that Emily's prose rhythms might be lost if her pointing is not preserved. On the other hand, having said this much for the need of revising the punctuation, we must recognize that this punctuation, inconsistent as it is and corrupted by a shoddy printer, often seems representative of the author's intent and is characteristic of her country and of her century. Certain intentions can be discerned, despite the author's inconsistencies and the printer's indifference. These intentions I have tried to recognize.[11] I have also retained Emily's paragraphing, for there is no reason to believe that Charlotte's drastic reduction in the number of paragraphs represented anything more than the publisher's desire to print three volumes as one.

1. See an exchange of letters between Newby and the editors of the *Examiner*, July 29, August 5, 12, 1848. See also *The Brontës: Their Lives, Friendships and Correspondence*, ed. Wise and Symington, Oxford, Shakespeare Head Press, 4 vols., 1932, II, 241–45.
2. *The Brontës*, II, 145; III, 160.
3. *Ibid.*, III, 156; II, 154–56; 165.
4. *Ibid.*, II, 165.
5. *Ibid.*, II, 142.
6. M. L. Parrish, *Victorian Lady Novelists*, Constable and Co., London, 1933, pp. 99–155.
7. See below, p. 273.
8. The text of the novels concludes on p. 468, followed by literary remains of Emily and Anne.
9. *Wuthering Heights* (World's Classics edition), Oxford University Press, London, 1961, p. vii. (Editor's Introduction dated 1930.)
10. *Brontë Society Publications*, Part XLII (No. 1 of Vol. VIII), 1932, p. 34.
11. For instance, the almost unrestrained use of the exclamation point; the frequent use of the colon when the sentence that follows is explanatory of the one that precedes; the use of the semicolon preceding a final participial phrase; and the use of the question mark in indirect questions which usually retain the word order of the direct form (e.g., *I asked, how was the baby?*).

NOTES TO THE TEXT

In each entry below, the numbers refer to the page and line of the present text where the word or phrase under discussion is located. The following abbreviations are used in these notes:

A: *Wuthering Heights*, 1847 (the first edition)

B: *Wuthering Heights*, 1850 (the second edition, revised by Charlotte Brontë)

B et al: The second edition and most of the later editions

C: *Wuthering Heights*, Vol. 1, 1847 (said to have corrections in Emily Brontë's handwriting. See p. 273).

C.B.: Charlotte Brontë

E.B.: Emily Brontë

S.H.: *Wuthering Heights*, 1931. (Vol. III of the Shakespeare Head Edition)

Shorter: *Wuthering Heights*, 1911 (Vol. II of *The Complete Works of Emily Brontë*, ed. Clement Shorter)

13.30 court—
In *A*, dialogue is introduced by a concluding semicolon, period, comma, or dash at the close of the preceding paragraph. Since *E.B.* most frequently used the dash, I have used this mark throughout.
17.12 chipping off
A: chipping of, surely a misprint.
17.24–28 On coming ° ° °—on mounting
A: "On coming up from dinner. * * * On mounting the stairs. * * *" I have punctuated this sentence so that the opening phrase may not stand as an awkward fragment.
18.11 Nor-ne me
In *A, nor-ne me* becomes *nor nuh me* on p. 117. At that point *C.B.* substitutes *none o' me.*

18.28 door
A: floor, when the sense requires *door*.
21.13 bordering on repulsive
C: "bordering on *the* repulsive."
24.44 Wisht
In *A, wisht* is used with comparative frequency and by several characters. It is a less common variant of *whisht* or *whish*, meaning *hush, be silent, hold your tongue.*
30.28 gripe
A variant spelling of *grip.*
32.27 access
B et al: *excess;* perhaps advisedly, but *E.B.* uses *access* in similar contexts on pp. 99 and 112, and may mean to do so.

32.34–35 his shadow's arm
B et al: "by the motion of his arm's shadow." The reading of *A* is more interesting.
42.11–13 our curate ° ° ° he
B et al: omits the colloquial *he* in this construction.
42.36 last
B: latter.
44.12 done so longer
A: done longer.
46.8 Heathcliff bore
A: "He bore"; *B:* "*Heathcliff* bore."
51.7–8 I removed ° ° ° shoes
A: "I removed the habit, and there shone forth, beneath a grand plaid silk frock, white trousers, and burnished shoes"; I have supplied the punctuation of *B*, for surely *E.B.* meant that three items—frock, trousers, and shoes—shone forth when the habit was removed.
51.28 counterpart of
A and *B:* counterpart *to*
57.5–6 the place was so full
A: "it was so full"; *C:* "*the place* was so full."
58.28 surface change
B: surface, change, but this punctuation changes the meaning and seems unwarranted.
59.38 when
A: then; B: when, advisedly.
60.11 I asked, how was the baby?
I have followed *E.B.'s* practice of using question marks in such indirect questions as *I asked, what was the matter?* But *A* at this point reads: *I asked, how was the baby?"* with a closing but no opening quotation mark. Modern editors frequently attempt to remedy matters by supplying an opening quotation mark: *I asked, "how was the baby?"* *E.B.* never resorts to this curious punctuation for indirect questions.
61.11 there was
A: "he had plenty of wickedness"; *C:* "*there was* plenty of wickedness," an improvement, perhaps, but the sentence is still an awkward one.
63.37 Pennistow
Probably not a misprint for *Penistone*, but a spelling to suggest a dialect sound.
69.5 Maker
A: maker; B: Maker, presumably to make the blasphemy more apparent.
75.40 Hathcliff's
B: Heathcliff's, but surely unwarranted.
77.33 the room filled
C: "the room *was* filled," an acceptable change, but of no real importance.
78.8 und bolt intuh th' hahs
A: "nud bolt intuh th' haks"; *C:* "and bolt intuh th' house." I have merely corrected the apparent misprints, *nud* and *haks.*

80.40 sizer's
An alternative spelling of *sizar*, retained in *B*.
82.1 It had got dusk
C: "It *was* dusk."
91.6 lugs
A: higs, a misprint; *C: ears.*
93.6 pining
B: dining, a misprint, changed by some modern editors to *dying!*
94.35 trembled
Shorter: "trembled *in* every limb," but the verb can take a direct object. Keats uses it as a transitive verb.
95.20 barn
B and *S.H.: bairn,* but *barn* is an alternative dialect spelling.
96.36 the art
Shorter: the *heart,* but why?
97.13 jealous of ° ° ° jealous for
A: "I'm not jealous of you" * * * "I'm jealous for you." *B:* italicizes *of* and *for,* and I have adopted this emendation.
102.9 rung
B: rang, but *C.B.* used *rung* as the past tense of *ring* in the first edition of *Jane Eyre* (1847), changing it (but not always) to *rang* in the second edition (1848). See M. L. Parrish, *Victorian Lady Novelists* (London, 1933), pp. 99–155. *E.B.* uses *sprung* instead of *sprang, sunk* instead of *sank.*
103.8 and while
A: "and she fasted pertinaciously"; *C:* "and *while* she fasted pertinaciously." By this change a firmer parallelism is established between this clause and the one that opens the sentence.
103.27 ate
A: eat, but *A* has *ate* for the past tense on p. 253. *C.B.* uses *eat* for the past tense in the first edition of *Jane Eyre,* changing later to *ate.* See Parrish, *op. cit.,* in note to 102.9.
105.29 Penistone
A: Peniston, a misprint. This natural phenomenon is usually referred to as Penistone Crags, but *E.B.* thinks of it sometimes as *it,* sometimes as *them,* and hence uses both Penistone *Crag* and Penistone *Crags.* I have followed her text with respect to the number of the noun, but have used the spelling *Crags* throughout, though she occasionally uses the alternative spelling *Craggs.* See note to 156.9. Ponden Kirk, a black gloomy rock, towering above the head of Ponden Valley, has been identified as "Penistone Crags."
110.29–30 suspended by a handkerchief
A: "suspended to a handkerchief"; *B:* "suspended *by* a handkerchief."
111.23 thick
C: friendly; B: intimate. Shorter, alone among modern editors, follows *C.*

112.7–8 if pursued instantly
In some modern editions (e.g., the Oxford World's Classics edition, p. 162, and the Rinehart edition, p. 139), this passage is revised to read "if *I* pursued instantly." But *E.B.* may have intended "if pursued instantly," that is, in effect, "if they were pursued instantly." *B* retains the reading of *A*.

113.16 mistake him, besides—
Shorter alone omits *besides*, perhaps on the authority of *C*. See p. 274.

127.18 one bit
A: "a bit"; *B:* "one bit."

128.45–129.1 and watch ° ° ° mischief
A: "and watch till I departed—your conscience quite calm, you would be hindering mischief." I think the meaning requires the punctuation I have adopted.

130.14 mother!
A: Vol. I ends here.

132.43 if you
A: "if you"; *B:* "if *you*."

135.25 westering
B: *western*, but *C.B.* uses *westering* in the first edition of *Jane Eyre*. See Parrish, *op. cit.*, in note to 102.9.

138.3–4 inhabitant
A and *B:* *inhabitants*, but surely the singular form is required.

139.33–34 The murdered ° ° ° on earth
A: "The murdered *do* haunt their murderers. I believe—I know that ghosts *have* wandered on earth." The punctuation I have adopted seems to secure *E.B.'s* meaning, to contrast what is believed with what is known.

140.26 grave; he
A: "grave; *and* he sent no excuse, but he never came." *B* deletes the *and* as I have done.

143.30 proceeded
A and *B:* "He was worked up * * * and *proceeding* to murderous violence"; I have followed later editions in changing *proceeding* to *proceeded*.

145.12 for a sympathy
A: "searching in my eyes, a sympathy"; *B:* "searching in my eyes *for* a sympathy."

148.7 Heathcliff was not
A: "he was not"; *B:* "*Heathcliff* was not."

148.12 his opponent was ignorant
A: "he was ignorant"; *B:* "*his opponent* was ignorant."

152.28 there were
A: there *was*.

156.9 Penistone Crags
A: Penistone Crags, but *E.B.* immediately refers to the Crags as "it." Later, in the same conversation, she writes: "*they* are not worth the trouble."

159.23 Hareton offered
A: "*But* Hareton offered"; *B:* "Hareton offered."

164.28 were sorrow
B et al: "*was* sorrow."

168.27 If he have
B et al: "If he *has*."

175.33–34 Are you Linton?
A: Are you, Linton?; *B et al:* Are you Linton?. This change in punctuation seems to secure the intended meaning.

186.1 tenure
A: tenour: *B:* tenor.

189.38 hadn't the skill to
A: hadn't skill to, retained by *B*.

190.16–17 if the master were in?
B et al: "if the master *was* in?"

208.15 she changed
A: "and changed"; *B:* "*she* changed."

215.16 vivisection
A: vivifisection, possibly a misprint.

222.42 store every tear
B follows *A* with "store every tear." Some later editions read "store *up* every tear."

242.23 Ee
E.B. usually employs *Aw* for *I* in rendering dialect, but here she uses *Ee* and on p. 252 she uses *E*. *Ee* is the usual dialect form for *eye*, and *E* the usual form for *he*.

252.10 wisely
Unwisely might be expected.

253.23 ate
See note to 103.27.

253.44 thick again
B: "*friends* again." See p. 111 and note to 111.23.

256.1–3 he was ° ° ° healthy
A: "he was neither in danger of losing his senses, nor dying, according to my judgment he was quite strong and healthy." The punctuation here leaves the meaning in doubt. Mine secures what seems the likeliest meaning.

258.25–26 rare and pleased
B: *rarely pleased*, which distorts the meaning.

260.14 imaging
B: *imagining*, but *C.B.* uses *imaging* in the first edition of *Jane Eyre*, revising for the second edition. See Parrish, *op. cit.*, in note to 102.9.

265.21 Nab
E.B. spells *Nab* with a small *n* on earlier pages. See p. 174, for example.

APPENDIX I. A NOTE ON EMILY BRONTË'S SPELLING AND CAPITALIZATION

Since Emily Brontë's corrections in proof were ignored by her printer, we cannot be sure which misspellings were printer's errors and which were Emily's. I have silently corrected such errors as *to* for *two*, *moddled* for *modelled*, *dam'n* for *damn*, *staunchily* for *staunchly*, *whose* for *who's*,

Linton's for *Lintons*, and *her's* for *hers*. Beyond this, I have adopted the accepted spelling or capitalization for the following words which appear in two forms in the text. Those words marked with an asterisk appeared in the less conventional form in the first edition of *Jane Eyre* and were changed by Charlotte Brontë either in the second or third edition of her novel (M. L. Parrish, *Victorian Lady Novelists*, London, 1933, pp. 99–155). Perhaps neither sister was very sure of herself.

awhile, a while: *a while*	methodist, Methodist: *Methodist*
*bible, Bible: *Bible*	miss, Miss: *Miss*
*christian, Christian: *Christian*	mistress, Mistress: *mistress*
christmas, Christmas: *Christmas*	parlor, parlour: *parlour*
dose, doze: *doze*	*ribband, riband: *riband*
*eat, ate [past tense]: *ate*	satan, Satan: *Satan*
*good bye, good-bye: *good-bye*	soliloquise, soliloquize: *soliloquize*
*heaven, Heaven: *heaven*	staid, stayed: *stayed*
hell, Hell: *hell*	teazing, teasing: *teasing*
him, Him [God]: *Him*	up stairs, up-stairs: *upstairs*
lighted, alighted: *alighted*	wont, won't: *won't*
mama, mamma: *mamma*	

The following words I have changed as indicated. When used more than once, they are used in the same form. Some may be misprints.

affected: *effected*	in doors: *indoors*
bannister: *banister*	journies: *journeys*
changling: *changeling*	no where: *nowhere*
confidant: *confident*	quaker: *Quaker*
down stairs: *downstairs*	sometime: *some time*
every body: *everybody*	tormenter: *tormentor*
every thing: *everything*	transcient: *transient*
gallopped: *galloped*	visiter: *visitor*

Charlotte Brontë changed *bannister* to *banister* for the second edition of *Jane Eyre*, and she never quite made up her mind about *upstairs*.

APPENDIX II. THE YORKSHIRE DIALECT

When Charlotte Brontë was preparing the second and revised edition of *Wuthering Heights*, she wrote to her publisher: "It seems to me advisable to modify the orthography of the old servant Joseph's speeches; for though as it stands it exactly renders the Yorkshire dialect to a Yorkshire ear, yet I am sure Southerns must find it unintelligible; and thus one of the most graphic characters in the book is lost on them" (*The Brontës: Their Lives, Friendships and Correspondence*, ed. Wise and Symington, 4 vols., Oxford, 1932, III, 165). Charlotte's method of modifying the orthography I have commented on in my preface. She is probably right in saying that to a Yorkshire ear the dialect would be intelligible, though few of the words are specifically Yorkshire. Christopher Dean, who is well informed about these matters, says that the "dialect used is northern in which there are no elements foreign to the West Riding" of Yorkshire ("Joseph's Speech in 'Wuthering Heights,'" *Notes and Queries*, N.S. VII, February, 1960, 73–76), though he qualifies the statement in one respect, which I shall point out below. Most of the words are marked in the *New English Dictionary* and in Joseph Wright's *English Dialect Dictionary* as Scottish and north of England.

It has been generally assumed that Emily Brontë became familiar with the dialect largely through a servant of the Brontës, Tabitha (Tabby) Aykroyd, who, according to a fragment of Emily's diary written when she was sixteen, said, "Ya pitter pottering there instead of pilling a potate"— Emily's early attempt at rendering dialect (*The Brontës*, I, 124). Tabby is reported to have sung "the children ballads and told them tales of the 'fairish' (fairies) which lived in the Bottom before machinery drove them away, stories of 'the graves under the rectory back-kitchen,' of witches running red-hot needles into human flesh" (Romer Wilson, *All Alone: The Life and Private History of Emily Jane Brontë*, London, 1928, p. 65).

Emily Brontë seems to have been surprisingly successful in rendering the sounds of the northern dialect, though her method is not always consistently employed, and occasionally her words are directed to the eye and not the ear as when, for example, she uses *wer* for *were*, *ses* for *says*, and *holld* for *hold*. Christopher Dean points out that sometimes her spelling suggests a sound not common to the north of England but suggestive of Irish, as when she uses *spake* for *speak*, *clane* for *clean*, *stale* for *steal*, *dacent* for *decent*.

The reader will soon become familiar with the use of such forms as *t'* for *the*, *'t* for *it*, *i* for *in*, *nut* for *not*, *tuh* for *to*, *on* for *of*, *soa* for *so* or *therefore*.

APPENDIX III. EMILY BRONTË'S COPY OF WUTHERING HEIGHTS

When Clement Shorter edited *Wuthering Heights* in 1911 (Vol. II of a two-volume edition of *The Works of Emily Brontë*), he said in his preface (p. xi) that his text was "set up in type from Emily Brontë's own copy of *Wuthering Heights*, which was carried by Mr. Arthur Bell Nicholls [Charlotte's husband] from Haworth to his later home in Banagher in Ireland, where it rested on his shelves for more than forty years." His declared intention "to present the book here as it left its author's hands" was not fully realized, as has been pointed out in Frederick Page's textual notes to the World's Classics edition (Oxford University Press, 1930). But Page did not record all the changes made by Shorter and failed to note some interesting instances in which Shorter provided readings that differ from the first edition and from all other reprintings of the text. Shorter himself gave no authority for these variant readings, but Thomas J. Wise in his *Bibliography of the Writings in Prose and Verse of the Members of the Brontë Family* (1917) says that Clement Shorter's copy of *Wuthering Heights*, "formerly the property of Emily Brontë herself," has fifteen corrections in Vol. I "marked in pencil in her own handwriting" (p. 101). Wise lists nine of these fifteen corrections, and Shorter silently introduces these nine (and perhaps the six others) into his edition. After Shorter's death in 1926, this copy was sold at Sotheby's to Walter Spencer, a London bookseller, for £26 (*Book Auction Records*, XXV, 359, Sale of June 18, 1928) and in 1952 was acquired by J. E. Kite, then of Hove, Sussex. My efforts to locate Mr. Kite have finally proved successful, and he would have graciously permitted me to examine Emily's copy had it still been in his library. He had, however, sold it at Sotheby's in 1964, where it was purchased by Horace G. Commin, a bookseller at Bournemouth, presumably for a private collector (Sale of July 28, 1964, and *Book Auction Records*, Vol. 61, where the price was given as £420). I have not been able to secure from Mr. Commin any information about the present location of the copy.

Conflicting evidence abounds as to the number of corrections in Vol. I. Wise, as I have said, counted fifteen but listed only nine. In 1954 Mr. Kite reported that there were twelve corrections "in her own unmistakable writing" (*The Sunday Times*, September 26). When the copy was sold at Sotheby's, it was described as having "twenty-three corrections written in pencil, in her hand," those on the nine pages listed by Wise and on twelve other pages. Since nine and twelve add up to only twenty-one, there must have been more than one correction on one or two of these pages to make up the sum of twenty-three noted by Sotheby's. To make matters worse, Sotheby's reports that pp. 163–168 of Vol. I are missing, as are the title-pages in both volumes.

Shorter, as I have said, failed to identify any of the variants that he introduced. Even more inexplicably, Wise, when he edited the novel for the Shakespeare Head Edition (1931), failed to introduce the variants which he himself had listed in 1917. I have indicated in my textual notes the nine revisions listed by Wise and silently introduced by Shorter (see notes to 21.13, 57.5–6, 61.11, 77.33, 78.8, 82.1, 91.6, 103.8, and 111.23). For my text, however, I have adopted only three of these nine changes, since only these three make for greater clarity. A laborious collation of Shorter's text with the other modern editions might serve to locate other corrections found by Wise and by Sotheby's for their catalogue of 1964. But I suspect that if found they would prove of little significance. A casual collation of Shorter revealed only such variants as the following: Shorter (173.9) omits the *besides* in my edition on 113.16; he substitutes a *these* (174.2) for the *those* on 113.38, and a *here* (190.34) for the *there* on 124.11.

Contemporary Reviews
and Essays in Criticism

Contemporary Reviews

Emily Brontë preserved five reviews of *Wuthering Heights*, which eventually found their way into the Brontë Parsonage Museum at Haworth as part of the contents of her writing desk. Four of the five have been identified as having appeared in the *Atlas*, in *Douglas Jerrold's Weekly Newspaper*, in the *Examiner*, and in the *Britannia* (*The Brontës: Their Lives, Friendships and Correspondence*, ed. Wise and Symington, Oxford, Shakespeare Head Press, 4 vols., 1932, II, 280; Charles Simpson, *Emily Brontë*, London and New York, pp. 168–179). When Charlotte Brontë edited the second edition of her sister's novel (1850), she or her publisher prefixed to that edition extracts from the reviews in the *Atlas* and the *Britannia*, and a somewhat longer portion of an essay by Sydney Dobell (1824–1874), the English poet and critic. This essay had been published in the *Palladium* in September, 1850, almost three years after *Wuthering Heights* was published. It was singled out by Charlotte in her "Biographical Notice" (see above, p. 3) as the work of the only critic who had recognized her sister's "very real powers." The justice of Charlotte's sweeping attack on Emily's critics can be assayed only after sampling some of the early reviews, and her choice of Sydney Dobell as the only "true seer" can be better understood if we know something about the essay from which she selected his comments on Emily's novel.

The critical reception of *Wuthering Heights* has been generally assumed to have been unsympathetic, and so of course it seems in the light of the extraordinary tributes that have later been paid to the novel. But if we compare what Charlotte herself said of the novel in her "Preface" (see above, p. 9) with what many of the early critics said, we should perhaps conclude that both Charlotte and the critics were finding it difficult to come to terms with a strangely different piece of fiction. If we read Dobell's essay, we may conclude that Charlotte had certain reasons of her own for being so conspicuously impressed by what he had to say about *Wuthering Heights*. Dobell was not reviewing a novel, but writing a literary essay on what he thought to be the four works of a single novelist, "Currer Bell" (Reprinted in *The Life and Letters of Sydney Dobell*, ed. Jolly, London, 2 vols., 1878, I, 163–186). He thought that Charlotte Brontë had written *Wuthering Heights*, *The Tenant of Wildfell Hall*, *Jane Eyre*, and *Shirley* in this order, and he considered *Wuthering Heights* as "at once the earlier in date and ruder in execution," though the author of *Jane Eyre* "need fear nothing in acknowledging [her] immature creations." Charlotte must have been pleased by Dobell's tribute to her, but she might have had some doubts about the critical acumen of a man who could not distinguish her work from that of Emily and who thought the author of *The Tenant of Wildfell Hall* wrote *Jane Eyre* and *Wuthering Heights*. And so should those who later cited Dobell as the critic who surprisingly anticipated the cult of Emily Brontë. Without impugning Charlotte's motive, we should not forget that she was under a strong temptation to speak well of Dobell, and that she later admitted that she had not intended to single him out from all others. The *Examiner*, reviewing her edition of Emily's novel (December 21, 1850), pointed out that its review of the first edition did not materially differ from Charlotte's preface in "explaining what was faulty as well as what was excellent" in *Wuthering Heights*. Charlotte wrote: "The 'Examiner' is very sore about my Preface, because I did not make it a special exception in speaking of the mass of critics. The soreness is unfortunate and gratuitous, for *in my mind* I certainly excepted it." (*The Brontës*, III, 191–192). The italics are mine.

Wuthering Heights must have seemed to Emily's contemporaries an English novel without ancestors, and it seems now to be almost without descendants. But its power, its "genius," its freedom from affectation, its sombre truth were all recognized, along with what seemed to some to be its faulty structure, its awkward use of narrators, its stark brutality, its lack of relief. Praise was never unqualified and in some instances only grudgingly granted. Henry Fothergill Chorley in the *Athenaeum* (December 25, 1847) dismissed the novel as a "disagreeable story," appearing in a period in which England needed "sunshine more than ever" (See Leslie A. Marchand, *The Athenaeum*, Chapel Hill, N.C., 1941, p. 192 for identification of the reviewer. For Charlotte Brontë's opinion of Chorley, see *The Brontës*, III, 62, 66). The majestic *Quarterly Review* (LXXXIV [December, 1848], 175) did not acknowledge its existence until a year after publication and then said that "with all the unscrupulousness of the French school of novels it combines that repulsive vulgarity in the choice of its vice which supplies its own antidote," that it could not have been written by a woman, or if by a woman, then only by one who had "long forfeited the society of her own sex." The *Spectator*, a periodical that described *Moby Dick* as "rhapsody run mad," found Emily's "incidents and persons * * * too coarse and disagreeable to be attractive," but concluded: "The execution, however, is good: grant the writer all that is requisite as regards matter, and the delineation is forcible and truthful" (December 18, 1847). The *North American Review* (LXVII, [October, 1848], p. 356) thought that the work of the Brontës was an "attempt to corrupt the virtue of the sturdy descendants of the Puritans." But many of the reviewers were more temperate, and many of the periodicals devoted space to their reviews far in excess of what most first novels are accorded in this century. The assumption that posterity alone recognizes genius is an assumption that posterity finds it only too easy to make.

From the *Palladium*†

["*The Flight of an Impatient Fancy*"]

* * * We look upon ["Wuthering Heights"] as the flight of an impatient fancy fluttering in the very exultation of young wings; sometimes beating against its solitary bars, but turning, rather to exhaust, in a circumscribed space, the energy and agility which it may not yet spend in the heavens—a youthful story, written for oneself in solitude, and thrown aside till other successes recall the eyes to it in hope. In this thought let the critic take up the book; lay it down in what thought he will, there are some things in it he can lay down no more.

That Catherine Earnshaw—at once so wonderfully fresh, so fearfully natural—new, 'as if brought from other spheres,' and familiar as the recollection of some woeful experience—what can surpass the strange compatibility of her simultaneous loves; the involuntary art with which her two natures are so made to co-exist, that in the very arms of her lover we dare not doubt her purity; the inevitable belief with which we watch the oscillations of the old and new elements in her mind, and the exquisite truth of the last victory of nature over education, when the past returns to her as a flood, sweeping every modern landmark from within her, and the soul of the child, expanding, fills the woman?

Found at last, by her husband, insensible on the breast of her lover, and dying of the agony of their parting, one looks back upon her, like that husband, without one thought of accusation or absolution; her memory is chaste as the loyalty of love, pure as the air of the Heights on which she dwelt.

Heathcliff *might* have been as unique a creation. The conception in his case was as wonderfully strong and original, but he is spoilt in detail. The authoress has too often disgusted, where she should have terrified, and has allowed us a familiarity with her fiend which had ended in unequivocal contempt. If 'Wuthering Heights' had been written as lately as 'Jane Eyre,' the figure of Heathcliff, symmetrised and elevated, might have been one of the most natural and most striking portraits in the gallery of fiction.

---

† An extract from an essay entitled "Currer Bell," reprinted from *The Life and Letters of Sydney Dobell*, ed. Jolly (London, 2 vols., 1878), I, 169–71. It originally appeared in the *Palladium* for September, 1850.

Not a subordinate place or person in this novel but bears more or less the stamp of high genius. Ellen Dean is the ideal of the peasant playmate and servant of 'the family.' The substratum in which her mind moves is finely preserved. Joseph, as a specimen of the sixty years' servitor of 'the house,' is worthy a museum case. We feel that if Catherine Earnshaw bore her husband a child, it must be that Cathy Linton, and no other. The very Jane Eyre, of quiet satire, peeps out in such a paragraph as this:—'He told me to put on my cloak, and run to Gimmerton for the doctor and the parson. I went through wind and rain, and brought one, the doctor, back with me: the other said, *he would come in the morning.*' What terrible truth, what nicety of touch, what 'uncanny' capacity for mental aberration in the first symptoms of Catherine's delirium. 'I'm not wandering; you're mistaken, or else I should believe you really *were* that withered hag, and I should think I *was* under Penistone Crags: and I'm conscious it's night, and there are two candles on the table making the black press shine like jet.' What an unobtrusive, unexpected sense of *keeping* in the hanging of Isabella's dog.

The book abounds in such things. But one looks back at the whole story as to a world of brilliant figures in an atmosphere of mist; shapes that come out upon the eye, and burn their colours into the brain, and depart into the enveloping fog. It is the unformed writing of a giant's hand: the 'large utterance' of a baby god. In the sprawling of the infant Hercules, however, there must have been attitudes from which the statuary might model. In the early efforts of unusual genius, there are not seldom unconscious felicities which maturer years may look back upon with envy. The child's hand wanders over the strings. It cannot combine them in the chords and melodies of manhood; but its separate notes are perfect in themselves, and perhaps sound all the sweeter for the Æolian discords from which they come.

We repeat, that there are passages in this book of 'Wuthering Heights' of which any novelist, past or present, might be proud. Open the first volume at the fourteenth page, and read to the sixty-first. There are few things in modern prose to surpass these pages for native power. We cannot praise too warmly the brave simplicity, the unaffected air of intense belief, the admirable combination of extreme likelihood with the rarest originality, the nice provision of the possible even in the highest effects of the supernatural, the easy strength and instinct of keeping with which the accessory circumstances are grouped, the exquisite but unconscious art with which the chiaro-scuro of the whole is managed, and the ungenial frigidity of place, time, weather, and persons, is made to heighten the unspeakable pathos of one ungovernable outburst.

* * *

From the *Examiner*†

["A Strange Book"]

This is a strange book. It is not without evidences of considerable power: but, as a whole, it is wild, confused, disjointed, and improbable; and the people who make up the drama, which is tragic enough in its consequences, are savages ruder than those who lived before the days of Homer. * * * Heathcliff may be considered as the hero of the book, if a hero there be. He is an incarnation of evil qualities; implacable hate, ingratitude, cruelty, falsehood, selfishness, and revenge. * * * Like the Corsair, and other such melodramatic heroes, he is

"Linked to one virtue and a thousand crimes;"

and it is with difficulty that we can prevail upon ourselves to believe in the appearance of such a phenomenon, so near our own dwellings as the summit of a Lancashire or Yorkshire moor. * * *

We are not disposed to ascribe any particular intention to the author in drawing the character of Heathcliff, nor can we perceive any very obvious moral in the story. There are certain rough dashes at character; some of the incidents look like real events; and the book has the merit, which must not be undervalued, of avoiding common-place and affectation. * * * We detest the affectation and effeminate frippery which is but too frequent in the modern novel, and willingly trust ourselves with an author who goes at once fearlessly into the moors and desolate places, for his heroes; but we must at the same time stipulate with him that he shall not drag into light all that he discovers, of coarse and loathsome, in his wandering.

† Emily Brontë left us no indication of how she felt about her critics, but Charlotte liked the *Examiner* and said she was willing to be judged by it. She seemed to think that John Forster, the biographer of Dickens, wrote its reviews of fiction (*The Brontës*, III, 33, 59, 62). Forster had been the chief critic of literature for the *Examiner* in its early years when Albany Fonblanque was editor. On the retirement of Fonblanque in 1847, Forster took over the editorship.

Generous portions of the reviews preserved by Emily Brontë are reprinted in *Brontë Society Publications*, Part LVII (No. 2 of Vol. XI), 1947, pp. 89–95. Extracts from two of these reviews, in the *Examiner* and the *Britannia*, are reprinted here; this one appeared in the *Examiner* for January 8, 1848.

From the *Britannia*†

["*Humanity in Its Wild State*"]

There are scenes of savage wildness in nature which, though they inspire no pleasurable sensation, we are yet well satisfied to have seen. In the rugged rock, the gnarled roots which cling to it, the dark screen of overhanging vegetation, the dank, moist ground and tangled network of weeds and bushes,—even in the harsh cry of solitary birds, the cries of wild animals, and the startling motion of the snake as it springs away scared by the intruder's foot,—there is an image of primeval rudeness which has much to fascinate, though nothing to charm, the mind. The elements of beauty are round us in the midst of gloom and danger, and some forms are the more picturesque from their distorted growth amid so many obstacles. A tree clinging to the side of a precipice may more attract the eye than the pride of a plantation.

The principle may, to some extent, be applied to life. The uncultured freedom of native character presents more rugged aspects than we meet with in educated society. Its manners are not only more rough but its passions are more violent. It knows nothing of those breakwaters to the fury of tempest which civilized training establishes to subdue the harsher workings of the soul. Its wrath is unrestrained by reflection; the lips curse and the hand strikes with the first impulse of anger. It is more subject to brutal instinct than to divine reason.

It is humanity in this wild state that the author of "Wuthering Heights" essays to depict. His work is strangely original. It bears a resemblance to some of those irregular German tales in which the writers, giving the reins to their fancy, represent personages as swayed and impelled to evil by supernatural influences. But they give spiritual identity to evil impulses, while Mr. Bell more naturally shows them as the natural offspring of the unregulated heart. He displays considerable power in his creations. They have all the angularity of misshapen growth, and form in this respect a striking contrast to those regular forms we are accustomed to meet with in English fiction. They exhibit nothing of the composite charac-

† The section of the review given here is substantially that portion which was selected for reprinting as preliminary matter in the second edition of the novel. The review appeared in the issue of January 15, 1848.

ter. There is in them no trace of ideal models. They are so new, so wildly grotesque, so entirely without art, that they strike us as proceeding from a mind of limited experience, but of original energy, and of a singular and distinctive cast. * * *

We do not know whether the author writes with any purpose; but we can speak of one effect of his production. It strongly shows the brutalizing influence of unchecked passion. His characters are a commentary on the truth that there is no tyranny in the world like that which thoughts of evil exercise in the daring and reckless breast.

Another reflection springing from the narrative is, that temper is often spoiled in the years of childhood. "The child is father of the man." The pains and crosses of its youthful years are engrafted in its blood, and form a sullen and a violent disposition. Grooms know how often the tempers of horses are irremediably spoiled in training. But some parents are less wise regarding their children. The intellect in its growth has the faculty of accommodating itself to adverse circumstances. To violence it sometimes opposes violence, sometimes dogged obstinacy. The consequence in either case is fatal to the tranquillity of life.

From the *North American Review*†

["*Power Thrown Away*"]

He [Acton Bell] appears to think that spiritual wickedness is a combination of animal ferocities, and has accordingly made a compendium of the most striking qualities of tiger, wolf, cur, and wildcat, in the hope of framing out of such elements a suitable brute-demon to serve as the hero of his novel. Compared with Heathcote

† This long-lived Boston magazine (1815–1939) was in 1848 a quarterly on the order of the great English quarterlies. Its reviewer had read the American edition of *Wuthering Heights*, published by Harper and Brothers, 1848, as "by the Author of Jane Eyre." He decided that Acton, Currer, and Ellis Bell were two brothers and a sister, and that Acton Bell had written *Wuthering Heights*. At second hand, we have a brief note on Emily's response to the critic's attack. "To-day, as Emily appeared a little easier," Charlotte wrote within the month of Emily's death, "I thought the 'Review' would amuse her, so I read it aloud to her and Anne. As I sat between them at our quiet but now somewhat melancholy fireside, I studied the two ferocious authors. Ellis, the 'man of uncommon talents, but dogged, brutal, and morose,' sat leaning back in his easy-chair drawing his impeded breath as he best could, and looking, alas! piteously pale and wasted; it is not his want to laugh, but he smiled half-amused and half in scorn as he listened" (*The Brontës*, II, 287). Charlotte is quoting the review from memory, but she adequately represents its tone. The notice appeared in Volume LXVII (October, 1848), pp. 358–59.

[sic], Squeers is considerate and Quilp humane. * * * As he [Acton Bell] is a man of uncommon talents, it is needless to say that it is to his subject and his dogged manner of handling it that we are to refer the burst of dislike with which the novel was received. * * * His attempt at originality does not stop with the conception of Heathcote, but he aims further to exhibit the action of the sentiment of love on the nature of the being whom his morbid imagination has created. This is by far the ablest and most subtle portion of his labors, and indicates that strong hold upon the elements of character, and that decision of touch in the delineation of the most evanescent qualities of emotion, which distinguish the mind of the whole family [of Bells]. For all practical purposes, however, the power evinced in Wuthering Heights is power thrown away. Nightmares and dreams, through which devils dance and wolves howl, make bad novels.

From the *Leader*†

["*We Cannot Deny Its Truth*"]

Critics, we are told, failed to do them [*Wuthering Heights* and *Agnes Grey*] justice. But to judge from the extracts given of articles in the *Britannia* and *Atlas*, the critics were excessively indulgent, and we take it the great public was the most recalcitrant, and would *not* be amused with these strange wild pictures of incult humanity, painted as if by lurid torchlight, though painted with unmistakeable power—the very power only heightening their repulsiveness. * * * And yet, although there is want of air and light in the picture we cannot deny its truth: sombre, rude, brutal, yet true * * * such brutes we should all be, or the most of us, were our lives as insubordinate to law; were our affections and sympathies as little cultivated, our imaginations as undirected. And herein lies the moral of the book, though most people will fail to draw the moral from very irritation at it. * * *

The power, indeed, is wonderful. * * * It is in the treatment

† This periodical began publication in March, 1850, under the direction of Thornton Leigh Hunt and George Henry Lewes. The excerpt below was written on the publication of the second edition of *Wuthering Heights*, in the issue of December 28, 1850. Lewes had exchanged a few letters with Charlotte, beginning in 1847, when he advised her of his intention of reviewing *Jane Eyre*. He was literary editor of the *Leader*, and Charlotte thought he wrote its reviews (*The Brontës*, II, 151, III, 111). The "extracts" referred to in this review were those prefixed to the second edition.

of this subject that Ellis Bell shows real mastery, and it shows more genius, in the highest sense of the word, than you will find in a thousand novels. * * * Creative power is so rare and valuable that we should accept even its caprices with gratitude.

Essays in Criticism

The order in which these essays are printed is by no means inevitable. The first essay, identified for many years only by the initials of its author, C.P.S., is by Charles Percy Sanger, whose qualifications to discuss Emily Brontë's extraordinary knowledge of the laws of property and inheritance can now be attested by his *Rules of Law and Administration relating to Wills and Intestates*, London, 1914; 2nd edition, 1925. Sanger's essay and that of Lord David Cecil, which follows, have held the admiration of many readers since they first appeared, though they are radically different in intent. I have included only Part I of Lord David's long essay, but he states his position very clearly in this part and uses the remainder largely to support his contentions. In the multifaceted essay by Q. D. Leavis, "A Fresh Approach to *Wuthering Heights*," she exposes the specious reasoning in attempts to prove the novel flawless and points out misinterpretations that have resulted from a failure to recognize "its relations to the social and literary history of its own time." But she also discloses the novel's affinities with such modern works as D. H. Lawrence's *Women in Love* and—strikingly—with Henri-Pierre Roché's *Jules et Jim*. The next essay is from Inga-Stina Ewbank's study of the three Brontë sisters as early-Victorian female novelists. I have titled it—appropriately, I hope—"The Structure and Pattern of the Whole Novel." John Mathison and Carl Woodring address themselves to the question of the role and function of the narrators, a question that has aroused considerable interest in the last twenty-five years or so. The selection from Mary Visick's book *The Genesis of Wuthering Heights* provides an intelligent estimate of Edgar Linton, who usually gets less than justice from Emily Brontë's critics. Mark Schorer's essay provides a highly original approach to our understanding of the novel. Because many readers have been curious about a possible relation between Emily Brontë's poems and her novel, I have provided a brief discussion of conjectures that have been proposed. The authors of these essays have drawn their quotations from texts of *Wuthering Heights* that do not coincide in all details with that of the present edition.

CHARLES PERCY SANGER

The Structure of Wuthering Heights†

By common consent *Wuthering Heights* is a remarkable book. I do not propose to discuss its literary merits, but to confine myself

† This essay was published as by C.P.S., but the author has been identified as Charles Percy Sanger (1871–1930). The essay was a paper read to the Heretics, a society at Cambridge University. A version of the chronology of the novel, differing slightly from San-ger's, was written by Charles Travis Clay and published in the *Brontë Society Transactions*, Part LXII (No. 2 of Vol. 12), 1952, 100–105. Reprinted by permission of the copyright holder, Mrs. H. M. Lucas.

to the humbler task of investigating its structure, which presents certain peculiarities. Whether this is worth doing I do not know, but I found that it added to my interest in the book and made the tale much more vivid for me.

The main theme is how a sort of human cuckoo, called Heathcliff, sets out with success to acquire all the property of two families, the Earnshaws and the Lintons. The tale is a fairly complicated one, and the incidents extend over a period of more than thirty years. Stated as baldly and shortly as I can, the plot is as follows: Mr and Mrs Earnshaw live at Wuthering Heights, a farm-house on a Yorkshire moor. They have two children, a son called Hindley and a daughter Catherine. One day Mr Earnshaw, who has been to Liverpool on business, brings home a waif he has picked up there. This waif, Heathcliff, is brought up at Wuthering Heights. Not long after, Mrs Earnshaw dies. Heathcliff is Mr Earnshaw's favourite; he is also great friends with Catherine, but Hindley, who is older, bullies him. At last, Hindley is sent off to college. When Mr Earnshaw dies, Hindley returns for the funeral, bringing with him a young wife. He takes possession, ill-treats Heathcliff, thrusts him into the position of a mere servant, and allows him no more education. But Catherine and Heathcliff have remained great friends, and one Sunday they go for a walk, and out of curiosity look at Thrushcross Grange, a gentleman's house in a park four miles off where Mr and Mrs Linton live. Catherine and Heathcliff peep in through the drawing-room window and see the two Linton children—Edgar and Isabella. The Lintons, hearing Heathcliff and Catherine and taking them for robbers, let the bulldog loose on them; the dog seizes Catherine and hurts her ankle badly. She is taken in and looked after at Thrushcross Grange for five weeks, and returns to Wuthering Heights elegantly dressed. Heathcliff, who is very dirty and untidy, is ashamed. The next day the two Lintons come to dinner; Heathcliff behaves ill and is punished by Hindley. The next year Hindley's wife gives birth to a son—Hareton. She, however, is consumptive and does not survive long. In despair at her death Hindley takes to drink. When Catherine is fifteen Edgar Linton proposes to her. She accepts him, feeling all the time that she is doing wrong because she loves Heathcliff. She tells Hareton's nurse, Ellen Dean, about it; Heathcliff overhears part of the conversation, runs off and vanishes. Catherine is distracted by this, gets fever, and when convalescent goes to stay at Thrushcross Grange. Her host and hostess, Mr and Mrs Linton, both catch the fever and die. This may be considered the end of the first stage of the story. The elder generation are all dead. The next generation are all alive—Hindley and Catherine at Wuthering Heights, Edgar and Isabella at Thrushcross Grange. Hindley's wife is dead, but his son Hareton—the only representative of the third generation

—is alive. Heathcliff has disappeared. His passion for Catherine and his revenge is the main theme of the root of the story.

Catherine in due course marries Edgar and goes to live at Thrushcross Grange. After six months of happiness, Heathcliff, who has meanwhile mysteriously got some education and money, reappears. He sets himself to ruin Hindley, who gambles and drinks. He also finds that Isabella is in love with him, and decides to marry her to get her money. One day, after a violent scene between Heathcliff and Edgar, Catherine goes on hunger strike and gets brain fever. Isabella elopes with Heathcliff, who treats her abominably, and finally brings her back to Wuthering Heights. One Sunday while Edgar is at church, Heathcliff comes to see Catherine. There is a passionate scene. That night Catherine gives birth to a daughter and dies. On the night after the funeral, Hindley tries to kill Heathcliff but is nearly killed by him. Isabella escapes from Wuthering Heights and goes to the South of England, where she gives birth to a sickly child named Linton Heathcliff. Soon after this Hindley dies of drink, and Heathcliff is left in possession of Wuthering Heights with Hareton, whom, out of revenge for the way he was treated as a boy, he brings up as a mere brute. At this stage there is a long gap in the story. Edgar's daughter, who is also called Catherine, lives with him at Thrushcross Grange; Isabella's son, Linton, lives in the South of England with her. Catherine is kept in ignorance of both her cousins Linton and Hareton.

Edgar hears that Isabella is dying and goes to see her. Catherine in his absence goes to Penistone Crags, and in doing so has to pass Wuthering Heights, where she sees Hareton. On Isabella's death, Edgar comes home with Linton, but Heathcliff claims him, and he is taken to Wuthering Heights. Catherine is not allowed by Edgar, her father, to go there. One day, after some time, Catherine on a walk meets Heathcliff and Hareton and goes to Wuthering Heights, where she sees her cousin, Linton. Catherine and Linton correspond secretly. The correspondence is detected and stopped. Catherine's father, Edgar, becomes ill. Heathcliff meets Catherine and tells her that Linton is seriously ill. She goes to see him, and many times visits him secretly. One day, just before her father dies, she is kidnapped by Heathcliff and forced to marry Linton. Soon after Linton dies, having made a will leaving all his personal property to his father, Heathcliff. Heathcliff takes possession of Thrushcross Grange, and lets it to Mr Lockwood, who tells the story. But Heathcliff dies soon after, and Hareton and Catherine marry.

How is a long story like this to be told? How is the reader's interest to be excited? How is the tale to be kept together? How are we to be made to feel the lapse of time without being pestered by dates? How far did the authoress accurately visualise the ages of the characters in the different incidents, the topography, and so on?

And how did Heathcliff succeed in getting the property? These are the questions I attempt to answer.

The most obvious thing about the structure of the story which deals with three generations is the symmetry of the pedigree. Mr and Mrs Earnshaw at Wuthering Heights and Mr and Mrs Linton at Thrushcross Grange each have one son and one daughter. Mr Linton's son marries Mr Earnshaw's daughter, and their only child Catherine marries successively her two cousins—Mr Linton's grandson and Mr Earnshaw's grandson. See the following pedigree:—

In actual life I have never come across a pedigree of such absolute symmetry. I shall have to refer to this pedigree again later. It is a remarkable piece of symmetry in a tempestuous book.

The method adopted to arouse the reader's interest and to give vividness and reality to the tale is one which has been used with great success by Joseph Conrad. But it requires great skill.

After Edgar Linton's death, Mr Lockwood, the narrator, takes Thrushcross Grange for a year. He goes to call on his landlord, Heathcliff, at Wuthering Heights, and is puzzled to find there a *farouche* young woman and an awkward boor. At first he supposes Catherine to be Heathcliff's wife; when told she is his daughter-in-law, he then supposes that Hareton is Heathcliff's son, and has again to be corrected. He, and the reader, are naturally puzzled at this strange trio. Lockwood calls again, and is forced to spend the night because of a heavy fall of snow. In his room he finds some books with the name Catherine Earnshaw and Catherine Linton, and a sort of diary of Catherine's in a childish hand which gives a vivid picture of the situation just after her father's death. Mr Lockwood has a nightmare in which Catherine's spirit comes to the window, and he also witnesses a strange scene of Heathcliff imploring Catherine's spirit. Our interest cannot fail now to be excited. What is this strange man and this strange menage? Who was this Catherine who died years before? What were her relations with Heathcliff? Naturally, Lockwood is much intrigued. On his way back next day he catches a chill and becomes ill. To pass the time he asks Ellen Dean, the housekeeper at Thrushcross Grange, what she knows about the family at Wuthering Heights. She, who was first Hareton's nurse and then the younger Catherine's, tells him the story of the past thirty years in considerable detail. So that during the major part of the book Mr Lockwood is telling us what Ellen Dean told him, but sometimes, also, what Ellen Dean told him that someone else—for instance, Isabella—had told her. Only a small part, perhaps one-tenth of the book, consists of direct narrative by Lockwood from his own knowledge. But such a scheme may be confusing, and it is easy to muddle the time. Did Emily

Brontë realise and let us know the dates when each event happened? She did, but not by giving them directly. Look again at the pedigree. The dates there have all been derived from the book, yet only one is directly stated. What first brought me to study the book more closely was when I noticed that the first word in the book was a date —1801. I thought this must have some significance. Similarly, the first word of Chapter XXXII is 1802. Apart from this, only one other date is given directly. In the last sentence of Chapter VII, Ellen Dean says, "I will be content to pass on to the next summer—the summer of 1778, that is, nearly twenty-three years ago." This gives no further information, as 1801 is twenty-three years after 1778, but in the first sentence of the next chapter she tells us that Hareton was born in June. This is how I get June 1778 for Hareton's birth in the pedigree. But what about the rest of the dates, not only those in the pedigree but of all the incidents in the story? There are a considerable number (perhaps nearly a hundred) indications of various kinds to help us—intervals of time, ages of characters, the months, the harvest moon, the last grouse, and so forth, and we learn, incidentally, that the younger Catherine's birthday was on 20th March. Sometimes, too, we know the day of the week—thus Ellen Dean will remember something which happened on a Sunday, or on a Christmas Eve. Taking all these indications, it is, I think, possible to ascertain the year, and, in most cases, the month of the year in which every event takes place—also the ages of the various characters, except, naturally, there is a slight doubt as to Heathcliff, because no one knows his exact age when he was found by Mr Earnshaw. But one has to go warily and consider all the indications together, for there is a curious subtlety that sometimes the characters are described as *looking* some ages which are not exact. Thus Lockwood when he first describes them says that Heathcliff was about forty and Catherine did not look seventeen. In fact, Catherine was seventeen and three-quarters and Heathcliff cannot have been more than thirty-eight. It would be too tedious to state the process by which I have discovered each date (see Appendix). But I will give one or two illustrations. We already know that Hareton was born in June 1778; we are told that he was nearly five when Catherine Earnshaw married Edgar Linton, so that the marriage was before June 1783. But Heathcliff returned in September after they had been happily married for six months. Thus the marriage was in April 1783. We are told that the scene that led to Catherine's death was a Sunday in the March after Heathcliff's return, and that her daughter, Catherine, was born about midnight, and the mother died two hours after. Later on we learn that Catherine's birthday was the 20th (and that this was also treated as the day of her mother's death). Hence Catherine died at 2 a.m. on Monday, 20th March 1784.

I will give only one other instance. Lockwood begins his account in 1801; it is snowy weather, which might be in January or February or in November or December. But he returns in 1802 before his year's tenancy is out. Hence the story begins at the end of 1801. A Michaelmas tenancy begins at the 10th October—not on 29th September—because when the calendar was reformed eleven days were left out. Therefore, the story begins after 10th October 1801. Now after Lockwood has been ill three weeks Heathcliff sends him some grouse, the last of the season. Since the Game Act, 1831, grouse may not be shot after 10th December, so we may take this as about the date for the last grouse. Thus the story begins about the middle of November, and this fits pretty well with the later indications. That is sufficient to illustrate the process. Sometimes it is only by fitting together several indications, each rather vague, that one can find the month. There is, however, one curious fact. We can ascertain Hindley's age. Now Ellen Dean was of the same age. She was his foster sister, and the doctor also refers to her as being of the same age as Hindley. Yet she makes two mistakes about her own age. Middle-aged people do, of course, make mistakes about their age, and these slips may have been intentional on the part of Emily Brontë, but, if so, it seems to me a little over-subtle.

The topography is equally precise. On going from Thrushcross Grange to the village of Gimmerton a highway branches off to the moor on the left. There is a stone pillar there. Thrushcross Grange lies to the south-west, Gimmerton to the east, and Wuthering Heights to the north. The distance from Thrushcross Grange to Wuthering Heights is four miles, and Penistone Crags lie a mile and a half farther on. It was half an hour from Gimmerton to Thrushcross Grange.

The botany is sure to be correct. Emily Brontë loved the country. I was a little surprised to find an ash tree in bud as early as 20th March, but then I realised that it was not on the moor but in the park at Thrushcross Grange, which lay low and was no doubt sheltered.

I now come to the final problem. Heathcliff schemed to get all the property of both the Earnshaws and the Lintons. How did he do it? Emily Brontë clearly had a considerable knowledge of the law. We know the source of George Eliot's use of a base fee for the plot of Felix Holt. We do not know the source of Jane Austen's unerring grasp of the law of real property; but she lived among people who had settled estates and could easily have obtained it. But how Emily Brontë acquired her knowledge I cannot guess. There is also this difficulty. *Wuthering Heights* was written in the eighteen-forties. It was published in 1847. But the period of the

tale is from 1771 to 1803. The Inheritance Act of 1834, the Wills
Act of 1837, and, I think, the Game Act of 1831, had changed the
law. Did Emily Brontë apply the law at the time she wrote or that
at the period of the tale? In one case, as we shall see, she used the
earlier law.

Novelists sometimes make their plots depend on the law and
use legal terms. But they frequently make mistakes and sometimes
are absurd as Trollope is in *Orley Farm*. What is remarkable about
Wuthering Heights is that the ten or twelve legal references are,
I think, sufficient to enable us to ascertain the various legal processes
by which Heathcliff obtained the property. It is not a simple matter.
There was a fundamental difference between the law of land (real
property) and that of money and goods (personal property).

Let us begin with Wuthering Heights. The Earnshaws were
farmers and not likely to have their estate settled. The property
had been in their family since 1500. We may take it then that Mr
Earnshaw was owner in fee-simple, that is in effect absolute owner,
of Wuthering Heights, and was not likely to have possessed any
investments. It is more likely that there was a mortgage on the
house and farm. On Mr Earnshaw's death the land descended to
Hindley as his heir-at-law. There is no mention of a will. The
personal property, which, probably, was only the farming stock
and the furniture, would go equally to his children, Hindley and
Catherine, subject to the payment of his debts out of it. On Catherine's marriage Edgar would have become entitled to her personal
property. Now Hindley drinks and gambles away all he has, and at
his death the property is mortgaged up to the hilt. Heathcliff we
find is the mortgagee. The personal property would also be liable
to the debts. So that Heathcliff is mortgagee in possession and, for
practical purposes, owner of all the Earnshaw property except any
personalty that had gone to Catherine. This is all fairly simple; but
it is more difficult when we come to the Linton property. They
were landed gentry; they had a park, they had tenants. Mr Linton,
and Edgar after him, was a magistrate. Such people, generally, had
a settlement of their land, and we find, in fact, that Mr Linton had
settled it by his will. To understand what happens it is necessary
to go into the intricacies of real property law and to look at the
pedigree.

I must explain very shortly the law of entails. What is called an
estate tail is an estate which descends according to the following
rules: (1) Males are preferred to females; (2) males take in order
according to seniority of birth, but females take equally; (3) descendants represent their ancestor. In case of a conflict between
them, rule (3) prevails. A tenant in tail of full age in possession
could by means of a fictitious action (for which a deed was sub-

stituted by the Fines and Recoveries Act, 1833) bar the entail and obtain the fee-simple, which practically amounts to absolute ownership. By his will a testator could settle his land on living persons for life, but could not give life estates to the children of such persons who were not alive at the testator's death. Consequently, if he wanted to tie up his estate as long as possible, he gave life estates to such of his descendants as were living at his death, followed by estates tail to their children.

Now the settlement made by Mr Linton's will must have been as follows: The estate was devised to Edgar, his only son, for life, then to Edgar's sons in tail; Edgar's daughters were passed over in favour of Mr Linton's daughter, Isabella, who, presumably, had a life interest with remainder to her sons in tail. This is the usual form. Thus on Edgar Linton's death, Linton Heathcliff became tenant in tail in possession during the few weeks he survived his uncle. As a minor he could not bar the entail. It is most improbable that he had an estate in fee-simple; that would have been too unusual. Isabella might have had an estate tail instead of a life interest. This is most improbable, but if she did, her son, Linton Heathcliff, would have become tenant in tail by descent, so the result is the same. Heathcliff claims the property—by what right? Ellen Dean says that he claimed and kept the Thrushcross Grange estate in his wife's right and in his son's also. She adds: "I suppose, legally at any rate, Catherine, destitute of cash and friends, cannot disturb his possession." She is quite right in her suspicions. Even if Isabella had had an estate tail, or even an estate in fee-simple, Heathcliff would not have had any right as husband to an estate for life—the estate known as an estate by courtesy—because Isabella was never in possession. And even if, which to my mind is not possible, Linton Heathcliff had had an estate in fee-simple, his father would not have been his heir before the Inheritance Act, 1833, because it was considered unnatural that an inheritance should ascend directly; and, as Ellen Dean knows and states, Linton Heathcliff as a minor could not dispose of his land by will. There is no difficulty as to the personal property. Whatever Isabella had Heathcliff got by marrying her. There was no Married Women's Property Act in these days. They eloped, so there was no question of a marriage settlement. Edgar Linton had saved out of his rents to make a provision for his daughter, Catherine. When dying he decides, in order to prevent Heathcliff getting at them, to alter his will so as to settle them on Catherine for life and then for her children. The attorney for whom he sends is, however, kept from going by Heathcliff, and Edgar dies before his will is altered, so the money passes to Catherine and then to her husband, Linton. He, though a minor, could (before the year 1838) make a will of personalty. He is induced or forced to do so, and leaves it all to Heath-cliff.

Thus, at Heathcliff's death, the position seems to be that he has acquired all the personal property of both families: he is mortgagee in possession of Wuthering Heights, and is, though wrongfully, in possession of Thrushcross Grange, which he has let to Lockwood. He thinks of making a will but does not do so. What then happens on his death? He has no relations, so that his real property will escheat, and his personal property will go to the Crown as *bona vacantia*. What then becomes of Hareton and Catherine who, when the tale ends, are to be happily married on New Year's Day, 1803? At one time I thought this was the climax of the tragedy. These young people, ill-educated and incompetent, were to be left desti-tute. But that would be going too far. Catherine, as you will see from the pedigree, is the sole living descendant of Mr Linton. In some way or other, I need not go through the various alternatives, she must have become entitled to Thrushcross Grange, which is plainly by far the most valuable property. Heathcliff had been mortgagee in possession of Wuthering Heights for eighteen years, but this was not long enough to obtain an absolute title by adverse possession. Hareton, as Hindley's heir, would be entitled to the equity of redemption. Now if Heathcliff, who managed well, prop-erly accounted for his profits during the eighteen years as he could be made to do, it may well be that they were sufficient, if he was charged a proper occupation rent, to pay off the mortgage. So that Hareton would get the house and land unincumbered or, at any rate, only slightly burdened. The personal property was compara-tively unimportant, and we can only hope that the Crown did not insist on its rights, if it knew of them, or that if it did insist, the happy couple could buy out the Crown's claim out of the rent which Lockwood, as we know, paid.

There is, so far as I know, no other novel in the world which it is possible to subject to an analysis of the kind I have tried to make. This in itself makes the book very unusual. Did the authoress carry all the dates in her head, or did she work with a calendar? Was 20th March 1784, for example, on a Monday? According to my calculations it was not, it was a Saturday, but I should like to have this confirmed by some competent chronologist; for if I am right, it shows that Emily Brontë did not use a calendar, and that nothing will be gained by finding out, for instance, the date of Easter in 1803.

However dull and technical the above details may be, they do, I believe, throw a light on the character of Emily Brontë and her book. German romances can hardly have been the source of her knowledge of English law. A great critic has spoken of the passionate chastity of the book; but the extreme care in realising the ages of the characters at the time of each incident which is described seems to me a more unusual characteristic of a novel. It demonstrates the vividness of the author's imagination.

Appendix: Chronology of Wuthering Heights

CHAP.

	1757,	before September.	Hindley Earnshaw born.
	1762,	,,	Edgar Linton born.
	1764,	,,	Heathcliff born.
	1765,	summer.	Catherine Earnshaw born.
	,,	late.	Isabella Linton born.
IV.	1771,	summer, beginning of harvest.	Heathcliff brought to Wuthering Heights.
	1773,	spring or early summer.	Mrs Earnshaw dies.
V.	1774,	October.	Hindley sent to college.
	1777,		Hindley marries.
	,,	,,	Mr Earnshaw dies.
VI.	,,	,,	Hindley returns with his wife.
III.	,,	October or November.	The scene described by Catherine.
VI.	,,	November, third week, Sunday.	Catherine and Heathcliff go to Thrushcross Grange.
VII.	,,	Christmas Eve.	Catherine returns to W. H.
	,,	Christmas Day.	The Lintons visit W. H.
VIII.	1778,	June.	Hareton Earnshaw born.
	,,	late.	Frances Earnshaw dies.
	1780,	summer.	Edgar Linton calls at W. H. and proposes to Catherine.
IV.	,,	,,	Hindley returns drunk.
	,,	,,	Catherine tells Ellen about Edgar.
	,,	,,	Heathcliff goes off.
IV.	1780,	summer.	Catherine gets wet through and catches fever.
	,,	autumn.	Catherine, convalescent, goes to Thrushcross Grange. Mr and Mrs Linton catch the fever and die.
	1783,	April.	Edgar marries Catherine.
X.	,,	September.	Heathcliff returns and sees Catherine.
	,,	autumn.	Isabella falls in love with Heathcliff, who visits Thrushcross Grange from time to time.
XI.	,,	December.	Ellen Dean sees Hareton.
			Heathcliff kisses Isabella.
	1784,	January 6, Monday.	Violent scene at Thrushcross Grange. Heathcliff is turned out and Catherine goes on hunger strike.
XII.	,,	January 10, Friday.	Catherine delirious.
	,,	,, ,, 2 a.m.	Isabella elopes with Heathcliff.

CHAP.			
XIII.	„	March 13, Monday.	The Heathcliffs return to W. H.
XIV.	„	March 15, Wednesday.	Ellen Dean goes to W. H.
XV.	„	March 19, Sunday.	Heathcliff sees Catherine: violent scene.
XVI.	„	„ midnight.	Catherine Linton born.
	„	March 20, Monday, 2 a.m.	Catherine (the elder) dies.
	„	March 21, Tuesday.	Heathcliff puts a lock of hair in Catherine's locket.
	„	March 24, Friday.	Catherine's funeral.
XVII.	„	same day, midnight.	Heathcliff nearly kills Hindley, who tried to kill him.
	„	March 25, Saturday.	Isabella runs off.
XVII.	1784,	September.	Linton Heathcliff born.
	„	September or October.	Hindley Earnshaw dies. All his property is mortgaged to Heathcliff.
XVIII.	1797,	early June.	Catherine goes to Penistone Crags and meets Hareton.
XIX.	„	June.	Isabella dies. Edgar brings back Linton Heathcliff.
XX.	„	„	Linton Heathcliff is taken to live at Wuthering Heights.
XXI.	1800,	March 20.	Catherine and Ellen meet Hareton, and go to Wuthering Heights where they see Linton.
	„	March or April.	Catherine and Linton correspond.
XXII.	„	late October or November.	Catherine sees Heathcliff, who says that Linton is seriously ill.
XXIII.	„	late October or November.	Catherine and Ellen go to see Linton. Ellen catches cold and is ill for three weeks.
XXIV.	„	November.	During Ellen's illness Catherine visits Linton secretly.
XXV.	1801,	March 20.	Edgar too ill to visit his wife's grave.
	„	June.	Edgar declining.
XXVI.	„	August.	Ellen and Catherine go to meet Linton.
	„	August, Thursday, a week later.	They are kidnapped.
	„	Monday?	Catherine and Linton marry.
XXVII.	„	August or September.	Ellen is let out.
	„	next Tuesday.	Edgar is dying; he sends for Mr Green, the lawyer, who does not come.
XXVIII.	1801,	Wednesday, 3 a.m., harvest moon.	Catherine escapes and comes to Thrushcross Grange.
			Edgar Linton dies.
XXIX.	„	September, evening after the funeral.	Heathcliff comes to Wuthering Heights and takes off Catherine.

CHAP.

XXX.	„	October.	Linton Heathcliff dies. Hareton tries to please Catherine.
I.	„	late November.	Lockwood calls at W. H.
II.	„	next day.	He calls again and has to stay the night. He finds Catherine's diary and sees Heathcliff's outburst.
	„	next day.	Leaves at eight. Catches cold.
IV.	„	„	Ellen Dean begins her story.
X.	„	three weeks later.	Heathcliff sends grouse.
	„	one week later.	Heathcliff calls.
XV.	1802,	January, one week later.	Lockwood continues his account.
XXXI.	„	January, 2nd week.	Lockwood calls at W. H.
XXXII.	„	beginning of February.	Ellen goes to live at W. H.
	„	March.	Hareton has an accident.
	„	Easter Monday.	Catherine is nice to Hareton.
XXXIII.	„	Easter Tuesday.	Scene about altering garden.
	„	(after March 18.)	Heathcliff getting odd.
XXXIV.	„	April.	Heathcliff goes on hunger strike.
	„	May.	Heathcliff dies.
	„	September.	Lockwood visits Thrushcross Grange and Wuthering Heights.
XXXIV.	1803,	January 1.	Catherine and Hareton marry.

DAVID CECIL

Emily Brontë and Wuthering Heights†

Wuthering Heights—the very name is enough to set the imagination vibrating. We hear it perhaps spoken in a London street, for a moment the intricate roar of traffic and chattering people fades into stillness: and instead our mental ear is filled by the rush of streams, the shock and reverberation of thunder, the whistling of the wind over the moors. Nor is the sound fainter to us than it was to its contemporaries. Alone of Victorian novels *Wuthering Heights* is undimmed, even partially, by the dust of time. Alone it stirs us as freshly today as the day it was written.

Yet Emily Brontë has never been generally appreciated as she deserved. In her own time she was hardly appreciated at all: and though since she has slowly pushed her way to the front rank of Victorian novelists, she is still regarded, even by admirers, as an unequal genius, revealing some flashes of extraordinary imagination, but remote from the central interests of human life, often clumsy

† From *Early Victorian Novelists* by Lord David Cecil; copyright © 1935 by The Bobbs-Merrill Company, Inc., 1962 by Lord David Cecil; reprinted by special permission of The Bobbs-Merrill Company, Inc., and Constable & Company, Ltd. Pp. 147–59.

and exaggerated, and incapable of expressing her inspiration in a coherent form.

As a matter of fact she is a great deal more than that. Yet it is not odd that people should have failed to realize it. We tend to judge a work of art by a preconceived standard drawn from the masterpieces of the form and school of which it is representative. We take for granted that an author writing a novel in the Victorian age is trying to write an orthodox Victorian novel; and we estimate it accordingly. Now by any such criterion there is no doubt that Emily Brontë is a very imperfect novelist indeed. If *Wuthering Heights* was meant to be the same sort of novel as *Vanity Fair* or *David Copperfield*, it is a lamentable failure.

But it was never meant to be anything of the kind. The first fact to be realized about Emily Brontë, if we are ever to appreciate her properly, is that her achievement is of an intrinsically different kind from that of any of her contemporaries. Like that of Dickens, indeed, it is specially distinguished by the power of its imagination. And like his, hers is an English imagination. There is nothing exotic about Emily Brontë. *Wuthering Heights* is not like *Esther Waters*, a French novel written in English, in accordance with French ideals and with French limitations. The imagination that informs it is characteristically English, violent, unself-conscious, spiritual. And the mode in which it expresses itself is wholly the product of native influences. Its every fiber smells of the northern soil where it had its root. But though Emily Brontë is characteristic of England, she is not characteristic of Victorian England. No generalization that is true of Thackeray and Dickens, Trollope and Mrs. Gaskell, is true of her. She writes about different subjects in a different manner and from a different point of view. She stands outside the main current of nineteenth-century fiction as markedly as Blake stands outside the main current of eighteenth-century poetry.

For one thing she writes about a different world from the other novelists of her age. She spent her short tense aloof life almost entirely in her father's parsonage in Yorkshire. And Yorkshire, in those days of slow infrequent communications and before the industrial revolution, was pretty well cut off from the influence of those forces that shaped the main trend of the time. Its life remained essentially the same as it had been in the days of Queen Elizabeth; a life as rugged and unchanging as the fells and storm-scarred moors and lonely valleys which were its setting: a primitive life of confined interests and unbridled passions, of simple earthly activities and complex demon-haunted imaginings; where feuds endured for generations, and a whole existence could concentrate itself with fanatical frenzy upon a single object.

Nor did she, like her sister Charlotte, ever turn from this life to contemplate the world outside. She drew mankind only from the grim race who inhabited the land of her childhood and from her own grimmer relations. So that if we are accustomed to the picture presented by Dickens or Thackeray, hers seems, to say the least of it, odd. That bustling, prosaic, progressive world of nineteenth-century middle-class England, which is the background of their whole picture, simply does not come into her view at all. Finally, since she was unconscious of this world, she did not, as all the other Victorians did, write to please it. So that its conventions and preoccupations and moral preferences left as little mark on the world of her creation as if she had lived and died in China.

But even if she had lived and died at Brighton, her books would still have been essentially unlike those of Dickens or Thackeray. For she looked at the human life which was their common subject from a different point of view. I have said that she stood outside her age as Blake stood outside his. It is for the same reason. Like Blake, Emily Brontë is concerned solely with those primary aspects of life which are unaffected by time and place. Looking at the world, she asks herself not, how does it work? what are its variations?— but what does it mean? None of the other Victorian novelists are concerned with such a question. And the fact that she is so occupied makes Emily Brontë's view of life essentially different from theirs. For it means that she sees human beings, not as they do in relation to other human beings, or to human civilizations and societies and codes of conduct, but only in relation to the cosmic scheme of which they form a part. Mrs. Brown appears not as to Jane Austen in relation to Mr. Brown, or as to Scott in relation to her ancestors, or as to Trollope in relation to her place in the social structure, or as to Proust in relation to herself; but in relation to time and eternity, to death and fate and the nature of things. Nature plays a much larger part in Emily Brontë's books than it does in most novelists'. On the other hand those individual and social aspects of life which fill their canvasses do not appear on hers. Her great characters exist in virtue of the reality of their attitude to the universe; they loom before us in the simple epic outline which is all that we see of man when revealed against the huge landscape of the cosmic scheme.

This does not make her unique even in English literature; Hardy is primarily interested in man's relation to the universe. And, as a matter of fact, she is more like Hardy than anyone else. But she is not very like him. Essentially, her view of human nature is more unlike his than his is unlike that of Thackeray or Dickens. For though she was concerned with the same aspects of it as he was, she looked at them from a different angle. Hardy sees man and nature in a different proportion to one another from Thackeray and Dickens, but they have the same significance for him. Hardy's heroes were concerned with fate and free will, Dickens' with their marriages and their careers; but fate and free will meant much the same thing to them as they would have to Dickens' heroes if they had happened to consider them.

Not so the heroes and heroines of Emily Brontë. It is here we come to the determining factor in her personality. She was—once more like Blake—a mystic. She had on certain occasions in her life known moments of vision—far and away the most profound of her experiences—in which her eyes seemed opened to behold a transcendental reality usually hidden from mortal sight. And it is in the light of these moments of vision that she envisages the world of mortal things; they endow it with a new significance; they are the foundation of the philosophy on which her picture of life rests. What precisely this philosophy was she never tells us in explicit terms. She was an artist, not a professor. Moreover, founded as it was on sporadic flashes of vision, she seems never to have made it wholly clear even to herself. And any attempt to state it explicitly reveals it as full of dark places and baffling inconsistencies of detail. However, its main features are clear enough.

The first is that the whole created cosmos, animate and inanimate, mental and physical alike, is the expression of certain living spiritual principles—on the one hand what may be called the principle of storm—of the harsh, the ruthless, the wild, the dynamic; and on the other the principle of calm—of the gentle, the merciful, the passive and the tame.

Secondly, in spite of their apparent opposition these principles are not conflicting. Either—Emily Brontë does not make clear which she thinks—each is the expression of a different aspect of a single pervading spirit; or they are the component parts of a harmony. They may not seem so to us. The world of our experience is, on the face of it, full of discord. But that is only because in the cramped condition of their earthly incarnation these principles are diverted from following the course that their nature dictates, and get in each other's way. They are changed from positive into negative forces; the calm becomes a source of weakness, not of harmony, in the natural scheme, the storm a source not of fruitful vigor, but of disturbance. But when they are free from fleshly bonds they flow unimpeded and unconflicting; and even in this world their discords are transitory. The single principle that ultimately directs them sooner or later imposes an equilibrium.

Such convictions inevitably set Emily Brontë's view of human life in a perspective fundamentally different from that presented to us by other English novelists. For they do away with those antitheses which are the basis of these novelists' conceptions. The antithesis between man and nature to begin with: Emily Brontë does not see animate man revealed against inanimate nature, as Mrs. Gaskell does. She does not even see suffering, pitiful, individual man in conflict with unfeeling, impersonal, ruthless natural forces, like Hardy. Men and nature to her are equally living and in the same way. To her an angry man and an angry sky are not just metaphorically alike, they are actually alike in kind; different manifestations of a single spiritual reality.

" 'One time, however,' "—it is Catherine Linton speaking of Linton Heathcliff—" 'we were near quarrelling. He said the pleasantest manner of spending a hot July day was lying from morning till evening on a bank of heath in the middle of the moors, with the bees humming dreamily about among the bloom, and the larks singing high up overhead, and the blue sky and bright sun shining steadily and cloudlessly. That was his most perfect idea of heaven's happiness: mine was rocking in a rustling green tree, with a west wind blowing, and bright white clouds flitting rapidly above; and not only larks, but throstles, and blackbirds, and linnets, and cuckoos pouring music on every side and the moors seen at a distance, broken into cool dusky dells; but close by great swells of long grass undulating in waves to the breeze; and woods and sounding water, and the whole world awake and wild with joy. He wanted all to lie in an ecstasy of peace; I wanted all to sparkle and dance in a glorious jubilee. I said his heaven would be only half alive; and he said mine would be drunk; I said I should fall asleep in his; and he said he could not breathe in mine.' "

In this passage Linton's and Catherine's choices represent no chance preference, but the fundamental bias of their different natures. Each is expressing his or her instinctively felt kinship with that aspect of nature of which he or she is the human counterpart. When Linton says that he could not "breathe" in Catherine's heaven he is stating a profound truth. He draws the breath of his life from a different spiritual principle.

Again, and more important, Emily Brontë's vision of life does away with the ordinary antithesis between good and evil. To call some aspects of life good and some evil is to accept some experiences and to reject others. But it is an essential trait of Emily Brontë's attitude that it accepts all experience. Not that she is an optimist who believes that the pleasant parts of life are its only real aspects. The storm is as much part of her universe as the calm. Indeed, she is peculiarly aware of the storm: she makes out the harsh elements of life to be as harsh as they can be. Her characters set no bridle on their destructive passions; nor do they repent of their destructive deeds. But since these deeds and passions do not spring from essentially destructive impulses, but impulses only destructive be-

cause they are diverted from pursuing their natural course, they
are not "bad." Further, their fierceness and ruthlessness have, when
confined to their true sphere, a necessary part to play in the cosmic
scheme, and as such are to be accepted. Emily Brontë's outlook is
not immoral, but it is pre-moral. It concerns itself not with moral
standards, but with those conditioning forces of life on which the
naïve erections of the human mind that we call moral standards
are built up.

In consequence that conflict between right and wrong which is the
distinguishing feature in the Victorian view of life does not come
into her view. Human nature, to her, is not a mixture of good and
bad elements, as it is to Thackeray. It cannot be grouped into the
virtuous and the wicked, as it is by Charlotte Brontë or Dickens. The
conflict in her books is not between right and wrong, but between
like and unlike. No doubt she herself did find some characters more
sympathetic than others. But this did not lead her to think them
"better," in the strict sense of the word. Sympathetic and unsympathetic alike, they act only according to the dictates of the principle
of which they are the manifestation; and are not, therefore, to be
blamed or praised. Even when one of her characters undergoes a
change of heart, she never represents this as a moral process. Catherine Linton is first cruel to Hareton, and then kind: but she shows
no remorse for her cruelty; nor does her creator give any sign that
she thinks she ought to have.

Emily Brontë's attitude to human emotion is equally different
from that of her contemporaries. Her characters have extremely
intense emotions, the most intense in English fiction. They are
implacable and irresistible as the elemental forces they resemble;
unchanging as the hills, fierce as the lightning; beside them, even
Mr. Rochester's passions seem tame and tea-party affairs. But they
are not awoken by the same causes as the emotions in other Victorian novels. Emily Brontë's heroes and heroines do not love each
other because they find each other's personalities pleasant, or because they admire each other's characters. They may be superficially
attracted for such reasons, as Catherine Earnshaw is attracted to
Edgar Linton. But their deeper feelings are only roused for someone for whom they feel a sense of affinity, that comes from the
fact that they are both expressions of the same spiritual principle.
Catherine does not "like" Heathcliff, but she loves him with all
the strength of her being. For he, like her, is a child of the storm;
and this makes a bond between them, which interweaves itself
with the very nature of their existence. In a sublime passage she
tells Nelly Dean that she loves him—" 'not because he's handsome, Nelly, but because he's more myself than I am. Whatever
our souls are made of, his and mine are the same, and Linton's is

as different as a moonbeam from lightning, or frost from fire. . . . My great miseries in this world have been Heathcliff's miseries, and I watched and felt each from the beginning: my great thought in living is himself. If all else perished, and *he* remained, *I* should still continue to be; and if all else remained, and he were annihilated, the universe would turn to a mighty stranger: I should not seem a part of it. My love for Linton is like the foliage in the woods: time will change it, I'm well aware, as winter changes the trees. My love for Heathcliff resembles the eternal rocks beneath: a source of little visible delight, but necessary. Nelly, I *am* Heathcliff! He's always, always in my mind; not as a pleasure, any more than I am always a pleasure to myself, but as my own being.' "

The quality of these emotions is as remote from that of the ordinary lover's passion as its origin. For all its intensity, Catherine's love is sexless; as devoid of sensuality as the attraction that draws the tide to the moon, the steel to the magnet; and it is as little tender as if it were hate itself. Catherine does not care whether her death will make Heathcliff unhappy or not. She fears only lest it may break the bond between them. If inconsolable anguish will keep him faithful to her, she is glad of it.

"'You and Edgar have broken my heart, Heathcliff! And you both come to bewail the deed to me, as if *you* were the people to be pitied! I shall not pity you, not I. You have killed me—and thriven on it, I think. How strong you are! How many years do you mean to live after I am gone? . . . I wish I could hold you till we were both dead! I shouldn't care what you suffered. I care nothing for your sufferings. Why shouldn't *you* suffer? I do! Will you forget me? Will you be happy when I am in the earth? Will you say twenty years hence, "That's the grave of Catherine Earnshaw? I loved her long ago, and was wretched to lose her; but it is past. I've loved many others since: my children are dearer to me than she was; and, at death, I shall not rejoice that I am going to her: I shall be sorry that I must leave them!' "

Finally, Emily Brontë does away with the most universally accepted of all antitheses—the antithesis between life and death. She believes in the immortality of the soul. If the individual life be the expression of a spiritual principle, it is clear that the mere dissolution of its fleshly integument will not destroy it. But she does more than believe in the immortality of the soul in the orthodox Christian sense. She believes in the immortality of the soul *in this world*. The spiritual principle of which the soul is a manifestation is active in this life: therefore, the disembodied soul continues to be active in this life. Its ruling preoccupations remain the same after death as before. Here she is different from other Victorian novelists: and, as far as I know, from any novelists of any time. Emily

Brontë does not see human conflict as ending with death. Catherine Earnshaw dreams that she goes to heaven, but is miserable there because she is homesick for Wuthering Heights, the native country of her spirit. Nor is this a parable: it is a sort of prophecy. For when in fact she comes to die, her spirit does take up its abode at Wuthering Heights. And not just as an ineffective ghost: as much as in life she exerts an active influence over Heathcliff, besieges him with her passion.

Thus the supernatural plays a different part in *Wuthering Heights* from that which it does in other novels. Most novelists, intent on trying to give a picture of life as they know it, do not bring in the supernatural at all. Those who do, either use it as a symbol, not to be believed literally, like Nathaniel Hawthorne—or like Scott, as an extraneous anomaly at variance with the laws of nature. With Emily Brontë it is an expression of those laws. It is, in truth, misleading to call it supernatural: it is a natural feature of the world as she sees it.

Her characters hold this view of death as much as she does. They may regret dying, but it is only because death means a temporary separation from those with whom they feel an affinity. For themselves they welcome it as a gateway to a condition in which at last their natures will be able to flow out unhampered and at peace; a peace not of annihilation, but of fulfillment. " 'And,' " cries the dying Catherine, " 'the thing that irks me most is this shattered prison, after all. I'm tired of being enclosed here. I'm wearying to escape into that glorious world, and to be always there: not seeing it dimly through tears, and yearning for it through the walls of an aching heart: but really with it, and in it. Nelly, you think you are better and more fortunate than I; in full health and strength: you are sorry for me—very soon that will be altered. I shall be sorry for *you*. I shall be incomparably beyond and above you all.' " And Nelly, gazing on her dead body, has the same thought. " 'I see a repose that neither earth nor hell can break, and I feel an assurance of the endless and shadowless hereafter—the Eternity they have entered—where life is boundless in its duration, and love in its sympathy, and joy in its fulness.' "

* * *

Q. D. LEAVIS

A Fresh Approach to *Wuthering Heights*†

After its initial adverse reception ('too odiously and abominably pagan to be palatable to the most vitiated class of English readers' —*The Quarterly Review*) and its subsequent installation as a major English classic (of such mystic significance that while its meaning transcends criticism adverse comment on any concrete features would be in the worst taste), *Wuthering Heights*, to my knowledge as a university teacher of English literature, seems to be coming under attack from a new generation. To those who find the novel mainly melodrama, complain that the violence is factitious or sadistic, or object (with justice) to the style as often stilted and uneven, and to those who can see no coherent intention but find incompatible fragments and disjointed intentions at different levels of seriousness, an answer that the novel's greatness is unquestionable is useless. Some of these charges cannot be altogether refuted, though they can be generally accounted for as inevitable features of the kind of undertaking by such a writer at such a date, and some agreement reached about the nature of the success of the book on the whole: for that *Wuthering Heights* is a striking achievement of some kind candid readers can and do feel. The difficulty of establishing that a literary work is a classic is nothing compared to the difficulty of establishing *what kind* of a classic it is—what is in fact the nature of its success, what kind of creation it represents. One has only to read the admiring critics of *Wuthering Heights*, even more the others, to see that there is no agreed reading of this novel at all. Desperate attempts to report a flawless work of art lead to a dishonest ignoring of recalcitrant elements or an interpretation of them which is sophistical; other and more sustained sophistry has resulted from such academic bright ideas as the one confidently asserted to me in an American university by a professor of English Literature who had discovered that 'The clue to *Wuthering Heights* is that Nelly Dean is Evil'.

Of course, in general one attempts to achieve a reading of a text which includes all its elements, but here I believe we must be satisfied with being able to account for some of them and concentrate on what remains. It is better to admit that some of the difficulties

† From F. R. and Q. D. Leavis, *Lectures in America* (New York: Pantheon Books, 1969), pp. 85–138. Reprinted by permission of Pantheon Books and Chatto & Windus Ltd. Mrs. Leavis has graciously consented to the omission of portions of her essay.

of grasping what is truly creative in *Wuthering Heights* are due to the other parts—to the author in her inexperience having made false starts, changing her mind (as tone and style suggest) probably because of rewriting from earlier stories with themes she had lost interest in and which have become submerged, though not assimilated, in the final work.[1] Another source of confusion to the reader is that she tried to do too much, too many different things (a common trouble in first novels and in most Victorian novels) and that some of these interfere with her deeper intentions—though of course this is also one source of the richness of this novel and we wouldn't care to sacrifice many of these, I think. The novel has all the signs of having been written at different times (because in different styles) and with varying intentions; we must sort these out in order to decide what is the novel. In spite of the brilliantly successful time-shifts and what has been called, not very happily, the 'Chinese box' ingenuity of construction, it certainly isn't a seamless 'work of art', and candour obliges us to admit ultimately that some things in the novel are incompatible with the rest, so much so that one seems at times to find oneself in really different novels.

* * *

I would first like to clear out of the way the *confusions* of the plot and note the different levels on which the novel operates at different times. It seems clear to me that Emily Brontë had some trouble in getting free of a false start—a start which suggests that we are going to have a regional version of the sub-plot of *Lear* (Shakespeare being generally the inspiration for those early nineteenth-century novelists who rejected the eighteenth-century idea of the novel). In fact, the Lear-world of violence, cruelty, unnatural crimes, family disruption and physical horrors remains the world of the household at Wuthering Heights, a characteristic due not to sadism or perversion in the novelist (some of the physical violence is quite unrealized) but to the Shakespearian intention. The troubles of the Earnshaws started when the father brought home the boy Heathcliff (of which he gives an unconvincing explanation and for whom he shows an unaccountable weakness) and forced him on the protesting family; Heathcliff 'the cuckoo' by intrigue soon ousts

1. Mr Justice Vaisey, giving a legal opinion on the text ('The Authorship of *Wuthering Heights*', Brontë Society Publications, 1946), notes such a distinction in 'diction, style and taste' between 'the introductory portion' and the rest of the book, that he believed it to indicate two authors; which would give ground to an old theory or tradition that Emily worked from a manuscript of Branwell's at the start (joint composition being probably a practice of the Brontë children, and Emily and Patrick are said to have written practically indistinguishable minute hands). Writing at two different periods by Emily alone, and at the earlier under the influence of Branwell or in deliberate imitation of his style (as Lockwood) would, however, account for such a disparity.

the legitimate son Hindley and, like Edmund, Gloucester's natural son in *Lear*, his malice brings about the ruin of two families (the Earnshaws and the Lintons, his rival getting the name Edgar by attraction from *Lear*). Clearly, Heathcliff was originally the illegitimate son and Catherine's half-brother, which would explain why, though so attached to him by early associations and natural sympathies, Catherine never really thinks of him as a possible lover either before or after marriage;[2] it also explains why all the children slept in one bed at the Heights till adolescence, we gather (we learn later from Catherine (Chapter XII) that being removed at puberty from this bed became a turning-point in her inner life, and this is only one of the remarkable insights which *Wuthering Heights* adds to the Romantic poets' exploration of childhood experience). The favourite Romantic theme of incest therefore must have been the impulsion behind the earliest conception of *Wuthering Heights*. Rejecting this story for a more mature intention, Emily Brontë was left with hopeless inconsistencies on her hands, for while Catherine's feelings about Heathcliff are never sexual (though she feels the bond of sympathy with a brother to be more important to her than her feelings for her young husband), Heathcliff's feelings for her are always those of a lover. As Heathcliff has been written out as a half-brother, Catherine's innocent refusal to see that there is anything in her relation to him incompatible with her position as a wife, becomes preposterous and the impropriety which she refuses to recognize is translated into social terms—Edgar thinks the kitchen the suitable place for Heathcliff's reception by Mrs. Linton while she insists on the parlour. Another trace of the immature draft of the novel is the fairy-tale opening of the Earnshaw story, where the father, like the merchant in *Beauty and the Beast*, goes off to the city promising to bring his children back the presents each has commanded: but the fiddle was smashed and the whip lost so the only present he brings for them is the Beast himself, really a 'prince in disguise' (as Nelly tells the boy he should consider himself rightly); Catherine's tragedy then was that she forgot her prince and he was forced to remain the monster, destroying her; invoking this pattern brought in much more from the fairy-tale world of magic, folk-lore and ballads, the oral tradition of the folk, that the Brontë children learnt principally from their nurses and their servant Tabby.[3] This element surges up in Chapter XII, the

2. The speech (Chap. IX) in which Catherine explains to Nelly why she couldn't marry Heathcliff—on social grounds—belongs to the sociological *Wuthering Heights*. But even then she intends, she declares, to keep up her old (sisterly) relations with him, to help him get on in the world—'to *rise*' as she significantly puts it in purely social terms.

3. Tabby had, Mrs Gaskell reports, 'known the "bottom" or valley in those primitive days when the faeries frequented the margin of the "beck" on moonlight nights, and had known folk who had seen them. But that was when

important scene of Catherine's illness, where the dark superstitions about premonitions of death, about ghosts and primitive beliefs about the soul, come into play so significantly; and again in the excessive attention given to Heathcliff's goblin-characteristics and especially to the prolonged account of his uncanny obsession and death. That this last should have an air of being infected by Hoffmann too is not surprising in a contemporary of Poe's; Emily is likely to have read Hoffmann when studying German at the Brussels boarding-school and certainly read the ghastly supernatural stories by James Hogg and others in the magazines at home. It is a proof of her immaturity at the time of the original conception of *Wuthering Heights* that she should express real psychological insights in such inappropriate forms.

In the novel as we read it Heathcliff's part either as Edmund in *Lear* or as the Prince doomed to Beast's form, is now suspended in boyhood while another influence, very much of the period, is developed, the Romantic image of childhood,[4] with a corresponding change of tone. Heathcliff and Catherine are idyllically and innocently happy together (and see also the end of Chapter V) roaming the countryside as hardy, primitive Wordsworthian children, 'half savage and hardy and free'. Catherine recalls it longingly when she feels she is dying trapped in Thrushcross Grange. (This boy Heathcliff is of course not assimilable with the vicious, scheming and morally heartless—'simply insensible'—boy of Chapter IV who plays Edmund to old Earnshaw's Gloucester.) Catherine's dramatic introduction to the genteel world of Thrushcross Grange—narrated with contempt by Heathcliff who is rejected by it as a plough-boy unfit to associate with Catherine—is the turning-point in her life in *this* form of the novel; her return, got up as a young lady in absurdly unsuitable clothes for a farmhouse life, and 'displaying fingers wonderfully whitened with doing nothing and staying indoors'[5] etc. visibly separates her from the 'natural' life, as her inward succumbing to the temptations of social superiority and riches parts her from Heathcliff. Heathcliff's animus against his social degradation by his new master Hindley is barbed by his being made to suffer (like Pip

---

there were no mills in the valleys, and when all the wool-spinning was done by hand in the farm-houses round. "It wur the factories as had driven 'em away", she said.'
4. I am referring to the invaluable book, *The Image of Childhood*, by P. Coveney, though this does not in fact deal with *Wuthering Heights*.
5. This very evident judgment of Nelly's on the gentility with which Catherine has been infected by her stay at Thrushcross Grange (lavishly annotated in the whole scene of her re-

turn home in Chap. VII) is clearly endorsed by the author, since it is based on values that are fundamental to the novel and in consonance with Emily's Wordsworthian sympathies. It is supplemented by another similar but even more radical judgment, put into Joseph's mouth, the indispensable Joseph who survives the whole action to go on farming the Heights and who is made the vehicle of several central judgments, as well as of many disagreeable Calvinistic attitudes. Resenting the boy Linton Heathcliff's contempt for

at the hands of Estella in *Great Expectations*)[6] taunts and insults
—mainly from Edgar Linton—based on class and externals alone.
They are suffered again (thus making Emily Brontë's points inescapable) in the second half of the novel by Hindley's son Hareton
at the hands of Catherine's and Edgar's daughter Cathy as well as
from his other cousin Linton Heathcliff, Isabella's son. And this
makes us sympathetic to Heathcliff as later to Hareton; we identify
here with Nelly who with her wholesome classlessness and her spontaneous maternal impulses supports Heathcliff morally while he is
ill-used (and even tries to persuade Catherine not to let Edgar sup-
plant him in her life)—she retains this generous sympathy for him
until she transfers it to her foster-child Hareton when in turn he
becomes a victim (of Heathcliff's schemes). Her sympathy for
Heathcliff's hard luck, even when she sees that his return is a threat
to the Lintons' happiness, is at odds with her loyalty to her new
master Edgar, and leads her to consent to some ill-advised interviews between Catherine and the desperate Heathcliff—though she
also feels that to consent to help him there is the lesser of two evils
(as it probably was), and she has no doubts about her duty to protect Isabella from becoming Heathcliff's victim.

* * * It follows from this 'social' development of the theme
that Heathcliff should go out into the world to make his fortune
and come back to avenge himself, 'a cruel hard landlord', 'near,
close-handed' and given over to 'avarice, meanness and greed', plot-
ting to secure the property of both Earnshaws and Lintons and also
to claim equality with them socially—we are now in the Victorian
world of *Great Expectations* where money, as Magwitch the convict
learnt, makes a gentleman. Emily Brontë took no trouble to explain
the hiatus in Heathcliff's life—irrevelant to her purposes—and in
fact it is enough for us to gather that he comes back a professional
gambler at cards; a real flaw however is wholly inadequate illustra-
tion of the shared life and interests of himself and Catherine that
makes it plausible that on his return she should be so absorbed in
conversing with him as to cut out immediately and altogether her
young husband. After all, we reflect, they couldn't always have been
talking about their childhood escapades—that is to say, we recognize a failure in creative interest here in the novelist; nor do we ever

---

the staple food, porridge, made, like the
oat-cake, from the home-grown oats,
Joseph remembers the boy's fine-lady
mother: 'His mother were just soa—
we wer a'most too mucky tuh sow
t'corn fur makking her breead.' There
are many related judgments in the
novel. We may note here the near-
caricature of Lockwood in the first
three chapters as the town visitor continually exposing his ignorance of coun-

try life and farming.
6. A regular Victorian theme, springing
from the consciousness and resentment
by creative artists of a new class snob-
bery and expressed in such widely different novels as *Alton Locke*, *North
and South*, *Felix Holt*, *Dombey and
Son*, *Great Expectations*, as well as
Wuthering Heights which is earlier than
all these.

hear what they talk about till Catherine attacks him over Isabella
and they quarrel, when it becomes clear even to Catherine that he
can be only the monster he has been made by his history. This
aspect of him is kept before us from now till the end and accounts
for his brutalities and violent outbreaks. For various reasons, therefore, after envisaging several alternative conceptions of Heathcliff,
Emily Brontë ended by keeping and making use of them all, so that
like Dostoievski's Stavrogin he is an enigmatic figure only by reason
of his creator's indecision, like Stavrogin in being an unsatisfactory
composite with empty places in his history and no continuity of
character. (And like Iago and Stavrogin, Heathcliff has been made
the object of much misdirected critical industry on the assumption
that he is not merely a convenience.) There is nothing enigmatic
about either Catherine, we note, and this points to the novelist's
distribution of her interest.

There are various signs that the novelist intended to stress the
aspect of her theme represented by the corruption of the child's
native goodness by Society and to make this part of the explanation
of Catherine's failure in life. She evidently had in mind the
difficulties and dangers inevitable in civilizing children to enter the
artificial world of class, organized religion, social intercourse and
authoritarian family life. This is the point of Catherine's childhood
journal that Lockwood reads, which gives a caricature of the torments suffered by children in the enforcement of the Puritan Sabbath, and another caricature is the account given by the boy Heathcliff of the parlour life of the broken-in Linton children as seen
from the other side of the window by a Noble Savage whose natural
good instincts have not been destroyed like theirs. More impressive
is the beautifully rendered exemplary relation between the child
Catherine and the adults as reported by Nelly in Chapter V. Her
father's attempts to improve her, or tame her to an approved pattern,[7] resulted only in 'a naughty delight to provoke him: she was
never so happy as when we were all scolding her at once, and she
defying us with her bold, saucy look, and her ready words; turning
Joseph's religious curses into ridicule, baiting me, and doing just
what her father hated most'—'Mr. Earnshaw did not understand
jokes from his children', Nelly notes, 'he had always been strict and
grave with them'.

'After behaving as badly as possible all day, she sometimes
came fondling to make it up at night. "Nay, Cathy" the old
man would say, "I cannot love thee; go, say thy prayers, child,
and ask God's pardon. I doubt thy mother and I must rue that
we ever reared thee!" That made her cry, at first; and then,

7. Significantly, because old Joseph
'was relentless in worrying him about
ruling his children rigidly', as religion
required.

being repulsed continually hardened her, and she laughed if I told her to say she was sorry for her faults, and beg to be forgiven. . . . It pleased the master rarely to see her gentle—saying "Why canst thou not always be a good lass, Cathy?" And she turned up her face to his, and laughed, and answered, "Why cannot you always be a good man, father?" '

We note that the child is allowed the last word—and a very telling rejoinder it is. Emily Brontë, the girl in the family most sympathetic to the black-sheep brother, was the most recalcitrant to the domestic training of her rigid aunt, to schooling, and to orthodox religion; she had plainly thought about the psychological effects of conventional disciplines and taken this opportunity to report adversely in the strongest terms a novelist can use—by showing their part in destroying the possibilities of a happy childhood and maturity.

But this originally naïve and commonplace subject—the Romantics' image of childhood in conflict with society—becomes something that in this novel is neither superficial nor theoretic because the interests of the responsible novelist gave it, as we have seen above, a new insight, and also a specific and informed sociological content. The theme is here very firmly rooted in time and place and richly documented: we cannot forget that Gimmerton and the neighbourhood are so bleak that the oats are always green there three weeks later than anywhere else, and that old Joseph's Puritan preachings accompany his 'overlaying his large Bible with dirty bank-notes, the produce of the day's transactions' at market, and we have a thoroughly realistic account of the life indoors and outdoors at Wuthering Heights as well as at the gentleman's residence at the Grange. In fact, there would be some excuse for taking this, the pervasive and carefully maintained sociological theme which fleshes the skeleton, for the real novel. This novel, which could be extracted by cutting away the rest, was deliberately built, to advance a thesis, on the opposition between Wuthering Heights and Thrushcross Grange, two different cultures of which the latter inevitably supersedes the former. The point about dating this novel as ending in 1801 (instead of its being contemporary with the Brontës' own lives)—and much trouble was taken to keep the dates, time-scheme and externals such as legal data, accurate[8] —is to fix its happenings at a time when the old rough farming culture based on a naturally patriarchal family life, was to be challenged, tamed and routed by social and cultural changes that were to produce the Victorian class consciousness and 'unnatural'

8. *V. C. P. Sanger's *The Structure of 'Wuthering Heights'* (a Hogarth Press pamphlet).

ideal of gentility.[9]

* * *

But if we were to take the sociological novel as the real novel and relegate the Heathcliff-Catherine-Edgar relationship and the corresponding Cathy-Linton-Hareton one, as exciting but ex-centric dramatic episodes, we should be misconceiving the novel and slighting it, for it is surely these relationships and their working out that give all the meaning to the rest. For instance, though Cathy has in the second half to unlearn, very painfully, the assumptions of superiority on which she has been brought up at the Grange, this is only part of her schooling; it is only incidental to the process by which we see her transcend the psychological temptations and the impulses which would have made her repeat her mother's history; and this is not a question of sociology or social history but is timeless.

* * *

The focus of the first half of the novel is most certainly Catherine, and it is her case that is the real moral centre of the book. This case is examined with wonderful subtlety and conveyed in a succession of brilliantly managed dramatic scenes with complete impersonality. Charlotte Brontë rightly defended her sister against allegations of abnormality by pointing out that, as well as what Charlotte justly describes as 'the perverted passion and passionate perversity' of the first Catherine, and Heathcliff's 'warped nature', Emily had created the wholesome, maternal Nelly Dean, Edgar Linton's touching devotion and tenderness, and the 'grace and gaiety' of the younger Cathy—she might have instanced much more. And what precisely is this case, in which—and not in the sociological novel, which is more a matter of course in its age—lies the real originality of *Wuthering Heights?* Here I think we can draw very usefully on a remarkable modern novel, *Jules et Jim* by Henri-Pierre Roché. The film is more widely known that François Truffaut made from it—so intelligently that the film can serve the purpose for those who haven't read the book.[1] I should have thought the resemblance of

9. Other pre-Victorian novelists noted and resented the effects on children too. In the original preface to her children's classic *Holiday House* (1839), Catherine Sinclair wrote: 'In these pages the author has endeavoured to paint that species of noisy, frolicsome, mischievous children, now almost extinct, wishing to preserve a sort of fabulous remembrance of days long past, when young people were like wild horses on the prairies, rather than like well-broken hacks on the road.'

1. In general, the film wipes out inessentials and makes the theme inescapable; it telescopes with advantage, translates intellectual elements successfully into dramatic forms while wherever possible exactly reproducing the original, and interpolates very little. It is a faithful rendition which shirks almost nothing—unlike the usually over-praised 'film of the novel,' or dramatised version (contrast the film of the novel *Saturday Night and Sunday*

the plot and theme of the film to the core of the first half of *Wuthering Heights* was very striking, but the novel is still more like, while providing, in its challenging modernity and absence of all that makes it possible to describe *Wuthering Heights* as a regional novel, a means of showing critically why the older novel is more important and interesting. I must therefore use not the film but Roché's novel (pub. Gallimard, 1953). After a diffuse start it becomes the record of relations developing between two men and a woman (Kate, though confusingly—for *Wuthering Heights* purposes—named Catherine in the film). Kate answers exactly to Charlotte Brontë's description above of Catherine Earnshaw as well as in nearly all other essentials—it seems not to matter that, living in a sexually permissive society (twentieth-century Germany and France) she takes full licence, for she ends in Catherine's situation, and endures and causes similar suffering. Jules whom she marries is gentle, with bookish and philosophic leanings, like Edgar Linton, while Jim, a writer, is passionate, hard and violent, providing for Kate something that she needs to keep her alive and whole that her husband lacks—though she can't do without what Jules stands for either. Acquiescent as Jules inevitably is, considering the sophisticated society in which they live, and even by choice since his deep friendship with Jim antedates their meeting with Kate, and also because he hopes that, Jim being for Kate a lover who supplements himself in temperament, his marriage will be saved (he has two little girls)—yet the situation is inherently disastrous and ends with Kate's destroying herself and dragging the not unwilling Jim with her, while Jules survives, like Edgar Linton, only to foster his little daughters.

Except for the bond between the two men, the likeness to the first part of the English novel is obvious—and enlightening as to Emily Brontë's intentions in developing out of a simple sociological conflict an original psychological exploration. * * *

There are no distractions in *Jules et Jim* to prevent us seeing that it is a psychological drama written with an almost clinical detachment; both it and the film (in which Kate is fairly adequately embodied by Jeanne Moreau) achieved notoriety as an astonishing case-history. No mystical explanation is needed for Kate, and we can therefore see that none is needed for Catherine Earnshaw— though it is natural that at that date Emily Brontë should feel obliged to provide something of the kind, and inevitable that it should take the form of not very impressive rhetoric (in Chapter IX, ' "If all else perished and *he* remained" ' etc., and elsewhere).

Morning, which both softens and shirks, or the dreadful play *The Heiress* which misinterprets and denatures *Washington Square*). Nevertheless, this film omits the physical violence of the novel and is thus more suave and less disturbing than Roché's work.

Natural too that Emily Brontë should have had difficulty in explaining even to herself her genuine insights and that she should be driven to attach, to the delicately truthful notation of them in action and dialogue, explanations of them as 'poetry', a prose rhetoric of declamation which is in resonance with much that is unsatisfactory in the rhetorical verse of the Gondal cycle. It is very unfortunate that the brief, and on the whole misleading, 'metaphysical' parts of *Wuthering Heights* should have been not only overrated but universally seized on as a short cut to the meaning, the significance of the novel (to the virtual exclusion of the real novel enacted so richly for us to grasp in all its complexity). * * *

Inevitably, since the Romantics had made Love between man and woman the focus of values, succeeding novelists were led to ask what in terms of daily life does love become. Roché's novel, though consummations of love frequently occur in it, is not about sex, any more than *Women in Love* is: it is entirely an examination, in Jim's words, of 'what people call love'. Emily Brontë seems to have been equally occupied with this problem though as a much finer artist she saw it in all its complexity. Kate is a woman who uses her exceptional attractions to dominate men, humiliate them, punish them, or reward them if they obey her, and is jealously possessive of their persons and their inner selves too while demanding the right to retain complete liberty herself. Like a child, she assumes she is the centre of the world and has no sense of responsibility. Her power lies not in crude sex but in being, like Catherine Earnshaw, a dazzling original character whose personality enchants because she is able to make sunshine and happiness for everyone around her if she can only be kept contented.[2] Though there are in the background of Roché's novel other women, they are all neutralised by or summarized in her (Jules and Jim call her 'the queen bee'), so that we conclude that Kate is not offered as a perverse or dangerous woman but as WOMAN in essence, a menace to masculine stability and man's achievement of a civilized code, and yet indispensable to any life worth living—I take it this is the point of that 'archaic smile' which gets such a lot of stress in the novel and symbolizes the archaic characteristics which in spite of the dangers they imply are what Roché thinks men seek in a woman and which are seen to be stronger than men's civilized selves. Kate is shown as absolutely

2. Catherine Earnshaw is well in line here, e.g. 'Mr. Linton ventured no objection to her taking Isabella with her to Wuthering Heights in the afternoon; and she rewarded him with such a summer of sweetness and affection in return, as made the house a paradise for several days; both master and servants profiting from the perpetual sunshine.' And even in the first phase of the marriage: 'It was not the thorn bending to the honeysuckles but the honeysuckles embracing the thorn. There were no mutual concessions: one stood erect, and the others yielded . . . I observed that Mr Edgar had a deep-rooted fear of ruffling her humour. He concealed it fom her; . . . and for the space of half a year, the gunpowder lay as harmless as sand, because no fire came near to explode it. . . . It ended. . . .'

hostile to man-made rules: she cheats, steals without any reason, tells lies shamelessly, rejoices in violent scenes, acts on intuition always, refuses to admit any moral law except a childish tit-for-tat which always has to work in her own interest, and has no patience with the masculine world of logic, reason and impersonal justice (though she is no fool and has literary and artistic ability). When she is ill, generally through her wilful bouts of passion, she demands devotion from men, but is unfeeling and irritated when they fall ill. What she cannot and will not bear is that men should escape from her into their world of intellectual interests. It is the first meeting between the friends after her marriage when they insist on discussing their work, ignoring her, that makes her take the desperate step of jumping into the Seine and swimming underwater to alarm her husband into submission (tough-minded Jim is unmoved except by admiration)—this is also a forecast of her last desperate bid for power when seeing Jim about to escape from her by marriage she deliberately drives their car into the Seine to drown him with her.

* * * Catherine deliberately foments trouble between [Heathcliff and Edgar] as part of her need for violence and domination; and the scene where she locks the three of them in and then throws the key on the fire, putting her delicate (though by no means cowardly) husband at the mercy of the brutal Heathcliff, and humiliating him by her insults, disloyalty and indifference to what happens to him, is extremely painful reading. She has no moral sensibility to comprehend that he is stricken not by cowardice but by her attitude to him. In these ways she behaves quite as insufferably as Kate but unlike her she is offset in the context of the novel by many other and very different feminine natures and dispositions,[3] this point being driven home in the second half where the younger Catherine, with similar drives and temptations to her mother's, is able to profit by experience and get a moral education from her sufferings because she is also her father's daughter. It is the men who strike one as making a consistently poor showing in *Wuthering Heights*—not only Heathcliff and his odious son Linton but the generally callous Joseph, the misguided older Earnshaw, his drunken son Hindley, the crude youth Hareton, the conceited narrator Lockwood, and even Edgar Linton who is imprisoned in class and for all his civilized virtues ineffective. But in spite of these inevitable differences in prejudice by a male and a female novelist, there is a wide agreement in Roché's and Emily Brontë's investigations into 'what people call love'. Both isolate the striking irrationality that impels the heroine of each to destroy her own possibility of happiness, both note that the only kind of love a woman like Cath-

3. In *Wuthering Heights* there is a much greater range of feminine types than in either *Jules et Jim* or *Women in Love*, for example.

---

erine or Kate can feel is death-centred. A surprising insight of Emily Brontë's is that apportioning moral blame is impossible. Nelly Dean after describing the precarious nature of the Lintons' married happiness says:

> ' "It ended. Well, we *must* be for ourselves in the long run; the mild and the generous are only more justly selfish than the domineering; and it ended when circumstances caused each to feel that the one's interest was not the chief consideration in the other's thoughts." '

This is a basic truth, that the identification of interests in marriage is the only way of getting over the conflict of egos. Heathcliff's return is the spark that set off the train of gunpowder, but something else would have done so otherwise. Later on, in Edgar's tender devotion to Catherine in her final illness and even mental decay, we get another answer to the inquiry, "What is it that people call Love?"; this answer is not cynical. But Catherine, like Kate, is shown to be incapable of love in this sense—' "I care nothing for your sufferings. Why shouldn't you suffer? I do," ' she says to Heathcliff in their last interview—and Heathcliff justly says of her haunting spirit, as her husband might equally have done: ' "She showed herself, as she often was in life, a devil to me." ' Even when Heathcliff is taking farewell of the dying Catherine he upbraids her with her 'infernal selfishness'. In fact, the scenes between Catherine and Heathcliff after his return are the climax of the novel as regards establishing this theme; so thoroughly is the author determined to develop them that she hardly troubles to bring them about naturally, thus exposing Nelly to charges of connivance or worse.

* * * Why does one feel that in spite of its intensely painful scenes—painful in a great variety of ways—*Wuthering Heights* always repays rereading? * * * Take the sequence (Chapter VIII) when Catherine at fifteen is transferring her interest (unintentionally) from the now degraded Heathcliff to Edgar Linton, who besides being a desirable match does genuinely represent standards she must admire, even though it is a strain for her to have to appear to share them. We are actually shown her suffering from this strain and what the consequences are. Expecting Edgar, she has ungraciously to get rid of Heathcliff who hangs about her, and so she is already out of temper because uneasy about her treatment of her childhood friend. Consequently she is spitefully cross with Nelly who (on orders from the master) thwarts her desire to be alone with Edgar, is driven to defend herself to Edgar by a patent fib, then to laying hands in temper on her little nephew who naturally supports his foster-mother, and then when Edgar interferes to rescue the child she instinctively boxes *his* ear, in an irresistible progress of passion. Edgar, 'greatly shocked at the double fault of falsehood and violence which his idol has committed', reasons with her, but to reason she has no answer.

Catherine was mute.
'And you told a deliberate untruth!' he said. 'I didn't!' she cried, recovering her speech; 'I did nothing deliberately.'

To him, telling a lie and striking him in a most unladylike way are serious offences, as well as quarrelling with a servant (Nelly—to him always 'Ellen') and ill-treating a child. To her (as to Roché's Kate) that her behaviour was spontaneous justified it ("I did nothing deliberately"). She is not ashamed of being herself, having no such standards and no image of correct behaviour as he has which he feels obliged to sustain. She continues: ' "Well, go if you please—get away. And now I'll cry—I'll cry myself sick" ', and she proceeds to do so. If he is unjust enough to blame her for what she can't help she will punish him by making herself ill, a child's revenge and self-protective technique—' "She set to weeping in serious earnest" ' Nelly reports then. What is pardonable at fifteen becomes, however, the pattern of her mode of domination ('Falsehood and violence'), leading her when married to starve herself into delirium, threaten suicide, and look forward to death as a release from an intolerable self as well as from an intolerable situation, destroying also in effect both the men who love her. And this self is not archaic Woman like Roché's Kate but is shown in growth as the product of strains in social and emotional life in childhood and adolescence. * * *

And this episode (Chap. VIII, that is) not only leads inevitably to Catherine's self-destruction; it is recalled by contrast when we read the scene in Chapter XI where Nelly goes up to the Heights to see how her foster-child Hareton is getting on and to warn his father, her old playmate Hindley, against Heathcliff. Full of tender reminiscences of their joint childhood, she comes on the child Hareton, whom she at first takes for his father a generation ago, to find, to her horror and ours, that he has forgotten his foster-mother completely and, schooled by Heathcliff, greets her with curses and stones. With the most admirable restraint she suppresses her natural reactions, even grief, to try to do something for the child's welfare. Recalling Catherine's behaviour ('wicked aunt Cathy') to the same child, we realise that Catherine's kind of femininity is neither exhaustive of the possibilities of Woman nor really typical. And Nelly's adult and selflessly maternal behavior prepares us for her foster-child's, the younger Catherine's, evolution away from the possibilities of repeating her mother's disaster, though Cathy is shown to have similar impulses and in some ways nearly as unfortunate an upbringing (she is everyone's idol at the Grange). Cathy achieves the self-knowledge and wisdom that bring her to a successful coming of age as a woman with which the novels ends. * * *

Wuthering Heights is highly (though never obtrusively) schematic and the demonstration of the corrective case-history of the second part is not just a matter of winding up the story and restoring the land to the legitimate heirs. If it had stopped with the death of Catherine and the virtual withdrawal from life of Heathcliff and Edgar (the point at which *Jules et Jim* ends) it would have been unsatisfactory. *Jules et Jim*, we can see in comparison, doesn't tell us enough about women to show that Kate does not represent a general truth, as its author seems to imply, or one to which there is no alternative. The second half of Emily Brontë's novel however contains much that is indispensable to the true reading of the first half. The young Cathy's first visit to the farmhouse where her innocent ideas about her status are seen to be ridiculous, as well as offensive to the workers there who serve only their chosen master and are not servile, is characteristically conveyed through spirited dialogue: ' "What's the matter? Get my horse, I say." "I'll see thee damned before I be *thy* servant!" growled the lad (Hareton) . . . "How dare he speak so to me? Mustn't he be made to do as I ask him? You bring the pony," she exclaimed, turning to the woman. "Softly, Miss, you'll lose nothing by being civil. . . . I was never hired to serve you." ' Cathy has had that Linton education which is seen to be finally purged when, having recognized Hareton's merits and her own needs, she freely chooses him as her husband, to become Catherine Earnshaw like her mother; but she has moved in the opposite direction from her mother who, born Catherine Earnshaw, became Catherine Linton of Thrushcross Grange—even though, with the progress of social history, they have to abandon Wuthering Heights to be farmed by old Joseph and settle at the Grange as gentry. Cathy's mother had abandoned the degraded Heathcliff but her daughter generously takes the lad he has formed on that very pattern for revenge, thus righting the wrong. Another stage in her development is seen in Chapter XXIV where accepting Linton Heathcliff's apologia (that he cannot help being what he is) she says: 'I felt I must forgive him'. But the forgiveness carries with it the recognition that she is committed to him and has 'learnt to endure his selfishness and spite with nearly as little resentment as his sufferings'. The hard road begun when she refused to enter into competition with Linton in unkindness is completed when she has tended him till his death, and gone through the pangs of rebirth. Our attention is focussed on this in one of the most memorable passages in the book. Cathy has roused the unwilling Zillah to bid her tell Heathcliff his son is dying at last.

> I delivered Catherine's message. He cursed to himself, and in a few minutes came out with a lighted candle, and proceeded to their room. I followed. Mrs Heathcliff was seated by the bed-

side, with her hands folded on her knees. Her father-in-law went up, held the light to Linton's face, looked at him, and touched him; afterwards he turned to her.

' "Now—Catherine", he said, "how do you feel?"

'She was dumb.

' "How do you feel, Catherine?" he repeated.

' "He's safe, and I'm free," she answered: "I should feel well—but," she continued with a bitterness she couldn't conceal, 'you have left me so long to struggle against death, alone, that I feel and see only death! I feel like death!"

'And she looked like it too.' Zillah reports.

Cathy has still a long spell to serve before she is really free, however. The admirable resistance the thoroughly masculine Hareton puts up to her inherited impulses (she also is a Catherine) to torment and manipulate him as soon as she sees he loves her, helps her on the way to maturity. The last sign of the old Eve in her is the attempt to provoke a battle between Hareton and Heathcliff—' "If you strike me, Hareton will strike you" she said'—(just as her mother had deliberately provoked the fight between Heathcliff and Edgar). Her first instinct after securing Hareton's friendship and affection is to prove and show her power by making a violent scene to break the attachment between Hareton and Heathcliff (which exists in spite of all that has gone before, is completely convincing, and not the least of the proofs of Emily Brontë's genius). But on finding that Hareton has loyal feelings towards Heathcliff that are filial and make a tie beyond reasoning with, 'which it would be cruel to attempt to loosen', Nelly notes that 'She showed a good heart thenceforth, in avoiding both complaints and expressions of antipathy concerning Heathcliff; and confessed to me her sorrow that she had endeavoured to raise a bad spirit between him and Hareton.' She shows herself, unlike her mother, capable of self-education and not least in such remarkable restraint where her enemy was concerned; even more perhaps in tolerating a relation between men that excludes herself, but which, it seems to be implied, is essential to their being men (Roché and D. H. Lawrence both make this point more clearly). Cathy brings gaiety into Hareton's life, 'sticking primroses into his plate of porridge' and planning a garden with him by importing plants from the Grange, effective symbolic gestures, like the present of books she has made Hareton to express her repentance and change of heart towards him. She even accepts the necessity for replanting the fruit-bushes and relegating her flower-garden to an unwanted corner (Chapter XXXIV).

Cathy's selfless devotion to her tormenting husband Linton reminds us of Edgar's tenderness to his broken wife in *her* decline: this combination of inheritances from both sides in Cathy is clearly offered as something ponderable about the nature of the human family in general and an assertion of the novelist's belief in free-will as well as in psychological and sociological determinism.[4] * * *

I would make a plea, then, for criticism of *Wuthering Heights* to turn its attention to the human core of the novel, to recognize its truly human centrality. How can we fail to see that the novel is based on an interest in, concern for, and knowledge of, real life? We cannot do it justice, establish what the experience of reading it really is, by making analyses of its lock and window imagery, or by explaining it as being concerned with children of calm and children of storm, or by putting forward such bright ideas as that '*Wuthering Heights* might be viewed at long range as a variant of the demon-lover motif' (*The Gates of Horn,* H. Levin) or that 'Nelly Dean is Evil'—these are the products of an age which conceives literary criticism as either a game or an industry, not as a humane study. To learn anything of this novel's true nature we must put it into the category of novels it belongs to—I have specified *Women in Love* and *Jules et Jim* and might add *Anna Karenina* and *Great Expectations*—and recognize its relation to the social and literary history of its own time. The human truths *Wuthering Heights* is intended to establish are, it is necessary to admit, obscured in places and to varying degrees by discordant trimmings or leftovers from earlier writings or stages of its conception; for these, stylistic and other evidence exists in the text. Nor could we expect such complexity and such technical skill to have been achieved in a first novel otherwise; it is necessary to distinguish what is genuine complexity from what is merely confusion. That there is the complexity of accomplished art we must feel in the ending, ambiguous, impersonal, disquieting but final. And when we compare the genius devoted to creating Nelly Dean, Joseph, Zillah, Frances, Lockwood, the two Catherines, and to setting them in significant action, with the very perfunctory attention given to Heathcliff and Hareton as wholes (attention directed only when these two are wheeled out to perform necessary parts at certain points in the exposition of the theme to which—like Isabella and Edgar Linton—they are subsidiary) then we can surely not misinterpret the intention and the nature of the achievement of *Wuthering Heights.*

4. In this, as in the combination of convincing realism and symbolic action in which the belief finds expression, *Wuthering Heights* is remarkably similar to *Great Expectations.* The latter too is a work of art which also contains a sociological novel on the surface.

INGA-STINA EWBANK

[The Structure and Pattern of the Whole Novel]†

* * * What is outstanding about *Wuthering Heights* is the sense of form displayed by Emily Brontë—a sense which, before her, had been shown only by Jane Austen. Like Jane Austen, she achieves a structure which, in every part, is the visible embodiment of the theme, by the exclusion from the novel of anything not necessary, anything that would dissipate concentration. No more than in Jane Austen do we, in *Wuthering Heights*, have any references to the historical period of the novel, to the goings on at the time in the world at large. But here the similarity stops, for what Jane Austen includes—'parties, picnics, and country dances' (Virginia Woolf)—is just what Emily Brontë excludes.

The concentration on the world limited geographically by Wuthering Heights to the north and Thrushcross Grange to the south-west, with the chapel, churchyard and Gimmerton brook between them, is complete. We never follow anybody outside it. Hindley just reappears on his father's death, with a wife whom he has found somehow, somewhere. For three and a half years Heathcliff is just gone, and nobody is told where he has been or what he has done. There is not one word about where Isabella and Heathcliff go on their ghastly honeymoon; we pick up their story again with a characteristic sentence: 'The sun set behind the Grange, as we turned on to the moors', and all we hear of it from Isabella is that her heart 'returned to Thrushcross Grange in twenty-four hours after I left it'. Isabella herself vanishes, except for the barest account of facts, as soon as she leaves the Grange carrying the unborn Linton. The events in the novel stem from the moment that old Mr. Earnshaw brings Heathcliff into that world, carried under his coat from the streets of Liverpool; the central conflict from the moment that the first Catherine and Heathcliff peep in through the parlour window at the Grange. The novel is resolved with the second Catherine and Hareton going to live at Thrushcross Grange, leaving the Heights to 'the use of such ghosts as choose to inhabit it'. There is no sense of a geographical or social world outside this—it never occurs, for example, to Edgar Linton that his daughter might find a

† From Inga-Stina Ewbank, *Their Proper Sphere: A Study of the Brontë Sisters as Early-Victorian Female Novelists* (Cambridge, Mass.: Harvard University Press). Copyright 1966 by I.-S. Ewbank. Pp. 128–141. Reprinted by permission of Harvard University Press and Edward Arnold (Publishers) Ltd.

husband other than Linton Heathcliff.

For all its exclusiveness, this world is also inclusive. It has everything that matters: birth, death, love, hatred, nature, the seasons. And so it gets a larger than naturalistic significance, becomes a microcosm of the human condition. Despite the Yorkshire dialect and the moor-land setting, it is not really a regional novel—or, rather, its regionalism is a means, not an end. This is not to say that the world of the novel exists only on a symbolical level, for its every incident has a perfectly realistic plot validity as well as a symbolical validity. Thus, for example, the narrowing down of the social world is one for which the people themselves are responsible. In the early chapters there are hints at the existence of neighbours (they gossip when Hindley brings home a wife) and some social intercourse (there is a visit of the Gimmerton band who 'go the rounds of all the respectable houses . . . every Christmas'). Hindley's behaviour after his wife's death makes the Earnshaws socially unrespectable; all the servants, except Nelly and Joseph, vanish; also 'the curate dropped calling, and nobody decent came near us, at last.' After Catherine's marriage, Heathcliff's return sets the seal on the social seclusion of the Heights. A similar development takes place at the Grange. The Lintons, to start with, have a place in society: old Mr. Linton is a magistrate, and on his death Edgar takes over his duties; but after the death of Catherine, Edgar, too, becomes a recluse, resigns his office, and the second Catherine, until she goes to the Heights, has never entered another building than her own home and Gimmerton chapel. Yet, there is none of the trivia of social visiting, business, etc., that was the stock-in-trade of the conventional novelist. (This is where film and stage-versions of *Wuthering Heights* tend to commit one of their greatest outrages, showing us a ball at the Grange or letting Edgar and Catherine talk of their recent visit to the seaside.) Everything not bearing on the main action is as ruthlessly pruned as in a Racinian tragedy, and the result are characters who do not have professions but feelings, who do not *do*, but *are*.

Related to this is the exclusion of all the trivia of plot machinery. We are not told *why* Old Earnshaw has to go to Liverpool: the only important function of that marathon walk is to bring Heathcliff to Wuthering Heights. Cathy 'by some means' gets messages to Edgar where a conventional novelist would have expatiated on the means used (Charlotte Smith in *The Old Manor House* spends the best part of the novel working out ways for her young lovers to have chaste midnight meetings). The correspondence here is inessential, it is getting Edgar to the Heights that matters. On the other hand, the clandestine correspondence between the second Catherine and Linton, via the boy who carries the milk, is carefully described, for here it is an important mesh in the net that Heathcliff is weaving to catch Catherine and revenge himself on the Lintons.

Together with the exclusion of irrelevant details, there is an extraordinarily meticulous attention to such details and facts as matter. It is here that the deliberate nature of Emily Brontë's workmanship is most clearly revealed. In his interesting and useful pamphlet, *The Structure of Wuthering Heights*, C. P. Sanger has shown the accuracy of every detail of timing, pedigree and legal procedure and arrived at the conclusion that the structure is truly remarkable for the degree to which it seems to have been artificially constructed, with minute attention paid to details of apparent irrelevance. Such a detail, to take only one example from outside the important aspects covered by Sanger, is the embalming effect of the soil in Gimmerton churchyard. We first hear about it, very unobtrusively, in Lockwood's account of his dream about the interminable sermon in the chapel; later on it is a material fact in the preservation of Catherine's dead body for eighteen years: Heathcliff finds that her face is 'hers yet'.

Careful workmanship is shown, too, in the way apparently irrelevant details are woven together with images and incidents to form a developing symbolical pattern. The first hint that an elopement has taken place is Nelly's discovery of 'Miss Isabella's springer, Fanny, suspended to a handkerchief, and nearly at its last gasp'. In Chapter XIV Heathcliff tells Nelly how the first thing he did when eloping with Isabella was

> 'to hang up her little dog; and when she pleaded for it, the first words I uttered, were a wish that I had the hanging of every being belonging to her'.

As often in the novel, an incident is shown us through the eyes of first one person, then another, its significance gradually expanding. This particular episode marks the sudden disillusioning of Isabella, who, the moment she abandons herself to Heathcliff, loses her romantic infatuation and discovers what his real feelings for her are. Thematically, it echoes back to the image used by Catherine in trying to talk Isabella out of her growing infatuation: 'I'd as soon put that little canary into the park on a winter's day, as recommend you to bestow your heart on him.' Isabella's world is the cosy and artificial world of the cage-bird, or the lap-dog; Heathcliff, as Catherine knows, is a 'fierce, pitiless, wolfish man'. Isabella wilfully and disastrously blinds herself to the incompatibility of the wild and the tame. So the irony is the more powerful when the dog-image comes back in Heathcliff's words the first time we see him and Isabella together after their marriage; and now it is applied directly to Isabella:

'Now, was it not the depth of absurdity—of genuine idiocy, for that pitiful, slavish, mean-minded brach to dream that I could love her? . . . I've sometimes relented, from pure lack of invention, in my experiments on what she could endure, and still creep shamefully cringing back!'

Later, the son of this marriage is seen by Nelly as a frightened and fawning dog before his father. And another incident, at first sight a vignette of unnecessary gruesomeness, falls into place here: Isabella's last glimpse of Wuthering Heights, as she finally escapes from Heathcliff, is Hareton 'who was hanging a litter of puppies from a chairback in the doorway'. Presumably these puppies were not as lucky as Isabella's own dog. It would be absurd to say that these details add up to a symbol which clearly stands for something else: that is not how the symbolism in the novel works. On the other hand they do act as structural unifiers—one action reminding us of another—at the same time as they define and universalise oppositions between characters and their behaviour; their effect is both dynamic and complex.

In looking at this particular pattern of happenings and images, we have already touched on one of the main structural devices in the novel: its use of opposites and of repetition. In her poems Emily Brontë often achieves an eighteenth-century kind of balance and control through the use of antithesis. Even such an ecstatic poem as 'Aye, there it is! It wakes to-night' is held within a firm and simple structure, ending on an antithesis:

> Thus truly when that breast is cold
> Thy prisoned soul shall rise,
> The dungeon mingle with the mould—
> The captive with the skies;

and quite early (November, 1838) she controls a Gondal poem of passionate love-hatred ('Light up thy halls!') by the same means:

> Unconquered in my soul the Tyrant rules me still;
> *Life* bows to my control, but *Love* I cannot kill!

The same habit of mind, it would seem, is reflected in what we might call the skeleton of *Wuthering Heights*, in the opposition between the Heights and the Grange. The antithesis is repeated in terms of locality as well as of the people respectively identified with that locality, so that the whole action could be noted down in outline as a series of clashes between opposites. This is probably why it is so tempting to read the novel as a storm-calm allegory; but at this point, on the evidence of the poems as well as the novel, one ought to remember, as Eliot reminds us in his essay on Baudelaire, that a highly organised and restrained external form in a work of art may reflect a *wish* for inner order rather than an *achievement* of such order. The schematic structure of *Wuthering Heights* gives Emily Brontë the means to explore human material about which she has ambivalent feelings, while at the same time holding it in firm control. Again, the sets of opposites do not add up to a simple contrast; they intertwine into a complex pattern. To begin with, as the windy Heights on the moors are contrasted with the Grange, sheltered in the leafy valley, so the Earnshaws are contrasted with the Lintons. Interior decoration is made symbolical here, as the farm house with its stone floor,

> ranks of immense pewter dishes . . . towering row after row, in a vast oak dresser . . . the chairs, high-backed, primitive structures, painted green: one or two heavy black ones lurking in the shade,

is opposed to the description of the Grange, in which poetry is made out of early-Victorian tastes in a way comparable to Mick's dream of 'teal-blue, copper and parchment linoleum squares' in Pinter's *The Caretaker:*

> a splendid place carpeted with crimson, and crimson-covered chairs and tables, and a pure white ceiling bordered by gold, a shower of glass-drops hanging in silver chains from the centre, and shimmering with little soft tapers.

The Earnshaws have dark eyes and complexion, the Lintons are fair and blue-eyed. The Earnshaws ride to church in winter, the Lintons roll up in the 'family carriage, smothered in cloaks and furs'. With Catherine's attraction to that soft and bright world of the Grange, there develops the opposition of Heathcliff and Edgar, repeatedly contrasted in appearance, manners and character. As Heathcliff goes out and Edgar comes in, the contrast, Nelly thinks, resembled

> what you see in exchanging a bleak, hilly, coal country, for a beautiful fertile valley.

And the first crisis in the book is pivoted on Catherine's analysis of the two kinds of love she has for Edgar and Heathcliff, respectively:

> 'My love for Linton is like the foliage in the woods: Time will change it, I'm well aware, as winter changes the trees—my love for Heathcliff resembles the eternal rocks beneath—a source of little visible delight but necessary. Nelly, I *am* Heathcliff!'

The geographical opposition between Heights and Grange has here developed into natural imagery which defines character opposition. Despite her knowledge that

> 'whatever our souls are made of, his and mine are the same, and Linton's is as different as a moonbeam from lightning, or frost from fire,'

Catherine marries Edgar, and the quality of her relationship with the Lintons is defined by the image of 'the honeysuckles embracing the thorn'. Heathcliff comes back, and in revenge woos Isabella; and these two are the next pair of opposites. Isabella thinks Heathcliff is 'a rough diamond' when Catherine knows he is 'an arid wilderness of furze and whinstone'. To Heathcliff Isabella is 'a strange repulsive animal'; to Cathy, offering Isabella to Heathcliff would be like 'offering Satan a lost soul'. In the confrontation between Heathcliff and Edgar which leads to Catherine's fatal illness, Edgar is in Heathcliff's eyes 'a lamb' which 'threatens like a bull'—'the slavering, shivering thing you preferred to me'. When Edgar asks Catherine to choose between him and Heathcliff, Catherine contrasts herself with him: 'Your veins are full of ice-water—but mine are boiling, and the sight of such chilliness makes them dance.' In the delirium that follows this scene, Catherine recalls the Heights–Grange opposition, as she frets for the moors:

> 'And that wind, sounding in the firs by the lattice. Do let me feel it—it comes straight down the moor—do let me have one breath!'

Out of the two sets of opposites are born the second Catherine and Linton Heathcliff; and much of the second half of the novel is balanced on the opposition, yet relentless bringing together (in which Edgar Linton in his goodness and Heathcliff in his wicked scheming are both agents), of these two. Like her mother, the second Catherine is aware of the opposition, and in a famous passage she is made to develop the antithesis in natural imagery:

> 'One time . . . we were near quarrelling. He said the pleasantest manner of spending a hot July day was lying from morning till evening on a bank of heath in the middle of the moors, with the bees humming dreamily about among the bloom, and the larks singing high up over head, and the blue sky, and bright sun shining steadily and cloudlessly. That was his most perfect idea of heaven's happiness—mine was rocking in a rustling green tree, with a west wind blowing, and bright, white clouds flitting rapidly above; and not only larks, but throstles, and blackbirds, and linnets and cuckoos pouring out music on every side, and the moors seen at a distance, broken into cool dusky dells; but close by great swells of long grass undulating in waves to the breeze; and woods and sounding water, and the whole world awake and wild with joy. He wanted all to lie in an ecstasy of peace; I wanted all to sparkle and dance in a glorious jubilee.
>
> 'I said his heaven would be only half alive, and he said mine would be drunk. I said I should fall asleep in his, and he said he could not breathe in mine.'

Thus people are, throughout the novel, schematically contrasted— 'My love for Linton . . . my love for Heathcliff . . .', 'I said his

heaven . . . he said mine . . .'—with verbal antitheses acting out, as
it were, the successive disasters of the Edgar–Catherine, Isabella–
Heathcliff and Linton–Catherine unions. Over this outline of opposites is laid another, equally schematic, pattern: that of repetitions.
Heredity is used both realistically (Emily Brontë here anticipating
the later nineteenth-century interest in heredity which was to culmi-
nate in *Buddenbrooks*) and as an image which becomes symbolical
through iteration. The second Catherine has traits of both her
mother and her father:

> a real beauty in face—with the Earnshaws' handsome dark eyes,
> but the Lintons' fair skin, and small features, and yellow curling
> hair. Her spirit was high, though not rough, and qualified by a
> heart sensitive and lively to excess in its affections. That capacity
> for intense attachments reminded me of her mother; still she
> did not resemble her; for she could be soft and mild as a dove,
> and she had a gentle voice, and pensive expression: her anger
> was never furious; her love never fierce; it was deep and tender.

Linton Heathcliff has inherited the softness and the weakness of
the Lintons; yet he also has the sadism of Heathcliff, as Joseph
points out:

> 'That's father! We've allas summut o' either side in us.'

Most notable is the use of heredity in the case of Hareton and the
complex of emotions which Heathcliff feels for him—'the thousand
forms of past associations, and ideas he awakens, or embodies'.
Heathcliff must hate Hareton in so far as he is the son of Hindley,
and in revenge he deals with Hareton as he himself was dealt with
by Hindley. At the same time, just because of this, he must see in
Hareton a repetition of himself—good material brutalised and suppressed—and therefore to be sympathised with. But Hareton is also
a repetition of Catherine—his eyes, particularly, being the same
Earnshaw eyes—to be loved and feared. And in reply to this para-
doxical combination of emotions, Hareton gives Heathcliff a kind of
filial love which will not tolerate even the second Catherine speaking ill of him.

The case of Hareton shows how behaviour or action is repeated,
as well as hereditary features; interrelationships, too, are echoed,
with a difference, until ultimately the second Catherine and Hareton are seen as a parallel to the first Catherine and Heathcliff, and
yet different because of all the intervening interrelationships which
have shaped them, literally and metaphorically.

What produces both these patterns is, of course, the curiously
artificial symmetry of the pedigree of the Earnshaws, Lintons and
Heathcliffs:

Old Earnshaw = Mrs E.   Old Linton = Mrs L.   ? = ?

Hindley = Frances   Catherine I = Edgar   Isabella = Heathcliff

HARETON ←(2)—CATHERINE II—(1)→ LINTON

Thus the novel can be inspected like an equation where, all the other terms cancelled out, the second Catherine and Hareton must be united. The effect of this almost mathematical symmetry is like the effect of a metaphor: we get a sense of mastery by seeing the connections, the linkages, the order—emphasised here by the distribution of Christian names—imposed on the flux of time and experience. Fascinated by Catherine and Heathcliff, and yet aware of the dangers of such characters and such a relationship, Emily Brontë has created a pattern which gives her the chance to try out various combinations and permutations of them and their relationship. To see the novel in these terms is once again to throw emphasis on the second Catherine and Hareton as the integral resolution of the novel.

Yet, it is human material Emily Brontë is working on, not figures, and so instead of proceeding along the straight line of an equation or an allegory, *Wuthering Heights* grows cumulatively, like a snowball. Or, to change the metaphor, in this novel, and particularly the second half, one is very conscious of an added dimension which comes through Emily Brontë realising and reminding us of the presence of the past. Often the past rushes in as a visual shock. This is so, for example, at the beginning of Chapter XI, where Nelly, worried by rumours of wild drinking and gambling up at the Heights, sets out to go there and passes on the way the old sign-post round which she and Hindley used to play twenty years earlier. So powerful is the 'gush of child's sensations' which floods Nelly that

> as fresh as reality, it appeared that I beheld my early playmate seated on the withered turf; his dark, square head bent forward, and his little hand scooping out the earth with a piece of slate.
> 'Poor Hindley!' I exclaimed involuntarily.
> I started—my bodily eye was cheated into a momentary belief that the child lifted its face and stared straight into mine!

In agitation she hurries to the Heights, where

> the apparition had outstripped me; it stood looking through the gate. That was my first idea on observing an elf-locked, brown-eyed boy setting his ruddy countenance against the bars.

Only on further reflection does she realise that this must be Hareton and not his 'devil daddy', as the child has been taught by Heathcliff to call his father. Other such moments of shock are, of course, particularly important in Heathcliff's relation to the second Catherine—in Chapter XXXIII, for example, he is 'ready to tear Catherine in pieces', when 'of a sudden, his fingers relaxed, he shifted his grasp from her head to her arm, and gazed intently in her face'—and to Hareton, through whose Cathy-like eyes the past suddenly impinges on the present.

This device of suddenly 'seeing' the past is, I think, part of a larger feature of construction in the book. At moments, and usually critical moments in the action, Emily Brontë will crystallise a situation into a striking visual image which, as it were, arrests the narrative flow and makes us see a character and its context afresh—the 'film of familiarity' torn off. Usually this is done by way of a few, economically handled details which etch themselves on to the mind's retina. There is Lockwood looking in through a Heights window to see Catherine bending over Hareton and his book. There is Isabella looking through the window at Heathcliff whom Hindley has locked out of Wuthering Heights:

His hair and clothes were whitened with snow, and his sharp cannibal teeth, revealed by cold and wrath, gleamed through the dark.

There is Nelly Dean, running to close Heathcliff's window and coming upon him, dead, under it:

His eyes met mine so keen, and fierce, I started; and then, he seemed to smile. I could not think him dead—but his face and throat were washed with rain; the bedclothes dripped, and he was perfectly still. The lattice, flapping to and fro, had grazed one hand that rested on the sill—no blood trickled from the broken skin, and when I put my fingers to it, I could doubt no more.

Sometimes this visual moment is no more than an aside, as when Isabella runs away from the Heights, pushing aside Hareton who is hanging a litter of puppies over a chairback; or when later Nelly, escaping from imprisonment at the Heights, passes Linton 'on the settle, sole tenant, sucking a stick of sugar-candy.' Sometimes it is more elaborated, defining a character by placing him in the natural setting. Nelly goes into the garden to tell Heathcliff that Catherine has died:

He was there—at least a few yards further in the park; leant against an old ash tree, his hat off, and his hair soaked with the dew that had gathered on the budded branches, and fell pattering round him. He had been standing a long time in that position, for I saw a pair of ousels passing and repassing, scarcely three feet from him, busy in building their nest, and regarding his proximity no more than that of a piece of timber.

We are dealing here with that poetical quality which gives a kind of visual clarity to even the most abstract of Emily Brontë's poems— as, for example, the vision of Hope in the poem of that title, seen through the bars of the poet's 'grated den'—and which is most obvious in her nature poems, most of all in those fragments which are imagistic gems. Thus these lines from 1837:

> Only some spires of bright green grass
> Transparently in sunshine quivering;

or these from 1838:

> Still as she looked the iron clouds
> Would part, and sunlight shone between,
> But drearily strange and pale and cold.

Already in this early poetry there is the sharp visual definition by a combination of unexpected details and, in the second example, an approach to an identification of person and landscape. In the novel this quality is put to use to concentrate experience within a scene, much as in the over-all pattern of the book action is concentrated into short dramatic scenes, with the intervening time slid lightly over.

In the handling of descriptive moments in the novel, the principle of repetition with a difference again comes in. The structure is cemented and its meanings (often ironies) are pointed by the same image or situation being repeated with a partly different content. There is the first Catherine lying dead with Edgar asleep beside her, his head on the same pillow, to be repeated in Heathcliff's dreaming of himself and Catherine side by side in the grave, 'my cheek frozen against hers'. There is Edgar lying dead with the second Catherine sitting beside him:

> Whether Catherine had spent her tears, or whether the grief were too weighty to let them flow, she sat there dry-eyed till the sun rose;

and, only a few weeks later, there is Linton lying dead, and the same Catherine, again emotionally paralysed but now for very different reasons, 'seated by the bedside, with her hands folded on her knees'. Sometimes the parallelisms are pointed out to us, as when Heathcliff comes to claim the second Catherine and to take possession of the Grange:

> It was the same room into which he had been ushered, as a guest,

eighteen years before: the same moon shone through the window;
and the same autumn landscape lay outside.

Because of the schematic organisation of characters and location
practically every move between the Heights and the Grange, or
reversely, is an echo or an anticipation, or both, of another or
others. The first movement from Wuthering Heights to Thrushcross Grange is Catherine's and Heathcliff's escape, on a damp
Sunday evening, from the tyranny of Hindley and Joseph; the last
—only foreshadowed—will be the removal of the second Catherine
and Hareton to the Grange. But in between Edgar Linton has
ridden across to the Heights as a suitor and Heathcliff has come to
the Grange to see Catherine and woo Isabella; and later Edgar's
daughter has ridden across to the Heights again, in the unfortunate wooing of Heathcliff's son. The first Catherine has broken her
heart longing to escape back to the Heights and the second Catherine, imprisoned at the Heights, has broken hers to escape back to
the Grange. In this way, situations gradually accumulate around
them more than naturalistic significances; they become symbolic.
The same holds true for objects in the novel, which are naturalistic
enough on the surface, but are made symbolic by iteration in important contexts. An instance of this is the inscription over the door to
Wuthering Heights. On his first visit, Lockwood notices 'the date
"1500", and the name "Hareton Earnshaw"', and at this stage the
inscription does little more than whet our curiosity about the Earnshaws. But later on, it is to point the various stages in the relationship between the second Catherine and Hareton: in Chapter XXI
Catherine and Linton ridicule Hareton for not being able to read
the inscription; in Chapter XXIV Hareton has learnt to read the
letters but suffers more ridicule for being unable to interpret the
figures. Hareton's troubles are resolved by his becoming literate,
which is so closely tied up with the love between him and Catherine; at the same time this love leads to their departure from the
Heights, which becomes more momentous as we realise that the
departure of *this* Hareton Earnshaw means the end of over three
hundred years of Earnshaws at Wuthering Heights.

Most obviously made part of and pointer to a particular complex
of feelings is the quaint old closet-bed with its window. We are
alerted to its significance in Chapter III by Lockwood's nightmare
(anticipated in an early Gondal poem, 'A sudden chasm of ghastly
light') and Heathcliff's passionate call through the window. Later,
in her delirium, Catherine dreams that she is back in that bed and
begs to have the window thrown open:

'Oh, if I were but in my own bed in the old house! . . . And that
wind sounding in the firs by the lattice. Do let me feel it—it

comes straight down the moor—do let me have one breath!'

Eighteen years later the second Catherine flees through that very same window back to the Grange and Edgar's death-bed, using the same fir tree branch that knocks and disturbs Lockwood's sleep. And finally Heathcliff dies in that bed, under the opened window. (Clearly we must here again beware of the tendency to allegorise: the second Catherine's escape has around it a very different set of feelings from the first Catherine's wild longings to return to that bed and window.) In her delirious dream Cathy is miserable because it takes her back to the first time she was 'laid alone'. At this stage in the novel, the bed and its window has grown into a symbol of the time when Heathcliff was Cathy's 'all in all'. After Heathcliff's death, perhaps neither of them is laid alone? We do not know: the image reminds us how Emily Brontë stops short of the final mystery, but also how she uses her images to explore human situations and emotions right up to it.

* * *

JOHN K. MATHISON

Nelly Dean and the Power of "*Wuthering Heights*" †

The memorable quality of *Wuthering Heights*, its power, has often been mentioned; numerous elements of the work have been considered the source of this power. No one element can be expected to account completely for it, and no combination of causes is likely to produce an answer that is fully satisfying. But examinations of the various elements in the structure of the novel have suggested clear connections between method and results, between technique and meaning.[1]

† Copyright © 1956, by The Regents of the University of California. Reprinted from *Nineteenth-Century Fiction*, Vol. XI, xx (September, 1956) by permission of The Regents. Pp. 106–29.
1. I shall make no attempt to refer to previous studies of *Wuthering Heights* in the course of my essay. The essays listed below, as well as others, have all given readers valuable help in elucidating various causes of the power of the novel. My own essay does not in-tend to challenge or refute any of them, but to make one further suggestion toward this elucidation, through the consideration of one other aspect in detail. For criticism of *Wuthering Heights* from the time of its publication until 1948, one may consult Melvin R. Watson, "*Wuthering Heights* and the Critics," *The Trollopian*, III (1948), 243–263. Another article by Mr. Watson, "Tempest in the Soul: The Theme and Structure of *Wuthering Heights*," *NCF*, IV (1949), 87–

In this essay I am attempting a partial explanation of the power of the book through a detailed examination not of the general question of the use of a narrator but specifically of the fully developed character of Nelly Dean. Nelly Dean is not a mere technical device: we cannot forget as the story progresses that we are hearing it from her rather than from the author. She is a minute interpreter. She tells us what events mean, what is right or wrong, what is praiseworthy or despicable or unforgivable behavior. Her morality is a result of her training, experiences, and reading, combined with her native temperament. The reader's degree of acceptance of her explanations and moral judgments determines his understanding of the meaning of the story and its power over him.

Nelly is an admirable woman whose point of view, I believe, the reader must reject. She is good-natured, warmhearted, wholesome, practical, and physically healthy. Her interpretation of her reading and her experiences, her feelings on various occasions, are, to a large extent, the consequence of her physical health. When the reader refuses to accept her view of things, which he continually does and must do, he is forced to feel the inadequacy of the normal, healthy, hearty, good-natured person's understanding of life and human nature. He is consequently forced into an active participation in the book. He cannot sit back and accept what is given him as the explanation of the actions of the characters. He must continually provide his own version.

For the reader to disagree with Nelly would be easy, if Nelly were not admirable. But to prevent the reader's turning Nelly into a cliché of simple and narrow piety, Emily Brontë has provided

100, in comparing the structure of the novel to that of an Elizabethan play, and in considering Nelly Dean technically valuable as a means of dividing the action into convenient acts, has a closer bearing on my essay. Other essays which give some consideration to Nelly Dean are: William E. Buckler, "Chapter VII of *Wuthering Heights:* A Key to Interpretation," *NCF*, VII (1952), 51–55; Boris Ford, *"Wuthering Heights,"* Scrutiny, VII (1939), 375–389; and Dorothy Van Ghent, "On *Wuthering Heights,"* The English Novel, Form and Function (New York: Rinehart, 1953), pp. 153–170. Two other essays particularly valuable in the elucidation of *Wuthering Heights* are G. D. Klingopulos, "The Novel as Dramatic Poem (II): 'Wuthering Heights,'" *Scrutiny,* XIV (1947), 269–286, and Mark Schorer, "Fiction and the Matrix of Analogy," *Kenyon Review,* XI (1949), 539–560. Mr. Klingopulos asserts that "the author's preferences are not shown, do not reveal themselves unambiguously even to analysis" (p. 271). Mr. Schorer, in a very convincing demonstration of the consequences of the metaphorical language in a work of fiction, believes that Emily Brontë reached a conclusion she did not quite intend. "At the end the voice that drones on is the perdurable voice of the country, Nelly Dean's. No more than Heathcliff did Emily Brontë quite intend that homespun finality" (p. 549). It is not necessary to explain the ways in which my analysis differs from these in this note. Finally, three other essays should be mentioned: Richard Chase, "The Brontës, or Myth Domesticated," *Forms of Modern Fiction,* ed. William Van O'Connor (Minneapolis: University of Minnesota Press, 1948), pp. 102–119; C. P. Sanger, "The Structure of *Wuthering Heights,"* The Hogarth Essays, XIX (London: Hogarth Press, 1926), 24 pp.; and Dorothy Van Ghent, "The Window Figure and the Two-Children Figure in *Wuthering Heights,"* NCF, VII (1952), 189–197.

Joseph. He makes clear through his actions and his explicit state-
ments to Nelly that she is not conventionally or rigidly pious. Her
condemnations and approvals do not result from an unintelligent
or fanatical acceptance of rigid rules of conduct. Joseph is sure she
is destined for hell because of her warmth and human kindness,
and because of her enjoyment of such pleasures as folk song and
dancing. Joseph's strictures intensify the reader's favorable impressions of Nelly, the favorable impressions that make his rejection of her views more intense and significant.

And enough other servants are introduced to increase still further
our realization of Nelly's superiority, intellectual and moral. Her
pipe-smoking successor at the Grange[2] is apparently what might
be expected of a servant. One need not more than mention Zillah,
who has some mental alertness, to be made strongly aware of
Nelly's superiority.

But more strongly than her superiority is shown by contrast with
Joseph, with Zillah, or with the servant Lockwood finds at the
Grange on his return, it is shown by the affection of the major
characters, including Heathcliff, for her, as seen not in their words
but in their behavior to her. And of course there is her narrative,
full as it is of her ideas. In spite of all her fine qualities, nevertheless, she fails to understand the other characters and, more important, fails in her behavior in important crises of the action. From
the emphasis on her admirable qualities, and from her final inadequacy, the reader is led to see that the insight of the normal, wholesome person cannot penetrate into all feelings justly: the reader
becomes the active advocate of the extremes of passion of Cathy
and Heathcliff, troublesome as they are to a peaceful, domestic
routine.

Emily Brontë could not have succeeded in a direct attempt to
demand our sympathy for or understanding of two such characters as Heathcliff and Cathy. Approached directly, the reader would
not have to exercise his own perceptions; he would remain passive.
Some readers might say that such violent behavior is exciting
enough to read about in romantic novels, but that in real life it
would not do to encourage such people as Cathy and Heathcliff.
To other readers, the novel might have appeared merely as a tremendous protest against conventional standards, but the interest
in it would be merely biographical, sociological, or psychological.

By indirection, Emily Brontë has produced not a personal protest
but a work of art. The reader's reaction is not, of course, the precise
opposite of any of those mentioned above, not a simple stamp of
approval bestowed on Heathcliff and Cathy, but a realization that

2. *Wuthering Heights,* p. 241. The page
references in this essay have been altered to refer to pages in the present
edition. The quotations, therefore, do
not coincide in all details [*Editor*].

the "normal" person is often incapable of feeling for the tortured, emotionally distraught person, and that the latter's tortured failure to understand himself and the sources of his misery partly results from the failure of imagination of the majority. The question is not whether Heathcliff and Cathy are good or bad. They are the result of psychological isolation and misunderstanding working on a particular native temperament, and the "good" are as much the doers of the damage as the "bad," either Hindley or Joseph.

The better we come to know Nelly, the more we recognize her lack of understanding of the principals. To know her we need to watch her character as it is revealed through her opinions, and, even more, through her reports of her own actions. It is this person, whom we come to know well, whose judgments we finally interpret. Not abstract judgments of a merely nominal narrator, they are the particular limited judgments of a person of a distinct emotional and intellectual viewpoint. Knowing the judge, or interpreter, knowing the giver of advice as well as the advice given, we realize the inadequacy of the interpretation, the advice, and the judgments; we become as we read active interpreters, protesters, explicators, and possibly judges.

II

Nelly's physical vigor is emphatically part of her character. Impressing us generally from her account of her actions throughout the novel, her abundant good health is specifically alluded to as well. Her one illness, a bad cold after she had been obliged to sit for a long while in "soaked shoes and stockings," was a great surprise to her; up to the time of the narrative it is the only indisposition in her life that she can recall. By this accident, which most would accept as in the course of things, her spirits were depressed: "It is wearisome, to a stirring active body—but few have slighter reasons for complaint than I had" (p. 196). Elsewhere, responding to the terrors of Cathy, who fears that everyone she knows may die and leave her alone, Nelly confidently boasts: ". . . I am strong, and hardly forty-five. My mother lived till eighty, a canty dame to the last" (p. 186). Numerous examples of illness, decline, wasting away, and death in her experience make little impression on her, who feels herself so strong. Although she once remarks "I am stout and soon put out of breath" (p. 216), this reference confirms rather than contradicts her feeling of "ruddy" health; the picture is that of the Shepherd's wife in *The Winter's Tale*:

> when my old wife liv'd, upon
> This day she was both pantler, butler, cook;
> Both dame and servant; welcom'd all, serv'd all,
> Would sing her song and dance her turn; now here,
> At upper end o' the table, now i' the middle;

> On his shoulder, and his; her face o' fire
> With labour and the thing she took to quench it . . .
>
> (IV, iii, 55–61)

Her own health makes her a poor sympathizer with the illnesses of others; she tends to view even those illnesses in the novel
which end in death as partly willful, partly acting. The physique
and the temperament which goes with it of the weak or sick she
cannot really believe in. An early example is her view of Hindley's
consumptive wife; throughout the book further examples abound,
to the last case of the frail son of Isabella whom she finds revolt-
ing largely because he will not exert himself and be vigorous. But
to resume, of Hindley's wife, who had expressed fear of dying, she
says:

> I imagined her as little likely to die as myself. She was rather
> thin, but young, and fresh complexioned, and her eyes sparkled
> as bright as diamonds. I did remark, to be sure, that mounting
> the stairs made her breathe very quick, that the least sudden noise
> set her all in a quiver, and that she coughed troublesomely some-
> times: but, I knew nothing of what these symptoms portended,
> and had no impulse to sympathize with her. We don't in general
> take to foreigners here, Mr. Lockwood, unless they take to us
> first (p. 45).

Since Nelly regards the idea of her own death as absurd, she sees
no reason that Hindley's wife should be entitled to a fear of death.
Such nonsense is just what one expects of foreigners (from a different county of England). This passage, very early in the novel,
makes the reader aware of Nelly's fallibility of judgment combined with her satisfaction with her own attitudes. It conditions
our expectations regarding her probable actions in later episodes,
and helps us know her and hence discount her judgments and
substitute our own. These early suspicions are confirmed when
Cathy becomes ill:

> . . . Mr. Kenneth, as soon as he saw her, pronounced her dan-
> gerously ill; she had a fever.
> He bled her, and he told me to let her live on whey, and water
> gruel; and take care she did not throw herself down stairs, or out
> of the window; and then he left. . . .
> Though I cannot say I made a gentle nurse, and Joseph and
> the master were no better; and though our patient was as weari-
> some and headstrong as a patient could be, she weathered it
> through (p. 78).

Why should Cathy have chosen to come down with a fever, become dangerously delirious, and consequently be "wearisome" to
healthy, reasonable people?

If we knew less of Nelly we might be able to sympathize with her jogging of Lockwood during his illness: " 'You shouldn't lie till ten. There's the very prime of the morning gone long before that time. A person who has not done one half his day's work by ten o'clock, runs a chance of leaving the other half undone' " (p. 58). As it is, however, we know her advice is little more than justification of her own natural urges to be "busy and stirring" always; it is her failure to grasp the possibility of people's being less vigorous than herself.

Most serious is her deficiency in Cathy's later illness and delirium, foreshadowed by the illness already mentioned. Inevitably, she views it as an act:

> "Catherine ill?" he [Edgar Linton] said, hastening to us. "Shut the window, Ellen! Catherine! why . . ."
> He was silent; the haggardness of Mrs. Linton's appearance smote him speechless, and he could only glance from her to me in horrified astonishment.
> "She's been fretting here," I continued, "and eating scarcely anything, and never complaining, she would admit none of us till this evening, and so we couldn't inform you of her state, as we were not aware of it ourselves, *but it is nothing*" [italics mine] (pp. 108–109).

One might suppose Ellen's "it is nothing" were a well-meant if unsuccessful effort to cheer Edgar, if the scene ended at this point, and if we had not begun to know Nelly rather well, but as it continues, it becomes clear that she really considers the illness both willful and minor:

> "Her mind wanders, sir," I interposed. "She has been talking nonsense the whole evening; but let her have quiet and proper attendance, and she'll rally. Hereafter, we must be cautious how we vex her."
> "I desire no further advice from you," answered Mr. Linton. "You knew your mistress's nature, and you encouraged me to harass her. And not to give me one hint of how she has been these three days! It was heartless! Months of sickness could not cause such a change!"
> I began to defend myself, thinking it too bad to be blamed for another's wicked waywardness! (p. 109).

As Edgar Linton says, Nelly had had a lifetime of experience with Cathy, but the last quoted sentence alone makes clear the triumph of constitution and temperament over experience. Nelly never will grasp the less wholesome, physically or emotionally.

It may need to be said that objectively it would be possible for the reader to find Cathy a difficult person. But the healthy Nelly's complacent self-justification and lack of surmise of stronger passions and more highly strung temperaments, make the reader Cathy's advocate in the context, and while he reads they lower his enthusiasm for the vigorously normal and, it appears, consequently obtuse.

Nelly's health is only one, though a significant, feature of the total character. Her "philosophy" on all sorts of matters is presented in detail. It is primarily a matter of avoiding any really strong passions, but continually encouraging a good deal of "natural affection." Children must "take to her." On a visit to the Heights she encounters the five-year-old Hareton near the building, and he begins to throw stones at her, and curses, distorting "his baby features into a shocking expression of malignity" (p. 95). Her reaction is unperceptively conventional.

> You may be certain this grieved, more than angered me. Fit to cry, I took an orange from my pocket, and offered it to propitiate him.
> He hesitated, and then snatched it from my hold, as if he fancied I only intended to tempt and disappoint him (p. 95).

Here, too, she is clearly more concerned with her picture of herself as affectionately motherly, than with understanding.

She believes in forgiving one's enemies, but she herself, not having to struggle hard in this respect, does not realize that for others placid domestic normality may not be the strongest drive. After a serious crisis in which Hindley had confined Heathcliff (during childhood) fasting in the garret for more than twenty-four hours, she broke Hindley's commands by letting him into the kitchen to feed him: "he was sick and could eat little . . ."; he remained "wrapt in dumb meditation."

> On my inquiring the subject of his thoughts, he answered gravely—
> "I'm trying to settle how I shall pay Hindley back. I don't care how long I wait, if I can only do it, at last. I hope he will not die before I do!"
> "For shame, Heathcliff!" said I. "It is for God to punish wicked people; we should learn to forgive."
> "No, God won't have the satisfaction that I shall," he returned. "I only wish I knew the best way! Let me alone, and I'll plan it out: while I'm thinking of that, I don't feel pain."
> But, Mr. Lockwood, I forget these tales cannot divert you. I'm annoyed how I should dream of chattering on at such a rate . . . I could have told Heathcliff's history, all that you need hear, in half a dozen words (p. 57).

Nelly is sorry for Heathcliff and sneaks him some supper. As usual she compromises, helping Heathcliff a little and disobeying

Hindley a little. Perhaps that is what was possible. But in her role as narrator she looks back upon the event, having seen the whole history of the subsequent years, and takes it in stride, still blaming Heathcliff conventionally for his lapses, still blaming others moderately, and still keeping her picture of herself as normally affectionate and good. Heathcliff should have listened to her and forgiven his enemies.

She allows, of course, for normal selfishness. Since the marriage of Cathy to Edgar Linton does take place, she hopefully finds signs that there is a "deep and growing happiness" in their union. At least she is able to be a bustling housekeeper; there are no domestic storms. But this happy period ended. "Well, *we must* be for ourselves in the long run; the mild and generous are only more justly selfish than the domineering—and it ended when circumstances caused each to feel that the one's interest was not the chief consideration in the other's thoughts" (p. 81). To her this situation is normal. No allowance is made for the enduring passion of Cathy and Heathcliff. No doubt Cathy's marriage would have appeared more successful had she forgotten Heathcliff, but it is too easy for Nelly to take this stand for the reader to go along with her. He begins to sympathize with the course that Cathy and Heathcliff did take.

Later when the reader might have been exasperated with a tantrum of Cathy's, Nelly's stolidity makes him take Cathy's part against the printed interpretation:

> The stolidity with which I received these instructions was, no doubt, rather exasperating; for they were delivered in perfect sincerity; but I believed a person who could plan the turning of her fits of passion to account, beforehand, might, by exerting her will, manage to control herself tolerably even while under their influence; and I did not wish to "frighten" her husband, as she said, and multiply his annoyances for the purpose of serving her selfishness (p. 101).

For Nelly to control "fits of passion" and "manage to control herself while under their influence" have never required a struggle. She is too ruddy, healthy, physically busy and emotionally placid to know what such a struggle would be. When a few pages later she confidently announces that "the Grange had but one sensible soul in its walls, and that lodged in my body" (p. 103), we agree, but the value we place on being "sensible" is far lower than hers.

Nelly is as much opposed to cold lack of visible affection as to violent passion. Normally approving of Edgar Linton, she fails to understand the feeling behind his apparent coldness and is quite ready to condemn him in his treatment of Isabella:

"And you won't write her a little note, sir?" I asked imploringly.

"No," he answered. "It is needless. My communication with Heathcliff's family shall be as sparing as his with mine. It shall not exist!"

Mr. Edgar's coldness depressed me exceedingly; and all the way from the Grange, I puzzled my brains how to put more heart into what he said, when I repeated it; and how to soften his refusal of even a few lines to console Isabella (p. 123).

She is "depressed" by "coldness," although all she wants from Edgar is a few futilely affectionate, meaningless, brotherly words not calculated to achieve any helpful result. That there is more "heart" in his coldness than in her superficiality does not occur to her. To make things well, and it really seems so to those like her, she will soften his refusal, in some compromising way, and thus receive the congratulations of her own conscience. On arriving at the Heights a few minutes later, she is actually able to say, "There never was such a dreary, dismal scene as the *formerly cheerful* house presented" [italics mine] (p. 124).

The reader's first view of the house had been Lockwood's on his first visit, the history Nelly has told started with the discord resulting from the introduction into the house of the orphan Heathcliff (and the reactions to this say little enough in favor of the Earnshaws), and he has subsequently been concerned with Heathcliff, Cathy, and their agonized growing up in the house, not to mention Hindley, Joseph, and Hindley's consumptive wife. The reader, consequently, cannot help placing a low value on the judgment of the wholesome Nelly, and he reassesses her narrative with quite a different emphasis.

Edgar, except for his coldness to Isabella, is admired by Nelly. No unleashed and distressing passions are usually his, but a sensible and quiet affection, comforting to the housekeeper. Referring to Edgar's mourning for his deceased wife, Nelly approvingly says: "But he was too good to be thoroughly unhappy long. *He* didn't pray for Catherine's soul to haunt him: Time brought resignation, and a melancholy sweeter than common joy. He recalled her memory with ardent, tender love, and hopeful aspiring to the better world, where, he doubted not, she was gone" (p. 151). How much of this is Nelly's attribution, and how much was Edgar's real state remain doubtful; surely the part about "melancholy sweeter than common joy" is something she picked up from her boasted reading in the Linton library, but much is her natural wholesomely sentimental feeling about the decorous way for a bereaved husband to act. Possibly, too, Emily Brontë is indicating a tendency in Nelly to show off her elegance to impress Lockwood, a gentleman.

Of those aspects of experience which threaten to upset her out-

look she forbids discussion, admitting her uneasiness, but willing
to push aside the difficulty. Cathy, wishing to reveal a seriously
troubling dream to Nelly is abruptly halted: " 'Oh! don't, Miss
Catherine!' I cried. 'We're dismal enough without conjuring up
ghosts and visions to perplex us. Come, come, be merry, and like
yourself! Look at little Hareton—*he's* dreaming nothing dreary.
How sweetly he smiles in his sleep!' " (p. 72). Apart from the
unwillingness to hear the dream, for Nelly to characterize Cathy
as "merry and like yourself" is a stretch in making the desired
the actual at any time during Cathy's adolescence, and her preference for babies is again apparent. Cathy replies: " 'Yes; and how
sweetly his father curses in his solitude! You remember him, I
dare say, when he was just such another as that chubby thing—
nearly as young and innocent' " (p. 72). Nelly interrupted her
story to explain the situation to Lockwood:

> I was superstitious about dreams then, and am still; and Cathe-
> rine had an unusual gloom in her aspect, that made me dread
> something from which I might shape a prophecy, and foresee a
> dreadful catastrophe.
> She was vexed, but she did not proceed. Apparently taking up
> another subject, she recommenced in a short time.
> "If I were in heaven, Nelly, I should be extremely miserable."
> "Because you are not fit to go there," I answered. "All sinners
> would be miserable in heaven."
> "But it is not for that. I dreamt, once, that I was there."
> "I tell you I won't hearken to your dreams, Miss Catherine!
> I'll go to bed," I interrupted again (p. 72).

Little help can the distracted girl get from the only one from
whom she can even try to get it. Nothing must interfere with
Nelly's determination to impose her own meaning on events, and
that meaning must be ordinary and cheerful. But Cathy and
Heathcliff persist in a fatal tendency to try to confide in Nelly.
Even at the end of his life Heathcliff confesses to her, although,
dreading to hear anything unsettlingly appalling, she half refuses
to listen.

The customary always triumphs with Nelly. Admirable feelings
in Heathcliff, if strange or uncustomary, are shut out of her mind.
Far from admirable attitudes in Edgar are approved without question, if they would be shared by most normal people in his station. When Isabella is attracted to Heathcliff, Nelly observes it
merely as a new trouble to Edgar: "Leaving aside the degradation
of an alliance with a nameless man, and the possible fact that his
property, in default of heirs male, might pass into such a one's
power, he had sense to comprehend Heathcliff's disposition . . ."
(p. 88). No reader can approve such merely conventional objec-

tions, introduced without a qualm. Such attitudes had been responsible for much of the maiming of Heathcliff already. And Heathcliff is here blamed, as often, merely for not knowing his place.

Nelly is similarly imperceptive when Isabella, who has really suffered from Heathcliff, reviles him. Nelly's attempt is simply to "hush" her railings. To Isabella's "would that he could be blotted out of creation, and out of my memory!" Nelly replies, "Hush, hush! He's a human being . . . Be more charitable; there are worse men than he is yet!" (p. 143). What appears is her hatred of extremes; she does not want even Heathcliff to be unique, but merely a normally bad man, one of the well-known class of sinners. What she advocates is some conventional verbal charity and to forget, to proceed as if nothing had happened.

Nelly is a woman whom everyone in her circle, employers, the children of employers, the other servants in the neighborhood, the people of Gimmerton, and Lockwood have recognized as superior, and admirable. How superior to Joseph, Zillah, and to various other characters the reader readily perceives. To insist that she should have shown a fuller understanding of Cathy and Heathcliff would be to show a lack of understanding of what is possible or probable. From day to day she did her best, with regard to her own welfare and peace of comfort; few would have done better.

Nonetheless, her character, a representation of the normal at its best, is inadequate to the situation. As will be shown, failing to understand them, she advises them poorly, and her actions in relation to them are also harmful. Emily Brontë does not plead for them. She lets us see them as they were seen and dealt with by a good woman. The reader must progressively lower his estimate of the value of the normal and healthy, develop a comprehension of and sympathy for genuine emotions however extreme and destructive, and in so doing become an active interpreter of the meaning of the novel. The reader's active involvement and sympathy with the conventionally despicable makes the power of the book.

III

Resulting from qualities in themselves admirable, Nelly's judgments based on her understanding of events and other people result in advice and action which are parts of the total harm done to Cathy and Heathcliff. Describing the first days of Heathcliff in the Earnshaw household, she makes it apparent to the reader that her presence there will do nothing to better the little Heathcliff's situation. Speaking of the child's silent endurance of Hindley's torments, she says:

This endurance made old Earnshaw furious when he discovered his son persecuting the poor, fatherless child, as he called him. He took to Heathcliff strangely, believing all he said (for that matter, he said precious little, and generally the truth), and petting him up far above Cathy, who was too mischievous and wayward for a favourite.

So, from the very beginning, he bred bad feeling in the house . . . (p. 40).

Heathcliff is, at this early point in the story, obviously blameless, yet Nelly sides with the persecutors, concerned with the trouble caused by an unusual, and hence somehow wrong situation. Looking back through the years, she can only suppose that all would have been well had Mr. Earnshaw never had so freakish a notion as to introduce a waif into the neighborhood, not that the waif become warped through continued mistreatment and helpless suffering. The parenthetical words, whose significance she disregards, reveal the almost inevitable obtuseness of interpretation by a person of her type.

One page further on, another anecdote makes a point opposite from what Nelly intends it to. Heathcliff's colt (a gift from old Earnshaw) becoming lame, the boy tries to exchange it for Hindley's sound one. " 'You must exchange horses with me; I don't like mine, and if you won't I shall tell your father of the three thrashings you've given me this week, and show him my arm, which is black to the shoulder' " (pp. 40–41). The result is that Hindley "cuffs his ears," then threatens him with an iron weight, which he finally hurls at him, hitting him in the chest. Nelly prevents Heathcliff from revealing this blow to old Earnshaw, and Hindley suddenly says: " 'Take my colt, gipsy, then! . . . And I pray that he may break your neck; take him, and be damned, you beggarly interloper! and wheedle my father out of all he has, only afterwards show him what you are, imp of Satan—and take that, I hope he'll kick out your brains!' " (p. 41). Of the words or blows, which were more damaging to young Heathcliff may be debated, but Nelly's actively taking the part of Hindley certainly contributes to the harm. And beyond that, she teaches Heathcliff to lie about the episode: "I persuaded him easily to let me lay the blame of his bruises on the horse; he minded little what tale was told since he had what he wanted. He complained so seldom, indeed of such stirs as these, that I really thought him not vindictive—I was deceived, completely, as you will hear" (p. 41). From the beginning, Nelly deals with Heathcliff through a policy of expediency, preserving outward tranquillity, preventing "stirs" in the family. Later when events demand even more of her, we recollect her habitual patterns of behavior, and know she will continue to fail, with increasingly serious results.

After old Earnshaw's death when Hindley becomes "Master," Nelly is not much troubled by the resulting deliberate degradation of Heathcliff. "He bore his degradation pretty well at first, because Cathy taught him what she learnt, and worked or played with him in the fields. They both promised fair to grow up as rude as savages . . ." (p. 46). More surprising is her assumption that the fanatical Joseph's discipline would have been successful unless there was something basically wrong with Heathcliff and Cathy: "The curate might set as many chapters as he pleased for Catherine to get by heart, and Joseph might thrash Heathcliff till his arm ached; they forgot everything the minute they were together again, at least the minute they had contrived some naughty plan of revenge . . ." (p. 46). Another of her methods of helping Heathcliff is seen slightly later in a reproof: " 'You are incurable, Heathcliff, and Mr. Hindley will have to proceed to extremities, see if he won't' " (p. 50).

Dramatically, with no recourse to the essay technique of Fielding as he restores the wayward Tom Jones to the favor of the reader, the reader's sympathies are being directed powerfully toward Heathcliff, and Cathy. More powerfully, perhaps, because unless he is making a deliberate analysis of the book he does not feel his sympathies being directed by a device of the author. Fielding's reader, directly exhorted, may argue back; Emily Brontë's reader reacts spontaneously in favor of Heathcliff.

The most Nelly can admit is that Hindley was a bad "example" for Heathcliff. This way of going to ruin—evil companions showing the way to vice—is familiar, and she makes allowance for Heathcliff in this way. It is a qualified allowance, for Heathcliff, she says, seemed "possessed of something diabolical at that period" (p. 61). Her evidence is that Heathcliff rejoiced to see Hindley degrade himself. But the portrait of Heathcliff is far from the depravity suggested in miscellaneous remarks:

In the first place, he had, by that time, lost the benefit of his early education: continual hard work, begun soon and concluded late, had extinguished any curiosity he once possessed in pursuit of knowledge, and any love for books or learning. His childhood's sense of superiority, instilled into him by the favours of old Mr. Earnshaw, was faded away. He struggled long to keep up an equality with Catherine in her studies, and yielded with poignant though silent regret: but he yielded completely; and there was no prevailing on him to take a step in the way of moving upward, when he found he must, necessarily, sink beneath his former level (pp. 62–63).

It is hard to see how Nelly could account for Heathcliff's behavior at the same time both by diabolical possession and as she does here, but her ability to describe accurately, and yet disregard the facts in favor of explanation by a conventional formula, is a major feature of her character and her inadequacy as a counselor.

Usually, of course, Cathy and Heathcliff are being simultaneously influenced. When Cathy returns from her stay at Thrushcross Grange, Nelly is deceived by the surface improvement in her manners (p. 51). But Heathcliff's consequent desire for reform and self-improvement gets discouragingly brisk treatment:

> "Nelly, make me decent, I'm going to be good."
> "High time, Heathcliff," I said; "you have grieved Catherine; she's sorry she ever came home, I dare say! It looks as if you envied her, because she is more thought of than you" (p. 53).

Nelly, complacently quoting herself in such passages, still realizes no shortcomings in herself (her questions to Lockwood on moral problems from time to time never touch such failings). Had Heathcliff told his story, excusing all his actions through harsh portraits of these adults, the effect would be reversed: the reader would excuse the adults and blame Heathcliff, saying that they were no worse than most normal conventional people, and that others have survived better in worse circumstances.

Nelly's major failure (though few could have done better) is in the decisive episode during which Cathy reveals her intention of marrying Linton, despite her lack of love for him, and her intense love for, her identity with, Heathcliff. Nelly dissembles her knowledge of Heathcliff's presence, but worse, her knowledge of his departure at the worst possible moment: "Having noticed a slight movement, I turned my head, and saw him rise from the bench, and steal out, noiselessly. He had listened till he heard Catherine say it would degrade her to marry him, and then he stayed to hear no farther" (pp. 72–73). And when Catherine wants to be assured that Heathcliff, unlike herself, does not know what deep love is, Nelly answers equivocally, " 'I see no reason that he should not know, as well as you . . . and if *you* are his choice, he'll be the most unfortunate creature that ever was born!' " (*ibid.*), automatically putting Cathy in the wrong, getting herself over a difficult moment. What this moment has done is let Heathcliff overhear and leave, and the plans for marriage to Edgar go forward; Nelly has not let Cathy know that Heathcliff has heard her say that it would degrade her to marry him, but has not heard her say the words describing her real feelings, leading up to "I am Heathcliff." Nelly's view of the scene, in which her own inconvenience is more important than either Heathcliff's or Cathy's sufferings, is summarized by herself at the conclusion of Cathy's tremendous confession: "She paused, and hid her face in the folds of my gown; but I jerked it forcibly away. <u>I was out of patience with her folly!</u>" (p. 74).

The reader, prepared by earlier passages in which Nelly has shown, on lesser occasions, her inevitable adherence to expediency or her own comfort, is not surprised by the major failure here: moral habits are not likely to be overcome in a crisis where there is little time for struggle and deliberation. Heathcliff enters and leaves while Cathy is talking and Nelly cannot but act from habit, on the spur of the moment, but the defects revealed in this scene are her customary ones. Here, perhaps more than anywhere, the reader is sharply aware not only of her failure as an interpreter of the past, but more important, of her failure as a counselor at the time of the action. Both failures co-operate to affect the reader and produce the power of the scene.

The following page, on which Nelly admits that Heathcliff had heard much, confirms the disaster: Cathy searches for Heathcliff during the storm, and stays up all night in wet clothes while Nelly, at one here with Joseph, is chiefly concerned about the interruption in the household routine, even after Heathcliff is clearly gone and Cathy has come down with a serious illness. This whole passage, too well remembered to need detailed citation, is the turning point. We see it as Nelly tells it. Our necessity of disagreeing completely with the narrator's version, made very easy owing to the great detail, gives our total sympathy to Cathy and Heathcliff. We give, perhaps, more than they deserve; we become unduly severe towards Nelly, but to make us feel powerfully the inadequacy of the "steady reasonable kind of body," Emily Brontë's technique could not be improved. Neither a direct plea nor a narrator who was a moralizing, narrow-minded, hypocritically pious guardian could have placed us so completely with Heathcliff and Cathy. It needs above all Nelly's admirable qualities including particularly the affection she arouses in both Cathy and Heathcliff, and the awareness that her failure is the result of them. Heathcliff and Cathy would have fared better with worse parental guidance. The failure of the ordinarily good being made apparent, the reader, attempting to supply the fuller comprehension, becomes fully involved in the novel.[3]

3. A very different case of the same fundamental problem is shown with Lady Russell in *Persuasion*. Lady Russell is admirable but has certain qualities (dislike of wit and cleverness, and veneration of position) which cause her to fail as an adviser to Anne. Unless an admirable character in Anne's original social group had been shown wanting, it would not be clear that Anne was correct in emotionally and intellectually abandoning her family and their values. (Her one regret on marriage is that she has no friends or relations to introduce to Wentworth who will add to his social pleasures.) If she were only abandoning the stand of her absurd father and sister, she could still have accepted the

To emphasize the significance of the whole scene, Emily Brontë
has Nelly sum up her attitude:

> One day, I had the misfortune, when she provoked me exceed-
> ingly, to lay the blame of his disappearance on her (where indeed
> it belonged, as she well knew). From that period for several
> months, she ceased to hold any communication with me, save
> in the relation of a mere servant. Joseph fell under a ban also;
> he *would* speak his mind, and lecture her all the same as if she
> were a little girl . . . (p. 79).

Later on, a dialogue between Heathcliff and Nelly emphasizes
this superficiality of hers by contrasting her explanation with his.
To his inquiry, after Cathy's marriage and illness, concerning her
condition, Nelly first replies, "I blamed her, as she deserved, for
bringing it all on herself," and continues, "the person [Edgar]
who is compelled, of necessity, to be her companion, will only sustain his affection hereafter, by the remembrance of what she once
was, by common humanity, and a sense of duty!" She is speaking
not out of any true knowledge of Edgar, but out of her determination to edify Heathcliff. His refusal to be edified produces his reply
and reveals once more Nelly's inadequacy: " 'That is quite possible,' remarked Heathcliff, forcing himself to seem calm, 'quite
possible that your master should have nothing but common humanity and a sense of duty to fall back upon. But do you imagine
that I shall leave Catherine to his *duty* and *humanity*? and can you
compare my feelings respecting Catherine, to his?' " (p. 125).

Heathcliff finally forces her to agree to arrange an interview
between him and Cathy; her motives are not a genuine feeling
for the two, but the desire to avoid an "explosion":

> Was it right or wrong? I fear it was wrong, though expedient. I
> thought I prevented another explosion by my compliance; and
> I thought, too, it might create a favourable crisis in Catherine's
> mental illness: and then I remembered Mr. Edgar's stern rebuke
> of my carrying tales; and I tried to smooth away all disquietude
> on the subject, by affirming, with frequent iteration, that that
> betrayal of trust, if it merited so harsh an appellation, should be
> the last (p. 129).

Worse is the smugness in reporting the actual meeting when
she sarcastically remarks "it seemed Heathcliff *could* weep on a
great occasion like this" (p. 135). And conventionally, she weeps
herself for Heathcliff after Cathy's death:

> "She's dead!" he said; "I've not waited for you to learn that.
> Put your handkerchief away—don't snivel before me. Damn you

group as Emma did in marrying Knight-
ley. But with the inclusion of Lady
Russell, the best type that the group
can offer, Anne's revolt from the group
itself is complete.

all! she wants none of *your* tears!"

I was weeping as much for him as her: we do sometimes pity creatures that have none of the feeling either for themselves or others; and when I first looked into his face, I perceived that he had got intelligence of the catastrophe; and a foolish notion struck me that his heart was quelled, and he prayed, because his lips moved, and his gaze was bent on the ground.

"Yes, she's dead!" I answered, checking my sobs, and drying my cheeks. "Gone to heaven, I hope, where we may, every one, join her, if we take due warning, and leave our evil ways to follow good!"

"Did *she* take due warning, then?" asked Heathcliff, attempting a sneer. "Did she die like a saint? Come, give me a true history of the event. How did . . ." (pp. 138–139).

The death of Cathy and its repercussions, however, do not end Nelly's failures that result from the great good fortune, for her own survival, of her native endowments. There remain young Cathy and the sickly son of Isabella for her to fail to comprehend. Dealing with them, she reveals her unimpaired self-confidence. Suspecting that young Cathy is corresponding with Linton, rather than question Cathy as might seem her duty as a guardian, she automatically uses the method of trying all her household keys on Cathy's locked drawer:

. . . I emptied the whole contents into my apron, and took them with me to examine at leisure in my own chamber. . . .

Some of them struck me as singularly odd compounds of ardour and flatness; commencing in strong feeling, and concluding in the affected, wordy way that a schoolboy might use to a fancied, incorporeal sweetheart.

Whether they satisfied Cathy, I don't know, but they appeared very worthless trash to me.

After turning over as many as I thought proper, I tied them in a handkerchief and set them aside, re-locking the vacant drawer (pp. 182–183).

Catherine's agony on realizing that the letters have been discovered is great, but Nelly sympathizes with her not at all, since to her both the letters and their author are contemptible.

Still harsher is her treatment of Cathy after the revelation of the visits to Wuthering Heights:

"Now, Ellen, you have heard all; and I can't be prevented from going to Wuthering Heights, except by inflicting misery on two people—whereas, if you'll only not tell papa, my going need disturb the tranquillity of none. You'll not tell, will you? It will be very heartless if you do."

"I'll make up my mind on that point by to-morrow, Miss Catherine," I replied. "It requires some study; and so I'll leave you to your rest, and go think it over."

I thought it over aloud, in my master's presence; walking straight from her room to his, and relating the whole story, with the exception of her conversations with her cousin, and any mention of Hareton (p. 204).

Though Edgar, no doubt, should know of the activities of his daughter, Nelly's methods are shown first in her promise to Cathy to consider the problem (the easy and immediate way of "smoothing over" that difficulty), second, in her immediate and unreflective revelation to Edgar, and third, in her holding back from Edgar those items that might cause her some trouble with him. Most revelatory of all, of course, is the more than satisfied manner in which she narrates the whole episode to Lockwood.

One can also contrast the superficiality of Nelly's understanding even with that of young Cathy in two passages very close together (pp. 228 and 230). Cathy, now his daughter-in-law, says in the former,

"Mr. Heathcliff, *you* have *nobody* to love you; and, however miserable you make us, we shall still have the revenge of thinking that your cruelty arises from your greater misery! You *are* miserable, are you not? Lonely, like the devil, and envious like him? *Nobody* loves you—*nobody* will cry for you, when you die! I wouldn't be you!"

The realization of cruelty as the consequence of misery is beyond Nelly who had once explained his character as due to the evil example of Hindley. To emphasize Nelly's inability to understand, immediately after the passage just quoted, Emily Brontë has Heathcliff tell Nelly of his opening of Cathy's grave, and the reader is more than ever aware of the torments he has suffered, especially when he ends, "It was a strange way of killing, not by inches, but by fractions of hairbreaths, to beguile me with the spectre of a hope, through eighteen years." To this she comments to Lockwood:

Mr. Heathcliff paused and wiped his forehead—his hair clung to it, wet with perspiration; his eyes were fixed on the red embers of the fire; the brows not contracted, but raised next the temples, diminishing the grim aspect of his countenance, but imparting a peculiar look of trouble, and a painful appearance of mental tension towards one absorbing subject. He only half addressed me, and I maintained silence—*I didn't like to hear him talk* [italics mine].

And while he had been talking, she had interrupted him with, " 'You were very wicked, Mr. Heathcliff!' I exclaimed; 'were you not ashamed to disturb the dead?' " (p. 229), quick to register

conventional horror at a breach of custom, but apparently oblivious
of the overwhelming torment that had caused the breach. Here,
with particular intensity, the reader revolts from accepting the
wholesome, normal person as a criterion of thought and behavior,
and tends to accept any passion so long as it is real, and in so
doing becomes his own active interpreter of the true state of affairs and is powerfully affected by the genuine insight into human emotion.

Yet he may not be allowed to forget that Nelly is a fine woman
nevertheless; she is once more contrasted with Joseph when Lockwood finds both of them together on his unexpected visit in September 1802, just after, furthermore, he had encountered her clod-
dish successor at the Grange (see pp. 241–242):

> . . . at the door, sat my old friend, Nelly Dean, sewing and sing-
> ing a song, which was often interrupted from within, by harsh
> words of scorn and intolerance, uttered in far from musical ac-
> cents.
> "Aw'd rayther, by the haulf, hev 'em swearing i' my lugs
> frough morn tuh neeght, nur hearken yah, hahsiver!" said the
> tenant of the kitchen, in answer to an unheard speech of Nelly's.
> "It's a blazing shaime, ut Aw cannut oppen t' Blessed Book, bud
> yah set up them glories tuh sattan, un' all t' flaysome wickednesses
> ut iver wer born intuh t' warld. . . . O Lord, judge 'em, fur
> they's norther law nur justice amang wer rullers!"
> "No! Or we should be sitting in flaming fagots, I suppose,"
> retorted the singer. "But wisht, old man, and read your Bible
> like a christian, and never mind me. This is 'Fairy Annie's
> Wedding'—a bonny tune—it goes to a dance" (pp. 243–244).

With this picture of Nelly's natural attractiveness and gaiety in
mind we reach her narration of Heathcliff's end, his "queer" end,
as she calls it (p. 245).

As any reader of the novel will have guessed, Nelly was taken
by surprise at Heathcliff's death: as with all the other now dead
characters, she had supposed him sound in all ways:

> "But what do you mean by a *change*, Mr. Heathcliff?" I said,
> alarmed at his manner, though he was neither in danger of losing
> his senses, nor dying; according to my judgment he was quite
> strong and healthy; and, as to his reason, from childhood, he had
> delight in dwelling on dark things, and entertaining odd fancies.
> He might have had a monomania on the subject of his departed
> idol; but on every other point his wits were as sound as mine
> (pp. 255–256).

Such phrases as "delight in dwelling on dark things," "monomania on the subject of his idol" are perhaps a climax in Nelly's
brushing aside of all powerful emotion, and above all, it should

be noted that the only thing that here alarms her is Heathcliff's unwholesome manner.

As his death approaches, Nelly finally begins to worry about him; she fears for a short time, as the only way of explaining him, that he must be some "ghoul, or a vampire" (p. 260) but rejects that explanation and tries to conjure up some type of parentage that would account for his nature, but concludes by turning her attention aside to a serious abnormality, that he will not be able to have a proper tombstone, since his age and true name are unknown: "We were obliged to content ourselves with the single word, 'Heathcliff.' . . . If you enter the kirkyard, you'll read on his headstone, only that, and the date of his death" (p. 260). Her final words show how well for her own tranquillity she has settled the whole violent tale, when in response to Lockwood's half jest that the ghosts of Cathy and Heathcliff will be the future inhabitants of Wuthering Heights, " 'No, Mr. Lockwood,' said Nelly, shaking her head. 'I believe the dead are at peace, but it is not right to speak of them with levity' " (p. 265).

We have received the story almost entirely from Nelly, a representative of an admirable type of person, a character developed in great detail and with great skill, no obvious technical device, but a genuinely memorable character. In the circumstances in which she has been forced to live, she has revealed the futility of a tolerant, common-sense attitude which is the result of a desire merely to avoid trouble, to deny serious problems, and of a failure to grasp genuinely the emotions of others; the futility of compromise which is a mere improvisation from day to day in the interest of averting "explosions," of the futility of a constant attempt to preserve surface decorum and tranquillity on the grounds that what does not appear will not do any harm, and she has made the reader feel that her action has been throughout the best that can be expected of the type she represents. The reader continually decreases in sympathy with a type that he would usually admire, as she goes healthily and happily singing about her household duties and amusing the babies, since her so consistently emphasized good qualities turn out to be of so little use.

Thus, constantly rejecting her explanations, the reader substitutes his own, based always on the available evidence which she supplies but does not take into account or understand, and he becomes through his own perceptions increasingly sympathetic with the thoughts, feelings, and deeds of Heathcliff and Cathy. The engaging of the reader actively as one who does a large part of the work of comprehending is an important cause of the power of the novel. As Nelly contentedly provides her superficial interpretations of motive, and contentedly recounts her inadequate parental behavior, we are constantly directed toward feeling the inadequacy of the wholesome, and toward sympathy with genuine passions, no matter how destructive or violent.

CARL R. WOODRING

The Narrators of *Wuthering Heights*†

Since the seminal study by C. P. Sanger in 1926, the structure of *Wuthering Heights* has been further illumined by a host of laudatory critics, notably Paul M. Fulcher (1929), Lord David Cecil (1934), Boris Ford (1939), G. D. Klingopulos (1947), Melvin R. Watson (1949), Mark Schorer (1949), Royal A. Gettmann (1950), Bruce McCullough (1950), Dorothy Van Ghent (1952), B. H. Lehman (1955), and V. S. Pritchett (1956). Reprintings of the Oxford World's Classics edition preserve an older view in H. W. Garrod's resolute assertions, dated 1930, that the story, suffering from "inferior technique," is in parts "uncertainly conceived" and "in general ill constructed." Although most laudatory critics have noticed the debt owed by the structure of the novel to its use of two presumed narrators, more remains to be said about the utility of Lockwood and Nelly Dean.

The earlier scholar, learned in Gothic romances and tales from *Blackwood's,* found in Nelly's narrative within narrative the misfortune of inherited inconvenience; the later critic, familiar with selected masterworks, hails the use of contracting narrators as a wonder of creative intuition. Let us accept the method as borrowed from inferior tales, but chosen rather than inherited. What other method could have better provided the reader with the interlocking of familiar details concerning two generations and a stranger's astonishment over the beginning, the middle, and the end of Heathcliff's story? Nelly alone, Heathcliff himself as Jamesian or Austenian register, omniscient author, a series of actors or servants speaking independently—none of these as narrative authority could have provided the union of intimacy, intensity, interpretation, and detached admiration that Emily Brontë needed and achieved. Lockwood, the stranger, shares the reader's wonder at the characters and events; Mrs. Dean, the intimate, has long supped with wonders; stranger and intimate combine to certify the general facts.

† Copyright © 1957, by The Regents of the University of California. Reprinted from *Nineteenth-Century Fiction,* Vol. XI, xx (March, 1957) by permission of The Regents. Pp. 298–305.

The double narration is a convention and must be accepted as a convention. Much in *Wuthering Heights*, including characters as well as techniques, rests upon transformed conventions. Swept with the surge of demonism and quieted with purgation and repose at the end, the reader need not be disturbed because the conventions allow Nelly to linger overlong at various doors or Lockwood to report what Nelly said Zillah said the second Catherine said to Hareton. If, however, the critical reader becomes disturbed, if he demands a logic in the deviousness by which soliloquies reach him, he has no justification for exclaiming that Lockwood must have memorized Isabella's unlikely letter to Nelly verbatim. The logic he unnecessarily demands lies in this: ultimately all the words come to us from Lockwood. As after accepting the illusion of memory in a flashback, we may believe on critical reflection that the letter from Isabella as read by Nelly contained a briefer summary than Lockwood reports to us. Like his creator, Lockwood understands the value of first-person narrative; after 1784 in the events related by Nelly, he continues the story "in her own words, only a little condensed." That the events occurred, their impact makes us believe; Lockwood's intervention can account for similarities between the styles of Nelly, Isabella, and Zillah through which the events make their impact. If we hesitate to believe that Nelly remembers what Heathcliff said the Lintons said to each other some twenty-five years ago (Chapter VI), we can believe that Lockwood has supplied the appropriate words. To a protest that the author clearly thought of each scene as resting on the authority of its original narrator, the answer is that each scene does still so rest and that no justification exists for hanging critically suspended between these narrators and Lockwood, who is characterized by the author as a man who did in fact compose the book as we have it. The self-taught Nelly may mimic Joseph; so may Isabella; always it is the tenant of Thrushcross Grange who records Joseph's dialect.

Lockwood is an educated diarist from the city who records in course the remarkable events of his first two days among moors and boors. By dreaming in Cathy's paneled bed, he comes to pursue less palpable wilds. Emily Brontë may seem to allow him four days to transcribe the first nine chapters, a day for Chapter X, four weeks altogether (ill as he was) to hear and record the story through Chapter XIV, another week to report the urgency of Chapters XV through XXX, and at last the leisure of a possible three months to compose the subdued descent from Chapter XXXII to the final meditation over "the sleepers in that quiet earth." A qualification seems necessary. Without hesitation the author sacrifices strict consistency for immediate effect, but Lockwood's diary entries, as in Chapters III, IX, X, XV, and XXXI, especially the bored remarks in the present tense, may be taken as his immediate record during illness and convalescence when he resisted the appeal of violent rusticity. We may suppose that increased understanding and physical distance from the moors greatly stimulated his memory of the narrated details and permitted lengthy insertions when the story became meaningful to him. Observe the tenses in the following passage in Chapter X:

> I am too weak to read; yet I feel as if I could enjoy something interesting. Why not have up Mrs. Dean to finish her tale? I can recollect its chief incidents, as far as she had gone. Yes: I remember her hero had run off, and never been heard of for three years; and the heroine was married. I'll ring: she'll be delighted to find me capable of talking cheerfully. Mrs. Dean came.

At first Lockwood parades before us as a brittle ironist; slowly his irony mellows and finally dissolves. Quoted against himself, he has been called misanthropic. He is not. A reticent man, he comes to Thrushcross embittered because his chilly reticence has cost him the love of an attractive girl. In an unsociable mood, he nonetheless finds Heathcliff disgustingly unsociable. So gregarious is he that he soon craves conversation with his unpromising housekeeper, Mrs. Dean. If he seems inane, he suffers from the inanity his author attributes to the average London reader into whose hands her book will fall. In his introduction to the Rinehart College Edition, Mark Schorer follows Garrod in interpreting the original plan of the novel as the edification of a sophisticated and sentimental prig, Lockwood, in the natural human values of grand passion. Rather, Lockwood reacts for the normal skeptical reader in appropriate ways at each stage of the story and its unfolding theme. Within the action, he plays a more individual role. As actor, he tries to protect his "susceptible heart" (Chapter II) from attachment to the widowed Catherine; by March (Chapter XIV), he feebly resists the fascination of her eyes because he fears a "second edition" of her mother. By such self-restraint he thinks to "extract wholesome medicines from Mrs. Dean's bitter herbs." He reveals in Chapter XXV that he has fallen, he has asked that her portrait be hung over his fireplace, but he hesitates to act precipitately lest Catherine not return his love. Here the author intends Lockwood to replace Linton in the reader's mind as the active rival of Hareton. The suspense of this rivalry is to imbue Mrs. Dean's last words in the spring: ". . . I can see no remedy, at present, unless she should marry again; and that scheme it does not come within my province to arrange" (Chapter XXX). Always the sentimentalist, Lockwood feels pain when Catherine fails to perceive the value of dining with him instead of with "clowns and misanthropists" (Chapter XXXI). In September, he reports, "I bit my lip, in spite, at having thrown away the chance I might have had" (Chapter XXXII), and at the very end he admits to grumbling at the complacent love of Catherine and Hareton. The author manipulates and tolerates Lockwood much more for structure and plot than for theme.

Prefiguring Conrad's use of Marlow, Nelly's oral language sets itself off from Lockwood's prose by such simple phrases as "really, you know, Sir" and "well, Mr. Lockwood." Again an adequate convention, productive of immediate credibility and pleasure. Verisimilitude of narration gives way, happily, before binding detail. Cathy returned from her five weeks at Thrushcross Grange a neat little lady: "I was all over flour making the Christmas cake, and it would not have done to give me a hug; and, then, she looked around for Heathcliff" (Chapter VII).

As judge, Nelly pronounces Heathcliff a "black villain" and "evil beast"; Cathy a "wild, wicked slip" who "meant no harm"; and Joseph the "wearisomest, self-righteous pharisee." Cathy, she decrees, must be "chastened into humility." As interpreter, Nelly calls Heathcliff's a cuckoo's story—although she avoids assigning such a label to the later spiritual cuckoldry. As chorus, she lays aside superstition to proclaim happiness in the tranquillity of Cathy's death-chamber. In interviews, as attorney, she asks questions the reader wants asked. As in *The Brothers Karamazov*, the intensity of the passion lends credibility to the compulsive confessions; Nelly is the natural recipient of natural and unnatural confession.

She also acts. Attentive witness, narrator, and elucidator of past events, Mrs. (that is, Miss) Dean not only plays an active role economically designed, but also commands interest as a personality considerably beyond any of Thackeray's justly admired servants. Alert, observant, prying, gossipy, slightly superstitious, bold, saucy, tolerant, motherly, she has a very suspicious array of traits. Firm at the center, her character seems conveniently amorphous at the periphery. Even more than Lockwood's, her actions and utterances fit the immediate needs of the situation before the reader; she is no Mrs. Gamp to steal either attention or consistency from the central characters. This malleability makes her seem more complex. Heathcliff must be complex; Nelly may merely seem so. Superstitious enough to foreshadow with presentiments, she is skeptic enough to acknowledge her superstition. She remains a credible and canny witness by doubting the supernaturalness of the characters and events that certainly are, she has convinced us, supernatural. With placid disapproval, she can feel and communicate the basic distinction, expounded by Heathcliff and his Cathy, between demonic love and civilized emptiness.

In Nelly, Emily Brontë ingeniously produced the exactly needed combination of servant, companion, and saucy antagonist. With personal dignity, she keeps secrets; as a respected nurse, she tattles; she intercepts letters between young culprits; she scolds; she watches pots; she dances with the ungentle gentlefolk when needed (Chapter VII). Her removal in 1783 from Wuthering Heights to Thrushcross Grange had to be conceived before composition began; perception of her wonderful capacities as a catalyst could not have been long delayed. As witness and chorus, she must take part in nearly every scene in the book. We become accustomed to her interference from the time she admits putting the waif Heathcliff on the land to encourage his running away (Chapter IV). Soon deciding to scrub his person and manners, she plants in him the germinal suggestion that he might be an Oriental mogul, able to buy Wuthering Heights (Chapter VII). She provokes Cathy to show violence before Edgar (Chapter VIII); she unloads Hindley's gun (Chapter VIII); after her tattling to Edgar of Heathcliff's insolent acts results in an open clash, she lies to avoid further violence (Chapter XI). Yet even when she combines instigation of acts with explicit judgment of those acts, her author scrupulously prevents Nelly's actions from seeming to modify in any way either the personalities of the more important characters or the major directions of the plot. Nelly is allowed, not to advise Cathy on accepting or rejecting Edgar, but to catechize her after the acceptance (Chapter IX). Her own admissions of guilty responsibility make the reader the more ready to distribute blame among the principals. Locked inside Wuthering Heights in August 1800, she uttered and then withdrew a confession:

> I seated myself in a chair, and rocked, to and fro, passing harsh judgment on my many derelictions of duty; from which, it struck me then, all the misfortunes of all my employers sprang. It was not the case, in reality, I am aware; but it was, in my imagination, that dismal night; and I thought Heathcliff himself less guilty than I (Chapter XXVII).

Most scenes in the novel receive some imprint from Nelly's character or position. Her catalytic instigations gather strength almost imperceptibly from the many times when her actions help build portraits of herself and of the principals but otherwise merely provide a way of stating what occurred, as when she innocently supplies little Catherine with provisions for a ride to Wuthering Heights (Chapter XVIII). The frequency with which her character helps to determine the nature of immediate acts helps to support

the rarer occasions when she influences the action without moti-
vation, as when her one prolonged illness makes possible the meetings between Cathy and Linton (Chapter xxiii). Occasionally she
acts with inadequate motive to gain and communicate information
for her author; more often adequate motives impel her. She softens
toward Heathcliff the waif because measles make him quiet and
lead him to praise her for nursing him; soon, therefore, Heathcliff
can deceive her by his silence at mistreatment from Hindley
(Chapter iv). It is a condition of both respectability and fore-
handedness that she chaperone the final meeting of Heathcliff with
Cathy, who is about to die in childbirth. That the unearthly lovers
show awareness of her presence merely emphasizes their undimin-
ished passion (Chapter xv). Even here Nelly is up to her usual
trick: by her own actions, in character or credible for the moment, she reveals the character of others.

Acknowledged as narrators and interpreters, Mrs. Dean and
Lockwood have been slighted as actors in the plot. Lockwood
does not merely hear the tale in a tavern in Leeds; he dreams in
the paneled bed beside the ghostly window and himself threatens
to interrupt the final purgation and the happy-ever-after. As Heathcliff intrudes from some netherworld, Lockwood intrudes from the
city. Mrs. Dean belongs. From the time she takes Hindley's knife
between her teeth, she perfects the symbols. She interweaves
Heathcliff's hair with Edgar's for Catherine's locket; at the end
she combs the hair of the dead Heathcliff and closes the window.

MARY VISICK

[Catherine Earnshaw and Edgar Linton] †

Let us consider first the figure of Catherine Earnshaw. In Gondal
the heroine betrays and deserts both Julius the sun-man and Alfred
the moon-lover. These two events have no psychological connection; they simply portray the kind of woman A.G.A. is. But in
the novel the desertion of Heathcliff and then the spiritual for-
saking of Edgar become almost a single incident. Catherine betrays
her childhood love and then, realizing what she has done, is driven

† Reprinted from *The Genesis of
Wuthering Heights* (1958) by permission of the publishers, The Hong Kong
University Press, and the author. Pp.
42–60. Mrs. Visick considers the principal characters of *Wuthering Heights*
as transformed from the Gondal people
of Emily's poems.

With her permission I have omitted
her brilliant reconstruction of the
Gondal Saga, which precedes her comments on Catherine and Edgar.
"A.G.A." is the name Mrs. Visick gives
to the heroine of the Saga. Her full
name is Augusta Geraldine Almeda.
The Gondal hero is Lord Alfred.

to repudiate her husband. Unlike A.G.A. she cannot return to her first love and take up life with him again: her betrayal of Heathcliff cannot be cancelled out by a later betrayal of Edgar. A.G.A. is a falcon-eyed, imperious being, torturing men but herself no more than a leaf in the storm of her own passions. Emily Brontë had to fit this being into a normal social world.

Out of the simple ballad-figure she drew the complexities of Catherine. Her 'wrong' is far deeper than A.G.A.'s. It is a violation of her nature, and she cannot right it; she can only cry for release from the prison of her body. It is no longer possible to say:

> I know that I have done thee wrong—
> Have wronged both thee and heaven—
> And I may mourn my lifetime long,
> Yet may not be forgiven—

but 'if I have done wrong, I'm dying for it'.[1]

As long as Catherine[2] is in control of herself she does not voice her suffering; it is only suggested in the intensity of her reunion with Heathcliff. But in her delirium conscious control is relaxed and her agony, clothing itself in the symbols of her childhood, is made plain. Only thus could she be shown expressing what social convention, mild affection for her husband, and, not least, rationalization of her own conduct, would cause her to repress in her waking life. The device has plain affinities with Shakespeare's use of madness to reveal the springs of personality. Conscious, Catherine is as full of rectitude and self-justification as Lear when we first see him; she imposes a considerable strain on the gentle, long-suffering Edgar. Delirious, she has the status of a tragic heroine; everyday life no longer obscures her agony. In full possession of herelf she externalizes her conflict, reproaching the men whom her love has made wretched because they will not fit into the pattern of life she has tried to make—a pattern which has no justification save in her own mind. But delirious she faces herself. No wonder she says that she is afraid to go to sleep because her dreams 'appal' her. The carefully sustained role of Mrs Linton breaks down; and her deeper, more primitive self manifests itself in her haunted vision of the Heights:

> 'Look!' she cried eagerly, 'that's my room with the candle in it and the trees swaying before it—and the other candle is in Joseph's garret—Joseph sits up late, doesn't he? He's waiting till I come home that he may lock the gate. Well, he'll wait a while yet. It's a rough journey, and a sad heart to travel it; and we must pass by Gimmerton Kirk, to go that journey! We've

1. *Wuthering Heights*, Chapter XV.
2. I shall call Catherine Earnshaw 'Catherine' throughout, as Nelly does, reserving 'Cathy' for her daughter, Catherine Linton.

braved its ghosts often together, and dared each other to stand among the graves and ask them to come. But Heathcliff, if I dare you now, will you venture? If you do, I'll keep you. I'll not lie there by myself: they may bury me twelve feet deep, and throw the church down over me, but I won't rest till you are with me. I never will!' [3]

Yet she is not mad; the truth of her exile cannot be thrust aside:

'I remember being in the parlour after [Edgar and Heathcliff] had quarrelled, and Edgar being cruelly provoking, and me running into this room desperate . . . I thought as I lay there, with my head against that table leg, and my eyes dimly discerning the grey square of the window, that I was enclosed in the oak-panelled bed at home; and my heart ached with some great grief which, just waking, I could not recollect. I pondered, and worried myself to discover what it could be, and, most strangely, the whole last seven years of my life grew a blank! I did not recall that they had been at all. I was a child; my father was just buried, and my misery arose from the separation that Hindley had ordered between me and Heathcliff. I was laid alone, for the first time; and, rousing from a dismal doze after a night of weeping, I lifted my hand to push the panels aside: it struck the table-top! I swept it along the carpet, and then memory burst in: my late anguish was swallowed in a paroxysm of despair. I cannot say why I felt so wildly wretched: it must have been temporary derangement; for there is scarcely cause. But supposing at twelve years old I had been wrenched from the Heights, and every early association, and from my all in all, as Heathcliff was at that time, and been converted at a stroke into Mrs Linton, the lady of Thrushcross Grange, and the wife of a stranger: an exile, and outcast, thenceforth, from what had been my world . . . Oh, I'm burning! I wish I were out of doors! I wish I were a girl again, half savage, and hardy, and free; and laughing at injuries, not maddening under them! Why am I so changed? Why does my blood rush into a hell of tumult at a few words? I'm sure I should be myself again were I once among the heather on those hills.' [4]

Edgar, not unnaturally, thinks she is in love with Heathcliff; he has no insight into her real trouble. He would have understood her 'Nelly, I *am* Heathcliff' even less than Nelly. Catherine has no eyes for his distress; but as long as she is in control of herself she avoids saying the direct, the unretractable thing. When he tries to force her to see the situation as he quite understandably sees it, she breaks down:

'Remain where you are, Catherine', he said; without any anger in his voice, but with much sorrowful despondency. 'I shall

3. *Wuthering Heights*, Chapter XII.   4. *Wuthering Heights*, Chapter XII.

not stay. I am neither come to wrangle nor be reconciled; but I wish just to learn whether, after this evening's events, you intend to continue your intimacy with—'

'Oh, for mercy's sake', interrupted the mistress, stamping her foot, 'for mercy's sake, let us hear no more of it now! Your cold blood cannot be worked into a fever: your veins are full of ice-water; but mine are boiling, and the sight of such chillness makes them dance.'

'To get rid of me, answer my question', persevered Mr Linton. 'You *must* answer it; and that violence does not alarm me. I have found that you can be as stoical as any one, when you please. Will you give up Heathcliff hereafter, or will you give up me? It is impossible for you to be *my* friend and *his* at the same time; and I absolutely *require* to know which you choose.'

'I require to be left alone!' exclaimed Catherine, furiously, 'I demand it! Don't you see I can scarcely stand? Edgar, you—you leave me!'[5]

and she falls into a kind of swoon. Later she shuts herself away and when he goes to her she half deliriously repudiates him:

'I don't want you, Edgar: I'm past wanting you. Return to your books. I'm glad you possess a consolation, for all you had in me is gone.'[6]

Nevertheless, she does feel some compunction for the trouble she is inflicting on Edgar. She cannot put it into words; but once she feels clearly an impulse of gentleness towards him. It is when he has brought her flowers from the Heights, when she is recovering from her long breakdown: he understands her sense of exile, though not how deeply her feeling for Heathcliff is involved with it:

The first time she left her chamber was at the commencement of the following March. Mr Linton had put on her pillow, in the morning, a handful of golden crocuses; her eye, long stranger to any gleam of pleasure, caught them in waking, and shone delighted as she gathered them eagerly together. `

'These are the earliest flowers at the Heights,' she exclaimed. 'They remind me of soft thaw winds, and warm sunshine, and nearly melted snow. Edgar, is there not a south wind, and is not the snow almost gone?'

'The snow is quite gone down here, darling,' replied her husband; 'and I only see two white spots on the whole range of moors: the sky is blue, and the larks are singing, and the becks and brooks are all brim full. Catherine, last spring at this time, I was longing to have you under this roof: now, I wish you were a mile or two up those hills: the air blows so sweetly, I feel that it would cure you.'

5. *Wuthering Heights*, Chapter XII.   6. *Wuthering Heights*, Chapter XII.

'I shall never be there, but once more,' said the invalid; 'and then you'll leave me, and I shall remain for ever. Next spring you'll long again to have me under this roof, and you'll look back and think you were happy today.'

Linton lavished on her the kindest caresses, and tried to cheer her by the fondest words; but, vaguely regarding the flowers, she let the tears collect on her lashes and stream down her cheeks unheeding.[7]

The facile tears of the convalescent speak of her unutterable remorse.

She returns in fantasy to childhood not because she is really incapable of living in an adult world but because it was only as a child, before her personality was split, that she lived with her whole being. In Gondal Julius reproaches his unfaithful love with having betrayed their early happiness; in both poems and novel that moorland happiness is her deepest self and her 'spirit's home'. So in our first sight of Catherine, the nightmare child at Lockwood's window, she is not only a child shut out from the Heights, but she is also Mrs Linton, the lady of Thrushcross Grange. The dreamer sees a child's face at the window, and touches 'a little ice-cold hand':

'Who are you?' I asked . . . 'Catherine Linton', it replied shiveringly (why did I think of *Linton?* I had read *Earnshaw* twenty times for *Linton*).'I'm come home: I'd lost my way on the moor' . . . 'Begone!' I shouted. 'I'll never let you in, not if you beg for twenty years.' 'It is twenty years', mourned the voice: 'twenty years. I've been a waif for twenty years'.[8]

But it is not a childish ghost that Heathcliff sees; and the little boy at the end of the book sees not a child but 'Heathcliff and a woman'.

At the age of twelve Catherine is taken in hand by the Lintons and transformed from a 'wild, hatless little savage' into a young lady, careful of her clothes and of her manners. From that moment the strain is laid on her. Her new friends, Edgar and Isabella, with their fair hair, and gentle, querulous ways, are socially approved; her old friend Heathcliff is considered most unsuitable to her newly-acquired gentility. Nelly, watching her closely through that calamitous Christmas Day at the Heights, sees that under her hostess-like manner she is 'in purgatory' at being separated from Heathcliff, who is in disgrace. The conventional world of the rural young lady is being opened for her by the Lintons; and she never understands that this will drive out the older, rougher world of the Heights. A.G.A. deserted Julius out of 'ambition': here, as usual, the situation is more closely studied and more realistically

7. *Wuthering Heights,* Chapter XIII.   8. *Wuthering Heights,* Chapter III.

developed in the novel.

So Catherine is perfectly developed from the lonely child, now neglected, now spoiled, into the marriageable girl whom Hindley cherishes simply because he hopes she will make a 'good' marriage. Her powerful emotions, cramped in a lonely and miserable life, find vent often in sheer bad behaviour, as when she strikes Edgar in the face. In the great scene with Nelly, in which she weighs up the love of the two young men and talks, for the first and only time, of her real feeling for Heathcliff as 'more myself than I am', the usually hidden self looks out, and we know what she really is. But Nelly, the audience, is unfriendly. She pours on Catherine's elaborate rationalization of her decision to marry Edgar a cold douche of common sense:

'. . . Nelly, I see now, you think me a selfish wretch; but did it never strike you that if Heathcliff and I married, we should be beggars? whereas, if I marry Linton, I can aid Heathcliff to rise, and place him out of my brother's power.'
'With your husband's money, Miss Catherine?' I asked. 'You'll find him not so pliable as you calculate upon: and though I'm hardly a judge, I think that's the worst motive you've given yet for being the wife of young Linton'.[9]

Catherine's reply is the great outburst of protest against the idea that she can ever be separated from Heathcliff:

'. . . if all else perished, and *he* remained, I should still continue to be; and if all else remained, and he were annihilated, the universe would turn to a mighty stranger: I should not seem a part of it. My love for Linton is like the foliage in the woods: time will change it, I'm well aware, as winter changes the trees. My love for Heathcliff resembles the eternal rocks beneath: a source of little visible delight, but necessary. Nelly, I *am* Heathcliff! He's always, always in my mind: not as a pleasure, any more than I am always a pleasure to myself, but as my own being. So don't talk of our separation again: it is impracticable; and—'
She paused, and hid her face in the folds of my gown; but I jerked it forcibly away. I was out of patience with her folly!
'If I can make any sense of your nonsense, Miss,' I said, 'it only goes to convince me that you are ignorant of the duties you undertake in marrying; or else that you are a wicked, unprincipled girl'.[1]

The solidity of Nelly's stern common sense in this scene confers on Catherine's outburst a naturalistic as well as a poetic reality. In terms of the significance of the novel, two views of 'reality' clash; in terms of its success as a novel, Catherine is seen as a strange girl, whose inner life is lived habitually on another plane

9. *Wuthering Heights*, Chapter IX.   1. *Wuthering Heights*, Chapter IX.

than the 'normal', and as one whose last confidante and counsellor has lost patience with her. It is the great achievement of Emily Brontë as a novelist that if we, like Lockwood, 'take sides' here we lose the point of the book; but she never loses sight of the case, based on common sense and common ethics, that Nelly makes against Catherine.

Charlotte Brontë seems to miss the point when she implies in her preface to the second edition of *Wuthering Heights*, in 1850, that Catherine is an unsatisfactory heroine, lacking in what we might call human appeal. 'A certain strange beauty in her fierceness . . . honesty in the midst of perverted passion and passionate perversity' is all that Charlotte grants her. To reply that Catherine is a transformation of A.G.A., who was apparently much worse, is of course pointless, if Charlotte is right; and any reader who could see *Wuthering Heights* as an immature work by the author of *Jane Eyre* might well agree with her. However, it is not necessary to dive into the recesses of Gondal to say that Emily Brontë's intention is totally different from Charlotte's. The elder sister seems to be misled because she herself is a novelist with quite different aims. She commands sympathy for her lonely heroines, Jane or Lucy; for Catherine the appropriate emotion is tragic pity. Hers is the solitude not of Jane Eyre who has no one to talk to, but of Ophelia or Phaedra: it is absolute, and its existence in a normal world—the world where Nelly is 'out of patience with her folly'—heightens it. To Charlotte, Nelly, the novel's human norm, is wholly admirable. Her 'true benevolence and homely fidelity' lighten the gloom. Charlotte's criticism seems to imply that she sees no further than Nelly sees, that the tragic Catherine makes no appeal to her. When Nelly says 'I own I did not like her', is the reader, Lockwood-wise, to be careful how he commits his sympathies? He can only understand by realizing that before such desolation liking or dislike are irrelevant.

Such presentation is not common in the great English novels. In *Middlemarch*, when Dorothea at last breaks out to Will that she hates her money—that money which prevents him from speaking of his love for her—she says she has never been afraid of poverty: 'I want so little—no new clothes—and I will learn how much things cost.' Her words, beside her eager, naïve but real intellectual power, are moving by their humanly childish inadequacy. But when Catherine speaks, we are in a world where

> Double the vision my eyes do see,
> And a double vision is always with me;
> To the inward eye, 'tis an old man grey,
> To the outward, a thistle across my way.[2]

2. William Blake, *The Double Vision*.

'Don't *you* see that face?' she enquired, gazing earnestly at the mirror.

And say what I could, I was incapable of making her comprehend it to be her own; so I rose and covered it with a shawl.

'It's behind there still!' she pursued, anxiously. 'And it stirred. Who is it? I hope it will not come out when you are gone! Oh! Nelly, the room is haunted! I'm afraid of being alone!'

I took her hand in mine and bid her be composed; for a succession of shudders convulsed her frame, and she *would* keep straining her eyes towards the glass.

'There's nobody here!' I insisted. 'It was *yourself*, Mrs Linton: you knew it a while since.'

'Myself!' she gasped, 'and the clock is striking twelve! It's true, then! that's dreadful!'[3]

Is this tragic treatment of Catherine disabling to the novel? Emily Brontë has achieved something unique in fiction, but is it at the cost of violating the accepted frontiers of the form? In *Wuthering Heights,* and in the accounts of Catherine particularly, we miss the revealing trivial remark, of which George Eliot, for example, is a master ('I should not like to marry a clergyman, but there must be clergymen', says Rosamond Vincy in *Middlemarch*). Yet Catherine is completely realized. Like D. H. Lawrence (the novelist who in many ways most closely resembles her) Emily Brontë rarely chooses to show her characters in relaxed or trival moments. Like his, her characters live with an emotional violence which leaves the reader exhausted. Yet it is impossible to imagine a formula for the treatment of novel-characters which could include, say, Miss Havisham, or, for that matter, Mr. Bounderby, and omit Catherine Earnshaw.

Edgar Linton is a less extraordinary person; but he still retains enough of his Gondal past to make him a counterweight to Heathcliff. Lord Alfred was a suicide, an unquiet ghost, whereas Edgar is gentle and orthodox; but he is as capable of passionate devotion as any Gondalian. No less than the others, he is a creature of fate. Nelly considers him as he comes creeping back to Catherine, whom he wants to marry, after her cruel and unedifying outburst of rage:

The soft thing looked askance through the window. He possessed the power to depart, much as a cat possesses the power to leave a mouse half killed or a bird half eaten. Ah, I thought, there will be no saving him: he's doomed, and flies to his fate![4]

It is a mistake to think of him as a very ordinary person caught up in the whirling sweep of Catherine's passion: the ordinary per-

3. *Wuthering Heights,* Chapter XII.   4. *Wuthering Heights,* Chapter VIII.

son, as indicated by Nelly, would have walked out and left her to her frenzy. He is 'doomed' by the strength of a passionate devotion which Nelly—by one of those deliberate misdirections of sympathy for which her creator uses her—terms merely infatuation.

In spite of Nelly's continuous advocacy, he is by no means to be regarded as an angel of light. Lord David Cecil, indeed, calls him 'a poor creature'[5]: but that view, too, is inadequate. On one level, that on which Lockwood looking through Nelly's story sees him, he is the much-wronged husband of a termagant who is little better than unfaithful to him: a bookish, agreeable country gentleman whose life is laid waste by his love for his neurotic wife. On another level, he is simply not of Catherine's world at all. It is no fault of his; but Heathcliff is not entirely unjust when he says:

> 'If he loved with all the powers of his puny being, he couldn't love as much in eighty years as I could in a day. And Catherine has a heart as deep as I have: the sea could be as readily contained in that horse-trough as her whole affection could be monopolised by him. Tush! he is scarcely a degree dearer to her than her dog, or her horse. It is not in him to be loved like me: how can she love in him what he has not? . . . And that insipid, paltry creature attending her from *duty* and *humanity*! from *pity* and *charity*! He might as well plant an oak in a flower-pot, and expect it to thrive, as imagine he can restore her to vigour in the soil of his shallow cares!'[6]

It is Nelly's Linton that Heathcliff trounces so vigorously, and Nelly only thinks she understands him and his personality. She presents a picture of him as idealized gentleness; the half-truth of Heathcliff's attack implants another view of Edgar. We cannot ignore either of them. It is true that Catherine speaks to her husband abominably, and that in front of Heathcliff. But this is to neither of their condemnations; he simply rouses in her a very human and un-Gondalian emotion—he irritates her.

He is capable of spitefulness and petty jealousy. His first appearance in the book is in the child Heathcliff's tale to Nelly of his escape with Catherine from the Heights, and of their looking through the window of the Grange at the comfortable, petted Linton children:

> 'Isabella—I believe she is eleven, a year younger than Cathy—lay screaming at the farther end of the room, shrieking as if

5. In *Early Victorian Novelists*.
6. *Wuthering Heights*, Chapter XIV. These words, and others in the novel, suggest that Emily Brontë may have read Tennyson's *Locksley Hall:*

> He will hold thee, when his passion shall have spent its novel force

Something better than his dog, a little dearer than his horse.

The poem concerns 'the social wants that sin against the strength of youth', as Catherine's 'social wants' have made her betray Heathcliff.

witches were running red-hot needles into her. Edgar stood on the hearth weeping silently, and in the middle of the table sat a little dog, shaking its paw and yelping; which, from their mutual accusations, we understood they had nearly pulled in two between them. The idiots! That was their pleasure! to quarrel who should hold a heap of warm hair, and each began to cry because both, after struggling to get it, refused to take it. We laughed outright at the petted things; we did despise them! When would you catch me wishing to have what Catherine wanted? or find us by ourselves, seeking entertainment in yelling, and sobbing, and rolling on the ground, divided by the whole room?' [7]

Catherine and Heathcliff are passionately egotistical, but they are not pettish. Edgar is neither a noble character basely betrayed nor an insignificant fool. It is his tragedy that his faults are just those which put him in the worst light beside Heathcliff, and turn his virtues to nothing in his wife's eyes. His nervous trembling before Heathcliff, his nervous reproaches to Catherine, exasperate her and bring on the crisis in their relationships. Even Nelly, who is devoted to him and dislikes Catherine, feels his petulance and coldness towards the returned Heathcliff, and tries to warn him to welcome Heathcliff for Catherine's sake:

'What! the gipsy! the plough-boy!' he cried. 'Why did you not say so to Catherine?'
    'Hush! you must not call him by those names, master,' I said. 'She'd be sadly grieved to hear you. She was nearly heart-broken when he ran off.'

His irritation finds vent in a standing on his social dignity which Catherine is quick to take up:

'Shall I tell him to come up now?'
    'Here?' he said, 'into the parlour?'
    'Where else?' she asked.
He looked vexed, and suggested the kitchen as a more suitable place for him. Mrs Linton eyed him with a droll expression— half angry, half laughing at his fastidiousness.
    'No,' she added, after a while: 'I cannot sit in the kitchen. Set two tables here, Ellen: one for your master and Miss Isabella, being gentry; the other for Heathcliff and myself, being of the lower orders. Will that please you, dear?'

Apparently it does not; his next utterance is to call Heathcliff a runaway servant—a rather mean half-truth. [8]
    In her repudiation of the Lintons' snobbery Catherine immediately sets herself at a distance from her husband, on terms which win her the reader's sympathy. (All the Lintons are snobs; Cathy is disgusted to learn that the boorish Hareton is her cousin,

7. *Wuthering Heights*, Chapter VI.   8. *Wuthering Heights*, Chapter X.

and of Isabella Linton old Joseph says 'we were a'most too mucky to sow t' corn for making her bread'). But Catherine's gesture is made at the expense of the truth. She is certainly not of 'the lower orders', since the Earnshaws have farmed their own land at the Heights since the sixteenth century. Edgar unhappily hits on the one remark which is certain to drive her into revolt.

As she introduces the story of Heathcliff's return after Catherine's marriage Nelly makes one of the moral generalizations of which Emily Brontë is so sparing. The comment is essential to our judgment of Edgar: it is carefully placed and phrased:

> Well, we *must* be for ourselves in the long run: the mild and generous are only more justly selfish than the domineering; and [the happiness of Catherine and Edgar] ended when circumstances caused each to feel that the one's interest was not the chief consideration in the other's thoughts.[9]

'Only more justly selfish . . .'; it is eminently fair. Lord Alfred, the Gondal hero, was involved in a much cruder situation, to which the rather tritely-turned expressions of the autonomy of passion—'I could not rend another heart, Not even by blessing thee'—were adequate. Edgar is the result of Emily Brontë's rethinking and re-experiencing the Gondal situation which itself developed, as we have seen, out of an earlier and simpler story. For all his faults, Edgar is 'big' enough to fit into the story, even if he is shut out from understanding his wife and Heathcliff.

In Gondal the gentle lover is religious, and even converts A.G.A. by his love to 'adore' a spiritual heaven as well as the blue heaven of the natural world. The poem in which A.G.A. expresses this sentiment has a sugary and slightly unpleasant quality; nevertheless, in this characteristic which she had bestowed on Lord Alfred, Emily Brontë found a suggestion of the source on which she might draw in giving Edgar some strength and stature. He does not, of course, 'convert' Catherine to anything—that would be a piece of crudity more suited to Gondal than to the novel—but her being, in Nelly's eyes, 'almost over-fond' of Linton in the early days of their marriage[1] is the nearest possible equivalent to A.G.A.'s temporary conversion to a religion of love.

Edgar's personal religious faith is at one end of a scale of which the other end is old Joseph the farm-servant, who is no mere piece of local colour. Joseph sees the personages of the story simplified in the lurid light of hell fire; Edgar sees Catherine, at least, bathed in the radiance of a heavenly immortality. The one belongs to the Heights, the other to the gentler world of the Grange; but they are not equivalents. Neither has any power over Catherine, and

9. *Wuthering Heights*, Chapter X.   1. *Wuthering Heights*, Chapter X.

after his death Edgar's spirit does not 'walk' with Catherine's; nevertheless, his unorthodox charity of mind cancels out his occasional human pettiness.

He has a steadfast assurance that in spite of her sins—against him more than anyone else—the wild, stormy, amoral Catherine is at peace. Joseph, on the other hand, makes almost the first allusion to what has gone and what is to come, when Lockwood hears him mutter to Cathy, 'Yah'll go raight to t'devil like yer mother afore ye'. Emily Brontë knew the hell-fire evangelicalism of the moors, its canting joylessness and its vengefulness; 'she held' wrote Charlotte, 'that mercy and forgiveness are the divinest attributes of the Great Being'. It is to underline Edgar's goodness that Joseph's religion is given such prominence. Joseph is, of course, observed with a satiric eye; Nelly explains his perverse devotion to Heathcliff and his continuing to live at the Heights by remarking that 'it was his vocation to be where he had plenty of wickedness to reprove'.[2] This treatment might well serve to forestall any criticism of *Wuthering Heights* from the unco' guid. Joseph, the orthodox, is a repellent character; Edgar, whose conviction of Catherine's happiness in the next world might be thought, as Lockwood says, 'somewhat heterodox', has his own charm. To adopt a narrowly 'moral' attitude to the story would place the reader in the company of either Lockwood or Joseph.

There are thus positive values expressed through the personality of Edgar, some of which are hinted at in the Gondalian Lord Alfred. It is the reality of these values which make his love, whatever Nelly may say of 'infatuation', a counterweight to the other love of Heathcliff. Gentle and 'well brought up' (and perhaps less intrinsically interesting to his creator) he must make a third fit for the other two, and yet be set apart from them. He might have been, as Nelly sees him, a suffering, heroic soul; he might simply have appeared besotted and contemptible, losing all trace of his Gondal origin. Either would have wrecked the novel. He had to have stature and reality, if only for the plot's sake—Catherine's desertion of Heathcliff must have threatened to become a really weak point. The solution was to give him spiritual strength but of a different order from Heathcliff's; and thus he is distinguished by gentle, persistent, Christian faith and love. He is no Charles Bovary, on whom Flaubert could conceive the terrible verdict:

'Pour lui plaire, comme si elle vivait encore, il adopta ses prédilections, ses idées: il s'acheta des bottes vernies, il prit l'usage des cravates blanches, il mettait du cosmétique à ses moustaches, il souscrivait comme elle des billets à ordre. Elle le corrompait par delà le tombeau'.[3]

2. *Wuthering Heights*, Chapter VIII.   3. *Madame Bovary*, Chapter XI.

In the second half of *Wuthering Heights* we feel that Edgar's life, no less than Heathcliff's, has been laid waste. Both are sustained only by their sense of communion with the dead woman. Heathcliff turns to violence, Edgar to settled melancholy. At thirty-nine he is already an old man. Nevertheless, such is Emily Brontë's achievement that we do not see him as hopelessly deluded about Catherine's nature. He may be ineffectual but he is not small.

It is a technical flaw in the book that Edgar is not presented in quite the same way as any of the other major characters. He is treated more nearly in the mature George Eliot manner, and this involves a slightly jarring change of texture. In him the author reveals her power, which we think of as most specifically the novelist's gift, of making a small remark or a minute change of tone indicate what is hidden in the depth on which the minutiae of every day float. 'Catherine, unless we are to have cold tea, please to come to the table' cuts into that rapt exchange between his wife and the returned Heathcliff. They do not see how completely they are giving themselves away; and he is too well bred to voice direct resentment. Again, his dismissal of Heathcliff from the Grange— 'three minutes' delay will render [your departure] involuntary and ignominious'—has just that quality of premeditation which suggests weeks of exasperation boiling up at a half-longed-for legitimate grievance. He is a fully realized character, and represents a fine solution of the problem which the translation of this part of Gondal into a novel set the author; but he is not absolutely satisfactory. Whether by design or not, he is the only major character who is never shown confiding in Nelly: to have afforded a glimpse of him opening his heart to her, if it could have been done, might have been one way of closing the gap between his presentation and that of Heathcliff. As it is, the gap is not large, but it is there; and it adds to the impression we have of Catherine and Heathcliff blazing with a vitality denied to the other characters. This may be a false impression, but it has been made on so many readers that we cannot deny it altogether.

MARK SCHORER

Fiction and the "Analogical Matrix"†

If the novel, as R. P. Blackmur recently proposed, is now to enjoy the kind of attention from criticism that for the past twenty years has been the privilege of poetry, criticism must begin with the simplest assertion: fiction is a literary art. It must begin with the base of language, with the word, with figurative structures, with rhetoric as skeleton and style as body of meaning. A beginning as simple as this must overcome corrupted reading habits of long standing; for the novel, written in prose, bears an apparently closer resemblance to discursive forms than it does to poetry, thus easily opening itself to first questions about philosophy or politics, and, traditionally a middle-class vehicle with a reflective social function, it bears an apparently more immediate relation to life than it does to art, thus easily opening itself to first questions about conduct. Yet a novel, like a poem, is not life, it is an image of life; and the critical problem is first of all to analyze the structure of the image. Thus criticism must approach the vast and endlessly ornamented house of fiction with a willingness to do a little at a time and none of it finally, in order to suggest experiences of meaning and of feeling that may be involved in novels, and responsibilities to and for their style which novelists themselves may forget.

To choose, more or less at random and without premeditated end, one novel by each of only three novelists, and to examine in each only one element in the language, the dominant metaphorical quality—this, positively, is to work piecemeal, and merely to suggest. I emphasize not *metaphor* but *quality*, intending not only the explicit but the buried and the dead metaphors, and some related traits of diction generally, that whole habit of value association suggested in Scott Buchanan's phrase, the "analogical matrix." The novels are *Persuasion*, *Wuthering Heights*, and *Middlemarch*.

* * *

The style of Jane Austen is so entirely without flamboyance or gesture, the cited illustrations are so commonplace, so perfectly

† "Fiction and the 'Analogical Matrix' " was originally presented in longer form as a lecture before the English Institute at Columbia and the Kenyon School of English. It was first printed in the *Kenyon Review* XI (Autumn, 1949), and is reprinted here by permission of the *Kenyon Review* and the author.

within the order of English idiom, that, unless we remind ourselves that our own habits of speech are even more intimately involved in the life of cash than Jane Austen's, no case at all may appear. Yet the inevitability of individual imaginative habit, the impressive fact that every mind selects its creative gamut from the whole range of possible language, and in thus selecting determines its insights and their scope, in short, its character and the character of its creations, is at once apparent when we open some other novel. Emily Brontë is very different from Jane Austen, yet both were unmarried provincial women, living in the same half of the same century, speaking the same language, both daughters of clergymen, and one might reasonably expect to encounter, even in *Wuthering Heights*, some of those perfectly normal figures with which *Persuasion* abounds. There are, I think, none of the same kind. Emily Brontë does not "divide the time" but, on the first page, "the desolation"; "time," when she mentions it, "stagnates," and "prudence" is "diabolical." If there are any figures of the same kind, they are so few, and in their own metaphorical context, function so differently, that the total quality owes nothing to them. Where Wentworth speaks of the "crown" of "all my other successes," Lockwood speaks of the "copestone on my rage and humiliation." Both *crown* and *copestone on* mean climax, but "crown" is drawn from rank and money, "copestone" from earth and building. If Nelly Dean's phrase, "the crown of all my wishes," suggests a kingdom at all, it is a heavenly kingdom, quite different from "all my other successes." The difference signifies. *Wuthering Heights* has its own sphere of significant experience, and its metaphors, like its epithets and verbs, tell us different things. They tell us, too, of a special problem.

Wuthering Heights, as I understand it, means to be a work of edification: Emily Brontë begins by wishing to instruct her narrator, the dandy, Lockwood, in the nature of a grand passion; she ends by instructing herself in the vanity of human wishes. She means to dramatize with something like approval—the phrase that follows is from *Middlemarch*—"the sense of a stupendous self and an insignificant world." What her metaphors signify is the impermanence of self and the permanence of something larger.

To exalt the power of human feeling, Emily Brontë roots her analogies in the fierce life of animals and in the relentless life of the elements—fire, wind, water. "Wuthering," we are told, is "a signicant provincial adjective, descriptive of the atmospheric tumult to which its station is exposed in stormy weather," and, immediately after, that "one may guess the power of the north wind blowing over the edge, by the excessive slant of a few stunted firs at the end of the house; and by a range of gaunt thorns all stretching their limbs one way, as if craving alms of the sun." The application of this landscape to the characters is made explicit in the second half of the novel, when Heathcliff says, "Now, my bonny lad, you are *mine!* And we'll see if one tree won't grow as crooked as another, with the same wind to twist it!" This analogy provides at least half of the metaphorical base of the novel.

Human conditions are like the activities of the landscape, where rains *flood*, blasts *wail*, and the snow and wind *whirl wildly* and *blow* out lights. A serving woman *heaves* "like a sea after a high wind"; a preacher "*poured* forth his zeal in a *shower*"; Mrs. Dean *rushes* to welcome Lockwood, "exclaiming *tumultuously*"; spirits are "at high-water mark"; Linton's soul is as different from Heathcliff's "as a moonbeam from lightning, or frost from fire"; abuse is *lavished* in a *torrent*, or *pours forth* in a *deluge*; illnesses are "*weathered* . . . through"; "sensations" are felt in a *gush*; "your veins are *full* of *ice water*; but mine are *boiling*"; hair *flies*, bodies *toss* or *tremble* like reeds, tears *stream* or *rain down* among ashes; discord and distress arise in a *tumult*; Catherine Linton "was *struck* during a *tempest* of passion with a kind of fit" and "*flew off* in the *height* of it."

Faces, too, are like landscapes: "a *cloud* of meditation" hangs over Nelly Dean's "*ruddy* countenance"; Catherine had a "suddenly *clouded* brow; her humor was a mere *vane* for constantly varying caprices"; "the surface of" the boy Heathcliff's "face and hands was dismally *beclouded*" with dirt; later, his face "*brightened* for a moment; then it was *overcast* afresh." "His forehead . . . *shaded* over with a heavy *cloud*"; and "the *clouded* windows of hell," his eyes, "*flashed*." Hareton, likewise, grows "black as a *thundercloud*"; or *darkens* with a frown. The older Catherine experienced whole "*seasons* of gloom," and the younger Catherine's "heart was *clouded* . . . in double *darkness*." Her "face was just like the *landscape—shadows* and *sunshine* flitting over it in rapid succession; but the *shadows* rested longer, and the *sunshine* was more transient." Sometimes "her eyes are *radiant* with *cloudless* pleasure," and at the end, Hareton shakes off "the *clouds* of ignorance and degradation," and his "*brightening* mind *brightened* his features."

Quite as important as the imagery of wind and cloud and water is the imagery of fire. In every interior, the fire on the hearth is the center of pictorial interest, and the characters sit "*burning* their eyes out before the fire." Eyes *burn* with anguish but do not *melt*; they always *flash* and *sparkle*. Fury *kindles*, temper *kindles*, a "*spark* of spirit" *kindles*. Catherine has a *fiery* disposition, but so do objects and states: words *brand*, shame is *burning*, merriment *expires* quickly, fevers *consume* life; hot coffee and basins *smoke*, they do not steam; and Isabella shrieks "as if witches were running *red-hot* needles into her." Sometimes fire is identified with other elements, as when a servant urges *flakes* of *flame* up the chimney," or when Isabella complains that the fire causes the wound on her neck, first stopped by the icy cold, to stream and smart.

Metaphors of earth—earth takes more solid and durable forms than the other elements—are interestingly few. Twice Heathcliff is likened to "an arid wilderness of *furze* and *whinstone*"; there is a reference to his "*flinty* gratification"; and once he speaks scornfully of "the *soil* of" Linton's "shallow cares." Earth and vegetation sometimes result in a happy juxtaposition of the vast or the violent and the little or the homely, as when Heathcliff says of Linton that "He might as well plant *an oak in a flowerpot*," or when he threatens to "crush his ribs in like *a rotten hazelnut*," which is like his saying that Catherine's passion could be as readily encompassed by Linton as "*the sea* could be . . . contained in that *horse-trough*."

Most of the animals are wild. Hareton's "whiskers encroached *bearishly* over his cheeks," and Heathcliff denies the paternity of "that bear." Hareton had been "cast out like an unfledged *dunnock*," and Heathcliff is a "fierce, pitiless, *wolfish* man." He is also "a *bird* of bad omen" and "an evil *beast*" prowling between a "stray *sheep*" and the fold, waiting his time to spring and destroy. He has a "*ferocious* gaze" and a *savage* utterance; he *growls* and *howls* "like a beast," and is many times named "a brute," "a beast," "a brute beast." He struggles like a *bear*, he has *sharp cannibal teeth* which *gleam* "through the dark," and "*basilisk* eyes . . . *quenched* by sleeplessness." He *gnashes* his teeth and *foams* like a *mad dog*. He is "like a *bull*" to Linton's "*lamb*," and only at the very end, the exhausted end, "he breathed as fast as a *cat*."

For the domestic and the gentler animals are generally used for purposes of harsh satire or vilification. Edgar, "the soft thing," "possessed the power to depart, as much as a *cat* possesses the power to leave a *mouse* half killed, or a *bird* half eaten." He is "not a *lamb*" but "a sucking *leveret*," and his sister is a "pitiful, slavish, mean-minded *brach*," she is among those *worms*, who, "the more they writhe, the more" Heathcliff yearns "to crush out their entrails." Hindley dies in a stupor, "snorting like a *horse*"; "flaying and scalping" would not have roused him, and when the doctor arrives, "the *beast* has changed to *carrion*." Hareton is "an infernal *calf*," and young Linton is a "*puling chicken*" and a "*whelp*." Like a dying dog, he "slowly *trailed* himself off, and lay down," or, like a cold one, he "*shrank* closer to the fire." He "had *shrunk* into a corner of the settle, as quiet as a *mouse*"; he is called "a little perishing *monkey*"; and "he achieved his exit exactly as a *spaniel* might." He is also "an abject *reptile*" and a "*cockatrice*." Hareton, who is capable on occasion of gathering "*venom* with reflection," is once called a "*magpie*," and once said to be "obstinate as a *mule*"—one of the few kindly animal references in the novel. To be sure, Isabella describes herself as though she were a deer: "I *bounded, leaped* and *flew* down the steep road; then . . . *shot* direct across the moor, *rolling* over banks, and *wading* through marshes." And Catherine, on the whole, is not abused. She is a "cunning little *fox*" and she runs "like a *mouse*," but chiefly she is "soft and mild as a *dove*."

Emily Brontë's metaphors color all her diction. As her epithets are charged with passion—"jealous guardianship," "vexatious phlegm," "importunate branch"—so her verbs are verbs of violent movement and conflict, both contributing to a rhetorical texture where everything is at a pitch from which it can only subside. The verbs *demand* exhaustion, just as the metaphors *demand* rest. And there is an antithetical chorus in this rhetoric, a contrapuntal warning, which, usually but not only in the voice of Nelly Dean, says, "Hush! Hush!" all through the novel, at the beginning of paragraph after paragraph. At the end, everything *is* hushed. And the moths *fluttering* over Heathcliff's grave and "the soft wind *breathing* through the grass" that grows on it have at last more power than he, for all his passion. These soft and fragile things paradoxically endure.

The passions of animals, if we may speak of them as passions, have meaning in that they are presumably necessary to survival; Heathcliff's passion destroys others, himself, and at last, itself. The tumult of the elements alternates with periods of peace, and the seasons are not only autumn and winter. The *fact* of alternation enables nature to endure. The singleness of Heathcliff's tempestuous and wintry emotional life dooms it. Thus there is a curious and ironic contrast between the condition and the destiny of Heathcliff, and the full facts of those areas of metaphor. When, at the end of the novel, Nelly remarks that "the same moon shone through the window; and the same autumn landscape lay outside" as eighteen years before, she is speaking with metaphorical accuracy; but Heathcliff is *not* the same. He has not indeed come into a "sober, disenchanted maturity"—that will be the privilege of Hareton and the second Cathy; but he has completely changed in the fashion that Joseph described much earlier—"so as by fire" ". . . there is a strange change approaching: I'm in its shadow at present," he declares when he has found that nothing is worth the feeling of it. At last, after all the windy tumult and the tempests, he says, "I have to remind myself to *breathe.* . . ."

If his life, exhausted at the end, has not been, as he once said of it, "a moral teething," and the novel, therefore, no tragedy, the story of his life has been a moral teething for the author. Lockwood is instructed in the nature of a grand passion, but he and Emily Brontë together are instructed in its final fruits: even roaring fires end in a bed of ashes. Her metaphors instruct her, and her verbs. That besides these rhetorical means (which in their functioning make tolerable the almost impossibly inflated style), she should have found structural means as well which give her whole narrative the remote quality of a twice-told tale, the property of an old wife (and so make its melodrama endurable), should reinforce the point. At the end, the voice that drones on is the perdurable voice of the country, Nelly Dean's. No more than Heathcliff did Emily Brontë quite intend that homespun finality. Like the older Catherine, Emily Brontë could have said of her book, "I've dreamed in my life dreams that have stayed with me ever after, and changed my ideas: they've gone through and through me, like wine through water, and altered the color of my mind." Her rhetoric altered the form of her intention. It is her education; it shapes her insight.

WILLIAM M. SALE, JR.

Emily Brontë's History of Gondal

Over a period of years Emily Brontë and her sister Anne wrote a kind of history in prose of the lives of imaginary characters on the imaginary islands of Gondal and Gaaldine. This history paralleled a story of events in Angria and Glasstown written by Charlotte and her brother Branwell. The prose history of Angria survived but that of Gondal has been lost or was destroyed. Miss Fanny Ratchford grew to believe, however, that an outline of the Gondal history could be found in the large number of poems that Emily wrote during the years 1836–1848, years in which she and Anne were writing Gondal's history in prose. Miss Ratchford finally concluded that the prose Gondal was a "compact and well-integrated whole," with the poems "highlighting such incidents and moods of the familiar Gondal world as stirred her imagination at the moment."[1] In consequence she presented the poems with her own narrative links in a volume which she called *Gondal's Queen, A Novel in Verse*, from which I have just quoted. She believed that Gondal's history was essentially the life story, from birth to death, of Gon-

---

1. Fanny Ratchford, *Gondal's Queen* (Austin: University of Texas Press, 1955), pp. 23, 28.

dal's queen, known variously as Augusta Geraldine Almeda (A.G.A.) and Rosina. The two principal male characters in Augusta's life were the Emperor Julius and Lord Alfred. Inevitably critics were to speculate on the possibility that these three characters were prototypes of Catherine Earnshaw, Heathcliff, and Edgar Linton.

Miss Ratchford, however, is not disposed to find in the Gondal poems close connections with characters and events in *Wuthering Heights*, though she is prepared to speculate that "a boy of dark and tragic aspect" in one of Emily's poems was a prototype of Heathcliff and that Angelica in another poem, who is found pitying a lonely boy, suggests the young Catherine Earnshaw.[2] Other critics have not been so cautious. Mary Visick, for example, feels that "the story they [the poems] can be shown to tell is the story of *Wuthering Heights*," and that "the central Gondal people themselves were reborn as Catherine, Heathcliff and Edgar. . . ."[3] In Miss Ratchford's *Gondal's Queen* Augusta first loves Julius, then abandons him for, among others, Lord Alfred, and finally leaves Alfred to return to Julius. It seems obvious to Miss Visick that we have here a sketch of the relations between Catherine, Heathcliff, and Edgar, though she recognizes that in the Gondal poems the narrative is revealed only in a series of lyric moments.

Either in *Gondal's Queen* or in C. W. Hatfield's edition of *The Complete Poems of Emily Jane Brontë* (New York, 1941), the poems are available for any reader who wants to judge for himself to what extent the poems foreshadow Emily's novel. What some of these poems have meant to some critics may be seen in excerpts such as the following.

A dark boy and a fair girl as original projections of Catherine and Heathcliff, or perhaps more persuasively, of Catherine Linton and Hareton Earnshaw:

> Heavy looms the dull sky,
> Heavy rolls the sea—
> And heavy beats the young heart
> Beneath that lonely tree.
>
> Never has a blue streak
> Cleft the clouds since morn—
> Never has his grim Fate
> Smiled since he was born.
>
> Frowning on the infant,
> Shadowing childhood's joy,

2. Ratchford, pp. 71, 74.
3. Mary Visick, *The Genesis of Wuth-* *ering Heights* (Hong Kong: University of Hong Kong Press, 1958), pp. 11, 38.

> Guardian angel knows not
> That melancholy boy.

And the girl:

> I, the image of light and gladness
> Saw and pitied that mournful boy,
> And I swore to take his gloomy sadness,
> And give to him my beamy joy.
>
> . . . .
>
> Guardian angel, he lacks no longer;
> Evil fortune he need not fear:
> Fate is strong, but Love is stronger;
> And more unsleeping than angel's care.[4]

An anticipation of the passage in the novel which concludes with Catherine's "Nelly, I *am* Heathcliff" (p. 74):

> O God within my breast
> Almighty ever-present Deity
> Life, that in me hast rest
> As I Undying Life, have power in Thee.
>
> . . . .
>
> Though Earth and moon were gone
> And suns and universes ceased to be
> And thou were left alone
> Every Existence would exist in thee.[5]

Augusta's love of Alfred as an earlier description of Catherine's mood in the first days of her marriage to Edgar:

> At such a time, in such a spot,
> The world seems made of light;
> Our blissful hearts remember not
> How surely follows night.
>
> I cannot, Alfred, dream of aught
> That casts a shade of woe;
> That heaven is reigning in my thought,
> Which wood and wave and earth have caught
> From skies that overflow.
>
> That heaven which my sweet lover's brow
> Has won me to adore,
> Which from his blue eyes beaming now

4. Ratchford, pp. 74–76; *The Complete Poems of Emily Jane Brontë*, ed. C. W. Hatfield (New York: Columbia University Press, 1941), pp. 229, 230. 5. Ratchford, pp. 173–174; Hatfield, p. 243.

Reflects a still intenser glow
Than nature's heaven can pour.

. . . .

Then art thou not my golden June
All mist and tempest free?
As shines earth's sun in summer noon
So heaven's sun shines in thee.[6]

Augusta's betrayal of Alfred as a foreshadowing of Catherine's betrayal of Edgar:

I know that I have done thee wrong—
Have wronged both thee and Heaven—
And I may mourn my lifetime long
Yet may not be forgiven.

. . . .

Till far beyond earth's frenzied strife
That makes destruction joy,
Thy perished faith shall spring to life
And my remorse shall die.[7]

Augusta's lament for the death of Julius as comparable to Heathcliff's mourning for the death of Catherine:

Cold in the earth, and fifteen wild Decembers
From those brown hills have melted into spring—
Faithful indeed is the spirit that remembers
After such years of change and suffering!

Sweet Love of youth, forgive if I forget thee
While the World's tide is bearing me along:
Sterner desires and darker hopes beset me,
Hopes which obscure but cannot do thee wrong.

No other Sun has lightened up my heaven;
No other Star has ever shone for me:
All my life's bliss from thy dear life was given—
All my life's bliss is in the grave with thee.[8]

An epitaph for Augusta as a suggestion of the peace of the graves at the end of *Wuthering Heights*:

The linnet in the rocky dells,
The moor-lark in the air,
The bee among the heather-bells
That hide my lady fair:

6. Ratchford, pp. 69–70; Hatfield, pp. 143–144.
7. Ratchford, p. 85; Hatfield, pp. 197–198.
8. Ratchford, p. 126; Hatfield, pp. 222–223.

The wild deer browse above her breast;
The wild birds raise their brood;
And they, her smiles of love caressed,
Have left her solitude!

. . . .

They thought the tide of grief would flow
Unchecked through future years,
But where is all their anguish now,
And where are all their tears?

. . . .

Blow, west wind, by the lonely mound,
And murmur, summer streams,
There is no need of other sound
To soothe my Lady's dreams.[9]

9. Ratchford, pp. 159–160; Hatfield, pp. 204–205.

Selected Bibliography

[NOTE: *Articles reprinted in this edition are not included.*]

EMILY BRONTË

Bentley, Phyllis. *The Brontë Sisters*, London, 1950.
Hartley, L. P. "Emily Brontë in Gondal and Gaaldine," *Brontë Society Transactions*, XIV, v (1965), 1–15.
Hatfield, C. W., ed. *The Complete Poems of Emily Jane Brontë*, New York, 1941.
Hinkley, Laura L. *The Brontës: Charlotte and Emily*, New York, 1945.
Lewis, C. Day. "Emily Brontë and Freedom," *Notable Images of Virtue*, Toronto, 1954, pp. 1–25.
Ratchford, Fannie Elizabeth. *The Brontës' Web of Childhood*, New York, 1941.
———. *Gondal's Queen; A Novel in Verse by Emily Jane Brontë*, Austin, Tex., 1955.
Simpson, Charles. *Emily Brontë*, London and New York, 1929.
Spark, Muriel and Stanford, Derek. *Emily Brontë, Her Life and Work*, London, 1953.
Wise, Thomas J. and Symington, J. A., eds. *The Brontës: Their Lives, Friendships and Correspondence*, 4 vols., Oxford, 1932.

WUTHERING HEIGHTS

Adams, Ruth M. "*Wuthering Heights:* The Land East of Eden," *Nineteenth-Century Fiction*, XIII (June, 1958), 58–62.
Allott, Miriam. "*Wuthering Heights:* the Rejection of Heathcliff?" *Essays in Criticism*, VIII (January, 1958), 27–47.
Bradner, Leicester. "The Growth of *Wuthering Heights*," *PMLA*, XLVIII (March, 1933), 129–46.
Chase, Richard. "The Brontës, A Centennial Observance," *Kenyon Review*, IX (Autumn, 1947), 487–506. Reprinted in *Forms of Modern Fiction*, ed. William Van O'Connor, Minneapolis, Minn., 1948, pp. 102–19. The essay is here titled "The Brontës, or Myth Domesticated."
Collins, Clifford. "Theme and Convention in *Wuthering Heights*," *The Critic*, I (Autumn, 1947), 43–50.
Dodds, M. Hope. "Heathcliff's Country," *Modern Language Review*, XXXIX (April, 1944), 116–29.
Ford, Boris. "*Wuthering Heights*," *Scrutiny*, VII (March, 1939), 375–89.
Gose, Elliott B., Jr. "*Wuthering Heights:* The Heath and the Hearth," *Nineteenth-Century Fiction*, XXI (1966), 1–19.
Hafley, James. "The Villain in *Wuthering Heights*," *Nineteenth-Century Fiction*, XIII (December, 1958), 199–215.
Hawkes, Jacquetta. "Emily Brontë in the Natural Scene," *Transactions of the Brontë Society*, Part LXIII (No. 3 of Vol. 12), 1953, pp. 173–86.
Jordan, John E. "The Ironic Vision of Emily Brontë," *Nineteenth-Century Fiction*, XX (1965), 1–18.
Kettle, Arnold. "Emily Brontë: *Wuthering Heights*," *An Introduction to the English Novel*, 2 vols., Harper Torchbooks, New York, 1960, I, 139–55.
Klingopulos, G. D. "The Novel as Dramatic Poem (II): *Wuthering Heights*," *Scrutiny*, XIV (September, 1947), 269–86.
Lettis, Richard and Morris, William E., eds. *A Wuthering Heights Handbook*, New York, 1961.
Maugham, W. Somerset. "Emily Brontë and *Wuthering Heights*," *Ten Novels and Their Authors*, London, 1954, pp. 204–33.
McCullough, Bruce. "The Dramatic Novel: *Wuthering Heights*," *Representative English Novelists*, New York, 1946, pp. 184–96.
Shannon, Edgar F., Jr. "Lockwood's Dream and the Exegesis of *Wuthering Heights*," *Nineteenth-Century Fiction*, XIV (September, 1959), 95–109.

Sonstroem, David. *"Wuthering Heights* and the Limits of Vision," *Publications of the Modern Language Association*, 86, 1 (January, 1971), 51–62.

Swinburne, A. C. "Emily Brontë," *Miscellanies*, London, 1886, pp. 260–70.

Turnell, Martin. *"Wuthering Heights," The Dublin Review*, CCVI (January–June, 1940), 134–49.

Van Ghent, Dorothy. "The Window Figure and the Two-Children Figure in *Wuthering Heights," Nineteenth-Century Fiction*, VII (December, 1952), 189–97.

———. *"On Wuthering Heights," The English Novel: Form and Function*, New York, 1953, pp. 153–70.

Volger, Thomas A., ed. *Twentieth-Century Interpretations of Wuthering Heights*, Englewood Cliffs, N.J., 1968.

Watson, Melvin R. *"Wuthering Heights* and the Critics," *The Trollopian*, III (March, 1949), 243–63.

———. "Tempest in the Soul: The Theme and Structure of *Wuthering Heights," Nineteenth-Century Fiction*, IV (September, 1949), 87–100.

West, Rebecca. "The Role of Fantasy in the Work of the Brontës," *Transactions of the Brontë Society*, Part LXIV (No. 4 of Vol. 12), 1954, 255–67.